The World's
Finest Mystery and
Crime Stories

Fourth Annual Collection

**Forge Books Edited by
Ed Gorman and Martin H. Greenberg**

The World's Finest Mystery and Crime Stories
First Annual Collection

The World's Finest Mystery and Crime Stories
Second Annual Collection

The World's Finest Mystery and Crime Stories
Third Annual Collection

The World's Finest Mystery and Crime Stories
Fourth Annual Collection

The World's Finest Mystery and Crime Stories

*Edited by Ed Gorman
and Martin H. Greenberg*

A TOM DOHERTY ASSOCIATES BOOK

NEW YORK

THE WORLD'S FINEST MYSTERY AND CRIME STORIES:
FOURTH ANNUAL COLLECTION

Copyright © 2003 by Tekno Books and Ed Gorman

This book is printed on acid-free paper.

Edited by James Frenkel

A Forge Book
Published by Tom Doherty Associates, LLC
175 Fifth Avenue
New York, NY 10010

www.tor.com

Forge® is a registered trademark of Tom Doherty Associates, LLC.

ISBN 0-765-30848-7 (hardcover)
ISBN 0-765-30849-5 (trade paperback)

First Edition: September 2003

Printed in the United States of America

0 9 8 7 6 5 4 3 2 1

Copyright Acknowledgments

To Tom Doherty, a man whose taste, intelligence, and skill have made
him a publishing icon

Acknowledgments

As always, to the Tekno Books staff, who do most of the work.
—Ed Gorman

Contents

The Year in Mystery and Crime Fiction: 2002

Jon L. Breen

In any field of endeavor, transition is a constant, but for mystery fiction 2002, more than most, was a Year of Transitions. Early in the year, shortly after being named cowinner (with Janet Hutchings) of the Ellery Queen Award by Mystery Writers of America, Cathleen Jordan, widely admired and respected editor of *Alfred Hitchcock's Mystery Magazine* since 1982, died, to be succeeded by Linda Landrigan. *Mystery Scene,* an essential source of news and opinion in the genre since 1985, moved its headquarters from Cedar Rapids to New York when sold to Kate Stine and Brian Skupin by publisher Martin H. Greenberg and editor Ed Gorman (cofounder with Robert J. Randisi). Walker and Company, a steady mystery market for many decades, first for British imports (including the American debuts of John Le Carré and Robert Barnard) and later for developing American writers (Edgar winners Julie Smith and Aaron Elkins, among many others), closed its venerable crime fiction line. Meanwhile, nontraditional markets outside the New York publishing mainstream continued their growth spurt.

Some known for mystery fiction made at least a temporary transition into true crime. Otto Penzler and Thomas H. Cook co-edited *The Best American Crime Writing* (Pantheon), which deserves to be an annual tradition. On the other hand, Patricia Cornwell, based on her unconvincing case against British impressionist painter Walter Sickert in *Portrait of a Killer: Jack the Ripper Case Closed* (Putnam), would be well advised to stick to fiction.

The year's happiest transition, though its permanence remains in doubt, was American television's newfound ability to accomplish something British TV has been doing for years: make strong and faithful adaptations of detective fiction classics. While viewers throughout the world have enjoyed meticulous small-screen versions of Agatha Christie's Poirot and Miss Marple, Colin Dexter's Inspector Morse, and many other famous British sleuths, American TV for some reason (perhaps not trusting the strength of the material and/or the intelligence of its audiences) didn't have the knack. True, there have been those series about Mike Hammer, Ellery Queen, Spenser, Father Dowling, and other print sleuths, with varying degrees of success, but they were usually comprised of TV originals. For a reasonably faithful American adaptation of a series of novels, you'd have to go back to the Perry Mason series with Raymond Burr in the fifties and sixties. In 2001, A&E began its fine series of dramatizations of Rex Stout's Nero Wolfe novels. The sad news that the Wolfe series was being cancelled in 2002 was followed by the much cheerier fact that Tony Hillerman's series about the Navajo Tribal Police had found a home on PBS's Mystery series, so long the territory of British imports. *Skinwalkers,* well cast with some accomplished Native American actors (notably Wes Studi as Joe Leaphorn and Adam Beach as Jim Chee), directed by Native American filmmaker Chris Eyre, and adapted by Jamie Redford, showed the same confidence and respect for its material as the best of the British adaptations. It is hoped this heralds a long small-screen life for the Hillerman series and leads producers to do the same service for other American classics.

BEST NOVELS OF THE YEAR 2002

The following fifteen were the most impressive crime novels I read and reviewed in 2002. The usual disclaimer applies: I don't pretend to cover the whole field—with today's volume of new books, no single reviewer does. But try to find fifteen better.

Max Allan Collins, *The Lusitania Murders* (Berkley). S. S. Van Dine sets sail on the great ship's final voyage and finds a surprising model for Philo Vance in the fourth of the author's masterfully conceived and executed disaster series.

Thomas H. Cook, *The Interrogation* (Bantam). Big-city cops circa 1952 have eleven hours to get a confession in a powerful and unpredictable gem from one of our best active writers.

Michael Dibdin, *And Then You Die* (Pantheon). One reviewer compared Dibdin to Agatha Christie, Ian Fleming, and Elmore Leonard, but the creator of Italian cop, Aurelio Zen, defies pigeonholing.

Ed Gorman, *Save the Last Dance for Me* (Carroll & Graf). The fourth case for Sam McCain, lawyer sleuth of 1960s Iowa, is the best yet in plot, prose, and period detail.

Parnell Hall, *A Puzzle in a Pear Tree* (Bantam). What better holiday present than a Puzzle Lady mystery, with the author's trademark humor and a plot in the grand tradition of clue-planting and misdirection?

Reginald Hill, *Dialogues of the Dead* (Delacorte). With much to offer the lover of elaborate wordplay, offbeat psychology, and literate narrative, the creator of Yorkshire cops Dalziel and Pascoe jostles with Martin Cruz Smith (see below) for the year's top honors.

Laurie R. King, *Justice Hall* (Bantam). The latest account of Sherlock Holmes and wife, Mary Russell, is the rare pastiche that can be recommended to those who dislike pastiches.

Rochelle Krich, *Blues in the Night* (Ballantine). Don't let the depressing subject matter—infanticide and postpartum psychosis—put you off this expertly crafted and often humorous case for a new Orthodox Jewish sleuth, true crime writer, Molly Blume.

Peter Lovesey, *Diamond Dust* (Soho). Bath detective Peter Diamond investigates the murder of his wife in the latest from a master of smooth narrative and reader manipulation.

Bill Pronzini, *Bleeders* (Carroll & Graf). It's good to report this is not the final book about San Francisco's Nameless Detective, as was rumored at the time of its publication, and it is one of the best in the series.

S. J. Rozan, *Winter and Night* (St. Martin's Minotaur). The private eye team of Bill Smith and Lydia Chin, whose relationship is as complex as the ornate plot, encounter some people who take high school football much too seriously.

Alice Sebold, *The Lovely Bones* (Little, Brown). Not all runaway best-sellers are distinguished novels, but this hard-edged fantasy, told by a teenage murder victim, certainly is.

Martin Cruz Smith, *December 6* (Simon & Schuster). This suspenseful and vividly detailed view of Japan on the brink of World War II, from the viewpoint of an American con man almost equally influenced by the two cultures, tied with Reginald Hill (see above) for my best of the year.

Richard Stark, *Breakout* (Mysterious). Another caper for professional thief Parker shows Stark (the grimmer face of humorist Donald E. Westlake) at the top of his game.

Laura Wilson, *My Best Friend* (Delacorte). In her third novel, Wilson again displays her knack for the time- and viewpoint-shifting saga, from the World War II British home front to 1995, the year of VE Day's fiftieth anniversary.

SUBGENRES

Private eyes. Among the sleuths for hire I enjoyed in 2002 were Dana Stabenow's Alaskan, Kate Shugak, in *A Fine and Bitter Snow* (St. Martin's Minotaur); Sue Grafton's Californian, Kinsey Millhone, in *"Q" is for Quarry* (Putnam); Paco Ignacio Taibo II's Mexican, Hector Belascoaran Shayne, in *Frontera Dreams* (Cinco Puntos); Max Allan Collins's Midwestern, Nate Heller, in the mid-century *Chicago Confidential* (New American Library); and Stuart M. Kaminsky's 1940s Hollywoodian, Toby Peters, in *To Catch a Spy* (Carroll & Graf/Penzler).

Amateur sleuths. The charming cozy meddlers could be divided into those who detected from real clues—e.g., wedding planner, Carnegie Kincaid, in Deborah Donnelly's *Died to Match* (Dell) and caterer, Faith Fairchild, in Katherine Hall Page's *The Body in the Bonfire* (Morrow)—and those who did not—e.g., gardening broadcaster, Louise Eldridge, in Ann Ripley's *The Christmas Garden Affair* (Kensington) and Emily Toll's travel-agent-cum-tour-guide, Lynne Montgomery, in *Murder Will Travel* (Berkley).

Police. Some favorite cops were active in solid cases, including James Lee Burke's Dave Robicheaux, in *Jolie Blon's Bounce* (Simon and Schuster); Michael Connelly's Harry Bosch, in *City of Bones* (Little, Brown); and Tony Hillerman's Leaphorn and Chee, in *The Wailing Wind* (HarperCollins). Andrea Camilleri's Sicilian Police Inspector Montalbano made an impressive American debut in *The Shape of Water* (Viking), first published in Italy in 1994, while Mat Coward's London team of bipolar Inspector Don Packham and Constable Frank Mitchell had an excellent second outing (or innings?) in *In and Out* (Five Star). Manhattan's Ben Stack and Rica Lopez sought a serial killer in John Lutz's masterful *The Night Watcher* (Leisure).

Historicals. The length of this paragraph reflects both this reviewer's taste and a steadily growing trend. A long-standing British series starring a team of detectives in fourteenth-century Devon continued to gain an American foothold in Michael Jecks's *The Sticklepath Strangler* and *The Devil's Acolyte* (Headline/Trafalgar Square). Other deep-in-the-past sleuths in strong form included Steven Saylor's ancient Roman, Gordianus the Finder, in *A Mist of Prophecies* (St. Martin's Minotaur); Kate Sedley's fifteenth-century itinerant, Roger the Chapman, in *The Saint John's Fern* (St. Martin's Minotaur); and Viviane Moore's twelfth-century Frenchman, Chevalier Galeran de Lesneven, in *A Black Romance* (Orion). Anne Perry's late Victorian, Thomas Pitt, was reliable as ever in *Southampton Row* (Ballantine), while her slightly earlier London private eye, William Monk, was in improved form in *Death of a Stranger* (Ballantine). The year's best new Sherlock Holmes case, aside from the King title on my list of fifteen, was Barrie Roberts's *Sherlock Holmes and the Crosby Murder* (Carroll & Graf). A Scotland Yard detective solves a case in 1922 India, in Barbara Cleverly's first novel *The Last Kashmiri Rose* (Carroll & Graf/Penzler). Other twentieth-century historical sleuths in action included Carola Dunn's 1920s journalist, Daisy Dalrymple, in *The Case of the Murdered Muckraker* (St. Martin's Minotaur); Michael Pearce's British functionary in 1910 Egypt, the Mamur Zapt, in *The Camel of Destruction* (Poisoned Pen); and Michael Kilian's Jazz Age art dealer, Bedford Green, in *The Uninvited Countess* (Berkley).

Thrillers. Val Davis's historical archaeologist, Nicolette Scott, had another harrowing outing in *Thread of the Spider* (St. Martin's Minotaur). Michael Connelly's second book of the year, *Chasing the Dime* (Little, Brown), was a riveting piece of technological suspense. Tales of professional criminals are not my usual meat, but I make an exception with novels as intriguing as Ken Bruen's *London Boulevard* (Do-Not/Dufour), a homage to Billy Wilder's great film, *Sunset Boulevard*.

SHORT STORIES

Single-author short-story collections continue to burgeon satisfactorily. Ian Rankin's 1992 John Rebus collection, *A Good Hanging* (St. Martin's Minotaur), finally saw American publication, while a second volume, *Beggars Banquet* (Orion), appeared in Britain. Among the year's other highlights were Donald Thomas's *Sherlock Holmes and the Voice from the Crypt* (Carroll & Graf), his second group of stories involving the Baker Street sleuth with real-life crimes; Peter Lovesey's varied and polished *The Sedgemoor Strangler and Other Stories of Crime* (Crippen & Landru); Nero Blanc's *A Crossworder's Holiday* (Berkley), about a puzzle-editor and private eye team; Jan Burke's *18* (A.S.A.P.), with an introduction by Edward D. Hoch; Michael Collins's early-career retrospective *Spies and Thieves, Cops and Killers, Etc.* (Five Star); and the first full English translation of Georges Simenon's *The 13 Culprits* (Crippen & Landru), published in France in 1932 as *Les 13 Coupables*.

Crippen & Landru's new Lost Classics series brought a new generation of readers to some great writer/detective teams of the past, including Peter Godfrey's *The Newtonian Egg and Other Cases of Rolf le Roux;* Craig Rice's *Murder, Mystery, and Malone;* Stuart Palmer's *Hildegarde Withers: Uncollected Riddles;* Charles B. Child's *The Sleuth of Baghdad,* about Inspector Chafik; and Christianna Brand's *The Spotted Cat and Other Mysteries from Inspector Cockrill's Casebook.* In its partnership with Black Mask Press, Crippen & Landru presented the first short-story collection of legendary pulp writer Raoul Whitfield, *Jo Gar's Casebook.*

In a semireverse on mystery fiction's venerable tradition of disguising short-story collections as novels, several recent Five Star products marketed as collections have reprinted novels as the majority of their contents: Robert Colby's *The Last Witness and Other Stories,* K. K. Beck's *The Tell-Tale Tattoo and Other Stories,* Susan Dunlap's *Karma and Other Stories,* Carolyn G. Hart's *Secrets and Other Stories of Suspense,* Joan Hess's *Death of a Romance Writer and Other Stories,* and Graham Masterton's *Charnel House and Other Stories.* This is not an objection, you understand: think of it as a novel reissue with a bonus.

For the permanent shelf were Lawrence Block's eighty-four-story retrospective, *Enough Rope* (Morrow), similar but not identical to his 1999 British volume, *Collected Short Stories;* and Patricia Highsmith's *Nothing That Meets the Eye: The Uncollected Stories* (Norton).

The bumper crop of original theme anthologies included several illustrating the growing popularity of historical mysteries: *Murder, My Dear Watson* (Carroll & Graf), another set of new Sherlock Holmes pastiches edited by Martin H. Greenberg, Jon Lellenberg, and Daniel Stashower; *Much Ado About Murder* (Berkley), Shakespearean mysteries edited by Anne Perry; *The Mammoth Book of Egyptian Whodunits* (Carroll & Graf), edited by Mike Ashley; and *White House Pet Detectives* (Cumberland), edited by Carole Nelson Douglas. Though not specifically designated as historical, tales set in the distant or recent past were prominent in *Murder Most Catholic* (Cumberland), edited by Ralph McInerny; the Alaskan-themed *The Mysterious North* (Signet), edited by Dana Stabenow; and *Measures of Poison* (Dennis McMillan), the publisher's twentieth-anniversary anthology.

Guns of the West (Berkley), edited by Ed Gorman and Martin H. Greenberg, illustrated the considerable crossover of western and crime fiction, including contributions of several writers familiar to mystery readers: Bill Pronzini, Bill Crider, L. J. Washburn, Gary Phillips, James Reasoner, Kristine Kathryn Rusch, and editor Ed Gorman.

Among the nonhistorical theme anthologies were two strong collections of erotic noir stories, one of them mostly (but not entirely) from a male perspective, *Flesh & Blood: Dark Desires* (Mysterious), edited by Max Allan Collins and Jeff Gelb, and the other, *Tart Noir* (Berkley), edited by Stella Duffy and Lauren Henderson, entirely from a female perspective. Other notable theme anthologies included the International Association of Crime Writers' *Death Dance* (Cumberland), edited by Trevanian; the Adams

Round Table's *Murder in the Family* (Berkley); and Otto Penzler's football anthology *The Mighty Johns and Other Stories* (New Millennium).

No less than three volumes published in 2002 gathered their editors' choices as best short crime fiction of 2001: *The World's Finest Mystery and Crime Stories* (Forge), edited by Ed Gorman and Martin H. Greenberg, the present volume's predecessor hereafter called GG; *The Best American Mystery Stories* (Houghton Mifflin), edited by James Ellroy (guest editor) and Otto Penzler (series editor), hereafter EP; and the newest and smallest, my own *Mystery: The Best of 2001* (ibooks), hereafter JLB. Clearly, there is room for all three in the mystery marketplace and on the shelf of any reader with an enthusiasm for what Anthony Boucher called "the short shudder." There is zero crossover between EP's twenty selections and JLB's fifteen. GG's thirty-nine have only two stories in common with JLB and none with EP. Of the prestigious Mystery Writers of America Edgar Awards nominees, only the winner (S. J. Rozan's "Double-Crossing Delancy") appears in GG and none of the other four nominees appear in any of the collections; only one of the Private Eye Writers of America's Shamus nominees is selected (Clark Howard's "The Cobalt Blues" in EP); none of Mystery Readers International's Macavity Award nominees appear in any of the anthologies; and only one of the Bouchercon's Anthony Award nominees appears (that same Rozan story in GG). With only two awards candidates getting any attention at all, a whole fourth best-of-the-year volume could be comprised of otherwise unselected nominees.

So what does this all prove? If you assume (as I do) that all these editors and all the members of awards committees (of the above, the Edgars and Shamuses are juried) have good taste, it simply shows the wide range and generally high quality of today's short mystery fiction.

As always, for the full story on the year's anthologies and single-author collections, I commend to you Edward D. Hoch's bibliography.

REFERENCE BOOKS AND SECONDARY SOURCES

Reference book of the year for the general mystery fan was Mike Ashley's *The Mammoth Encyclopedia of Modern Crime Fiction* (Carroll & Graf), the most up-to-date and one of the most accurate single-volume references on the field, emphasizing writing since about 1960. The more specialized book of the year was the revised and much improved edition of *The Sound of Detection: Ellery Queen's Adventures in Radio* (OTR) by Queen expert Francis M. Nevins and old radio authority Martin Grams, Jr.

Similarly, two notable "companions" were published, one for a very large market, George Beahm's *The Unofficial Patricia Cornwell Companion* (St. Martin's Minotaur), and one for a much smaller circle of connoisseurs, *From A to Izzard: A Harry Stephen Keeler Companion* (Ramble House), edited by Fender Tucker.

Prospective writers of mystery fiction (who sometimes seem more plentiful than readers) had available to them the new edition of *Writing*

Mysteries: A Handbook by the Mystery Writers of America (Writer's Digest), edited by Sue Grafton, along with Jan Burke and Barry Zeman. For marketing advice, more important than ever in the increasingly fragmented world of mystery publishing, writers could turn to Jeffrey Marks's *Intent to Sell: Marketing the Genre Novel* (Deadly Alibi).

Trafalgar Square, that fine importer of British books to the American market, made available two books by Mark Campbell, *The Pocket Essential Agatha Christie* and *The Pocket Essential Sherlock Holmes,* both with critical and informational value that belies their small size. That same distributor also brought over a much larger volume to delight the Irregulars, Alan Barnes's excellent *Sherlock Holmes on Screen.*

Other secondary sources worthy of mention included Stephen M. Murphy's interview collection *Their Word is Law: Bestselling Lawyer-Novelists Talk About Their Craft* (Berkley); *They Died in Vain: Overlooked, Underappreciated, and Forgotten Mystery Novels* (Crum Creek), a great source of reading tips edited by Jim Huang; and the second and third volumes of *The Anthony Boucher Chronicles* (Ramble House), completing the cornerstone reprint of Boucher's reviews and columns of the 1940s from the *San Francisco Chronicle.*

Again, see Ed Hoch's bibliography for the full story.

A SENSE OF HISTORY

Apart from Crippen & Landru's lineup of oldtimers (see Short Stories above), there were many other gestures of respect to the genre's past. Best news may have been the revival in print of Fredric Brown (1906–1972), one of the mid-century writers most celebrated by his fellow professionals in two genres. Brown's first four novels about Ed and Am Hunter were reprinted in the omnibus volume *Hunter and Hunted* (Stewart Masters), while his five science fiction novels were revived in *Martians and Madness* (NESFA).

Prominent reprint series devoted to general literature paid plenty of attention to detective fiction during the year. Everyman Library presented Raymond Chandler's *Collected Stories,* the first gathering of all the short fiction by Philip Marlowe's creator, with an introduction by John Bayley, who reveals that his late wife Iris Murdoch was a Chandler fan. Penguin Classics brought out scholarly paperback editions of several landmark works, including Horace Walpole's pioneering gothic novel *The Castle of Otranto,* Charles Dickens's unfinished *The Mystery of Edwin Drood,* and two volumes from Conan Doyle, *The Adventures and Memoirs of Sherlock Holmes* and *The Valley of Fear and Selected Cases.*

Meanwhile, Rue Morgue Press continued its rediscovery of past crime fiction with new editions of Craig Rice's *Home Sweet Homicide* (1944), Norbert Davis's *Sally's in the Alley* (1943), and additional books by Juanita Sheridan and the team of Constance and Gwenyth Little.

AT THE MOVIES

Crime film of the year for this observer was *Road to Perdition,* an atmospheric gangster drama destined for classic stature. It was directed by Sam Mendes from David Self's script, based on the graphic novel by Max Allan Collins and Richard Piers Rayner. (In an interesting third-generation twist, Collins wrote a prose novelization of Self's screenplay, published by Onyx.) Another possibility for landmark status, though its early box-office returns were disappointing, was Martin Scorsese's visually and dramatically arresting epic of nineteenth-century Manhattan, *Gangs of New York,* adapted by Jay Cocks, Steven Zaillian, and Kenneth Lonergan from Herbert Asbury's 1928 nonfiction book.

The degree of Asbury's devotion to literal truth has been questioned. Other films ostensibly based on real-life crimes included Paul Schrader's morbidly interesting and probably quite accurate biography of ill-fated *Hogan's Heroes* star Bob Crane, *Auto Focus,* written with Michael Gerbosi and Trevor Macy from Robert Graysmith's 1993 book; and *Cat's Meow,* a fanciful speculation on the alleged murder of Thomas Ince on William Randolph Hearst's yacht, directed by Peter Bogdanovich from Steven Peros's script and most notable for its period feel and Kirsten Dunst's performance as Marion Davies.

Michael Connelly's *Blood Work* was turned into a pretty good film, albeit with a change of murderer, by screenwriter Brian Helgeland and director/star Clint Eastwood. *Minority Report,* a science fictional crime drama from Philip K. Dick's short story, directed by Steven Spielberg from a script by Jon Cohen and Scott Frank, was entertaining though not up to the expectations of many fans. No less than three films gave Robin Williams a chance to play a deranged actual or potential murderer: Mark Romanek's *One Hour Photo;* the satirical *Death to Smoochy,* directed by Danny DeVito from Adam Resnick's script; and (best of all) *Insomnia,* directed by Christopher Nolan from Hillary Seitz's adaptation of a Swedish film written by Nicolaj Frobenius and Erik Skjoldbjaerg. Brian De Palma's *Femme Fatale* was a lively and tricky addition to the erotic thriller genre.

Some of the best crime and mystery films available to American audiences in 2002 came from France. Director Francois Ozon's *8 Women,* which he wrote with Marina De Van and Robert Thomas, was a witty spoof of classical whodunits that showcased an octet of French actresses, from Danielle Darrieux to Catherine Deneuve to Emmanuelle Beart. On a more realistic level, Claude Chabrol's *Merci pour le Chocolat* was an effective adaptation, written with Caroline Eliacheff, of Charlotte Armstrong's novel *The Chocolate Cobweb.* (My wife, who read the novel after admiring the film, found the print version much richer, reminding me that Armstrong is a giant of suspense fiction who needs to be rediscovered.) Claude Miller's *Alias Betty* also turned to an English-language source, Ruth Rendell's *Tree of Hands.* Also subtitled at the art houses was a great con man film from Argentina, Fabian Bielinski's *Nine Queens.*

AWARD WINNERS FOR 2002

Generally, these were awarded in 2002 for material published in 2001. Awards tied to publishers' contests, those limited to a geographical region smaller than a country, those awarded for works in languages other than English (with the exception of Crime Writers of Canada's nod to their French members), and those confined to works from a particular periodical have been omitted.

Edgar Allan Poe Awards

(MYSTERY WRITERS OF AMERICA)

Best novel: T. Jefferson Parker, *Silent Joe* (Hyperion)

Best first novel by an American author: David Ellis, *Line of Vision* (Putnam)

Best original paperback: David Chavarria, *Adios Muchachos* (Akashic)

Best fact crime book: Kent Walker with Mark Schone, *Son of a Grifter* (Morrow)

Best critical/biographical work: Dawn B. Sova, *Edgar Allan Poe: A to Z* (Facts on File)

Best short story: S. J. Rozan, "Double-Crossing Delancy" (*Mystery Street,* Signet)

Best young adult mystery: Tim Wynne-Jones, *The Boy in the Burning House* (Farrar, Straus & Giroux)

Best children's mystery: Lillian Eige, *Dangling* (Atheneum)

Best episode in a television series: Terence Winter, "The Pine Barrens," story by Tim Van Patten and "Winter" (*The Sopranos,* HBO)

Best television feature or miniseries: William Ivory, *The Sins* (BBC America)

Best motion picture: Christopher Nolan, *Memento* (Newmarket Films)

Grand master: Robert B. Parker

Robert L. Fish award (best first story): Ted Hertel, Jr., "My Bonnie Lies" (*Mammoth Book of Legal Thrillers,* Carroll & Graf)

Ellery Queen Award: Janet Hutchings and Cathleen Jordan

Raven Award: Charles Champlin; Anthony Mason and Douglas Smith

Mary Higgins Clark Award: Judith Kelman, *Summer of Storms* (Putnam)

Special Edgar: Blake Edwards

Agatha Awards

(MALICE DOMESTIC MYSTERY CONVENTION)

Best novel: Rhys Bowen, *Murphy's Law* (St. Martin's Minotaur)

Best first novel: Sarah Strohmeyer, *Bubbles Unbound* (Dutton)

Best short story: Katherine Hall Page, "The Would-Be Widower" (Malice Domestic X, Avon)

Best nonfiction: Tony Hillerman, *Seldom Disappointed* (HarperCollins)
Lifetime Achievement Award: Tony Hillerman

Anthony Awards

(BOUCHERCON WORLD MYSTERY CONVENTION)

Best novel: Dennis Lehane, *Mystic River* (Morrow)
Best first novel: C. J. Box, *Open Season* (Putnam)
Best paperback original: Charlaine Harris, *Dead Until Dark* (Ace)
Best short story: Bill and Judy Crider, "Chocolate Moose" (*Death Dines at 8:30,* Berkley)
Best critical/biographical: Tony Hillerman, *Seldom Disappointed* (Harper-Collins)
Best young adult mystery: Penny Warner, *The Mystery of the Haunted Caves* (Meadowbrook)
Best cover art: *Reflecting the Sky* by S. J. Rozan, cover design by Michael Storrings from a photograph by Josef Beck/FPG (St. Martin's Minotaur)
Special Award for Service to the Mystery Community: Doris Ann Norris

Shamus Awards

(PRIVATE EYE WRITERS OF AMERICA)

Best novel: S. J. Rozan, *Reflecting the Sky* (St. Martin's Minotaur)
Best first novel: David Fulmer, *Chasing the Devil's Tail* (Poisoned Pen Press)
Best original paperback novel: Lyda Morehouse, *Archangel Protocol* (ROC)
Best short story: Ceri Jordan, "Rough Justice" (*Alfred Hitchcock's Mystery Magazine,* July)
The Eye (life achievement): Lawrence Block
Friends of PWA award: Jan Grape

Dagger Awards

(CRIME WRITERS' ASSOCIATION, GREAT BRITAIN)

Gold Dagger: Jose Carlos Somoza, *The Athenian Murders* (Abacus)
Silver Dagger: James Crumley, *The Final Country* (HarperCollins)
John Creasey Award (Best First Novel): Louise Welsh, *The Cutting Room* (Canongate)
Best short story: Stella Duffy, "Martha Grace" (*Tart Noir,* Pan Macmillan)
Best nonfiction: Lillian Pizzichini, *Dead Man's Wages* (Picador)

Diamond Dagger: Sara Paretsky
Ellis Peters Historical Dagger: Sarah Waters, *Fingersmith* (Virago).
Ian Fleming Steel Dagger: John Creed, *The Sirius Crossing* (Faber)
Dagger in the Library (voted by librarians for a body of work): Peter Robinson
Debut Dagger (for unpublished writers): Illona Van Mil, *Sugarmilk Falls*

Macavity Awards

(MYSTERY READERS INTERNATIONAL)

Best novel: Laurie R. King, *Folly* (Bantam)
Best first novel: C. J. Box, *Open Season* (Putnam)
Best critical/biographical work: G. Miki Hayden, *Writing the Mystery* (Intrigue)
Best short story: Jan Burke, "The Abbey Ghosts" *(Alfred Hitchcock's Mystery Magazine,* January)

Arthur Ellis Awards

(CRIME WRITERS OF CANADA)

Best novel: Michelle Spring, *In the Midnight Hour* (Ballantine)
Best first novel: Jon Redfern, *The Boy Must Die* (ECW Press)
Best true crime: (tie) Stevie Cameron and Harvey Cashore, *The Last Amigo* (Macfarlane Walter & Ross); Andrew Nikiforuk, *Saboteurs* (Macfarlane Walter & Ross)
Best juvenile novel: Norah McClintock, *Sacred to Death* (Scholastic Canada)
Best short story: Mary Jane Maffini, "Sign of the Times" *(Fit to Die,* RendezVous Press)
Best crime writing in French: Anne-Michèle Lévesque, *Fleur invitait au troisième* (Vents d'Ouest)
Derrick Murdoch Award for Lifetime Achievement: James Dubro

Ned Kelly Awards

(CRIME WRITERS' ASSOCIATION OF AUSTRALIA)

Best novel: Gabrielle Lord, *Death's Delights* (Hodder)
Best first novel: (tie) Bunty Avieson, *Apartment 255* (Pan); Emma Darcy, *Who Killed Angelique?* (Pan)
Best true crime: (tie) Larry Writer, *Razor* (Pan); Mike Richards, *The Hanged Man* (Scribe)
Best teenage/young adult: Ken Catran, *Blue Murder* (Lothian)

Crime Factory Magazine Readers' Vote: Bunty Avieson, *Apartment 255* (Pan)

Lifetime achievement: Patrick Gallagher

Herodotus Awards

(HISTORICAL MYSTERY APPRECIATION SOCIETY)

Best Historical Mystery: Miriam Grace Monfredo, *Brothers of Cain* (Berkley)

Best First Historical Mystery: Rhys Bowen, *Murphy's Law* (St. Martin's)

Best Short Story Historical Mystery: Max Allan Collins, "Kiss of Death" *(Kiss of Death,* Crippen & Landru)

Lifetime Achievement Award: Max Allan Collins

Barry Awards

(*DEADLY PLEASURES* MAGAZINE)

Best novel: Dennis Lehane, *Mystic River* (Morrow)

Best first novel: C. J. Box, *Open Season* (Putnam)

Best British novel: Stephen Booth, *Dancing with Virgins* (HarperCollins)

Best paperback original: Deborah Woodworth, *Killing Gifts* (Avon)

Don Sandstrom Memorial Award for Lifetime Achievement in Mystery Fandom: Gary Warren Niebuhr

Nero Wolfe Award

(WOLFE PACK)

Linda Fairstein, *The Deadhouse* (Scribner)

Dilys Award

(INDEPENDENT MYSTERY BOOKSELLERS ASSOCIATION)

Dennis Lehane, *Mystic River* (Morrow)

Hammett Prize

(INTERNATIONAL CRIME WRITERS)

Alan Furst, *Kingdom of Shadows* (Random House)

A 2002 Yearbook of Crime and Mystery

Edward D. Hoch

COLLECTIONS AND SINGLE STORIES

ALLYN, DOUG. *The Hard Luck Club*. Waterville, ME: Five Star. Eight stories from various sources, 1988–2000.

BATORY, DANA MARTIN. *The Federation Holmes*. Shelburne, Ontario, Canada: The Battered Silicon Dispatch Box. Thirteen stories, one new, which transport Sherlock Holmes to the twenty-second century. Twelve were first published in a fanzine, *The Holmesian Federation*, 1978–91.

BECK, K. K. *The Talltale Tattoo and Other Stories*. Waterville, ME: Five Star. A novel, *Peril Under the Palms* (1989), and four short stories, 1992–2001, all but one about Beck's 1920s sleuth Iris Cooper. Introduction by Elizabeth Foxwell.

BEGBIE, HAROLD. *The Amazing Dreams of Andrew Latter*. Ashcroft, B.C., Canada: Ash-Tree Press. Six adventures of an occult detective, from *London Magazine,* 1904. Edited and introduced by Jack Adrian.

BLANC, NERO. *A Crossworder's Holiday*. New York: Berkley. Five crossword mystery stories.

BLOCK, LAWRENCE. *Enough Rope: Collected Stories*. New York: Morrow. Eighty-four stories, virtually all of Block's short fiction to date, an expanded version of *The Collected Mystery Stories*. (London, 1999) with thirteen stories added.

BLUE, J. MICHAEL. *3 Lady Blues + 12*. Mystery and Suspense/iUniverse (publication on demand). Fifteen stories, three about blues singer Lady Blue.

BOWLES, PAUL. *Collected Stories & Later Writings*. New York: Library of America. Fifty-eight stories, 1939–90, some criminous, one reprinted by *EQMM*.

BRAND, CHRISTIANNA. *The Spotted Cat and Other Mysteries from Inspector Cockill's Casebook*. Norfolk, VA: Crippen & Landru. Nine stories, one previously unpublished, and the previously unpublished three-act title play. Edited by Tony Medawar.

BURKE, JAN. *18*. Mission Viejo, CA: A.S.A.P. Publishing. Eighteen stories, some new, two fantasies. Introduction by Edward D. Hoch.

CHANDLER, RAYMOND. *Collected Stories*. New York: Everyman's Library. The first complete collection of all twenty-five stories and novelettes, including two fantasies. Introduction by John Bayley.

CHILD, CHARLES B. *The Sleuth of Baghdad: The Inspector Chafik Stories*. Norfolk, VA: Crippen & Landru. Fifteen stories from *Colliers* and *EQMM,* 1947–69, about Inspector Chafik of the Baghdad CID.

CICIARELLI, RICHARD. *Thy Brother's Blood and Other Stories*. New Concepts Publishing. Three novellas about a private eye and a blind armchair detective, sold on a diskette for reading by computer.

COHEN, STANLEY. *A Night in the Manchester Store and Other Stories*. Waterville, ME: Five Star. Fifteen stories, 1973–2000, from various sources.

COLBY, ROBERT. *The Last Witness and Other Stories*. Waterville, ME: Five Star. A full-length novel *The Deadly Desire* (1959) and four short stories.

COLLINS, MICHAEL. *Charlie Chan in the Temple of the Golden Horde*. Holicong, PA: Wildside Press. A single pastiche novella from the short-lived *Charlie Chan Mystery Magazine,* May 1974, first published under the house name of "Robert Hart Davis." (See also Pronzini and Wallman below.)

———. *Spies and Thieves, Cops and Killers, Etc.: Stories*. Waterville, ME: Five Star. Seventeen stories, 1962–99, from various sources.

DANIELS, ELIZABETH. *The Liz Reader.* Johnson City, TN: Silver Dagger Mysteries. A mixed collection containing six detective stories about Peaches Dann.

DAWSON, JANET. *Scam and Eggs: Stories*. Waterville, ME: Five Star. Ten stories, 1991–2002, three new. Includes two stories about series P.I. Jeri Howard.

DOYLE, ARTHUR CONAN. *Sherlock Holmes's Greatest Cases*. London: Orion. One of countless Holmes collections, this one contains the twelve stories from *The Adventures* plus a complete novel, *The Hound of the Baskervilles*.

———. *The Sir Arthur Conan Doyle Reader: From Sherlock Holmes to Spiritualism*. New York: Cooper Square. Novel excerpts, short stories, and nonfiction conveying the full range of Doyle's writing. Includes the first half of *A Study in Scarlet* and all of *The Poison Belt*. Edited by Jeffrey Meyers and Valerie Meyers.

DUBOIS, BRENDON. *By the Light of the Loon*. Norfolk, VA: Crippen & Landru. A single new short story in a pamphlet accompanying the limited edition of *The Dark Snow*.

———. *The Dark Snow and Other Mysteries*. Norfolk, VA: Crippen & Landru. Eleven crime tales, 1986–2000, including the Edgar-nominated title story.

———. *Tales From the Dark Woods*. Waterville, ME: Five Star. Ten stories from various sources, 1986–2001.

DUNLAP, SUSAN. *Karma and Other Stories*. Waterville, ME: Five Star. A full-length novel *Karma* (1981) and two previously collected short stories.

EVANS, FRANK HOWELL. *"Old Pawray": The London Adventures of Monsieur Jules Poiret, Late of the French Secret Service*. Shelburne, Ontario, Canada: The Battered Silicon Dispatch Box. Five stories from the *New Magazine,* 1909. Preface by Margaret Osoba, introduction by Robert Adey.

GEORGE, ELIZABETH. *I, Richard*. New York: Bantam. Five suspense stories and novelettes, one newly revised about Inspector Lynley. Each has an introduction by the author about the story's origins.

GILBERT, MICHAEL. *The Curious Conspiracy and Other Crimes*. Norfolk, VA: Crippen & Landru. Twenty previously uncollected stories, 1950–90, some about Inspectors Hazlerigg and Petrella.

———. *Old Mr. Martin: A Patrick Petrella Story.* Norfolk, VA: Crippen & Landru. A single short story from *Argosy* (UK), April 1960, accompanying the limited edition of *The Curious Conspiracy.*

GODFREY, PETER. *The Newtonian Egg and Other Cases of Rolf le Roux*. Norfolk, VA: Crippen & Landru. Ten stories, 1948–86, by the late South African writer, mainly from

EQMM but four published for the first time in the U.S. First in a series of Crippen & Landru Lost Classics.

GRAPE, JAN. *Found Dead in Texas*. Waterville, ME: Five Star. Nine stories from various sources, 1989–98, five about Austin private investigators C. J. Gunn and Jenny Gordon. Introduction by Marcia Muller.

HANSEN, JOSEPH. *Bohannon's Women*. Waterville, ME: Five Star. Six stories from mystery magazines, 1992–2000, five about California ex-sheriff Hack Bohannon.

HART, CAROLYN, *Secrets and Other Stories of Suspense*. Waterville, ME: Five Star. A novel, *A Settling of Accounts* (1976), and three short stories, 1999–2001.

HESS, JOAN. *Death of a Romance Writer and Other Stories*. Waterville, ME: Five Star. Four stories, 1988–99, and the full-length novel *The Night-Blooming Cereus* (1986) originally published under the name of "Joan Hadley."

HIGHSMITH, PATRICIA. *Nothing Meets the Eye: The Uncollected Stories of Patricia Highsmith*. New York: Norton. Twenty-eight stories, 1938–82, mainly criminous, twelve previously unpublished. Afterword by Paul Ingendaay, story notes by Anna von Planta.

HILLERMAN, TONY. *Chee's Witch*. Norfolk, VA: Crippen & Landru. First separate edition of a story from *The New Black Mask 7, 1986*, in a pamphlet for distribution at Malice Domestic XIV.

HORNSBY, WENDY. *Nine Sons: Collected Mysteries*. Norfolk, VA: Crippen & Landru. Ten stories, two new, and one article, 1991–2002, including the Edgar-winning title story.

————. *Why Vanessa Jumped*. Norfolk, VA: Crippen & Landru. A single new short-short story in a pamphlet accompanying the limited edition of *Nine Sons*.

JAMES, P. D. *Murder in Triplicate*. London: Belmont Press. A limited edition of three short stories from various sources, one about Adam Dalgliesh, with a new introduction by the author.

KIDD, A. F., & RICK KENNETT. NO. 472 *Cheyne Walk: Carnacki: The Untold Stories*. Ashcroft, B.C., Canada: Ash-Tree Press. Twelve fantasy pastiches, six new, continuing the adventures of William Hope Hodgson's occult detective.

KING, STEPHEN. *Everything's Eventual: 14 Dark Tales*. New York: Scribner. A mixed collection of horror and crime stories and novelettes, including a long tale of John Dillinger's last days.

L'AMOUR, LOUIS. *With These Hands*. New York: Bantam. A final collection of the late author's early pulp stories, mainly mystery and adventure, one western.

LEONARD, ELMORE. *When the Women Come Out to Dance*. New York: Morrow. Nine stories and novelettes, two new.

LITTLE, BENTLEY. *The Collection*. New York: Signet. Thirty-two stories, some new, mainly horror, some fantasy.

LUPOFF, RICHARD A. *One Murder at a Time: The Casebook of Lindsey & Plum*. Cosmos/ Wildside. Six stories, four about Lindsay and/or Plum, one new.

MACLEOD, CHARLOTTE. *It Was an Awful Shame and Other Stories*. Waterville, ME: Five Star. Nineteen stories, 1963–91, three previously uncollected.

MALONE, MICHAEL. *Red Clay, Blue Cadillac: Stories of 12 Southern Women*. Naperville, IL: Sourcebooks. A mixed collection of twelve stories, three new, more than half criminous, including "Red Clay," 1997 MWA Edgar winner.

————. *Christmas Spirit.* New York: The Mysterious Bookshop. A single new short story in a Christmas pamphlet for customers of a mystery bookstore.

MASTERTON, GRAHAM. *Charnel House and Other Stories.* Waterville, ME: Five Star. The title novel (1979) and three short stories, 1995–99, mainly horror-fantasy.

MORTIMER, JOHN. *Rumpole Rests His Case.* New York: Viking. Seven new legal stories.

MOSLEY, WALTER. *Six Easy Pieces: Easy Rawlins Stories.* New York: Pocket Books. Six stories, collected after first publication in the six Easy Rawlins novel reprints, September–November 2002, one story per book, plus a seventh new story.

PALMER, STUART. *Hildegarde Withers: Uncollected Riddles.* Norfolk, VA: Crippen & Landru. Eleven stories, 1933–48, mainly from *Mystery* magazine. Introduction by Jennifer Venola, the author's widow.

PARETSKY, SARA. *V.I. Times Two.* Chicago: Sara & Two C-Dogs Press. A pamphlet containing two uncollected V. I. Warshawski stories, 1996–2000.

POE, EDGAR ALLAN. *The Murders in the Rue Morgue and Other Stories.* London: Orion. One of countless Poe collections, this one contains his complete detective stories, the three Dupin tales, plus "The Gold Bug" and "Thou Art the Man."

POST, JUDITH. *Twisted in the Dark: Four Short Mysteries.* Upwey, Australia: Wormhole Books. A fifty-page chapbook of four new stories. Introduction by Edward Bryant.

PRONZINI, BILL. *All the Long Years: Western Stories.* Unity, ME: Five Star. Fourteen western stories, 1971–2000, several criminous, one from *AHMM*.

PRONZINI, BILL, & JEFFREY M. WALLMAN. *Charlie Chan in The Pawns of Death.* Holicong, PA: Wildside Press. A single pastiche novella from the short-lived *Charlie Chan Mystery Magazine*, August 1974, first published under the house name of "Robert Hart Davis." (See also Michael Collins above.)

RANKIN, IAN. *A Beggar's Banquet.* London: Orion. Twenty-one stories from various sources, seven about Inspector John Rebus.

RICE, CRAIG. *Murder, Mystery and Malone.* Norfolk, VA: Crippin & Landru. Twelve previously uncollected stories, 1947–60, ten about attorney John J. Malone and two about private eye Melville Fairr. Edited and introduced by Jeffrey A. Marks. (One of the stories, "Hard Sell," was later revealed to have been ghosted by Lawrence Block.)

ROBERTS, LES. *The Scent of Spiced Oranges and Other Stories.* Waterville, ME: Five Star. Ten stories from various sources, 1991–2000, three about his actor/detective Saxon and one about Cleveland sleuth Milan Jacovich.

SAYERS, DOROTHY L. *The Complete Stories.* New York: Perennial. All forty-four of Sayers's short stories, including twenty-one about Lord Peter Wimsey, eleven about Montague Egg, and ten non-series. Introduction by James Sandoe.

SIMENON, GEORGES. *The 13 Culprits.* Norfolk, VA: Crippen & Landru. Thirteen stories from the French magazine *Detective,* 1930, collected in a French edition in 1932 but never before in English. Translation by Peter Schulman. (The limited edition includes a pamphlet of twelve photographs from the French edition.)

SMITH, ALEXANDER MCCALL. *The No. 1 Ladies' Detective Agency.* New York: Anchor Books. A 1998 novel published for the first time in America, consisting of closely connected stories, some criminous, about Precious Ramotswe, a native woman who opens a detective agency in Botswana. It was followed by two more books about the character, closer to true novels, *Tears of the Giraffe* and *Morality for Beautiful Girls*.

THOMAS, DONALD. *Sherlock Holmes and the Voice From the Crypt, and Other Tales*. New York: Carroll & Graf. Five new novelettes in which Holmes becomes involved in actual Victorian crimes.

WEBER, KEN. *Five-Minute Mysteries*. London: Allison & Busby. Thirty-nine brief mystery puzzles.

WHITFIELD, RAOUL. *Jo Gar's Casebook*. Norfolk, VA: Crippen & Landru. All eighteen Jo Gar short stories, 1930–37, sixteen from *Black Mask*. Edited by Keith Alan Deutsch with introductory essays by E. R. Hagemann. First in a series of Tales from the Black Mask Morgue.

———. *Scotty Scouts Around*. Norfolk, VA: Crippen & Landru. A pamphlet containing a single story from *Black Mask,* April 1926, accompanying the limited edition of *Jo Gar's Casebook*.

YAFFE, JAMES. *Mom Lights a Candle*. Norfolk, VA: Crippen & Landru. A holiday pamphlet containing a new Mom story by Yaffe, for friends of the publisher.

ANTHOLOGIES

ADAMS ROUND TABLE. *Murder in the Family*. New York: Berkley. Twelve stories, all but one new, in the seventh volume of a continuing anthology series. Introduction by Mary Higgins Clark.

ASHLEY, MIKE, ED. *The Mammoth Book of Egyptian Whodunnits*. New York: Carroll & Graf. A history of Egypt from ancient times, as traced through nineteen stories, all but one new.

BLOCK, LAWRENCE, ED. *The Best American Mystery Stories 2001*. Boston: Houghton Mifflin. Twenty stories from the year 2000 in an annual collection. Series editor: Otto Penzler.

BREEN, JON L., ED. *Mystery: The Best of 2001*. New York: ibooks/Simon & Schuster. Fifteen stories from a variety of sources.

BROWNING, ABIGAIL, ED. *Murder Most Merry: 32 Christmas Crime Stories from the World's Best Mystery Writers*. New York: Gramercy Books. Stories from *EQMM* and *AHMM*, 1942–97, plus Conan Doyle's "The Blue Carbuncle."

COLLINS, MAX ALLAN, & JEFF GELB, EDS. *Flesh & Blood: Dark Desires: Erotic Tales of Crime and Passion*. New York: Mysterious Press. Eighteen stories, all but one new.

———. *Crimes of Passion*. Toronto: Worldwide. Four new novellas of love and murder.

DOUGLAS, CAROLE NELSON, ED. *White House Pet Detectives: Tales of Crime and Mystery at the White House from a Pet's Eye View*. Nashville, TN: Cumberland House. Fourteen stories about presidential pets, all but one new.

DUFFY, STELLA, & LAUREN HENDERSON, EDS. *Tart Noir*. New York: Berkley. Twenty new crime stories by women writers.

EDWARDS, MARTIN, ED. *Crime in the City*. London: The Do Not Press. Twenty-one stories, all but two new, in the annual anthology from Britain's Crime Writers Association. Foreword by Lindsey Davis.

ELLROY, JAMES, ED. *The Best American Mystery Stories 2002*. Boston: Houghton Mifflin. Twenty stories from 2001 in an annual collection. Series editor: Otto Penzler.

GEORGE, ELIZABETH, ED. *Crime from the Mind of a Woman*. London: Hodder & Stoughton. Twenty-six stories by twentieth-century women writers. Individual story notes by Jon L. Breen.

GORMAN, ED, & MARTIN H. GREENBERG, EDS. *The World's Finest Mystery and Crime Stories: Third Annual Collection*. New York: Forge. Thirty-nine stories, with reports and checklists by Jon L. Breen, Edward D. Hoch, Maxim Jakubowski, David Honeybone, Edo van Belkom, Thomas Wörtche, and George A. Easter.

GREENBERG, MARTIN, JON LELLENBERG, & DANIEL STASHOWER, EDS. *Murder, My Dear Watson: New Tales of Sherlock Holmes*. New York: Carroll & Graf. Ten new stories and three Sherlockian essays.

HEALD, TIM, ED. *Great Stories of Crime and Detection*. London: Folio Society. A four-volume set containing 104 stories, one new, with volume titles "Beginnings to 1920," "The Twenties and Thirties," "The Forties and Fifties," and "The Sixties to the Present." Individual volume introductions by H. R. F. Keating, Robert Barnard, Priscilla Ridgeway (who co-edited volumes II and III), and Tim Heald.

How Still We See Thee Lie. Toronto: Worldwide. Four original Christmas novelettes by various authors.

JAKUBOWSKI, MAXIM, ED. *The Mammoth Book of Comic Crime*. New York: Carroll & Graf. Forty-two stories, ten new.

JAKUBOWSKI, MAXIM, & M. CHRISTIAN, EDS. *The Mammoth Book of Tales from the Road*. New York: Carroll & Graf. Thirty-three stories and excerpts, all but ten new, some criminous, a few fantasy.

KRICH, ROCHELLE, MICHAEL MALLORY, & LISA SEIDMAN, EDS. *Murder on Sunset Boulevard*. Los Angeles: Top Publications. Fourteen stories by members of the L.A. chapter of Sisters in Crime.

LANE, JOEL, & STEVE BISHOP, EDS. *Birmingham Noir*. Birmingham, England: Tindal Street Press. Twenty-three new crime stories.

MCINERNY, RALPH, ED. *Murder Most Catholic: Divine Tales of Profane Crimes*. Nashville: Cumberland House. Fourteen new stories.

MCMILLAN, DENNIS, ED. *Measures of Poison*. Tucson, AZ: Dennis McMillan Publications. Twenty-four new stories written in 1930s pulp style, plus an unpublished screenplay by Howard Browne.

PENZLER, OTTO, ED. *The Mighty Johns*. Beverly Hills, CA: New Millennium Press. An anthology of fourteen new football mysteries, including the title novella by David Baldacci.

PENZLER, OTTO, & THOMAS H. COOK, EDS. *Best American Crime Writing*. New York: Vintage. Seventeen true crime stories from American magazines. Introduction by guest editor Nicholas Pileggi.

PERRY, ANNE, ED. *Much Ado About Murder*. New York: Berkley. Seventeen new stories based on Shakespeare's plays.

RANDISI, ROBERT J., ED. *First Cases, Volume 4: The Early Years of Famous Detectives*. New York: Signet. Thirteen stories, one new, in the fourth volume of the "First Cases" series.

——, ed. *Most Wanted: A Lineup of Favorite Crime Stories*. New York: Signet. Twelve past presidents of the Private Eye Writers of America choose a favorite from among their stories. Eight reprints, four new.

SLUNG, MICHELE, ED. *Stranger: Dark Tales of Eerie Encounters*. New York: HarperCollins. Twenty-two stories, five new, mainly fantasy but some criminous.

SPILLANE, MICKEY, & MAX ALLAN COLLINS, EDS. *A Century of Noir: Thirty-Two Classic Crime Stories*. New York: NAL/Putnam. Stories from various sources, 1933–99.

STABENOW, DANA, ED. *The Mysterious North*. New York: Signet. A dozen new crime stories set in Alaska.

TREVANIAN, ED. *Death Dance: Suspenseful Stories of the Dance Macabre*. Nashville, TN: Cumberland House. Fourteen stories, twelve new, in an anthology from the International Association of Crime Writers.

TUCKER, FENDER, ED. *Fakealoo! Pastiches of Harry Stephen Keeler's Inimitable Style Taken from the Keeler News*. www.ramblehouse.bigstep.com: Ramble House. Eight pastiches from a fanzine edited by Richard Polt.

Unveiled. Toronto: Harlequin. Three new novellas of romantic suspense.

NONFICTION

ASHLEY, MIKE. *Algernon Blackwood: An Extraordinary Life*. New York: Carroll & Graf. A biography of the fantasy writer and creator of occult detective John Silence.

————. *The Mammoth Encyclopedia of Modern Crime Fiction*. New York: Carroll & Graf. Some five hundred detailed entries on mystery writers from the 1950s to the present, plus sections on television series, films, award winners, and mystery magazines. Indexed by key characters and series.

BARNES, ALAN. *Sherlock Holmes on Screen*. North Pomfret, VT: Trafalgar Square Books. A guide to film and television versions of Holmes in all languages.

BARNETT, COLLEEN. *Mystery Women: An Encyclopedia of Leading Women Characters in Mystery Fiction, Vol. 2 (1980–1989)*. Scottsdale, AZ: Poisoned Pen Press. A continuation of a reference work first published in 2001.

BEAHM, GEORGE. *The Unofficial Patricia Cornwell Companion*. New York: St. Martin's. The life and works of the creator of Kay Scarpetta.

BISHOP, DAVID. *The Complete Inspector Morse*. Richmond, Surrey, UK: Reynolds & Hearn. A guide to Colin Dexter's novels and television adaptations.

BOUCHER, ANTHONY. *The Anthony Boucher Chronicles: Reviews and Commentary 1942–1947. Volume II: The Week in Murder*. Shreveport, LA: Ramble House. Boucher's review columns from the San Francisco Chronicle, edited by Francis M. Nevins.

————. *The Anthony Boucher Chronicles: Reviews and Commentary 1942–1947. Volume III: A Bookman's Buffet*. Shreveport, LA: Ramble House. Miscellaneous reviews by Boucher, edited by Francis M. Nevins.

CAMPBELL, MARK. *The Pocket Essential Sherlock Holmes*. North Pomfret, VT: Trafalgar Square Books. A brief guide to all the novels and stories, with an essay on parodies and pastiches, and a directory of actors who have played Holmes.

CLARK, MARY HIGGINS. *Kitchen Privileges: A Memoir*. New York: Simon & Schuster. A memoir, with photos, from the author of twenty-seven bestselling mysteries.

EARWAKER, JULIAN, & KATHLEEN BECKER. *Scene of the Crime*. England: Aurum. A guide to the landscapes of British detective fiction. Introduction by P. D. James.

FEASTER, SHARON A. *The Cat Who . . . Companion.* New York: Berkley. Revised third edition of a guide to Lilian Jackson Braun's mystery series, including an interview with Braun.

GRAFTON, SUE, WITH JAN BURKE & BARRY ZEMAN, EDS. *Writing Mysteries: A Handbook by the Mystery Writers of America,* second edition. Cincinnati, OH: Writer's Digest Books. Revised and expanded from the 1992 edition.

HAINING, PETER. *The Classic Era of Crime Fiction.* Chicago: Chicago Review Press. An illustrated history of crime fiction, from Poe to John le Carré.

HAUT, WOODY. *Heartbreak and Vine: The Fate of Hardboiled Writers in Hollywood.* England: Serpent's Tail. A study of the experiences of twenty-nine crime writers in Hollywood.

HUANG, JIM, ED. *They Died in Vain: Overlooked, Underappreciated and Forgotten Mystery Novels.* Carmel, IN: Crum Creek Press. Brief essays by booksellers, writers, and editors recommending 103 mystery novels, 1878–2000.

KRAFT, JEFF, & AARON LEVENTHAL. *Footsteps in the Fog: Alfred Hitchcock's San Francisco.* Santa Monica, CA: Santa Monica Press. An illustrated guide to the city's sights as used in Hitchcock films.

MALLING, SUSAN, & BARBARA PETERS, EDS. *AZ Murder Goes . . . Professional.* Scottsdale, AZ: The Poisoned Pen Press. Revised edition of a 1998 collection of papers from the previous year's Scottsdale conference on mystery writing.

MARKS, JEFFREY. *Intent to Sell: Marketing the Genre Novel.* Vancouver, WA: Deadly Alibi. Tips for writers, by the novelist and biographer of Craig Rice.

MORRELL, DAVID. *Lessons from a Lifetime of Writing: A Novelist Looks at His Craft.* Cincinnati: F&W Publications. Helpful information from the author of *First Blood* and sixteen other thrillers.

MULLER, EDDIE. *The Art of Noir.* New York: Overlook Press. Posters and graphics, with commentary, from the era of film noir.

MURPHY, STEPHEN M., ED. *Their Word Is Law: Bestselling Lawyer-Novelists Talk About Their Craft.* New York: Berkley. Interviews with thirty-one lawyer-novelists, first published in San Francisco Attorney, 1988–2000. Introduction by Steve Martini.

NEVINS, FRANCIS M., & MARTIN GRAMS, JR. *The Sound of Detection: Ellery Queen's Adventures in Radio.* Churchville, MD: OTR Publishing. A revised and expanded edition, more than twice as long as the original 1983 book, with new information on Anthony Boucher's contributions to the Queen radio show.

PENZLER, OTTO. *Rex Stout's Nero Wolfe, Part I.* New York: The Mysterious Bookshop. A booklet for collectors, containing a descriptive bibliography and price guide, covering the series from 1934 to 1955.

———. *Rex Stout's Nero Wolfe, Part II.* New York: The Mysterious Bookshop. A continuation of the above bibliography and price guide, covering the remaining books through 1977.

SERVER, LEE. *Encyclopedia of Pulp Fiction Writers.* New York: Checkmark. Entries on more than two hundred pulp and mass market writers, mainly in the mystery field.

SOTER, TOM. *Investigating Couples: A Critical Analysis of The Thin Man, The Avengers and The X-Files.* Jefferson, NC: McFarland & Co. Analysis and background information on three popular television series.

TERRACE, VINCENT. *Crime Fighting Heroes of Television: Over 10,000 Facts from 151 Shows, 1949–2001.* Jefferson, NC: McFarland & Co. Alphabetical entries plus an index of performers.

TUCKER, FENDER, ED. *A to Izzard: A Harry Stephen Keeler Companion.* Shreveport, LA: Ramble House. Ten essays about Keeler and his screwball mysteries, with seven stories and articles by Keeler, four pastiches by other writers, and a bibliography of Keeler's work.

OBITUARIES

DOUGLAS ANGUS (1909–2002). Author of a single suspense novel, *Death on Jerusalem Road* (1963).

EDWARD L. BEACH (1919–2002). His writing about submarines includes a single suspense novel, *Cold Is the Sea* (1978).

MILDRED BENSON (1905–2002). Writer for the *Stratemeyer Syndicate,* best known for having written the earliest Nancy Drew books, twenty-three of the first thirty titles beginning with *The Secret of the Old Clock* (1930) under the house name of "Carolyn Keene."

LLOYD BIGGLE, JR. (1923–2002). Founding secretary/treasurer of the Science Fiction Writers of America, whose work included twelve mystery novels (1963–94), five set in the future and two others featuring Sherlock Holmes. His Grandfather Rastin series appeared in *EQMM,* and a series of Victorian mysteries ran in *Alfred Hitchcock's Mystery Magazine.*

JANIE BOLITHO (c. 1950–2002). British author of at least eight novels about Inspector Ian Roper, starting with *Kindness Can Kill* (1993), and at least three about painter and photographer Rose Trevelyan, starting with *Snapped in Cornwell* (1997).

MALCOLM BOSSE (1926–2002). Historical novelist whose work included three suspense novels, notably *The Man Who Loved Zoos* (1974).

DAN BRENNAN (1917–2002). Journalist and press secretary to Hubert Humphrey, author of twenty-five paperback novels, eight of them criminous, 1961–77.

DEE BROWN (1908–2002). Well-known western historian and novelist who published a single suspense novel, *They Went Thataway* (1960).

LOUIS A. CAMPANOZZI (c. 1943–2002). Retired Rochester, New York, policeman who authored two mystery novels, *The Killing Cards* (2000) and *Ground Lions* (2001).

PATRICIA CARLON (1927–2002). Australian author of fourteen mystery novels between 1961 and 1970, many unpublished in America.

ALIXE CARTER (1912–2002). Canadian author of two mysteries, 1979–89, featuring Sergeant Mark Baldwin.

CURTIS W. CASEWIT (1922–2002). Author of a single suspense novel, *Accent on Treason* (1966), and contributor to *Mike Shayne Mystery Magazine, Mystery Digest,* and other publications.

R(ONALD) V(ERLIN) CASSILL (1919–2002). Mainstream novelist who wrote seven paperback crime novels, 1954–59, as well as the hardcover *Doctor Cobb's Game* (1970).

DAVID CHARNAY (1912–2002). Television executive who wrote a political thriller, *Target 1600* (1980).

R. CHETWYND-HAYES (1919–2001). British author of seven thrillers and a short-story collection, *Terror by Night* (1974).

CHARLES BAXTER CLEMENT (1940–2002). Author of a single suspense novel, *Limit Bid! Limit Bid!* (1986).

DAVID C. COOKE (1917–2000). Original editor of *Best Detective Stories of the Year, 1947–60,* and author of four suspense novels, 1967–70.

GWEN DAVENPORT (1910–2002). Mainstream novelist, contributor to *EQMM* and coauthor with Gustav J. Breuer of a single suspense novel, *A Stranger and Afraid* (1943), under the pseudonym of Michael Hardt.

GEORGE ALEC EFFINGER (1947–2002). Science fiction writer who penned six suspense novels, one in collaboration with Gardner Dozois. At least four had futuristic settings, notably *When Gravity Falls* (1987).

MICHAEL ERLANGER (1915–2002). Author of a single suspense novel, *Mindy Lindy May Surprise* (1969).

TIMOTHY FINDLEY (1930–2002). Mainstream Canadian author of twelve novels and three plays, including five novels and one play in the mystery-suspense genre, notably *The Telling of Lies* (1988), MWA Edgar winner for best paperback novel.

THOMAS FLANAGAN (1923–2002). Historical novelist who contributed seven stories to *EQMM,* 1949–58, including the first prize winner in the magazine's 1951 contest.

ROBERT L. FORWARD (1932–2002). Well-known science fiction writer who published a single suspense novel *The Owl* (1984).

LEONARD GERSHE (1922–2002). Playwright whose work included a single suspense drama, *Miss Pell Is Missing* (1963).

BARTHOLOMEW GILL (1943–2002). Pseudonym of columnist Mark McGarrity, author of some fourteen mysteries about Irish detective Peter McGarr, notably the Edgar-nominated *The Death of a Joyce Scholar* (1989). He also published two suspense novels under his own name.

ROBERT GILLESPIE (1917–2000). Author of eight suspense novels, 1979–90.

GORDON GORDON (1906–2002). With his late wife, Mildred, he produced eighteen novels as "The Gordons," notably *Campaign Train* (1952), *Operation Terror* (1961), and *Undercover Cat* (1963). In a final 1983 novel he collaborated with Mary Dorr.

WILFRED GREATOREX (1922–2002). Author and screenwriter whose work included four mysteries, 1976–90.

RICHARD GRENIER (1933–2002). Washington journalist who wrote a single suspense novel, *The Marrakesh One-Two* (1983).

VIRGINIA HAMILTON (1936–2002). Well-known African-American children's writer, winner of the 1969 Edgar for best juvenile novel, *The House of Dies Drear.*

MARILYN HARRIS (1931–2002). Author of two suspense novels, 1974–76.

ISABELLE HOLLAND (1920–2002). Author of teenage novels who also published eighteen Gothic mystery novels, 1967–89.

JAMES A. HOWARD (1922–2000). Author of nine suspense novels, 1954–81, plus one under the pseudonym of Laine Fisher.

ROY HUGGINS (1914–2002). Well-known television and screenwriter who published three mystery novels, notably *The Double Take* (1946), and a collection of three locked-room novelettes, *77 Sunset Strip* (1959), the basis of his scripts for that series.

LAURENCE M. JANIFER (1933–2002). Science fiction writer who published three mystery novels and a story collection, *Knave and the Game* (1987), as well as two novels under his original name of Larry M. Harris, one of which, *The Pickled Poodles* (1960), continued Craig Rice's John J. Malone series. He also collaborated with Randall Garrett as "Mark Phillips" for three paperback novels about a telepathic spy.

CATHLEEN JORDAN (1941–2002). Editor of *Alfred Hitchcock's Mystery Magazine* for the past twenty years and author of a single mystery novel, *A Carol in the Dark* (1984). Posthumous recipient of MWA's Ellery Queen Award.

LAWRENCE KAMARCK (1927–2001). Author of four suspense novels, 1968–79.

AUSTEN KARK (1926–2002). Husband of British author Nina Bawden who published his first novel, the thriller *The Forwarding Agent* in 1999.

DAMON KNIGHT (1922–2002). Well-known science fiction author who published two mystery short stories in the 1950s.

FREDERICK KNOTT (1916–2002). Well-known playwright, Edgar-winning author of *Dial M for Murder* (1953), *Wait Until Dark* (1967), and other suspense plays.

OLIVER KNOX (1923–2002). Nephew of Monsignor Ronald Knox who published a single mystery, *Asylum,* in 1977.

VINCE KOHLER (1948–2002) Journalist and mystery reviewer who published four novels about reporter Eldon Larkin, starting with *Rainy North Woods* (1990).

ROBERT W. LENSKI (1926–2002). Winner of the 1979 television Edgar for his adaptation of Hammett's "The Dain Curse."

FRANCO LUCENTINI (1920–2002). Prolific Italian thriller writer whose collaboration with C. Fruttero, *The Sunday Woman,* was published in the United States in 1973.

WALLACE MARKFIELD (1926–2002). Mainstream author of a single suspense novel, *Radical Surgery* (1991).

JOHN McGRATH (1935–2002). Author of a 1973 suspense play, *Bakke's Night of Fame,* as well as the screenplay for Len Deighton's "The Billion Dollar Brain" (1966).

JAMES MITCHELL (1926–2002). British author of eighteen espionage and suspense novels under his own name, 1957–93, plus four others under the pseudonym of "James Munro."

B(ETTY) J(ANE) MORISON (1924–2001). Author of five novels about Elizabeth Lamb Worthington, set in Maine, starting with *Champagne and a Gardener* (1983).

DOUGLAS MUIR (190?–2002). Movie and television director who published four thrillers, 1985–89.

JOHN MIDDLETON MURRY (1926–2002). British author who published science fiction and a single suspense novel, *Shades of Darkness* (1986), under the name "Richard Cowper."

IAN NIALL (1916–2002). Pseudonym of John McNeillie, author of two mysteries, notably *No Resting Place* (1948).

HELEN NIELSEN (1918–2002). Author of eighteen mystery novels, 1951–76, notably *Obit Delayed* (1952), as well as numerous television scripts and stories in *EQMM, AHMM,* and elsewhere.

VIRGINIA NIELSEN (1909–2000). Author of two romantic suspense novels, 1961–62.

JOEL OLIANSKY (1935–2002). Television writer and 1974 MWA Edgar winner for the TV film *The Law.*

JACK OLSEN (1925–2002). Author of five suspense novels, 1976–82, and winner of the MWA Edgar Award for his 1989 true crime book, *Doc: The Rape of the Town of Lovell.*

LOUIS OWENS (1948–2002) Writer of fiction and nonfiction about Native Americans, who authored four mysteries starting with *Wolfsong* (1991).

LOIS PAXTON (1916–2002). Best-known pseudonym of Lois Dorothea Low, British author of three novels as Paxton, three as Zoe Cass, notably *The Silver Leopard* (1976), and six as Dorothy Mackie Low.

JOHN LEONARD PIERCE, JR. (1921–2002). Under the pseudonym of John Bramlett, he authored two paperback mysteries, 1960–67.

ERNEST PINTOFF (1931–2002). Author of a single suspense novel, *Zachary* (1990).

BARRY C. REED (1927–2002). Trial lawyer who authored a number of novels, notably *The Verdict* (1980).

REGINALD ROSE (1920–2002). Noted television writer, best known for his jury room drama *Twelve Angry Men* (1955).

ALVIN SAPINSLEY, JR. (1921–2002). Winner of the 1956 television Edgar for *A Taste of Honey.*

WILLIAM A. S. SARJEANT (1935–2002). Geologist and fantasy writer who wrote a number of Sherlockian articles and coauthored *Ms. Holmes of Baker Street* (1989).

CHARLES SHEFFIELD (c. 1935–2002). Well-known science fiction author and former president of SFWA, who published a collection of historical mystery novelettes, *Erasmus Magister* (1982), and a collaborative suspense novel, *The Judas Cross* (1994), as well as short stories in *AHMM* and elsewhere.

HENRY SLESAR (1927–2002). Well-known television writer who published seven novels starting with his MWA Edgar winner, *The Gray Flannel Shroud* (1959), and nearly five hundred short stories, many in *AHMM* and *EQMM*. He contributed several stories to *The Alfred Hitchcock Show* and nineteen were collected as *Death on Television* (1989). Slesar won a second Edgar for his daytime TV drama series *The Edge of Night* (1981). More than two-dozen of his early short stories appeared under the pseudonym "O. H. Leslie," one in collaboration with Jay Folb. A collaboration with Harlan Ellison appeared as by "Sley Harson."

JERRY SOHL (1913–2001). Science fiction writer who wrote five suspense novels, notably the futuristic *The Altered Ego* (1954). He also published a film novelization as "Sean Mei Sullivan" and other novels as "Nathan Butler."

JOHN SPENCER (1944–2002). British author of six mystery novels, 1984–2003, two about Charlie Case.

RAYMOND STEIBER (1938–2001). Author of two mystery novels, plus more than a dozen stories in *EQMM*. Posthumous Edgar winner.

JESS STERN (c. 1914–2002). Journalist who wrote on occult subjects and published a single crime novel, *The Reporter* (1970).

J. LEE THOMPSON (1914–2002). Well-known movie director who published a single mystery play, *Murder Without Crime* (1943).

PETER TINNISWOOD (1936–2002). Author of a single suspense novel, *Shemerelda* (1981), published in England.

FRED S. TOBEY (1908–2001). Short story writer who published a single collection, *Never Hit a Lady* (1984).

DAVE VAN ARNAM (1935–2002). Collaborator, with Ted White, on a single suspense novel, *Sideslip* (1968).

ROBERT VAN SCOYK (1928–2002). Television writer and producer of the CBS series *Murder, She Wrote* and several others. His first story won a prize in *EQMM*'s 1957 contest, and he won the 1979 MWA Edgar Award for an episode of *Columbo*.

MARGOT WADLEY (1936–2001). Author of a single novel, *The Gripping Beast* (2001), winner of the St. Martin's Press Malice Domestic Contest in 2000.

JOHN WEITZ (1923–2002). Well-known fashion designer who authored several histories and novels including one suspense title, *Friends in High Places* (1982).

MARY WESLEY (1910–2002). Popular British author whose novels include a futuristic mystery, *The Sixth Seal* (1969).

CHERRY WILDER (1930–2002). Publication name of Cherry Wilder Grimm, New Zealand science fiction author who published one crime novel, *Cruel Designs* (1988).

MARITA WOLFF (1918–2002). Mainstream author whose brief career included a best-selling crime novel, *Whistle Stop* (1941), filmed in 1946.

World Mystery Report: Great Britain

Maxim Jakubowski

It was a year in which, for the second time in a row, a foreign novel in translation won the coveted Crime Writers' Association Gold Dagger award, when, to much surprise (even to the CWA press liaison officer who actually misspelled the Cuban author's name in the immediate press release, as well as ascribing Spanish nationality to him), Jose Carlos Somoza's *The Athenian Murders* scooped the prize. Last year, of course, the award was won by Swedish writer Henning Mankell. Does this mean that the parochial world of Anglo-Saxon mystery writing is changing? Maybe. In fact, a remarkable number of crime novels in translation did make their appearance on British and American lists, usually to solid critical acclaim.

Although there was sadness that Harvill Press, Mankell's British publishers and one of the most admirable British literary independent houses, lost their autonomy, their buyout by Random House benefited the marketing efforts behind Mankell's ensuing promotion and saw him skirt the lower reaches of the bestselling lists. Elsewhere, the other independents involved in crime and mystery writing had a tough time, with distribution problematic and a lack of financial resources. No Exit Press cut their output rather considerably, cutting short their previous efforts to impose new British and American voices. Jim Driver's hardy The Do-Not Press continued to expand the readership base of their main authors: Bill James, Jerry Raine, Russell James, Paul Charles, Carol Ann Davis, and myself, and took on the annual CWA anthology, helmed by Martin Edwards. Arcadia published Nicolas Freeling and translations, while Serpent's Tail had relative success with Danny King's Burglar series and the final installment of David Peace's final volume in his ferocious Red Riding Quartet (only for the author to move on to established house Faber & Faber, just as he was selected for the prestigious new Granta list of Best British Writers Under 40!). Meanwhile, Allison & Busby became the refuge of all the esteemed British mid-list authors who were systematically being dropped by the larger companies and conglomerates for lack of mega-sales: Robert Barnard, Roy Lewis, Edward Marston, Joyce Holmes, Jonathan Gash, etc. . . . .

With the big boys, Orion still leads the pack with the success of Ian Rankin and their many U.S. buy-ins (Connelly, Pelecanos, Burke, Hoag), and are cultivating the development of Graham Hurley, Caroline Carver, Sarah Diamond, Laura Wilson, and other home-grown talent. But the manifold attraction of mystery writing means that all major houses have a solid crime list and are regularly taking chances on new talent, even if the survival quota of writers who don't score immediate hits is dicey and too quickly dictated by sales figures and marketing imperatives.

The Silver Dagger this year, runner-up to Somoza's intriguing blend of historical and meta-sleuthing with a clever dash of philosophy, went to James Crumley's *The Final Country*. Two other Brits made the shortlist: Minette Walters for *Acid Row,* and ex–stand-up comedian Mark Billingham's second psycho thriller, *Scaredy Cat* (his debut effort, *Sleepyhead,* achieved impressive sales in paperback and marks him as an important voice for the future). The John Creasey Memorial Dagger for best first novel went to Scottish author Louise Welch's gritty *The Cutting Room* (from independent Scottish publisher Canongate, who are slowly growing a good crime list, albeit with U.S., Australian, and New Zealand talent so far). Shortlisted for the same award were Alan Glynn's thriller, *The Dark Fields,* and Jim Kelly's *The Water Clock.* The CWA Macallan Short Story Dagger was lifted by Stella Duffy for her story "Martha Grace," from the ladies of determined noir anthology, *Tart Noir,* which she coedited with Lauren Henderson. The Ellis Peters Historical Dagger went to Sarah Waters for her romp, *Fingersmith,* which also made it onto the shortlist of the Booker Prize, and the new Fleming Thriller Dagger was won by John Creed (a pseudonym for Irish author Eoin McNamee) for *The Sirius Crossing.* Earlier in the year Sara Paretsky won the Cartier Diamond Dagger for lifetime achievement, and the Dagger in the Library, the more populist of the awards, deservedly went to Peter Robinson, who has enjoyed enormous commercial success after a decade or so of knocking at the door of an assortment of publishers, thanks to concerted support from Pan Macmillan.

On the social side, the year's Crime Scene literary and film festival had its third year at London's National Film Theatre, an event and celebration of crime that keeps on steadily growing. With a focus on Sherlock Holmes and Richard Widmark as film guest of honor, the three days' event saw the crème de la crème of British crime writing debate, meet, and perform in three of the NFT's auditoriums, with sterling appearances by Anne Perry, Martina Cole, John Connolly, Robert Barnard, Nicci French, Tony Strong, Jane Jakeman, Mark Timlin, Minette Walters, Fidelis Morgan, Stephen Booth, Lindsey Davis, Sarah Strohmeyer, Gary Phillips, and fifty or so others. The 2003 edition of Crime Scene is already set and will take place July 10–13, with the annual focus this year on Georges Simenon (whose centennial it is) and American guests to include Janet Evanovich, Walter Mosley, and Elizabeth Peters. In addition, Peter Robinson is also expected, together with the majority of British crime writers. *Sherlock Magazine* will also give out its annual awards at Crime Scene. Dead on Deansgate had another edition but with the CWA no longer involved, the event was on a smaller scale and within the walls of Waterstone's Manchester store.

Like any year, we lost some good people: Ronald Chetwynd-Hayes, Janie Bolitho, James Mitchell, Richard Cowper, John B. Spencer, and bookseller Mike Hart all took their last bow.

Despite a sluggish book market, there was as ever a plethora of books to read and choose from, which brings me to my inevitable list-making, which, I hope, offers an abbreviated X ray of the British crime and mystery scene in 2002. To reiterate that the following overview is a selective one will only serve to emphasize the robust strength of crime and mystery writing in Britain, despite the many problems that publishing and mid-list authors keep on encountering. But then for every writer who somehow disappears from sight, a handful of new ones appears from left of field when you least expect them. And so it should always be.

Books by some authors are always eagerly expected and the following did not fail their fans: Catherine Aird (*Amendment of Life*), Mark Billingham (*Scaredy Cat*), Simon Brett (*The Torso in the Town*), Christopher Brookmyre (*The Sacred Art of Stealing*), Lee Child, a British author if resident in the U.S.A. and situating his books there. (*Without Fail*), Martina Cole (*Maura's Game*), John Connolly (*The White Road*, the third in the U.S.-based Charlie Parker dark thrillers), Lindsey Davis (*The Jupiter Myth*, the annual Falco Roman adventure), Michael Dibdin (*And Then You Die*, marking the return of his Italian cop protagonist Inspector Aurelio Zen), Paul Doherty (*Domina; The Godless Man; A Haunt of Murder; The Plague Lord*, as prolific as ever . . .), Ben Elton (*Dead Famous*, a mischievous murder mystery on a reality TV program set by a notorious Brit comedian), Nicolas Freeling (*The Janeites*), Jonathan Gash (*Bone Dancing*), Reginald Hill (*Death's Jest Book*, with his familiar Dalziel and Pascoe duo), H. R. F. Keating (*Detective Under Fire*), Lynda La Plante (*Royal Flush*), Peter Lovesey (*Diamond Dust*), Michael Marshall (*The Straw Men*, a powerful U.S.-set thriller by speculative master Michael Marshall Smith), Denise Mina (*Sanctum*), Iain Pears (*The Dream of Scipio*), Anne Perry (*Southampton Row; Death of a Stranger*), Ian Rankin (*Resurrection Men*, the new Rebus), Ruth Rendell (*The Babes in the Wood*), Peter Robinson (*Aftermath*, the breakthrough book for Inspector Banks), Barbara Vine (*The Blood Doctor*), Jill Paton Walsh and Dorothy L. Sayers (*Presumption of Death*, inspired by Sayers notes and featuring Wimsey and Harriet), and Minette Walters (*Fox Evil*).

But there is a horde of talent and thrills and spills biting at the ankles of the A-list, and the following writers also published new titles in 2002. Jane Adams (*Angel Eyes; Mourning the Little Dead*), Andrew Arden (*The Programme*), Campbell Armstrong (*Last Darkness*), Vivien Armstrong (*Beyond the Pale; Smile Now, Die Later*), Jeffry Ashford (*Truthful Injustice*), Andrea Badenoch (*Loving Geordie*), John Baker (*The Meanest Flood*), Jo Bannister (*True Witness*), Colin Bateman (*Horse with No Name*), Pauline Bell (*A Swansong*), Nicholas Blincoe (*White Mice*), Janie Bolitho (*Killed in Cornwall; Lessons in Logic; The Slaughterhouse*), Michael Bond (*Monsieur Pamplemouse on Vacation*, the return of a popular series), Hilary Bonner (*A Moment of Madness*), Stephen Booth (*Blood on the Tongue*), David Bowker (*Rawhead*), Ken Bruen (*The Killing of the Tinkers; Blitz*), Gwendoline Butler (*Coffin Knows the Answer*), Paul Charles (*I've Heard the Banshees Singing*), Alys Clare (*The Faithful Dead*), Jon Cleary (*Easy Sin*), Barbara Cleverly (*Ragtime in Simla*), Neil Cross (*Holloway Falls*), Clare Curzon (*Dangerous Practice; Body of a*

Woman), Judith Cutler (*Dying in Discord; Hidden Power*), Eileen Dewhurst (*No Love Lost; Easeful Death*), Maureen Duffy (*Hanging Matter*), Alan Dunn (*Payback*), Marjorie Eccles (*Killing a Unicorn*), Martin Edwards (*Take My Breath Away*), Kate Ellis (*Painted Doom*), Ron Ellis (*Singleshot*), John Francome (*Inside Track*), Anthea Fraser (*Fathers and Daughters*), Philip Gooden (*The Ion*), Paula Gosling (*Ricochet*), Anne Granger (*A Restless Evil*), Susanna Gregory Pale Compan (*Summer of Discontent*), Christine Green (*Deadly Echo*), J. M. Gregson (*A Little Learning; Death on the Eleventh Hole*), Jeff Gulvin (*The Procession*), Patricia Hall (*Death in Dark Waters*), Gerald Hammond (*Grail for Sale*), Victor Headley (*Seven Seals, Seven Days*), Juliet Hebden (*Peland and the Nickname Game*), Veronica Heley (*Murder by Suicide*), Joanna Hines (*Surface Tension*), Hazel Holt (*Leonora*), Lesley Horton (*Snares of Guilt*), Graham Hurley (*Angels Passing*), Graham Ison (*Working Girl*), Jane Jakeman (*In the Kingdom of Mists*), Maxim Jakubowski (*Kiss Me Sadly*), Bill James (*Double Jeopardy; Middle Man; Naked at the Window*), Russell James (*Pick Any Title*), Quintin Jardine (*Head Shot; Poisoned Cherries*), Michael Jecks (*The Devil's Acolyte; The Mad Monk of Gidleigh*), Roderic Jeffries (*Seeing Is Deceiving; An Intriguing Murder*), Paul Johnston (*A Deeper Shade of Blue*, a new Greek set series), Susan Kelly (*Little Girl Lost*), Alanna Knight (*Dangerous Pursuits*), Bernard Knight (*The Grim Reaper*), Deryn Lake (*Death at St. James's Palace*), Janet Laurence (*Canaletto and the Case of Bonnie Prince Charles*), Caroline Lawrence (*The Pirates of Pompeii; Assassins of Rome*, a young adult Roman historical series with a growing following), John Lawton (*Sweet Sunday*), Roy Lewis (*Ways Of Death; Phantom*), Gillian Linscott (*Dead Man Riding; The Garden*), Gaye Longworth (*Dead Alone*), Phil Lovesey (*The Screaming Tree*), Lury and Gibson (*Blood Data*), Jim Lusby (*Serial*), Barry Maitland (*Babel*), Jessica Mann (*A Voice from the Grave*), John McCabe (*Big Spender*), Ken McClure (*Wildcard*), Marianne Macdonald (*Die Once*), Jill McGown (*Births, Deaths and Marriages*), Bob Marshall–Andrews (*Man Without Guilt*), Andrew Martin (*The Necropolis Railway*), J. Wallis Martin (*Dancing with the Uninvited Guest*), Priscilla Masters (*Disturbing Ground*), Gwen Moffatt (*Retribution*), Fidelis Morgan (*The Ambitious Stepmother*), J. M. Morris (*Fiddleback*, a crime debut for horror writer Mark Morris), Fiona Mountain (*Pale as the Dead*), Margaret Murphy (*Darkness Falls*), Barbara Nadel (*Deep Waters*), Hilary Norman (*Twisted Minds*), Maureen O'Brien (*Unauthorised Departure*), Gemma O'Connor (*Following the Wake*), Pat O'Keeffe (*Burn Out*), Nick Oldham (*Substantial Threat*), Stuart Pawson (*The Laughing Boy*), Jenny Pitman (*Double Deal*), Julian Rathbone (*A Very English Agent*), Danuta Reah (*Bleak Water*), Mike Ripley (*Angel Underground; Double Take*), Barrie Roberts (*Crowner and Justice*), David Roberts (*Hollow Crown*), Rosemary Rowe (*The Chariots of Calyx*), Denise Ryan (*Betrayed*), David Scarrow (*When the Eagle Hunts*), Kate Sedley (*The Lammas Feast*), Zoe Sharp (*Riot Act*), Simon Shaw (*Selling Grace*), Carol Smith (*Grandmother's Footsteps*), Sally Spedding (*Cloven*), Sally Spencer (*Red Herring; Death of an Innocent*), Cath Staincliffe (*Towers of Silence*), Veronica Stallwood (*Oxford Proof*), Marilyn Todd (*Dreamboat; Dark*

Horse), Peter Tonkin (*One Head Too Many*), Rebecca Tope (*Sting of Death*), Peter Tremayne (*The Haunted Abbott*), M. J. Trow (*Maxwell's Match*), Peter Turnbull (*After The Flood; Dark Secrets*), Gillian White (*Devil's Spawn; Refuge*), David Williams (*Unholy Writ*), Derek Wilson (*Tripletree*), David Wishart (*White Murder*), and Elizabeth Woodcraft (*Babyface*).

Among a crowded group of newcomers the following stood out, although only the future will be able to confirm their staying power. In the meantime, their debut efforts found a grateful audience. Michelle Berry (*Blur*), Stephen Burgen (*Walking the Lions*), Sean Burke (*Deadwater*), Vivian Chern (*Homicidal Intent*), Jonathan Davies (*The Bird Table*), Meg Gardiner (*China Lake,*) an impressive first outing by a Britain-based U.S. debutante), Janet Gleeson (*The Grenadillo Box,* a striking historical novel by an acclaimed nonfiction author), Alex Gray (*Never Somewhere Else*), Mandasue Heller (*The Front*), Philip Jolowicz (*Towers of Silence,* heavily hyped thriller that I found morally ambiguous to a tee), Simon Kernick (*The Business of Dying,* a delectable slice of London noir that should have won the Creasey Dagger, in my opinion), David Lawrence (*The Dead Sit Down in a Ring*), Ed O'Connor (*The Yeare's Midnight*), William Rhode (*Paperback Raita*), Christian Thompson (*That Which Does Not Kill You*), Louise Welch (*The Cutting Room*), and John Hartley Williams (*Mystery in Spiderville*).

With echoes of the Cold War disappearing faster by the day, most thriller authors are essaying new grounds or seeking for the truth behind past headlines. Notable were Ted Allbeury (*The Networks*), Geoffrey Archer (*The Burma Legacy*), Michael Asher (*Rare Earth*), Murray Davies (*The Devil's Handshake*), Michael Dobbs (*At the Right Hand*), Daniel Easterman (*Maroc*), Paul Eddy (*Mandrake,* the second Grace Flint adventure), Clive Egleton (*Cry Havoc*), Giles Foden (*Zanzibar*), Brian Freemantle (*Ice Age; The Watchmen*), John Gardner (*Bottled Spider; Day of Absolution*), Jack Higgins (*Midnight Runner*), Peter May (*Snakehead*), Glenn Meade (*Resurrection Day*), David Michie (*Expiry Date*), James Mitchell (*Bonfire Night*), Chris Petit (*The Human Pool*), and Michael Shea (*Endgame*).

On the magazine and anthology front, *Crime Time* changed formula and size again but still appears regularly, each issue focusing on a specific author or theme and still offers much in the way of columns, interviews, and informed reviews, and no longer features fiction, but *Shot* fell by the wayside and only survives online. *Crime Wave* continues, if irregularly, but with a high quality of short stories. *CADS* survives on the amateur but critical front, with its wonderful emphasis on Golden Age crime and fervent readers' letters. There were few anthologies during the course of the year, but those that made their way to the light all had some wonderful material. They were Stella Duffy and Lauren Henderson's *Tart Noir,* Martin Edwards's *Crime in the City,* Joel Lane's *Birmingham Noir,* and my own *Mammoth Book of Comic Crime* and *Mammoth Book of On The Road* (not all criminous but drawing some fine stories from within the field). Single-author collections were also few and far between, for sadly commercial reasons, and were limited to Michael Gilbert's *The Curious Conspiracy,* John Harvey's revised version of *Now's the Time,* Peter Lovesey's *The Sedgemoor Strangler,* John Mortimer's *Rumpole Rests His Case,* and Ian Rankin's *Beggars Banquet.*

A good vintage, methinks.

World Mystery Report: Canada

Edo van Belkom

2002 was a rocky year for Canadian crime and mystery, with the first blow coming early in the year with the bankruptcy of General Distribution. General's downfall left many small publishers (and a few big ones) tottering on the verge of bankruptcy themselves, being owed tens-of-thousands of dollars by what had been one of the largest books distributors in the country. But small publishers in Canada (as they do all over the world) soldiered on, producing many of the year's award-winning works of mystery.

The ceremony for top prize in Canadian crime-writing, the Arthur Ellis Awards, was held in Toronto on June 12, while a west coast celebration of the Arthurs was held simultaneously in Victoria, B.C. Winners were: Novel Category: Michelle Spring, *In the Midnight Hour* (Ballantine); True Crime: (tie) Stevie Cameron and Harvey Cashore, *The Last Amigo* (Macfarlane Walter & Ross), and Andrew Nikiforuk, *Saboteurs* (Macfarlane Walter & Ross); French-Language: Anne-Michèle Lévesque, *Fleur invitait au troisième* (Vents d'Ouest); First Novel: Jon Redfern, *The Boy Must Die* (ECW Press); Juvenile: Norah McClintock, *Scared to Death* (Scholastic Canada); Short Story: Mary Jane Maffini, "Signs of the Times" in *Fit to Die* (RendezVous Press). The Derrick Murdoch Award, for contributions made to crime and mystery writing in Canada, went to James Dubro for serving as the Arthur Ellis Award chair for seven years, and to Caro Soles for creating the successful Bloody Words Conference.

In other award news, Margaret Atwood's Booker Prize–winning novel, *The Blind Assassin,* earned another honor in 2003, being named to the shortlist for the IMPAC Dublin Literary Award, the richest prize for a single piece of fiction in English, 100,000 Euros. Among other prizes, *The Blind Assassin* previously won the Hammett Prize. Eric Wright's *The Kidnapping of Rosie Dawn* received the Barry Award for Best Paperback Original Mystery of the year. The novel was also short-listed for the Edgar, Arthur Ellis, and Anthony Awards. Andrew Nikiforuk's *Saboteurs,* which tied for the AE Award in the nonfiction category, was also honored with the Governor General's Award, Canada's highest literary honor. And, finally, Tim Wynne-Jones, a previous AE Award winner, won the Edgar Award for best young adult novel with *The Boy in the Burning House.*

In media news, work began on television film adaptations of Maureen Jennings's novels, *Except for the Dying* and *Poor Tom Is Cold,* for broadcast on the Canadian stations City-TV and Bravo. *Poor Tom* was also selected as one of the best books of 2001 by the editors of *Drood Mystery Review.* Meanwhile, the audio CD, *Fears for Ears,* was released in October (with coop television advertising on the digital channels Scream and the Mystery Channel), featuring full dramatizations of five stories, including Peter Sellers's "The Vampires Next Door" and Edo van Belkom's AE- and Bram Stoker–nominated "The Rug." In other media news, Nigel Tappin's stories for *The Clue Mysteries* and *More Clue Mysteries,* set in the fictitious Clubholm Manor in Devonshire and featuring clues and weapons from the Hasbro board game, *Clue,* had been accepted by publishers The Running Press, but were ultimately turned down by Hasbro for being a bit too graphic and unsuitable for children. The books were then assigned to writer Vicki Cameron, and the new *Clue Mysteries* is scheduled for publication in 2003.

The Bloody Words mystery conference was held in Toronto, June 14–16, with guests Walter Mosely and Peter Robinson. It was the last year for the event in Toronto, as in 2003 Bloody Words will be moving to Ottawa. August 24 saw the launch of the Scene of the Crime Festival on Wolfe Island, near Kingston, Ontario, where Canada's first mystery writer, Grant Allen, was born in the mid-nineteenth century.

In magazine publishing news, *Storyteller,* Canada's short story magazine and publisher of previous Arthur Ellis Award–winning stories, has now become a paying market. Meanwhile, the mystery magazine, *Over My Dead Body,* published its first all-Canadian issue. The Crime Writers of Canada published its fifth edition of *In Cold Blood,* written by Jim McBride. *In Cold Blood* is a 120-page perfect-bound directory-style reference guide to Canadian crime and mystery writing and writers. Copies can be ordered through the CWC Web site, www.crimewriterscanada.com, or at 3007 Kingston Road, Box 113, Scarborough, Ontario, M1M 1P1. To inquire by E-mail, write to: info@crimewriterscanada.com.

Finally, the roller coaster of 2002 took an upward turn in December of 2002 as production began on a new half-hour show about the mystery genre called "Mystery Ink." Hosted by Montreal radio personality John Moore and produced in Montreal by Fairplay Productions for the Global Broadcasting Network's digital cable Mystery Channel, each edition of "Mystery Ink" features an interview with a Canadian mystery author, a Max Haines Crime Flashback, and interviews with experts on various true and historical Canadian crimes. The show is set to debut on the Mystery Channel in 2003.

World Mystery Report: Germany

Thomas Wörtche

The Retro Year: In "popular culture," Halle Berry as a quotation of Ursula Andress was the most significant picture of the year. No new kids on the block, but the old ones in brand-new, sexy outfits. And it's also exactly what happened on Germany's crime and mystery scene in 2002. No promising new name, no new idea, no innovation at all.

It may sound more devastating than it actually is. At the very least, a market lacking the new names must cede space to forgotten old quality. Indeed, it was a pleasure to see a comeback of authors like Robert Littell (with Scherz), Alan Furst (with Ullstein), or Bill Pronzini (with Fischer paperback)—who had all been absent for years or even decades. The deceased Charles Willeford enjoyed a new edition with Alexander Verlag; Gerald Kersh, the great Brit noir author of the thirties is finally published in German by Pulp Master; Ernest Tidyman's *Shaft* novels are available for the first time in a complete and new translation (Pendragon Verlag). Distel Verlag bravely continues the project of publishing all of French noir master Jean-Patrick Manchette's work, to be completed in 2003. Unionsverlag metro started the relaunch of the Japanese classic by Masako Togawa, *Lady Killers* from 1963, an outstanding psycho-thriller as fresh as if it was written yesterday. A movie, based upon this novel, directed by Harold Becker, will be out soon in the States. Swiss publisher Diogenes came up with journalist Stefan Howald's biography of Eric Ambler. It is the first worldwide attempt to acknowledge the life and times of this great founding father of the modern political-thriller genre. The house also published the complete works of Patricia Highsmith, including some unknown texts, in an excellent edition.

This wave of relaunches, new editions, and comebacks reflects the nervousness of the crisis-shaken publishing industry—nobody dares to put too much money into experiments. The blockbusters of the past years—Henning Mankell, Donna Leon, Patricia Cornwell—more and more turned from money earners into money movers. It requires enormous amounts of money to keep the media hype boiling. And one can see why by monitoring keenly the crime-fiction chat rooms on the Internet. They gain importance by the day, not only as a forum for advertising and marketing, but offering insight for professionals into what the (in)famous "nonprofessionals" like and dislike, and why. Here you see how tired of the respective formulas the "average reader" (and buyer) is.

This leads us to a second remarkable trend: replicas "made in Germany." Smart publishing seems to follow the motto: why should we spend money for translations and travel expenses for foreign authors if we can easily have their ideas, plots, and characters copycatted by locals who cost less and can add some petty "German-ness" to them? As a result, the German language bookshelves are overcrowded with German amateur sleuths or—even more bizarre—German cops investigating crime abroad. Preferably in Italy, because fake-Italian grounds are well prepared by Donna Leon's fairy tales, and Italy is always easy to combine with fine food and dubious crooks. The latter, mistaken as the Mafia, which seems to be something so mysterious that the author doesn't even try to know anything about it.

The second popular option of some publishers: Take all the patterns of the serial-killer-profiler-novel à la U.S. and bury German settings under them. Petra Hammesfahr (with Wunderlich), for instance, started off very successfully in this sub-genre, but then exaggerated it a little bit: her German cops behaved like even FBI agents would never dare to, and so, after a couple of weeks, the author was forgotten again. The sheer economic calculation, however, worked perfectly—because replicas are less expensive than the originals. Cheap thrills indeed.

Of course, there was the one exception to the rule: Manuela Martini's first novel, *Outback* (Bastei-Lübbe)—a classic cop novel set in Australia, with Australian cops and criminals, and written in a style that could have been translated from English into German. The novel works because Martini lives in Australia and just happens to write in German.

Nevertheless, there is no real future for this "buy German" campaign. The market is already beginning to get tired. This is also true for the so-called regional mysteries. By now Grafit and a lot of other small publishers have overburdened the capacities of the respective regional sub-markets. Every tiny region (Upper Moselle river, Middle Moselle river, Lower Moselle river, and so on) has its own crime writers and crime novels meanwhile, and nobody outside of the region seems to care about it. It is a question of mathematics of when this market segmenting will be gone. To avoid misunderstandings: there are brilliant novels that tell real dark stories about the countryside, but they are not easy to find among the plethora of regional mysteries. But the avalanche (about 120 novels settled in the small Eifel mountains, not bigger than New York City but without a major town) did a lot of damage to good books.

Another tendency that will do harm to the genre, at least for some time, is the mania for marketing crime fiction by "funny events": 2002 saw trillions of candlelight dinners with murder, riverboat tours with murder, silly live quiz-shows with murder (with questions like "What was the shoe size of Dr. Watson?"), coiffeur sessions with murder. . . . Of course, you'll always find audiences who enjoy this kind of event, stubbornly determined to have fun. But if you create the need, you have to bring the offer: Authors who are willing to sit on those stages and read from their books without feeling like the whipped cream on a cup of coffee. It can only be "local heroes" who perform easy reading for easy listening. In other words: irrel-

WORLD MYSTERY REPORT: GERMANY | 51

evant stuff that will be forgotten by the curfew hour. Still, this trend will soon starve for a new incursion by some other genre (coming up: erotic novels or juvenile books).

It is tragic—or ironic?—that the German crime fiction community, notoriously lamenting about not being taken seriously by the serious media, does everything to deliberately demonstrate its own inferiority. It is even more difficult to imagine that any creative step forward will come out of this.

As to the department of scandals, we also had our little storm in the water glass: for reasons unclear so far, there are no reliable reference books about crime fiction in the German language. Perhaps because Germans have no problems using the ones available in English. But now, Reclam Verlag—a very renowned and well-established publisher of excellent encyclopedias and dictionaries, famous since the eighteenth century and almost a monopolist in the area of libraries, both public and private, high schools and universities—decided to fill the gap and presented *Reclams Krimi-Lexikon*— *Reclam's Crime Fiction Lexicon*. Immediately it was followed by an outcry of outrage. Amazingly enough, both professionals and consumers agreed: This is the worst lexicon ever made—errors, failures, no information about important authors, irrelevant facts about no-names, a grotesque selection of who is mentioned and who is not (try to find Elmore Leonard, for example). The funniest—or most scandalous—part of the story: Reclam played a total duck-and-cover act and refused to discuss the item, let alone withdraw the sad pamphlet.

And here are Germany's remarkable books of the year. They were, like in 2001, stand-alone novels not necessarily to be labeled mysteries or thrillers. The Crime Authors Award, Glauser, was given to Austrian author Thomas Glavinic for *Der Kameramörder* (Volk & Welt), a complicated, even bulky piece of prose about the sick voyeurism associated with serial killing, both in fiction and in reality. We are all Peeping Toms, is what Glavinic's excellent novel makes clear to us. It is a meta-novel, reflecting in literature the consequences of media interest for true crime cases. Closer to a genuine crime novel is an extraordinary period piece: *Wer übrig bleibt, hat recht*, from Eichborn Verlag, by authors Roland Birkefeld and Göran Hachmeister. It is set in Berlin, 1943–1945, with a detective protagonist who is an SS officer tracking down an escapee from a concentration camp taking bloody revenge on his foes. It may sound tasteless at first sight, but the book is grounded in brilliant recherché and fact-finding, not just fake history like Philipp Kerr's novels about Nazi Berlin, and the authors, both professional historians, manage to tell a dark and bitter tale about how there was no true "Zero Hour" after World War II, but a specific "German continuity." Like the characters in this novel, Nazis—police and civilians—had no problems finding new jobs in Cold War Germany—on both sides of the Iron Curtain. *Wer übrig bleib, hat recht* is not only a very thrilling novel, it tells a very true tale of crime and society.

The rest of the year's production offered some good routine stuff without big surprises, by Austrian authors Kurt Lanthaler and Wolf Haas, and German authors Uta-Maria Heim, Astrid Paprotta, and Irene Rodrian.

In short, the general economic crisis in Germany unfortunately did not generate fresh energy for crime fiction. Germany, like Switzerland and Austria, seemed to cultivate its nervousness in the face of crisis. The general feeling was that the fat years may be over forever. But actually, that is grounds for hope. Because fat years are bad times for a sensitive genre feeding on social and political turmoils and the state of reality. So the economic downturn, while hard on everyone, may at least create an atmosphere in which strong crime novels will be written.

The World's
Finest Mystery and
Crime Stories

Fourth Annual Collection

Clark Howard

To Live and Die in Midland, Texas

CLARK HOWARD is the author of several nonfiction books and more than ten novels in the action-adventure and crime genres, along with numerous short stories and magazine articles. His fiction has been praised for its taut pacing and well-crafted suspense. His nonfiction works include *Six Against the Rock,* about an abortive escape attempt from Alcatraz, and *Zebra,* about racially motivated killings by a fanatic religious sect. Both are noteworthy for the author's meticulous research and his ability to recreate the mindset that led to the commission of the crimes. He is generally regarded as one of the two or three best writers of short crime fiction in the world. In "To Live and Die in Midland, Texas," which appeared in *Ellery Queen's Mystery Magazine,* he's writing about folks on the wrong side of the law and just how dangerous that position can be.

To Live and Die in Midland, Texas

Clark Howard

Frank Raine wasn't supposed to drink alcoholic beverages. He had been out on parole from the Texas penitentiary up in Huntsville for just a week, and he knew full well that the Tanqueray and tonic in front of him on the bar could put him back in the place they called The Walls for another two, maybe three years. He wasn't supposed to associate with known felons, either, but he was about to break that rule, too, waiting as he was in a small Houston bar to meet his old cellmate, Jesus Ortega. Because the Spanish pronunciation of Ortega's given name was *hay-soose,* everyone called him "Soose." Raine had not seen him since Soose made parole some eight months earlier, but when Frank walked out of the joint a week ago, a message from a gate trusty had been passed to him, a phone number on a scrap of paper, and when he called it a couple of days later, Soose answered. Now, as Frank Raine took his first tangy sip of the T-and-T, Soose walked in the door and Frank rose to greet him. The two men embraced and exchanged *amigos.* Soose was carrying about thirty extra pounds, and Frank patted the Latino's belly. "Who's the father, man?"

"Very funny," Soose replied, unoffended. "It's hard not to put on weight living with my mother, man; she never cooks small. Come on, let's get a booth in the back." Soose bobbed his chin at the bartender, who was also Hispanic. "Double Jack Daniel's, *carnal,*" he said. *Carnal* meant street brother; all Hispanic males understood it.

The two men sat in a back booth and made small talk until Soose's drink had been set in front of him. Then Soose got down to business.

"Man, you getting out last week was like the answer to a prayer. How'd you like to split a cool two million four ways?"

"What kind of cool two million?" Raine asked.

"Dollars, baby," Soose replied with a dazzling smile. "Greenbacks. Currency. And all *unmarked.*"

"If you're talking an armored truck or something like that, I'm not interested," Raine told him. "I'm waiting for Stella to get out next week so's we can get back together. I'm not looking for anything high-risk right now—"

"It ain't high-risk, Frankie," his friend assured him. "That's the beauty of it. The cash ain't even gonna be in a vault; it's gonna be in a footlocker, just like one of those you buy at Wal-Mart. Only this one is painted gold. There'll be maybe two, three, four security guards or local redneck cops looking after it. You, me, and one other guy can take 'em down with no sweat." Soose smiled again: two rows of the kind of teeth you see in toothpaste ads. "Interested now, *amigo?*"

"Maybe," said Raine. "Let's hear the rest of it."

Soose leaned forward on the table, his dark face becoming grave. "How much you know about Texas, man?"

Raine shrugged. "Good cops. Lousy prisons."

"No, I mean about Texas history."

"Not much. My people stole it from your people."

"Yeah, but besides that." Soose took a sip of his Jack Daniels. "Let me give you a little history lesson. After the *gringos* stole it from the Mexican people, Texas was annexed as a state in 1845. For a long time, it didn't have no real borders; it jus' went on forever. Because of its size, some smart *gringos* decided to put in the state's charter that it could be divided into *five* smaller states if the people living here voted for it."

Raine frowned. "Five different states?"

"Yeah. Think about it. Today it would mean *ten* U.S. senators instead of two."

"Whoa," Raine said quietly, pursing his lips in a silent whistle.

"Whoa is right," Soose agreed. "Anyway, when the Civil War came along, Texas went with the Confederacy, so it was no longer part of the United States and its original charter was no good no more. Then, after the war ended, Texas was readmitted to the Union in 1870 under a new state charter. This one left out the right of Texas to divide itself up. But there's a lot of feeling around that with a vote of the people, it could still be done. Not into five states, but into two: North Texas and South Texas. Just like North and South Carolina, North and South Dakota."

"What's all this got to do with a two-million-dollar score?" Raine asked.

"I'm getting to that," Soose told him. "You ever hear of an oil burg named Midland?"

Raine frowned. "Sounds familiar, but I'm not sure why."

"It's over in West Texas, in the middle of a huge wasteland that just happens to have an ocean of oil under it. 'Member about twelve, fifteen years ago, a little girl fell in a well? Baby Jessica . . ."

"Yeah, I remember that. It was front-page stuff for two or three days. They got her out, right?"

"Yeah. Everybody that could read knew about it. Midland is famous for it. That and the fact that President Bush started in the oil business there.

He calls it his hometown, says he wants to be buried there."

"You're not working up to something that involves the President and Secret Service, are you?" Raine asked prudently. "Because if you are—"

"No, man, you think I'm crazy?" Soose demurred. "Jus' listen, okay? There's this big private building in Midland called the New Petroleum Club. All the big-shot oilmen are members. They hold private parties there, business meetings, political powwows, that kind of stuff. A week from now there's gonna be a big fund-raising luncheon there to start piling up money to run a slate of independent candidates in the next state election who will support a movement to divide Texas into two states, north and south. They're gonna call themselves the Partition Party. A hundred of the wealthiest men in the state are behind it. I'm talking oilmen from central Texas, cattlemen from the panhandle, telecommunications people from Houston, natural-gas pipeliners from El Paso, millionaire cotton farmers from the Rio Grande valley, shipping big shots from Galveston, you name it. There's money from all over Texas behind this idea. A hundred of the wealthiest men in the state are gonna meet in Midland for this fund-raising luncheon and kick in twenty thousand bucks apiece to put the first two million into this new political party's campaign chest."

"Yeah, but they won't bring cash," Raine said, "they'll bring checks—"

"Wrong. They *will* bring cash. This is all under-the-table money. These guys don't want any record of their donations. This is how they get around the federal limit on political donations. You've heard politicians talking about 'soft' money? Well, this is what they call *quiet* money."

Raine was staring almost in disbelief at his friend. "All one hundred of these guys are bringing twenty grand to this luncheon—in *cash?*"

"You got it. Fresh currency, mixed bills, from different banks all over the state, unmarked, and—"

"Untraceable," Raine finished the sentence for him.

"Right. And it all gets dropped into that Wal-Mart footlocker that's painted gold and sitting in front of the head table. When everybody's dropped their money in, those hick cops I tol' you about will put it in the back of a station wagon to drive it to a local bank to be put in a vault. But between the club and the bank—"

"It's exposed," Frank Raine said quietly. He drummed his fingertips silently on the table. Slowly his expression morphed into the set, steady look of a man who had just established for himself an irrepressible goal. "How'd you hit on this?" he asked.

"I worked in the oil fields over in Midland while I was on parole. Me and this *gringo* kid named Lee Watts worked for an old-timer named J. D. Pike. The guy's an old wildcatter, been rich three or four times, married three or four times, gone broke three or four times. Right now he's supposed to have enough money to be on the list of oilmen invited to the luncheon, but fact is he's almost flat busted. He's got some oil leases over in Louisiana that he's sure are gonna hit, but he needs a stake. He could go out and borrow the dough, but then he'd have to share the profits if he hit a gusher. So he asked Lee if he knew anybody who might be interested in a quick and easy score for big bucks. Lee came to me with it."

"And now you're coming to me," Raine said. "Why?"

Soose looked chagrined. "Come on, Frank. I'm small-time compared to you. I can go along on a score like this, but I can't plan it. I can't pull it all together. It needs a *jefe.*" Soose pronounced the last word *hef-fey.* It meant chief.

"Who all's in on it?" Raine asked.

"Just the guys I tol' you about: old man Pike, Lee Watts, an' me."

"What kind of split you figuring on?"

"I already talked that over with the others, without mentioning your name, just your reputation. We agreed to give you forty percent, eight hundred grand, to engineer the whole job. The rest of us would split a million-two even: four hundred grand each."

"What about front money? Guns, getaway car, other expenses?"

"Old man Pike said he still has a little cash left for that."

Raine sat back and chewed on a piece of hard, dead skin next to one of his thumbnails. He was an ordinary-looking man, some good features, some poor, not the kind that many women looked at twice, but those who did were serious about it. He was graying at the temples and had a not unattractive scar above his right eyebrow where he'd been hit with a bottle once. It was his eyes that told the most about him: they said don't lie to me and I won't lie to you. It was best to believe them.

"When is this big luncheon planned for?" he asked Soose.

"A week from Wednesday."

Today was Tuesday, Raine thought. That gave them seven days before the day of the job. Stella would be getting out on Thursday; that would give Raine enough time to work on her, to give her the "one last job" routine. And it would give him time to check out the others on the job: an old man, a kid from the oil fields—it might be too thin from a personnel aspect.

"What about this guy who brought it to you?"

"Lee? He's okay. Texas poor, you know, but not trash. Good kid. Got a steady girl but they ain't married yet. Wants to buy a motorcycle shop with his end of the take."

"And the old man?"

"A little shaky," Soose admitted, "but tough. You prob'ly wouldn't want him in on the actual heist, just before and after."

"Can you set up a meet for Saturday?"

"Sure, perfect time. Everybody comes to Midland on Saturdays; nobody'll notice us."

"Not in Midland. The old man must be known there; the kid, too, maybe even you. Make it someplace else."

Soose thought a moment, then said, "We could meet in Odessa, about

twenty-five miles away. Just south of town there's a public park called Comanche Trails. There's picnic tables around. I could pick up some tostados
and salsa and beer; we could eat while we talk."

"Good. Make it this Saturday, three o'clock. Listen, I need a car."

"You can take mine, *carnal*. It's a sweet little ninety-one Chrysler with
leather, runs like a dream. I'll use my mother's car and she can use my
sister's car. My sister's expecting; she's eight months along and don't drive
much anyhow." Soose's expression firmed. "So, we're set for Saturday, *ca-
marada?*"

"Yeah," Raine nodded. "We're set for Saturday. In Odessa."

On Thursday morning, early, Raine got out of bed in a Holiday Inn south
of the main drag in Waco. He showered, shaved closer than usual, and
dressed in new slacks, a pullover Izod, and new loafers. He had bought
some Alberto VO5 the previous night to color the gray streaking his temples, but decided against using it. He figured what the hell, Stella would be
older, too; as practical and right-on as she had always been, she would
expect him to be different, too.

At a Denny's out on the highway, he had a heart-attack-on-a-plate for
breakfast—eggs, sausages, biscuits and gravy, and coffee. Then he got into
Soose's car and drove the eighteen miles out to Gatesville, where the
women's prison was.

Stella came walking out with two other discharges, both Hispanic, at
ten o'clock. She was wearing a plain cotton dress that buttoned up the
front, low-heel oxfords with white socks, and carried a brown paper bundle
with her personal items in it. Raine walked up and took the bundle from
her.

"I've got a car over here," he said. "And a room for a couple of nights
in Waco."

She merely nodded. Raine put an arm around her shoulders and
walked her to the car. He could tell she had tears building up in her eyes,
but she held them back. In the front seat of the car, she took a tissue from
the pocket of her dress and dabbed her eyes dry. Then she forced a smile
and brushed two fingertips across the hair at his temples.

"You're getting gray."

Raine smiled self-consciously. "You aren't."

"I color mine," she said.

"Can you do that in there?" he asked, surprised. Stella threw him a
cynical look.

"You can do anything you want to on the inside. You should know
that."

He shrugged. "I guess I thought things were different in a women's
prison."

"Inside is inside," she said quietly.

He asked how her mother and sisters were, she asked how his father
was.

"Dead," he told her. "Finally drank himself to death."

She asked him about his parole, told him about hers. He asked if she wanted to stop and get something to eat; she said no, but asked him to pull over somewhere and park. He turned off on a dirt road. She opened the bundle on her lap and handed him a small school photograph.

"She's fourteen now, Frank. This is her eighth-grade graduation picture."

Unlike Stella, Raine could not keep all the tears in; one escaped from each eye and stung his freshly shaved cheeks. "My God, she's you all over again—"

"I think she's got your eyes," Stella said. "So direct and serious."

After a while, they drove on.

"Mother says she's a good kid," Stella told him. "Gets good grades. Bags groceries at a Kroger store on weekends. Runs around with a good crowd."

"That's important," Raine said solemnly.

"Don't we know it now," Stella agreed. "Lord, it seems like a hundred years ago when we left that little Tennessee town on a Greyhound bus to set the world on fire. What a couple of crazy kids we were. I'm glad Lucy's not like us."

"Yeah, me, too," Raine replied softly.

They were silent for the rest of the drive to Waco.

When they got to the motel and he unlocked the door for her, Raine said, "You need some clothes. There's a big mall just down the road—"

"Clothes aren't the only thing I need," Stella told him, putting down her bundle and unbuttoning her dress.

Raine watched her. She was heavier than he remembered, as Soose was, as he knew he himself was; but the thighs had the same roundness, the hips the same sensual jut, the breasts the same buoyancy, the lips the same unspoken invitation and promise. When they got into bed, the familiarity of all the places he began to kiss and lick and bite made him able to ignore the stale prison smell of her.

After she shopped for clothes and changed into something new, they went to a steakhouse for dinner. While they ate, Stella said all the things Raine knew she would.

"I want to go home, Frankie. I want to go back to that little hick town in Tennessee and get a job in some store uptown and come home every night and fix supper. I want to be a mother to Lucy for these last few years before she's all the way grown up. I haven't held her in my arms since she was six years old, Frankie—"

Her voice broke and Raine took her hands across the table. "I know, honey, I know—"

"Do you, Frank? Do you really?"

"Sure I do. But *how*, Stel? How can we go back? Everybody in town knows us, everybody will remember us. They know what we've been, *where* we've been. You might be able to get a job, but what about me? You think anybody would hire me? I'm a two-time loser: the Tennessee reformatory and now the Texas pen. I couldn't get a job delivering newspapers."

"There must be *some* way, Frank." Stella's voice had pleading in it, and desperation. "Just because we've made mistakes shouldn't mean we have to pay for them forever. There's *got* to be a way to start over."

"There is," he told her. "Change our names. Get new identities. It's not hard to do. Then find a place to settle down, buy a home. Florida maybe, or California. Get a little business of some kind. A franchise, maybe. Like a video rental store, something like that." He paused a beat, then added carefully, "Only to do those things we'd need a stake, money to get us started—"

"What if we could both find work somewhere new? We could start saving and—" Her hopeful words stopped suddenly, broken off by the reality of the moment. A knowing look clouded her face. "A stake, you said. You've already got something lined up, haven't you?"

"Not exactly lined up, but a good possibility. A guy I celled with in Huntsville brought it to me. It sounds quick and clean, plus the money is serious. But I'd have to take a closer look at it."

"How serious—the money?"

"Eight hundred grand. Cash. Untraceable."

"Suppose we get it—what then?" Stella asked. "Head for Mexico? Lease some lavish villa in Acapulco or Puerto Vallarta? Buy a new boat? Clothes, jewelry? Live like rich people for a few months, a year, until we're broke again? That's the usual plan, isn't it, Frank?"

"No," he said quietly, eyes lowered as if the suggestion were shameful. "No, not this time." He looked up at her. "I'm tired, Stel. I want to go home, too."

"Don't lie to me about this, Frank."

Anger flashed across his face. "I don't lie to you about anything, you know that."

Now Stella lowered her own eyes. "I'm sorry."

They finished dinner and walked a pier that bordered Lake Waco until the mosquitoes became too much for them and they headed back to the motel.

"Let's talk about this tomorrow," Stella said, her arm in his as they walked. "You always told me it was better to talk about serious things in the morning, when your mind was fresh. Remember?"

"Yeah, I remember."

On the way they came to a liquor store. "Want me to get us a bottle of Tanqueray?" he asked.

"Why not?" Stella said. "Be like old times."

They spent Thursday and Friday nights at the motel in Waco, then got up at dawn on Saturday and started driving west across Texas. At nine o'clock they stopped in San Angelo for gas and breakfast. Then they covered the remaining 130 miles and drove into Odessa from the south just after one o'clock. They checked into another Holiday Inn and Stella went for takeout food while Raine washed up and changed shirts. During the trip, Raine had told Stella all about the job and what he knew about the men involved.

"I'll get a better handle on things after the meet," he said as they sat on the bed and ate Big Macs and fries. "Then you and I can decide if we think it's worth the risk. If we decide it isn't, we'll back off, just like you want."

They had talked incessantly about their options during their hours in the car: their goal was to make a life with their daughter Lucy before it was too late; their choices—try it the honest way, tough it out, see if it could be done; or do it the easy way, a quick, clean job, a good take, and *this* time play it smart, don't blow all the cash on the good life. No. Instead, use it slowly to build a *new* life, a respectable life, one they could bring Lucy into.

There was now a tacit agreement between them. Frank would not go in on the heist unless it was a sure thing—a *really* sure thing—or at least as close to one as thieves ever got. It had to be too good to pass up.

But if they went for it, and it came off okay, and they were in the clear, they would hole up somewhere—somewhere *modest*—and start putting together their new life. There would be *no* Mexican villa, *no* high life, *no* boat—nothing like that.

And this would be their last job.

Their very last.

Raine picked up a city map at the motel desk and located Comanche Trails Park. He got there early and took up a parked position where he could watch the others arrive. It was one of those hot West Texas days when the air was heavy and your lips got puffy and dry if you stayed outside too much. Only about half of the picnic tables were in use, mostly by young Hispanic families. Soose had picked a good place to meet; Hispanics tended to notice little, mind their own business, and forget everything that did not concern them.

The kid, Lee Watts, got there first, driving a beat-up old Dodge Ram pickup. He had a gawky, oil-field-roustabout look to him: deeply tanned, buzz-cut blond hair, tight Wranglers, white shirt with the cuffs rolled up a couple of turns, pack of cigarettes in his shirt pocket. He looked around for the others, didn't see them, and walked to a picnic table to wait. The table was in the far corner, off to itself. Smart, Raine thought.

Next came the old man, J. D. Pike, thin as a whip under a tan Stetson, ancient face as leathery as a work saddle, eyes concealed by mirrored sunglasses, Western shirt closed at the neck with a Bolo tie. As he emerged from his pickup, which was much newer than Lee's, he saw the younger man at once and ambled over to him.

Soose showed up in an older-model Chevy sedan and got a large restaurant takeout box from the trunk. When he was halfway to the table, Lee went out to meet him.

"There's an ice chest of beer in the backseat." Soose bobbed his chin toward the car, sending Lee to get it.

While Soose was opening the box of food and dealing out paper plates, Raine got out of the car and walked casually over to them. Lee and old man Pike turned their attention his way, studying him as he approached.

"Hey, *carnal!*" Soose said when Frank walked up. The two ex-convicts embraced. Soose introduced the others to Raine, then waved his arm over the table. "Tostados, tacos, taquitos, tamales—the works. And some good Cerveza to wash it down."

As they began to eat, Raine said quietly, "Well, it's your job, Mr. Pike. Why don't you tell us about it, start to finish, just like we don't know nothing at all."

Pike laid it out for them, pretty much the same way Soose had laid it out for Raine in the bar. It gave Raine an opportunity to scrutinize and evaluate the old man, to scope him out: the way he talked, how his eyes moved, how steady his hands were while proposing armed robbery. By the time Pike had finished, Raine was convinced that the old man was solid. Lee he would check out later, with Soose. But for now, when Pike asked, "Well, what do you think?" Raine nodded approval.

"Sounds good. I'll check the layout this afternoon. If it *looks* good, we're on."

Soose and Lee smiled broadly, while Pike pursed his lips and clasped his hands together on the table, relieved.

"We're going to have to work fast," Raine said. He was eating little, since he had eaten lunch earlier with Stella. The others, appetites apparently whetted by the job looking to be on, were wolfing down the food. "We'll need front money right away," he told Pike.

"I've got five thousand in my pocket right now," Pike said. "And I can get more, not much, but a little." The old man was being flat-out honest, Raine felt, which was good.

"I don't think we'll need that much," Raine said. "I'll take a grand for personal expenses. Give Soose three grand." To Soose, he said, "Pick up a couple of good, cold, throwaway pieces for you and Lee. Nothing big and bulky, no long barrels, no automatics. Thirty-eight Specials with four-inch barrels if you can get them. No hollowpoint cartridges; if we have to shoot anybody, I don't want them to die. And pick up an AK-47 for me, just for show; I'll need it to cover the guards while we get the footlocker into our car. Also pick up three big bandanas for masks." Raine turned to Lee. "I want you to go back to Houston with Soose. He'll get you a fake driver's license. Next Tuesday you'll use it to rent a car at Houston International. Pay cash and get something ordinary-looking, four-door sedan, but with a boss engine—a Buick or an Olds. Have it back here by five o'clock Tuesday afternoon. You can follow Soose back and you two can get a motel room somewhere on the other side of Odessa for the night." Raine drummed his fingertips on the table. "That's all I can think of right now. Mr. Pike, let us have the money and give me a phone number where I can reach you."

While Pike counted out hundred-dollar bills from a roll he took from his pocket, Raine noticed that Lee was cleaning off their picnic bench and taking the refuse to a nearby trash can. When he saw Raine watching him, the younger man grinned sheepishly. "Can't litter," he said, almost in embarrassment. "Got to keep Texas beautiful."

Raine gave him a thumbs-up in approval.

The next day, with Soose driving, he, Raine, and Lee headed for Midland, twenty-five miles north. Stella stayed behind in the Odessa motel. Raine had told her at dinner the previous evening that the job appeared good on the surface, but he wanted to check out every last detail of it before making a final commitment. Stella was pleased that Raine was being so cautious; in the past he had pulled jobs on the spur of the moment if they looked even passably good. That, of course, was what had caused them to draw six-to-ten in the Texas pens.

The drive north was along a girder-straight highway across a parched, yellowish-gray land that was the surface of the Permian Basin caprock. It would have looked like some lifeless planet far away except for the skeleton-scaffolded oil-well pumps bobbing up and down in endless monotony to suck up some of the millions, perhaps billions, of barrels of crude that had been discovered when the first gusher popped nearly eighty years earlier.

When they got to Midland, they drove through Old Town first, then cruised slowly through a mostly deserted downtown section that looked like it was just stoically waiting out the dry, heavy-heated day until closing time. The only activity was in a small plaza where people sat on park benches eating ice cream cones, and young mothers in pairs and trios pushed their toddlers in strollers and gossiped.

"Wasn't always like this," Lee said from the backseat. "Time was, when crude was thirty-five dollars a barrel, this ol' town was jumping seven days and nights a week. People had so much money, they broke sweat trying to think up new ways to spend it. Hell, we used to have a *Rolls-Royce* dealership right here in town. And just about ever'body who had a producing well owned an airplane." He grunted softly, remembering. "Fancy country clubs all over the place. Big parties all the time. But not no more. Big things now for most folks is shopping at Wal-Mart and going to the high school football game on Friday night."

"You lived here all your life?" Raine asked.

"Yeah, mostly. My old man was a rigger; tried to put together enough money to buy some mineral rights and put in a well of his own, but he never made it. We never was dirt poor, but we was definitely part of the lower class in Midland. In high school I never got invited to no swim parties or dances that the rich kids had at the country clubs. Never wore nothin' to school but old hand-me-down jeans and work shirts from my old man and brothers. Believe me, it weren't no fun living like that in Midland, right in the middle of a town full of rich oil people and their kids. We wasn't but a step up from the Mexicans." Lee glanced uneasily at Soose. "Nothin' personal, man."

Soose said nothing, but seated next to him Raine noticed a slight clenching of his jaw. Cellmates learned to recognize little things like that about one another. Soose had not liked the remark, but it was not important enough to make an issue of it. The job came first.

"Soose tells me you want to buy a motorcycle shop," Raine said, changing the subject.

"Yeah. I figure a small Suzuki dealership somewheres, not in no big city, and not around Midland for sure, but maybe up in the panhandle. Amarillo or thereabouts."

"And you've got a girl, right?"

"Yeah. Name's Wendy. She comes from the same kind of fam'ly I do: got nothin' and gettin' nowhere. She works out at the Dairy Queen right now. We plan on gettin' married soon's we can get out of this dead-end town."

"What does Wendy think of you being in on a job like this?" Raine asked casually.

"She don't know about it," Lee replied earnestly. "She wouldn't put up with nothin' like that. You don't think I'd—" Abruptly the younger man stopped talking and, where he had been leaning forward to converse, now sat back and grinned knowingly. "I get it. That was a test, right?"

"Sort of," Raine admitted. "Where you gonna tell her you got the money to buy that shop?"

"I figure to find a place for sale and tell her the owner's bringing me in as a partner to run it and pay for it in, like, five years. She won't know the difference."

"You won't be leaving Midland right away, will you?"

"No, sir. I figure that might look suspicious. We'll wait awhile. People hereabouts know I been looking for a shop; they won't think nothin' of it if we leave in six months or so."

"Good thinking," Raine told him. "It's a good plan. Just stick to it. Don't let the money go to your head."

"I don't aim to," Lee Watts assured him.

After Lee guided them on a general tour of the area, Raine had him show them the New Petroleum Club. On the way, they passed the original Petroleum Club. "That's the old place," Lee said. "Goes back to the days of the wildcatters. Inside, it's like being on the *Titanic*. Got this huge grand staircase leading to the dining room. People who belonged there weren't just worth millions, they was worth *billions*. But it's kind of been going downhill for quite a while now."

"But this isn't where the big fund-raising luncheon's being held, right?" asked Raine.

"No, sir. That's at the *New* Petroleum Club. Hang a right at the next corner, Soose."

The New Petroleum Club sat on a low mound of manicured rye grass, a cobblestone drive leading to it from the highway north of town. It was a high-tech building, all glass and chrome and polished tile, valet parking under a modernistic porte cochere, huge U.S. and Texas state flags flying from tall silver poles.

"This here was built by the younger crowd that missed the big bonanza," Lee said. "They come along later: high-level people with Mobil and Conoco and Texaco—the ones that've got millions but not billions. There's a back road over behind it where Mr. Pike says they'll be bringing the money out. . . ."

From a narrow, blacktopped farm-to-market road running several hundred yards behind the club grounds, Frank Raine could see the less impressive rear façade of the building. There was a small loading dock off to one side, backed by service doors that he guessed accessed the club's kitchen, food lockers, and service facilities. The other side of the lower rear was a blank wall. The upper part of the rear wall had cantilevered windows floor to ceiling all the way across the structure. At the moment they were closed by horizontal blinds.

"That the dining room?" Raine asked, anxiety rising in him at the thought of a hundred Texans gathered up there watching the robbery. But Lee relieved his mind.

"No, sir. Mr. Pike said that was a big conference room that won't be in use the day of the luncheon. The actual luncheon will be around t'other side where the dining room faces a big duck pond. Mr. Pike says won't be nobody here 'cept kitchen help. Mostly, uh . . ." He nodded toward Soose.

"Hispanics," Soose said.

"Yeah," said Lee. "Mr. Pike figures when all the cash has been tossed in, the footlocker will be closed up and security guards from the Permian Basin Merchant's Bank will carry it out back to a van or SUV—he don't think they'll go to the expense of an armored truck, not for just a two-mile drive. Anyhow, there'll also be a couple or three local cops out back, maybe city, maybe county, for an escort. The footlocker's to be driven straight uptown where the president of the bank will be waiting to put it in the vault. Mr. Pike says they'll prob'ly be extra alert for an ambush 'tween here and town—but he don't think they'll expect nothing right here at the back door."

"He's right," Raine agreed. "They'll be concentrating on loading the locker into whatever kind of transportation they've got. This is the place to do it, all right."

Raine's eyes darted around the back of the building. Two kitchen workers, wearing white culinary coats, came onto the dock and emptied trays into disposal cans. Raine studied them, then turned his attention to two rows of cars between the club and where they were parked.

"What are those cars over there?"

"That's club employee parking."

As they were looking, a new Lincoln drove in and parked in a reserved space nearest the club. Two men got out, one short, wearing a sport coat, the other tall and lanky, in a red Western shirt.

"The short guy is Mr. Sims," Lee said. "He runs the club. Other fellow's Ross Tabb. He organizes big hunting trips up to Canada and down to Mexico for the rich men. He's a professional rifle and pistol shot, too; got lots of trophies and stuff. Ever'body calls him 'Red' 'cause he don't never wear nothin' but red shirts."

"Will he be at the luncheon?" Raine asked.

"Oh, hell no. He ain't in the same league with these oil men; he's just hired help."

Good, Frank Raine thought. Last person he wanted around during a big heist was some hotshot hip-shooter who liked to show off.

Soose drove them back to Odessa. On the way, Raine was quiet, contemplative. At one point he said to Soose, "Pick up three of those white coats the kitchen workers wear, one for each of us." Later he said, "Get a box of surgical gloves, too."

When they got back to Odessa, they dropped Lee at his pickup, then Raine and Soose went to a local bar and had a drink.

"Well, what do you think, *carnal?*" Soose asked.

Raine shook his head. "I don't know. It looks almost *too* good." Briefly he bit his lower lip in thought. "I keep looking for some weak spot, something that can glitch up on us, but I can't find anything. One thing I've learned is that there's no such thing as a completely *perfect* heist—but this one sure looks close to it."

"Maybe this is our once-in-a-lifetime shot, *carnal.* Guys like us don't get many chances in life. There's things I want to do for my mother before she dies, you know? Get her a nice house. Take her on a trip back to Mexico to see her sisters and brothers. She's had a hard life, an' a lot of it's been my fault. I want to give her a few good years, you know? Maybe this is my chance to make it." He paused a beat, then added, "Yours too, *amigo.*"

"Yeah," Raine agreed quietly. "Maybe this one is it. Maybe this is the one every thief looks for in life. The dream job."

After several moments of silence, Soose said, "So? Do we go?"

Frank Raine nodded solemnly.

"Yeah. We go."

The next morning, after eating breakfast at a Denny's, Raine said to Stella, "I want to take you up to Midland, honey. I want you to see where this job is going down, and I want to find a spot where you can hook up with Pike, the old man who's bankrolling the job. You'll take him to a place where Soose, Lee, and I will come directly after the job. We'll dump the getaway car and all five of us will head back to the motel in Odessa in the car you're driving. That's where we'll cut up the take."

"Why not just have the old man come to the motel and wait there with me?" Stella asked.

"Because I don't trust him," Raine said evenly. "I don't trust anybody anymore, except you. And I don't want you trusting anybody either, hear me? Nobody."

"Sure, baby," Stella replied quietly. "Whatever you say, Frankie." The tone of his voice had somehow frightened her for a moment. She had never heard him talk like that before a job. He was, she realized for the first time, a lot harder, colder, than before he went to prison. Texas pens, she had heard, did that to a man.

After breakfast, they drove up to Midland and cruised around the area for a while. Raine showed Stella the New Petroleum Club and the escape route he had planned. "As soon as we score, we leave the club and hang a left on this farm-to-market road so we can skirt around downtown Midland to pick up Interstate Ten back to Odessa. We'll find a place uptown for you to meet old man Pike, and someplace to go on the farm-to-market road for all of us to hook up."

They scouted the farm-to-market road first and located a cornfield about two miles from the robbery site. There was a dirt road that gave tractor access to the field, but fifty yards off the paved road a car could not be seen from there or from the farmhouse far across the field. From the dirt road to the Midland city limits it was exactly four-point-three miles. "Can you remember that?" Raine asked.

"Sure," Stella said quietly. "Four-three. April third. That's Lucy's birthday, Frank."

He glanced at her, chagrinned. "Yeah, that's right. I guess I wasn't thinking."

Uptown in Midland, they selected Centennial Plaza, a once-popular park for rollerbladers and skateboarders until a city ordinance banned them, and now just a lazy location for people to sit on benches or stroll in the thick summer air. They parked and got out and entered the plaza, sitting down on the first bench they came to. "How about this spot for picking up the old man?" Raine asked.

"Suits me," Stella agreed, shrugging.

As they were sitting there, a bright green older-model pickup truck, gleaming in mint condition, pulled up and parked. A boy and girl about sixteen got out and went across the street to an ice cream parlor. Several minutes later they came back out again with large double-dip cones and walked laughing and teasing into the park, where they sat across from Raine and Stella. They sat there, bumping shoulders, nudging each other, whispering and giggling, catching ice cream drips on their tongues, while Raine and Stella watched them in amusement. The boy's name, they overheard from the banter between them, was Jerry, and the girl's name was Sue. After they had been sitting there a short time, the young couple became aware that Raine and Stella were staring at them. Jerry blushed and looked down at the sidewalk, but Sue confronted the situation.

"Is there something wrong, ma'am?" she asked, in a not unfriendly tone.

Stella smiled and shook her head. "I'm sorry, hon. We didn't mean to be rude. It's just that you two remind us of ourselves. You know, back when we were your age."

"Oh." Now Sue blushed as Jerry had. "Well, we're not really this silly all the time."

"I know. Being silly is just having fun." Stella squeezed Raine's knee. "Isn't that right, hon?"

"Yeah, sure, right," Raine replied appropriately. He patted Stella's hand. "Well, we'd best be going along," he added.

As they were leaving, Stella threw the young people a parting smile. "You kids have a fun day. Time enough to be serious when you get older."

But when she and Raine were back in their car, Stella's smile faded and a cheerless expression replaced it. "Where in the hell did our lives go, Frank?" she asked dolefully.

Raine did not answer.

Late in the morning on the day of the job, Soose pulled up to the motel in his mother's car, with Lee right behind him in a rented gray Buick Century four-door. As they were parking, Stella was just driving away to go pick up J. D. Pike, whom Raine had called the night before to set up the meeting. Raine watched Stella driving off, then hung the DO NOT DIS-TURB sign on the door, and along with Soose got into the Buick with Lee.

"Got everything?" Raine asked without preliminary.

"All in the trunk," Soose told him.

"Okay," Raine said. "Let's go."

All three men were quiet on the drive north. Getting ready to steal, *seriously* steal, with guns, was, Frank Raine imagined, a lot like going into ground combat in a war. It was a tight time, a nervous time, a time to be mindful. It was no time for idle conversation. None of the three men said a dozen words the entire trip.

When they arrived at the entrance drive to the New Petroleum Club, Raine saw that the member parking lot was filled with Lincolns, Cadillacs, BMWs, and an array of other high-ticket automobiles. "Looks like a nice crowd," he said evenly.

He had Lee drive back to the employee lot and park where they could see the rear loading dock. A station wagon was parked at the dock, its tailgate down. Two overweight men in khaki uniforms, wearing gun belts, were lounging against one fender, smoking and talking.

Raine and the two men with him got out of the Buick and opened the trunk. Each of them tied a blue and white bandana around his neck and tucked it down under the front of his shirt where it could not be seen. Then they slipped into white cotton coats like the club's culinary workers wore. They pulled on surgical gloves and took rags to wipe down the interior of the car and the guns they would use. Soose and Lee each stuck a pistol in his waistband; Raine, after checking the magazine and safety, slipped the AK-47 under the right side of his white coat and held it in place with the fingertips of his right hand. Then they loitered at the open trunk as if engaging in idle conversation before leaving for the day. Inside them, they felt like frogs were loose in their stomachs.

The footlocker of cash was carried out onto the loading dock by two other men uniformed in khaki, escorted by Mr. Sims, the man whom Lee had pointed out as the manager of the club. The two guards at the station wagon moved toward the loading-dock steps to help them.

"Let's go," Frank Raine said. "Nice and easy."

Raine and Soose began walking toward the loading dock, keeping the station wagon between them and the dock. Lee closed the trunk and got back into the Buick. He swung it around and drove slowly across the lot toward the club. As Raine and Soose got close to the dock and Lee drove up near the station wagon, all three pulled their bandanas up over the lower part of their faces. Raine and Soose stepped around from opposite sides of the station wagon. It dawned on the guards just a second too late what was happening. As the two nearest the tailgate reached for their holstered pistols, Soose clubbed one of them in the temple with his gun, and Raine butt-stroked the other across the jaw with the AK-47. Both of the men dropped like sandbags. Raine swung the AK-47 around on the other three.

"Be smart, boys," he warned tensely. "Don't get killed protecting somebody else's money."

"We hear you," the club manager said, voice wavering.

Lee stopped the Buick near them and popped the trunk from inside.

"Put that footlocker in the trunk." Raine gestured with the AK-47. "Put your guns in there, too—very carefully."

As the guards were doing what they were told, Lee hurried around and snatched the ignition keys from the station wagon, and Soose relieved the two fallen men of their sidearms. The guards set the footlocker in the trunk, along with their guns, and Soose tossed in the two extra pistols he had. Lee came hurrying back around to get behind the wheel of the Buick. Just as he started to get in, a single rifle shot split the air and a .30-30 slug hit him dead-center in the middle of the forehead.

Shocked by the suddenness of it, all five men at the tailgate of the station wagon dropped into a reflexive crouch. Raine's eyes swung like searchlights, trying to find the source of the shot. Soose stared in horror at the ugly, walnut-size hole in the fallen Lee's forehead. Brain matter was already slowly mushrooming out. Then both Raine and Soose detected movement close to them and swung to see Sims, the club manager, pulling a chrome automatic from under his coat. Raine quickly brought the AK-47 around to firing position, but Soose was a split second ahead of him and shot the man twice in the chest. Then there was another single rifle shot and Soose had a hole in his forehead just like Lee did.

Now Frank Raine saw a flash of red and knew where the shooter was, and in the same split instant knew what the glitch was in this dream robbery of theirs. Lee's words came back to him: ". . . Ross Tabb . . . organizes big hunting trips . . . professional rifle and pistol shot . . . don't never wear nothin' but red shirts . . ."

The flash of red Raine had seen was in the cantilevered window on the second floor of the club, above the loading dock. A red shirt. A professional rifleman. The glitch in their dream job. A backup sniper.

Raine moved in a crouch behind the station wagon. The faces of both standing guards were paper-white, with visible sweat running down from under their hats. "You two drag your friends over there under the loading dock," Raine ordered. One of them glanced tentatively at the club manager, who was on the ground, clutching at his chest, the heel of one foot digging spastically at the asphalt. "Never mind him!" Raine said harshly. "He chose to die, now let him! Get your friends and move!" Each guard grabbed one of the unconscious men and began dragging him to the shelter of the dock.

Raine's eyes riveted on the second-floor window, waiting for the flash of red he knew would come again. When it did, seconds later, he rose and raked the upstairs with a long burst from the AK-47. The man in the red shirt spun completely around and pitched backward through the cantilevered window, falling with a heavy thud to the concrete dock, then lying still as a shower of glass rained down on him.

A dozen men burst out onto the dock from the kitchen. Raine fired a quick burst of rounds over their heads and they fought like slaughterhouse sheep to get back inside.

Suddenly it was very quiet behind the New Petroleum Club. Raine tossed the AK-47 into the trunk of the Buick, grabbed two of the four pistols taken from the guards, and stuck them on each side under his belt. Slamming the trunk lid, he stepped over to Lee and took the keys to the station wagon from his lifeless hand. The heavy circulation of gunpowder in the air somehow got under the bandana covering his face and made him sneeze twice, heavily. Behind the wheel of the Buick, engine still running, he threw the car into gear and sped around to the front of the building. It did not surprise him that no one was in sight out front; everyone, even the valet parking attendants, had probably run to the rear of the club to see what all the shooting was about. Heading down the cobblestone drive to the road, Raine pulled down the bandana and exhaled what he was sure was the deepest breath he had ever taken. Maybe, he thought, he had beaten the glitch after all.

At the road, he swung right and accelerated. There was a quick catch in his chest, but he ignored it. He checked the odometer as his mind drew up the numbers he needed: two miles to the cornfield where Stella waited with old man. Pike; change cars; four-point-three miles from there into Midland; then pick up Interstate 10 to Odessa—

Another quick catch seized his chest. He frowned. What the hell—?

Then he found out. At the two-mile point, there was no cornfield. There was nothing on either side of the highway except flat, gray dirt, parched by an eternity of sunlight, then sucked dry by grasshopper pumps, and finally left to die under patches of scrubby mesquite.

Raine's head began to throb. *Wait a minute.* Did he have the distances reversed? Was it four-point-three to the field, then two miles to Midland—? Pulling to the side of the road, he shook his head violently. *No.* He had the distances correct. Come out of the New Petroleum Club drive, hang a left on the farm-to-market road—

Hang a *left.* He had turned *right.*

Son of a bitch! He could not believe it. A stupid wrong turn and now he was in an identifiable car on the wrong side of the meeting place.

He couldn't go back; the law would be coming toward him from Midland. He couldn't go forward; that would mean leaving Stella behind. Anyway, every little jerkwater town in that direction would soon have its deputies out watching for the Buick. Maybe he could hide the footlocker someplace, ditch the car, and hoof it back to the cornfield; plan things from there—

Just then, something caught his eye. Far off across one of the gray flats. It was bright green, like an artificial oasis in a wasteland. Where had he seen it before? As he watched, he could make out two figures moving about—

The two kids from town that he and Stella had briefly talked with. The green oasis was the boy's shiny pickup truck. Jerry, that was his name. The girl was Sue.

There was a tractor road leading out to where they were. Putting the Buick in gear, Raine drove up to it and turned in. When he was halfway to them, he heard the crack of a small-bore rifle, and made out what they were doing: target practicing at tin cans and bottles. Jerry was probably teaching Sue how to shoot. Memories of himself and Stella from years back flooded his mind.

When Raine drove up, the two teenagers walked over to the car. He got out, smiling. "Doing a little shooting, huh?"

"Yessir," Jerry said. He was holding a .22 lever-action Winchester. A bird gun. "We ain't trespassing or nothing," Jerry assured him. "This here's open land."

"I didn't stop because I thought you were trespassing," Raine said easily. "I want to buy your truck."

"Buy my truck?" Jerry and Sue exchanged surprised looks.

"Yeah. I'm kind of a collector of old-model vehicles. I remembered yours from the other day in town."

"Oh, yeah," said Sue. "That's right. In the park."

"Yeah. I've been driving around looking for you. I'll give you twenty thousand for it. Cash."

"Twenty thousand! Why, mister, the book on this here model ain't but about six—"

"Anyhow, we don't want to sell it," Sue said. "This truck is special to us. For a special reason."

Jerry blushed beet red. "What she means," he quickly amended, "is that her and me's been restoring this pickup together since we was freshmen in high school. It means a lot to us."

"Fifty thousand," Raine said.

"Fifty thousand! Are you crazy, mister?" Jerry's mouth was hanging open.

"We don't want to sell it," Sue said firmly. "At no price." She linked arms with Jerry. "Like I said, it's special." She squeezed his arm.

"She's right, mister," Jerry said, though a little reluctantly now. "It's not for sale."

Raine drew one of the pistols from under his coat. "Look, kids, I need that truck and I ain't got time to argue with you." He bobbed his chin at Jerry's rifle. "Lay that bird gun on the ground." Jerry did as he was told. "Give me the keys."

"They're in the ignition," Jerry said.

Raine backed over to the truck and looked inside; the keys were there. Stepping over to the Buick, he removed those keys, put them in his pocket, and popped the trunk with the dashboard button. "Okay, kid," he said to Jerry, "grab one handle of this footlocker and help me set it in the back of your pickup." They moved the locker of cash into the truck bed, up close to the cab so it could not easily be seen by oncoming traffic. Raine reached in, flipped up the buckle latches, and opened the lid. Both he and Jerry momentarily stared in awe at the contents: stacks of currency, sheaves of hundred-dollar bills, banded in bundles of fifty. Bank-stamped in red: five thousand dollars. Fingering out ten of them, Raine tossed them on the ground at Jerry's feet.

"Fifty thousand dollars, kid, and nobody'll know you've got it. All you've got to do is say I stole your truck—"

"We don't want your damned money, mister! And you're not taking our truck, neither!"

It was Sue speaking. She had picked up Jerry's rifle and had it leveled at Raine, who was still holding the pistol, but had it down at his side.

"Look, miss, put the rifle down," Raine said patiently. "We both know you're not going to shoot me—"

"Oh, no?" the girl said—and squeezed the trigger, exactly as Jerry had taught her.

Frank Raine felt a .22 short round rip into his right side. He staggered back two steps but did not fall; the slug had missed his hip bone.

"Lord, Susie, you shot him!" Jerry shrieked.

Raine stared at the girl. A thought surfaced of his own daughter, Lucy, fourteen, back in Tennessee. This kid couldn't be more than a year or two older than her—

"Oh, my God!" Sue bawled. "What did I do? Oh, Lord—!" She threw the rifle away from her as if it were a rattlesnake. Turning, she ran crying across the barren flat. Jerry looked apprehensively at Raine, and the gun he held.

"Go on," Raine said, bobbing his chin at the fleeing girl. Jerry bolted and ran after her.

Shoving the pistol into his coat pocket, Raine twisted his arm around his back, feeling for blood and an exit wound. He found none. Pulling his coat back, he pulled up his shirt and looked at the hole in his side. It was small, puckered, bleeding slowly. Taking a sheaf of currency from the open footlocker, he pressed it over the wound and hitched up his trousers to tighten his belt and hold it in place. A five-thousand-dollar pressure bandage.

Securing the lid of the footlocker, he got into the green pickup and drove away, leaving the Buick and fifty thousand dollars on the ground behind him.

On the way to the meeting place, Raine passed the entrance drive to the New Petroleum Club. He could see two police cruisers with light bars flashing in front of the place. In the next two miles before he got to the cornfield turnoff, a third cruiser, siren wailing, sped past him without a glance.

Raine's side burned like it had a lit highway flare shoved into it. He knew that every bump along the rutted tractor road was pumping an extra spurt of blood out of him, but he was sure he could make it. All he had to do was get to Stella and she would take care of him. When they got back to the motel in Odessa, she could swab it with iodine, pull the slug out with a pair of tweezers, squeeze a tube of antibacterial ointment into the wound, and pack it with gauze pads to stop the bleeding.

He would give old man Pike the green pickup and his share of the take at the cornfield. After Stella cleaned Raine up at the motel, the two of them would head south on some of the hundreds of back roads that covered southwest Texas like dusty veins.

Pike was pacing back and forth when Raine drove up. At the sight of the green pickup truck, he pulled a chrome pistol from under his coat; he put it away when he saw that the driver was Frank Raine.

Stella blanched at the sight of Raine's blood as he got out of the truck. "My God, Frankie—!"

"Never mind," he said sharply. Then to Pike, "Get the tailgate down and drag that footlocker back."

"Where's the other boys?" Pike asked as he did what Raine wanted.

"Dead. They had a sniper at the second-floor window."

"Son of a bitch," said Pike. "Was he wearing a red shirt?"

"Yeah. And I made it a lot redder." To Stella, he said, "Open the locker and count out four hundred grand for Mr. Pike." Raine leaned on the side of the truck and pulled out the other pistol he still had in his waistband, holding it loosely at his side.

"What about the eight hundred thousand them other two boys was gonna split?" Pike asked.

"I'm taking that," Raine said flatly. "You get the share that was agreed on. Everything left over is mine."

Pike hooked both thumbs over his belt buckle and nodded thought-fully. "That slug you take come out the back?" he asked casually. Raine shook his head. "No? Then I'm afraid you ain't gonna make it, son," the old man said quietly. Stella stopped counting and stared at him. "Look at the color of that blood you're losing," Pike said. "It's damn near black. If that bullet didn't go all the way through you, then it's in your liver. You ain't gonna live an hour, if that."

As the old man spoke, Raine's vision blurred and his throat went dry and constricted. He lost all feeling in his right arm and hand; the gun he held dropped to the ground. Five seconds later, Raine dropped to the ground, too. Stella rushed over and knelt beside him. "Oh, baby—"

Pike stepped over and picked up Raine's pistol.

"Sorry, honey," Raine whispered, and closed his eyes.

"Well, little lady, looks like it's just me and you now," Pike said. "You know, you ain't bad-looking. There was a time I'd've taken you *and* the money. But at my age, I tend to look less at younger women and more at older whiskey. So I reckon I'll just have to end it for you like it ended for him."

"Can't we talk it over?" Stella asked. She was still kneeling beside Raine, her hands on his body, one of them slowly working into his coat pocket for what she felt there. Pike was shaking his head.

"Sorry, little lady, but my mind's made up."

"Have it your own way," Stella said, and started working the trigger of the pistol in Raine's coat pocket. She fired four times, right through the pocket, and hit Pike with all four shots, in the chest, every one of them in a six-inch pattern. Just like the young Frank Raine had taught her years ago.

Pike was thrown back half a dozen feet and fell like a tree. Stella pulled the bandana from around Raine's neck, took the gun from his pocket, wiped off her fingerprints, and then put it back. She leaned over and kissed him on the lips.

"Good-bye, baby," she said.

At the footlocker, she took several bills out of a number of sheaves until she had counted out fifty thousand dollars. If they thought all the money was still there, they wouldn't come looking for anybody else. Fifty thousand was enough for her to get home to her mother, and to Lucy, to get settled and start over.

In the car she had come in, Stella circled around Midland and got on the interstate back to Odessa. Once there, she would wipe off her prints, abandon the car, and buy herself a Greyhound ticket. She would go back home on the bus.

Just like she left.

Kate Wilhelm

Rules of the Game

After a varied career as a model, switchboard operator, and insurance company underwriter, KATE WILHELM became a full-time writer in 1956. She received the Hugo and Jupiter awards for her 1976 novel *Where Late the Sweet Birds Sang,* an exploration of the consequences of human cloning. Unlike many authors, she does not limit herself to just one genre of fiction. Her mysteries featuring Constance and Charlie are well known, as are her science fiction/mystery thrillers starring attorney Barbara Holloway. The first in this series, *Death Qualified* (1991), fuses courtroom drama with conjecture about chaos theory. A mainstay with critics and readers alike, her literate fiction has been a staple of year's best lists in both science fiction and mystery. We're pleased to present "Rules of the Game," also first published in *Ellery Queen's Mystery Magazine,* where mystery and fantasy intersect in a most unusual way.

Rules of the Game

Kate Wilhelm

I was watching a senator give a speech a couple of years ago. "They say it's not about money, it's about money. They say it's not about politics, it's about politics. They say it's not about sex, it's about sex."

Then Harry comes in and says, "Hey, so the guy plays around a little. What's the big deal?"

Eleven months ago I kicked Harry out, after six years of being married. He talked me into calling it a trial separation, and agreeing to let him keep this office in our house because he had a year's supply of letterheads and cards with this address. He even had an ad in the Yellow Pages with this address and phone number: Computer Consultant, On Site. He hung out here, ate my food, drank my coffee, and was gone by the time I got home from work. Too late I realized that what he gained from our agreement was rent-free office space and freedom. He never paid a cent of our mortgage after he moved out.

Four months ago I left him a note in his pigsty of an office telling him I wanted a divorce. He never got around to answering. I left the divorce papers on his desk; they vanished. He was as elusive as a wet fish when I tried to reach him.

Two weeks ago I buried him.

And now here he is, Harry Thurman, as big as life, if not as solid. I can see a lamp through him. He's like a full-color transparency.

I drop the coffee-crusted mugs I'm carrying and he lets out a yelp and disappears.

"And stay out!" I yell at the lamp.

I step over the mess on the floor, leave the office, and close the door behind me. I'm shaking, not from fear but from anger. My fury ignited when I opened his apartment to clean it out and found expensive suits, a huge flat-screen television, DVD system, Chivas Regal. . . . He drove a two-year-old BMW. For a year I lived in near poverty, meeting our mort-gage payments, insurance, his and mine, taxes. . . . I cashed out my 401K to meet payments, since I couldn't sell the house without his cooperation. A small inheritance from my aunt had made the down payment; I would have lost everything if I'd failed to pay up every month. My fury increased when I found two gift boxes in his bureau, one addressed to *My darling Marsha*. That was a bracelet with semiprecious gems and pearls. The other was to *Dearest Diane*, a heavy gold chain. I also found four credit-card bills totaling twenty-seven thousand dollars, for which I would be responsible since I was his widow and my name was on them along with his.

"Let it go," I tell myself, taking a gin and tonic into the living room where I sit and regard the bracelet and gold chain on the coffee table.

"Pretty, aren't they?" Harry says, and he's mostly there again, blinking on and off like a Christmas-tree light.

I close my eyes hard. "Either come in all the way, or go out, but stop that blinking!"

"I'm doing the best I can."

When I look up again, he's still there, no longer flickering, and I can still see through him.

"You're not hallucinating," he says. "I'm really here, or mostly here."

I take a long drink. "Why?" My voice is little more than a whisper.

"I don't know why. I just found myself here. You scared the shit out of me when you suddenly saw me, by the way."

"What do you mean? How long have you been here?"

"When did that real estate agent come?"

"This morning."

"I was here then. Two hundred seventy-five thousand for this place! Wow! You'll make out like a bandit. Didn't I tell you that mortgage in-surance was a good idea? And double indemnity for my insurance, plus the BMW. Beautiful rich young widow. What are you going to do with all that dough?"

"Harry! Stop this. Why are you here? What do you want?"

"Aren't you scared?"

"No. I don't believe in ghosts."

After a moment, looking surprised, he says, "Neither do I."

"Isn't there someplace you should be? Report in or something?"

He shrugs expressively. He's very handsome, even if he is dead. Thick black hair just curly enough, wonderful dark blue eyes with makeup-ad lashes, cleft chin. He's wearing pale blue sweats, possibly the clothes he had on when a hit-and-run maniac clipped him and ran.

"You never used to drink alone," he says, eyeing the gin and tonic as if he's longing for one just like it.

"I never used to sit talking to my dead husband."

He reaches for the gold chain. His fingers pass through it. "Ah well," he says. "Diane ran a credit check on me and said get lost. And Marsha wanted to get married and I said there was a little complication, namely you. She got sore. If you can find the receipts, you probably can return them. Be worth your while."

I need a therapist. It's one thing to hallucinate but quite another to hold a conversation with a hallucination. It could even be a serious disorder. I drink the rest of the gin and tonic.

"Did you find the pictures?" he asks.

"What pictures?"

"Oh. Well. What are you going to do with the furniture and things?"

"Garage sale, auction. I don't know."

"You might want to look in the desk drawer. Bottom lifts out, and there's a file folder. . . . I'd get them myself, but . . ." He passes his hand through the bracelet and looks at me with what I used to think was an appealing expression, like a boy caught stealing a cookie.

I go back to his office, step over the broken mugs on the floor, and head for his desk. There are pencils, pens, computer disks, miscellaneous office stuff. I dump it out and there really is a fake bottom. The folder has Polaroid shots of seven different naked women, including me. Just one among many.

I take the folder, pick up a newspaper in the kitchen, and head for the patio and the grill.

"Hey!" he says. "They're worth something, you know."

If he were not already dead, how satisfying it would be to hit him myself with a car, or a train, or a sledgehammer.

My lawyer said that if they found the guy who ran him down, we'd sue him for a million for wrongful death. Rightful death, I think, watching the Polaroid shots writhe, blacken, and curl up, emitting clouds of foul-smelling smoke.

He doesn't walk exactly, just drifts along, near me when I go out to the patio, near me when I go back inside.

"Why are you haunting me?" I demand in the kitchen. "I never did anything to you."

"I'm not haunting you," he says a bit indignantly.

"Then get out, go away, and don't come back."

"I can't," he says. "See, I'm doing my morning run, down by the river, the way I always do, and *whammo,* just nothing. Then I'm here and you're talking to the real estate agent. And neither of you seems to see me or hear me even though I'm yelling my head off."

"Who hit you? Do you know?"

"Nope. Came out of nowhere behind me."

"Have you even tried to find out what you're supposed to do now? Someone to ask what the rules are or something?"

"What rules?"

"I don't know. There must be a protocol, something you're supposed to do, someplace to check in. There are always rules."

"Maybe," he says. "I used to think there'd be a rosy-cheeked cherub waiting to take your hand and guide you, or maybe an old guy with a long white beard and a staff, maybe even a beautiful girl in a flowing white gown, something like that. But like I said: nothing, then here.'"

"A little guy in a red suit with a white-hot trident," I mutter. It's another bureaucratic snarl. I know something about bureaucracy, working for a law firm as I do, or did. I quit a week ago. There are always rules and procedures, routines to follow, and there are always some things that fall through the system and get lost. Like Harry.

"Look," I say, "I believe you're supposed to haunt the person or persons who did you in. You know, revenge, something like that. Or are you haunting the house? If I leave, do you stay with the house, like the refrigerator and stove?"

"I believe," he says, "the people who wrote those rules weren't the ones who knew much about it."

"Well, I'm going out now, and you stay here. Okay?" I pick up my purse, fish out the car keys, and walk out, with him close enough to touch, if there were anything to touch besides a draft of cool air.

My neighbor Elinor Smallwood comes over to say hello, and it's apparent that she doesn't suspect that he is there; neither does her dachshund. "Lori, I hope you're bearing up. Was that a Realtor I saw leaving this morning? Oh, dear, I hope if a buyer turns up, it will be someone compatible who speaks English. You know what I mean?"

I nod and return to the house. He doesn't need doors; he flows inside while I'm still working with the key.

"It isn't fair!" I yell at him. "I don't deserve this! Get out of here! Let me get on with my life."

He flickers for a moment, then spreads his hands helplessly. "I'm as stuck as you are," he says.

I swallow hard as the realization hits me: He really won't, or can't, leave. No matter what I do, he'll be there watching, commenting. I haven't been to bed with a man in a year; I dated a few times but I never let things get out of hand. After all, I was still married. Now I'm not married; I'm thirty years old, and whatever I do, there will be my audience of one.

"Oh, God, what about Carl?" I say out loud. He's the attorney from the office who is helping with my legal affairs. He suggested a quiet dinner in a discreet restaurant, and I know he intended to seduce me afterward, and I intended to let him.

"Aha!" Harry says gleefully. "You have a boyfriend!"

I head for the telephone to break my date with Carl. Actually, he never gave me a second glance until I became a fairly-soon-to-be-rich widow.

After the call I sit on the bench by the wall phone, my gaze on Harry, who is trying to pick up a salt shaker on the table. He swoops like a striking snake and his hand goes through it without causing a tremor; then he sneaks up on it stealthily, with the same effect. Over and over. God help me. If he learns to materialize completely, what then?

I start down a list of friends and family, trying to decide if there is anyone I can confide in. There isn't. Who would believe me? Jo Farrell might, but she would find it exciting and want to hold a séance or something. I can imagine telling Super Iris; she thinks we mean like Superwoman, but it's really Superior Iris, who always knows more than anyone else and is free with opinions and advice. I can hear her voice in my head: "Surely you understand that it isn't about ghosts. . . ." Wherever she starts, it always ends the same: It's really your own fault.

It isn't my fault, I think then, but it certainly is my problem. I remember a little red phone book in the drawer with the false bottom. Why that when he had a Rolodex?

We go back to the office where I pick up the phone book. He tries to grab it, but the only effect is that of a cool breeze blowing across my hand.

In the kitchen I sit at the table and look over the names in the little red book. Eight women! I even know one of them, Sheila Wayman.

Maybe, I tell myself, maybe one of those women still cares, maybe she'll want him back, or maybe I can just dump him on one of them. Transfer him. Turn over custodial care . . . I can feel hysteria mingling with fury now, and I draw in a deep breath. *Eight!* I pick up the Portland phone book and look up Sheila and Roger Wayman. Southwest Spruce. A twenty-minute drive. Halfway to the door I stop. What will I say to her? I snatch up a paperback book from an end table, scrawl her name on the inside cover, and leave. He drifts along at my side.

"Where are we going?"

He oozes between molecules or something and gets in the passenger seat as I get behind the wheel. For the first ten minutes or so he comments on the beautiful June day, or the heavy traffic, or criticizes my driving, whistles in a low tone at a woman walking a dog. . . . I ignore him. When I turn onto Spruce he leans forward, looking around, and now there's a note of uneasiness in his voice when he asks again, "Where are we going?"

A minute later, when I slow down to examine house numbers, he says, "This is crazy. She might not even be home. She was a long time ago. She won't even remember me. What's the point? What are you going to do, make a scene, pick a fight with her?"

I continue to ignore him. At her house I pull into the driveway and get out holding the book. He is close behind me all the way. If she isn't home, I'll sit in the car and read and wait for her, I think grimly, but she answers the doorbell. A small boy on a tricycle is by her side, and she is fifteen pounds overweight.

"Sheila?"

She gasps, recognizing me, and her face pales. "What do you want?" she whispers.

"I'm cleaning out the house and I came across this. I was in the neighborhood and decided to drop it off." I hand the book to her.

"Wow! She's turned into a tub," Harry says at my side. Sheila doesn't even glance in his direction.

In the car again, I say, "One down, seven to go." Harry lets out a ghostly type of moan, and tries to grasp my purse. He's in the passenger seat with my purse on the same seat, where his crotch would be if he had any substance; he is looking at the purse cross-eyed as he makes a quick snatching grab, draws his hand back, and tries with the other one. I start to drive.

At home, I make myself an omelette and salad and he practices. "It's like having a muscle that you can't find exactly," he says. "Like wriggling your ears. I'll get it," he adds confidently. I'm very afraid that he will.

I plot out the following day, using a map, listing the women in the order of proximity, the closest ones on to the most distant. I had all day Saturday, when they might be home, and if not, then Sunday, on into the next week or however long it would take. I would track them down at their offices or schools or wherever they spent their time and see each one, give each one the opportunity to see Harry.

And if none of them claims him? No answer follows the question.

I don't bother with an excuse again. When Hilary Winstead comes to the door, I say, "I'm Lori Thurman. I was cleaning out Harry's office and I came across your pictures. I burned them. I just wanted you to know."

Behind me Harry says, "She makes a mean martini."

Hilary Winstead stares at me, moistens her lips, and then slams the door.

Bette Hackman is tall and willowy, very beautiful. Harry sighs when she says, "What do you mean? I paid for those pictures. He swore that was all he had. That bastard!"

On Southeast Burnside I detour a few blocks and park at the cemetery. A few people are around, none paying any attention to us as I walk to the new grave of Harry Thurman.

"That's where you planted me?"

"That's where you belong. Get in there and go back to sleep."

He shudders and drifts backward. "You're out of your mind."

I guess I am. What I was hoping was that a guy with a long beard and a staff, or a cherub, or even a beautiful woman would cry out, "Harry! We've been looking everywhere for you. Come along now." We return to the car and I drive on.

No one answers the doorbell at Wanda Sorenson's house.

Diane Shuster says, "I could care less."

"Shrewd, but nearly illiterate," Harry comments. "Great ass, though."

I am ready to give it up. No one sees him, or notices a cold breeze, or anything else out of the ordinary.

Then he says, "How it goes is, they'd call for help with the new computer, or new software, and I'd go in and find things screwed up royally. So I'd fool around and get things working, and accidentally log on to a porn site, something like that, and then . . . One thing leads to another."

I grit my teeth and look at the next name: Sonia Welch. He nods when I turn onto River Drive. "Ah, wait until you see that house! Gorgeous place! Sonia broke it off before I was ready, actually. Afraid her old man would find out."

He sounds regretful when he says, "That was part of it, of course, the fear of discovery, a mad husband with a gun, something like that. A little added spice."

My lips are clamped so hard they hurt. I am determined to ignore him until he gets so bored he'll find a way to go somewhere else. He'll find someone who knows the rules.

"That's it," Harry says, pointing to a tall gray house nearly hidden behind shrubbery. It *is* beautiful, with bay windows, stained-glass panels, professional landscaping. . . . A heavyset man in shorts, holding a can of varnish, is touching up a motorboat in the driveway.

"Hello," I say, getting out of the car. "I'm looking for Sonia. Is she home?"

The man looks me over as if I am up for auction.

"The husband. He's a shrink," Harry says. "Would you tell him your innermost secrets?"

I have to admit, although silently, that I would not. His eyes are as cold and fathomless as black ice.

"She's back on the terrace," Welch says. "Go on around." He motions toward a walkway and returns to his boat repair.

I walk under a lattice covered with roses in bloom. The fragrance is intoxicating. I see the woman before I step onto the terrace; she is dozing, apparently, with a magazine over her face against the late afternoon sun.

"Sonia?" I say.

With a languid motion she moves the magazine and looks around over her shoulder. Then she jumps up and jams both hands over her mouth, staring wide-eyed, not at me but at my side, at Harry.

"No," she cries then, and begins to back up, nearly falls over the chaise behind her, catches her balance, and continues to back up around a glass-topped table, staring, paler than death.

"I didn't mean to, Harry," she whispers. "It was an accident. Don't come closer, stay back! Please, don't come closer!"

Harry is flickering wildly, moving toward her like a cloud fired with lightning. Then he goes out. Sonia keeps backing up.

"Harry, stay away! I had to do it. I told you he was suspicious! I told you to stay away! I had to do it! You should have stayed away! Don't touch me! Oh, God, don't touch me!"

I don't think she even saw me. I turn and retrace my steps under the roses and out to the car.

"Wasn't she there?" Welch asks, looking up.

"I think she's sleeping. I didn't want to disturb her. I just wanted to thank her for a favor she did me. It isn't important."

I knew there were rules, I tell myself, driving away. There are always rules.

Val McDermid

The Wagon Mound

VAL MCDERMID, a former journalist, is the author of sixteen mysteries, including three series starring Kate Brannigan, Lindsay Gordon, and the team of Tony Hill and Carol Jordan. *A Place of Execution* (1999) won the Macavity, Anthony, Dilys, and *Los Angeles Times* awards for best novel. Lately, her books have become not only genre favorites but international bestsellers as well. Her most recent work is *The Last Temptation,* published in 2002. Along the way she has written the occasional short story, such as "The Wagon Mound," from *Ellery Queen's Mystery Magazine,* in which the simple desire for revenge comes back to haunt the person who was wronged in the first place.

The Wagon Mound

Val McDermid

Nothing destroys the quality of life so much as insomnia. Ask any parent of a new baby. It only takes a few broken nights to reduce the most calm and competent person to a twitching shadow of their normal proficiency. My wakefulness started when the nightmares began. When I did manage to drop off, the visions my subconscious mind conjured up were guaranteed to wake me, sweating and terrified, within a couple of hours of nodding off. It didn't take long before I began to fear sleep itself, dreading the demons that ripped through the fabric of my previous ease. I tried sleeping pills, I tried alcohol. But nothing worked.

I never dreamed that I'd rediscover the art of sleeping through the night thanks to a legal precedent. In 1961, the Privy Council heard a case concerning a negligent oil spillage from a ship called the *Wagon Mound* in Sydney Harbour. The oil fouled a nearby wharf, and in spite of expert advice that it wouldn't catch fire, when the wharf's owners began welding work, the oil did exactly what it wasn't supposed to do. The fire that followed caused enough damage for it to be worth taking to court, where the Privy Council finally decreed that the ship's owners weren't liable because the *type* of harm sustained by the plaintiff was not, as the law required, reasonably foreseeable. When Roger, the terminally boring commercial attaché at the Moscow embassy, launched into the tale the other night in the bar at Proyekt OGI, he could never have imagined that it would change my life so dramatically. But then, lawyers have never been noted for their imagination.

Proximity. That's another legal principle that came up during Roger's lecture. How many intervening stages lie between cause and effect. I think, by then, I was the only one listening, because his disquisition had made me think back to the starting point of my sleepless nights.

Although the seeds were sown when my boss in London decided to invite the bestselling biographer Tom Uttley on a British Council tour of

Russia, I can't be held accountable for that. The first point where I calculate I have to accept responsibility was on the night train from Moscow to St. Petersburg.

I'd been looking after Tom ever since he'd landed at Sheremetyevo Airport two days before. I hadn't seen him smile in all that time. He'd lectured lugubriously at the university, glumly addressed a gathering at the British Council library, done depressing signings at two bookshops, and sulked his way around a reception at the Irish embassy. Even the weather seemed to reflect his mood, gray clouds lowering over Moscow and turning April into autumn. Minding visiting authors is normally the part of my job I like best, but spending time with Tom was about as much fun as having a hole in your shoe in a Russian winter. We'd all been hoping for some glamour from Tom's visit; his Channel Four series on the roots of biography had led us to expect a glowing Adonis with twinkling eyes and a gleaming grin. Instead, we got a glowering black dog.

Over dinner on the first evening, he'd downed his vodka like a seasoned Russia hand, and gloomed like the most depressive Slav in the Caucasus. On the short walk back to his hotel, I asked him if everything was all right. "No," he said shortly. "My wife's just left me."

Right, I thought. *Don't go there, Sarah.* "Oh," I think I said.

The final event of his Moscow visit was a book signing, and afterward, I took him to dinner to pass the time until midnight, when the train would leave for St. Pete's. That was when the floodgates opened. He was miserable, he admitted. He was terrible company. But Rachel had walked out on him after eight years of marriage. There wasn't anyone else, she'd said. It was just that she was bored with him, tired of his celebrity, fed up with feeling inferior intellectually. I pointed out that these reasons seemed somewhat contradictory.

He brightened up at that. And suddenly the sun came out. He acted as if I'd put my finger on something that should make him feel better about the whole thing. He radiated light, and I basked in the warmth of his smile. Before long, we were laughing together, telling our life stories, swapping intimacies. Flirting, I suppose.

We boarded the train a little before midnight, each dumping our bags in our separate first-class compartments. Then Tom produced a bottle of Georgian champagne from his holdall. "A nightcap?" he suggested.

"Why not?" I was in the mood, cheered beyond reason by the delights of his company. He sat down on the sleeping berth beside me, and it seemed only natural when his arm draped across my shoulders. I remember the smell of him: a dark, masculine smell with an overlay of some spicy cologne with an edge of cinnamon. If I'm honest, I was willing him to kiss me before he actually did. I was entirely disarmed by his charm. But I also felt sorry for the pain that had been so obvious over the previous two days. And maybe, just maybe, the inherent Dr. Zhivago romance of the night train tipped the balance.

I don't usually do this kind of thing. What am I saying? I *never* do this kind of thing. In four years of chasing around after authors, or having them chase after me, I'd not given in to temptation once. But Tom penetrated all of my professional defenses, and I moaned under his hands from Moscow to St. Petersburg. By morning, he swore I'd healed his heart. By the time he left St. Pete's three days later, we'd arranged to meet in London, where I was due to attend a meeting in ten days' time. I'd been out of love for a long time; it wasn't hard to fall for a man who was handsome, clever, and amusing, and who seemed to find me irresistible.

Two days later, I got his first E-mail. I'd been checking every waking hour on the hour, wondering and edgy. It turned out I had good reason to be anxious. The E-mail was short and sour. "Dear Sarah, Rachel and I have decided we want to try to resolve our difficulties. It'll come as no surprise to you that my marriage is my number-one priority. So I think it best if we don't communicate further. Sorry if this seems cold, but there's no other way to say it. Tom."

I was stunned. This wasn't cold, it was brutal. A hard jab below the ribs, designed to take my breath away and deflect any possible comeback. I felt the physical shock in the pit of my stomach.

Of course, I blamed myself for my stupidity, my eagerness to believe that a man as charismatic as Tom could fall for me. Good old reliable Sarah, the safe pair of hands who second-guessed author's needs before they could even voice them. I felt such a fool. A bruised, exploited fool.

Time passed, but there was still a raw place deep inside me. Tom Uttley had taken more from me than a few nights of sexual pleasure; he'd taken away my trust in my judgment. I told nobody about my humiliation. It would have been one pain too many.

Then Lindsay McConnell arrived. An award-winning dramatist, she'd come to give a series of workshops on radio adaptation. She was impeccably professional, no trouble to take care of. And we hit it off straightaway. On her last night, I took her to my favorite Moscow eating place, a traditional Georgian restaurant tucked away in a courtyard in the Armenian quarter. As the wine slipped down, we gossiped and giggled. Then, in the course of some anecdote, she mentioned Tom Uttley. Just hearing his name made my guts clench. "You know Tom?" I asked, struggling not to sound too interested.

"Oh, God, yes. I was at university with Rachel, his wife. Of course, you had Tom out here last year, didn't you? He said he'd had a really interesting time."

I bet he did, I thought bitterly. "How are they now? Tom and Rachel?" I asked with the true masochist's desire for the twist of the knife.

Lindsay looked puzzled. "What do you mean, how are they now?"

"When Tom was here, Rachel had just left him."

She frowned. "Are you sure you're not confusing him with someone else? They're solid as a rock, Tom and Rachel. God knows, if he was mine I'd have murdered him years ago, but Rachel thinks the sun shines out of his arse."

It was my turn to frown. "He told me she'd just walked out on him. He was really depressed about it."

Lindsay shook her head. "God, how very Tom. He hates touring, you know. He'll do anything to squeeze out a bit of sympathy, make sure he gets premier-league treatment. He just likes to have everyone running around after him, Sarah. I'm telling you, Rachel has never left him. Now I think about it, that week he was in Russia, I went around there for dinner. Me and Rachel and a couple of her colleagues. You know, from *Material Girl*. The magazine she works for. I think if they'd split up, she might have mentioned it, don't you?"

I hoped I wasn't looking as stunned as I felt. I'd never thought of myself as stupid, but that calculating bastard had spun me a line and reeled me in open-mouthed like the dumbest fish in the pond. But, of course, because I'm a woman and that's how we're trained to think, I was still blaming myself more than him. I'd clearly been sending out the signals of needy gullibility and he'd just come up with the right line to exploit them.

I was still smarting from what I saw as my self-inflicted wound a few weeks later at the Edinburgh Book Festival, where we British Council types gather like bees to pollen. But at least I'd finally have the chance to share my idiocy with Camilla, my opposite number in Jerusalem. We'd worked together years before in Paris, and we'd become bosom buddies. The only reason I hadn't told her about Tom previously was that every time I wrote it down in an E-mail, it just looked moronic. It needed a girls' night in with a couple of bottles of decent red wine before I could let this one spill out.

Late on the second night, after a particularly grueling Amnesty International event, we sneaked back to the flat we were sharing with a couple of the boys from the Berlin office and started in on the confessional. My story crawled out of me, and I realized yet again how foolish I'd been from the horrified expression on Camilla's face. That and her appalled silence. "I don't believe it," she breathed.

"I know, I know," I groaned. "How could I have been so stupid?"

"No, no," she said angrily. "Not you, Sarah. Tom Uttley."

"What?"

"That duplicitous bastard Uttley. He pulled exactly the same stunt on Georgie Bullen in Madrid. The identical line about his wife leaving him. She told me about it when I flew in for Semana Negra last month."

"But I thought Georgie was living with someone?"

"She was," Camilla said. "Paco, the stage manager at the opera house. She'd taken Uttley down to Granada to do some lectures there; that's when it happened. Georgie saw the scumbag off on the plane and came straight home and told Paco it was over, she'd met someone else. She threw him out, then two days later she got the killer E-mail from Tom."

We gazed at each other, mouths open. "The bastard," I said. For the first time, anger blotted out my self-pity and pain.

"Piece of shit," Camilla agreed.

We spent the rest of the bottle and most of the second one thinking of ways to exact revenge on Tom Uttley, but we both knew that there was no way I was going back to Moscow to find a hit man to take him out. The trouble was, we couldn't think of anything that would show him up without making us look like silly credulous girls. Most blokes, no matter how much they might pretend otherwise, would reckon, *Good on him for working out such a foolproof scam to get his leg over.* Most women would reckon we'd got what we deserved for being so naïve.

I was thirty thousand feet above Poland when the answer came to me. The woman in the seat next to me had been reading *Material Girl* and she offered it to me when she'd finished. I looked down the editorial list, curious to see exactly what Rachel Uttley did on the magazine. Her name was near the top of the credits. *Fiction Editor, Rachel Uttley.* A quick look at the contents helped me deduce that as well as the books page, Rachel was responsible for editing the three short stories. There, at the end of the third, was a sentence saying that submissions for publication should be sent to her.

I've always wanted to write. One of the reasons I took this job in the first place was to learn as much as I could from those who do it successfully. I had half a novel on my hard disk, but I reckoned it was time to try a short story.

Two days later, I'd written it. The central character was a biographer who specialized in seducing professional colleagues on foreign trips with a tale about his wife having left him. Then he would dump them as soon as he'd got home. When one of his victims realizes what he's been up to, she exposes the serial adulterer by sending his wife, a magazine editor, a short story revealing his exploits. And the wife, recognizing her errant husband from the pen portrait, finally does walk out on him.

Before I could have second thoughts, I printed it out and stuffed it in an envelope addressed to Rachel at *Material Girl.* Then I sat back and waited.

For a couple of weeks, nothing happened. Then, one Tuesday morning, I was sitting in the office browsing BBC on-line news. His name leapt out at me. TOM UTTLEY DIES IN BURGLARY, read the headline in the latest news section. I clicked on the "more" button.

> Bestselling biographer and TV presenter Tom Uttley was found dead this morning at his home in North London. It is believed he disturbed a burglar. He died from a single stab wound to the stomach. Police say there was evidence of a break-in at the rear of the house.
>
> Uttley was discovered by his wife, Rachel, a journalist. Police are calling for witnesses who may have seen one or two men fleeing the scene in the early hours of the morning.

I had to read the bare words three or four times before they sank in. Suddenly, his lies didn't matter anymore. All I could think of was his eyes on mine, the flash of his easy smile, the touch of his hand. The sparkle of wit in his conversation. The life in him that had been snuffed out. The books he would never write.

Over a succession of numb days, I pursued the story via the Internet. Bits and pieces emerged gradually. They'd had an attempted burglary a few months before. Rachel, who was a poor sleeper, had taken sleeping pills and stuffed earplugs in before going to bed. Tom, the police reckoned, had heard the sound of breaking glass and gone downstairs to investigate. The intruder had snatched up a knife from the kitchen worktop and plunged it into his stomach, then fled. Tom had bled to death on the kitchen floor. It had taken him awhile to die, they thought. And Rachel had come down for breakfast to find him stiff and cold on the kitchen floor. Poor bloody Rachel, I thought.

On the fifth day after the news broke, there was a large manila envelope among my post, franked with the *Material Girl* logo. My story had come winging its way back to me. Inside, there was a handwritten note from Rachel.

Dear Sarah,

Thank you so much for your submission. I found your story intriguing and thought-provoking. A real eye-opener, in fact. But I felt the ending was rather weak and so I regret we're unable to publish it. However, I like your style. I'd be very interested to see more of your work.

Gratefully yours,
Rachel Uttley

That's when I realized what I'd done. Like Oscar Wilde, I'd killed the thing I'd loved.

That's when my sleepless nights started.

And that's why I'm so very, very grateful for Roger and the case they call Wagon Mound (No. 1). And for an understanding of proximity. Thanks to him, I've finally realized I'm not the guilty party here. Neither is Rachel.

The guilty party is the one who started the wagon rolling. Lovely, sexy, reckless Tom Uttley.

Janice Law

Ghost Writer

JANICE LAW was one of the first authors to use a female detective when *The Big Payoff,* featuring Anna Peters, was published
in 1975. Since then, the intrepid Peters has appeared in eight other
novels. Law is an instructor at the University of Connecticut,
from which she received a Ph.D., and is also the author, under
the name of Janice Law Trecker, of several nonfiction works. She
writes short stories, as well as contributing to academic journals
and popular magazines. We are pleased to include her September
contribution to *Ellery Queen's Mystery Magazine,* "Ghost Writer,"
a simple, chilling tale about the hazards of the writing business.

Ghost Writer

Janice Law

Marvin was excited when his agent called. It had been awhile since he'd heard from Audrey, whose soft, raspy voice was permanently, if hopelessly, associated in his mind with sales and contracts, and the possibility of fame, if not fortune. Some foreign rights? A chapter in an anthology? Ready cash?

"Can you stop by today?" Audrey asked.

Of course, Marvin said he would, clearing out time that would otherwise have been spent in a fruitless perusal of his notebooks or in research on-line for a now overdue article or in sharpening pencils and tidying his desk and probably, the way things had been going, quitting early to hit the beach. Instead, he fought the traffic down I-95 through blizzards of snowbirds and the mind-numbing exhaust of heavy trucks to Audrey's blue glass office building in the center of Lauderdale.

Audrey Striker had been his agent for six years. Three books, U.K. rights on one, a modest movie option on another: not bad, not great, about par for the course for a midlist author of more ambition than talent and more talent than luck. What else is new? Another agent might have done better for him but would just as likely have done worse. Besides, he liked Audrey's throaty, world-weary voice, her greed, her toughness.

She was waiting for him, that was surprise number one, and number two, Cindy, her secretary, was nowhere to be seen. He was being allowed an unprecedented private audience. "Come in, Marv," Audrey called when her office door beeped. She was sitting with her back to the blue-tinged panorama of pastel condo and hotel towers, her large, well-shaped head awkwardly balanced on her small twisted frame. Her spindly legs were propped up on a footstool. Her cane was beside her, the motorized wheelchair she used for longer distances parked in the corner.

"I've been looking at your latest royalty statements," she said.

Marvin's heart sank. He hoped she had not called him all the way downtown just to tell him that his career was in the toilet. He took one of the handsome leather chairs and angled it away from the bright pastel towers of the cityscape toward the comforting expanse of close-packed bookshelves. He could see the slender spines of his own novels.

"I think we need to make a move in a slightly different direction, and I think you might be right for a proposal I've received."

"What sort of proposal?"

"Completion of a dark-fantasy trilogy. I have the contract in hand."

"Sorry," said Marvin, disappointed in spite of himself, "that's hardly my field."

Audrey was undeterred. "We already have a fairly detailed plot outline of the first novel, and rough—I'll be honest—*very* rough outlines of the second and third. However, with the exception of two characters . . ." She scrambled among her notes. "Ah, here we go. Someone called Lord Ostrucht and the Lady Fergaine must be spared at all costs. Otherwise, you would have almost complete freedom. And," she added, seeing Marvin was about to interrupt, "if the first novel proves successful, as I'm sure it will, you would have even more freedom with the later books. The key, Marv, dear, is speed and quality. Write me a good book fast and we can make a lot of money."

"Look, Audrey, not that I don't appreciate it, but I write literate contemporary novels. I don't want a reputation for swords and fantasy."

Audrey gave a smile that marred rather than enhanced her fine, clean features. Nature, Marvin thought, had had a grand design in mind with Audrey and then, at the last moment, smashed it. "Your last two novels earned mid-four-figure advances," she said. "You can't live on that. Think of this as work to support your serious writing. Also, I can assure you, Marv, dear, that your name will never be mentioned. Will never be, must never be; that is a most important condition."

Interesting! Marvin racked his brain to think of who could command serious advances on the basis of rough outlines. The only possibilities were names big enough to scare him just a little. It was one thing to dismiss certain popular works; it was quite another to invent the same sort of audience-pleasing junk. "How much?"

"The whole package is two-point-five million. I am authorized to give you a partial advance of fifty thousand dollars on signing. On completion of each novel, you and the writer whose name will appear on the jacket split the profits, advance, royalties, everything, fifty-fifty."

The sum was a shock, almost a physical shock, and it took Marvin a moment to digest the possibilities of repairing the Datsun, paying off his credit cards, leaving the Sun 'n Surf apartments.

"Are you on?" Audrey asked.

He could feel a little bubble of exhilaration growing around his heart, but he didn't quite trust himself to decide yet.

"I know you can do it," Audrey said, "and I think you can do it quickly."

"How fast and how long?"

"I need a manuscript of no less than six hundred pages; a little longer would be better, but six hundred would do."

"Whew!" said Marvin.

"We have a full year. I was able to get an extension," Audrey added a trifle grimly, "on the grounds of ill health."

"And are we sick?" Marvin asked.

"We are drunk, if you must know." Audrey's tone was drily sarcastic. "We have developed multiple addictions and responsibility issues and a damn bad attitude! I need you to do this, Marv, dear," she said in a different tone. "You and I will earn every penny, but it's a pretty penny, and having invested twenty years of work in—our author—I'm not about to lose the best contract I've ever negotiated."

"All right," said Marvin, "but I'd better have a look at the outline and I'd better read some of the the the other books—there are others, right?"

"The proverbial five-foot bookshelf." Audrey levered herself to her feet, grabbed her cane, and limped to the nearest bookcase. She came back with a handful of novels that she laid facedown on her desk. "There will be a confidentiality statement for you to sign," Audrey said. "All the usual. Basically, you promise never to reveal your authorship."

"As if I'd want to," said Marvin.

"But understand, Marv, dear, only your best work will do for this project."

"My best work, my heart and soul." Marvin could already feel himself adjusting to prosperity.

Audrey produced a thick folder of legal documents. She offered the confidentiality statement first. "In case, Marv, dear, you should change your mind." This document was as near to ironclad as dozens of "to wits," "whatsoevers," and "to whomevers" could make it.

Marvin signed with a flourish, then turned over the first novel in the stack on the desk. "Ah," he said in surprise; he had read some of Hilaire LaDoux's novels and liked them. "I thought LaDoux did sci-fi."

"All the work is on the border of the genres," Audrey said. "Alternate worlds, alternate futures—same old human nature."

"Here's to human nature," Marvin said and held out his hand for the contract.

"You're sure?" Audrey asked. "Please be sure, Marv, dear, because there won't be time to get another writer if you change your mind."

"Worry not, sweet Audrey!" He flipped to the end of the document and signed his name. "I'm your ghost."

He left with a stack of LaDoux's novels in a Burdine's shopping bag and stopped at his local liquor store on the way home for some really good beer and a bottle of vintage Bordeaux. I'm going to be rich, if not famous, he told himself, and better by far to be at least one or the other.

Marvin sat down on his minuscule balcony, poured a Bellhaven, and opened *The Cave of the Winds,* the first novel in LaDoux's Galatan Trilogy.

He read for three hours, making notes occasionally on a yellow pad as he picked out favorite vocabulary, sentence structures, the little tricks like adjectives grouped in threes and a fondness—a weakness in Marvin's eyes—for beginning with participial phrases.

After dinner, he checked the outline for *Dragon in the Sun*. It was, as Audrey had promised, thoroughly detailed. Ten single-spaced pages outlined an epic and dynastic struggle that he found intimidatingly inventive until he realized that most of the events had been lifted from the Hundred Years War in France and the English Wars of the Roses. Okay!

Marvin made a note to himself to begin some serious historical reading—the Borgias should be good for a plot or two, and the Russians for a series. He was sure that the various Ivans and Peters, not to mention the licentious Catherine the Great, could help flesh out the skimpy notes for *Dragon* II and III.

Though Marvin normally worked in fits and starts as inspiration took him, he was at his desk early the next morning. He had a year to produce six hundred pages, which meant, he calculated, roughly two pages a day, the other two months left over for the inevitable mishaps that afflict manuscripts as well as man. He was slightly daunted at the prospect of working up scenes and characters that were not his own, and he dawdled, as he usually did, straightening his desk and hopping up to water the plants and take out the garbage. It was on this latter errand that Marvin had the happy inspiration of imaging not the novel but Hilaire LaDoux.

He sat down at his computer and told himself that this new book would be the contrivance of an invented character, a bestselling novelist of considerable talent and an unerring popular touch named Hilaire LaDoux. His LaDoux invariably started early in the morning, well before time for the first drink of the day, and tapped out exactly two—no, better make it four—pages a day, as good genre writers were known for their productivity.

Hilaire LaDoux would work to something ancient, Marvin decided, and he rejected several possibilities before selecting Monteverdi, his *Orpheus*. Unlike Marvin, who liked to write sitting on his balcony, LaDoux would keep the shades drawn and would wear something elegant and unusual, something Marvin would have to acquire. But for now, semidarkness and *Orpheus* would have to be good enough. He slid the CD into his computer, heard the chords, exotic with the everlasting strangeness of genius, and began typing: "Trotting along the long, weary, dry road into Balson, Lord Ostrucht saw clouds black as serpents darkening the horizon and laid his hand on the Blade of Zermain. He was alone now, he was the only one left. . . ."

Although Marvin took some time to settle into this routine, so different from his own, novelty proved potent. Day after day, Lord Ostrucht struggled with warriors and wizards, with dragons and other chimeras of the mind, searching always for the Lady Fergaine. At first, Marvin stayed close to the original design, but very soon Ostrucht began to develop some new and interesting habits.

Marvin knew that he was really on his way when he discovered one morning that the cliché dragon of one of the planned set pieces had evolved into a yellow-tinged mist, so faint as to be almost subliminal. This scarcely noticed alteration in the atmosphere gradually disturbed perception, causing its victims to see the world as horror, as such unrelieved and dreadful ugliness that they were driven to despair.

"That's very good," Audrey said, looking up from the latest installment of the manuscript. "That's very good, indeed." Like all authors, Marvin needed compliments and reassurance, particularly during composition, and she had learned the right way to do this: Praise only the book and never, by so much as a syllable, hint that he had a genuine flair for this sort of thing. In fact, Audrey was convinced that Marvin was writing better than ever, that a sort of literate action was his true métier. Instead, she said, "Very LaDoux. Hyper LaDoux."

Marvin smiled. "The creation of the character was the key thing— and unexpectedly inspiring."

"Lord Ostrucht," Audrey said.

"No, no, he's quite an interesting fellow, but I meant Hilaire LaDoux."

Audrey looked at him. Yes, now that he mentioned it, she could see some changes, which she had registered without attaching importance to them. An expensive haircut and good clothes were only to be expected from sudden prosperity, but she would not have expected Marvin's choices: a cerise silk shirt, and an Italian silk and wool sweater patterned in mustard, lavender, and sienna, worn with khakis and sandals. Marvin had always been a jeans and T-shirt kind of guy who owned a blue suit for good. He'd added a pair of tinted glasses, too, which shadowed his eyes and made him look subtly different, enough like the real LaDoux to give Audrey a little frisson, because no image of Hilaire LaDoux had been published for years. Well, she wasn't going to worry about that! Whatever works, she thought, and congratulated herself on spotting Marv's potential. "We'll have no problem completing the book," she said.

"No problem at all, and, Audrey, I'm getting so many ideas for volumes two and three. I've started to plan material for future books. Now this scene . . ." He turned the pile of manuscript around and ruffled through the pages. "Here, in chapter sixteen where I've introduced Ranoch, the squire . . ."

"I like Ranoch," said Audrey.

"I'm glad you do, because I see an important role for him in the second volume."

She pulled out a yellow pad and began making notes. When they were finished, she assured Marvin that the publisher would be thrilled, then shook his hand and saw him out of the office herself, as Cindy, who was apparently not privy to the arrangement with Mr. LaDoux, had been sent on an errand.

Marvin supposed that was only prudent, though in his own mind Hilaire LaDoux came into existence when he put on the very handsome silk jacket that Hilaire wrote in, added the blue-tinted spectacles, and slid

the Monteverdi *Orpheus* into the CD player. During the less and less frequent days when Marvin took off, wore his own clothes, listened to Talking
Heads, drank beer, and loafed on the beach, Hilaire LaDoux, Esquire, simply ceased to exist, leaving Marvin to enjoy the fruits of his labor and of
LaDoux's reputation.

And after the first volume was published to acclaim and profit, there
seemed no reason why Marvin couldn't continue writing about Lord Ostrucht and the Lady Fergaine and their ilk virtually forever. The second
volume was finished and Marvin was well into the third before the first
cloud appeared.

He was in Audrey's office for one of their now routine private meetings. The latest chapters of *The Dragon's Child* lay on the desk between
them, and Audrey was running her delicate fingers nervously over the pages.
"Quite brilliant," she said, tapping the manuscript. "Everyone agrees, and
you know, Marv, dear, I'd be the first to tell you if the books weren't up
to par."

He did know that.

"So you'll know this is none of my doing. I'm thoroughly satisfied,
and so is everybody at the publishing house."

"What's the matter?" Marvin asked, sensing a problem without really
being troubled by it. He had money—and people like Audrey—to sort
problems out for him. Since the great success of the *Dragon* books, their
relationship had undergone a sea change: Now she waited for his calls and
arranged her schedule to suit him. Now it was her plans and her strategy
that came under scrutiny as much as his manuscripts.

"Well, it's Hilaire, of course. Jealousy, I'm sure. If I'd thought, Marv,
dear, I'd never have let *Dragon* be nominated for any award whatsoever.
Never."

"Hilaire?" It took Marvin a moment to remember that there was such
a person with volition of his own, a real person whose desires could not
be altered by a few lines of type. "He's unhappy? Fifteen weeks on the
bestseller list, foreign rights, a pot of found money—what more does he
want?"

"He's feeling creative again. He feels—well, Marv, dear, he feels he
doesn't need you anymore."

Marvin's first reaction was fury, modulating into shock. "He can go
to hell! I've got another three novels plotted out, plus some terrific new
characters!" It was illogical, inconceivable, grotesquely and monstrously un-
fair. And besides, he'd been counting on the money.

"He's got an ironclad contract. Look, Marv, dear, I've tried to talk to
him, but he claims he's inspired. And more important, he's determined to
cut back on the drinking."

"Great for him. All right, let him write. I still have three good plots
and half a dozen new characters."

"His characters," she said. "All his. You know that, Marv."

"So I change the names and we're still in business."

"And who are you?" she asked. "Do you think I can get as good a contract as you can get from selling the outlines to Hilaire? Be real."

Marvin swore there must be some way to indicate that he was the writer behind LaDoux's latest bestseller, and Audrey raised the confidentiality agreement. But she promised to hold LaDoux up for plenty. "I think even a credit isn't out of the question. Something along the lines of 'based on a story by,' which will do you good later, Marv. Besides, you can get back to your own writing now, and with what you'll make from the plot outlines . . ."

Marvin was furious, but though he had a lawyer friend go over the contract not once but twice, there was no way out. LaDoux had all rights to the books. As far as the publishing world went, it was Marvin, not Hilaire LaDoux, who was an imaginary character, or rather, what was worse, a middling author with no real prospects.

For consolation, he had a good whack of money for the work he'd done on *The Dragon's Child,* but he absolutely refused to sell anything more, causing Audrey to roll her eyes and to wonder aloud why she hadn't taken to representing sensible people like stuntmen and professional wrestlers. Then she sighed and told Marv that he might perhaps change his mind.

"After all," she added, accurately, but somewhat unkindly, "now you have what you've always said you wanted: time and money to do your own writing."

So he got busy. He opened his old notebooks and took up a plot he'd begun then set aside, a story about a talented man down on his luck in paradise: a.k.a. South Florida. Marvin struggled with it for several months, but the story was dead in the water. Oh, the writing was good; Marvin had an easy style that rolled from one paragraph to the next without the slightest hitch, but also without the oddity and flare that can illuminate old stories and make familiar characters fresh.

The very smoothness that had rendered Lord Ostrucht, the Lady Fergaine, and a host of supernatural entities plausible worked against Marvin's contemporary characters. They were just a little bit boring, and, realizing that, he began to find new and creative ways to delay his stints at the computer. When he got fed up with procrastination, he'd throw on his swim trunks and head for the beach: As far as writing went, Marvin was stymied.

Then, one depressing morning, just as an experiment, he got up early, put on Hilaire's silk writing jacket, and dropped *Orpheus* in the CD player. When he sat down to work at the keyboard, Lord Ostrucht was waiting for him, sitting melancholy on the back of his black charger, reading a farewell letter from the Lady Fergaine. Marvin almost wept with joy.

Two days later, when he'd at last obtained LaDoux's address from an unwary new editorial publicist, Marvin was surprised to find that the novelist lived not more than five miles away, along a swanky stretch between the inland waterway and the ocean. Marvin drove out that same night, burdened with a bottle of expensive white French Burgundy and uncertain intentions.

Decorative lights lined the waterway side of the narrow street, illuminating boat slips and gazebos and freestanding decks where the big spenders could sip cocktails and contemplate hundreds of thousands of dollars' worth of marine horsepower. The ocean side was dark with overgrown trees and ambitious plantings. Only a few discreet lights punctuated the shadows, revealing heavy metal gates across nicely tiled driveways or else big signs indicating that trespassing on a job site is a felony in Florida. Since the neighborhood seemed full of folks constructing hurricane bait, there were plenty of these posted warnings.

LaDoux's house was of an older, less ostentatious vintage, well screened by live oaks, bamboos, and a variety of large and thriving palms—*My kind of place,* Marvin thought. The flat-roofed building was coated with a scabbed and cracked rust-colored stucco, vaguely Mexican in inspiration and adjoined by a massive screen made of blocks interwoven with a bright climbing vine. Several soft yellow lights, perhaps candles, glimmered behind this screen, and a weak bulb illuminated the weathered front door. Otherwise, the house, which was handsome in conception, but clearly neglected, remained in darkness.

Marvin stepped out of his car to the sound of surf and of cars and motorcycles passing. He rang the intercom buzzer on the gate several times, and he was ready to give up when a voice, quite loud and very close to him, asked what he was doing and what the hell he wanted. Marvin gave a start. Someone about his own height and weight was standing half hidden by the dappled purple and ocher leaves of a rampant ornamental shrub. The man wore a white shirt and an ascot, like a country-house extra in an English movie, but what sent the evening lurching in a direction Marvin had not expected was the man's appearance. Marvin immediately recognized their surprising resemblance. "I was hoping to see Hilaire LaDoux," Marvin said. "I'm a big fan of his books."

"Take a look and get out," said LaDoux, starting to turn away. Marvin noticed that he carried a drink in one hand.

"You might want to take a look at me, too," Marvin said. "I wrote your last two novels."

"What are you doing here?" LaDoux demanded, his voice rising. "You're not supposed to have any contact with me. That was in the contract!"

"No," said Marvin, "that was about the only thing that wasn't."

"Audrey should have thought of that," LaDoux said querulously. "Did she give you my address? I'll fire her if she did. No one's supposed to have my address."

"I acquired it elsewhere," Marvin said. "Look, I thought we might work out a deal. Something beneficial to us both."

LaDoux eyed him suspiciously. "What's Audrey been telling you? She's wrong to give you any hope at all. I'll get back on schedule."

Marvin decided that he was probably drunk. "This has nothing to do with Audrey. I've constructed some interesting plot outlines, and I want to talk to you about them."

LaDoux's eyes glittered. "Plots, plot ideas, used to be my forte," he remarked. "But no more. The Muse has shown me her backside lately."

"So we should talk," Marvin repeated.

"Audrey said you were being difficult. Audrey said you didn't want to sell anything."

"Well, now I need the money."

"Where is this material?"

Marvin tapped his breast pocket. He had a diskette, plus an envelope with a few printed pages from one of his detailed outlines.

"Pull your car in," LaDoux said. He opened the gate and waved Marvin up the short drive and into the dark and empty garage.

The door clattered down behind them, giving Marvin a moment's trepidation before his host switched on a light. Marvin stepped out with the bottle of wine. He followed LaDoux through the hall and a book- and paper-strewn dining room that opened onto the terrace and a rustling jungle of palms and banyans. On the west side, a heavy flowering vine cut off the lights and noise of the street with a cascade of foliage and deep red blossoms, while the east was open to the coal-black sea, fringed white with breakers along the sand. The place struck him as absolutely perfect.

"For me?" LaDoux asked when Marvin held out the bottle. "Naughty. I'm reformed, on the wagon, learning abstinence." He gave a sour laugh. "We're at the mercy of mysterious forces. That's the reality of it."

Marvin agreed; he certainly felt that way at the moment.

" 'Course, a certain awareness of mysterious forces is what pays our bills." LaDoux opened the bottle expertly and poured the wine into two large and ornate glasses. He raised his glass silently and took a long drink. "Not bad."

Marvin said nothing.

"And your problem?" LaDoux asked, after he'd refilled their glasses for a second time. "I assume there is a problem."

"I can't do my own work anymore. The only ideas I get now are for the *Dragon* novels, for Ostrucht and his lady. Even your beautiful terrace with the sound of the sea suggests . . ." Marvin sighed. "I've been ruined after writing your novels."

"You wrote them rather well, the critics say. Of course, my reputation provided a leg up there," he added.

Marvin nodded. He knew the ways of the literary world.

"So?"

"I thought we might collaborate," said Marvin.

"But I don't need you know, and it's time for you to depart—in the literary sense, I mean." He splashed more wine into each glass. "There's no reason for you to leave this nice Burgundy."

"Yet you were willing to buy the outline for the second trilogy."

"The flesh is weak," LaDoux admitted.

"Perhaps you'd like to see a sample."

Doux looked up with an eager expression and stretched out his hand. He needed help, whatever he said. "Let me see."

"One page." Marvin opened the envelope and handed over the synopsis of the first five chapters.

LaDoux put on a pair of tinted glasses and scanned the copy. "Like this wine, not *grand cru,* but very nice. And the rest?"

"Good. Audrey knows. She wanted to buy them for you."

"Audrey has somewhat lost confidence in me," LaDoux said. In the silence that followed, Marvin listened to a rustling in the shrubbery and the night wind in the palms. Perhaps Lord Ostrucht should be sent on a sea voyage to some hot, tropical land. "What do you want?" LaDoux asked abruptly.

"To write some of the books," Marvin said.

"But not all of them?"

"Not all of them."

LaDoux stared at him for a minute. "We'll drink to that," he said. "But now I want to see the rest of the plots."

"They're on this diskette." Marvin drew the floppy out of his pocket and dropped it back in. "We'll call Audrey, shall we? Have her come over and draw up a contract."

LaDoux hesitated, then smiled. There was an avidity about him that both encouraged and disgusted Marvin. "Right. We'll call Audrey. To whom we owe so much. Including this whole bloody situation." He stood up. "My office is upstairs. I never do business on the terrace."

Inside, LaDoux switched on the weak hall light and started upstairs. Marvin saw old woodwork, Mexican tiles, cracked and dirty plaster. The main stairs made a steep run to a landing, then turned left. A full moon was shining through the tall window at the top, and Marvin was about to remark on its bright beauty when LaDoux suddenly pivoted on the landing and kicked him square in the gut. Marvin gasped, his lungs suddenly airless, and grabbed the banister to keep from falling. LaDoux struck him again, in the face this time, sending Marvin tumbling backward down the stair to land flat at the bottom.

He was quite helpless. His lungs were deflated, and he couldn't make his legs work. The stair rose above him like a monstrous wave, down which LaDoux dropped toward him like a surfer. Marvin waved his arms, trying to pull air into his lungs, trying to strike LaDoux, who, clearly not as drunk as he'd appeared, caught Marvin under the arms and dragged him down the back hall. He kicked open the French door and pulled Marvin onto the grass and then, to his rising horror, toward the shore. Out of shock and surprise rose an awareness that he was very likely going to die.

Marvin tried to shout, but his voice was a cracked whisper, lost in the wind and surf. LaDoux hauled him through a low hedge and unceremoniously dropped him over the sea wall onto the sand. Marvin tried to get to his feet, but his whole body was focused on acquiring air and his limbs refused to cooperate.

LaDoux grasped him again and started toward the water, but here Marvin began digging his heels and his hands into the soft, deep sand, causing LaDoux to swerve and stagger. It was dark on the beach, too, the few lights dazzling and confusing rather than illuminating. Twice LaDoux dropped to his knees, but though Marvin could impede their progress he could not stop it. Drops of spray landed on his shirt as he was dragged through a fishy, salty-smelling band of wrack. Then LaDoux splashed into the surf, and cold water shocked Marvin's back.

There were crushed shells underfoot. Unsteady, LaDoux slipped both left and right, stumbling on every step. Waves broke over Marvin's head and sloshed down his legs. "The diskette," he managed to gasp. "It's in my pocket."

LaDoux stopped and released one of Marvin's arms, dropping him halfway into the water. Marvin jerked up his head, took a great gulp of air, and, as LaDoux fumbled in his shirt pocket, threw himself sideways, pulling LaDoux under with him.

They weren't in more than a foot of water, but the shore was at once soft and gritty, the band of ground-up shells unstable beneath them. Thrashing and struggling, they got a little farther out, then farther yet, and as they swallowed more water and took more blows, they found it harder and harder to get back on their knees, to find their feet.

At last, they floundered into chest-deep water, and they were half swimming, half wrestling, each trying to hold the other under, when a big roller crashed into them, separating them and turning Marvin head over heels. As he felt himself dragged out by the current, he forgot LaDoux, forgot everything but the shore, dry land, air. He paddled forward, clawing for ground, and after a second wave broke over his head felt the rough band of shells under his hands and lurched onto the shore, gasping for breath and shaking with cold and shock.

He crawled onto the beach and fell forward on his face. The waves whooshed and thundered behind him, his lungs burned, the night wind chilled his sore back. He had nearly died; someone had tried to kill him; he had possibly drowned a man. With this, he remembered his danger and scrambled painfully to his feet, but he could not see LaDoux.

Marvin called softly: nothing but the sea and the rattle of palm fronds, and somewhere far away, the sound of traffic, of civilization. He limped to the water's edge and peered into the darkness for what seemed a long time before he saw a whitish something as inert as a log rising and falling in the surf. Marvin waited until he was sure of that inertia before wading out into the water and hauling LaDoux's body to shore.

Once he had wrestled the corpse up onto the sand, he laid his hand on LaDoux's chest and felt for a pulse. When all signs proved negative, Marvin sat down, put his head between his knees, and vomited on the sand.

"You've killed the golden goose," said a voice in his mind.

And another, even less welcome thought followed: Hilaire LaDoux was someone whose death would be investigated, whose loss would be news. Marvin's own version of events, so implausible and peculiar that even he had trouble crediting what had happened, would come under scrutiny. He had been attacked, there had been a struggle, and Marvin had survived without anything to prove his story. It did not take a novelist's imagination to see big difficulties, both professional and legal, ahead for Hilaire LaDoux's fired ghost writer.

Marvin stood up, washed off his mouth with salt water, and began to undress, dropping his sodden clothing on the sand beside the corpse. Next he turned to LaDoux, though the body already felt cold and the slippery feel of the skin, as well as LaDoux's unsettling resemblance to himself, turned Marvin's stomach and made his hands shake.

Finally, after an exhausting struggle, he managed to get his own clothes onto the body and jammed his sneakers on its feet. The diskette, ironically, was still in the pocket of his shirt. Marvin retrieved it and set it on the sea wall before dragging LaDoux back to the water. He towed the body out as far as he dared, and when he felt the first signs of a rip current, he let it go.

Back on shore, he bundled up the novelist's wet and sandy clothes. One shoe was missing, and he made a futile search of the sand before returning to the house. The clothing went into the washer, the remaining shoe in a plastic bag. Up in LaDoux's bedroom, Marvin found a change of clothes and dry sneakers. After he composed a brief note for Audrey, he drove north to the public beach, where he abandoned his car, keys, and wallet. He discarded LaDoux's incriminating shoe in a trash barrel. Then Marvin went down to the surf, took off his borrowed sneakers, and slogged back along the shore to the house. He let himself in, found a bottle of scotch, and went up to bed.

A day later, Marvin saw a brief report about his abandoned car, and within a week read an account of the recovery of his body. He waited a few days before calling Audrey. By then he knew a great deal more about his new identity: debts, alcoholism, dubious investments, an estranged family, and the absolute impossibility of ever holding a driver's license again.

On the other hand, he had a fair-sized bank balance, a spectacular if deteriorated house, and more important than all the rest, Lord Ostrucht and his lady, for whom Marvin, or Hilaire, as he must now call himself, had wonderful plans. He reached for the desk phone and dialed. "Audrey?"

"Yes, Audrey Striker speaking." Her response seemed tentative; voices are, after all, hard to disguise.

"Hilaire LaDoux. I'm really flying on the new novel, and I wondered if you'd like me to send you the finished chapters."

Again, the hesitation. He could almost hear the wheels turning. "Of course, I would," she said with a fair show of enthusiasm. "But, Hilaire, you're working? You're really working? Because I understood you wanted me to find someone to replace poor Marvin—you heard about that?"

"Yes, I did. I can't help feeling a little guilty. He sold me his last outlines, you know. Yes, yes, he cut you out, the naughty boy. But poor fellow! The writer's life is not always a happy one."

"I'd actually found someone—tentatively, you understand. I thought perhaps a woman writer this time . . ." In truth, Audrey had been nearly at her wit's end.

"Quite, quite unnecessary," he said briskly. "I've had a genuinely life-changing experience. You might say I met a ghost, Audrey, and I can assure you I foresee no more writing problems from here on in."

Susan Isaacs

My Cousin Rachel's Uncle Murray

SUSAN ISAACS, a New York native, writes bestsellers featuring ordinary people whose lives are transformed by extraordinary events. She renders her fiction with sharp wit, dead-on social observation, and page-turning narrative skills. Her first novel, the consummately hilarious *Compromising Positions,* was a mystery, with Judith Singer investigating the murder of her lusty periodontist. The (long-awaited) sequel, *Long Time, No See,* was published in 2001. In addition to her novels, Ms. Isaacs has written screenplays, book reviews, and the nonfiction volume *Brave Dames and Wimpettes: What Women Are Really Doing on Page and Screen.* In "My Cousin Rachel's Uncle Murray," which first appeared in the Adams Round Table anthology *Murder in the Family,* a young female lawyer tries to answer that age-old question: is blood thicker than water?

My Cousin Rachel's
Uncle Murray

Susan Isaacs

Family.
My mother. Phyllis Lincoln. In 1971, shortly before my first birthday, she ran off with a Mr. Maumoon Fathulla Hussain, bodyguard for the Consul of the Permanent Mission of the Republic of Maldives to the United Nations whom she had met at a hot dog stand outside a B. B. King concert at the Fillmore East. That was about five blocks from home, two rooms on the Lower East Side. My father had declared it an apartment; my mother, a slum. From what I have heard, we shared the premises with a heavyset rodent. My father said, *Oh, a cute little mouse,* and called it Mickey; my mother called it a rat. In any case, my mother took off and I never saw her again.

My father. Eugene Lincoln. Back then, my father was employed as a part-time driver by Frank ("Clockwork") Lombardini, a *caporegima* in the Gambino family who had originally retained him in the mistaken belief that all Jews are smart.

Our surname, Lincoln. Maybe the family legend is actually true and in the penultimate year of the nineteenth century, some Protestant clerk on Ellis Island with an antic sense of humor wrote down "Samuel Lincoln" when my great-grandfather—full of beard, dark of eye, and great of nose—stepped before him. More likely, Great-grandpa Schmuel Golumbek heard the names "Washington" and "Lincoln" while hanging out around the pickle barrel in downtown Minsk listening to stories about the Golden Land. Flipping a kopek, he got tails. Could he truly have believed that by being a Lincoln, no one in New York would notice his six extant teeth and ten words of English? Very likely. By and large, my relatives have never been prone to analytical thought.

Anyhow, my father. When I was four, he was dispatched to the Downstate Correctional Facility for five to seven. On one of my semiannual visits, when I was nine, Dad raised his right hand: "I swear on my mother's grave, Amy, baby, I'm innocent."

"Grandma's still alive," I pointed out.

"That's okay. Listen." He explained he'd merely been the driver of the Fleetwood Brougham that had transported Clockwork, Sick Vinny DeCicco, and some poor schnook of a restaurateur to a remote section of Van Cortlandt Park in the Bronx. "It was Clockwork and Sick Vinny that roughed up the guy. I was, you know, sitting behind the wheel. Listening to a Doobie Brothers tape. I was minding my own business."

" 'Roughed up'?" I repeated. "Dad, the guy was in a coma for three weeks."

"Yeah. And what did he prove in the end? He could've gotten his tablecloths and aprons and crap from Lombardini's Linen Service and not wasted all that time in the hospital."

After my father went up the river to Downstate, I was sent to live with his mother. Grandma Milly looked a little like Mrs. Potato Head, with giant ruby lips, over-wide eyes, and stick-out ears. She was one of those unctuous individuals whom other people, who can't stand them, feel obliged to call "well-meaning." Grandma worked a day or two or three a week as a substitute waxer, ripping the hair off the lips, legs, and the random chins of the famous and the merely rich at Beauté, an uptown, upscale salon.

From the jet set and celebrity clientele, Grandma learned about the finer things of life, which she felt obliged to pass on to me, mainly because no one else she knew would listen. "Always be nice to the help," she told me when I was ten. She held up her finger in a hold-on-a-second gesture. Then, with a hop-step that looked like the opening of an obscure Slavic folk dance, she clunked her foot down on a bloated cockroach; it made a barely audible crunching sound. "I heard about how this guy James who owns a catering business—I told you what catering is?"

"Yeah," I said.

"Don't say 'yeah.' Say 'yes.' "

"Yes."

"Anyways, this James guy is such a shit to his waiters that one of them actually spit on the cheese straws and, like, half the guests at a hemophilia benefit saw him do it!"

"What's a cheese straw?" I asked. I already knew what hemophilia was and could figure out benefit.

"Who the hell knows? Something rich goyim eat. So, Amy, the motto of the story is, treat your help good and they'll be good to you."

So I learned what to do from Grandma. As well as what not to do: I sensed that saying *"Ciao, bella"* in a breathy voice, as she did, while flapping fingers rearward as one dashes toward Delancey Street to get to the subway, was not the way to endear oneself to one's neighbors in one's low-income housing project.

And so I grew. By age fourteen, I sensed a change of scenery might be salutary. My father, who'd been out of jail for a year and a half, was back in. This time, it was for stealing a black Lincoln town car in order to become a self-employed limo driver. Within months of Dad's second trip to the Big House, two of my good friends from school dropped out to have their babies. Another left to support her family; she earned fifty bucks a head performing fellatio on homebound New Jersey commuters who would have otherwise gotten irritable during the usual half-hour wait to get into the Holland Tunnel. Another girl, a year ahead of me, died from a crack overdose.

Though my guidance counselor at Intermediate School 495 said "I don't know if you'd be comfortable at a place like that, sweetie," I applied for a full scholarship at Ivey-Rush Academy, a boarding school for young ladies in the Connecticut Valley that Grandma had reported was the "best of the best of the best." I signed her name to the application and request-for-scholarship form in a round, shaky hand to simulate old age (Grandma was fifty-three) and semiliteracy (a promotion). I sensed she might not want me to go, as that would mean not only losing my company, but the eighty-seven bucks a week from the City of New York's Human Resources Administration.

I also submitted a heart-wrenching essay about visiting Dad in prison; "Father's Day" was full of shocking language (in quotation marks) as well as graphic descriptions of nauseating smells, oozing sores, and piercing wails from junkie girlfriends pleading for money. Ivey-Rush was mad for such a well-phrased account of degradation. Graciously, they offered me a more-than-full scholarship. And they were so genteel that when they discovered that Amy Lincoln, the year's Fahnstock Scholarship winner—the traditional black face in the class photograph—was white, they did a reasonably good job of hiding their dismay.

At Ivey, I quickly decided trying to fit in would be a waste of my efforts. I could get far more mileage out of my New Yorkese "tamayta" rather than mimicking the "tamahto" crowd. My accent—"sooo refreshing"—to say nothing of my biography featuring runaway mother and imprisoned father, took me places where the F train didn't go. Like Capri and Chamonix. I learned to mesmerize a dinner party in Palm Beach with now-appalling, now-amusing vignettes of the mean streets. By the time I got to Brown University and then to Harvard Law School, I was an accomplished guest. During most vacations, my friends' families—rich, poor, in-between—took me in. I'd go from Thanksgiving in Aspen to Christmas in Bedford-Stuyvesant to spring break in Circleville, Ohio.

As for my own *mishpochah,* Grandma Milly began exhibiting symptoms of vascular dementia in my junior year at Brown. She decided I was my mother and would screech "Fucking Phyllis" and try to shove me out the door whenever I came to see her. She died during my second year at law school. The few times I couldn't sponge a free Presidents' Day weekend in Hobe Sound, I stayed in Canarsie with my father's long-estranged sister.

To make a long story shorter, I grew fond of my aunt Linda and her husband, Uncle Patrick. They were a pleasant, ordinary couple (except for a curious predilection for Velveeta cheese) who had a daughter a year older than I. My cousin Rachel.

Rachel looked like a better me. Her hair was a glossier black, her eyes a more chocolaty brown, her body more supermodel than lacrosse defense. Instead of my coloring, which tends toward cirrhotic without great brushfuls of blush, she had inherited her father's O'Toole strawberries and cream complexion. If I was passably pretty, she was a knockout. She had a beautiful face, an inferior intellect, a glorious figure, the kindest heart. And what a live wire! At least half her sentences ended in exclamation points, so even her most banal utterance had an air of excitement. Excitement!

Rachel taught me the secrets of applying multiple layers of mascara and informed me I looked exactly like Salma Hayek—if Salma had been Jewish and a tiny bit big-boned. Better than Salma Hayek, as a matter of fact, because "you look younger and between me and you, Amy, Salma probably couldn't have gotten into Harvard Law. Next time you see a picture of her, look close. There's no Harvard in those eyes."

I loved my cousin Rachel in that elemental way one ought to love one's family: without reason, simply because of that mysterious blood tie. The two of us had nothing in common except our mindless admiration for each other. When I went off to college, Rachel went off to a job at the men's fragrances counter at Saks Fifth Avenue. She didn't stay there long. Just before her nineteenth birthday, she sold a bottle of *Boucheron Pour Homme* to Danny Glickstein, the thirty-year-old executive vice president of Gladstone Motor Cars, a Mercedes dealership on the Upper East Side. Within two months Rachel O'T. Glickstein was living in a ten-room co-op twenty blocks due north of Saks.

After law school, I moved back to New York, first to clerk for a United States district judge and then to become a federal prosecutor. Rachel and I would meet for lunch every few months. She also insisted I attend her dinner parties. Clearly, she had hopes of matching me up with one of Danny's chums, men with deep golf tans who comported themselves as if intent on refuting Freud's assertion that sometimes a cigar is just a cigar. So when she called me at the office one April morning I was not at all surprised to hear from her. But instead of Rachel's usual spirited "Hi!" (which actually was a prolonged honk of "Hoy!"), she murmured: "Amy, it's me, Rach," in a funeral voice.

"What's wrong?" I demanded. I often worried that Aunt Linda and Uncle Patrick would suffer myocardial infarctions from Velveeta-clogged aortas.

"It's Danny's uncle Murray. Remember him from the wedding?" Rachel asked. "Uncle Murray Glickstein?" As Rachel's maid of honor, I had been mamboed and fox-trotted around the floor by a gaggle of Glicksteins, a clan who resembled ambulatory mailboxes. Most of them sang along as they danced. However, I could not recall if any of the gents crooning moistly into my ear had been a Murray. "He's the big jeweler," she added.

I decided not to say all the Glicksteins seemed big to me, including her husband, Danny, and their two sweet, cube-ish children, Brianna and Ryan. "I'm not sure which one Uncle Murray was," I replied. "Has anything happened to him?"

"He's being questioned."

"By whom?"

"You always know when to say 'whom,' Amy! Prep school, right?"

"Who's questioning him, Rachel?"

"Questioning him? I don't know. The cops, I guess. But he's a very, very important jeweler! Uncle Murray's the G of B and G Gems."

"Right," I said respectfully, while I doodled a diamond ring in the margin of a motion to suppress, not that I felt any pressure to find a husband, even though as Aunt Linda so diplomatically pointed out: *You're twenty-eight, Amy, and in two more years you won't be no spring chicken anymore. Look, me and Uncle Pat love it that you're a lawyer—we're so proud—but what can I tell you? I worry about you being too smart for your own good, guy-wise.* "What are the cops questioning Uncle Murray about?" I inquired.

"About his partner," Rachel said. "Barry Bleiberman."

"The B of B and G," I observed.

"He's one dead B!"

I took a deep breath and slowly let it out. "Let me get this right. Barry Bleiberman is dead and they're questioning Uncle Murray. . . . Why? Do they think Barry might have been the victim of foul play?"

"He was! He was stabbed!"

"Where?"

"In the heart. With his own letter opener! It had his initials!"

"I mean, where was Barry when he was stabbed?"

"In his office at B and G. The safe was open and some really, really fine jewels were G-O-N-E. Gone!"

"Well, Rachel, I'd say Uncle Murray definitely needs to get a lawyer before he even says 'Good morning' to the cops and—"

"He *has* a lawyer. A very classy criminal lawyer that came with the highest recommendations from B and G's accountant. Nick Schwartzman. He's also Danny's accountant. I trust his judgment totally!"

"Excellent."

"But Danny and I would like you personally to look into this. I mean, Amy, you're not just a Harvard lawyer. You're *family!*"

Once again, as I had done the five or six times Rachel had asked me to fix a parking ticket as well as the once she'd pleaded with me to sue her dry cleaner, I explained I was not in private practice. And not with the district attorney's office. "I'm an assistant United States attorney in the Southern District of New York. That means I prosecute *federal* crimes: securities fraud, narcotics cases, taking potshots at a bald eagle." I didn't bother mentioning that what with the contretemps between my father and the criminal justice system (to say nothing of Dad's organized crime associations), all that had gotten me an FBI clearance was the unstinting support of the judge for whom I had clerked, an incandescent letter from a senator on the Judiciary Committee whose wife had been an Ivey-Rush girl, stellar grades since kindergarten, having been an editor of *The Harvard Law Review*—plus God smiling down on me. Gem though he might be, I was not going to risk all for Uncle Murray. "The Bleiberman homicide is a state crime, Rachel. I cannot represent Murray Glickstein. I wish I could help you, but—"

"Sweetie, I'm not asking you to do anything illegal—or that other thing."

"Immoral? Unethical?"

"Whatever. Please, please, Amy, please. Just look into it."

"What if I conclude that it was Uncle Murray who did the dastardly deed?" I asked. Rachel's answer was a peal of girlish laughter: *Oh, you're being silly!*

At first all I did was check out the reputation of the lawyer representing Uncle Murray. A former assistant DA, he was said to be tough and smart. Splendid. I went back to my two-buy junk case. However, by seven that night, recognizing a major Uncle Murray distraction, I gave up and called my cousin Rachel.

One hour later, as I found myself sitting on a settee in her living room, Aunt Vivian, Murray's missus, was informing me: "We've heard *so* much about you, dear." Obviously, my gray suit, which even I thought was tacky, was causing Aunt Viv to try and suppress a shudder. So I suspected her cordial "dear" was evoked less by the fact of me than by the Ivey-Rush-and-her-roommate-was-a-Collier-of-*the*-Colliers briefing she'd clearly gotten from Rachel. As for appearance, Vivian Glickstein of Park Avenue pretty much resembled a just-budding eleven-year-old. Well, an eleven-year-old got up in a sleek brown-and-black Carolina Herrera ensemble. Except what was going on above her neck, while unlined, was not youthful: Aunt Vivian had the fish face wealthy women in their late fifties wind up with by the time they are on a first-name basis with their plastic surgeons. "You're . . ." She paused for an instant. "What can I say, Amy? You're family."

With a hasty smile, I acknowledged what I assumed was a compliment. Uncle Murray, a multichinned man who seemed to have been born with a paisley ascot rather than a neck separating his head and chest, smiled also. The Glicksteins and I sipped Montrechet and nibbled on shiitake fritata squares and seared foie gras on brioche toast in the Vivian and Murray Glickstein Eclectic Living Room with a Heavy Emphasis on Louis Quatorze. Judging from the amount of ormolu, to say nothing of the elaborately framed Dutch still lifes on the glazed vermilion walls, business at B and G Gems had been thriving.

The third Glickstein, Ken, son of Vivian and Murray, a man about my age, sat to my left in a gilt chair upholstered in deep blue brocade that looked royal enough for the Sun King himself. Not that anyone would call Ken Glickstein regal. He had inherited his mother's dainty frame and Uncle

Murray's oversized head, so he resembled a lollipop, albeit a lollipop dressed in a snazzy black silk shirt. Lost in the vast luxury of the chair, Ken peeped: "Uh, can I get . . . is there, uh, anything else you want?"

Out. But I said: "No. I'm fine, thanks." I held up my three-quarters full wineglass as proof. I wasn't sure if Viv and Mur had trotted Ken out for me to interview or marry, and it seemed either prospect was making him dreadfully anxious. He kept crossing and uncrossing his legs, as if seeking the best position for protecting his privates. So I turned to Uncle Murray. "Your partner, Barry Bleiberman, was stabbed?" Uncle Murray nodded once, twice, and then seized by some head-bowing frenzy, could not seem to stop. Ken, clearly perturbed, turned toward his mother. She responded to her son's discomfort by ignoring him and fingering her pearls—each one of which looked large enough to have come from a fowl rather than an oyster.

"Stabbed three times in the chest," Murray finally said, slapping his own hand against his chest, Pledge of Allegiance–style.

"Tell me a bit about B and G, Mr. Glickstein."

"Murray, please." At last his head stopped its manic bobbing. "I mean, we're family."

"Murray," I said.

"Well, first and foremost, so to speak, we're jewelry *manufacturers*. Let's say Harry Winston or Tiffany's, and of course some smaller"—he stopped to chortle—"but equally elegant vendors will hand us a design and say, 'Here, B and G. Make it!' We employ two master gem-cutters from Belgium, and of course we've trained some of our own boys. *And* we have a fine, fine staff who can take a model of a design and bring it to—how shall I put it?—fruition. A piece of jewelry *any* woman in the world would be proud—might I even say honored?—to wear." I was praying he would go back to mere nodding, but no, he kept spouting: "And of course we have our own private customers, some of *the* most discriminating people worldwide. If I named names, you'd say 'Oh, my God!' Anyhow, they'll give us a description of what they want and say 'B and G, make my wildest dream come true.' Or some others will say 'B and G, do something magical with this eight-carat sapphire.' "

I tried to get a "Riveting!" expression on my face, but I'd been working fifteen hours a day for the past two weeks preparing for trial, so I probably looked somewhere between merely blinky and stupefied. However, the sight of Uncle Murray's pale peach Egyptian cotton shirt clinging and turning orange from Rorschach-like patches of perspiration suggested he might be getting so enthused he would keep pontificating, from sapphires down through rubies to all that glittered between amethysts and zircons. So I inquired: "Were all your company's gemstones and jewelry in that open safe in Barry's office?"

Uncle Murray's moon-face flushed darkly, as though he were being strangled by his own ascot. "No, no." He glanced toward his wife and son, but Aunt Viv was still diddling a pearl and Ken was engrossed in exploring the weave of his herringbone slacks just above his knee. "We have the main safe in the back, behind the cutters' workroom. But both Barry—may he rest in peace—and I have smaller safes in our own offices, which are the floor above. This way, if one of our clients is looking for, let's say, a diamond necklace, we can keep certain pieces in our own safe and also some loose stones to show them. It's much more . . . civilized. I mean, sitting in a more, shall we say, comfortable environment with a cup of perfect coffee. Or a glass of lovely wine."

I was curious to learn what constituted perfect and/or lovely, but, on the other hand, I was afraid he might actually tell me. "The safe was open?" I asked instead.

Vivian and Ken peered up. Uncle Murray didn't notice because he was gazing directly into my eyes, the way people do when they are trying to appear honest. "Yes."

"Was anything missing?"

"Stones," he said sadly. Sadly as in no big deal, like when the travel section is missing from the Sunday paper, not like when hundreds of thousands of dollars of gems have been heisted.

"Stones? Like diamonds? Those kinds of stones?"

"In this case, a few diamonds and—how shall I put it?—more emeralds than I care to think about."

"Rings? Bracelets?"

"No, no. Loose stones."

"There was no actual jewelry in the safe?" I asked.

"The jewelry wasn't taken," Ken interjected. Both Uncle Murray and I turned in time to see Ken's lollipop of a face turn cherry. His lips looked as though they were sorry for parting and were dying to stick together, but he pried them apart because he knew he had to offer something more. "I mean, the pieces that were in the safe . . . they weren't . . . stolen. But the stones are gone."

"Do you work at B and G?" I asked.

"Yes," Ken said, "I'm—"

"He's a senior vice president," Uncle Murray declared. Since Ken did not turn red this time, I could not tell if his father's speaking for him was business as usual or if Uncle Mur had been trying to shut up his son before he spilled some B and G beans.

"Who found Barry Bleiberman's body?" I asked Ken, just to see who would answer.

Murray obliged. "His daughter." I waited. Long before I became a prosecutor, in the school yard of P.S. 97, I understood that the most efficient way to get the facts was to offer a potential informant nothing. And then more nothing. Few people can bear silence. "Her name's Gabrielle. She's a twin." I waited some more. "Gabrielle and Garrett," Murray went on. "Boy-girl. So they're not identical. I mean, not just counting the boy-girl differences. They're both . . . They're both at B and G." Murray's upper body was wriggling either with unease or the desire to separate skin from the sweaty cling of his shirt. "They're a year younger than Ken. Garrett's a vice president. So is Gabrielle."

"Senior vice presidents?" I inquired.

"In their case, 'senior vice president' is an honorary title," Aunt Vivian murmured. "Not like with Ken."

As far as I can recall, I have never been the sort of person who gets surprised. Thus, let me simply say I was mildly unsettled to discover how unlikeable this particular branch of the Tree of Glickstein was. Rachel's husband, Danny G., while a tad too extroverted for my own taste—given as he was to huggy greetings and uproarious laughter at his own jokes—was a friendly and generous soul. His mother and his father (brother to Uncle Murray), too, were a benevolent couple. They sent me birthday cards with watercolors of pups or kitties or rosebuds on the front, I think in part because they viewed me first as a motherless child and only second as Rachel's adult cousin.

"So until Barry's death, the company was technically BBB and GG," I remarked. No response, though Viv did lay her hand over her sternum; most likely her gesture for "I'm aggrieved." However, she could have been protecting her pearls. Or preparing to burp. In any case I ignored her and concentrated on her (slightly) better half. "Why do the police want to question you, Murray?" I tried.

"I guess . . . I was in my office at the time, but like I told them"—he cleared his throat—"through my attorney: Our offices are soundproofed. Our clients, and us . . . We don't need noise from the workrooms. Like the grinding." A brief chuckle. "You'd think you were at the dentist, which is *not* how you get someone about to spend a couple of hundred thou to relax."

"So, in other words, you didn't hear anything? No arguments? No cries for help?"

Uncle Murray's head began bobbing again, saying, *That's right, That's right, That's right,* until Aunt Vivian commented sharply: "And he didn't see anything, either."

I glanced away. Ken's head was hanging, his jaw drooping. He looked utterly dispirited. For an instant, he peered up toward the hall outside the living room. I sensed he wanted to scurry off, back to his room, where he could get consolation from some ancient teddy bear, probably the only source of comfort in that house. But he turned back to me. "We *all* didn't see anything. My mother, my father . . ."

"Vivian," I said in honeyed tones, "do you work at B and G?"

Startled, she pulled back her head. "No, of course not. I just happened to be there that morning."

"Really?"

"I wanted to pick up a lapis and diamond brooch to wear with my suit to a luncheon." Auntie Viv's voice was harder than diamonds. She then became busy clearing her throat, making much ado about mucus. When that business was taken care of, her nostrils dilated. I surmised all this was an overture to a withering remark directed to me. I silenced her with the disdainful *grande dame* gaze Ivey girls learn in Mademoiselle Charpantier's French class long before the *passé antérieur.*

Ken, realizing his mother was less than overjoyed at his reporting her presence at B and G, added: "Nadine Bleiberman was there that morning, too. We're all on the videotape. See, we have a security camera at the door."

I turned back to Murray. "If the police seem eager to keep in touch with you, may I assume they heard rumors that you and the late Mr. Bleiberman were on the outs?"

"The usual stuff two partners have," Murray remarked before nervously inserting a couple of seared foie gras canapés into his mouth.

"I see," I said, trying to sound pleasant. "In this case, what particular kind of 'stuff.' "

"Lines of responsibility," he declared through a fair amount of goose liver.

"Yours and his?"

"More . . ." He held up his index finger in a wait-while-I-swallow gesture. "More the kids."

"Ken here and Garrett and Gabrielle Bleiberman?" I asked. This time he offered just a single nod. "What seems to be the problem?"

"Garrett's a bully," Vivian snapped. I focused on her shiny, pulled-tight cheeks so I would not humiliate the bully's inevitable target, poor Ken, by looking at him. "And Gabrielle's a tramp," she went on. "Always was, always will be."

"Are the Bleiberman twins productive?" I asked.

"Work-wise?" Murray inquired. "To be perfectly honest, they're not bad."

"Tha*t* is no*t* the poin*t!*" Vivian said, spitting her Ts. "The poin*t* is, Murray, legally B and G is and was a fif*t*y-fif*t*y operation." She paused, possibly weary from expectorating so many Ts. "All of a sudden when Ken came into the business—mainly so clients wouldn't start thinking, 'Oh, B and G has been taken over by a fraternity moron and a slut who never wears a bra'—Barry Bleiberman started supposedly kidding around: 'Well, there's three of us now, so we can outvote you.' I mean, is that unmitigated gall?" She inhaled and exhaled one of those deep relaxation breaths women learn at thousand-dollar-a-day spas. "Not that I'm not mourning Barry's loss. And murder, no less! Although I don't know why the authorities haven't considered suicide."

"Perhaps because he was stabbed three times in the heart and was very likely dead before the last two thrusts occurred," I suggested.

Vivian Glickstein, still on a roll, crossed her ankles to give me a better view of her brown alligator pumps and kept talking: "I call the twins 'The Untalented Twain.' Of course you know twain means two. Between the two of them, they don't have half of Ken's intellect—if that. It's not just the future of the business Barry was going to sabotage. It was—"

I stood. "I know how important all of you are to my cousin Rachel, and I'd love to help you. I cannot in any way represent you, of course. I am sure Rachel has explained my position. But I'll be more than happy to look into the matter informally and let you know if I find anything." Now all three were nodding in what I optimistically assumed was appreciation. I grabbed my handbag and restrained myself from hurling my body at the door. Out! Liberated, I would gambol down Park Avenue, shout "Hosanna!" as I flagged down a taxi. I was nearly free of the Glickstein Three!

And then Uncle Murray muttered: "Whatever you can do." His shoulders slumped. And his voice tightened. "The cops . . ." He sounded on the verge of tears. "They said something to my attorney about maybe, you know, having to arrest me."

Because I had a stack of discovery material to read the following morning, when Rachel called I agreed that: 1) Uncle Murray was a doll, 2) Aunt Vivian's taste was quietly elegant, and 3) Ken was a teeny-weeny on the shy side. When I asked her how bitter the dispute between Bleiberman and Glickstein was, she told me: "Don't ask!"

"Rachel, I'm asking."

"Very, very, *very* bitter." As usual, I waited. "See, Ken isn't what you'd call a firecracker. He probably should have some calmer job. Like some science thing with a clipboard. He could do that. No pressure, no people. I hate to say this, but he's a major dork, personality and looks-wise. Unfortunately. I mean, put him in total Armani and he's still a schlepper. Speaking of looks: like, Gabrielle Bleiberman looks like a ho—That means, you know, like a hooker."

"Right."

"Except for her jewelry. Huge gold cuff on her right wrist. Gorgeous. Man's gold Rolex on her left, which looks stunning with the cuff! Diamond studs so big, her earlobes'll be hanging down to her shoulders in a few years. But a mind? Amy, like a steel trap! Anyhow, Garrett's nicer but he never got as far as nice, if you know what I mean. He's okay. Good-looking in a sort of Keanu Reeves way if Keanu didn't come from Hawaii and have that permanent tan. Except he's got a schnozz big enough for two. Garrett, not Keanu. He's engaged. And he's smart. They both are."

"Garrett and the fiancée?"

"No, Garrett and Gabrielle. They went to one of those smart little colleges. You know, Ivy League, but not Ivy League. Like whatever that place is . . . Amherst! Except if they're so smart, why aren't they?"

"Why aren't they in the Ivy League?" I asked.

"Yeah."

Best not to begin, I concluded. With Rachel, any well-reasoned response more complex than a single, simple declarative sentence would induce glazed eyes or, occasionally, a remark like: God, you really *are* an intellectual!

"So essentially," I said, "Gabrielle and Garrett have it in them to be successful in business and Cousin Ken does not."

"Right!" However dismissive my cousin might have been of actual thought, she did have the gift of sounding enraptured at the most elementary deduction. The miracle of it was she wasn't just exercising a talent for being effusive; she was genuinely thrilled with me. "That's the problem!"

"Was Barry Bleiberman putting any pressure on Uncle Murray to get rid of Ken?"

"Yes. But it was like this awful double whammy because while he was putting the pressure on Murray, Gabrielle and Garrett were making Ken's life a living hell!"

"In what way?"

"To tell you the God's honest truth," Rachel conceded, "I don't know."

"Oh."

"But it's what Uncle Murray told my father-in-law."

"When?"

"I guess a month or two ago. And Dad—Dad Glickstein, not Daddy O'Toole—told Danny about it and naturally Danny told me. That the twins were making poor Ken's life a living hell!"

After I got off the phone with Rachel, my first thought was that if I were in the DA's homicide unit, I, too, would be inviting Murray Glickstein for a chat, and, later in the day, perhaps requesting the pleasure of Ken's company as well. Then I banished all contemplation of Glicksteins and reached for the top document on the mountain of discovery material for my upcoming trial, the report of the defense psychiatric expert whose conclusion would inevitably be that Bernard Charles Lee could not be held responsible for selling five hundred grams of cocaine because inefficacious parenting had resulted in a lacuna of his superego.

Less than a minute later, I tossed it to the far side of my desk and meandered out into the hallway. Unfortunately, out of approximately two hundred assistant United States attorneys in the Southern District of New York, I was forced to poke my head into the office of the one I liked least.

Larissa Corrigan had come in second in Louisiana's 1986 Junior Miss Contest. Now, at age thirty-one, she remained the same ponytailed moppet she had been when she'd almost succeeded in capturing the crown by doing gymnastics on a vaulting horse while lip-synching Anne Murray's "You Are My Sunshine."

Periodically Larissa would come into my office and inquire where she could go to get the "true flaaa-va"—which I assumed meant flavor—of the Lower East Side or assorted other impoverished neighborhoods. Every so often she seemed to get the urge to visit areas filled with Americans darker than she whom she so genuinely admired fo' desirin' to make a bettah life fo they-ah chil'ren. (Quite in the same way, she'd let me know that when she had first heard about me she was truly, truly touched by larnin' how Ah'd pulled myself up bah mah bootstraps.)

"Why, Amy!" As usual, Larissa sounded close to ecstasy, her usual greeting for someone she did not particularly like.

Before she could drawl *Come on in and set a spell!* and give me yet another reason to rejoice that the Confederacy had lost, I sauntered in and sat in the chair in front of her desk. It was the standard government issue, with uneven metal legs and a leatherette seat that had retained a vague scent of some forgotten lawyer's lower intestinal turmoil that had occurred a decade earlier. "Didn't you recently have a possession of stolen diamonds case?" I inquired.

"Oh my, did I! Their defense was they had a secret process to quote cook unquote the diamonds, which would add to their value, so if they'd stolen hem, they'd have cooked them and—" Enraptured by her skill as a raconteur, Larissa gave a tinkly Junior Miss laugh. "So the defense gave this demonstration. The jury sat fo' five hours watching the diamonds cook and in the end, you know what? My chemist said 'My gosh, those diamonds are worthless now!' "

I managed to emit a relatively convivial har-har. Then, before she could resume, I inquired: "Besides the chemist, did you have any other expert witnesses? I need someone who knows the players and the ways of the jewelry business."

"They've given you a case involving the jewelry business?" If one's Pearly Dawn–glossed lips are going to offer a falsely congenial smile, I was tempted to advise her, one should not display all thirty-two teeth and adjacent gums at once. Larissa clearly considered Jewelryland, the area that stretched from Forty-seventh Street uptown to Van Cleef & Arpels, hers alone. In truth, she was a fairly good lawyer and she ought to have been more confident.

"No!" I assured her, flicking my hand to dismiss utterly the idea of my putting even a toe onto her turf. "A friend of a cousin needs some kind of a jewelry expert."

My smile, far more false than hers, was so credible that she quickly typed *diamond* on her keyboard and then read from her database: "Jonah Bergman. And, Amy, tell him Larissa Corrigan sends her warmest, warmest regards!" She jotted down a phone number for me. From her ardent "warmest, warmest" I sensed old Jonah must be, in Larissa-ese, totally, totally adorable.

He was. And not old. So I was pleased I had accepted his offer of a drink after work. (His work, not mine: From the cut of his suit to the deliberately dulled gleam of his shoes to his first-name ease with the waiter, Jonah Bergman looked to be one of the scions of wealthy families who toiled for toil's sake, because not to work would be a prescription for personal anarchy.) In any case, at about five-thirty in the afternoon, there we were in the yellow damask lounge of the University Club sitting on English furniture a couple of centuries older than we. At first glimpse, Jonah was not much more than ordinary, with standard-issue nose and chin, dark brown hair, and a generic early-thirties urban male body. However, his eyes were the dazzling blue of exam books. They were fringed with such thick black lashes that he came across as handsome, or at least wildly dashing.

He raised his martini glass to me in an affable toasting gesture. Clearly, Jonah came from a world in which actually to say *Skäl, L'Chaim,* or *Banzai* was to risk being deemed gauche, a fate not merely worse than death but also as irreversible. "Cheers!" I proclaimed, just to see if he would flinch or cast sideways glances to check if anyone he knew had heard me. He did neither. After elevating a glass of vodka capacious enough to do laps in, I told him: "I appreciate your taking the time to talk to me." Then I took a too-large sip to choke back the Ivey-Rush accent that kept trying to take possession of my tongue—and thereby wow Jonah with my refinement. So, as usual, I wound up being me, sounding like a herring peddler. "I appreciate your meeting with me."

"Glad to help you." He had one of those deep, pleasing voices that called for violins and candlelight. "You're a federal prosecutor?"

I nodded. "But this is thoroughly unofficial. I need some background information on the jewelry business—a favor for a relative."

"So you couldn't say no."

"Not without a process comparable to excommunication by the Grand Inquisitor followed by auto-da-fé." Like most native New Yorkers I talk fast, perhaps in the hope that the next sentence will be more spellbinding than the last. Jonah blinked his glorious lashes at my fusillade of words. Nonetheless, I kept going. (Sadly, while excelling academically, shining at sports and occasionally sparkling in court, I had never mastered flirtation, never even learned to turn on the charm when face-to-face with a man I found attractive. Indeed, in that situation I would become so apprehensive that when quiet sensuality was the ticket, I'd babble, less coquette than locker room buddy.) "Larissa Corrigan said your knowledge of the jewelry business and the people in it is vast and that your family has been in the industry so long your DNA is more diamond-shape than double helix. Well, in truth, what she said, very southernly, was that you knew a lot."

"What are you interested in?"

Ah, I reflected, gazing into his luminous eyes. I told him: I need some background on B and G Gems. The company that Barry Bleiberman—" He nodded. "Within your world, what was the general opinion of the operation?"

"Good. As manufacturers, first rate. They do quality work, on time. They bargain hard but don't try to pull any funny stuff." Jonah fell silent.

"I hear an unspoken 'except.' "

"Except," he said slowly, "this has to be strictly off the record. I mean, to testify about the art of diamond cutting or where the highest quality emeralds come from is one thing, but to sit here and discuss personalities is another." His accent was New York private school, where vowels are round and elongated enough to sound clearly sophisticated and vaguely upper-class, but not draaaawn ooout enouuuugh to communicate the supercilious cool of a student from a New England boarding school. "Can I assume you're not going to subpoena me and ask—"

"Of course not." I transferred my vodka to my left hand and raised my right. "You have my word."

"It's like this," Jonah began. "There are some very worldly types in this industry, but there are also a lot of provincial people, from the guys with the pinky rings. . . ." Perhaps thinking I could be the child of a pinky ring wearer, he hesitated. I was tempted to tell him to relax, that my father's taste in jewelry ran more to handcuffs, but he continued: ". . . to the Hasidic Jews. You get used to dealing with an enormous range of people. So you get to be able to judge them pretty well. Not on the superficial level, like whether they wear a gold chain and have their shirts open to show their chest hair or whether they dress very Savile Row—custom-tailored and all that. Character counts. Like honesty. The industry is built on trust. You let a guy show a few ten-carat diamonds to his customer and you trust he'll return the same stones to you—all of them."

"Was Barry Bleiberman trustworthy?" I asked.

"Absolutely."

I set down the vodka on a small mahogany table that no doubt cost quadruple my monthly salary. "What was the problem with him, then?"

Jonah leaned back his head to think. I noticed he had a beautifully sculpted jaw. "He was respected as a businessman. He was a fund-raiser for a couple of big charities. He made all the right moves. But he wasn't . . . I know this must sound stupid, but the fact is, Barry wasn't nice. Not likeable. It wasn't just a matter of him having a big ego. Plenty of guys in the industry think they're hotshots, so that's no big deal. It's that Barry had nothing else: no humor, no generosity, no kindness." He sipped his martini in the perfunctory manner of a man who drinks not because he enjoys it, but to be sociable. "I never articulated this before," he went on, "so I'm kind of thinking while I'm talking. I guess what was wrong with Barry Bleiberman was that . . . If you looked into his window, no one was home."

"What about his family? His twins were in the business."

"Well, I guess he was home for them. I mean, I heard talk of some tension at B and G over kids."

"On whose part?"

"Both. Barry brought his two in and Murray Glickstein brought in his son. But in this industry, where companies are largely family-held, there's often tension. Fathers and sons at each other's throats, uncles and nephews plotting against each other, that kind of thing."

"Tension? That seems a pretty mild word."

"Well, call it loathing, then, or maybe just acrimony."

"How about plain old hatred?" I inquired, picking up my vodka again. We alumnae of Ivey-Rush, I had noticed, wind up with fingers perpetually curved, trained as we were to being ever ready to grasp either tennis racquet or glass, depending on whether it was before or after five P.M.

"Okay." He smiled agreeably. "Hatred." Nice teeth. They would have looked even more dazzling except for being eclipsed by the brilliance of his blue eyes. "Murray was about as likeable as Barry, except in his case it was because he's never been shy about letting everyone know he's smarter than they are. Plus he's . . ."

It looked as if Jonah was looking for a nice way to say "A pretentious jerk," so I said it for him.

"You've met Murray?" Jonah asked.

"Briefly. Do you know his son?"

"Ken? Yes, we went to school together."

"And?"

"I never knew him that well. He's on the shy side."

"Since this meeting is off the record, is he bright enough to take over the business?"

Jonah shrugged. I waited. "I don't know, at least IQ-wise. Maybe he is. But even years ago, when we were nine, ten, he struck me as kind of . . . Well, now I would call it emotionally fragile. I don't think he's up to it."

"And the twins?"

"Tough and Tougher. Sure, they seem like they could run the business, providing they stick around a few more years, learn more, stay on the up-and-up. They look a little slick, but I've never really dealt with them."

"What's their mother like?"

"I have no idea. If I ever met her, she didn't make any impression."

"If Barry hadn't been killed, do you think he and Murray could have worked out their differences?"

"If he hadn't been murdered, I would have said 'Not without blood being spilled.' But now I'll say probably not. Not unless Murray was willing to abandon all hope for Ken, and I hear that even if he finally came to that, his wife—"

"The lovely Vivian," I said.

Jonah would have won the Talleyrand Diplomatic Trophy for his circumspect nod. "The lovely Vivian would have forced him to back Ken to the death—and beyond."

"If you had to bet, well . . . perhaps the family jewels is an infelicitous expression, but let us say ten dollars. Who would you say stabbed Barry Bleiberman to death?"

"An intruder?"

"His safe was open. Would he have opened it if someone was threatening him?"

"He probably had a discreet silent alarm button on a small section of carpeting under his desk. And maybe a remote panic button on a key chain. My guess? If no one heard an alarm, then the safe was open because Barry felt it was probably all right to open it."

While I waited for Jonah to ask me to join him for dinner—the sort of flagrant female passivity one picks up along with one's teacup at a New England school for young ladies—I mused that an intruder would probably not stab Barry Bleiberman three times. Once. Maybe twice for certainty. Thrice seemed rather mean-spirited.

Alas, Jonah did not ask me to dinner. I wound up buying a hot dog and a Coke from the first street vendor who didn't look as if he were incubating bubonic plague, then took the subway back to the office. I attacked my cocaine case with fervor in order to boot Young Blue Eyes from my consciousness and also because I deemed it advisable to have at least one other sentence to follow "Ladies and gentlemen of the jury." So it wasn't until the next afternoon that I realized I still hadn't done my family duty in the matter of my cousin Rachel's uncle Murray.

"I beg your pardon?" my friend Tatiana Hayes Damaris Collier inquired. (Before her twenty-fifth birthday she had been Tatiana Hayes Damaris Collier Patterson as well as Tatiana Hayes Damaris Collier Martinez, but she had dropped those surnames as hurriedly as she dropped those husbands.) Although my age, born and raised on Beekman Place, she sounded as if she were auditioning for Lady Bracknell. Her voice was cured by expensive tobacco, then filtered through her aristocratic nose.

"I'd like you to pay a condolence call," I told her. "I will go with you."

"Might I ask . . . ?"

"I'm doing a favor for a relative."

"Oh," she murmured, which came out more like *eewwww.* "How considerate of you. Am I to dribble the milk of human kindness on behalf of one of your little people in obscure boroughs, all of whom speak like Groucho Marx?"

"No. All you have to do is go in and be yourself—upperclass and contemptuous."

"I should be delighted." Tatty had been my roommate at Ivey. We had been best friends from the second day, about twenty hours after she'd called me "rude, crude, and unattractive" in front of a group of girls on our floor and I'd punched her in the mouth, knocking out her left lateral incisor and splitting her lip.

"We'll be going to the shiva of the late Mr. B. of B and G Gems. B and G, by the way, is Bleiberman and Glickstein."

"What fun!" Tatty enthused. "Virtually a walk on the wild side."

The very next day, we went to offer our condolences to the Bleibermans of Central Park West.

"So nice of you to drop by," Gabrielle said to us. She was in mourning clothes, which in her case meant a low-slung black leather miniskirt, black fishnet stockings, and a black sweater small enough so that a moment later when she raised her arm in order to dab at her tearless eyes, you caught a glimpse of navel. Should this description suggest some hot little number, it should be noted that her figure, while fine, was full, rather like those inflatable female sex toys from whom misguided men seek solace.

Gabrielle seemed a bit tense in her sun-bronzed skin, though to be fair she was probably merely overstimulated, being suddenly in the company of an unknown WASP her own age who kept murmuring "My dear," as in "My dear, shocking. Your loss. Not just shocking. *Profoundly* shocking, my dear." In all the years I had known Tatty, the words "my dear" had never escaped her lips; she was high-toned, not condescending. Clearly, though, she was reveling in her role as stereotypical post-debutante.

Meanwhile, Gabrielle was torn between her functions of hostess and jewelry maven, trying to look Tatty directly in the eye while simultaneously estimating the price of the aquamarine and pearl rope twirled several times around Tatty's neck. Personally, I thought the rope with its matching earrings, bequeathed by some Jazz Age Collier, was a bit over the top for a one P.M. shiva call. But my friend had called me an ignoramus for not knowing that aquamarines were semiprecious stones and therefore *only suitable for daytime wear.*

The aquamarines and pearls must have dinged Gabrielle's mental cash register, because in two seconds not only did she ask if we wanted something to eat or drink, she immediately led us over to meet her brother and mother. "Mommy, Garrett, this is one of Daddy's oldest customers' daughters, uh, Tatiana, uh . . ."

"Collier." She elongated her vowels and muttered her consonants until the name was almost unintelligible—in case either of the twins decided to look it up in B and G's records. "And my dear friend Amy." We'd also agreed to drop my Lincoln, just in case, in more felicitous times, the Bleibermans had heard of my rags-to-slightly-better-rags saga from the Glicksteins. "Mother's tied up in Paris, but she asked that I drop by and offer our family's deepest sympathy." Tatty's mother, actually, was in the mental institution in Connecticut where she had been for the past fifteen years after having suffered irreversible brain damage from too many of what she had called her happy pills. "Mother said—and these were her exact words— 'Who in the *world* would want to lay a finger on my Mr. Bleiberman?' "

Could she have shoveled the shit higher and faster? Truly, no. Yet not a single Bleiberman looked askance. Watching her, I could understand why. Though built along the dainty lines of a wood nymph, Tatty had masses of blond-on-blond-on-blonder hair that looked as if it came from years of riding to the hounds or sunning at Cap Ferrat, which of course it did not. Her hollowed cheeks, her pale eyes that appeared blue or gray or white depending on the light, her high-bridged nose, her indecently expensive clothes, her I've-seen-it-*all*-my-dear drone of a voice announced blue blood and silk stockings, a woman not merely not to be trifled with, but to be accommodated.

"I appreciate . . ." Nadine Bleiberman, wife of the late Barry and mother of the twins, was so moved or intimidated by Tatty that the rest of the sentence disappeared as she swallowed hard, making the sort of noise that in comic books is rendered *Gulp!!* Unlike her daughter, her black skirt covered not only her thighs, but her knees as well. Her black silk blouse, while tissue-thin, revealed not even a hint of cleavage. Everything that should be covered was, indeed, modestly hidden beneath a simple black camisole. After Vivian Glickstein's designer clothes and alligator shoes, I had expected a widow fabulously clad in black. However, Nadine's outfit actually looked like something I could afford. The black emphasized her milk-white skin. Her hair was the color of strawberry Jell-O, the sort of tone the maladroit wind up with when they try to become glamorous at home.

Garrett, beside his mother on an endless modular sofa, had her pallor, but not her frame. Like his twin, he came in XL. Like her, too, he had dark hair as well as a thick-lipped mouth kind people would describe as generous. Unlike her, he obviously had no personal trainer; Gabrielle's triceps were in a realm beyond buff while Garrett's biceps would probably dimple like a stale marshmallow. With his black curls hanging over his pale forehead and the tops of his ears, he resembled the bust of some degenerate Roman emperor.

To the Bleibermans' amazement (to say nothing of mine) Tatty somehow fit herself on the three inches of couch that lay between Garrett and Nadine. She took Nadine's blue-veined hand in hers. "He was a splendid man, my dear," she said softly to the air directly in front of her. Both mother and son nodded their thanks. Gabrielle, not to be left out, hastened across the room for two small folding chairs with dark orange seats that could have been the work of some superchic designer as an homage to the fifties. Nevertheless, I suspected they had been left over from someone's grandmother's canasta game. She and I sat, completing a tight little circle that effectively excluded the five or six other callers in the room. For a moment none of us spoke. I glanced around. Unlike the Louis XIV–loving Glicksteins, the Bleibermans' taste was modern—and surprisingly modest: a reproduction of a Mies Van der Rohe Barcelona chair done in pale blue leather instead of the usual brown; a vast royal blue modular sofa that was slightly overstuffed, like the twins.

"Why," Tatty asked, "was his safe open?" Naturally, I wanted to take her swanlike neck and wring it; this had been the final question she was supposed to ask, not the first.

However, instead of gasping, Garrett gave a manly shrug—as in, *Beats the hell out of me.* And Gabrielle declared: "We keep asking ourselves that." Their mother seemed to have found not only her words, but her saliva, as she turned toward Tatty and sprayed: "He didn't have any appointments that afternoon."

"His secretary said he was alone the whole time!" Gabrielle added, fussing with something at her waist. I glanced over and saw she was adjusting a navel ring to hang over the waistband of her skirt. Tatty, of course, was by nature and breeding too stiff-upper-lip to act appalled, though it could be that she thought the ring was some Jewish mourning apparatus I had failed to mention.

"I'm trying to recall his office," Tatty mused. "I'd been there a couple of times—perhaps more—with Mother." She glanced at me. "The time she bought that glorious diamond spaniel with the ruby collar." She closed her eyes, then opened them an instant later. "Did the room have a window?"

"No," Garrett finally spoke, albeit slowly, as if he wished he didn't have to part with the words. "For security. Inner office. Cuts insurance rates."

"How interesting."

"Well lighted," Garrett mumbled.

"Of course. One wants to see the cut and color of the gem one is envisioning on one's finger."

Gabrielle was nodding eagerly. "About ten years ago Dad hired a famous lighting designer. A guy who does Broadway plays."

"Murray Glickstein," Garrett added. "Against it."

"Murray Glickstein was his partner," Nadine explained.

"Murray was, is, the G," Gabrielle explained. "In B and G. He didn't want it. See, Dad believed heart and soul in plowing profits back into the business. Like fertilizer. But instead of bigger, whatever, like roses, you come out with bigger sales. But he had to fight Murray tooth and nail on every capital investment."

"This Murray wanted to take all the profits out?" Tatty sounded scandalized.

Did it not occur to any of the Bleibermans that this was a bizarre conversation to be having with a total stranger just a few days after their father's/husband's murder? Obviously not, which is why I had enlisted Tatty. I could have borrowed her aquamarine and pearl gewgaws, put on the upperclass accent, even, if necessary, the hauteur. Over the years I had discovered I could go anywhere—from a longshoremen's bar to a yacht in the Mediterranean—and be accepted. What I could not fake, however, was Tatiana's assumption of privilege, that inborn assurance that puts the rest of the world on notice: *You must please me.* So, as I had predicted, questions that would have seemed presumptuous coming from me were taken as a kindness coming from Tatty. She *cares.*

"The wife," Garrett mumbled.

"This Murray's wife pushed him to take the profits out of the business?" Tatty's nostrils dilated, her I-am-appalled expression.

Gabrielle leaned forward so far, her head almost knocked Tatty's. "You should see how they live. Sumptuous is putting it mildly. Palatial."

"Gabrielle, it's really not palatial," her mother suggested, trying to cut off the conversation. Her voice was soft, hesitant. She was not a woman who enjoyed or even tolerated confrontation.

"It is too." Gabrielle dismissed her mother the way someone would brush a fly off his arm, not so much with contempt as mere annoyance; her mother, apparently, was a familiar nuisance. "Even if Murray *wanted* to plow back some more of the profits, he couldn't because he had to finance their lifestyle."

Tatty cocked her head. "I remember your father telling Mother and me that the two of you had joined him in the business. He was so proud." All three Bleibermans nodded at once. "Was it frustrating, to see the future of your business . . . ?"

When a second and a half passed and no answer was forthcoming, Tatty offered Garrett a small smile of encouragement. "Very, very," he answered immediately. What struck me was that, to look at them, the twins seemed tough customers. Overtanned Gabrielle in her leather tourniquet of a miniskirt. Pale, puffed-up Garrett doling out each word as if every syllable was a year deducted from his life. Yet both of them were so easily wowed by Tatty that it was hard to imagine them as the bullies making misery for Ken Glickstein.

"It was beyond the valley of upsetting," Gabrielle confided to Tatty. "Daddy and us . . ." She seemed to be hesitating over the *us,* thinking perhaps it might be a *we,* but then she went on. "We wanted to grow the business." The twins sighed in unison. Their mother was busy twisting her wedding band and its matching engagement ring.

"Must you now be partners with this spendthrift?" Tatty inquired. Her inquiries were posing the philosophical question: Can there be any end to chutzpah? The answer was: Obviously not.

"B and G," Garrett said. "Fifty-fifty." Tatty offered a consoling sigh. "Not the end of the world," he added.

"For now," his sister added. "I mean, we know the business as a business, a financial entity. But because Daddy was . . . well, Daddy, we don't know the regular customers all that well. They always asked for him. I mean, Daddy's middle name was Reliable."

"Richard," Nadine said softly, to no one in particular.

After the visit to the Bleibermans, late lunch or tea was called for. But being the new generation of Ivey alumnae we both went back to work— me to my cocaine case, Tatty to her second doctoral dissertation. She already had a Ph.D. in botany, with particular expertise in bryology, the study of mosses and liverworts. However, she had awakened one morning cosmically bored. Somehow her mind, always peculiar, made the leap that the cure for ennui was the study of medieval Italian politics. Now, as far as I could comprehend, she was writing about the traumatic effects of Savonarola's execution on Niccolò Machiavelli.

Sunday morning's cloudless sky was merely a cover for a cold, windy day. Nevertheless, I put on earmuffs and my old, stiff ski mittens and walked from my apartment in Little Italy uptown to Tatty's grand limestone townhouse on East Sixty-seventh Street. Technically it was her father's townhouse, but as he was usually traveling in foreign climes looking for new varieties of birds to shoot, she had all five floors to herself.

We sat at a giant butcher-block table in the kitchen, a room easily large enough to accommodate a staff of four, which it did on weekdays. "Well, shall we solve this murder?" Tatty demanded. "Or shall we go to the Pietro da Cortona exhibit at the Met?"

I mimed a large yawn, then wound up actually yawning. "Why do I sense Pietro will be a snore and a half? All right, we can figure out who killed Barry Richard Bleiberman, then I will keep you company." I put a dab of plum jam on my last piece of croissant and popped it into my mouth.

"What shall we talk of first?" Tatty asked.

"Chez Bleiberman," I suggested. "Didn't it strike you as being a little spare?"

"It did. Not simply spare. Bauhaus is not my period, but that yacht of a sofa and the blue leather chairs . . . they did not cry out 'less is more' to me. They were sadly unattractive. Unless a space is designed by someone with an exquisitely trained eye, less is invariably less." She stood and poured another cup of coffee from the pot the housekeeper had set up the night before. "But perhaps they are the sort of people who are oblivious to their surroundings."

"I don't know about that. They were all dressed fashionably—"

"*What?* Did you see the ring in that Gabrielle's navel?" Tatty demanded. "I thought I would retch. The mere notion of it! What if she had a large meal? Can you imagine it rubbing against the waistband of her skirt? And picture some poor man gagging in the midst of what might otherwise be a sensual liaison after spying that tawdry little hoop of metal that is probably gummed up with abhorrent navel secretions! How can you call that fashionable?"

"You know I don't mean fashionable à la Mainbocher of Givenchy. And if you would have let me finish my sentence you'd have heard me add: fashionable but not very expensive."

"Cheap." She reached for my cup, poured some more coffee for me, then joined me back at the table. The old white porcelain cups with their dainty traceries of aqua and gold looked even more fragile atop the sturdy wood table.

"Now, the night I went to visit Uncle Murray. If you sold off all the Louis Quatorze in their living room it could retire the national debt."

"The real thing?" Tatty inquired.

"It would have been discourteous to ask for the provenance of the settee," I explained. "Though the stuff looked pretty good to me. Real or not, I bet they paid a bundle. And Missus Murray—the lovely Vivian— was wearing Carolina Herrera and what looked like Manolo alligator shoes. Plus a really nice Upper East Side duplex. The Bleibermans' place may have been on Central Park West, but it wasn't facing the park."

"And it was a thoroughly undistinguished apartment. Someone had ripped down all the old moldings. And to have wall-to-wall carpet covering what must be beautiful old parquet floors. A desecration." She shook her head. "But all right. They lived modestly."

"Still," I said, "the two men were fifty-fifty partners, Tatty. Clearly Murray had the most power because he was able to pull out most of the profits from the business to keep his wife in Herrera and ormolu. Now, if he's doing this would it be sound business practice for Barry Bleiberman to have plowed back *his* cut?"

"No." She reached for a brioche, yanked off the top rather viciously, and popped it into her mouth. "Go on."

"So what was Barry doing with hundreds of thousands or, for all I know, millions of dollars *he* was taking out of B and G?"

"Not buying furniture," Tatty mused. "Although it is possible he was buying furniture for *someone*. Perhaps he was keeping a dominatrix with a taste for Chippendale."

"Perhaps. Or perhaps he had an offshore account in the Cayman Islands. Maybe he had a five-thousand-dollar-a-day drug habit. The point is"—I sipped my coffee—"all that money was not being conspicuously consumed by his family."

"Nadine's wedding and engagement rings are what I imagine a working-class man would buy," Tatty mused. "Nice. Tasteful enough. But ordinary."

"They are not what you would expect from a jeweler who dealt in big-ticket items," I agreed. "Even if Barry did not have much money when they got married, what would a conventional man of his current occupation and economic class do?"

Tatty shook her head at my asking a question with such an obvious answer. "Replace them with bigger and better, of course," she replied.

"Of course."

"Unless he was, as my mother so delicately referred to my father, a cheap fuck," Tatty pointed out.

"Hold that thought. Now, let us consider who would profit by Barry Bleiberman's death."

"Murray," she responded. "He still owns fifty percent of B and G. But the twins would be dependent on him, so he'd get to run things."

"Everything I heard from my cousin indicated that Gabrielle and Garrett would own their father's half."

"So then they would benefit from Mr. Bleiberman's death."

"Maybe ultimately, but if they were plotting, why would they kill their father now? They were pretty up front about not knowing the customers. That's why they were so accepting when you whirled in, Tatiana."

"I do not whirl. I glide. I have been called a sylph."

"You have been called many things. Now, does Ken Glickstein benefit if Barry B. checks out?"

"No," she said, "because that would leave him at the mercy of the twins."

"Vivian? Would killing Barry advance her cause of making her son more secure?"

"Only if she's a nincompoop."

"Well, I wouldn't swear she isn't, but she's a shrewd nincompoop. She understood it would be the Twain versus Murray—with her beloved little boy on the sidelines." I stood. "I am off to Rachel's."

"But you are going to the da Cortona exhibit with me."

"I might meet you there."

"You won't." Tatty sighed.

"I won't," I agreed.

• • •

Since I was already in the high rent district, I popped in on my cousin Rachel. She was otherwise engaged at the children's Sunday school, apparently helping first graders dip wicks for Hanukkah candles. But her husband, Danny, who resembled a Range Rover in a red V-neck sweater, was home trying to conquer all the sections of the Sunday *Times*. "Aaa-meee! Hey, great to see ya!" He gave me such an enthusiastic bear hug that I wound up getting red cashmere fibers embedded in my lip gloss.

When he let me go I breathed. Then I asked: "Dear Aunt Vivian: Before this little disagreement over the twins and Ken, was she friendly with Nadine Bleiberman?"

Danny laughed his hearty ho-ho football fan laugh and replied: "You've got to be kidding."

"They do seem an unlikely pair."

"Apples and oranges are at least fruit. Aunt Viv and Nadine . . . jeez, apples and lamb chops."

"Was there any competition between them?"

"How could there be? Aunt Viv has Uncle Murray wound around her little finger and gets whatever she wants. As far as I know, Nadine is one of those old-fashioned wives who, you know, is willing to wind herself around her husband's finger."

"So she didn't want elegant clothes and snazzy jewelry?"

Danny shrugged his bearish shoulders. "I really don't know her well enough to know what she wanted," he said. "But if it cost more than a buck and a quarter, she wouldn't have gotten it. Barry Bleiberman may have been one smart businessman, but he was a cheap, mean you know what."

I established that my cousin Rachel would be home late morning and accepted an invitation to dine *en famille* at six o'clock. Then I called my favorite FBI agent, a Mormon who alternately kept trying to convert me and bewitch me. I told him he could buy me lunch in Chinatown . . . and do me a small favor.

Although I had too many steamed vegetable dumplings and wound up in the agent's apartment listening to a Waylon Thibodeaux recording of Cajun music and profusely admiring the Choupique Two Step, he was happy to make a few phone calls. By the time I left to go back to the office to work on the opening in my cocaine case, I knew what I needed to know. Several hours later, I hied myself uptown to dinner, unfortunately not yet having digested lunch.

"This is the big question. Who benefits from Barry Bleiberman being . . ." I glanced over at Rachel's progeny, Brianna and Ryan, two thoroughly likeable children who, fortunately, had inherited their mother's dark, liquid eyes and their father's intelligence. Somehow, in the way of children, they sensed this was one adult conversation that had the potential to be interesting. So I began again: "The important question is this: Who benefits from Barry Bleiberman being nullified by three strikes with a desk implement?"

"What?" my cousin Rachel inquired, looking up from the single slice of turkey and mountain of salad she had allowed herself for dinner. She seemed perplexed, but then, the only three-syllable word in my question she probably recognized was Bleiberman.

"Kids," Danny decreed, "out. Grown-up talk. Doubles on Mallomars later if you make yourself scarce."

As they dashed from the dining room, Rachel sighed: The pediatrician says food should never be used as a bribe."

As this looked as if it could be the opening of a lengthy philosophical discourse between husband and wife, I turned to my cousin: "Zip it, Rach." I took a sip of expensive Italian water, and went on. "Before we talk about who benefits, a couple of off-the-record facts. A law enforcement friend of mine . . ."

Danny leaned forward to listen. Rachel leaned back. "Male friend?" she asked.

"Male friend," I replied. "Anyhow, he spoke with a colleague in the NYPD. The autopsy report indicated that any of the three stab wounds was sufficient to kill Barry Bleiberman."

"So why three?" Danny inquired.

"Certainty, perhaps. The killer wanted to feel sure Barry was done for. Either he or she wanted Barry dead very badly or was afraid of being identified if Barry lived."

Rachel stopped performing surgery on her slice of turkey and asked: "So it was someone he knew?"

"Not necessarily. It could have been a stranger worried about being recognized from a mug shot if Barry lived, or picked out of a lineup or caught from an artist's sketch." I took a wedge of lemon from the lemons and limes arranged starlike on a plate and squeezed it into my water. "But if I were a betting woman, I would say it was someone he knew. There was one entrance into B and G, which is on the fourteenth floor of a building on Fifth between Forty-seventh and Forty-eighth. There is a video camera that allows the receptionist to see who is outside the door. If it is someone who should be let in, she buzzes him or her into an anteroom. If the person has a legitimate reason for being at B and G, the receptionist—who is behind a bulletproof window—buzzes the person in to the office proper when the B and G employee whom the person is there to see physically comes down to receive him or her."

"Anybody suspicious come in that day?" Danny asked.

"No," I said. "And no one the day before . . . on the theory someone might have hidden there for the night, although that's highly unlikely: The alarm system has pretty sophisticated motion detectors."

"So *who?*" Rachel said. She was able to pause with her fork a tenth of an inch from her mouth. "Are we doing deduction or logic or something?"

"Rachel," I said, "why wouldn't Murray have killed Barry?"

"Because he's not a killer type."

"Why else?" I pressed.

"Bleiberman was a damned good rainmaker," Danny offered. "With him gone, all that business won't necessarily transfer to Murray."

"What about the other Glicksteins?" I asked. "Ken or Vivian."

"I give up," Rachel said.

"I can't see Ken doing it," Danny said. "He's such a nebbish." He paused and brushed a bread crumb off the Mercedes logo on his golf shirt. "Although it is true that you always hear about these crazy killers: 'He was such a quiet young man.'"

"As far as Ken goes, many of the employees saw him after the body was discovered, which was around one o'clock, when a gold dealer who'd made a working lunch appointment with Barry called to find out where he was. Anyway, neither the other employees nor the cops on the scene noticed any blood on him. Or blood on anyone, for that matter."

"He could have changed," Rachel said.

"You're right. He could have. But let's move on. No one really liked Barry Bleiberman. On the other hand, after all the interviews, there does not seem to be anyone who disliked him in any serious way." At almost the same instant, Rachel's and Danny's brows furrowed. "Okay, so the jewels are gone. Loose stones, not pieces of jewelry. Or at least no pieces of jewelry anyone knows about yet. So what does that tell you about the killer?"

"That he wasn't a rank amateur or a wandering junkie," Danny suggested. "He was someone who knew that when stones are in settings they can be easily identified."

"So what about the twins?" Rachel demanded. "Can you believe that Gabrielle? Wearing a tube top to her father's funeral and then taking off her jacket at the cemetery like it was ninety degrees? And not crying. And the brother not crying, either. Not one tear the whole time. That's what Uncle Murray told Danny." She glanced at her husband fondly. Danny nodded.

"What do the twins have to gain by getting rid of their father now? They are not seasoned enough to take over the business. And they are smart enough to know it."

"So who, Amy?"

I suppressed an urge for a Mallomar and took another sip of bubbly water. "What about Nadine?" I asked.

"The wife?" Danny appeared incredulous.

"She's like . . . so boring, she's not there," Rachel said. "I mean, I hate to be catty, but she's like the Invisible Woman." Her mouth dropped. "Oh."

"In fact, she was in the office that morning. About ten-thirty. Gabrielle was going out for dinner and the theater with a new man. She decided she wanted to wear flats because she was afraid of being too tall in heels. She asked her mother to bring over the shoes. Her mother did."

"Is there a video of Nadine leaving?" Danny asked.

"About fifteen minutes later, time enough to hand over shoes, drop in on husband, kill husband, then snatch jewels from the open safe. But why would she kill Barry?"

"Yeah. Why?" my cousin inquired.

And so I left. And made a phone call. And an hour later, met my father in an all-night coffee shop in Queens. "Amy, sweetheart! You're looking good."

"I am not. I am preparing for trial and I am sallow and dopey with fatigue. But thank you for lying, Dad."

"Would I lie?"

I smiled at him. He, at least, looked good, having successfully stayed out of the hoosegow for more than four years while maintaining a prisoner's weight-lifting regimen. Currently, he was living with a woman he referred to as Mary-the-rich-divorcey. By rich, I believe he meant his lady friend could afford to keep him in the style to which he was accustomed; as he had spent so many years incarcerated, his demands were not much more than a toilet with a door, cable TV, and access to barbells. I had never met Mary. She believed my father was an unmarried stud of thirty-six. It would have been awkward for him to have to explain the existence of a twenty-eight-year-old daughter. "You like your ice cream?" he asked.

"Thank you. It's lovely. Dad, I called because it has been months since I've seen you. But also: I need your professional expertise."

"You gotta be kidding." He laughed. His Adam's apple bounced around in his pumped-up neck.

"No. I am serious. I need some help."

"Tell me, sweetheart." So for the next half-hour, I told him all I knew about the murder of Barry Bleiberman. He asked a few questions, and said "Yeah" and "I get it" several times. While I cannot say he nodded sagely, at least he nodded.

"This is what I need from you, Dad: insight."

"Insect?"

"No. Insight. It is rather like wisdom. Why would a man like Murray kill Barry Bleiberman? Or why would he not kill him?"

My father pushed up the sleeves of his sweater, squeezed his fists, and watched his forearm muscles inflate. I assumed this was a prelude to deep thought, for he fell silent, staring into his vanilla malted. "Not," he said at last.

"Murray would not kill Barry Bleiberman?"

"You got it, Amy baby."

"Why not?"

"You gotta be shittin' me. Oh, sorry, sweetheart. You gotta be kiddin' me. You don't know?"

"That's why I came to you."

He smiled. It saddened me: Dentistry, as practiced in America's penal institutions, left much to be desired. "See, he wouldn't kill Barry because then what would he have?"

"Fifty percent of the business and two young partners who would be dependent on him."

"No, no, no. He'd have two pain in the ass kids who didn't know a pile of shit from a hot rock business-wise. Pardon my French. He could deal with a cheapo like Barry. Do you think he was so stupid he'd want to have to control that girl with the leather mini and that boy who's so constipated, he can't talk? So unless Murray was one big-time dumb schmuck, trust me, baby. He didn't stick no letter opener into the late Barry."

I was sickeningly behind in my preparations for my trial, but I was so tired, I dragged myself to my apartment rather than to the office. Before I fell into a near-lifeless sleep, I called my cousin Rachel. "Remember we were talking about Nadine?"

"Right. About how it wouldn't make sense for her to kill her husband."

"How about this, Rach? That although Barry dealt with wealthy people and was pretty well-to-do himself, the Bleibermans lived a life that was amazingly free of luxury. No fine furniture or rugs. No art. No designer clothes. No glorious jewelry." I regretted not having gone into Rachel's kitchen to get the Mallomar I had been lusting after. "The Bleibermans had no nothing, as it were. Well, Barry had money, but none of it was going to Nadine. What do you think it was like for her, seeing Aunt Vivian all decked out in furs and jewels? Going to the Glicksteins and seeing a small painting that cost more than everything in her own apartment?"

Two days later, after some prompting and threats from Uncle Murray's lawyer, Nadine Bleiberman was again read her rights and questioned, ostensibly to clear up what time she left B and G's offices. Then and there, she confessed to a kindly woman—who happened to be a sergeant in the NYPD's homicide unit.

"She said it was an accident," I told Tatty the following night. She was home reading Machiavelli and drinking Vernaccia. I, of course, was at the office with all my discovery material and an empty can of Diet Coke.

"An accident? Did she trip, grab the letter opener for support, and somehow in regaining her balance stab the man in the heart three times?"

"He had refused to give her money for a new outfit for some ladies' luncheon she was going to."

"A cheap fuck indeed," Tatty murmured.

"She went into his office to plead with him again. Vivian and all the other women she knew would be there. Alas, he refused. A magnificent strand of pearls happened to be on his desk just then, a box lined in ivory silk. She told the cop the sight of it made her momentarily lose her mind."

"I see."

"So although he knows nothing about you, Tatiana, Uncle Murray thanks you. My cousin Rachel, whom you met on the occasion of my swearing in, thanks you, as does her husband, Danny, Uncle Murray's nephew. And of course I am infinitely grateful to you."

"Does infinite gratitude include your buying me dinner tomorrow night?" Tatty inquired.

"Not tomorrow night."

"Have you a hot date?"

"With Uncle Murray and Aunt Vivian."

"No!"

"Yes. They sent over a Piaget watch completely covered with pavé set diamonds. Naturally I sent it back."

"Might I ask why?"

"I am your public servant. You would want me to be above reproach."

"I would. But I'll bet you also found it tasteless."

"I did. In any case, they asked to take me out for dinner."

"And you said yes?" Tatty gasped. "Are you an utter ass? Haven't you done enough for them?"

"What can I tell you?" I replied. "They invited my cousin Rachel and her husband. Auntie Viv said: 'Oh, Amy, it will just be the six of us. Murray and I. Rachel and Danny. Ken. And you. Family.' So I asked her, 'Family?' And in jewellike tones, she said 'Yes, family.' So I inquired: 'How about my father?' "

"To which she replied . . . ?" Tatty demanded.

"Well, at first there was utter silence: the universe just before the Big Bang. Then I heard her swallow. And finally she managed to say: 'Of course. Family.' "

Bill Crider

Top of the World

BILL CRIDER is a prolific writer in several genres, including westerns, mysteries, horror, and young adult fiction. Appearing in several of his novels is Truman Smith, a moody, introspective private investigator who lives on Galveston Island, Texas. Another series features Dan Rhodes, the colorful, folksy sheriff of Blacklin County, Texas. Crider is a professor of English and department chair at Alvin Community College in Alvin, Texas, and also the founder of *Macavity,* a fanzine of mystery fiction. He is long over-due for serious and wide recognition. In an era of illiterate bom-bast, he gives us plots that make sense, sentences to savor, and a panorama of characters who stick in the memory long after a story is finished. These include the wheelman in "Top of the World," which was first published in the anthology *Flesh & Blood: Dark De-sires,* a likeable guy who gets involved with the wrong woman—but not for the reason he thinks.

Top of the World

Bill Crider

I heard the song everywhere I went that spring. It was popular for months. It came out of the greasy jukes in the burger joints, and it was playing on every staticky station that the car radio picked up. "Sittin' on Top of the World," it was called, but at one point it surely sounded to me as if the woman singing it was saying "settin'." I knew that was wrong. Vicky always corrected my grammar, which I have to admit ain't—*isn't*— the best, and she'd never let me say a thing like that. "How many eggs are you setting on, you old hen?" That's what she'd have said to me if I'd made a mistake like that.

But it didn't seem to matter to the people who bought the records because, as I said, the song was everywhere. It was even playing on the cheap plastic radio in the little hotel room where Vicky and I were staying while Vicky sat on the edge of the bed and rolled her stockings down over those fine calves of hers, with her skirt pulled up so that I could see the flash of her white panties.

She knew I was watching. And I knew she liked for me to watch, even though it made me feel rotten inside, sweet and rotten at the same time, like a bruised, overripe peach lying in the sun.

It wasn't sunny outside. It was rainy and dark, and the lights were on in the buildings across from the hotel. The room we were in felt clammy and damp. I could smell the musty wallpaper.

And I could smell Vicky.

She knew that, too.

I felt my throat getting tight. I tried to swallow, but I couldn't. My throat was too dry. The blood was rushing in my head, and I couldn't hear the radio any longer.

Vicky kicked the rolled stockings off her feet, then stood up. She reached down and grabbed the hem of her dress, straightened up, and pulled the dress over her head. She tossed the dress on the bed and smiled at me.

"Not bad for an old broad, huh?" she said.

I couldn't answer, so I just nodded.

She unhooked her bra and threw it on the bed with the dress. Her breasts were round and firm, tipped with dark nipples that stiffened as I watched. Something else was stiffening, too, and I tried to turn away, but I couldn't. She knew I couldn't, and her smile grew wider. She hooked her thumbs in the elastic band of her panties, still smiling, and slid them slowly down over the burning bush, still a flaming red, though she'd dyed the hair on her head jet black. She kept right on smiling as she kicked the panties away from her and fell back on the bed.

"Come to Mama," she said, and, God help me, I did. It wasn't long before she was clawing at my back as I plunged between her legs, the rotten feeling welling up inside me, nearly choking me, but what we were doing was so sweet that I could ignore it until it burst from me and filled her and she cried out as I collapsed on top of her and lay there panting, wondering when she'd try to kill me.

Or whether the cops would get us first.

Sam Cobb was the one who introduced me to Vicky. He came in the shop early one day when I was lying on a creeper under a '50 Ford, putting a new muffler on it. He kicked my left foot, and I turned my head so I could see his shoes and the bottoms of his pants.

I knew who it was right off because nobody else I knew kept his shoes polished so bright or had such sharp pleats in his britches.

I rolled out from under the car and looked up at him while I wiped my hands on a rag. He was tall and thin, and he looked ever taller from down there on the floor. I sat up on the creeper and said, "Hey, Sam. What brings you in here? That Merc' of yours giving you trouble?"

I knew that wasn't it. He took better care of that Merc' than most people take of their homes.

"Might have a job," Sam said. "You want in?"

I looked around the shop. There was no one there but me and Sam and the oil and grease stains on the concrete floor. Which was a good thing, considering what he was talking about.

"Let's go in the office," I said.

I got up from the creeper, and Sam followed me into the little room that I called the office but which wasn't much more than some sheet metal siding put up like a couple of walls jutting out from the walls of the shop. There was a doorway but no door.

Inside there was an old desk covered with repair forms and receipts, a chair on rollers, and an old couch. Neither one of us sat down.

"What about a job?" I asked.

"Got it from a woman named Vicky." Sam looked at me speculatively. "She's got red hair like yours. Looks a lot like you, in fact. She's not your mother, is she?"

"I don't have a mother," I said.

"Everybody's got a mother."

"Not me. I was what they call a foundling. I grew up in an orphanage in Dallas."

"Sorry to hear it. My mother was an angel on earth."

I didn't want to hear about his mother.

"They taught me to work on cars at the orphanage," I said. "Tell me about the job."

He did, and it sounded sweet: a bank in a little cotton town that was taking in tons of dough while the farmers were selling their crops at the gin.

"Not a lawman in the whole town," Sam said. "Maybe not in the whole county."

I knew better than that, and so did he, but he was making it sound easy because he wanted me in.

"So you need a driver," I said.

"Yep. And you're just the guy for the job. What do you say?"

I'd driven for Sam before, and the money had always been good, just the way he promised. I figured that in a couple of years, I'd have enough money to open a really nice shop, hire some mechanics, and make a straight living. I might even be able to get a dealership. That's if we didn't get caught. But we'd never even seen a cop, not a single time. But then we'd never worked with anybody named Vicky before.

"She's okay," Sam told me. "I met her in church."

I thought he might even have been telling the truth. Sam was the kind of guy who met women everywhere. They liked him a lot, and he liked them.

But Vicky wasn't like anyone Sam had met before. Or anyone I'd met, either.

Sam and Vicky did the inside work at the bank, him with his hat pulled low and her wearing dark glasses, with a scarf tied over her red hair and a big floppy sun hat over that. Me, I just sat in the car and waited for them. I didn't have anything to do with what went on inside. I was just the driver.

When the two of them came running out and jumped in the backseat, I took off, fast at first and then just like a guy out for a pleasant drive. After all, I didn't want to get a traffic ticket.

Before long we were out of town and into the country. I'd scouted the dirt roads around there for a couple of days, and I knew no cops would ever find us now, not unless they got awfully lucky, which I didn't figure would happen.

What did happen was that my eyes met Vicky's in the mirror as I was driving along, and that was that. She grinned at me, and I grinned back, and we both knew what was going to happen between us without either one of us saying a word.

Two hours later we'd dumped the car, split the dough, and gone our separate ways. Or Sam had gone his separate way in the Merc', while Vicky and I had gone off together. I was supposed to drop her at her car, but we went straight to a little hotel I knew where the desk clerk never asked questions.

It didn't matter that she was a lot older than me or that we'd hardly spoken more than two words to each other. We both knew what we wanted, and it didn't take us long to find out that it was going to be even better than I'd thought it would. What she lacked in youth, she made up for in enthusiasm and experience. I rode her hard, and she wrung me dry.

"Slap me!" she said at one point, when I was too far gone to know any better.

She laughed when I did, and as the imprint of my fingers reddened on her face, she grabbed my hand with both of hers and bit it so hard that the blood ran out and over her chin and dripped on her breasts. But I didn't even feel it because all my feeling was concentrated so intensely somewhere else that my lips were peeled back in an insane grin.

Later we lay on the bed and smoked Luckies while we listened to the radio playing "Sittin' on Top of the World." My hand was throbbing, but it wasn't bleeding any longer, and I felt like the song was a good sign.

I was wrong about that, of course.

"Sam's going to be upset, you know," Vicky said, as she blew out smoke and watched smoke rise up toward the ceiling. "He thinks he owns me."

"It's not like Sam to get hung up on one woman," I said.

"He's hung up on me."

"Then what he don't know won't hurt him."

"*Doesn't* know," Vicky said.

"Huh?"

"*Doesn't*, not *don't*. What he *doesn't* know."

"Oh. I get it."

"And don't say *huh*. It's vulgar."

"Is this vulgar?" I asked, rolling toward her, and pinched the soft flesh between her legs. "How about this?"

"No. No. It's lovely. And don't stop."

I didn't, not until we were both too tired to move.

"Sam will find out," Vicky said, much later.

"I can handle Sam," I told her, and I was sure that I could.

"I know what's going on, son," Sam told me a month or so later.

I wasn't surprised. I'd been with Vicky more than a dozen times since the bank job. It would have been a miracle if Sam hadn't figured out what was going on by that time. I wondered what had taken him so long. Maybe he just didn't want to admit it to himself.

"I swear to God, I don't know what you're thinking about," he said. "You're a young guy. She's old enough to be your mother, for Christ's sake."

We were in the shop again, back in the office. I was leaned back in the chair with my feet up on the desk. Sam was standing there with his hat in his hands, turning it around and around.

"What difference does it make that she's older?" I asked.

He shook his head. "None, maybe. But it worries me, the way you look alike and the way she's been asking me things about you. Anyway, you stay away from her from now on. I've got another job lined up, and I don't need you thinking with the little head instead of the big one."

I swung my feet to the floor. "It's none of your business how I think."

"It is when you're doing a job with me. Or maybe you don't want to do that anymore. Maybe you want to spend your time in Sunday School."

"Fuck you," I said.

He shook his head again. He didn't look mad, just kind of sick, or maybe just sad, and he turned and left the garage, settling his hat down carefully on his head.

"He's going to kill you," Vicky told me.

We were lying in bed, which is where we usually were when we were together, buck naked, sweating like pigs, drained and drooping. Or at least I was. Vicky wasn't drooping, or drained, either. Just bruised a little, and she liked that. As far as I could tell, she never got tired.

"Sam?" I said. "What the hell would he kill me for?"

"Because he's jealous. He wants me for himself. I told you that."

"He won't kill me. He needs a driver."

"Anyone can drive."

"Not the way I can."

"I like a man with confidence."

I was confident enough about my driving, but not about other things. I didn't like guns, and I didn't like the people who used them, except for Vicky. That's why I was a driver. I'd never been inside a bank during one of Sam's jobs, and I never planned to be.

Vicky was different. She liked guns. I'd seen her running her fingers over the barrel of the .38 she carried in her purse, caressing it the way she sometimes caressed me.

"You're shivering," she said. "Are you cold?"

"No," I said. "I'm hot. Hot for you."

"I can see that," she said, looking down.

We didn't talk much after that.

Sam tried to kill me right after the next job. I let him out of the car at a deserted house in the country. No one had lived there for years. There was no paint left on the boards, and the windows were all broken. Sam's Merc' was in the dilapidated barn, and Vicky and I were going on to ditch the one I was driving in a city about fifty miles away. But Sam wanted Vicky to stay with him.

The wind was blowing dust down the road and tossing the trees near the old house. It was whipping Sam's suit coat, and he had to hold his hat down on his head with one hand.

He leaned down to the car window and said, "Get out, Vicky. You'll be going with me this time."

"We're not supposed to stay together," she said. "You've got the money. What more do you want?"

We always met later to divide the money, usually a week or two later, after the excitement had died down. I'd trusted Sam with the money before, though I wasn't so sure that I could do that anymore. But then I cared more about Vicky than the money by now.

"You know what I want," Sam said.

"You can't have it," Vicky said.

He opened the door and dragged her out before I could do anything about it. He twisted her arm when she struggled with him, and she raked his face with the fingernails of her free hand.

He let go of her arm, and she stumbled backward and fell to the road. Sam just stood there, his hand up to his face. I could see blood seeping around his fingers. His hat had blown off and was tumbling down the road, but he didn't even look to see where it was going.

I was out of the car by that time and heading around to the other side of the car. I couldn't let Sam manhandle Vicky like that, even if it didn't seem like she needed my help.

Before I got to him, though, Sam had his pistol out, and it was pointed right at me.

"Stay right there," he said. "Don't come any closer. There's something you have to know."

He didn't have to tell me twice to stay where I was. If there's anything I like less than a pistol, it's a pistol that's pointed at me.

But he didn't want me to stop because of anything he had to say. He just didn't want a moving target. I saw his eyes widen, and I knew he was going to shoot, but I couldn't move. It was like I was wearing concrete blocks on my feet instead of shoes. I remember wondering if the bullets would hurt me when they hit.

There were two shots, but neither one of them hit me. I kept my eyes closed, waiting for another one, but it didn't come. The next thing I heard was Vicky's voice. She was talking fast and breathlessly, as if she'd just run a couple of miles carrying a heavy suitcase.

"It's okay," she said. "You don't have to worry about Sam anymore, baby. I took care of him for you. It's okay."

I blinked my eyes and then opened them all the way. Sam was lying right about where he'd been standing. He was on his back, looking up at the sky. His jacket was flopped open, and there were two dark red stains on his white shirt. His gun was still in his hand, but he wouldn't be using it again.

I walked over and looked down at him. His eyelids flickered, and his lips moved. I couldn't quite make out what he was trying to say. It sounded a little like *Dallas*.

He didn't get a chance to say it again. Vicky stood beside me and shot him in the head.

"Get the money," she said, but I couldn't move. I just stood there, looking down at Sam, at the little round hole in his head, at the stuff that was leaking out the back of it onto the ground.

Vicky grabbed my arm and jerked me toward the car.

"Get in," she said. "I'll get the money."

I got behind the wheel and sat there, staring out through the windshield. The back door opened, and Vicky threw the money bag in the backseat. I didn't look around, but I knew it was a black leather bag, like the ones doctors carry.

"You have to help me," Vicky said. "We can't leave him lying there like that."

I didn't move.

"Do you hear me?" she asked. "We can't leave him, and I can't move him by myself."

I nodded and got slowly out of the car, moving like a very old man. I let her lead me over to Sam.

"You get his shoulders," she said.

I took a deep breath, knowing that sooner or later she was going to talk me into doing it. There was no use putting it off. So I grabbed Sam's shoulders and lifted. I tried not to let his head touch me, but it did. I didn't look down, but I knew I had blood on my clothes. Blood and maybe a little something else.

Sam was heavier than he looked, but between the two of us, we managed to get him into the barn and into his car. When we slammed the door on him, Vicky said, "Does anyone ever come here?"

"How would I know?" I said. Then I relented a little. "Sam wouldn't pick a place where anyone would stumble on his car by accident."

"Good. Then we don't have a thing to worry about."

Right, I thought. Not a thing. Not us. We're sitting on top of the world.

It's always the little things, the ones you never think of, that come back to bite you. This time it was something as small as a hat, the one I'd seen bouncing along the road when it blew off Sam's head and never thought of again.

It was the hat that led the cops to Sam, less than a day after we'd left him there in the barn. I should have thought about the hat, but after we left Sam, I wasn't thinking about anything at all. Seeing a man shot down and then having to drag him off to a barn will make you forget a lot of things.

Vicky couldn't complain. She hadn't thought about the hat, either. All she could think about was the money. She kept telling me over and over not to worry about Sam because we didn't need him anymore. We had plenty of money, and it was all for the two of us. Besides, she knew where Sam kept the rest of it.

"He doesn't spend it?" I managed to say.

"Well, he spent some of it on me," she said. "But not enough. I don't think he really liked having the money anyway. All he cared about was robbing banks. It gave him a thrill."

It had never given me a thrill. And it wouldn't be giving Sam one any longer. It thrilled Vicky, though. I could see that now, and I could see that killing Sam had been an even bigger thrill for her. She was so excited that she could hardly stop talking. She was bouncing around in the car seat like the steel ball in a pinball machine.

"You know what gives me a thrill?" Vicky asked.

I thought she'd been reading my mind, but that didn't seem possible. So I just shook my head as if I didn't have a clue.

"Fucking you," she said. "That's what gives me a thrill."

I was almost as shocked as I'd been when she killed Sam. I'd never heard a woman use that word before, not even in bed.

"As soon as we get that money, I'm going to fuck your brains out," she said.

But she wouldn't have to. She'd already done that, a long time ago.

I read all about the hat in the papers.

Some farmer was driving along the road, and he happened to see what looked like a really nice man's hat that had blown up against a fence post and hung there. He thought maybe it had blown off some guy's head, but he wondered why anybody would be driving on those back roads in a convertible. And he wondered why anybody would be so careless as to leave a nice hat like that behind. So he looked around a little, and he found the place where Sam had been killed. It wasn't hard to find, he said. There was a buzzard pecking at something on the ground.

I tried not to think too much about that, but the farmer thought about it, and he did a little more looking. When he found the Merc' and Sam's body, he drove to town and went straight to the police.

So now they knew about Sam. Which meant that they might also know about me. Sam and I had kept our business as secret as we could, and I'd certainly never told anybody that I was driving for a bank robber on the side. That didn't mean Sam hadn't told anybody, though.

And it didn't mean that the cops didn't know about Vicky. They found out about her within another day because of her connection with Sam, and there was her picture on the front page of the papers, along with her name and all the reporters could find out about her, some of which was very interesting. Especially the part about where she was from: Dallas. That was probably what Sam had been trying to tell me before he died. I had a feeling I knew why he'd wanted to tell me, a feeling that made me slightly sick and excited at the same time.

I didn't say anything about it to Vicky. Somehow I couldn't bring myself to talk about it.

We were staying at my place, and I was going in to the shop every day, working on cars the way I always had, even though there was more than twenty-five thousand dollars in a couple of black bags stuck under my bed.

Vicky wanted us to take it all and run away to Mexico.

"We can live for the rest of our lives down there with that kind of money," she said, and I knew she was right.

And I knew it was time to go when the cops found out about me.

I'd been careful not to let people see me with Sam, but Vicky and I hadn't been nearly so discreet. It took the cops awhile, but they're always patient. Someone finally must have told them about the young guy who'd been seen with Vicky. They got a description, I guess, and then they got more than that. And then they tracked me down one morning at the shop.

They weren't sure about anything even then, but they were persistent. I answered all their questions politely, and they left without arresting me, but I could tell they weren't satisfied. I waited around until lunchtime, just in case they were watching, and then I locked up and went to my place.

Vicky wasn't there, which was just fine with me. It was time we split up, long past time, and it would've been next to impossible for me to tell her that. She had a powerful hold over me, even though I knew it was wrong, and more than wrong.

If she wasn't around, though, I could just leave. It wouldn't be easy, and I couldn't have done it if I'd had to face her. I wasn't planning to take all the money, just half of it. I figured that was my share. I got one of the leather bags from under the bed, stuck some underwear, a couple of shirts, a toothbrush, and a razor in on top of it, and I was ready to go.

I was almost to the back door when Vicky came in.

"Where do you think you're going?" she said.

The bag felt like lead in my hand.

"Nowhere," I told her.

"The hell you weren't. You were running out on me."

"I left your half of the money."

"I don't give a damn about the money. I just care about you."

"I know," I said, and wished I hadn't.

She gave me a look that lifted the hair on the back of my neck, and I felt my eyes widen in fear and surprise, exactly the way Sam's had widened just before she shot him.

Two things occurred to me then. One was that Sam hadn't been afraid of me at all. The pistol might have been pointed in my direction, but only to threaten someone else. The second thing I realized was that Vicky may very well not have killed Sam to protect me from a bullet. She hadn't been afraid he was going to shoot me. She'd been afraid of what he was going to tell me.

She kept on looking at me. Finally she said, "I don't know what you mean, but I do know I'm coming with you."

I tried to keep my shoulders from slumping. Maybe I was even successful.

"Get your things," I said.

And that's how we wound up in that little hotel room on a rainy, musty spring day. Eight or ten more hours of hard driving and we'd be in Mexico, if the police didn't catch up with us or if Vicky didn't kill me. Because I knew now that she was crazy.

I'd seen the way she fondled pistols like a lover, and I'd seen her nearly delirious excitement after we did a job. I'd heard her voice, full of breathless exhilaration after she shot Sam. And then there was the way she acted with me, the way she talked, the things she made me do. It had finally dawned on me that what had taken me so long to figure out, well, that was something she'd known all along, or at least for a good while. I was sure Sam had told her what he knew about me, which wasn't much but which was enough.

She came out of the dinky little bathroom with a towel wrapped around her.

"Aren't you going to scrub my back?" she said.

I got off the bed, feeling as if I'd turned to stone. I was surprised my legs and arms would move.

"Sure," I told her, and I tried to smile. I don't think I managed it, though.

I followed her into the bathroom, and she dropped the towel to the floor before she stepped into the bathtub. The porcelain was cracked. The rust that had formed in them looked like dried blood.

I worked up a good lather on the washcloth and began soaping Vicky's back. She sighed and closed her eyes, and I worked my way around front to her breasts. There was a light coating of freckles across them, and I rubbed them gently. She sighed again and started to lean back in the tub. When she'd rested her head against the back of it, I climbed in on top of her, got my hands around her throat, pinned her arms and legs, and took her under.

She kicked and thrashed for a while, but not for long. I was a good bit heavier than she was. I tried not to look at her face when it was done.

I got out of the tub, took off my clothes, and toweled dry. I found myself talking to Vicky, explaining why I'd had to kill her. I'm sure she would have understood.

Then I changed clothes and packed the bags with everything in the room. I didn't want to leave anything that would identify either of us. We were in a small town a long way from where we'd killed Sam. The cops there might never make the connection.

When I left, I checked the map. I wasn't too far from Dallas, so I decided to make a stop at the old home place.

• • •

Nothing much had changed. The grounds were still neatly cut, and there were a few flowers already blooming in the beds. There'd be a lot more later on.

I didn't know the woman at the desk, but when I mentioned to her I was a former resident, she told me that one of my teachers was still around.

"Miss Arnold. She's in class now, but if you'd like to wait a few minutes . . ."

I said I'd wait, and I walked back into the classroom wing. It still looked and smelled the same. Maybe the floor had been worn a little smoother by all the feet passing up and down the hall. I stood by the wall until class was over and the kids came out the door. Then I went inside.

Miss Arnold hadn't changed much, either. She still wore her hair pulled back in a bun, though it was gray now instead of black, and she had a pair of little half-glasses on her sharp-featured face. She peered at me over the top of the glasses.

When I told her who I was, she said, "Of course. I remember you now. How could I forget that red hair?"

It wouldn't be red much longer, because I had Vicky's hair dye with me, but I didn't tell Miss Arnold that.

"I remember the day you came here," she said. "It must have been more than twenty years ago."

"It was," I said. "Do you happen to remember anything about my family?"

"We don't give out that kind of information," she said. "Besides, I don't have it."

"I didn't think so. I was just wondering."

Her face softened a little then, which surprised me. I don't recall that she'd ever softened when I'd been in her class.

"I do remember your father, though," she said. "I don't know his name, of course, but he had red hair, just like yours. I remember his saying that they'd never give you up if only they could afford to keep you."

I had an uneasy feeling.

"You said *they*. What did my mother look like?"

Miss Arnold stared off over my head as if the shadowy corner of the room might hold a preserved image of the past.

"She looked nothing like you. She was a cute little thing, short and blond, with pretty blue eyes. You do have the blue eyes, however."

I felt hollow inside, all the way down to my toes, and I stood there looking stupidly at Miss Arnold for a few seconds while she waited for me to make some kind of comment. But there was really nothing for me to say, except that I'd been wrong about Vicky, fatally wrong, and I wasn't going to mention that to Miss Arnold. Or to anyone. I left as soon as I could and got away from there.

• • •

Mexico isn't so bad. The climate's nice, and the ocean's pretty and blue where I am. I don't speak the language very well yet, but I have a lot of money, and that pretty much takes care of the language problem. There's plenty to drink, and there's—there *are*—plenty of women. Funny, but I can't seem to get interested in them. And when I do get interested, nothing happens, if you know what I mean. There's no shame in that, they tell me, and I guess they don't care, as long as I pay them. Maybe if they were redheads it would be different, but I try not to think too much about that.

So all in all, things are going great. I guess you could say I'm sitting on top of the world.

Anne Perry

Ere I Killed Thee

ANNE PERRY writes two distinctive series of detective novels set in Victorian England. In one series, Inspector Thomas Pitt works through official channels, while his wife, Charlotte, uses her highborn status to help solve crimes. In the second series, private detective William Monk and nurse Hester Latterly work together. Both teams employ female investigators who are well ahead of their time, both in their sleuthing and their interest in the motives behind human behavior. In addition, Perry exposes the rigidity and hypocritical pomposity of Victorian society with detail and wry humor. Her books are always stunningly plotted and compulsively readable; there has never been, nor is there ever likely to be, a bad Anne Perry novel. In "Ere I Killed Thee," her story from the aptly titled *Much Ado About Murder,* a collection of Shakespearean mystery stories, a troupe of Victorian actors must ferret out the truth when one of them turns to murder.

Ere I Killed Thee

Anne Perry

The audience rose to its feet and thundered applause. Oscar Wilde might be the sensation of the day, but there was nothing to excel the music of Shakespeare and the passion and tragedy of Othello. And of all the brilliant actors who had taken that role, there was no one who had invested it with more immediacy than Owain Glenconnor. There was no Iago more serpentine than Idris Evans.

Usually Owain's wife, Dierdre Ashbourne, had received standing ovations as well. Her Lady Macbeth was classic, but as Desdemona she was no more than good. Something of the fire and the luminosity was absent. As Owain stood on the stage next to her, taking the very last bow, he saw the shadow in her face and knew the bitter disappointment she felt. It happened to all actors sometime or another, but it had been many years since she had played second to anyone at all, certainly not to stand by graciously while a relatively minor actress like Idris's wife, Amelia Ryecroft, was thrown roses.

As soon as the curtain finally fell, they swapped brief words of enthusiasm, and then each returned to their dressing rooms. Dierdre had only to take off her gown and a little of the paint before being ready to go on to the party. She did not want or need a wig. Her own glorious tawny hair was perfect for the role and the public expected to see it. It was part of who she was. It only needed an expert twist and a few pins and it was ready for her appearance to celebrate.

Amelia was much the same. Idris had only to change his clothes and get rid of the jewelry of Iago and he was ready. Perhaps he should wash off a little of the extra color, but that was quickly done.

Owain had to get rid of every scrap of the black paint necessary for his part alone, not only from his face and neck, but from his hands as well. It was a long job, and as usual by the time he joined the rest of the cast, they were already sipping champagne and entertaining guests with stories of past performances, anecdotes about other plays, and hilarious stories of triumph and disaster on tour.

He stared across the room with its heavy pre-Raphaelite wallpaper, gas lamps he knew would be gently hissing but at the moment were drowned by the sound of voices and laughter and the clink of crystal. As usual, Dierdre was the center of a group of admirers. She stood on the lowest step of the stairs, her pale apricot skirts unshadowed by anyone else, catching the light like the center of a Rembrandt painting, making everyone else seem dull by comparison. By heaven, the woman knew how to draw the eye!

Owain walked in casually, a little swagger in his step. He was wearing his favorite loose white silk shirt with full sleeves, hardly conventional eveningwear but very flattering, very dramatic. He saw Idris grin at him and raise his glass. He read the scene exactly.

There was a drop in the buzz of conversation and half a dozen heads turned. Someone called out "Congratulations!" and others joined in. Immediately he was passed champagne and took it, relishing the sweet-sharp flavor. Someone had treated them to a very good vintage. He raised the glass high. "Thank you, whoever gave us this!" he said clearly. His voice was magnificent, dark and full of emotion. If he had not been a great actor, he might have sung at least well. But being one in a male voice choir, however good, had not the drama or the glory of a sublime solo performance.

Dierdre turned and looked at him, smiling with devastating charm. Most of the men in the room were watching her. That was not unusual, but tonight perhaps they were waiting to see how she would take having been upstaged by her husband and Iago, even Iago's young wife. If any imagined she would sulk, they did not know her. She was standing beside Idris now. She linked her arm through his and he responded gallantly. They had known each other for years, and ridden the crest of the waves and the troughs together.

Owain walked over to her and put his arm around her on the other side. "Who treated us to the champagne?" he asked casually. Better not to make any reference to the performance.

She glanced at Idris and away again quickly, and loosed herself from his arm, her face bleak for a moment before turning to Owain. "Kennedy," she answered, referring to Kennedy Williams, the theater manager. "And Idris." She looked awkward, as if it were a confession and something he might mind. Perhaps he did. He would like to have been included, and apparently they had not thought of him.

"I see," he said coolly. "Well, it's excellent." He upended the glass and drank all the rest of it, then signaled to the footman, who offered him another, which he took and then straightaway set it down on one of the small tables and ignored. He turned to Kennedy Williams and one of the supporting cast and began conversation with them.

Idris shrugged and looked back to Dierdre again, but instead of resuming their previous discussion, she moved away from him and stood beside Owain, smiling at him a little nervously.

"It really wasn't anything," she began, looking at him, then at Kennedy.

He did not answer.

"Owain, believe me!" she pleaded.

This was not the place to mention such a tiny, ridiculous matter. The only way to deal with it was to forget it. Talking about it in front of others, especially Kennedy, was embarrassing. He affected not to know what she was referring to. He stared at her blankly, but he knew his annoyance showed. "If whatever it was—wasn't anything, then we should dismiss it," he said coolly.

She handed him another glass, holding it out in a graceful gesture. She had beautiful hands and she used them marvelously, like a dancer. "The drink, darling . . ."

This was absurd. She was creating out of nothing a drama to be the center of. It was his own stupidity to have set the scene for her. The applause for Amelia must have hurt her more than he had appreciated. It was miserable to have an audience you thought was yours pass you by, even for one performance, for someone else younger, if not prettier. And Amelia was charming, but she would never have Dierdre's fire, or her grandeur. She could have been allowed this one triumph. A little generosity wouldn't hurt.

He took the champagne. "Of course." He sipped it, holding her gaze steadily. They had been married for over ten years. They could read each other so well. He could put warmth into his face, and it would deceive everyone else, but not her. "Thank you," he added, smiling back at her.

"And Idris?" she asked so softly only Kennedy would have heard her.

He held the glass up. "To his health!" It still sounded a little sharp.

She relaxed and turned to the others, ready for the next tale, the next remembrance and joke.

Owain forgot the matter altogether in a week of superb performances. The critics were enthusiastic, especially about his own final scene, and about the individual quality and power of Idris in the role of Iago. But of course no matter how good they were, there were always rehearsals, just to keep up the fluidity and polish. It was at one of these that he found himself unintentionally quarreling with Idris. He did not really know how it came about. One minute they were all standing together in the wings while Kennedy spoke to the man who was in charge of the limelights, a highly technical job, and one on whose skill their safety depended, the next minute Dierdre was walking across the boards in the light and putting her arm through Idris's.

Owain saw Amelia turn and the quick flash of displeasure in her face. She was young and still very much in love with Idris. She was in awe of

Dierdre's glamour, and Owain had noticed the vulnerability in her, the fear of being less interesting, less beautiful. She always played the second lead, not the first, except privately with Kennedy Williams. For him she was the first and the best, although she seemed quite unaware of it.

Owain stepped forward, intentionally interrupting them. "Dierdre, try that entrance again now that they have the lights correct," he ordered. It was rude and interfering, out of character for him, but it had the desired effect of breaking the scene. She looked at him with wide eyes, almost as if she were frightened. She glanced over at Kennedy Williams. Idris frowned.

"Yes, of course, Owain," Dierdre said meekly, and with downcast eyes she moved away.

"What the devil's the matter with you?" Idris demanded, his voice low, but the anger in his face unmistakable. "You've been playing Othello too long! Your imagination's overtaken you."

Owain was stunned. "Othello! Don't be ridiculous. It was nothing to do with me! Didn't you see Amelia's face?"

"What's Amelia got to do with it?" Idris was startled. "Dierdre's hurt, she needs a little compassion, a word of gentleness, and you don't seem to want to give it." There was criticism in his face and his dark eyes were cold.

"Compassion!" Owain said incredulously. "Don't be idiotic! There's nothing wrong with her that wouldn't be cured by a good notice or a little more applause."

Idris regarded him with total disgust. "I didn't think I'd hear you say anything so cold-blooded, Owain. I thought you had more humanity, and less selfish pride."

Owain was lost for words. His confusion must have shown in his face even before he spoke. "You're falling over yourself to give compassion to my wife, and leaving your own wife to wonder what's going on, and you despise me for it?"

The color washed up Idris's face, and embarrassment made him angrier. "Amelia knows perfectly well I have only friendship and admiration for Dierdre . . . as have all the rest of us."

"And compassion!" Owain said sarcastically. "Don't forget that! Your heart no doubt bleeds for her because your wife got the longer applause from the audience. I daresay Amelia wonders why you aren't proud of her. It's not as if she'd upstaged you."

"I'm not talking about applause, you fool!" Idris snarled, keeping his voice down only with difficulty.

Kennedy Williams was staring at them now, undecided whether to come over or not. He glanced at Amelia and his feelings were naked for an instant in his eyes.

"I'm talking about her sister!" Idris replied to Owain.

Owain was completely at a loss. "Sister?"

Idris's eyebrows shot up. "Her sister died last week, man! Don't stand there as if you don't know what I'm talking about. She must have been your sister-in-law. I think Dierdre has the superb courage and selflessness to go onstage every night, and all you can do is accuse her of being jealous because Amelia is getting recognition at last. I thought better of you." He turned away and took a step as if to leave.

Owain caught him by the shoulder and half spun him around.

Idris's whole body clenched as if he intended to strike back, and he restrained himself only when his fist was half raised.

"She hasn't got a sister!" Owain said between his teeth, still quietly enough for Kennedy Williams not to hear. "I don't know what the devil she's told you, but she's an only child!"

Idris stood motionless, his eyes wide. "What?"

"She's an only child!" Owain repeated.

Idris drew in his breath sharply as if to respond. Neither man was sure whether to believe the other or not.

The moment was broken by Dierdre returning, her face anxious. She glanced at Kennedy Williams, then smiled a little tentatively at Idris before turning to Owain.

"The lights are right. Please let's get on with the scene. Then we can go and"—she lifted her shoulder elegantly—"and have a pleasant afternoon doing whatever we wish. I need a little rest before tonight, don't you?"

He saw a moment of something like fear at the back of her eyes. But she was right, they all needed to leave the theater and have a break from work and a good meal before giving all the passion and concentration, even the physical effort, of a good performance this evening. He did more than anyone. Othello was an immense role.

"Yes, of course," he agreed, and without referring to anyone except Williams, he moved straight into the scene.

But a couple of days later the quarrel erupted again. Dierdre was playing the grand romantic lead, as she always had done. It was a dinner party with friends on a Sunday evening. There were perhaps a dozen people present. The chandeliers blazed on creamy shoulders, exquisite hair, and an array of jewels fit to grace the necks of duchesses. The table was set with crystal and porcelain. Roses spilled over the silver bowl in the center and sprays of honeysuckle twined around the silver cruet sets. Footmen waited discreetly by the side tables and maids in black dresses and white lace caps and aprons served each dish in its turn. Dierdre was flirting outrageously, particularly with Idris. Owain could see Amelia's face becoming more and more strained.

Four times he cut across the conversation, trying to draw Dierdre to speak to him, flirt with him, anything to break the sparkling bond between her and Idris, which must be becoming plainer all the time, not only to Amelia but to everyone else as well. He tried current events, other people's plays, Oscar Wilde was taking London by storm and his wit was becoming more and more outrageous. Owain even tried theater gossip, and comments on the music hall, but nothing worked until finally it became ridiculous and everyone was looking at him.

Afterward, when the ladies retired to the withdrawing room, he caught Idris alone in the hall, returning from the cloakroom.

"For God's sake, pull yourself together and stop behaving like a fool!" he said angrily. "You've got a wife who adores you, and you spend the entire dinner ignoring her! She may not be as much fun to show off with as Dierdre, but she's worth treating with a little dignity in public, whatever you do alone."

Idris colored scarlet, and Owain thought at first it was fury, then as he looked more closely he realized with a wave of relief that it was shame.

"I'm sorry," Idris said quietly. "Dierdre is so . . . so full of wit I forgot myself. I wish Amelia had more . . ."

"Confidence?" Owain said with an edge to his voice. "You don't give her much help, do you!" That was a criticism, not a question.

"You don't need to add to it," Idris replied. "It won't happen again."

At that moment Kennedy Williams came out of the dining room and Idris turned and walked away quickly, his face still scarlet.

Owain dismissed the matter from his thoughts until nearly a week later when he saw Amelia coming down the stairs of the hotel. It was late breakfast time, a meal not all of them took. She looked pale and unhappy. Dierdre came hurrying after her. She was wearing a loose robe over her nightgown and her hair was around her shoulders in a dark bronze wave. She was flustered and her cheeks were bright pink. She caught up with Amelia on the bottom step.

"It isn't what you think!" she said urgently. Her voice was something of a stage whisper, giving the impression of a desire for privacy, but actually carrying so far that even Kennedy Williams in the dining room entrance must have heard it.

"Isn't it?" Amelia said sarcastically, swiveling on the step and facing Dierdre. "If there is some alternative reason for you coming out of my husband's bedroom in your night-clothes, I should be interested to hear what it is? You are certainly giving a grandstand performance of being a whore!"

Owain took a step forward. This was going too far.

"Amelia, I swear . . ." Dierdre began, putting her hand on Amelia's arm.

But Amelia snatched herself away. "Don't insult us all!" she hissed. "You're a trollop. Owain may be prepared to put up with it. Maybe he's still enough in love with you he can't break free of you. But I certainly can, and I will!"

"Wait!" Dierdre cried out, her voice now carrying a note of real desperation. "Idris wasn't in there, and I knew he wasn't! I was looking for you!

I know how . . . how close you are! Idris adores you! I expected when you weren't in your own room that I'd find you there . . . where else would you be?"

Amelia stopped and turned back. She was struggling to believe. Owain could see it in her eyes, the trembling of her lips. Perhaps it was true . . . just conceivably? He believed it himself. What she wanted was drama, not passion. She had no use for Idris, except as a prop for her glamour.

"And what did you want me for?" Amelia asked huskily.

"A tisane," Dierdre said with an anxious smile. "I have a terrible head-ache and my maid has forgotten to get any more."

"I see."

Owain could not tell whether Amelia believed her or not. Perhaps she wanted to so badly she would not even ask Idris or attempt to find out. Or she might have cared too much not to put it to the test, and not allow herself the agony of ever afterward being tormented with doubt.

Now it was a matter of stopping the embarrassment.

"Dierdre!" he said firmly, taking her by the elbow. "For heaven's sake, get the hotel management to fetch you a tisane, and stop giving rise to the most awful speculation by half the dining room!"

As it happened, there was no chance for him to learn more of it. That evening just before the fourth act, he was alone in his dressing room, still looking for his favorite shirt, which either he or his dresser must have misplaced, and more importantly for his Moorish dagger, which he hung on the wall in every theater, whether he was playing Othello or not, when he heard a shrill and terrible scream. He knew immediately that it was not temper or someone caught by surprise—it was sheer and absolute horror.

He dropped the jacket in his hands and ran through the door and along the passage toward the sound. Cassio and Bianca were standing at Idris's door and it was she who was screaming, but even as Owain arrived, Cassio put both arms around her and pulled her back.

Owain pushed past him and saw Idris lying on the floor on his face, the Moorish dagger sunk into the middle of his back, where the scarlet blood spread wide and dark around its hilt. It was stupid to imagine he could still be alive with a wound like that, but it was a desperate instinct. Owain pushed past the other two and knelt down beside Idris, feeling for the pulse in his neck. He knew there would be nothing there, and yet he was suddenly sick with disappointment. He looked at Idris's face. His dark eyes were wide open and he seemed surprised, as if he had seen death coming.

Should Owain close his eyes in decency, or leave him exactly as he was for the police? There would have to be police. There was no possibility at all that this was anything but murder.

He stood up slowly, startled to find himself shaking. "You'd better tell Kennedy," he said awkwardly. "There'll be no conclusion to tonight's per-formance. He'll have to make an announcement." He pulled the door closed. "And get someone to guard this till the police come!"

It was less than thirty minutes before Inspector Morgan arrived, dark as Idris himself, a little overweight and with a voice like melted treacle.

"Well, now," he said grimly. "Idris Evans, is it? What a tragedy! A fine actor, but it's Iago he plays, isn't it?"

"Yes," Owain agreed.

Morgan raised one eyebrow. "And no need to ask you who you are, sir. I've watched you many a time. One of the best Othellos of your generation, they say. I'd say the best, and no mistake. What happened here, do you know?"

"No, I don't."

"After Act Four, they tell me. So you weren't on stage before the interval, and neither was Mr. Evans, poor soul. Nor Desdemona . . . that'd be Miss Ashbourne."

"That's right," Owain agreed.

"Well, well," Morgan said thoughtfully. "You'd better tell me everything you did from the time you left the stage, until you heard Bianca scream, if you don't mind. And then I'll have everyone else do the same."

It was a long and tedious job establishing where everyone was, but in the end the conclusions were plainer than might have been supposed. No one had come in through the stage door from the start, so whoever had killed Idris had of necessity been one of the cast or dressers, or a stagehand, or Kennedy Williams. Morgan was dogged and perceptive. He wrote everything down in tiny, scratchy writing with lots of little figures, and at shortly before one in the morning they were gathered in the greenroom, except for Amelia, who was lying down. He announced that the only people who were not accounted for by someone else were Kennedy Williams, who said he had been alone in the manager's office; Amelia, who was upset and had closed her dressing room door and, since she shared a dresser with Bianca, was alone at that time; and Owain himself, also in his dressing room alone. The only other person seen by no one was the stage doorman, and Dierdre said that she had gone to collect a note from an ardent admirer, and she had seen him.

"He was there, on his stool," she said in a whisper. She looked ashen and her hands were locked together as if to keep them from shaking. She seemed to find difficulty in speaking and kept looking from Owain to Inspector Morgan as if she dreaded something even more tragic happening but was helpless to prevent it.

Kennedy Williams stood limply against the door, leaning on it to support himself. The lines of his thin face all dragged downward. He looked as if he had been up for days, not hours.

"You're sure of that, Miss Ashbourne," Morgan asked, but not as if he doubted her. It was just one more fact to be ticked off on his list.

"Yes, Inspector," she replied, then hesitated.

"Was there something else?" Morgan asked.

"No!" she answered a trifle too quickly.

Morgan waited.

Still she said nothing, but looked more and more wretched.

"I think perhaps I should speak to you alone again, Miss Ashbourne," he said.

"No, I . . . I really have nothing else I can tell you," she assured him. "I don't know who killed Idris. He was a brilliant actor and a dear friend— to my husband as well as myself." She said the last directly, almost aggressively, as if she had already been challenged on it.

Kennedy Williams stared at the floor.

Morgan glanced at him, then back at Dierdre with his eyebrows raised ages. "Some friends can quarrel, Miss Ashbourne."

"Oh, of course!" she acknowledged. "And I expect you've heard that Owain and Idris did, but it was all just over misunderstandings. Nothing that mattered, I assure you. Oh, no! You can't . . ." Then she stopped and lowered her eyes. "If it's anybody's fault, it's mine. I was foolish, but no more than that, I swear. And Owain knows me better than to imagine otherwise."

"I've seen the play, Miss Ashbourne," Morgan told her. "I know Desdemona's innocent of everything."

She gave him a tearful smile.

"And it's Othello and Desdemona who end up dead!" Owain snapped. "Not Iago . . ."

"I always thought that was a pity, myself." Morgan looked at him coolly. "If anyone ever deserved a bad end, it was Iago. Terrible sin, jealousy, whatever it's of . . . power, money, honor, the love of a woman, anything at all. Can spoil more lives than almost anything else."

"I know," Dierdre whispered. She gulped and controlled herself with a visible effort.

Morgan looked across at Owain, and Owain saw the hostility in his eyes. For the first time Owain realized that he was in danger. It was preposterous, but Morgan really considered he might have killed Idris. His first instinct was to deny it, to point out that there was rivalry between himself and Idris, but it was constructive, each one helping the other's performance! Then he looked around the room and saw Kennedy's haggard face, full of guilt and apology. Dierdre beautiful and tragic, and Morgan who loved the theater and had seen him play Othello, indeed thought him the best in the part he knew. It was nothing to do with acting . . . it was Dierdre! With a churning sickness, he remembered the quarrels he and Idris had had over the last few weeks, all of them seen by Kennedy. He knew what Morgan had drawn from him, and knew Kennedy would see it from Amelia's point of view. He was a fine manager, but he was no actor, his feelings for her were an open book for anyone to read.

"That's all for tonight," Morgan said at last. "But I'll see everyone tomorrow. Don't leave the hotel, if you please."

Owain went back to the dressing room to change into his own clothes. He still couldn't find his favorite shirt and was obliged to seek out another. He came out and was told that Dierdre had already left for the hotel. He walked the half mile or so alone in the dark, trying to think. He had no time to grieve for Idris. That would have to come later, and it would— they had been friends most of their professional lives. Owain had loved his humor, his strength, and above all his intelligence. They had brought out the best in each other, both as actors and as friends.

Now he had to wrestle with what had happened and find his way out of the net of suspicion that was already a circle around him. He found it almost impossible to believe that either Kennedy or Amelia could have killed Idris and yet the facts seemed to leave no other answer. Why? Jealousy. Always it came back to jealousy. Either one of them might have believed for an insane hour or two that Idris and Dierdre were really having an affair. Amelia was young and in love, only married a couple of years. Until the last week or two she had been by Dierdre onstage, and now it looked as if Dierdre were taking her husband also. Perhaps there was more fire of passion in her than even Idris had known?

But why did she kill Idris and not Dierdre?

Who could know what quarrel had taken place between them?

Or Kennedy? Was he more in love with Amelia than any of them had guessed, and he had killed Idris for betraying her . . . and in turn to free her for himself?

Owain crossed the dark street under the gas lamps and walked toward the lights of the hotel. Either answer hurt him for people he cared about deeply, but he felt dangers closing in, and only the truth would save him.

He did not see Dierdre. She had apparently already retired. She preferred to sleep alone. She was a woman of personal mystery. Her vanity required she did not share the secrets of her toilette with anyone but her maid. He had understood, even approved. It allowed him a similar privacy, and since he often liked to learn his lines late at night, it suited him very well. They were together when they chose.

He slept badly and went out without breakfast to see if he could learn anything more at the theater. Morgan was already there, but he managed to avoid him. By eleven o'clock he had a thumping headache, but had succeeded in finding a stagehand who had seen him go into his dressing room and then spoken to Idris afterward. He had then been in sight of the door and seen Owain leave to go in the opposite direction at about the time Idris must have been killed.

Brimming over with relief, he half-dragged him to tell Morgan.

However, after a miserable luncheon the stagehand found Owain in the hotel lounge.

"I'm sorry, Mr. Glenconnor, sir," he said wretchedly, shifting from one foot to the other in his embarrassment. "But it wasn't last night that I saw you. It was the night before. I'd say that it was because I know you couldn't 'ave 'urt Mr. Evans for the world, but Miss Ashbourne saw me where I really were, an' she'd 'ave to tell the truth, like, 'cos she already 'as done. I'm terrible sorry, sir."

"Yes, of course you have to," Owain agreed, horrified to find himself shivering. He clenched his body and forced himself to look at the man. "Thank you for coming to me."

"I'm sorry, sir."

"It's all right."

But it wasn't. It was made plain how very wrong it was when Dierdre herself came to him an hour or so later. She was dressed in very sober black, her bright hair contrasting with the pallor of her face.

"Owain, I'm so sorry," she said urgently. "I'd already told that miserable policeman that I'd seen the stagehand, whatever his name is. Otherwise I would never have mentioned it. I didn't realize how much it was going to mean to you. I'd have lied, if I'd known!"

"You don't have to lie for me!" he said sharply.

She winced, almost as if he'd struck her. "I know!" She looked down, avoiding his eyes. "I know you would never have killed Idris no matter what you thought about him and me."

"I didn't think anything," he said, hearing his own voice rise with a desperate note in it. "Except that you were behaving selfishly, and Idris was being a fool! Idris was my friend!"

She looked up now. "And I'm your wife! Lesser men than you have been jealous . . . and discovered too late that their wives were innocent of any wrong greater than a little harmless flirting, a little high spirits. I know perfectly well you are innocent. . . . I just wish Inspector Morgan was as sure of it as I am." There was no conviction in her voice, only fear, and it settled like a coldness around Owain until he was almost paralyzed by it.

Then in the theater that afternoon he found the shirt, his own beautiful white shirt with the gathered sleeves. It was stuffed behind a piece of scenery, with only a white tip sticking out above the painted flat. He pulled it and saw with horror tight in the pit of his stomach the bloodstained sleeve, dark red-brown and caked together. The left sleeve, as it would have been if he had worn when killing Idris. He was the only left-handed one in the cast.

Had anyone else seen him? He stared around him in the dimly lit backstage peering into the shadows of the wings, and then up to the galleries where the drops were winched up. He saw no one. He could barely make out the shape so far up, but why would anyone be up there in the dark when there was no performance this evening?

He pushed the shirt under his jacket and hurried into the corridor, his hand shaking. Morgan was somewhere about. He must destroy the shirt when he had a chance, but he could not risk being found with it now. Where could he put it? Anyone would know it was his as soon as they asked. And yet it was perfectly obvious that whoever murdered Idris had worn it. Why? There was only one answer: to blame him.

Where would he put the thing now? he thought with a black humor of Macbeth. Blood . . . the blood of his friend already on his clothes. And yet he was guilty of nothing. But how could Morgan, or anyone else, believe that? Except whoever had worn his shirt to murder Idris.

Where would nobody look for anything? He must be quick. Morgan was not far away. He suspected him already. Behind a flat no one ever moved? Well, they certainly were not performing *Othello* again for a while, and the Venetian scene belonged to this theater. It did not travel with them. He stuffed it behind the painting of the palace backdrop against the canal and straightened up just as the constable came across the stage and spoke to him. He managed to answer almost normally, but his heart was pounding so violently he knew that were the footlights lit, the man would have seen him shake.

And of course, Morgan did have the theater searched, even though he was uncertain what he was looking for, only that whoever had killed Idris must have had blood on them, on their clothes. Something was missing, some garment. Had Owain's shirt remained where it was? Morgan would have to have found it. At least it was not visible where he had put it now, and unless someone removed the heavy flats altogether, it would not be. Owain had a breathing space until he could get back there unobserved and destroy it.

But that was not what caused the dark, cold terror inside him; it was the knowledge that whoever had taken his Moorish knife off the wall and driven it into Idris's back had also deliberately taken his shirt as well, and worn it to commit the murder. They could only have done it with the intention of blaming Owain. They had left the shirt where it would be seen. They wanted it found . . . and Owain hanged. He struggled and twisted his thoughts, tortured them into all kinds of unlikely paths, but every one of them led back to the same conclusion. Someone wanted him destroyed every bit as completely as Idris had been, in a way more so. Idris was a tragic victim. Owain would be remembered not as a great actor, the greatest Othello of his generation, but as the Othello who reversed the drama and murdered Iago . . . a miserable man who resented another man's talent and charm and in a fit of jealousy plunged a knife into his back.

Who?

Only Kennedy or Amelia. Amelia could have done it. It was physically possible. Did that quiet face and light, charming manner hide a woman of such deadly purpose?

They were all in the green room waiting when Morgan came back to tell them that the search was completed.

"Did you find anything, Inspector?" Dierdre asked quietly. She looked very tense this morning, and she kept glancing curiously at Owain. Sitting here now, waiting for Morgan to speak, he realized he had not seen her alone since the evening before, and that had been brief. She had left within minutes, claiming a headache, which was more than likely true, in the circumstances. He had thought little of it at the time.

Morgan was saying that he had found nothing that he knew to be of relevance to the murder, and they were free to move about the theater as they wished.

Owain looked across at Dierdre and saw the flash of surprise on her face masked almost instantly. Then he knew what Idris must have felt the moment the dagger pierced him from a hand he had thought to be that of a friend. Dierdre had expected Morgan to find the shirt, and she could not understand why he had not, because she had put it there!

Why? Had she and Idris really been lovers after all? A quarrel? Or had she pursued him and he had rebuffed her, and he had concealed it with lightness of touch, laughter, to spare Owain's feelings?

He was sitting perched on an old horsehair sofa in the familiar green-room like that in any of scores of theaters up and down the country, and he felt sick. Why would Dierdre, his own wife, beautiful, melodramatic Dierdre, try to have him hanged for a murder he had not committed?

Had she killed Idris herself? Or was it brilliant opportunism, a chance to blame him seen and taken on the spur of the moment?

And what could he do to save himself?

Someone came in with the newspapers. He forced his attention to them. It was Cassio, and his face was a mixture of horror and fascination as he read the accounts aloud. Some were simple reporting of the facts. Brilliant actor Idris Evans had been murdered in the theater during a performance of *Othello,* in which he played the villain Iago. Police were investigating, but so far had no clear leads as to who was responsible.

But others rehearsed the plot of *Othello,* the passionate jealousy that had destroyed a great man and resulted in one of the most powerful tragedies ever portrayed on the stage. There were photographs of Dierdre in costume as Desdemona, looking beautiful and radiantly innocent, but with a shadow across her eyes as if she already knew she was the unwitting catalyst of death.

She rose now and took the newspaper from Cassio and Owain watched her face as she looked at the photograph of herself. He saw the flush on her cheeks, her body straighten a little and the soft satisfaction in her eyes the moment before she lowered them. She was the star again. Idris might be dead and Owain cast as the villain, a true Othello, a man whose love for his wife, and his jealousy over her, had caused him to commit murder. But Amelia was forgotten, and Dierdre was in the center of the stage.

Now he knew why she had done it.

He looked away quickly. He must not meet her eyes. As long as she did not know he knew, he had one slender advantage. He must leave, before his face gave him away. He was one of the best actors alive, but even he could not control the ashen color of his skin or force from his mind the horror and the fear that must be somewhere in the stiffness of his movement, the clumsiness he felt, as if his arms and legs scarcely belonged to him.

He stood up and walked out, passing Kennedy Williams, who looked like his own ghost. Now, when Morgan had already just looked, would be the time to get the shirt and destroy it. It would be impossible ever to remove the stain. He knew blood was one of the hardest things to wash out. Cold water before it was dried was about the only way. Now he would have to burn the whole thing.

He went almost blindly up the passage, tripping on the step, lucky not to fall. He had always known Dierdre was vain, ambitious, fed on admiration. But then had she not had an element of that in her character, she would never have been the actress she was. He understood it. Heavens, had he not enough of it in himself? He loved to stand in the lights with a thousand faces toward him and how every heart and mind was feeling the emotion that rang in his voice or cried out in the physical energy of his being. To make them part of his dream, to carry them into passion and thought they had never known before, was the fabric of his life.

But so was friendship. So was love. How could he have been so desperately wrong about Dierdre? Had everything between them been an act for her? Or was this madness grown only since she had lost the limelight to Idris and Owain? And she had lost it, a little. It was slipping out of her grasp. He could see that more clearly now, looking over the last few months.

He reached backstage and went to the heavy flats where he had stuffed the shirt. He pushed his hand into the crevice and fished for the touch of silk. There was nothing there. He reached in farther. He had not thought he had put it so far! It was still not there.

He must stop shaking and keep control of himself. It had to be there. Morgan had found it, he would have said so. Owain would already be under arrest. It was his shirt, everyone knew it, and if they didn't, Dierdre would have told them.

But where was the shirt? He had pushed his arm as far as he could into the crevice. He was right up to the shoulder, and there was nothing there! There was nowhere it could have dropped to. His fingers were right to the end of the space, and he could feel the floorboards at the bottom.

Ice filled the pit of his stomach and the sweat broke out on his face. Someone had removed it. Dierdre! God in heaven . . . what had she done with it? And he knew the answer before the question was fully formed in his mind. She had put it where Morgan would find it.

He stood up slowly, stiffly. Where? Where had she put it? Would she lead Morgan to it, or was it somewhere Morgan would find it himself? If the latter, then why had he not found it just now?

Was there still time for Owain to get it and destroy it? Would Morgan look in the places he had already looked before? Perhaps not. That would be the one area it would be safe. Where? One of the dressing rooms. His? She would never dare on her own! Or would she? Yes—of course. She had the nerve for anything.

He started to walk quickly, lightly, along the open spaces into the corridor, up the narrow stairs, and along the passage, past his own room and into Dierdre's. There was no one there. Heaven only knew when there would be another performance. He closed the door and started to go through the rack of gowns. Nothing. Of course not. Too obvious. What about the cupboard? He pulled open the door and went through the contents—blouses, underwear, stockings . . . no shirt. He turned and stared around the room. Where else? There were two wigs on stands, not for the part of Desdemona. Dierdre was too proud of her own hair to cover it unless she had to. The wigs were not hers. He pulled one off its stand. It must belong to some other actress. He looked at the second, then pulled it off as well. It came off the pole easily. It was stuffed with a white silk shirt, blood-stained sleeve stiff and dark.

The door opened and Morgan stood in the entrance. Dierdre and Kennedy Williams behind him.

"Well, then, Glenconnor," Morgan said sadly. "Now I was really hoping it wasn't you, but that in your hand makes it impossible for me to go on holding on to that dream, doesn't it." He put his arm forward. "Give it to me."

There was no point whatever in arguing. Owain held it out and Morgan took the crumpled bundle.

"I hope you're not going to tell me it isn't yours, are you, sir?"

Owain had difficulty finding his voice. "No. But I didn't kill Idris, in spite of what it looks like." That was futile, but he said it from passion, not thought.

"Didn't you now. There's blood all over it, sir. Please don't tell me you cut yourself, and hid it here in Miss Ashbourne's room in case we thought you were guilty of Mr. Evans's murder. Because, you see, you must have hidden it before he was found, sir, which would be very difficult to explain, now, wouldn't it?"

"I didn't say the murderer wasn't wearing it," Owain answered him. "I said it wasn't me!"

"But, Owain, the blood is on the left sleeve!" Dierdre said huskily. "And you're the only one who is left-handed! Oh, God! I'm so sorry! I knew you were jealous, but I never dreamed it would come to this!" She covered her face with her beautiful hands and stood sobbing silently, a picture of womanly grief.

Morgan turned around very slowly to look at her. "Left sleeve, you say, Miss Ashbourne?"

She lifted her face, eyes wide. "That's right, Inspector. Owain is the only one of us who is left-handed. I'm . . . so . . . sorry!"

"I'm sure he is, ma'am," Morgan said very slowly, his face still sad, his brow furrowed. "But how did you know the shirt was stained on the left sleeve, seeing that we just found it?"

She looked bewildered, but Owain saw her stiffen. "What?" she breathed out. She was shaking now.

Morgan repeated the question. "How did you know it was the left sleeve that was stained, ma'am?"

"I . . ." she started to explain, then saw in Morgan's eyes that it was too late. She swung around to Kennedy Williams.

But understanding filled his face as well and he took a step backward away from her, shaking his head a little.

"Jealousy's a terrible thing," Morgan said softly. "Cruel as the grave. But I am not sure that the love of glory's any better. Anything that'd drive a person to kill one man and see another hanged for it has got to be a tragedy, any way you look at it."

Dierdre lifted her chin high and stared at him defiantly. She was magnificent. Owain felt a lurch of pity for her, for all that she had been in her best moments, the laughter and the hunger for life, and above all for what she could have been. But mostly he grieved for Idris, who had been just as alive, as gifted, as hungry to create the magic of theater and hold an audience in his spell.

Dierdre stood very stiff. This would be her last act, and she would be more Lady Macbeth than Desdemona, but at least she would be center stage, sharing the limelight with no one. It seemed that was what mattered more than all else.

Owain found there were tears on his face as he watched her walk out next to Morgan and disappear down the corridor, the light still bright in her burnished hair.

Gesine Schulz

The Panama Hen

GESINE SCHULZ is the first of a new crop of foreign mystery writers we're welcoming to the pages of this year's World's Finest edition. Crime and mystery stories are alive and well in other countries besides the United States and Great Britain. This short and undeniably effective story, translated by Edna McCown, comes to us from the German anthology *Die Stunde des Vaters,* and features a private detective trying to solve a mystery involving a cheating spouse, a reclusive novelist, and a tattoo of a chicken. Yes, you read that correctly. Now read on to see how she pulls it off.

The Panama Hen

Gesine Schulz

No, Frau Rutkowsky, I can't go to the police. Absolutely not. My husband goes bowling with our local policeman. You don't know how things are in a village. And if my husband were to find out . . ." Frau Papendieck shook her head. "I couldn't bear it. I'd rather kill myself."

Karo thought she would ask for double her advance, just in case. "And you don't think that your husband would believe you, if you assure him that—"

"No. Why should he? If I weren't sure myself that it couldn't possibly be me in the photograph, I wouldn't believe me either! Sometimes at night, when I think about it and my thoughts go around and around in circles, I'm afraid that I'm going crazy. Recently I got out of bed at two in the morning to look at the photo. Just to prove to myself that I hadn't imagined it all . . ." Frau Papendieck pulled a frilly handkerchief out of the pocket of her blouse and dabbed her eyes.

"Well," Karo said. "It does sound strange. Do you take drugs?"

"Never!"

"Have you ever experienced memory lapses?"

"No, at least not that I can remember. Well, I forget things now and then. My shopping list. Or a birthday. But I would never forget that I had slept with a stranger, believe me. And especially not in that position."

They both looked at the color photo that lay on Karo's desk.

"But that looks like your backside, right?"

"Yes. That's what makes it so terrible. Ever since our vacation to Panama last year my backside is unmistakable."

"Oh, so the hen is from Panama?"

Frau Papendieck smiled for the first time. "We were a bit sloshed and thought it was a funny idea. The drawing is from an ad for rum. We tore it out of a magazine that was lying around in our hotel. Dirk said it looked like such a happy hen. That's his nickname for me, sometimes. Because . . .

he says that I cluck like a happy hen when . . . uh, when, hmm, you know what I mean."

Karo nodded.

"Yes, well, so then we wandered through Old Town and stumbled on the tattoo shop. That's where it happened." Frau Papendieck shook her head. "I've told myself that it's not totally unthinkable that the tattoo artist used the image again, that there's another woman walking around with a hen on her right buttock . . . but that she would come to our village, to our farm, and be photographed like that, and that I would be blackmailed with the photo, that simply cannot be! It just can't. It's a nightmare. . . . Will you take my case, Frau Rutkowsky?"

Karo nodded. She would take the case. Even though the countryside wasn't exactly her thing. But the people lining up in front of the Lichtburg weren't waiting for her, they were in line for the new Tom Tykwer film. And only in her other job, as a highly paid cleaning woman in a few select villas in south Essen and a fabulous loft in Katernberg, could she be choosy about the work she accepted. She didn't enjoy that privilege as a private detective. Not yet.

Karo took the photo. The man was barely visible, the woman a bit more so. The kitchen table was made of old pine, the curtains were Laura Ashley. One of the clients she cleaned for, who loved the English country look, had the same curtains. "And this was taken in your home?"

"No, no! At our farm, yes. But not in our house. This was taken in the former worker's cottage. A little house behind the orchard. We've rented it out for a year now."

"Aha. To whom?"

"To someone from Cologne, Max Penk. He uses it primarily on the weekends."

"What sort of man is he? The photo was taken in his kitchen. Could he have something to do with this?"

Uli Papendieck hesitated. "He's a very nice man. Likeable. Only . . ."

"Only?"

"Well . . . I don't think he's the blackmailing sort. Because he's really too nice. And he has plenty of money. But . . . well, he writes mysteries, and I've asked myself whether a mystery writer might perhaps like to, you know, try something like that. But I don't really believe he did."

"Max Penk?" Karo asked. "I've never heard of him. He can't be very successful. Maybe he needs the money and would rather carry out a crime than write about one."

Uli Papendieck shook her head. "He really wouldn't need to. If you promise not to tell anyone . . ."

Karo raised her hand. "On my honor as a private detective!"

Frau Papendieck leaned over and whispered, "He's really Sophie Réchaud."

"Sophie Réchaud? No! Really?"

"That's what I said." Uli Papendieck nodded several times.

Sophie Réchaud was the new star of German country house mysteries! Rosamunde Pilcher meets Stephen King. Even Karo had heard of her. Him.

"Sophie Réchaud is a man. Well, well." A man with all the marks of a prime suspect. "Does he know about your tattoo?"

"Please! Of course not. Nor does anyone else."

Which couldn't be true. "Perhaps he climbed up on a ladder and looked into your bedroom?"

"Nonsense. We're not in Bavaria, after all! And Herr Penk is from Cologne. I already told you that."

"Then maybe you go to a sauna? Showed your best friend the hen? Or had a massage? A tanning session? Went to the doctor?"

"No. Believe me, I've racked my brains. I went to my gynecologist two months ago. But she's out of the question. She's over sixty and totally respectable. I've been seeing Dr. Forster, she's in Moers, for many years now. And my mother goes to her as well. My gynecologist could never do something like this! Never."

Karo was inclined to believe her, as she looked down at the gray head between her legs the next day.

"I can't find anything, Frau Rutkowsky. No sign of inflammation. Perhaps it was a passing irritation. Call me if it recurs."

Karo crossed the physician off her list of suspects. For the present. Her perp of choice was the mystery writer.

Konrad Krieger, the expert she had gone to with the photograph, told her it was authentic. "It's most unlikely that we're talking about a montage here. I'm almost one hundred percent certain that this is a genuine photo of a woman's tattooed buttock. In the midst of a fairly obvious act. I must say that I don't understand people's predilection for the kitchen table. Above all when it's an old table like this one. The danger of getting a splinter . . ."

"No one was injured," Karo had interrupted him, and took her leave. He was always helpful and an authority in his field, but so long-winded that one's only recourse was to beat a hasty retreat.

Karo left the gynecologist's office in Moers and drove on to Leeken. The surrounding countryside was nothing but flatland, with avenues of poplars` and villages like those in nearby Holland. "My husband is on the road today," Uli Papendieck had told her on the phone that morning. "He's on the committee organizing the tractor race in two weeks. I don't expect him back before four. But if he returns early and sees you . . ."

"Oh, if that happens, I'll think of something," Karo said. She always traveled with a collection of Dubber-Ware in her trunk. And all kinds of brochures on this "economical alternative for the price-conscious house-wife." Her mother sold them at Dubber-Ware parties, and Karo considered the role of saleswoman to be a useful cover.

The Papendiecks' farm was outside the village. The two-story brick building had white window frames and was decorated with window boxes lovingly planted with flowers. Next to the house was a vegetable garden behind a fence, with a barn and a number of stables behind it.

Karo was about to climb the steps to the dark-green front door when Uli Papendieck turned the corner of the house and walked toward Karo with a small ax in her hand. The ax, as well as her apron, was spattered with blood. Karo could see the headlines:

Young farm wife kills mystery writer to save her marriage!
Sophie Réchaud a man!
A blackmailer!
Dead!

"Hello," Uli Papendieck smiled. "I've just killed a couple of geese. Could you wait just a minute? And then I'll show you his house."

The former farmworker's cottage behind the orchard looked like a city dweller's dream of country life. Boxwood hedges enclosed the small front yard. A gravel path led up to the royal-blue front door, which was flanked by sky-blue wood containers planted with white rosebushes. Crown glass with pretty white curtains covered the panes. Inside there were terra-cotta tiles and carefully chosen country antiques, pillows and curtains in a rose pattern, and all the latest technological comforts in the kitchen.

Karo was holding an enlargement of the photo in her hand. There could be no doubt that it had been taken in this kitchen. With a self-timer. Karo studied the angle. "The camera must have been situated here, see?" She patted the freestanding butcher block table. It wasn't looking good for Sophie Réchaud.

"Could I see the picture again?" Uli Papendieck leaned against the window and studied the enlargement. "Hmm, you know what? It couldn't possibly have been Herr Penk. Oh, I'm so relieved. Because—"

"What? Why not?" Karo tore the photo from her hand.

Uli Papendieck pointed to a yellow blur that could be seen through the window in the photo. "Those are daffodils. In the front yard. He was traveling when they bloomed, in Italy. So he couldn't have anything to do with the photograph. Or with the blackmail. Because I picked the flowers, for our gospel choir's jubilee. Two big basketfuls. They looked wonderful."

Damn. Karo questioned her client closely once again, but she stuck by her story: No one here had seen her hen but her gynecologist. Karo sighed. Globalization or not, she simply didn't believe that the Panamanian tattoo artist was blackmailing his way across Europe.

Someone must have tattooed somebody else's buttock using an exact pattern. On orders from the blackmailer, male or female. And since then, some other woman was walking around with the same tattoo. At least three people knew about this: the tattoo artist and the couple in the photo. Only the couple was involved in the blackmail, Karo concluded. Or perhaps the woman alone?

Karo drank a beer at the local pub and then began checking out the tattoo parlors in the neighboring towns and villages. There were an astounding number of them. One was run by a retired needlework teacher, who specialized in cross-stitch tattoos. No one admitted to having tattooed this particular hen, or any hen at all. Woody Woodpecker, the German Eagle, Donald Duck, yes. But no hens. Until Karo arrived in Bickum, at the studio of Tom Duhley. He remembered the hen, the backside, the woman, and her companion. But he wasn't saying anything else. "Data protection, you understand."

Karo nodded and started sliding bills across the counter. At two hundred Euros it occurred to him that there was no data to protect, because he didn't have any names, he only knew that the blonde worked in the only bookstore in the county seat. "My girlfriend works in the café across the street. You can see right into the bookstore from there. I've spotted the blonde there often." His description of the man who had come with her, and paid in cash, was useful.

Shadowing the bookstore clerk wasn't difficult. During a long lunch break Karo trailed her like a dog, from the bookstore to the cleaner's to the Italian restaurant and back. That evening she followed her in the car to a two-story residential building. The next evening the woman from the bookstore received a visit from a man who fit the description Tom Duhley had given her. Karo wrote down his license plate number.

Unfortunately, Lutz Berner, her ex-boyfriend and the only policeman she had something on, wouldn't be back at work until the next morning. He'd apparently had a rough night, for his powers of resistance were running low when Karo reached him shortly after nine at police headquarters in Essen. Less than an hour later he told Karo to whom the car was licensed, and then it was her regrettable duty to inform her client that the case was solved. It was her husband Dirk who was the blackmailer—he'd been carrying on an affair with the bookstore clerk for some time now.

Uli Papendieck turned as white as milk and looked at the floor. "So," she said finally, unnaturally quiet. "So that's how it is."

"I'm sorry," Karo said. And, after a while: "Do you have a property agreement?"

"Yes, we do. You mean he wants to start a new life with her? He doesn't own anything. And bookstore clerks don't earn much, right? I've never understood why not. In that sense, blackmail wasn't a bad idea. I would have paid. My parents sold a few fields as building sites. That gave me a nice stock portfolio." She gave a quick nod. "Thank you. I'll take care of the rest."

Karo thought about the bloody ax. "You won't do anything stupid?"

Uli Papendieck shook her head. "Never again."

• • •

Several months later Karo was cleaning one of her villas when her eye caught a magazine lying on a glass coffee table. Time for a cup of tea, she decided, after a glance at the cover:

Exclusive in *Country & Elegance!*
A new mystery story by Sophie Réchaud,
queen of german country house mysteries

Karo put aside her dustcloth, prepared a pot of tea, and settled into a comfortable armchair. This guy knew how to write, but that wasn't the only reason Karo read faster and faster.

The story took place, naturally, in a country house. The wealthy and betrayed wife, who was being blackmailed, had let herself be talked into getting a swan tattoo during a vacation to Guadalupe, because in the eyes of her loving husband her neck was like a swan's neck. She then discovered the truth from a private detective, a good-looking but disillusioned former policeman. At first she had suffered in silence, then she wanted revenge. At the central train station of the nearest big city she bought used needles from three drug users who had AIDS. During a feigned bout of foreplay, she artfully tied up her husband, using hand-printed silk scarves. She filled the syringes with ink and slowly and painfully tattooed a crooked heart on his right buttock. In doing so, she told him where she had gotten the needles. Then she threw him out.

The tea had gotten cold. Karo read the story all the way through a second time. Then she called information for a number, and then the farm.

"The Papendieck residence, Penk speaking," a man's voice said.

Karo hung up very carefully.

She had to think about it.

What she needed now was hot water and brandy.

Ten minutes later she was relaxing in the white marble tub while letting brandy-filled chocolates melt slowly in her mouth, and the sound of Elgar's "Violin Concerto" floated down from loudspeakers mounted in the ceiling.

Karo had added a generous amount of cinnamon-scented oil to her bathwater. The house bar the owners of this villa kept was a joke, but the bottles and flagons in the bathroom left no room for complaint. She simply had to make sure that she didn't spray shaving cream under her arms as she had once before, thinking it was some new deodorant.

Gillian Linscott

Gracious Silence

GILLIAN LINSCOTT has had a long career as a journalist with various newspapers and the British Broadcasting Corporation. She has written numerous books featuring Nell Bray, a turn-of-the-twentieth-century suffragette and amateur detective, as well as other mysteries, radio plays, and short stories. She brings a singular British love of form to her fiction, making it exciting material indeed. The wife in "Gracious Silence," also from *Much Ado About Murder,* suffers from an overbearing mother-in-law in ancient Rome, and comes up with a remedy for the situation as novel as the one in Anne Perry's tale.

Gracious Silence

Gillian Linscott

My gracious silence, hail!
Wouldst thou have laugh'd had I come coffin'd home,
That weep'st to see me triumph?
—*Coriolanus,* Act II, Scene I

G racious silence. That's what he
called me in front of the whole re-
joicing city. I've always been silent by nature. The gracious part took longer,
but by that day when he came home in triumph with a crown of laurel on
his head and the crowd drunk on cheering and cheap wine, I'd had ten
years of working on graciousness under the best tutor in the history of
Rome. Dear Volumnia, noblest of mothers-in-law. I was a shy seventeen-
year-old when my education started. Caius Marcius—not Coriolanus yet—
arrived one summer evening with his friends at my father's house to carry
me off in the traditional way. By arrangement, of course, and all very
properly done. I know now that she must have chosen me as her son's bride
after careful consideration of my pedigree, constitution, temperament,
soundness of teeth, father's military service, and Adam's record of fertility.
Not quite good enough for Caius Marcius, of course, but then only Juno
freshly down from Mount Olympus might just about have matched up to
that high privilege, provided she'd minded her manners and been suitably
grateful. As for me, I suppose I was grateful. Over-awed, certainly. For one
thing, he was thirteen years older than I was and already Rome's most
famous soldier. His face was burned brown by the sun, except for two shiny
scar slashes, one across his forehead and right cheek just missing the eye,
one down the left side of his chin and neck. By no means bad-looking,
though. Broad-shouldered and muscular, thatch of black hair newly
trimmed for the wedding rites, surprisingly well-shaped lips almost as full
as a woman's. Eyes bright and very watchful. Like his mother's. As soon as
he brought me over the threshold, she was there to welcome me formally
to their home. My home how. I'd been well coached by my parents in the
little speech I must make in return but somehow when I needed it, it wasn't
there. She seemed pleased rather than otherwise by my silence and downcast
eyes. "Can't find your voice, Virgilia? Well, better that than a chatterer."

How could she know that there was a voice inside my head, speaking just to me? It was the first time even I'd heard it and in the beginning it was so quiet, so nervous and hesitant, that I could pretend it wasn't there at all.

Why isn't there any laughing? When my friends' husbands came to take them, there was laughter, people getting the words all muddled in the wedding songs, rose petals in the bridegroom's hair and down the neck of his toga. This time nobody got the words wrong, as if they'd been practicing all day, and if petals landed in his hair he must have brushed them off before anybody could see them, so there was nothing to laugh at. I'm never going to sleep in my own bed again, and perhaps I've already had all the laughing I'll ever be allowed to do. Help me, somebody. Help me.

Our son was born three years after the wedding. She didn't blame me for the delay—at least not entirely. After all, Caius Marcius was away campaigning for at least half the year and naturally he'd come back tired. There'd been a lot of work for the army over those three years because our old enemies, the Volsci, were in one of their more active phases. They'd always been there, roving around outside our walls from way back when the city was founded. Sometimes, they simply went in for a little cattle stealing and ambushing bands of travelers. But now and again a more than usually ambitious leader would emerge among them and Rome itself would be under threat. This was one of their surging times and the more nervous citizens scared one another with nightmares of the Volsci breaking down our gates, burning our homes, and carrying off the women over their saddle bows. So it was a good time to be a soldier and Caius Marcius had all the fighting he wanted.

Naturally he'd be tired when he came home and it was hard for him to adjust from a world of men and action, from sleeping on the muddy ground under a tent of stitched skins that let in the wind and rain (he was a good leader, you see, and shared his men's hardships) to this softer world of women and soft voices and baths with sweet smelling oils. Harder to get through the long evenings of political talk with the grayheads over the wine cups. "Another few years, Caius Marcius. Another year or two and a really decisive victory over Tullus Aufidius, and it's in the bag. You'll have our voices, the people's voices, the fund-raising will be no problem. You'll be unstoppable." Volumnia would sit drinking her wine and putting in her opinions like a man. I'd spin and listen and say nothing. He had no great taste for wine, no head for it, but he had to drink to be companionable because a man trying for high public office has to tread a careful line between being pleasure-loving or prudish, so naturally by the time we got to our room, he'd be drowsy. To be honest I think I liked him most, came nearest to loving him, those nights. Away from the grayheads, his soldiers, and his mother, he had a lost quality about him, like a puzzled child left on his own. One night he ruffled my hair, yawned, and said to me, "Why do we put ourselves through all this? Do I want the consulship so much?"

Well, I knew the answer: *No, but your mother wants it for you.* But I couldn't say it, of course, so I just kissed him, then we both turned over and went to sleep. So there was a delay, but when I duly produced a healthy boy, she quite forgave me. No question, of course, that it would be a boy. If it had started out otherwise, I think her determination would have reached into my womb and swapped its sex as it grew.

Life changes once you're a mother. For one thing, you're allowed to laugh again. I laughed at little Marcius cooing in his basket and he laughed back, waving pink fists no bigger than poppy buds. ("Looking for a fight already, bless him," his grandmother said. "He's the image of his father." As if I'd had nothing to do with it.) We laughed, he and I, as I taught him to take his first steps along the stone paths between the borders of herbs. She was always watching there before me when he fell over, but not to sympathize. "Roman soldiers don't cry, Marcius. Your father's been wounded nineteen times and he never cried." I suppose I should have known then, but I was happy for a few years, playing with him in the sun. It didn't dawn on me until the day of the butterfly, when he was five. He loved chasing butterflies, of course, as all children do, and hardly ever caught them. There was one day in late summer when a particular butterfly moved too slowly. Maybe the night had chilled it or its wings were wearing out. Anyway, he made a grab for it and for once got it in his hand. He came running to show it to me, tripped, opened his hand, and off it flew, unsteadily with one wing torn. His childish roar of rage brought her in a second. "Don't let it get away, Marcius. Get up and go after it." With her yelling him on, he chased that limping butterfly up and down the paths, over the vegetable beds, up the steps and down until he'd got it again, firmly crushed in his fist. "Now kill it, Caius. Pay it back for escaping." His eyes were locked on hers, hers on him, while he tore the creature into pieces until his fingers were clotted with the yellow ichor from inside it and the rainbow dust of its wings. When it was over she smiled her approval at him and he smiled back at her, not looking at me, leaving me out of it. I knew then, as I should have known from the start, that he wouldn't be left as mine for much longer. A few years—a few very short years—and he'd be campaigning with his father, learning to be a hero. I think I saw then what was going to happen—not the details of how we'd get there, of course—but where we'd be at the end. Sharp-eyed as ever, she noticed something in my face. "Virgilia, have you been crying?" Only from laughing, I said.

Another thing about becoming a mother is that your women friends feel they can talk to you about sex. Unmarried girls and young brides must blush and pretend not to understand the coded remarks over the spinning wheels or the bowls of watered wine, but a child in the cradle is your entrance fee to the school of double meanings. "You're looking a little tired, Flavia. Restless night?" Or, "A little tetchy today are we, Marcia, dear? How long has Marcus been away?" It took me a long time to realize that they envied me. Because Caius Marcius was such a famous warrior, they assumed that he must be more than usually rampant in bed. When I realized at last what they meant by the remarks about building up my stamina for when he got home and the warrior's return and so on, I didn't reply in kind. I'd blush and concentrate on my spinning or sewing and say nothing. Volumnia was always there, of course. I could see that she was pleased with the compliments to his virility, but she approved of my modest silence, implying that the pleasures of our marriage bed were too sacred for gossip.

> In fact, my spinning friends, you've no cause to feel jealous, really no cause at all. It isn't all you imagine in that department, being married to a famous soldier. The wounds, for one thing. Two or three more in every campaign and—he being a hero—all on the front, of course. If you think about it, you can see that hardly makes for joyful abandon. Then there's her, on the other side of the wall. Every creak of the bed joints, every whisper, and you imagine her lying awake and wondering if this is going to be the night that produces another little hero. And if not, what's the silly girl doing wrong? So please spare me the remarks about Venus and Mars. I wish you would, because you see they make me wonder what you and your husbands do in bed. Is it really fire and rushing waters, rose scents and beating wings like the poets say? I wish somebody would tell me.

It must have been around this time that I happened to catch the eye of a young man of about my own age, when I was walking with Volumnia to a friend's house. He was tall, with dark curling hair, and when he saw me looking at him, he smiled such a frank, open smile that I couldn't help smiling back. Back at home, she told me that it wouldn't do. I must understand that as wife to Caius Marcius, consul-in-waiting, I could not risk the slightest hint of gossip. My spotless reputation must be as important to me as his courage was to him. Then, with her eyes on my face and in a tone of voice as ordinary as if we were discussing household accounts, she said, "If I ever found you'd been unfaithful to Caius Marcius, I'd kill you. I'd kill you with my own hands. You understand that?" I nodded, bowed my head, and said nothing.

Or is it something different altogether? Not fires or perfumes or roses but simply something that two people can laugh about together, like a secret that can't be told to anybody else. Am I going to have to live my life without knowing?

The rats were particularly bad that summer. What made it worse was that every grain of wheat and drop of oil mattered because we expected any day to find Tullus Aufidius and his barbarian horde besieging us. Caius Marcius hardly came home at all, and when he did, he could hardly talk about anything except Tullus Aufidius. He was becoming obsessed by the man. Aufidius said this. Aufidius might do that. Aufidius has an almost-Roman grasp of military tactics. One night, when the grayheads were around for earnest conference, he said, "My only fear in the world is that somebody else will kill him." Then, when they asked why: "Because his head belongs to me." He said it in almost a loving way. Later, when we were alone, I asked him what Tullus Aufidius was like. "A fine soldier," he said. "I mean what does he look like?" That surprised him and he had to think about it. "Red hair, red beard. Quite tall for a barbarian." Then, trying hard. "Very white teeth when he smiles." "Young?" "Quite young, younger than I am, but a lot of military experience." Then he patted me on the shoulder and said I wasn't to worry. He would protect us all from Tullus Aufidius. Then he went back to his army and the bed was all mine again.

Come and rescue me, Tullus Aufidius. Come galloping through the city gates with your red hair flying in the wind and your white teeth smiling through your beard, sweep me up out of my white bed and ride away with me. She won't be able to stop us. We'll laugh at the look on her face and our laughter will trail behind us like a red comet's tail as we gallop over the flat fields with the full moon in the sky until Rome is just a misty wall in the distance and we'll lie down under an olive tree and make love all night until I beg you to stop then laugh and say I didn't mean it and you laugh too and press down on me with all your weight and make me forget him and her and Rome and everything. I'm your city, waiting here for storming. My gates are open to you. Come and take me.

Only he didn't, of course. What happened that summer was exactly what should have happened. Caius Marcius stormed their citadel, Corioli, and although Tullus Aufidius lived to fight another day, his defeat was so thorough that we thought Rome would be in no danger from his Volsci for years to come. We could all sleep safely in our beds again without fear of the barbarians coming to carry us off. And my husband—Coriolanus now—came home to a triumph the like of which the city had never seen. That was when he kissed me and called me his gracious silence. And that's when, with my gracious silence, I started killing him. It wasn't clear in my mind then. It isn't clear even now, but I suppose I must have had some warning again of what was going to happen because I started crying. He thought it was because I was so relieved to see him home safe, and made a joke of it. If I was crying to see him come home in triumph, would I have laughed if he came home in a coffin? That went down well with the part of the crowd that could hear him. Under her tuition, he was cultivating the art of seeming natural and easy in public. Of course, I said nothing, as if my feelings were too deep for the world to know. Which they were.

Well, my noble husband, since you've raised the subject, I have to admit that I have been wondering what I'd do if you came home dead. I wouldn't have laughed. Not exactly. Certainly not outwardly and in full view of the whole of Rome. Not laughed, no. I'd have been quite sorry—the way you feel if a pet bird dies, or an aunt who was quite kind to you sometimes, or a dog you didn't know but saw crushed under somebody's chariot wheels. But then I'd have gone away into my own room and thought to myself, "Well, that's over, then, so what next?" And I might have laughed then—shakily perhaps and without making a noise—but yes, I might have laughed. Well, you did ask.

So with the fighting over for a while, and before the effect of that welcome home could go cold on us, the political campaign began. The grayheads agreed that there'd never be an opportunity better than this one. The aristocrats, the common people, the money men were all in the camp of our genuine hero, still only forty with a lot of scars and a few gray hairs gained in the city's service, and a background and home life that were models of all that Rome expected. That was where I came in again. I'd thought at least I'd be left to myself while he and Volumnia got on with the politics, but not a hope of it. "We must visit as much as possible, Virgilia. The women's voice is essential." Surprised into argument for once, I said, "But they haven't got a voice. We don't vote." She smiled. She was pleased when I showed my naïveté. "We don't need to. In our homes we have a voice." So for weeks it was an endless round of visits, seven or eight of them a day, all over the city. Sitting there, sipping herb teas or spiced wine with the women, talking about nothing in particular with her eyes and ears on me all the time to make sure I didn't say a thing out of place. So, of course, I said as little as possible. Usually, Marcius Junior had to come with us to complete the picture. He was at the fidgety age by then and didn't like it, but though he argued with me, he couldn't stand out against his grandmother. My one consolation was that as soon as Coriolanus was safely elected—and it seemed a certainty—I could go back to my old life, dreaming and thinking my own thoughts in my rooms or along the herb walks in the garden. Then she put me right on that, too. All this was good training for the duties I'd have once I was the consul's wife. I didn't even belong to myself anymore. I belonged to Rome. There was no way out.

Only there was a way out and I found it. I swear by all the gods that I didn't mean it. If I prayed to them to save me—and yes, I suppose that other voice inside my head did pray to them—I didn't mean it to be that way. I didn't intend to kill my husband. I didn't intend to kill Coriolanus. It was my silence that did it. How could I help my silence? It was the thing I was good at, after all.

You know the story, I suppose. It's our custom in Rome that before a man can be elected consul he has to put on a ragged working man's tunic and cap and go into the marketplace to beg the commoners for their votes. It's really no more than a carnival, a break from the serious campaigning and a chance for the candidate to show his so-essential sense of humor and common touch. He buys a lot of wine, makes a comic speech written by a friend who's good at that kind of thing, making sure to put in a reference to the latest wrestling results. They cheer him to the echo and that's that, everybody is happy. Now, I know the way she's managed to rewrite what happened to make him look good, even in all this wreckage. Her version— Coriolanus was too proud, too noble to go along with this humiliating farce. So he loses his temper with the mob and is forced into exile. No, I'm sorry, Volumnia, but it wasn't quite like that. I come from a military family so even I know that you can't lead men unless you can share a joke with them, look at things through their eyes. He could have come through the ragged tunic business quite well, if he'd wanted to. Only, I think he was tired. It had been a long campaign after all and we were near the end of it. I know I was tired. The heat in the city was like a bludgeon, I had a sick headache and a list of eight visits to make that day and Marcius Junior was irritable, probably a touch feverish. I'd heard Volumnia's laughter from her room next door and him laughing, too, an unusual sound. Then he came into our room in his stained and torn tunic (borrowed from one of the slaves but well washed, naturally), holding an old squashy cap in his hand. Well, Virgilia, how do I look?" He struck an attitude in the doorway and squashed the hat on his head, still laughing. Now, I know I should have laughed, too, entered into the joke, told him he looked good or looked awful or anything. Just anything. Instead, I looked away and said nothing. "Oh," he said. Just that, but I could feel the confidence going out of him like air from a puffball when you tread on it. Why it should have mattered to him so much that day I've wondered and wondered. Why, when nobody cared much what I thought, should a few words not said have such consequences? Perhaps, all along he'd cared for me more than I thought but if so why didn't he tell me? Didn't she let him tell me in case tenderness made him less of a warrior? Whatever the reason, he should have said.

Anyway, the result was that he started the whole thing off balance, forgot his jokes, lost his temper, and got forced into exile. And killed, of course. Killed by Tullus Aufidius. Or by my silence.

He died among the barbarians so he had no grave in Rome. Volumnia decided to devote the rest of her life to putting up a statue to him. My life, too. This statue wouldn't be made out of stone or metal but of our lives, our visible and noble grief. In all we did from then onward, we were to be a reminder to Rome of the city's ungratefulness to its most deserving son, a souvenir of all the virtue that had gone out of the city the day they drove him away. We walked together through the forum, she and I and young Marcius, dressed in mourning clothes, eyes cast down on our daily journey to the temple of Mars. We did it for weeks, for months. At the end of a year I asked her how long we should go on with it. She looked at me with eyes as hard and dark as jet. "Forever," she said. At the end of two years a message came from my father asking if I had thought of marrying again. As a respectable widow, I was entirely free to marry if I wanted. My father had in mind a distant cousin I remembered and quite liked. When I raised the subject with her, very diffidently, I thought she was going to hit me. "What did I tell you? If you're ever unfaithful to Caius Marcius, I'll kill you with my own hands." "But he's—" "That makes no difference." Her face looked as if it had already willed itself halfway to stone. Her hair had grayed to the color of flint and her back was as straight as Minerva's on a temple frieze. She must have been in her sixties but age meant nothing. I knew she wouldn't let herself die, not for decades, because she was too busy making us his monument. I said nothing.

But I'm not ready to turn to stone like her. It would be a waste. My hair is still thick and dark and heavy. When I let it down, in my own room, it swirls around my body like the river around a willow tree. My toenails are pink like shells, my knees soft and rounded as those of Venus herself in the mosaic on her temple floor. But I'll be thirty next year. Soon it will be too late. Last night, I heard two of the slaves whispering and giggling under the window. I recognized the girl's voice, a little scrap of a thing, younger than I am but not pretty. I heard their whispers dying away and lay awake all night, imagining where they'd gone and what they were doing, and cried with envy.

All this morning I kept out of her way and made myself busy in the storerooms. Even living statues have to eat and drink. I checked the level of grain in the bins and the olive oil in the big jars. We were running short of oil so I sent the steward out with some slaves to buy more, warning them to be careful with it on the steep dark steps down to the storerooms. It was evening when I decided to go to her, with the low sun throwing a wash of copper-colored light over the courtyard and the corners of the rooms dusky. It wasn't quite dark enough to light the lamps yet. We've turned economical now that we don't have many guests. She was sitting there at her spinning wheel in the dusk of the living room, on a low stool, upright as ever. The only sound was the whirr of her wheel. I found another stool so that our eyes would be on the same level and positioned it carefully between her and the door. I said, "There's something I should tell you."

For the first time since I'd known her, the regular sound of the wheel faltered. She couldn't have guessed what was coming but she knew the sound of my voice was different. It was different in my ears, too, the secret voice of a silent woman but now speaking so that somebody else could hear it.

"It's about Caius Marcius."

I had to time it carefully, not let it out all at once.

"What about Coriolanus?"

She insisted on the title in spite of everything. She'd stopped spinning altogether. Outside I could hear the low tones of the steward giving orders to a slave. I was glad there were other people not far away.

I said, "You know he was away such a lot. That was why it happened."

"Why what happened?"

The judge beyond the River Styx probably sounds like that, a voice telling you there will be no mercy but you've got to confess in any case.

"My lover."

And I poured it all out, like a bird that knows it's only going to sing its song once. I looked her in the eye and told her about how my lover crept past the guards on hot summer nights and I let him in at my window. I told her about those other times when it was my turn to creep past the guards and meet him waiting for me on the other side of the walls with his horse so that we could gallop away and find a place to make love by a river under the trees. He was a wonderful lover, I said. I'd no idea of what love was until we found each other. All the time she stared at me without moving. If it hadn't been for her eyes, I'd have thought she really had finally turned to stone from hearing it. But the eyes were like rats' eyes, two glossy berries in what was left of the light, only black not red. And there wasn't much light left. I stood up, took two steps toward the door.

"What was his name?"

I looked at her over my shoulder.

"Your lover's name?"

"Tullus Aufidius," I said.

Then I threw myself at the door, opened it, and ran for my life. The screech that came after me as I ran into the corridor and along the side of the courtyard was like nothing I'd ever heard before. Some winged monster might have made it, diving on its prey, but nothing human. It came behind me, louder and louder, as she chased after me. I'd never guessed that she could run so fast, let alone scream at the same time. I didn't know then and I don't know now whether she believed me. If she'd thought about it for a moment, she'd have seen that I'd never had a chance to go galloping over the plains with a lover, not with her eyes and ears on me every minute of the day. But saying it was enough. I heard from behind me things crashing over, slaves and servants shouting to one another. They must have known that she'd kill me when she caught up with me. Perhaps some of them tried to stop her, but I don't know. I think probably not. Her word had been law for a long time, and if she chose to kill her daughter-in-law, that was her affair. I'd counted on having a good start, on being a lot younger than she was, but her vengeance was a force of nature and I thought, beginning to panic, that I hadn't given myself long enough. I lost a sandal, kicked off the other one, and heard that screech coming closer and closer until she was only a few strides away. Ahead of me, at the far side of the courtyard, was the door to our storerooms. I grabbed the latch, wrenched it open, then threw myself through and slammed it behind me. It was quite dark with the door shut. My heart was thumping but I made myself go down the steps slowly and carefully, keeping well to the side, with one hand against the wall. By the time I got down to the floor among the jars and bins, the screeching had stopped. The next sound was the door at the top of the steps grinding open. She stood there above me, a darker shape against the dark blue sky.

I said to her, quietly, "Even if you kill me, he was worth it."

The dark shape came down the steps at me. She came quite slowly at first, taking her time because she knew she had me cornered. Then suddenly the shape changed and she was flying at me, head first as if she really had changed herself into an avenging Fury and was hurtling at my throat, beak and claw. That was how it looked to me and I screamed, even though I knew that everything was happening just as I'd planned it, that she'd slipped on the olive oil I'd poured so carefully all down the middle of the steps and was falling headlong. She didn't scream. She landed at my feet and, apart from the snap of her neck breaking, died quite silently. Which was strange, because silence was my speciality, not hers.

In a while, I shall go upstairs. I have a funeral to arrange, a household to run. I shall make it very clear that the slaves must not be punished for the oil spilled on the steps. After all, accidents can happen in the best households. Young Caius and I will mourn properly for the appointed time, and I shall write to my father and tell him that the distant cousin might be worth thinking about. Unless, that is, anybody more interesting comes along. After all, I am a rich young widow and free as a bird. As for that other voice, the one that spoke in my head, I don't think I shall be needing it anymore. The rest is silence.

Stephan Rykena

Cold-Blooded

STEPHAN RYKENA makes a welcome return to our pages with his story, "Cold-Blooded," which was first published in the newspaper *Stadtanzeiger* (apparently the German public likes an occasional break from reality with their morning news). Although the locale and the characters are different, the story is as old as time itself, and could happen anywhere, from America to Japan. Trust Stephan, however, to give it a novel twist all his own.

Cold-Blooded

Stephan Rykena

Simon Polt had been a diver for many years and a lot of things had happened to him during that time, but he had never made such a mistake.

The moory waters of Lake Steinhude were no excuse at all. He should have worked more carefully. And now he could even read it in the local paper:

> "It was only shortly after the old Volkswagen had been pulled out of the muddy waters of Lake Steinhude that the firefighters found a skeleton inside the vehicle, which had possibly been on the bottom of the lake for some years."

"I didn't see it," said Simon, shaking his head in dispair. "I thought the car was empty."

Chief Inspector Karl Norman put his hand on Simon's shoulder.

"No problem, Karl," he mumbled calmly. "Those few minutes won't change anything about the case. Do you know how long the car has been in there?—At least five years! And the eels have done a good job, as you can see. Not one piece of flesh left for our pathologist. So, don't think too much about it."

At ten Norman was just reading the report from the forensic department, when the door opened and his partner, Sarah Toley, a very attractive red-haired woman in her twenties, came in.

"The car was stolen," she said immediately, without looking at him. "Five years ago. In January 1997. In Hamburg."

Norman looked at her and nodded.

"The corpse was male, not older than twenty," she said, and started to read some papers from her desk. "Six feet tall and rather delicate. The shape of the scalp and the fillings of the teeth could mean that he was of Baltic origin. But that's just a guess. Nothing special that could help us. The car was no help, either. The only interesting thing about it was that it had been started by its ordinary key."

She frowned and put a finger on her beautiful red lips.

"Was it freezing in that winter of 1997?" asked Norman. "I mean, was the lake . . ."

She grinned and showed her immaculate teeth.

"Frozen, you mean? Of course it was. How on earth do you think a car can sink down to the bottom of the lake two hundred meters away from the banks if the water was not frozen? There is no ferry or bridge or anything like that. The lake had been frozen for weeks that winter. But the funny thing about that lake is that there are always a few holes that don't freeze—because of the moory ground, you know. They are called dipes, as far as I know. Very dangerous for ice-sailing and skating."

Norman nodded again and bit his lower lip.

"Not bad for a start," he said. "So you mean that guy drove the car on the ice and broke through it. If it is as simple as that, I don't know why we are involved. Seems to have been a simple stupid accident."

Sarah shook her head.

"Unfortunately, it's not that easy," she said. "The car was stolen from the parking lot of a house for political refugees in Hamburg. And exactly that night a seventeen-year-old Bosnian called Trojan Delim, who was waiting to be sent back to Bosnia three days later, disappeared.

"Delim was the witness in a trial in Hanover. . . ."

Tatjana looked strained while she was reading the local page of the Hanover *Post* between the aircraft's narrow seats. The sun twinkled through the small window as the plane gained altitude.

The young female police officer beside her who had escorted her looked nervously at her fingers.

"Seems to be a calm flight," she said, rather to assure herself than to get an answer from Tatjana. "Will anybody be waiting for you in Sarajevo?"

Tatjana nodded and went on reading.

> "The dead person may possibly be a seventeen-year-old asylum seeker who disappeared from a house for political refugees in Hamburg on the 15th of January 1997.
>
> "Until recently it was assumed that the young man had fled from the house because his objection had been overruled. It is not clear how the body got into Lake Steinhude.
>
> "The proceedings are difficult, because only the skeleton is left."

Tatjana leaned back in her seat and closed her eyes.

So they have finally found him, she thought, after so many years!

Now it would be absolutely impossible for her to ever go back to Germany.

She had always hoped to find a way to return to Germany after her arrival in Sarajevo, even though she was just about to be deported.

But soon they would find out everything and Tatjana didn't want to go back to jail in that country she liked so much. Four and a half years had been enough.

She fell asleep for a minute and pictures of the past ran through her mind.

The horrible months together with her father and her little sister in the house in Hamburg.

Three people in a tiny room with that smelly sink and metal furniture. Three people among a hundred who had no work and no future. The permanent fights of the men in the house. The thrashings by her father. Those degrading thrashings by her father that had finally led to . . .

A hand on her arm woke her up. Surprised, she looked into the face of the young female officer. "Breakfast," her warm voice said. "You have to take your table down. Do you prefer tea or coffee?"

After the breakfast Tatjana looked silently through the little window at the mountains far below.

"When you look out of the windows on the right, you can see Lake Constance," said a friendly voice from the loudspeakers in the cabin. "At this time of the year it's covered by a thin ice-layer and . . ."

At the sight of the frozen lake Tatjana's thoughts drifted back to the newspaper article about the corpse of Lake Steinhude.

Trojan Delim—yes, Trojan Delim. He had been the only light in this horrible house in Hamburg. They had liked each other immediately and not only because he, too, had been from Bosnia. He had been the first man in her short life who had given her the feeling that she could tell him everything. And exactly he . . .

She bit her lower lip and her normally beautiful face became a strange mask.

He had deserved death, like her father.

In Skodja, the little village in Bosnia where she was born, nobody would have sent her to jail for something that had cost her four and a half years in a German prison.

Lake Constance disappeared under the wings of the plane and on the horizon you could see the snow-covered Alps.

For a few seconds life in Skodja came back to her mind. The poor little village in the mountains. The scenery of her childhood. In those days her father had still been very different, not so embittered and very optimistic that the Germans needed good carpenters and that he would find a job immediately.

He had collected every cent to be able to pay for the illegal transfer that had finally got them to the land of their dreams . . . where the dream had melted away after a short time.

And then, after her mother's death, Tatjana had taken her place in the eyes of her father.

Ice-cold shivers ran down her spine.

Those thrashings, those disgusting touches, the horrible smell of his sweat!

He had really deserved death! Nobody, no, really nobody would have sentenced her in Bosnia.

He had been the one who had wanted to kill her, after Trojan had told him about her plan.

She had had to be quicker than him. And unfortunately he had survived, even though he would have to spend the rest of his life in a wheelchair.

"Attempted murder" was the term they had used in the trial. Five years in prison. A high price for a just cause.

The police officer touched her hand gently. "I have to go to the toilet," she said, and smiled. "If you have to go, too?"

Tatjana shook her head. "No problem," she said, grinning. "I won't run away."

The officer looked a little embarassed and walked off down the aisle.

Tatjana took a chewing gum from her pocket and looked around the plane.

That was it, she thought. From now on you will have to stay away from Western Europe. No court there will understand that traitors have no right to live. They will call it murder and send you back to jail for many years, as soon as they get you.

But it hadn't been murder. Trojan had betrayed Tatjana and her sister. He had told their father about their plan to kill him, even though he knew that he beat them every day, that he had raped them. Even though he knew that this father wanted to sell Tatjana to a sex club in Munich.

She had trusted Trojan and he hadn't helped them. He and their father. Disgusting! He had betrayed them, and betrayal meant death. A simple philosophy. Even if the Germans didn't accept those rules. Trojan had died as a traitor and that was justice in her opinion.

The officer came back and took the newspaper from the seat pocket.

UNIDENTIFIED CORPSE FOUND IN LAKE STEINHUDE. It jumped up to Tatjana's eye.

Well, he could have known, she thought, that a simple excuse couldn't wipe out his betrayal.

He had come from Bosnia himself. He knew the rules and then he had thought . . . ?

Yes, okay, he had told her about the circumstances he had been in. Yes, he had asked her to forgive him, but that hadn't saved his life at all.

He had stolen a car in Hamburg to visit her in that mental hospital in Wunstorf near the lake, where she had spent some weeks so that the judge could find out about her criminal responsibility. He had wanted to explain everything to her. And she had played her role.

The nurses of the hospital had given her the opportunity to meet her "cousin" for a few hours in town, and she had talked to him as if she had forgiven him. And when it had become dark they had driven to a little wood near Lake Steinhude with a bottle of wine and she had looked at him as if he could expect something very promising.

But when they had reached the lake, Trojan had wanted to show her what a brilliant driver he was by driving on the ice of the frozen lake and performing a few tricks.

"Crazy, lovely, isn't it! Absolutely fantastic," had been his last words.

The screwdriver that she had stolen from a mechanic before she had left the mental hospital a few hours before had gone straight into his heart, very easily. Death had come within seconds.

She had jumped out of the slowly rolling car before, after a few meters, it had magicallly disappeared in the dark.

Later in the evening she had arrived back in the hospital with a plausible excuse.

"We will now leave our cruising altitude to land in a few minutes. . . ."

The voice from the loudspeakers jolted Tatjana back to where she was.

"Well, that's it, I think," she said, sighing to the young lady next to her who was smiling helplessly.

Karl Norman and Sarah Toley, the two investigators, were sitting in their office in Wunstorf. For them the whole case was not at all as spectacular as the press had described it.

Norman had phoned for hours and searched the computer but with hardly any results.

"The house for these political refugees in Hamburg was closed three years ago. The manager, the owner of the Volkswagen from the lake, died a year ago. He left no family. And the autopsy hasn't helped, either. Nobody knows anything about the teeth. A dead end.

"The only maybe helpful information as to why the dead man from the lake could be Trojan Delim is that a certain Tatjana Chesnic, who was accused of attempted murder in a case in Hanover, where Trojan Delim was to be heard as a witness, was in the mental hospital in Wunstorf exactly at that time in January 1997 when Trojan Delim disappeared. . . ."

Sarah shrugged.

"That's absolutely useless. The pathologist can't even say how the dead man really died. He had been in the water for five years and the eels . . ." She looked disgusted. "What if this stupid man just drove on that bloody ice and drowned in one of those dangerous holes we all know about? It's no case for criminal investigation, I think. You know that there is a lot of work waiting for us concerning the other cases on our desks. I think we should close this case. What do you think?"

Four weeks later Tatjana started a job in the kitchen of a Russian containership on its way to Hamburg.

Jac. Toes

Lead . . . Follow

Our next story is from JAC. TOES, an experienced Dutch author who enjoyed a restless youth that was followed by an even stormier career as a sailor in the Merchant Navy. Later, he graduated from the University of Nijmegen with a degree in literature and linguistics. He has taught secondary education in various colleges and in 1980 founded the broadcasting station "Radio City." He is the author of several crime novels, including *Twin-Tracks* and *Settling Accounts,* both nominated for the Golden Noose, the Dutch award for best crime novel, and *Fotofinish,* which won the Golden Noose for best crime novel of 1997. He is a full-time novelist who also works as a scriptwriter for various Dutch media.

For some mysterious reason there are certain themes that crop up in the mystery field year after year. Crime and dancing is one of them. In his story "Lead . . . Follow," first published in the Dutch edition of *Penthouse* magazine and translated by Hans van den Berg, Toes explores the maddening, seductive world of the Argentinian tango, and of a perfectly matched pair of dancers who work—and play—together, and wouldn't have it any other way.

Lead . . . Follow

Jac. Toes

A snippet of Piazzolla, wafting from a half-open door, lured me to a tango dancing in the city center. Just a few melancholy chords on a bandoneon, that was enough to bring back to life a period of half a year in Buenos Aires. Tango, a dancing teacher, and a gigantic, maddening crush. On both. The cocktail had kept me in a state of intoxication during those six months, and the hangover took just as long.

As far as my dancing teacher was concerned it was nothing new, another one of those wandering Europeans in search of those moments when passion, soul, and body would find one another. I trailed her to all the dancings and finally in some way-out dance hall I asked her if she would be prepared to come with me to *Holanda*.

"I couldn't possibly get mixed up in your life," was her definite answer. "You are just too . . . different."

"As man or as *tanguero?*"

She shrugged; it would be all the same to her.

Once back in the land of the wooden clogs and chilly feet she faded from my mind, eventually. Just like the dancing steps she taught me. At least that is what I thought, until the moment I swung around without any hesitation. The tango was still there, firmly settled in my subconscious.

Inside the dance hall, the heat was simmering below the rotating fans, in spite of the fact that the autumn weather had made short shift of the summer. Goodness me, the tango . . . the dance of God and the devil, of merriment and death, love and suffering; my Argentinian sweetheart repeatedly had tried to get this across, up until the moment when she made it obvious that I was expecting from her much more than she would ever be able to give me.

"And don't you ever confuse the Argentinian tango with that insipid concoction that the impotent English have made from it," she had added. "The ballroom tango that robbed the soul from the dance."

I stopped for a moment at the entrance and then allowed myself to be swept by the urging rhythm and the razor-sharp chords, which had made Piazzolla immortal. On the dance floor some dozen couples were dancing, concentrated and serious. The women, dressed in low-cut evening dresses, held their eyes closed, some of them showing a faint haze of transpiration between their shoulder blades. The gazes from the eyes of their male partners were firmly fixed on the floor, almost as if some light beam was showing them the right direction. They wore sharply pleated trousers, black shirts, some of them even sported black ties.

The barman came toward me, pointing at a space next to the entrance where I was able to find hanging space for my raincoat. A sign on the wall presented a special offer: daiquiris. I know that alcohol and tango do not mix, but somehow I decided to give the barman a chance.

"You are new around here, aren't you?" he observed while unscrewing a bottle of rum.

I nodded and watched how he squeezed a lemon into the glass and, with the help of a drinking straw, stirred it in the rum. He threw an ice cube in it, did not bother adding the customary resin syrup, and slid the glass in my direction. Using a shaker would probably disturb the music, I thought.

When the barman was obviously getting ready to start a chat, I turned away and chose an empty table on the edge of the dance floor. The first notes of *Hora Cero* stirred my blood and I decided I was going to have a dance, for the first time since Buenos Aires. I started looking for an experienced dancer, not some *tanguera* who would get her ankles in a knot. What I sought was a woman who demanded the necessary space to submit fully to the dance, and to me. The number ended in a slashing chord with most of the couples answering the finish with the prescribed stylized end-movement.

Across the floor three women were sitting at a table, their gazes scanning the dancing crowd, waiting for what would follow the short interval in the music, their spiked heels at the ready. I thought I would ask the woman who so openly had watched the dancing couples, while the other two were trying to fake some air of nonchalance by sporting a cigarette, held high. I put my glass down and got up.

The hand that forced me back on my chair rested on my shoulder for a short moment. Somebody I knew, here of all places? And I am not ashamed to admit: that joyous flash of the impossible, could it be my Argentinian *tanguera* . . . ? I noticed the wrist with the jangling armbands close to my face and then the bare arm. A woman was trying to worm her way past my chair, rejecting her dancing partner's proffered hand.

"I beg your pardon," she murmured, and continued toward the dance floor.

She had a rather low voice that somehow did not fit in with her frail body, the ponytail, and especially not with the ten centimeters of bareness between her top and her belly button.

The barman had selected a more traditional number, *Recuerdo,* a hit from the forties. I watched her left hand getting hold of her partner's upper arm, how her right hand entwined his fingers. She was wearing a dress that came to halfway between her knees and ankles, but with the first step a high split in the dress revealed a most shapely thigh. Her partner, a stocky character sporting a blond hairdo combed backward, allowed her to spin around her own axle at first and then took her in a number of sideward steps, smoothly moving from the hips. The performance showed obvious experience, their movements perfectly synchronized. And yet, in spite of their skilled technique, there seemed to be some tension in their dancing, an indefinable friction. I watched the couple until they disappeared behind a set of pillars. Other couples passed my table, some of them dancing without any direction, drifting like the autumn leaves outside, while others were clinging tightly to each other like sumo wrestlers, not allowing each other one inch. The less experienced were much more careful in their movements, still torn between the desire to become one with that other body and the fear of reaching that point.

The routine of a dance floor is just the same as that of a merry-go-round, and it took only a few minutes for the intriguing couple to come back into the line of my vision. A short delay further along in the procession forced them to improvise on the square meter they were occupying, using *giros* and *molinas*. Even though there was a lack of space, they stuck to their open style, keeping a distance from each other of about six inches. Pirouetting around each other, they appeared intensely involved and concentrated. And yet again I noticed that odd tension in their movements. When eventually the hold-up was dissolved and there was sufficient room again, the man seemed to hesitate as if he was not quite sure what step to take next. To gain time he swayed her up and down a few times. The woman's reaction was almost instant: her fingers formed into the shape of a claw, and with a push she thrust him backward into the open space in the center of the dance floor. Once there he still did not give any direction, and again it was she who took the initiative and forced him into the sandwich position, stroking the lower part of his leg with her ankle. All of a sudden I realized the reason for this remarkable mixture of experience and hesitance. It was she who led the dance all this time! All the impulses were initiated by her—he was no more than a marionette and she the puppeteer. Yet the mysterious thing about all this was that they both did their utmost to create the impression of the reverse.

Fascinated, I kept watching the way she circled around her partner and in the split second that her eyes caught mine, she gave me a penetrating look, as if to confirm my discovery.

In Europe the dance floor is like a marketplace. The man approaches a woman and asks if she is prepared during the following ten minutes to place her hands into his and to press her breasts against his chest. She either refuses or accepts his offer. He either loses or collects his prey.

In Buenos Aires man and woman seek eye contact. The slightest hint is sufficient. Separately they step on to the dance floor, giving the impression as if meeting purely by accident. They who do not find eye contact will not be dancing, but they are spared the humiliation of a refusal.

The intriguing couple had returned to their table, where they took their seats opposite each other. She leaned sideward, holding a cigarette in her mouth. He gave her a light and while she exhaled the first cloud of smoke, she uttered a few words. Straightaway the man got up to fetch her a glass of water from the bar. After that she stuck her feet out and ordered him to grease the sides of her dancing shoes with Vaseline, in order to ensure that her pumps would slide effortlessly against each other during the maneuver of closing her feet during the dance. My Argentinian *tanguera* certainly had educated me very thoroughly in the world of tango dancing.

I waited until they got up to go to the toilets.

On her way back, as she walked along the dance floor, I got up. She halted for a moment, raising a questioning eyebrow, her manner telling me that I was in her way. She lowered her eyes, but I kept staring at her with raised chin. Then she looked up again, giving a hint of a smile.

The next moment we started with a tango-waltz. I began quietly, using simple figures, no showing off, no speed-ups. She allowed a few swaying steps, showing amusement in her expression. Halfway through the number she closed her eyes and brought her face closer. Her chest touched my lapels, her left hand slid upward from my upper arm to the back of my neck. It surprised me. Most women would keep their distance, particularly during the first dance. Now and then she sought my support, especially whenever I led her in the cross-step. She never made any attempt to take the lead, and allowed herself to be directed like a true *tanguera*. She certainly knew the rules, the give-and-take of available space, the challenge and reaction, and the paradoxical leading and following. Yet her dancing was not completely relaxed: constantly there seemed to be a kind of hesitance, as if some under-the-surface protest bothered her.

I led her in a bracket of backward *ochos,* and again she sought support from my shoulder. After that I led her forward in double tempo, which I clearly gave her time to understand. She kept up easily with the increased pace, but toward the end she hesitated again. Was I going too fast? Were my steps too large? I looked at her face that showed a smile, almost an expression of ecstasy. Only a very slight trembling at the corners of her curved mouth betrayed tension.

The next thing I knew she pressed herself against me. Vicelike, even though there was plenty of space on the dance floor to allow for extensive fireworks. I smelled her breath—white Corona—and her perfume—sea and freesias. She concluded this gesture by lowering her head and letting her perspiration-covered cheek rest in my neck.

It was obviously a diversion trick to give her some leeway. When I executed a *Barrida,* the fast movement whereby the leader takes his partner's foot with his own, she got frightened and withdrew her leg abruptly. Without the intended resistance, my leg went from underneath me. I lost my balance and the fact that we did not finish up sprawled on the dance floor was thanks to the barkeeper who happened to be walking in the path of the dancers, toting a tray stacked with drinks.

The glasses crashed to the floor, bursting into shards.

Together with her escort, my dancing partner disappeared via the main entrance without as much as an apology, an explanation, not even a glance at the mess she had left behind.

I waited at the bar for the dance floor to be cleared and decided to regard the incident as pure bad luck, no reason to let my evening of dancing be spoiled. After I had ordered a second daiquiri, tipping the barman rather generously, I made my way to the three women who had been sitting at their table opposite me during all this disturbance. The first refusal I regarded as a misunderstanding, the second one with amazement, the third knock-back as a humiliation. I left the saloon under the sneering looks of the barman. Outside I let the autumn rain splash my red-hot face, before I stormed with angry steps out of the lane.

At the corner a white Mercedes was parked, two wheels on the footpath. As I was about to pass the vehicle, the back door swung open and a hand beckoned me to get in, armband jingling.

On the backseat sat the same woman who shortly before had made an utter fool of me, and who was responsible for making it impossible for me to ever dance there again. Her escort was sitting behind the steering wheel. He was wearing a chauffeur's cap and did not even glance at me through the rearview mirror when I got in. As I sat down beside her, she offered me her scarf to dry my face. Again I became aware of her scent, much stronger this time. I was on the verge of opening my mouth to ask her to explain her rude behavior inside the dancing hall, but she was already ahead of me—she burst out in a fit of raucous laughter. The beams of a streetlight flashed over the rings on her fingers as she bent forward to stroke my cheek with the back of her hand.

"My name is Elaine, that's what you wanted to know," she said.

"For a start," I answered. "And . . ."

She squeezed my upper leg.

". . . And that is Gerhard."

Gerhard turned his head and lifted the corners of his mouth a fraction. I acknowledged the greeting with a nod.

"Gerhard is much more than a lover, much more than a husband. Gerhard is my protector."

Gerhard remained staring ahead. She gave me a wink.

"My protector," she repeated.

I nodded quickly. After all, pimps, too, call themselves protectors.

"A kind of bodyguard?" I asked.

Again that burst of laughter.

"Very good! Indeed, Gerry guards my body."

She tapped him on the shoulder.

"Just take the long route back. We need some time."

She rummaged through her handbag and produced a silver-plated hip-flask.

"Yes, it's quite obvious. You are curious, you want to know more. I'll tell you in a minute how we conquered each other. Elaine and Gerhard. But first let me give you a decent drink. Those revolting daiquiris in there are enough to make the worst lush gag."

"Just the same, you did fix that barkeeper well and good."

She burst out laughing again while she unscrewed the flask.

"He asked for it. I've got no time for waiting staff getting in the way. Nowhere else in the world you'll find waiters swaggering among the dancing public."

She brought the flask to her mouth, took a quick sip, and then wiped the lipstick from the bottle top.

"Go on, have a drink."

I sniffed at the opening of the flask.

"Peat and sea," she said. "Whiskey doesn't need more than that."

While I took a decent swig, she watched me, smiling.

"Why do you two dance like that . . ." I started. "So . . ."

She took the flask back again and made herself more comfortable.

"So ambiguous, you mean," she said. "Because Gerry is so faithful. He has got many good qualities, but his fidelity comes head and shoulders over the other ones. Isn't that right, Gerry?"

Gerhard did not react. He kept his eyes glued to the wet road's surface. We drove through barren, dark countryside, pastureland around the city, here and there a few lights from farms, a streetlight at intersections, the outlines of a forest in the distance.

"Faithful to such an extent that he pretends to lead you on the dance floor," I said. "That he lets you hold the reins?"

Elaine let out a soft growl by way of approval. She moved closer to me and put her arm around my neck.

"Well observed," she said. "Gerry is an ideal follower."

She whispered as if she was sharing a secret: "Gerry was my colleague, you know. Earlier, before the accident."

She eased her head on my shoulder, putting the hipflask back in my fingers.

"The accident?"

"Gerry and I worked in security," she said softly. "Gerry and I, real pros. A golden future for a golden couple. We worked with armored vehicles, delivering money in special boxes. They are painted blue, like damned tanks. Money transports . . . how many millions have we delivered, Ger?"

Gerhard's silhouette shrugged slightly. Her fingers ruffled my hair, fondled my ear. We entered the forest, through a tunnel of brown-red leaves.

"We were very well equipped," she continued. "We were under constant surveillance, watched by video cameras, inside as well as outside. We chatted like mad on the mobile communication networks. We carried waterproof alarm transmitters. On our belts were walkie-talkies, hand torches, our personal alarm signals, the works. And the money was carried in bangboxes."

"Bangboxes?"

"Money cassettes with built-in explosive devices, filled with paint. They could be detonated by remote control. One push on the button and *whoosh!* You'll look like one of those modern paintings. Water-resistant. Even the banknotes would get a dash of paint."

She laughed once more and pressed herself against me. Her foot sliding along my leg, the whispering voice, her groping hands . . . what she actually was after, I didn't know, but just the same I did not resist her.

"We wore uniforms. Perhaps that was the moment I fell for Gerry, when we got those new uniforms. . . . We used to dance a lot at that time. Every moment we were at it. Even between training sessions. Remember, Ger? Visitations, explosives reconnaissance, wire-tapping, kidnap situations. Repeatedly we had to practice those alarm procedures. Staying for weeks in one of those swanky training centers."

She put a cigarillo between her lips. Gerry reached over to hand her the dashboard lighter.

"And yet, you know, everything went wrong. Right on our first consignment, we were confronted with an emergency situation. Really very messy! Two guys on motorbikes. Police motorbikes, police helmets, police uniforms. Either stolen or copied, who knows? Perfect planning. No alarm procedures can protect you against that. As a matter of fact, this took place on this very road, quite close by. Am I right, Ger?"

Her mouth was very close to my ear now. She began talking even softer and more quickly. She only paused to draw on her cigarillos now and then. I began to wonder how much longer she was going to have Gerhard drive us around.

"They directed us to the side of the road. Gerry thought—so did I, as a matter of fact—that we had copped a speeding ticket. He was always driving too fast. The two guys strolled over, taking their time. In fact, we were getting impatient. Gerry got out. He did not realize that they kept their visors down. "I'll smooth things over," he said. After all, Gerry had been a traffic cop himself. Ger, weren't you with highway patrol? But to get out! That was nowhere in the instructions."

Her cigarillo was glowing in the dark. Her face was close, and she blew smoke in my neck.

"They got Gerry straightaway."

"And what about you?" I asked.

"In fact, I opened the door for them, as they knew exactly what they were after. Gerry had to get the booty out of the safe. Fourteen money cassettes. They had been tipped off, they knew precisely how much we had onboard."

"And you acted correctly, according to the instructions?"

Her breasts were pressed hard against my upper arm, her hand wormed its way between the buttons of my shirtfront.

"They kept their guns leveled at me. But, of course, Gerry always wanted to play the big hero," she panted. "He refused them. That was his second mistake. The instructions state clearly: Do whatever they say. However, not so our Ger. All he had to do was to remove those stupid cases from the safe. Gerry messed the whole thing up for me!"

Suddenly she hissed out her words.

"That's the reason I dance the way I do. Gerry bolted, trying to get into the undergrowth. He was going to raise the alarm. To get him back they only fired one shot. One, mind you! So he came back and then he forgot to activate the explosive mechanisms. They made a clean getaway. The money was never traced."

We came to a halt outside a small villa. Her breathing became normal again. Gerhard switched off the engine and the headlights, but remained motionless in his seat, the windshield wipers swishing to and fro.

"Ger is a very loyal colleague. In fact, he is very good. He dances with me, he takes care of me, he takes me to where I want to go. He is at my disposal twenty-four hours a day. He'll never bolt again."

She placed her feet in my lap.

"Here, feel for yourself."

She took my hand and forced it under her dress. I could feel the top of her stocking, the bare skin farther along. . . .

"No, go down!"

My fingers slid along her thigh. With a sudden jerk she spread her legs, leaving me only to hold the right knee. I hesitated. Was she going to punish him by making a show of lovemaking here on the backseat of her car, right under his very nose?

"Go on!" she ordered.

I felt a sharp edge, a hard surface . . . was she perhaps wearing some sort of capsule, a shin protector? I withdrew my hand. My slowness infuriated her. Quickly she raised her frock and took her stocking off. In the dark I could only sense her jerky movements; in front of me I could see the immovable silhouette of Gerhard. There was the sound of a clasp, then a sucking sound, her foot swinging in front of my face.

"That is why I lead and not him."

I felt her laughter in my ear as she opened her door and turned away.

Gerhard was already outside, quite prepared. He knelt down in front of her, straightened her back, and lifted her out. She did not put her arms around his neck. Instead, with both hands she held the artificial limb.

Ger cradled her like a sleeping child as he carried her to the front door of the villa.

Gerhard came back after a few minutes, sprinting through the rain. In the meantime I had finished the cigarillos that Elaine had left behind. He started the car and for a short moment he was silent. Guilt always gnaws at self-respect. Gerhard would know this better than anyone, I guessed.

When he swung the car onto the forest road, I asked him if he went dancing very often . . .

"I don't keep track of it," he answered.

"Very sporting," I said, "not to leave your colleague in the lurch."

Gerhard eased the accelerator, took off his cap, and placed it on the passenger's seat. For the first time he looked at me through the rearview mirror.

"It took a lot more than that," he said briefly. He stopped the car on the side of the road and turned around.

"There never were policemen on motorbikes," he started. "Oh, yes, later on when the whole thing was over. You could not see the trees for all the uniforms running around. No, sir, there were no damned coppers, they were never there."

"But weren't there the videotapes?" I asked. He snorted and smiled a little.

"Of course there was that tape and there still is. She showed it to me once."

He shrugged and held up his thumb and index finger about two centimeters apart.

"Those cassettes fit in a cigarette packet. That's how small they are."

"There is digital technique for you," I remarked.

"Every sucker who has to handle large amounts of money is a liar if he tells you that he has never dreamed about the big haul," he continued. "Bank tellers, croupiers, security people—they all have their fantasies. But to actually carry out the deed . . . that needs more than just a dream."

"Somebody like Elaine, for instance?"

He nodded.

"It was on this deserted forest road . . . you have seen it for yourself how long it takes before somebody passes by. First we secured the money-boxes. Suspended them in a sewer, under one of these manholes in the center of the road, a few kilometers back. And after that, during the supposed raid, we sat down and had a sandwich. After that, the truck was to be set alight. Beforehand we had arranged for jerry cans with petrol at the ready. That was to destroy all the evidence and also to explain why we had not activated the alarm system. We tossed everything inside the truck: our personal alarm systems, our walkie-talkies, our mobile phones, even our watches. Just to show how they robbed us of everything. And then I was going to shoot myself in the leg, to add even more credence."

"Her idea . . ."

"Everything was her idea. But when it came to the point to pull the trigger, I couldn't make myself do it. To blow my leg to smithereens . . . I was going to be a cripple. At first she begged me, then started abusing me. We were sitting on the front seat arguing. There was only very little time left. . . ."

He looked me straight in the eyes.

"Then she decided to do the job herself. She grabbed my hand, I tried to push her away. Whoever pulled the trigger . . . perhaps it was me. The bullet struck her knee. She was most unlucky. The knee joint was destroyed, infection set in, complications. What possibly could go wrong, she got it. She eventually left the hospital in a wheelchair."

"But what about those videotapes?"

"She sure kept her mouth shut. When I had to go and get rid of the gun . . . yes, I did run into the undergrowth, but only for that, to make that damned gun disappear. During that time she managed to switch the tape with the takes for an empty cassette. Nobody noticed it, and neither did I. The fire destroyed everything."

"And now she is holding you at ransom?" I asked. "She has the evidence that you two set the whole thing."

"Well, from her point of view, that was logical," he said in a forgiving tone. "She was going to land in a hospital, while I had all the opportunity to lift the manhole, grab the booty, and disappear. She must have realized this at that moment and decided she was not going to run the risk."

He started the car engine and moved out onto the road.

"In other words, you are her prisoner. . . . How long do you think this can last?"

"The term of limitation is twelve years," he said. "We're halfway now."

"Why don't you leave? She also has everything to lose."

"Elaine is a kamikaze pilot. She'd rather see us both destroyed than risk the chance of letting me go. At times she provokes me, dances with some other guy. Like with you tonight . . . She is giving me to understand that I am here for her, not the other way around. That is why I got such a kick out of watching you, to see how much resistance she put up."

He chuckled with some glee. "Purely with your skill you did not make it, although I grant you, you are an excellent dancer. You obviously have been taught how to make a woman flow . . . but only with me she can dance without pain. Because I can follow, while giving the impression that I lead."

We got back to the city. It had stopped raining. He parked the car at the beginning of the lane, where the dancing hall was located.

"Come with me," I offered on impulse. "Shoot through. If it means that much to you, you could always dance with me."

Gerhard picked up his cap and put it on.

"Never," he said in a sudden temper. "A woman like Elaine . . . My God, she may have me in a vice, but I wouldn't have it any other way."

He got out and opened the rear door for me.

"Elaine was *my* dream. For a long, long time already. Long before she snared me to make her own dream come true."

Frauke Schuster

Two Sisters

The short-short mystery story is a time-honored tradition in the field, and, as such, is very difficult to execute successfully. There are those writers in America who write curt crime tales with style and panache, Ed Hoch being one of them, and to this admittedly short list we can now add German mystery writer FRAUKE SCHUSTER. Born in 1958 in southern Germany, she spent the greater part of her childhood in Egypt, then returned to her native land where she studied chemistry, was awarded the OBAG Cultural Prize for her doctoral thesis in 1984, and worked for a scientific magazine. She started her writing career with various short stories, and in 2002 her first crime novel, *Atemlos (Breathless),* was published by KBV, Germany. The second novel, *Toskanisches Schattenspiel (Tuscan Shadow Play),* will follow in May 2003. First published in the anthology *Moerderisch kalt* and translated by Emmy Muller, her tale, "Two Sisters," should be required reading for those who are looking for a short, painfully cold shock in their stories.

Two Sisters

Frauke Schuster

W hat a tragedy!" the preacher says, and Rita adjusts her hat. She just hates funerals, especially under that horrible eastern wind at minus-fifteen! Even the preacher, though delivering his speech solemnly and devoutly—there will be an ample donation, if the Stolze family is pleased with the ceremony—even the preacher seems numbed, as if escaped from the deep-freezer and not yet completely thawed.

"It all happened so fast," someone behind Rita sighs.

No, Rita thinks. Not really fast. Twenty minutes . . .

As usual, she had started on the trip with reluctance. And, like every year, she had been angry with herself that she hadn't been able to think of any plausible excuse, hadn't been able to free herself with the mention of an urgent business trip, like Marina always did when she wanted to avoid any nasty situation. Marina, always the brighter star, outshining her. Marina, of whom she had forever been envious, even for her name. . . .

She didn't drive fast, hadn't been able to, not with that old Fiat, date of construction Stone Age or earlier. And especially not on that slippery road, covered by ice and snow.

Unnerved, she tried for the umpteenth time to wipe the right window. You didn't have to do so in Marina's high-class Daimler, where the comfortable heater kept the windowpanes from taking such liberties and, in addition, your bottom didn't freeze off during the first half hour of a trip.

Naturally, Marina's luxurious green car already stood waiting in the driveway, taking up that much space that Rita, having finally maneuvered her battered Fiat into the narrow, remaining gap, had to wriggle like an eel to get out of the door.

And then Marina appeared, in a close-fitting, slim-cut green dress. Only she could wear that. There wasn't a single gram of fat on her hips, there wasn't the slightest trace of cellulite on her thighs, unlike with normal women her age. On her perfect body, blouses didn't hang listlessly and shapelessly like potato sacks; with her, they showed decoratively what should be shown. And stains of all kinds naturally kept out of her way. And her hair . . .

"Rita! At long last! We knew you would be late again! And how do you like Marina's hair dye? So beautiful, isn't it? Maybe you, too, should try—but no, it would never suit you, that reddish . . ."

Rita listened to her mother prattling on and on, but, luckily, no answer seemed necessary. She just had to deliver her birthday congratulations, which she got rid of with as little enthusiasm as if they had been worn-out socks.

It was Marina who had laid the table with Hutschenreuther china and luxurious silverware—Rita hadn't been in time, as was once more pointed out. "And just look what she has done with the napkins! Marvelous, isn't it? Well, she surely has got that streak of the artist. . . ."

Marina must have sacrificed at least ten minutes, ten minutes of her precious news editor time. Ten minutes to force lavender-colored napkins into a parody of modern art. Ten minutes, and her mother couldn't praise her enough for that silly paper performance.

But where had Marina been last summer, when her mother was in the hospital with her hip surgery? Who washed and ironed her nighties and underwear two times a week? Who carried enormous heaps of fruit and liters of juice up to where she lay helplessly? Second-class work, good enough for the second-class daughter, with her second-class life between her ABC learners and a husband who occasionally was untrue. Unacceptable, however, for brilliant Marina, who swept past the invalid's bed in her stretch miniskirt, leaving behind a dazzling cloud of Elizabeth Arden perfume, together with an impractically huge rose bouquet and a lasting impression on the senior surgeon and the rest of the male staff.

She had just shown up once, but her mother still praised her today, and talked of how difficult it must have been for hard-working editor Marina to take off even half a day. Was there nothing she wouldn't do for her mother?

And Rita and her dirty linen bags slowly faded from everyone's memory.

The birthday cake was that sumptuous that Rita's stomach started to churn, but she had a second slice because as long as she was eating she didn't have to look, to admire. And yet, in the midst of all that buttercream filling, Marina drew her ace of trumps?

"Haidmann is going to retire, in the middle of next year, did I tell you?" She knew she hadn't, the question was rhetorical, should stress the importance of her news, and Rita speared her cake with the silver fork in an unmistakably murderous mood.

"Well, can you guess who'll be chief editor next year?"

Marina leaned back in her chair, slim, triumphant, victorious. Her mother shrieked with delight and Rita had to make an effort to mumble something in the way of congratulations, though it sounded more like a curse.

Why had it always been that way? Marina, who effortlessly won the math competition, while Rita stumbled about, dumbly and helplessly, with the lowest grades. Marina, who floated home from every sports event laden with awards, while Rita had dropped the baton at the relay race. Marina, who had graduated first in her year and who now smiled in black-and-white from the daily newspaper, while Rita paddled somewhere in the no-name swamp.

Rita stole a glance at her watch. At least another hour until she could leave with the appearance of decency and return to the scribbled letters of her abecedarians. Chief-editor-to-be. Rita's simple job shied away from comparison, as tin cans dulled in the presence of glittering gold. Teaching the first letters to little kids, who afterward wouldn't even remember the effort—that wasn't spectacular in the least.

Finally, at long last! Five o'clock. For sheer decency Rita waited another seven minutes, then started the ritual good-bye ceremony. One kiss here, one kiss there. Marina's "remember to drop in some day," pure ritual, never meant in earnest.

The cold February air had turned the old Fiat into a grotto of ice. Icy rain froze on the outside of the windshield. On the inside it was Rita's breath that froze. But now she didn't mind any longer, now she was on her way home, back to her second-class life that wouldn't be so bad if there were no Marinas in this world and especially in her family. Now she just had to endure the last part of the show—Marina overtaking her in her Daimler, in the usual careless maneuver, another of those silly family rituals.

Marina, with her speedy car, always departed after Rita, just to pull over on her way, mostly on the road along the lakeside, before their roads and lives parted again.

And there it was, in the rearview mirror, Marina's Daimler, and Rita thought enviously of the superior heating system in her sister's car, while her own clammy fingers clung to a steering wheel that seemed to be cut of pure ice.

Marina drove fast, set the indicator, effortlessly overtook Rita's rust-bucket, waved, and pressed the horn three times, and Rita hooted back as always, though she thought her sister ridiculously childish.

And the Daimler returned to the right lane, the ice of the lake glittering in the light of the fading day, but the Daimler rolled on, straightaway to the shore, shot over the frozen grass like a late New Year's Eve firecracker. Noisily the car crashed through the ice—and then deathly silence reigned. The Daimler disappeared. Just a few irregular waves sloshed around in the hole, kept shards of ice dancing. Among them here and there was a bubble of air.

The Fiat stopped of its own accord. Rita's icy fingers started fumbling for the mobile. There was no time to lose, she must call for help—but her gaze wandered away from the keys to the hole in the ice. How long would someone be able to survive down there, in water and ice, in cold February?

She lit a cigarette, looked at her watch. How long? There might be a bubble of air in the car that would prolong the possibility of survival. She smoked and waited. Five minutes, seven, ten. A quarter of an hour. No other car came along; with all that ice on the roads people preferred staying at home to partying, even on carnival day.

Twenty minutes later, Rita dialed 110, reported the accident to the police. She didn't need any playacting. Her whole body shivered with cold.

"Her sister had found the car," some woman whispers. "Just imagine, what the shock must have been! Her own sister!"

Slowly, the small church choir begins a song. Solemnly the sounds rise up into the clear, blue sky, and to her surprise Rita discovers that she is still envious of Marina, for the noble ceremony and for the melodious name carved in stone.

Chris Rippen

Barefoot

CHRIS RIPPEN was born in Haarlem in the Netherlands in 1940. He studied Dutch language and literature at the University of Amsterdam, and currently teaches literature and writing in Amsterdam. He has published a collection of short stories as well as several crime novels, including *Playback,* which won the prestigious Dutch mystery award, the Golden Noose. A former president of the Society of Dutch/Flemish Crime Writers, he is also the chairman of the Dutch/Flemish branch of the IACW. His novels and short stories have also appeared in Germany, Spain, Bulgaria, Japan, and the United States, including the following story, "Barefoot," a classic police procedural that begins with a very unusual discovery, which was translated into English by Emmy Muller. The story appeared in the anthology *Mord und Steinschlag* (the unlikely title *Murder by Rockfall).*

Barefoot

Chris Rippen

They're ready for us," Detective Mook said. Though Dekker was only three steps away, he couldn't hear him. Mook put the mobile phone in his pocket and tapped the chief inspector on the shoulder. "Are you coming?"

Away from the shelter of the Land Rover the wind cut off their breath. The sand, blowing diagonally across the beach in irregular patterns, lashed their faces. Behind them the breakers roared. With their streaming eyes screwed up they stomped up the slope to the bunker. They caught their breath behind the tarp that had been hastily erected by the police technicians.

"Get away from the edge, please," one of the men yelled from the pit. "It isn't properly braced yet." He stepped aside and motioned to his colleague who was taking photographs. "Hold it a second, will you?"

Both policemen leaned forward. The excavated area was about a meter and a half deep, a pit measuring two by three meters at the bottom of a deep trench between the underside of the bunker and the bank on which they were standing. A niche had been dug in the opposite bank. In it lay the remains of a human body. Not much more than a skeleton, brownish, with white spots and scraps of clothing, paler than pale in the bright spotlights erected on the edge of the pit.

Pompeii, Dekker thought. It wasn't just the niche in the sandbank but also the fact that the skeleton was lying on its side that had triggered the association. Overtaken by death in sleep. He pushed the thought from his mind. This was a grave. What's more, he had to remember all its details now because they wouldn't be there later. He looked at the rivulets of sand flowing over the hard edge into the pit, at the layered soil; black lines of peat between ocher and pale white. This was dune land that had almost become beach. The coastline was still moving and there was erosion after every storm, particularly since the pier at IJmuiden had been extended. The bunker behind the pit, half-subsided and filled with sand, had originally been on the second row of dunes and probably about ten meters higher up. That's the way he'd seen them as a boy, near Zandvoort. Most of them had been cleared away. This one remained, an undermined giant from by-gone years, not built to withstand the constant movement of the sand, shifting, flowing, and piling up around and underneath it. That was how the lump on the leeside had got there. It looked like it had risen from the trench at a slant to the wind, the pulling wind uncovering more and more of the concrete foundations. And so the skeleton had been exposed and noticed by that early-morning hiker, coincidence determined by the ele-ments; one day later, a different wind direction and everything would have been different. A body deep underground. One and a half kilometers, as the crow flies, from Hierdum. Of all places. Dekker looked at the small crowd watching them from a distance. Not just hikers, surely. By tonight the entire village would know.

Suddenly, one corner of the tarp loosened and snapped sharply against the guy wires. "Look out!" Mook said. One of the spotlights toppled over the edge of the pit and was left dangling by its cord. A man rushed forward and hoisted the thing back up the bank.

"I'm going to have a look down there," Dekker said. He descended the small ladder into the pit. The calm was a relief. A police technician gave him a suspicious look over his shoulder.

"We're not finished yet."

"It's okay," Dekker said. "Any word from Dr. Schmitt?"

"He's called in the traffic police. If they can pick him up and get him past the rush hour traffic, he'll be here before dark. Otherwise . . ." The pathologist was stuck in traffic at the Velsertunnel. Because of an accident only one tube was available.

"I wouldn't hold my breath, if I were you." Mook had come down as well. "They'll have better things to do."

"And that tent?" Dekker asked.

"On its way. They're just not sure it'll hold in this storm."

"They'd better make sure it does."

Mook was getting irritated. He was chilled to the bone and his head was buzzing with the noise from the storm. "Anyway, things can't stay like this. Can you tell us anything yet?"

"We'd rather wait for the doctor."

Mook looked at him. "You've got eyes in your head, haven't you? Male, female, one year underground, ten years underground, visible damage to the bone structure. Say something."

Dekker gave him a warning glance. "What are these?" he asked. "Is this the way you found it?" He pointed at some boards sticking out of the sand above the body.

The other man nodded. "When we've removed the body we'll have to expose more of this. It looks like a partition. Two of the boards were stuck together. It could just be flotsam."

"We'll be at the Hierdum-Binnen police station," Dekker said, one foot on the ladder. "Call us in case of any new developments. Mook, you coming?"

"A German nurse, thirty-six years old, in a borrowed bikini and with a taste for marinated herring," the police technician said to Mook. "Mister detective. Go catch some crooks, that's your job. Get out of my pit."

Mook gave a scornful laugh. "You sound like a German tourist yourself. 'Get out of my pit!' "

"You just couldn't resist, could you?" Dekker yelled as they walked back to the SUV. "You'll never make it to chief inspector that way. I think he was right about one thing, though. It is a woman." He saw by the look on Mook's face that he hadn't heard half of his words.

It had to be Hierdum, Dekker thought. I'll never see the end of it. He greeted the sergeant on duty and walked to the back of the station. He could still draw a diagram, even of the room, from memory. Apparently there was only one.

"Hierdum," he said to Detective Mook after they'd sat down. "How much do you know about it?"

"The Trijnie Visser case," Mook said, thinking, as he rolled a cigarette. Mook was one of the few people in the force who still smoked. Another habit that might be in the way of his promotion, Dekker thought. But in all other ways he was highly competent. "Nineteen . . . ninety-five? Or a year later. Seventeen-year-old high-school girl doesn't come home after a night out at the village disco. Body found two days later in the dunes between Hierdum and Limmen, fifty meters from the road between the disco and the village, partially hidden under sand and shrubs. She was raped and then strangled. Perp never found. You were on the investigating team."

Dekker nodded. "Of course, there's no reason yet to assume that this new case is linked to the Visser case, or even whether this is a case at all. Still, the district commander immediately sent for me. You never know. Hierdum is still 'hot,' to coin a phrase."

Hierdum had made the national press for weeks. Smoldering irritation about the presence of an asylum seekers center just outside the village had fueled a vicious rumor campaign and a biased article in the local rag just after the disappearance of Trijnie Visser, followed by a witch hunt after the discovery of the body, led by worried parents and supported by right-wing nationalist sympathizers. Things had culminated into two meetings that had gotten so far out of hand that they'd made the national television news. After two years of investigation, three arrests and as many releases, and a few thousand voluntary DNA tests that yielded nothing, the team had been disbanded. Some of its key members, Dekker among them, had been on standby ever since.

Public opinion in Hierdum was still split. A small, hard-core minority still believed that the perpetrator was among the former inhabitants of the asylum seekers center, which had meanwhile been closed down. They saw its closing, three years ago, as proof that they were right. In direct opposition to them, just as irreconcilable, was a group that had taken sides with the foreigners from the start. They had taken the outcome of the investigations as confirmation of their belief. The large, fairly silent, and mainly orthodox majority between these two extremes wavered. The rift had paralyzed local politics ever since. At the time when the file had been temporarily closed, the investigation team believed that the culprit was more likely to be one of the villagers, maybe even one of the victim's acquaintances, than an outsider. However, there was no real evidence to support this. No one had believed three years ago that the asylum seekers center was being closed because of structural and technical reasons, as the government had stated. Dekker had driven past it later. It didn't look totally implausible.

"So, if this turns out to be a case, you have been warned," he told the detective.

"Hierdum is not just any village. On the other hand, you shouldn't let that influence you."

At 5:15 they got their first call from Dr. Schmitt. The remains were those of a non-Caucasian female in her early twenties. Further details would follow after he had examined the body in his lab. The body had probably been buried in the sand for two to three years. There was no visible damage to the skeleton. "One sad detail was that she was pregnant," said the pathologist.

"Can you tell me anything about the cause of death?" Dekker asked.

"Not yet. I may never be able to. Judging from the position of the body, the place where she was found, and the conditions, we can assume that the woman was lying quietly on her side when she was buried under the sand or the sand landed on top of her. She could have been either dead or alive at the time."

"Non-Caucasian?" Dekker asked. "What do you mean by non-Caucasian?"

"I'll have to investigate that further, too. Judging from the minute traces we found, we concluded that she had dark brown skin and slightly frizzy hair, which justifies the supposition that she is not of Asian descent."

The police technician only said his report would be on Dekker's desk no later than tomorrow morning. From the way the man sounded, Dekker could tell it was still cold on the beach.

Mook looked at the chief inspector. "Trijnie Visser was Caucasian, I take it?"

"Caucasian and blond," Dekker said. "But at this stage that difference doesn't tell me anything."

"You and your German tourist," Dekker said next morning.

"That wasn't me," Mook answered.

The investigation had shown that the woman had been naked. The fragments of textile next to and on the body were from a thin, pink cotton beach towel measuring 70 by 160 centimeters. The sand had also yielded a flip-flop but it didn't match the length of her feet. No other possessions had been found. Remarkably, during the excavation some sort of under-ground hut had been exposed—two sides of one, in any case—made of a variety of different types of rough boards. The loose boards they'd found lying around must have been from its collapsed roof. The bunker had served as a back wall; as they dug, the police had found an opening in the concrete that could have served as an entrance to the hut. A small hut. More like a lean-to. At no point longer than one and a half meters, nowhere wider than half that, and no more than half a meter high—but that was just the side boarding. The pit might have been deeper. The woman's body lay more or less diagonally, with the knees pulled up.

"The kind of hut boys build," Mook said. "Dig a hole, brace the sides, and when it's finished you cover the top. I used to do that, too."

"Sand on the roof?"

"If possible. Grass sods first or, if you didn't have any, a piece of plastic. Then cover it with earth or sand—that made it real. Make it invis-ible. That way, it became sort of a den. Entrances on two sides. One through the bunker and another on the beach side with stairs dug out in the sand. That's why there were only a few short boards at the front."

"How deep is the layer of sand on the roof?"

"Not too deep, about twenty centimeters, something like that. Thirty, tops, otherwise the boards wouldn't hold."

"Any idea what the woman was doing in there?"

"Could be anything. Sheltering from the rain, or the sun—it's hot as hell here on sunny days—and then falling asleep. But I think it's strange that she only had a towel with her. If she were a tourist and wanted to sunbathe in the nude, unseen and sheltered, you'd expect her to have kept her other belongings with her. Bathing suit, clothes, tanning oil, stuff like that."

Dekker nodded. That was why he had ordered the excavation to con-tinue in stages, enlarging the area by half a meter each time, to see if there was anything else buried in the sand.

"The woman herself," he continued. "About one-point-six-five me-ters tall, relatively long legs with a powerful foot bone structure. A slight deviation of the left hip joint, possibly caused by strain. Schmitt thought she might have been a sportswoman, an athlete, originating from the An-tilles or Central Africa maybe. He still owes me an explanation on that point, by the way. And approximately five months pregnant." His mouth pursed for a moment, Mook saw, as though he'd tasted something bitter.

"Anything else?" he asked. Dekker shook his head.

"Okay," Mook said. "So the hut collapses, she can't free herself and dies. And in spite of the popularity of this part of the beach in the summer, nobody notices anything, not even in the weeks after."

"I think you're wrong on one point, though. She was lying on her side. According to Schmitt, nothing in the position of the skeleton indicates there was any attempt to free herself. She was lying on her side as though she were asleep."

"As though she were already dead?"

"Could be."

"Has a colored athlete who also happened to be pregnant been missing for the last few years?"

"They're checking on that now," Dekker said. "And now let's talk about what we have so conveniently ignored so far. There are only two and a half kilometers of nature reserve between the hut and the A.C.H., the Asylum Seekers Center Hierdum."

"A.C.H. Terrible name, that," Mook said. "Spells trouble, if you ask me."

Did his boss have a gift for prophecy or was it that obvious? Mook wondered. Toward evening, below the entrance to the bunker, the excavators found a faded red T-shirt with the A.C.H. logo over the left breast. There was an *S* on the label in the collar. Dekker recalled from the former investigation that each newcomer to the center had been given such a T-shirt as a welcome gift.

"Her size," Mook said. "The information matches what we already know of her. What are the chances of it being her shirt?"

Dekker left the question unanswered. He'd been wondering all day whether to put an appeal with a description on the cable news. Half an hour ago he had finally decided to go ahead, and since then the switchboard had taken six calls, four of which were anonymous and not fit to be repeated. Things were still unsettled in Hierdum. The information from the other two calls was too vague to be of any use.

That night they went home feeling as though everything was slipping through their fingers, like sand. They didn't know anything, not even whether they had a case or not.

The following morning Dekker showed his colleague the former A.C.H. A desolate apartment building on top of one of the overgrown old dunes outside the village. Built just before the recession by a holiday resort builder while the planning authorities were looking the other way. After its inevitable bankruptcy it had fallen into the hands of a property developer who had bitten off more than he could chew and couldn't sell it. After a while, the state had rented it and used it as an asylum seekers center, and now, after four years of disuse it was not much more than a shell. "A building fit for nothing," Dekker said on the way back. "Architects who ruin the landscape with objects like that should be hanged. Tearing it down is the only answer for it now but the owner is still asking too much for it."

Mook shook his head. "Being a refugee already and then ending up here must have felt like jumping from the frying pan into the fire."

Then the car phone rang. They had a name. Dekker asked for the address of the person who phoned it in and they drove straight over.

Of course, she couldn't be sure, Hilde Damstra of the interchurch aid committee said, but the description roughly matched that of a woman she'd met a couple of times at their meetings, who had suddenly disappeared. It had happened the year before the center closed. In the living room area of her white bungalow in one of Hierdum's new housing estates, Hilde Damstra showed them the photo she'd gone to find after she'd read the appeal, as the coffeemaker spluttered.

"We'd gone on a day outing in a minibus. A trip to the IJsselmeer, if I remember correctly. I think this is April Gessesse. Her real first name was so difficult to pronounce that she came up with this herself. It's pronounced the English way. She was from Ethiopia."

The photo had been taken from too far away. Four women lined up in front of a souvenir shop. On the left, a lady who was clearly a committee member; beside her, smaller, darker, a little shy, her crew. "April is the one all the way on the right," Hilde Damstra said.

"Can we borrow this?" Dekker asked. Of course, they could. As he drank his coffee, Dekker looked at the woman in the photograph. She was the tallest of the three. A narrow, dark face with a high forehead and delicate features. A classical face. She was the only one of the refugees not smiling. "Is there anything you remember about her?" he asked.

Hilde Damstra put her cup down. She was nice, Dekker thought, a pleasant lady, brave enough to care about refugees even after the riots during the Visser case. "I've been thinking about that," she said. "I don't remember if she was married or not, or if she had a family, although she may have been a little young for that. But I do seem to remember she was a runner. And may I ask you something? How did she die?"

"Bingo!" Mook said as they were driving back, but Dekker thought that a bit premature. With the aid of the police computer and the naturalization authorities, they'd tracked down four Gessesses: two of whom had stayed at the Hierdum center for a while, but it became clear that April had been an adopted name that hadn't been registered anywhere. They compared the data. Woizero Gessesse, born 1969, living in the Netherlands since 1993, residing in Hierdum from 1993 until 1996, student. Registered as an economic refugee, residents permit not granted, married to a Swiss in 1996 and living in Basel since then. The other one, Alemenesh Gessesse, born in 1975, reported to immigration in 1995, stayed at the Hierdum A.C. as an economic refugee until the fall of 1997, was refused a permit and sent back to her country in October of that year.

They agreed that Alemenesh's data came closest to resembling those of the woman found in the sand, and who, according to Hilde Damstra, had adopted the name April and was a runner. It could have been so easy. But if Alemenesh had been put on a plane to Ethiopia in October 1997, it didn't make any sense.

"I had several dealings with the A.C.H. administrator during the Visser case," Dekker said. "Dries Kleinhout. I'll give him a ring. He's a nice man, very well informed, too."

But Kleinhout had moved and his name wasn't on file with the immigration and naturalization authorities. They found the address of Kleinhout's former boss, the ex-director of the A.C.H., though. He currently held some middle-management position in the justice department. "He was not very nice at all," Dekker said. "On the contrary, he was a real bastard." But he phoned him anyway and got a hold of him after dealing with umpteen underlings first. Miracle of miracles, he remembered who Dekker was and he even knew Kleinhout's current location. "He's the director of social services in the West Veluwe region. I only know because I met him at a reception recently. I even have his card here somewhere. Is this about the Visser girl homicide?"

"Well, that wasn't too bad," Dekker said as he put the phone down. "He was actually nice."

"There you go," Mook said. "There's hope yet, even for bastards. By the way, I noticed you didn't mention that you were calling about a body ID."

"You don't want to give people too much information," Dekker said.

He got through to Kleinhout at once. The exchange was businesslike but friendly. Even without looking at the paperwork the former administrator could remember how individual procedures had been dealt with. "If I remember correctly, there were two residents called Gessesse. Both came from Ethiopia, but they were not related. Which one are we talking about?"

"The athlete," Dekker said. He didn't quite know why.

"I didn't know them that well," Kleinhout said. "Is that the one who married a foreigner, I mean a European foreigner?"

"The other one."

"That is . . . I remember she called herself April, but her real name was . . . also started with an A . . . Alemenesh. That one?"

"Amazing!" Dekker said.

"Alemenesh Gessesse had reached the end of the procedural track in the summer of . . . hang on a minute . . . 1997 and was sent back home in October of that year."

"You could join the circus with that memory of yours," Dekker said. "Fantastic."

"My current job is kind of a circus. Are you prepared to tell me why you want this information?"

Dekker and Mook exchanged a glance. Mook nodded. "We're investigating the death of a woman, but now we're fairly certain we're looking in the wrong direction."

"Unless she came back," Kleinhout said. "That used to happen sometimes. Often on the next flight. But, to set your minds at rest, those were exceptional cases."

So the dead woman in the sand definitely wasn't April Gessesse. Unless what Kleinhout suggested at the end of their discussion had happened, but that was very unlikely. Why would she return to the village she had been removed from as a hopeless case and where people knew her? She'd more likely seek out the anonymity of a city like Amsterdam.

"There's one thing I don't understand," Mook said during lunch. "Why didn't the lady from the aid committee know April had been deported?"

When they got back to the police station, a man was waiting for them outside their office. He wanted to speak with Chief Inspector Dekker, he said. Dekker recognized the mixture of authority and measured respect in the man's voice from his time in the army. The man introduced himself as Gerard Berghuis.

"It's about the appeal you made," he said. "I've been away for a few days and just found an E-mail from Mrs. Damstra."

"Mrs. Damstra," Dekker said. "We were there this morning. Why would she send you an E-mail?"

"I was a volunteer sports teacher at the A.C.H. for a few years. I used to be a sports instructor with the army."

"Please, take a seat," Dekker said.

Berghuis remained standing. He was old school, Dekker noticed. A short, stocky man of about sixty with a weathered face and a supple efficiency in his movements. "I heard it's about April Gessesse?"

"Probably," Dekker said. "Did you know her?"

Berhuis's light eyes regarded him. "I would first like to know why you're looking for her."

Dekker nodded as if he found this a reasonable request. He'd come across this kind of solidarity before.

"It concerns an identification. We've found a body on the beach and are investigating possible causes of death."

"On the beach," Berghuis repeated. His eyes narrowed. Then he said: "I was her coach." He sat down as though the memory forced him to.

Sort of, he immediately added, nothing official. April had been at the center for six months when they'd met. He'd seen her running along the shoreline, a dark woman barefoot, wearing a T-shirt with the center's logo, who had moved with the natural grace of a born athlete. He'd waited for her the next day at the entrance to the A.C.H. grounds.

She'd told him she ran from the slope at Hierdum to the dike at Petten every day. Over thirty kilometers, sometimes even farther. Always across the beach, always barefoot. She'd been used to doing that at home. Home was a desertlike plateau in Ethiopia, where she'd run from home to school and back. Just as her idol Abebe Bikila, winner of the Olympic marathon and a national hero in her country had done. She'd come to Europe to get the training she couldn't get at home and, once she was good enough, she wanted to compete professionally in the marathon circuit.

"I didn't realize until later that her story didn't add up," Berghuis said. "If she'd been talented enough, she wouldn't have had to come to our country as a refugee. She could have run and won competitions in Ethiopia and drawn international attention to herself that way. A lot of Central African athletes do."

When April discovered he knew about athletics she'd latched on to him. He'd given her advice on running techniques and experimented with training schedules. He had had great difficulty in getting her to shorten her daily training program a little because she was convinced that more was always better. He'd also taught her the importance of interval training and rest. They'd communicated in a mixture of English and Dutch, augmented with sign language.

She'd fascinated him. Her drive, her willpower, and her beauty. "The haughty, closed face that would light up for you on rare occasions. Once she trusted you, her devotion was almost endearing."

After a few months he'd noticed that, despite specific training, she hadn't improved. When she'd run a race, usually middle-distance cross-country races, her movements would become labored toward the end. She rarely won. One day he'd noticed she was limping after her daily training. In spite of her objections he'd had a friend of his, a sports doctor, examine her. She turned out to have a hip deviation that was causing her pain when she got tired.

In all likelihood she'd had it from childhood. She'd ignored it because she'd had a dream. Which was partly why the dream remained out of reach.

"I felt very sorry for her, but that didn't help. After the examination she'd retreated into herself. She still ran every day but she didn't need me for that anymore. Sometimes I'd give her an invitation to race, if it wasn't too hard, and sometimes she'd even take it." He'd seen less and less of her. He'd also suspected she'd gotten into a relationship with someone at the center, one more reason to keep his distance. He knew her request for asylum had been rejected and that the appeal would not stand a chance. Unless, of course, she married to gain Dutch nationality. When she'd refused an invitation to compete in a beach race, which had taken him a lot of effort to get, he decided to break the connection. He hadn't seen her since.

Dekker and Mook exchanged a glance. "I am grateful for your detailed statement," Dekker said. "I would just like to go over the dates again. When was the last time you saw April Gessesse?"

Berghuis thought for a moment. "A week before the beach race. That would have been . . . the third or fourth of November 1997."

"Are you sure?"

"Yes."

"We know she was deported in October of that year."

Berghuis sat up. "Then you should check your information again. The St. Maarten race from Noordwijk to IJmuiden is run annually on or around November eleventh. The results are posted on the sports page of every paper the following day. One week before that April refused to enter."

"Where was that, at the A.C.H.?"

Berghuis gave them a wry smile. "No, appropriately enough, we met on the beach. She hadn't been training this time, she was wearing street clothes." His smile disappeared. "She even tried to pretend she didn't see me."

Early that evening Mook and Dekker drove to Woudenberg. Mrs. Kleinhout had told them her husband always got home around six, in time for dinner. Around seven-thirty would be fine.

"I'd like a job like that," Mook said, after Dekker had put the phone down. He'd wondered out loud whether this new piece of information was worth driving all that way for. October or November, it didn't make that much difference, did it?

Kleinhout lived in a prewar semidetached house with a cedar tree in the front garden. After they'd pushed the bell they saw the lights go on behind the little stained-glass windows and they heard someone call: "I'll get it."

The door swung open. "Gentlemen," former A.C.H.-administrator Dries Kleinhout said. "Do come in." He shut the door and looked at them. Then he went ashen and started to cry silently.

They'd had an affair starting in the winter of 1996. Kleinhout said he had fallen for the distant black woman who had pleaded her case at his office almost on a weekly basis. He was honest enough to say that he'd made the first move. He'd known he was taking advantage of his position and hers, had warned her that he would not be able to do anything about her status, and had then been swept up by what he called a fatal infatuation. He'd had no idea what her feelings were. Calculation, passion, love—all possible but also possibly not. After all those months she was still a mystery to him. Only when he'd tried to detach himself from her did one thing become clear: She was not going to let go of him.

He'd thought and hoped that her imminent deportation would solve the problem for him. In the week in which she was to be put on the plane, he and his wife had gone to Crete. When he'd returned to the office, the military police informed him that April had disappeared from the center before they could pick her up. Two days later, as he was driving away from the parking lot in the evening, she'd slid into the seat beside him. That night she'd told him she was pregnant.

Two nightmarish weeks followed. During the day she'd stayed in the bunker, sleeping in the hut she'd discovered a long time ago, under blankets she'd brought with her. She'd dug until the hut was a cave and she had reinforced its walls. She refused to move into the boardinghouse he'd offered to pay for. She'd been through worse and had slept in stranger places. She'd used caves and caverns to hide in all her life. He'd brought her food every day, leaving his car on the road to the beach and plowing through the dunes to the hut, because he'd draw too much attention to himself if he went across the beach. He'd once taken an afternoon off to talk to her, and had gotten nowhere. He'd visited her on the weekend. His life had turned into a total mess. It had been bizarre, frightening, and what had scared him most had been the change in her attitude toward him. He was her man now.

He'd considered turning her in, he'd considered turning himself in, but the possible consequences had been too much for him to even contemplate. By the end of the second week he was at his wit's end. There had been a two-day storm, the walls of the cave were soaked and the wind was howling through the bunker. April had been feverish and vomited bile. He'd gotten her things together and told her he was going to take her to the hospital. She'd refused, furious. They'd even fought. Then he'd given in.

The following day he'd dissolved a triple dose of sleeping pills in the broth he'd warmed up for her. When she was completely sedated, he'd put all her belongings into the bags he'd brought. He'd walked to the car and back twice. The last time he walked back from the car, he'd taken a shovel. He'd undressed her, wrapped her in her beach towel, and put her on her side. Then he'd taken the lamp outside, kicked in the roof and shoveled sand into and around the hut until only a lump showed, a small dune. The wind had done the rest.

Dekker told Berghuis the story as they were walking across the beach to the place where the woman had been found. He thought the other man had a right to know. They searched for a while but there was nothing left to see. The police technicians had leveled everything. The photos in Dekker's office were enough.

"Maybe someday," Berghuis said, "you'll ring somebody's doorbell about the murder of that other girl and the same thing will happen."

"Maybe," Dekker said.

As they walked back across the beach it was near tide. Gulls hung in the air over the tidal pools. The damp sand was hard and solid under their feet. Berghuis gestured. A small gesture that included the entire expanse of beach. "She always ran at low tide. The sand under her feet would feel just like it had on the plateau where she was born. If you run fast, you're flying, she'd say. Sand gives you wings."

Carole Nelson Douglas

Those Are Pearls That Were His Eyes

The miltigenre, multitalented CAROLE NELSON DOUGLAS has won a variety of awards for her newspaper reporting and her science fiction, fantasy, romance, and mystery books. She set the bar high for herself in 1990 with *Good Night, Mr. Holmes*—a novel-length adventure featuring Irene Adler, the only woman to ever outsmart Sherlock Holmes—and has never looked back. She is also the author of more than ten books detailing the adventures of Midnight Louie, a black tomcat who lets his human, Temple Barr, provide for him while he solves a variety of crimes in Las Vegas. She works in a style and voice all her own. Her story selected for this year's volume, "Those Are Pearls That Were His Eyes," published in *Much Ado About Murder,* draws on her experience in collegiate theater, and imparts a deadly twist to more than one of Shakespeare's plays.

Those Are Pearls That Were His Eyes

Carole Nelson Douglas

Prologue

Humility is only doubt,
And does the sun and moon blot out,
Rooting over with thorns and stems
The buried soul and all its gems.
This life's dim windows of the soul
Distorts the Heavens from pole to pole,
And leads you to believe a lie
When you see with, not thro', the eye.
—William Blake

"What's past is prologue."
—Antonio

Dramatis Personae

Prospero, right Duke of Milan
Miranda, daughter to Prospero
Ariel, an airy spirit
Caliban, a savage and deformed slave

Antonio, usurping Duke of Milan, brother to
Prospero
Ferdinand, son to the King of Naples
Gonzalo, an honest old counselor
Balthasar, a doctor of law from Rome

ACT I

"The wills above be done, but I would fain die a dry death."
—Gonzalo

Scene I. *On an island. Enter a* MONSTER.

The sea's soft fists beat upon the beach, its salty lips kiss the cool sand senseless. He hears murmur after murmur, a tide of whispers from the mermaids in Poseidon's deepest, watery dungeons.

You are alone, the mermaid voices hiss like sea snakes. *You are alone.*

He huddles in his cave, knowing naught else to do. *The island is my own again,* he answers the mocking voices. Perhaps it is not he they mock. Perhaps they do not mock, but he has never known anything but mockery and in some ways the taunting chorus brings sweet familiarity.

The island is his own again. His alone.

He tallies his solitary kingdom. Every blade of grass and upright sword of reed, each drop of dew, each thorn upon each briar and bramble. Each blast of wind and knife-flung dirk of rain. All that is called human has left. He had crouched among the lacerating froth of mermaid tongues to watch the ships's white-sailed masts joust with the clouds of heaven. The fleet had rocked upon the frothy breast of mother ocean until it vanished into her lapping, salt-laced sleeves.

He heard them speak before they left, those strangers, though they little marked him. Once shipwrecked, they now sail on fresh ships, bound to climes called Algiers, Milan, and Naples, fair-sounding names for unseen places.

He is bound to this unnamed island, cursing a god of whom he knows only his name, Setebos, remembering a long-dead mother he knows only from the old man's curses. She had named him Caliban and then died. The old man who came after had called her as many foul names as he called the son she left behind. The blue-eyed hag Sycorax, the old man had named her.

Caliban cannot say how old or hag-ridden his mother was, what color her eyes. Her memory was soon supplanted by the old man, Prospero . . . and by one other creature, the only fair thing he ever saw upon this island, the maiden Miranda. She the old man will wed to a prince, the son of his once-mortal enemy, the King of Naples.

They are all gone, enemies to each other no longer. And no longer will he, the one left behind, be called Caliban the slave, the monster. No more shall he be pinched blacker than pitch and given groaning cramps by the vexed and invisible spirits Prospero called to berate him. Nor shall he carry bruising burdens of wood and huddle apart in his foul cave, nor be called villain and misshapen knave and poisonous filth.

The island is his own again.

When the rain comes, drowning out the mermaid taunts, he ventures into its stinging curtains. He trudges the island's length and width as if to measure with his naked feet the rich cloths worn by the men of Milan and Naples. The old man saw that even when these, his bitter mortal enemies, were shipwrecked on this shore, not so much as their garments were salt-wracked and ruined. No harm to those who harmed him, but to Caliban who has harmed no one, all incivility.

Still, he howled when they left. So in the rain he runs to the island's every selvage edge. This lone rugged rock is his kingdom, as it was his mother's, and he howls at wind and water, who howl back like brothers.

He is not quite alone. The mischievous spirits his mother imprisoned in twisted pine trees around this island home scream their solitary agony in chorus as he passes their binding places. They do not sing as sweet as mermaids, but like wild pigs. Sometimes he joins them, as if they were all dogs of the same unlucky litter. At other times he laughs and curses them as Prospero cursed Caliban. Sometimes he is silent. And at other times he thinks that the ceaseless howls of trapped spirits will drive him mad.

The island is his own again. Yet the powers his hated mother had in full measure remain to him only as weak memories. When the storm has passed, he will huddle in his cave, whipped by wind and wave into a shivering cur, hiding from the unholy wails of helpless spirits.

Sun and moon are his only visitors.

He taught Caliban them, the old man. He had a long beard and hair that flowed like the white froth at the waves' rabid mouths. His eyes were the cold churning green of a wall of water tall enough to oversweep the isle entire. He told Caliban of the bigger light and the smaller light that come and go in dark and brightness above. At first he taught Caliban kind words. Sun. Moon. And at length he taught Caliban that he was a monster.

Caliban will still build the fire, which the old man taught him, though he eats only roots and sere fruits. There is nothing living on this island save him. Save Caliban.

And the whispering mermaids and the howling spirits trapped for eternity. Like Caliban.

Scene II. *Outside* CALIBAN's *cave.*

Enter ARIEL, *invisible, singing.*

> *"Ah, brothers, sisters, on this strand*
> *Take heed, take heart and then take hand,*
> *This free and ever dancing sprite*
> *will deliver thee from spite.*
> *So touch the earth and spring to air*
> *I banish foul and make all fair."*

ARIEL *darts into the cave.*

Caliban flees his only shelter, wincing beneath invisible blows. What madness is this? What dream, what nightmare? He is at last alone, yet the same pestilence that had beset him under the reign of Prospero bedevils him still.

"Away! I have done with invisible things, save the wind."

A spiteful funnel of dust shimmers in the salt air until a narrow, wild face surmounts it.

"You are not done with me, foul fiend!"

"Ariel, blasted spirit! You were freed. I saw the old man unleash you. You were free to serve the wind alone, and your own will."

"I have become the wind, and grew used to buffeting such foolish beasts as you hither and yon. Get thee to a woodpile, slave, or I shall pinch thee blacker than thy villainous heart!"

"Strike me not! You need obey no one now."

"None but my own willful nature. If you wish me gone, you will tell me how to free my brethren in the trees."

"Did not the old man tell you that I had no powers? Why else would I suffer his insults and blows, and yours?"

"You know the ways of your foul dam, the witch Sycorax, driven from Algiers to exile on this island, with sprites all her unwilling servants, until she treed us in fury at our disobedience. You told Prospero enough spells that he released me for his body servant."

"Softly, ungentle Ariel, who pinches and spits and tricks at another's command. You would not serve my mother, but you served the ill-usage of that old man. Even Prospero spoke to me softly at first and taught me words and warmth of the fire, all the better to charm the secrets of my dead mother's spells from me. Have you learned nothing from your former master but his cruelty?"

Have you learned even less, to think that you dare disobey a higher spirit? Away! To the trees that weep bitter sap. I will have my kin unleashed."

Scene III. CALIBAN *alone.*

He sits by the trees who wail with only the wind for company now. He has come to a sore state. He misses his old enemy and all his kind and even Prospero's cruel disembodied servants, even the eternal howls of the imprisoned sprites. But he was not completely cowed by the airy tormenter. This pine conceals one last bound sprite. He swallows, then croaks out a song that mimics Ariel's spell.

> *"Come to my bidding as I sing*
> *You shall fly to ev'ry unkempt thing,*
> *You shall do a task at my command*
> *When I call you forth with clutching hand."*

His gesture is crude, a fist not a flourish, but the tree splits as if peeled by lightning. From its raw, pale fissure swirls another disorder of air. A wicked face appears in the sulphurous mist.

Sprite, you must obey my command 'ere you fly free."

"Woe that I must heed a witch's hellish spawn!"

Before you take to air and cloud, you will follow foul Ariel's example. Blow me a tempest, Sprite, that will drive near shore a ship to take me far from here. No tricks. No shipwreck, no dead school of sailors stranded on my island's frothy petticoats. I will have an argosy to waft me to such shores as Naples."

Whirling into a blur like a water spout, the sprite vanishes into the kettle of thunder and lightning cooking above.

Caliban looks to the darkling sky. He can see no large light and no little light, no sun and no moon. The coming storm smells of human fear. This island soon will be as dead to him as is his mother and even now-distant Prospero. He offers a vow to the lightless heavens:

"I have been a monster and a slave." His knotted fist shakes as if it brandishes a weapon, but it is empty and any weapon is invisible. "Now I will try my hand at aping a man."

ACT II

"Let me live here ever; So rare a wondered father and a wife
Makes this place Paradise."
—Ferdinand

Scene I. *A market in Milan.*

Enter MIRANDA *and* FERDINAND.

Among the bustling citizens of Milan flourishing jeweled lengths of burnished silk and bright vessels of Venetian glass, the young couple strolls as if lost in a garden by themselves.

He wears velvet tunic and silken shirt. Her gown of sky-blue silk is full and plain, as if borrowed. Simplicity frames her features, both serene and struck with wonder, as richly as gold-leafed haloes embellish some Tuscan friar's latest fresco.

"What sights and sounds of joyous souls are these, Ferdinand?" she asks in fine Italian, but with an accent strangely innocent of the intonations of the region. "I blink in wonder to see a land thronged with people instead of my father's spirits and my fraught imagination. My island home now seems no larger than a wedding band."

He takes her hand, bare of any decoration. "An apt comparison, my sea-borne bride-to-be, for soon such a loving ring shall circle thy finger. But look about. Thy father bade you on the island to be sure I was the fairest man you did ever look upon, yet you had never seen none but his own venerable brow." He frowns with an unwelcome memory. "And, I trow, the shaggy, lowering head of that brute slave of his. Here you see the young noblemen that populate a dukedom. How stands Ferdinand now?"

"Oh, my love. First sight is best."

She has stopped to gaze into his eyes. Jugglers, pedlars, and the good wives of Milan flow around the island these twain have made of themselves.

He may be the son of the King of Naples, but since he has been shipwrecked on Prospero's island he marvels at seeing only one, while she stands shocked by multitudes.

"What kind of bold seafarer are you," he asks fondly, "to sail across half the salt ocean, and swear you need only Ferdinand for captain and crew?" The question is meant to have but one answer.

" 'Tis true. My sire did well by both of us when he his magic caused your father's fleet to stumble to its knees upon our island shore."

"O, happy accident! I have won a wife, but Prospero has won his dukedom back from his treacherous brother, Antonio. Now they are bosom brothers, or at least act so. It astonishes me that Prospero should forgive where he was so sinned against."

"I can only think he does it for the welfare of his child. His every thought was always of me."

"Prospero is truly a noble man. I almost bless the unjust exile that has brought you safe and unsullied to me. Blush indeed. You are not a bride yet."

"I had no cause to blush upon the island, save in one instance." She glances away to avoid a troublesome memory, then her smooth face lightens with delight. "Look, Ferdinand! What is the hue and cry over there? Is it a dancing bear?"

"We shall see at once. If so, we must engage him. Even the bears will dance at our wedding."

Moving nearer brings the maiden to a halt. "Ah, the poor beast is in a cage."

"I have never sensed a heart tenderer than yours."

"And it is dressed in satin foppery, poor brute, as if to mock its hairy soul."

"If the entertainment distress you, we shall leave."

"Distress me? Only in that I have come to think that another's misery is not entertainment. I have seen such civility in Naples and now in Milan as would shame the island."

"Naples is my father's seat, and he is a king. Civility is first courtier there, but the larger world is seldom such. Fine clothes may disguise the foulest intention."

"I begin to think back upon the island with dismay. Only now do I see my father's sorceries as strange and frightening. Were you not dismayed by them?"

"Your father spoke harshly on our meeting. I was dazed from swallowing half the salt sea. With my kin and party lost in the waves, I did fear his gruffness. Yet I had only to drown in your sweet eyes to grow brave again."

"And I yours. His harshness tested our swift enamorment, I think."

"A man of consummate wisdom."

"Look! Listen. Does the beast sing? What a harsh, rough tongue."

"Full fathom five thy father lies,
Of his bones are coral made;
Those are pearls that were his eyes,
Nothing of him doth fade."

"O, Ferdinand! So pale you grow. What has the beast done?"

"I heard those very syllables when first wandering on your island. I took them for a kind of death knell for my own father. I had feared our entire party drowned but I. Then I heard those dread words. I had forgotten that cruel song."

"And so you shall forget again, that mere ditty sung by that most mischievous spirit, Ariel. My father permitted him too much taunting. He was ever tormenting my father's slave and even myself on occasion. But he is free to mock the winds of the wide world now, and shall not bother us here."

"Then why has his cruel song followed us half a world away?"

"Can Ariel, freed from an island tree, have found another fettered lodging in the body of a beast? I must see for myself. But what fiend is this! Caliban!"

CALIBAN, *singing.*

"Full fathom five thy father lies,
Of his bones are coral made;
Those are pearls that were his eyes,
Nothing of him doth fade.
But doth suffer a sea-change
Into something rich and strange."

"This is not possible," Ferdinand says. "This is the unearthly burden I heard upon the isle, thinking it played the death knell for my drowned father. It was no mortal business then, and is not so now. I feel a chill. Will my father die soon, in Naples?"

"That city is far away, my love. Come with me. I feel the beast's stare. I will not have so fair a day darkened by a brutish scowl and a lying song."

Scene II. PROSPERO's *garden in Milan.*

Enter MIRANDA.

She moves through the garden like Eve through Eden, knowing herself alone, speaking to her only friend, herself.

"How it amazes me, that my father has ended as he begun, ruling a dukedom in this fruitful land amid a garden trained to flower in neat rows and trellises, where the only spirits on the wind are fragrance and unanchored petals like a fairy ship's sails.

"When all I knew was island, I was satisfied with every sight and sound. Now I see our safe anchorage as a harsh and unhappy land. Even my father's temper there was stern as some distant storm. I knew him not then for a deeply wronged man, nor knew his care of me, a toddling child. Yet his magic brought his enemies to his exile place. And some spirit other than Ariel stirred in him when he forgave the brother who had set us loose upon the sea without provision. So now we are returned to solid land and solid souls and cultivated gardens, to rank of place and myself to a bridal bed. I feel a fool among these city-bred folk and wonder if my eyes are opened yet."

Exit CALIBAN, *enter* FERDINAND.

"You grow pale as an April lily, Miranda," Ferdinand says, hastening to her side, an arm around her shoulders. "What ill thoughts turn your temper so cool in this warm and nurturing clime?"

"Memories."

"Memories are what the future will make. I remember nothing before I gazed into your eyes. I wonder if it was an enchantment of thy father's making."

"He harnessed many enchantments to make much happen on the is-land. Perhaps I am but another captive spirit of his powers."

"I did but jest, fairest maid! You require no enchantments but the level gaze of your honest eyes. I have never seen a truer pair. So smile, and let your cheeks warm to the regard of your lover."

"I will, most excellent Ferdinand. As my father forgave his brother Antonio his treachery, so I must forgive the past its mysteries. Perhaps I must even forgive. . . ."

Tumult without. GONZALO *enters, distraught.*

"Woe! Oh, woe. What perfidy is this? Death in the dukedom. Murder has struck. We must clothe ourselves in ashes and midnight stuffs. Dead. Drowned, as he had not drowned upon the island. What wreck of a man is this?"

Miranda seizes Ferdinand's hand, but her eyes cannot leave Gonzalo's woe-racked face.

"My father!" she cries. "He said that he came home only to die. But say not so soon!"

"No, no! Take her hand, good Ferdinand. She has naught so close to home to mourn. Prospero lives. It is Antonio who has been struck and felled, until the blood ran from his head into a ribbon of scarlet fishes in the pond not two minutes walk from here."

Shaking his white-locked head, Gonzalo leaves the pair. Miranda paces away from Ferdinand's loving custody, as if suddenly lost in this most civil garden.

"My heart rejoices and breaks in the space of one beat," she breathes. "How can grief and joy ride tandem in such a narrow alley of emotion?"

"When evil expectation becomes unexpected deliverance of one dear to us, yet at the cost of another, grief becomes guilt. Mourn not," Ferdinand counsels her. "Antonio died a shriven soul. He had confessed his crimes against your father and yourself and had been forgiven. Show me a finer surety of paradise upon this earth! Wait here, and I shall see to the sad event."

Kissing her hand, Ferdinand follows in Gonzalo's footsteps.

Miranda remains unmoving in the tranquil garden, unsoothed by the curried comfort of nature. Her thoughts form soft phrases that fall like strings of broken beads upon the heedless flowers.

"My heart still beats in twain." She approaches a small orange tree and almost seems to address it. As a child she had heard the moaning spirits pent in the island's trees and had regarded them as friendly winds and almost-playmates. This tree solaces her now. "Surely the beast Caliban has done more evil here." She paces away to a soldiering stand of sentry pines. "Yet doubt has entered into my house of memory, and I teeter upon the threshold of my own abode, afraid."

Shaking her head, Miranda strides to the carved marble bench at the center of the bower, and declaims loud words as if making a speech makes her words toll true. " 'Tis clear Caliban will stand for this crime and that I must bear witness to his recent presence in this garden, not many steps away from where Antonio fell dying. It is only fitting that the beast must pay."

Again she walks away from her own brave words, muttering, "Yet if I have learned anything since leaving my father's island, it is that all is not what it seems. Oh, woe indeed! What shall I do?"

Scene III. *A house in* VENICE.

Enter BASSANIO.

" 'A Daniel come to judgment' I seek! 'A Daniel come to judgment.' "

Laughing, the Venetian pauses to watch his wife set aside her fancy work. Her eyes widen as they move from stitches smaller than eyelashes to a well-clad canvas as large as a man, and they warm with new-made marriage.

"Good Bassanio, has my husband become the town crier? What paper bear you?"

"This? A trifle. A summons fresh brought from the dukedom of Milan for the learned Doctor Balthasar. It seems a murderous monster requires an advocate."

"I have done with masquerades and the sickening compromises of the law. When your good friend Antonio stood to lose a pound of flesh and thus his very life to the Jew, Shylock, I did not hesitate to don a doctor's robe and play at manhood for thy friend's sake. But we are wed now, and Venice is in good temper. Why should I venture to Milan to seek more travail? Besides, Nerissa has sworn never to visit court more."

"Still, my Portia, this old Bassanio beseeches aid for a new Antonio, my role this time played by the daughter of the long-lost Prospero, Duke of Milan, one Miranda. It seems the murdered man was her uncle, Antonio, and the monster thus accused, one Caliban, is a servant from an island she and her father were marooned upon for many years."

"The niece of this dead Antonio seeks counsel for the monster that slew him? What kind of monster is it? Or is she?"

"This creature, I understand, is a low beast cast up like Duke Prospero and Miranda upon the deserted isle, rough of skin and feature and speech, the very likeness of a monster within and without, Caliban by name, and by fact Prospero's servant upon the island. I have heard of Milan's lost duke, this Prospero, that he was a learned man."

"A Daniel come to judgment, doubt it not."

"Not so learned as thee, noble Balthasar."

"Flatter me no more, husband. 'Tis you should hie to Milan. And I must go in my doctor of law disguise, to do what, I ask you?"

"Evoke the right and wrong of it and preserve some ignorant savage from death if he is innocent."

"I will go, noble Bassanio, but not because I believe the golden shower of praise that slips from thy lips. So ducats escaped Shylock's grasp when his daughter took his treasure and hied off to wed a Christian and the Jew argued himself into losing even more. Willful, stubborn man! I tried every persuasion to urge mercy for his claim upon Antonio. He had been ill used in his own turn, and argued well himself: 'Hath not a Jew eyes, If you do cut us, do we not bleed?' and so on. And if you bleed then, Jew, answer this: should you bleed another?

"Yet my own arguments for mercy, my every plea, pelted ears of stone. In the end the court stripped him of all his wealth. I can still hear his plaint for his lost treasures, one soft posterity, one hard currency. 'My daughter and my ducats.' Now we have another daughter and the dark deed of murder. Will ducats weigh in the balance here as well?"

"Ducats, no doubt, always weigh in a court of law."

"But gold has no way with you. You stand here with me, husband, because your eyes were blind to the glitter of the chest of gold and the chest of silver. Where nobler suitors chased false gleams, you chose the casket of lead, wherein the real treasure lay, and thus gained my hand. My wealthier suitors chose the surface glister and went home poorer. The truth most often lies inside the leaden casket, Bassanio, and is always the heaviest of any burden. I think that truth is crueler than ever mercy was kind."

"Then if you venture into bearing such burdens again, fair Portia, I will accompany you as the learned Doctor Balthasar's humble clerk, and hope that Nerissa will pardon my usurping her role."

"No woman of sense would settle for a maid when she may have a man to wait upon her pleasure. 'Tis done. We are off to Milan, which is not so long a journey. I am most eager to meet this monster from a world of water far away."

ACT III

"And thence retire me to my Milan, where every third thought
shall be my grave."
—Prospero

Scene I. MILAN: *a court of justice.*

Enter PROSPERO, GONZALO, MIRANDA, *and* FERDINAND.

Prospero moves slowly under the weight of brocaded velvet robes, restored
in raiment to the nobility of his office and his heritage.

"I would I were not here, my friends and daughter. Murder is foul
enough a deed in its own person. To meet the beast that did it and know
him for the monster that he always was only further affronts my breast."

Gonzalo, accompanying the Duke, attempts to reconcile him to the
coming judgment. "Cruel it is to lose a land and a brother, then reclaim
both, only to lose the one again so soon."

Miranda gazes upon the ornate chair that her father will soon occupy
as judge. It is a thing of gilded elegance unseen upon the island.

"It is not certain that Caliban did the deed," she says.

Prospero assumes his seat. "O, my daughter, too long have you lived
on seaweed and bright air, on Ariel's songs and caperings. You saw every
day the scabrous underbelly of our island home, that stinking clod of animal
earth that threatened to cloud o'er all our joy. Can you doubt his guilt,
who was born thus?"

"I cannot doubt that he was born, and born upon the island we came
to as castaways. He was not wrong in claiming the island first. No matter
how we berate him then or now, Caliban was our Eden's only Adam."

"And you are not his Eve! Nothing Christian or fair ever dwelt within
that cankered hide. I have taught thee too well the finer things of life and
breath. You overflow with the honey of mercy, like hive in apple orchard.
Yet you have no sting to defend yourself."

Ferdinand joins hands with Miranda as she stands uncertain before her
father, like one seeking judgment.

"I would not change a jot of her, sir," he says, "and mercy is the
crown jewel of an unsullied mind."

Mind, King's son, that you are wed to your jewel soon. She shows a
sinew of stubbornness that would power a long-bow. Such does not make
for a meek wife."

"As long as she makes for my wife, I will not ask for meekness in the
maid."

Gonzalo comes to clap Ferdinand upon the back and restore peace.
His role has always been thus. "Well spoken, Prince. She much reminds me
of her mother, so soon taken from hence."

"You knew her, sir?" Miranda asks with eagerness. "I have heard so little of the one who bore me. Am I like her?"

"Enough." Prospero speaks gruffly, with the finality of a judge decreeing. "There is naught to say of her. In birthing, Miranda, she gave twin life to you and to her own death, and a ghost of my life perished with her."

"Forgive me, Father. I forget the losses that wreathe your brow: a wife, a land, and now a brother. I cannot allow a daughter to leave you also. Much as my soul leans toward my Ferdinand as the shadow of the sun-dial creeps 'round to tell each hour, following time like a faithful hound, I cannot leave you thus."

"All will be well once this fiend has been laid low for his crime. It is good that I have renounced the practice of my powers, or I would have the winds tear him gristle from sinew without the gentle intervention of a court."

Enter CALIBAN, *in chains, with two guards.*

"O, be thou damned, inexorable dog!" cries the Duke. "Ingrate spawn of an unhappy, unhallowed dam. I gave thee the sweet suckle of human knowledge, but thou art a beast from fangs to cloven feet and have moved from lust to slaughter like the wolf from lamb to shepherd in the winking of an evil eye."

"If I am wolf, then you be bear, old man, who stole sorceries I gave you as freely as air itself gives loft to the pinions of the eagle. And for your thanks you filled my island's ether with the screeching burdens of malicious spirit you called servants; though I was always but your slave."

"Did you not stand accused long ere this? Is not the roster of your savage wrongs longer than a fjord of forgotten Hyperborea? And does it not point as cold an accusing finger? You deny that you did lust after my girl-child?"

"I do!"

"Liar! I saw with my own eyes. And at the very moment of our delivery from the isle, whilst I was newborn in forgiveness of those who worked against me here in Milan, did you not conspire to murder me?"

"Not so! I was innocent of the ills that may hide in a bottle, and made drunk by those noble shipwrecked savages of Milan, the lords of your former land yet not too high to mislead one naked of all knowledge of the world from whence you had been driven by your own brother."

"This will not do," Gonzalo objects. "The beast is to be tried for Antonio's death, not his misdeeds in another place. The past is not meat for today's repast."

"What's past is prologue." Prospero pauses to pronounce his unofficial judgment. "And so shall Caliban pay the debt of past and present evil today."

Scene II. *Enter* PORTIA *and* BASSANIO, *clothed as doctor and clerk.*

"Who are these strangers?" Prospero asks.

"My master is a young doctor of Rome," answers Bassanio, "most esteemed by the learned Bellario, who oft assists in thorny matters of justice. In Venice this young solon overcame the bloodthirsty claim of the Jew Shylock for a pound of flesh from the merchant Antonio."

"I have heard of this case," Gonzalo says, nodding.

"He is young and bare of beard for such powers of judgment," Prospero notes doubtfully, settling into the cushions of his high seat.

"Youth is a disadvantage," Portia concedes, her voice low in tone and modest, "except in cases where it is an advantage."

"You speak like a well-tried doctor of law, at least, in paradoxes, Balthasar. Are you acquainted with the case before this court, the murder of my brother Antonio, previously Duke of Milan?"

"The dead I know, but not much of the living. Since you are judge, m'lord, and this creature Caliban is criminal, and you both are two of three persons to come from the distant island that was your home, your daughter, sir, is the only one left to play the witness. From her I will elicit the founding facts as to the history of this matter."

"There is no history!" Prospero says. "My brother lies but three days dead, struck down in his garden . . . my garden now and previously. That is the only history worth investigating."

"Ah," says Portia, bowing in agreement. "That is true. You and your dead brother have traded roles like actors in a play. First you were Duke of Milan, and then you were not, but were the exiled master of an unnamed island while Antonio duked it here in Milan. Then he became as you, shipwrecked and thrown up upon a foreign shore, a tiny strand where you were master. Master of more than earthly things, I gather. There two brothers came to see each other again as friends, and Antonio freely gave the dukedom back to you, so here he was again your subject. This is a very model of justice, save for Antonio's death."

"That is so."

"And is it not so, noble Prospero, that you used the strange powers you found upon the island to drive your brother's ship to your very feet? That you conjured the wind that united the brothers once riven?"

"Not I. A certain sprite I found upon the island."

"Enough. A judge should not play witness. I will ask the maiden Miranda to stand forward. Ah. I should have said the fair maiden Miranda. My apologies."

"You need not bow to me, learned doctor. I have no knowledge but the things my father taught me during our durance on the island."

"How long this servitude?"

"I was but three years old when we were cast upon the ocean's bosom in a boat with little water, and I mark but seventeen years now."

"Fourteen years upon a deserted island: the blood chills to think a well-born maid must grow in such an untamed place. Yet your father provided every comfort that he could."

"He did indeed, though little comfort was on the island save the presence of each other."

"Then you were alone except for servants?"

"I would not say we had such soft attendants as servants."

"Was not Caliban a servant?"

Miranda glances uneasily from the young doctor of law with his many questions to the figure of Caliban, still clad in gay raiment, but now decorated with chains.

"Perhaps that is a question," says Portia with the smooth command she has now employed in two courts of law, "that the creature Caliban may best answer. Let Caliban come forward."

He shuffles toward Portia, a huge and heavily burdened beast. As he moves forward, Miranda edges away.

"You speak?" Portia asks.

"Speak indeed, and walk upright when I am not laden with ropes of iron or pallets of firewood."

"There is no firewood here."

"There was wood aplenty on the island, and I carried it from one end to the other."

"Then you were a servant."

"I was a slave, for such old Prospero called me often enough that I forgot my given name."

"Hellhound!" the duke roars from his judgment seat. "The names I called thee were too fine by half and half again, though I called thee dog and cur and fiend and slave 'til the sea itself should dry and all its shells lie revealed from here to Gibraltar, like Neptune's treasury of pearls abandoned in the desert."

"So Caliban was your slave," Portia says, turning to Duke Prospero.

"Yes, and be damned to him! Slave was too good a word."

"And was this air spirit you commanded also a slave?"

"Ariel?" The Duke frowns. "My words and their usage are not on trial here. Ariel was a creature of that foul witch Sycorax, this monster's monstrous mother."

"This Sycorax had been in like straits to yourself, sir, and so came to the island under similar force, though sooner than yourself."

"Like to myself, young Balthasar? Thou art mad to draw parallel where there is only deep loathing. There was nothing like between Sycorax and myself, and besides, the witch was dead 'ere I came upon the island."

Portia strolls with deliberation toward the Duke's ornate throne, as though to consult a superior more closely, despite the listening ears all around.

"My lord, perhaps I am not informed as well as I should be. You must forgive my newness to the circumstances, even this cast, so to speak, of castaways."

" 'Tis true, for one small island, the place drew shipwrecked souls to it as if it were a last outlook of lost Atlantis."

"Indeed, my lord. So is it not a strange parallel, then, that the outcast witch Sycorax should be spared death in Algiers because her womb bore an unborn soul? That she was then left upon the island by sailors, long before you and your infant daughter were likewise spared assassination in Milan and given leave to take a boat to where the winds would send you?"

"You tell a tale rather than pose a question, young doctor of law. You will learn better soon. I suppose a stranger like yourself could draw some common line between our fates, that of this cursed Sycorax and her thrice-cursed son Caliban, and that of myself and my innocent daughter. But the circumstances are as opposite as the likeness of my angelic Miranda to this devilish whelp of a fiendish dam, this slave Caliban."

"And so too Ariel served, more slave than servant?"

"Ariel also was a malicious spirit, too headstrong to serve even Sycorax and thus punished with the cell of a tree trunk for eternity. With such harsh creatures only hardness will be heeded."

Portia nods as if well satisfied by this explanation, and returns to face Caliban.

"You claim, sir," she says with ironic dignity, as if the crouching, hairy beast is like unto a man, "that you are the heir and owner of the island, having been born there?"

"I was the only living thing upon that strand once my mother died."

"And did she die soon after your arrival, and hers?"

"I cannot say how long. I grew enough to walk, but she had always seemed weak. That is why she pent the spirits in the trees. She had not the will to control them and they would have played mischief until some unending tempest would have sunk our island."

"So your mother was ill, perhaps from the time of your birth?"

"I cannot say, but it would seem so."

Portia turns to Prospero. "Another strange coincidence, Duke. This creature's mother sickened and died of his birth."

"Not so strange. Look at the monster! If you were a woman, would you not have died of sheer fright from distaste at mothering that?"

Portia does not answer, but looks upon Caliban as Prospero had bade young Balthasar do. "Miranda's mother also died upon her birth, am I not right?" she says mildly. "Two motherless babes marooned upon the same lone island."

"Caliban was the elder, and never a fit object of pity!" Prospero cries, half-rising from his seat. "I tried to tutor the creature, as I did my daughter, using the library of books Gonzalo put as ballast in the leaky boat where our enemies had stored scant food and water. But we reached the island, and the books became our food. I taught that ingrate rascal to speak and then he turned upon the most precious pearl in my possession and sought to dirty it with his ragged claws."

"Is this true, Caliban?" Portia asks.

"I speak because he taught me, yes, but he only taught me so I could take him to the places where my mother penned the sprites and tell him the spells she used to seal and unseal them. Once he had Ariel free to obey his every whim, it was Caliban the slave, the dog."

"Then he was master of the island, and master of you and Ariel?"

"Oh, aye. And when Ariel tired of being his creature, the damned sprite put hedgehogs into my path to spear my feet, and adders to bite me into madness in my bed, and unseen demons to pinch me to a bruise as big as the moon."

"And no creature was kind to you upon the island?"

Caliban frowns and does not answer.

"No matter," Portia says, returning to a table to consult papers as high and thick as a plum pudding. "Kindness is not the issue here."

"At last," Prospero cries, "you come to the charge of murder."

"And so I must question . . . Ferdinand."

The young man starts, and almost drops Miranda's hand from the fond custody of his own. He had expected to be witness, not testifier.

But young Balthasar calls him forward. "You will answer true, all that I ask of you?"

"As true as man may talk."

"You are the son of the King of Naples, once Duke Prospero's bitter enemy, who conspired with the Duke's brother Antonio to exile Prospero and take his home and title?"

"Yes and yes to all. The sad tale is admitted by all, and all is forgiven and restored."

"More than restored, for not only does Prospero resume the Dukedom, but the shock of shipwreck brought Antonio to remorse. And did not Prospero oversee your island courtship of his own fair daughter, Miranda?"

Ferdinand smiles to find his testimony is on a subject so simple and dear to his heart. "He was quite canny in the way he first decried us to one another, yet forcing us closer, until it was clear our hearts had met and were meant to stay together."

"In short, Duke Prospero, then an exiled lord of only empty acres, acted as matchmaker between his daughter and his royal enemy's beloved only son and heir."

"Our love was our own idea."

"So love always claims, but I have reason to know that there is more wit and sense in it than one would believe." Portia takes a slow turn around the court, eyeing every witness.

"Thus comes a happy ending to all but Caliban. The Duke sails home, restored in every respect; the king's son sails home, with a lovely, unspoiled maiden for a bride, whose father has recently been named a duke. The island orphan shall wed a prince. Even Antonio merely retreats to his previous position of second to his brother.

"Only Caliban is left upon the island, with nothing, not even the company of his ancient enemy Ariel."

"O clever lad," cries Prospero. "You show how Caliban lay writhing on the beach, mad from lack of everything. How he conspired to fetch a ship to take him in the wake of those he'd known, there to wreak the ruin upon their lives that he had failed to do upon the island. Cruel envy, jealous wrath, and anger unmatched stirred his monstrous soul. And so he came to Milan and in the garden struck down the first of us to cross his crooked path: my brother Antonio."

The onlookers stir, and make angry mutterings, but Portia does not heed them. She again comes before the chained monster.

"You speak wisely, Duke. There is no bitterness on earth or island as bleak as losing all."

"Then the judgment is plain."

"Judgment is never plain. It is a gemstone of many facets, each of which may blink as bright as the sun, then shrink to a dark cinder of doubt. Soon another facet catches the fickle light of reason. This, we say, must be the fact the truth that shines like the sun upon us. But a cloud comes and our judgment darts behind it as beyond a curtain. What role shall Judgment play when next the curtain draws back to reveal . . . Dame Fortune, plump and shiny as a miser's purse? Or is it Sir Self-Deception, wearing ribboned tights upon his skinny shank and making courtier's bow to Lady Prevarication, whose starched collars quite obscure the expression on her face? I believe she would be smirking to see Judgment tricked up in so many costumes as we do view in court each day."

"Then forget this pointless questioning and declare what all must know to be true: Caliban has killed Antonio in revenge, and in revenge must pay the price with his own debased life."

"No life is debased, my lord, unless we let it be so. Caliban." Portia turns sternly to the prisoner. "You are an unwholesome thing to look upon and I do not doubt that the soul within is as deformed.

"You stand accused 'ere this of conspiring on the island to kill its departing lord, your admitted master, Prospero."

The creature's head bows as if under the weight of unseen chains.

"You do not deny it?"

"Two shipwrecked lords made me drunk, and I became their monster-servant, as they called me. They promised me fair treatment and we conspired together. I meant it not."

"Still, you cannot deny it and there were witnesses. So, Caliban. Even before you came here as a caged beast to amuse the people at market, you had been caged into servitude upon the island and held no love for Prospero."

"No," he mutters.

"Nor had you reason," Portia observes.

Prospero protests. "What excuse is this?"

"No excuse, mere fact, my lord. So, Caliban. You broke free of your cage and came straight to the ducal gardens, is that not truth?"

"Truth," the beast mutters.

"You came to kill Prospero."

The beast is silent.

"You came upon his brother Antonio in the garden, from behind, mistaking him for Prospero, and struck him down."

The beast is silent.

"Or you recognized him for Antonio, and still you struck him down, because he was brother to your enemy. Did not the King of Naples conspire to put Antonio in Prospero's place because he was brother to his enemy? So you unseated Antonio from the role of brother as he had been unseated from the role of Duke."

The beast is silent.

"Why else would you have come here, Caliban, but to kill your betters?"

The beast is silent.

"I call the royal bride," Portia says. "Miranda."

Ferdinand's hand tightens upon hers, as if to keep her by his side.

She does not move.

"I have spoken earlier," she whispers.

"I would have you speak more," Portia says, unswayed.

Miranda approaches, keeping well away from Caliban, looking neither up nor down, to one side or the other.

"This," says Portia, gesturing to the girl whose hair is golden wires, whose lips are coral, whose throat is alabaster, and whose skin is pearl, "is another of Caliban's would-be crimes called to testify against him. Murder is nothing to a creature who would violate his master's daughter, and she but a child upon the brink of girlhood then. Is that not true?"

"What? What is true?" Miranda cries.

Upon his judgment seat, Prospero writhes with swallowed action, but Portia has taken command of the courtroom and all eyes are upon the young doctor of law from Rome, Balthasar.

The gathered people hush in the presence of such vile intention, and Gossip slips among them and whispers until Miranda's skin is rose quartz.

"Is it true," Portia demands, "that this debased beast, this ugly, useless spiteful monster, did try to force himself upon you in the cavern on the island? That he did attempt this crime in those days when your father taught him to speak and took him around the island as a favorite child to learn from the pines with their moaning spirits?"

"I do not remember! I cannot remember. I cannot say!"

Gossip swells into a murmur like a spirit wind among the trees, and Miranda must answer the whispers.

"I remember my father descending up on us like Ariel from a storm-cloud, screeching, flailing in a tempest I had never seen before. Caliban was there, Caliban was—"

The beast is silent.

Miranda's cool palms chill her flagrant cheeks. She stares ahead, distracted. Ferdinand paces in his place as if on a leash. The merchant Bassanio from Venice has ceased to breath and move. The crowd sways against itself, whispering, conferring, leering at the maiden and the monster.

Prospero dares not speak.

Nothing stops Portia from speaking, from suggesting to Miranda . . . "Caliban was about to lay foul hands upon you, whisper lewd words in your ear, claw at your garments—"

"No!" Miranda's hands drop. Her head rises. "He had brought me stones to build a palace with. We used to play together. I had no other playmate and Ariel even then tormented him, and myself as well. Caliban taunted Ariel, so Ariel would forget me. Caliban was my playmate then." Miranda is thinking as a child, remembering as a child. "He was my only brother. I did not know he was ugly, who saw no other thing than Ariel, who was lithe and spiteful, and my father, who was wild of beard and hair as any wizard. Caliban . . . Caliban—"

"What did Caliban do?"

"He leaned toward me."

The crowd gasps.

"To kiss my cheek."

The beast is silent.

"And then?" Portia asks, so quietly it seems that Miranda is the only one who hears her, although the two words strike like small hissing serpents at every ear.

"My father coming. The noise. The blows. A tempest of fury I have never seen before. He is like an angry God. There is no answering him, no escaping him. I feel such fear. I have not recalled that day clearly until now."

Miranda looks at Caliban at last. "He did not attack me. He loved me."

"What does this nonsense matter?" a voice roars from on high. Prospero has stood before his throne. "She was a child. Her memories are worthless, deceptive. This has naught to do with the death of my brother Antonio."

Portia paces toward him, tilting her stern profile under its tasseled doctor's hat up toward the Duke. He is the figure of an Old Testament prophet, despite his rich robes, and now every eye in the courtroom sees the tempest that is within him.

"You studied many strange and magical matters when you were first a Duke," Portia says. "Had you not been lost in your studies, you might have noticed that the brother you allowed to rule the Dukedom in your stead wished to supplant you."

"I was bound to scholarship, yes. But a man should not lose his birthright from mere inattention, not if his kin are true."

"Even on your desert isle, kind Gonzalo had seen that your precious books followed you, along with some clothes and other stuffs. The books were all, except for your daughter."

"This is no crime, no matter to investigate."

"What's past is prologue." Portia tolls the words like a bell. "We have heard testimony that the first crime attributed to Caliban the monster is false. Why should the last crime attributed to him not be false as well?"

"Look upon him! He is a monster! He has always been a monster!"

"Sin seldom wears an obvious face, my lord. Methinks Caliban is too convenient a monster. I do not doubt that you saw what you saw. You saw this rough, unhandsome creature leaning toward your daughter in tenderness. And who should not lean toward the likes of Miranda in tenderness? You have made her for the world to love. But love is not lust, Duke Prospero, and you could not see the sibling kiss for the concealed guilt that sank its teeth into your soul."

"My guilt! I have always been the one sinned against!"

Portia's voice raises to match Prospero's. "There was no one on that island but Master and Slave. Two slaves, Caliban and Ariel. And your daughter Miranda. She you reared to be the best and gentlest of humankind. Him"—Portia gestures to Caliban as if accusing him, but her voice is directed at Prospero—"you reared to be beset, bullied, reviled, abused. And then you blame the beast: I am looking at the beast, my lord, and it sits upon the throne of judgment. Judgment is a bawd, my lord, and will paint on many faces, even yours."

Even Gossip purses her lips and is still. The courtroom is silent.

Finally Prospero finds his voice again. It is low, hollow. "What has this to do with the murder of my brother Antonio?"

"What's past is prologue. Does not the phrase echo with familiarity in thy ear? Gonzalo tells me that Antonio was fond of saying it. Poor Antonio, he gave me the clue to all in all, and never lived to know it."

"I do not understand," says a small voice behind Portia.

The false doctor of law turns with a smile. Miranda and Caliban stand side by side, not looking at each other, but unafraid of each other as well.

"I understand all too well," Portia tells Miranda with a warm but weary glance at Bassanio. "If my lord Duke will answer but a few more questions—?"

Prospero sinks back upon his seat, looking truly shipwrecked now, an old man with no more props for his seniority, not even the false truth he embraced like a lover.

"You knew of Sycorax of old," Portia declares as fact. "Your magical readings acquainted you with her powers."

"Yes," says the Duke.

"You sought her out to learn her charms."

"Yes," says the Duke.

"You brought her here to Milan in secret, or went in secret to Algiers."
The Duke is silent.

"She was the 'blue-eyed hag' from the North. Not such a hag, not until she had been ill served by you. When you were marooned upon the same island, you recognized her magic, you knew she had been with child and driven from Algiers with nothing but her empty life and swollen womb. You knew exactly who and what she was, though all that remained of her by then was her sole, barely surviving child. She was the mother of Caliban."

The Duke is silent.

"You are the father of Caliban."

Screams. Gasps. Shouts. Curses.

Portia stands against the storm like the Rock of Gibraltar. Sometimes Judgment wears the face of the mob. Sometimes Judgment kills.

Miranda swoons, but Ferdinand is there to catch her before a lock of her golden hair touches tile.

Caliban looks into Portia's eyes for the first time during his trial.

She strides toward him, takes the clumsy face into her hands, and tilts it to the Duke upon his high seat. She brushes the brutish eyebrows back from the rough brow, until the eyes that glint through the brambles of his face shine bright as sun and moon together.

"The eyes are the window of the soul, my lord. Sycorax had the sky-blue eyes of the North, but Caliban has the sea-green eyes of the South, as do you."

"I could not have spawned this, not even on an ancient witch who could assume any shape to suit her purpose."

"She was old, Sycorax, yes, but we only have your testimony that she was a hag, and perhaps she was after you were done with her and had leeched all the secrets you wanted from her bones. Was she hideous, or only so after you had made the memory of the woman you had used and abandoned into that of an ugly old hag? And no, you could not have spawned a son like Caliban, so you spelled him into the likeness of a repellent monster. Show us now Caliban's true likeness. You can conjure tempests and command sprites. You have bent the sea and kings and delinquent brothers to your will. You have married your daughter well and resumed your seat. Cast off your last, unworthy spell. Free this spirit from the husk you entrapped it within. Show us the son who is the fruit of your quest for power at all cost, whose very existence belies you, whom you had to turn into a monster to hold the ugliness of your own soul.

"Show us Caliban as he is, not as you needed him to be."

Prospero has shrunken into an old man, whom age and envy have bent into a hoop. He clings to his ducal seat. His snowy beard and hair hang like hoar frost around his sunken features.

"Ariel." His voice is a croak that could barely command a pond frog. "Ariel!"

The air bestirs itself in the gilded rafters of the chamber. It becomes a cloud, then a mist, then a disembodied face ever-youthful, ever-old.

"Free him from the last enchantment," Prospero asks, not commands.

Ariel's malicious features hesitate. He glances at his shrunken master and spite shines forth like a full moon. For once it pays him more to benefit Caliban than to harm him.

A sudden whirr of air, a shimmer of cloud.

Caliban rises, straightens, a brown-haired young man, straight and fair-skinned, with islands of sea-green eyes in the calm expanse of his face.

He lifts hairless hands, as if the iron manacles had fallen away, although they have not. Miranda gazes on him with amazement, and Ferdinand comes to join her.

"O brave new beast," she murmurs.

"It maddened you," Portia tells Prospero, "to see your son and daughter in fond embrace despite the lies you had erected like a wall between them. Knowing that they were half-brother and sister, you feared the worst, and thus saw the worst. The wrong was all yours."

"But he admitted it."

"Stung by pride and despair, he did not bow to give the lie to yours. You had left him nothing to be but your monster."

"And so all my spells and schemes have brought me only grief. Yet someone has killed my brother Antonio."

"And sometime Judgment dresses as a ghost, a teasing spirit that calls forth truth. Would it be justice, my lord Duke, if your maltreatment of your bastard son had made him into the monster you disguised him as?"

"No. No, not that. I never wished him ill. I simply thought that he was born to be evil in punishment for my sins. If he has done this murderous deed, I will serve the sentence for it."

Caliban steps forward, his face still slack and unaccustomed to its new geography. Yet there is something that might be called pity on it.

"Father!" Miranda cries, half protesting, half accusing still.

Portia spies Bassanio's knowing eyes among the crowd. It is now her turn to choose the right box, the chest of lead among the deceptive glitter of more apparent choices.

"Can we sentence the wind?" asks the wise young doctor Balthasar. "We have heard testimony how on the island Caliban was led astray time and again to his pain and suffering by an invisible enemy. Antonio indeed was mistaken for your self, Duke Prospero, and led down the garden path to a fatal misstep on the brink of a stone-edged pool."

"Ariel? My Ariel has killed him?"

"The sprite grew used to mischief and missed having a butt for his ill will. Shall he deliver himself now to our judgment? I ask you, spirit, will you come answer to us?" She looks around the courtroom and to the air above it. Not so much as a dust mote twinkles. "I think not. As with every ending, we answer only to ourselves. Beasts and sprites have fled this company and only mortal men and women remain to make what peace with past and present that they can.

"And now I must repair to Rome. Clerk, come take me hence. I grow tired of Judgment."

Epilogue

SPOKEN BY CALIBAN

Now my past becomes the present,
Turns my life from bleak to pleasant.
Prospero and his spells o'erthrown
Make any deceptions now mine alone.
I stand here like a new-made man
To sin or save as best I can.
To ev'ry spirit foul or fair
I offer this most savage prayer:
Handle souls within your power
As you would a precious flower.

Judge not lest ye be someday deemed
As one who is not what he seemed.
Give fellow creatures all you may
Of nature's sweetness and full sway
To some unspoken sense of justice
That gives the lie to what must us
Believe about each and ev'ry other,
As we bow to any unnamed brother.
I take my leave, no more a beast,
But what you will, I am at least.

Lillian Stewart Carl

A Mimicry of Mockingbirds

Multigenre author LILLIAN STEWART CARL, a former college history teacher, has been writing for as long as she can recall. Carl has traveled extensively in Britain, and uses some of the sites she's visited for her book settings. She has published many novels and short stories in multiple genres, ranging from fantasy novels, like the Sabazel series, to mystery, fantasy, and romance blends like *Memory and Desire* and *Lucifer's Crown,* the latter combining her love of mythology, history, and travel into one enchanting novel. More stories and novels are in the pipeline, but she's pretty much run out of new genres to conquer. Her latest novel, *Time Enough to Die* (2002), finds protagonist Matilda Gray investigating the stolen antiquities trade. Her novels are enjoying a steadily growing popularity. "A Mimicry of Mockingbirds," which first appeared in the anthology *White House Pet Detectives,* showcases her mystery short story skills, with President Thomas Jefferson turning sleuth to uncover a murderer.

A Mimicry of Mockingbirds

Lillian Stewart Carl

The evening was fine and warm in a last lingering imitation of summer. Through Tom's open window came a distant strain of harpsichord music, accompanied from time to time by a woman's voice. He would have preferred hearing the salutations of the muse of law, as he was at this moment preparing a difficult case. He pulled his candle closer to *Littleton's English Law with Coke's Commentaries.*

A song, an echo of the original, trilled from the tree outside. Tom looked up with a smile. He liked the voice of the mockingbird, *mimus polyglottos,* the American nightingale. Mockingbirds were clever little fellows, modest as widows in their silver and gray suits. . . . Voices shouted, the harpsichord and the woman's voice ceased abruptly, and with a flutter of wings the bird flew away.

Tom dipped his pen and turned to a fresh page in his commonplace book. "As our laws so have our vocabularies been shaped by the customs of our sovereign Britain. Such collective nouns as 'an ostentation of peacocks' or 'a parliament of owls' amuse our fancies and remind our intellects of the deep roots of our mother tongue. And of its insularity, that such a charming creature as a mockingbird has no such appellation. . . ."

A knock drew his attention. "Come!"

His landlady opened the door. "Mr. Jefferson, are you working still?"

"Indeed I am, Mrs. Vobe. My colleague Patrick Henry will soon argue a case of inheritance, for which I have promised him a complete brief."

"He does go on, Mr. Henry does. Why, you'd think he was preaching revolution!"

"So one might think," Tom returned, without venturing to express those grievances of which he as well as Mr. Henry were sensible.

Mrs. Vobe was wiping down a long-necked wine bottle with her apron, causing its blue glass to wink gaily in the light. "Here you are, Mr.

Jefferson. Shocking, the dust from the streets, but I reckon it repels the flies."

"Thank you." Tom placed the bottle at the far end of his desk, away from his books and papers, noting as he did so that despite Mrs. Vobe's best efforts with the apron, her own fingers, tacky with the baking and basting due her position, had left smudges upon the glass. "Did I hear voices exclaiming in the street just now?"

"Aye, that you did. Mr. Bracewell's been taken sick, very sudden, and his wife's sent for the doctor."

"Which Mr. Bracewell—Nicholas the merchant or his brother Peter?"

"Nicholas, the elder."

"I hope he recovers speedily."

"And if he don't, well, then, there's work for you in proving his will."

"Which is a duty I should gladly forgo, for I have quite enough work without wishing ill of one of my fellow citizens. There are greater matters at hand than such domestic ones as wills and properties. And yet"—Tom turned back to his books—"such domestic matters are as vital to those whom they closely affect as are the present debates on taxation to the citizens of all His Majesty's colonies."

He heard the door shut as Mrs. Vobe went on about her business and left him to his.

Raindrops sifted down the back of Tom's collar as he stood with his hat in his hand. But he took no more notice of them than he did of the odors of mortality—smoke and cooking food and ordure—which hung in the misty air. Beyond the churchyard the various buildings of the town seemed little more than suppositions, allowing him to imagine them as fine palladian structures, not the serviceable but disagreeably ramshackle houses of Williamsburg.

"Earth to earth," intoned the rector, "ashes to ashes, dust to dust . . ."

Eliza Bracewell attended the dark gash in the earth that was her husband's last resting place, her child clasped against her skirts. At her side stood Peter Bracewell and his wife. Nicholas had owned property and served his time as juror. If not representing the upper stratum of society, still he'd been of the solid middling sort. Now a goodly number of Williamsburg's citizens stood around his grave, eyes downcast in seemly sobriety.

To Tom's mind came the words of Cicero: "What satisfaction can there be in living, when day and night we have to reflect that at this or that moment we must die?"

A child was more likely to come to its funeral than to its marriage. Those souls who lived long enough to marry seldom made only one such contract. Tom's old school companion Bathurst Skelton, for example, had recently died, leaving his charming wife, Martha, a widow. Anne Bracewell, Peter's wife, had been the relict of James Allen, a planter from Surry County.

And now dire misfortune had deprived the other Mrs. Bracewell, Eliza, of her husband. Surely Peter, despite his reputation of caprice and instability, would remember his obligations to his nephew and provide for his education just as Tom's uncle had provided for his after the untimely death of his father. Although Eliza could be expected to marry again. She was a comely young woman, her complexion pale beneath the brim of her fashionable bonnet but of a pleasing plumpness.

"Amen," said the rector. In a soft wave of sound the gathered people echoed the word.

Eliza directed her steps toward the gate, awkward as a marionette, supported less by her brother-in-law on the one side than supporting her child on the other. Peter's wife walked just behind. By the draping of her skirts Tom perceived Anne was with child, and politely averted his eyes.

Every few steps Peter paused, inviting the socially select among the mourners to share the funeral feast at Nicholas's house. "Mr. Jefferson, we should be honored by your presence."

"Thank you, Mr. Bracewell. I should be honored to attend."

The rain thickened, dripping in resonant thuds down upon the coffin. Three mockingbirds perched along the wall of the churchyard, the notes of their song passing from the one to the next and then to the next in an avian symphonic composition. An exaltation of larks. A watch of nightingales. A mimicry of mockingbirds . . .

Tom found his creation pleasing, and promised himself he would write it down as soon as may be, after the funeral courtesies had been observed.

A cold wind blew dried leaves into the house. Hastily the servant closed the door and accepted Tom's hat, cloak, and gloves. Tom strode briskly through the hall, past the staircase, elegant in its austerity, to George Wythe's familiar office with its intoxicating scent of books.

"Mr. Jefferson, how very amiable of you to attend me." Wythe greeted his former pupil with a hearty handshake. His high forehead and eagle's-beak nose caused the lawyer and jurist to seem a veritable new world Aristotle, intellect personified.

"I always come to this house with great pleasure and fond memories, Mr. Wythe. How may I assist you? Is it a case of law?"

Wythe gestured Tom toward an empty chair and returned to his desk, stacked high with papers. "That is for you to tell me."

"I beg your pardon?"

"Allow me to set forth the facts of the matter, beginning with a question. How well were you acquainted with the affairs of Nicholas Bracewell, who was taken by death only two days since?"

"More by reputation and rumor than by actual discourse," Tom answered. "I confess it is his younger brother's reputation of which most rumor has reached my ears."

"There is no surprise in that," said Wythe, "when Peter has spent a rather longer time than most young men in sowing his wild oats."

"And so has found himself without the means to reap them?" Tom returned. "Mrs. Skelton, with whom I was conversing most amiably at the governor's palace last week, said she should not be surprised if Peter had married the former Mrs. Allen so that the property left to her by Mr. Allen might assist in the payment of his debts."

"Be that as it may—debts Peter has yet—many contracted upon the expectations of an inheritance from his brother."

"Have you read out Nicholas's will and made an inventory of his personal property, then? Has something gone amiss with one or the other?"

Wythe leaned forward. "Something has gone amiss, yes. Not with the will or the inventory, but with the heirs themselves. And with, I fear, the circumstances of Nicholas's death."

"Indeed?" Tom frowned, not caring for the direction of Mr. Wythe's conversation but intrigued nonetheless.

"Three days since, Nicholas sat at his desk tending to his accounts, as was his habit of an evening, when he was afflicted suddenly by a severe gastric fever. Mrs. Bracewell assisted him to his bed and summoned Dr. de Sequera, but the usual remedies availed nothing, and Nicholas died soon after dawn. May God rest his soul."

"Fevers are not infrequent this time of year."

"Neither are disputes between heirs, at any time of the year. This one, though, goes well beyond most such quarrels. Both Mrs. Nicholas Bracewell and Mr. Peter Bracewell have waited upon me, separately, each to accuse the other of murder by poison."

"Murder!" exclaimed Tom.

"Disagreeable as we may find it to be, that is the word exactly. At root, as you may expect, are the contents of Nicholas's will."

"And, I would presume, the contents of his last meal as well?" Tom smiled, thinly, as befit the circumstances. "Has Nicholas left Eliza less than her widow's third, so that she intends to renounce the will for her dower rights?"

"Not at all, no. He has left her the majority of the estate, property and business both, and Peter but a small settlement. Peter asserts, however, that Nicholas intended writing a codicil to his will that would insure him a full two-thirds of the estate. He suggests that Eliza killed her husband before he could do so. Eliza, in turn, asserts that Peter killed Nicholas believing that the codicil had already been written, reluctant to wait till nature had in the course of time worked its will upon his brother."

"Many a man has teased his family with implications of the contents of his will," offered Tom.

"True enough."

"But are these infamous charges true? Have you any evidence that such a terrible crime as murder was actually committed?"

"Not one jot or title of evidence, no. This is why I sent for you. I know how you enjoy digging into a case and discovering evidence."

"And yet no case is to be seen, Mr. Wythe, only the suspicions and accusations of dissatisfied heirs."

"As yet, yes. But if the citizens of Virginia are to live under the rule of law, as is their right, then such suspicions must be answered. I'm asking you to research the matter, Mr. Jefferson. Then if you believe that no case exists to be brought before judge and jury, the matter will rest."

"Very well," Tom returned. "As reason is the only sure guide that God has given to man, I shall apply my reason to the problem."

"Good," said Wythe. "I trust you to find its solution."

Tom made his way up Duke of Gloucester Street, envisioning himself a small boat tacking against the wind. His cloak fluttered like a sail. He secured his hat with one gloved hand. What he at first took to be a swirling red leaf settled upon a fence and revealed itself as a redbird.

So were man's senses deceived. Had the Bracewells allowed such distasteful motives as jealousy and greed to deceive them as well? Indeed, Tom himself had wondered at the stiffness between Eliza and Peter after Nicholas's funeral, each offering the other courtesies so exaggerated as to be mocking.

Death struck too easily and too swiftly to hasten anyone into his arms. Murder must out. Tom must not only prove a case of murder but bring its perpetrator to justice, lest doubt besmirch the community as surely as mist had smeared the streets the day of the funeral.

He turned into Dr. de Sequera's gate. There was the man himself, plucking globes of red, yellow, and green from several windblown bushes. "Doctor!"

De Sequera looked around. "Mr. Jefferson! What brings you out in such a gale?"

"A serious task. Eliza Bracewell and her husband's brother, Peter, are each accusing the other of the murder by poison of Nicholas."

"Well, well, well." De Sequera's thick black brows arched upward. He picked up a basket that was half-filled by smooth round fruits. "Come inside."

The two men walked up the steps and into the still silence of de Sequera's house. Tom looked about as eagerly as he always did when waiting upon his friend, finding great interest in the array of scientific instruments and medicines in their glass bottles. One of de Sequera's refracting lenses had so intrigued Tom he'd ordered a copy from England for himself, to magnify the vexatiously small print in his books. "What have you there?" he asked, indicating the basket. "Tomatoes?"

De Sequera held up a rosy red globe. "Yes. I eat them often."

"But are they not of the nightshade family?"

"They are, yes. And yet despite their mimicry of less salubrious fruits, they are tasty and nutritious. The food we eat determines our state of health.

And nowhere more so than with Nicholas Bracewell, it appears. Tell me what you have heard."

"Very little, in truth." Tom repeated what Wythe had told him, and concluded, "You treated Nicholas. What symptoms did you observe?"

"During the autumn I see many fevers of the remitting and intermittent kind. Nicholas was taken by a very sudden fit of gastric fever, with vomiting so severe I had no need for the usual vomits and purges. I administered snake root and Peruvian bark, but to no avail. This particular fever did run its course uncommonly swiftly, but each body is heir to its own."

"Vomits and purges. Those would also be the symptoms of some poisons."

"So they would."

"I should hate to ascribe to malice what could have occurred by accident. Could Nicholas have eaten food unsuitable for consumption? Not tomatoes, I warrant," Tom added with a smile.

"According to his relations, he took his dinner with friends at Weatherburn's Tavern, then supped lightly on the same bread and cheese eaten by his wife. If poison had been introduced into either meal, Nicholas should not have been its only victim. 'Tis more likely the poison found its way, by whatever means, into a cup or glass from which he and he alone drank, not long before he was struck down."

"I see." Tom nodded. "Arsenicum produces such symptoms, does it not? And antimony, the favorite of Lucrezia Borgia?"

"Both are elemental metals. Antimony, though, does not dissolve in food or water and tastes bitter. If Nicholas were indeed poisoned, I should think arsenicum a more likely means, as it readily dissolves and leaves no taste."

Tom knew he must not be afraid to follow the truth wherever it may lead. "Is it possible that Nicholas dosed himself, thereby taking his own life?"

" 'Tis possible. But if I were to make my own end, I should choose a method much quicker and tidier. 'Tis certainly against our deepest instincts to cause ourselves suffering."

"Yes," Tom agreed. "How unfortunate that it is not always against our deepest instincts to cause suffering to another. Thank you for your help, Doctor."

"If I can be of further assistance, please let me know." De Sequera hoisted his basket onto his arm. "Till then, I have a recipe to perfect, a sauce of tomatoes and herbs, served over fowl, perhaps. Will you join me in such a culinary experiment?"

"If you can eat tomatoes with a smile upon your face, then I shall gladly join you, and prove scientifically that they are a wholesome and delectable fruit." Shaking his head—the good doctor might be somewhat eccentric, but his methods were sound—Tom walked back out into the cold.

So Nicholas had indeed been hurried to his grave by poison. Now to discover whence the poison and how it was dispensed. Those considerations must, Tom hoped, bring him in due course to the hand that had dispensed it.

Nicholas Bracewell's parlor was small but in every particular fashionable. The porcelain figurines lining the mantelpiece were as superior a quality as any found in the best houses in Williamsburg. Tom doubted Nicholas, a pleasant but less than polished individual, had selected such tasteful furnishings. As the daughter of a planter possessing no more than an acre or two, it was Eliza who had by marrying a merchant risen above her origins.

Mrs. Bracewell's countenance was colored prettily now, but her fine dark eyes displayed a rigidity approaching haughtiness. In her black silk dress, its bodice softened by a white fichu, she reminded Tom of a magpie. "Allow me to offer you refreshment. Tea?"

Tom held that the present tax on tea was not so much an absurd expense as an affront to colonial rights. Bowing, he refused the tea but accepted a chair. After a few moments of polite conversation he came to the point of his visit. "Mr. Wythe has told me of your allegations against Mr. Peter Bracewell. And of his corresponding allegations against you."

Eliza flicked open her black-trimmed mourning fan and with it concealed her lips as she spoke. "He cannot even present you with a reasonable falsehood. Why should I kill my husband and render myself a *femme sole,* alone in the world?"

"Was the poison introduced into Nicholas's food, do you think?"

"No. No one else fell ill. I expect it was mixed with his wine."

"Wine?"

" 'Twas his custom to take a glass or two of wine in the evenings as he looked over his accounts. He fell ill with the bottle and the glass still before him, or so I found him when I answered his cries of distress."

"You were not with him when he was taken ill?"

"No. I was here, endeavoring to learn the words of a new song. My husband took pleasure in my singing, whether or not I had the advantage of tutors in music and deportment in my youth." Her voice took on a mocking edge.

Tom nodded. "May I see Nicholas's office, please, Mrs. Bracewell?"

"Surely." Furling the fan, Eliza led the way down a narrow hall to a closet at the back of the house.

A bookcase, a desk, and a chair filled the tiny room. Two ledger books lay upon the desk next to an inkwell and pen. A blue wine bottle and a glass occupied the far corner, beyond several bills of lading. A child's toy horse lay next to the door. "This is how the room appeared when Mr. Bracewell was taken ill?" Tom asked.

" 'Twas necessary to wash the floor," said Eliza.

"Ah." Tom had no wish to press Nicholas's wife as to the unfortunate details of his illness. He picked up the bottle, recognizing the same vintage he kept for his own use. 'Twas merchant Josiah Greenhow's best, evinced by Greenhow's seal, a glass medallion affixed to the bottle just beneath its shoulder. The cork that plugged the bottle's mouth was still damp and firm. A small amount of wine splashed back and forth inside. "This bottle is new, is it not?"

"I purchased it at Mr. Greenhow's store little more than an hour before my husband drank from it."

"Did you first draw the cork? Did you note whether it were sound?"

"I drew the cork, which was quite sound, with my own hands, to ease my husband's way for him."

And so was his way eased across the Styx, Tom said to himself. "Who, then, could have entered the room between the time you brought the bottle home and the time he drank from it?"

Eliza's plump face took on the appearance of a dried apple. "Our cook and housekeeper, Sylvia, was away that night. But Peter lives just there, on my husband's sufferance, and comes and goes in this house as though we lived here on his." She gestured toward the window.

It overlooked the house's dependencies—kitchen, dairy, smokehouse, and privy. Beyond the small structures lay a garden, set out with a trellis and a row of fruit trees in design very like the Wythe's garden. Over the few remaining leaves of the trees rose the roof of Peter Bracewell's cottage. A narrow path ran between the two properties, for the convenience of the servants, no doubt. "Nicholas owns the house where Peter and his wife make their home?"

"He did, yes. Now Peter owns it, for it and it alone was left to him in the will."

Tom set the bottle back down. "What, then, could be the motive for murder, Mrs. Bracewell?"

"My husband's other properties, not to mention his business, all of which have now come to me. Peter desires to live in leisured dignity but has not the means to do so. I must confess he is no stranger to the gambling tables, and in other ways lives well beyond his income. All is status and show to him."

Tom offered no response to that statement.

"The evening before the one my husband was taken from me, he and his brother fought most bitterly over Nicholas's refusal to pay Peter's debts. They spoke so loudly I could not help but overhear, walking as I was outside the door."

"Did Nicholas advise Peter that he intended to make his will more favorable to him?"

Eliza's chin went up. "Nicholas told him he had already made the change, hoping to encourage Peter to mend his ways and turn his hand to business."

"But Nicholas did not in fact write the codicil?"

"No. He did not. 'Twas Peter's pride and avarice that led him to believe Nicholas's ruse, as though Nicholas would compromise his own son's inheritance in favor of a blaggard such as Peter!"

"And so you believe Peter hastened Nicholas to his grave."

"I do not believe it, Mr. Jefferson. I know it."

"The facts of the matter have yet to be proved," Tom told her. "May I have the use of this bottle and its contents?"

"To pour away, I should hope, lest some other unfortunate soul should drink from it."

Tom's intentions were otherwise, but Mrs. Bracewell had no need to know his true purposes. "I should greatly appreciate the loan of a basket in which to carry the bottle. And may I interview your cook?"

Eliza, her color high, stared him up and down for a long moment, then quit the room.

Tom turned to the desk. Despite the sunlight outside, the room was dusky, and he had no means by which to light the lamp now sitting cold upon the desk. Still he inspected the desktop, books, and empty glass as best he could. Yes, by Jove, a few grains of a chalky white powder were caught in the hinges where the desktop could be folded away. Tom wet his forefinger at his lips and pressed it to the spot, so that a particle or two adhered to his flesh. Making a face indicative of doubt and caution mingled, he put his fingertip first close to his nostril, then passed it across his tongue. The substance had neither smell nor taste. It was neither sugar nor flour.

The light from the door was blocked by a woman's entrance into the room. By her simple calico garb, white headcloth, and ebon complexion, Tom deduced that she was the cook and housekeeper. She proffered a wicker basket filled with straw, her hands trembling so severely the straw rustled. "Mrs. Bracewell sends you this, Mr. Jefferson."

"Thank you," he said, and accepted the basket. "Sylvia is your name?"

"Yes, sir."

"Were you in the house the night Mr. Bracewell was taken ill?"

"No, sir. 'Twas my night out, so I went visiting with my daughter at Mr. Randolph's house. I was nowhere near this room, no, sir."

As this statement could be readily investigated, and as Tom was eager to ascertain the cause of the woman's agitation, he moved on to another question. "Do you have any knowledge of poisons, Sylvia?"

Her eyes widened, surpassing agitation and achieving outright fear. "No, sir. I never poisoned Mr. Nicholas. Why would I do that?"

"Indeed, Sylvia. An excellent question." As an enslaved person, Sylvia's testimony would not be allowed before a court of law, giving her no reason to lie about the circumstances in which she found herself. Indeed, to murder her master would have gone against her best interests, for even with her inheritance Eliza might have found herself obliged to make economies, and an experienced cook like Sylvia would bring a good price in that market for human flesh Tom found so troubling.

"Sylvia, you need fear no retribution if only you tell the truth. What do you know of Mr. Bracewell's death?"

"Nothing, sir," the poor woman stammered. "Only that he was taken terrible sick just after I brought arsenicum and soft soap into the house."

"Arsenicum and soft soap?"

"Mrs. Bracewell bid me buy them at the market, so as to clean the bedsteads and rid them of bedbugs. But within a day they was gone and Mr. Bracewell was dead."

"Did you by any chance overhear Mr. Bracewell and his brother in disputation over the younger gentleman's financial situation?"

"Oh, no, sir, I never heard anything of the sort. Not that I'd be listening, mind."

Nodding, Tom placed the wine bottle in the basket and slipped the handle over his arm. He found a small coin in his pocket and pressed it into Sylvia's hand. "Thank you. Please give my respects to Mrs. Bracewell, and tell her that I am continuing my investigations into the matter."

Her manner mollified, Sylvia showed Tom to the door.

Tom walked around the corner of the street toward Peter Bracewell's front door. Two households, as Master Shakespeare had said, both alike in dignity, and no less given to feuding, or so it seemed by Eliza Bracewell's testimony.

Black birds swirled like cinders in the wind, stooping over a field at the edge of town. Ravens or crows, most likely, although at this distance Tom could not ascertain which. An unkindness of ravens, he said to himself. A murder of crows.

The bottle and basket hung from his arm. He should not allow his next witness any knowledge of what the previous one had said. He concealed the basket behind a patch of tobacco which, despite the time of year, still flourished between the cottage and the street. Then Tom stepped up to Peter Bracewell's front door and in a matter of moments was seated in another parlor furnished à la mode, complete with an elegant French mirror above the mantel.

Peter himself, in truth only a half-brother of Nicholas, had always had more of a taste for culture than had the bluff merchant now deceased. Tom himself had recently spent a most agreeable musical evening in this house, playing his violin while Peter played the harpsichord and his wife sang like a lark. The cold supper had been the equal of one served at the palace itself, a calf's head displayed as the centerpiece of a veritable cornucopia of dishes.

Today Peter stood before the fireplace warming the tails of his coat, his handsome face soured by recent events. "Mr. Jefferson, I have given the matter much thought, and have concluded that my brother's death was an unnatural one. Fevers abound in these climes, yes, but for him to suffer one so conveniently defies belief."

"His fever and subsequent death were convenient?" Tom asked.

"On the day before his death, Nicholas stated his intention of paying my debts. He also informed me he'd added a codicil to his will leaving much of his property and his business to me, as a reward for my hard work in its pursuance. So Holy Scripture instructs us to welcome home the prodigal, he said, and congratulated me on mastering my baser appetites. But his wife has always been jealous of Nicholas's affection toward me, thinking it better directed to her own son."

"And who can blame a woman who wishes to protect her child?"

Peter's mouth twisted in a satirical smile. "No one at all. But not when she imposes upon Mr. Wythe, and through him upon you, the vilest of falsehoods—a charge of murder laid against an innocent man."

"Why, then, should Mrs. Bracewell accuse you?"

"If she were to eliminate me, then would not Nicholas's entire estate fall to their son and, through him, upon her? Who's to say she does not have her eye and her cap set already toward a new husband, one of greater property and therefore greater prospects than my poor brother?"

"What are you suggesting, Mr. Bracewell?"

"That Nicholas was indeed murdered. But by his own wife."

"How, then, do you think Mrs. Bracewell could have accomplished such an outrage?"

"With poison from her own kitchen. My own wife saw Nicholas's Sylvia purchasing arsenicum and soft soap, and remarked upon it, whereupon Sylvia admitted to the infestation she hoped to combat." Peter paced across the room, drew an arpeggio from the keyboard of the harpsichord, then looked out the window at Nicholas's roof. "Less than an hour before my brother's death I passed Eliza upon the street outside Mr. Greenhow's establishment, her basket upon her arm and the neck of a wine bottle protruding from it. Nicholas was accustomed to taking a glass or two before retiring. How easier to introduce a poison to him but to no one else?"

"You saw her carrying a bottle such as that one?" Tom indicated two blue glass bottles sitting in the corner cupboard, close beside several stemmed glasses.

"Very similar. Those, though, are my own private stock. Nicholas, with less of a palate than God saw fit to give me, drank from the common store." Peter presented one of the bottles for Tom's inspection.

The common store was quite acceptable for everyday consumption, in Tom's considered opinion. But he kept his own counsel and noted only that yes, the glass medallions on the bottles were indeed imprinted with Peter's name, not with that of merchant Greenhow.

"Surely you will not object to telling me, Mr. Bracewell, how you were employed between the time Mrs. Bracewell brought home the new bottle and the time her husband first felt the pangs of . . . his illness."

"I found employment just here, Mr. Jefferson, practicing the new minuet by Corelli, neglecting even to take my supper, for my wife and I intend to hold yet another musical evening very soon. We should be honored if you would join us. I shall," he added with a sly smile, "extend an invitation to Mrs. Martha Skelton as well."

Tom concealed his expression by inspecting his shoe buckles. Delightful as she was, blessed with a voice as lovely as her form, Mrs. Skelton was not party to this problem. "Thank you, Mr. Bracewell. I heard your playing myself that night, accompanied by your wife's most agreeable singing."

As though summoned by his words, Mrs. Anne Bracewell entered the room. She, too, had no doubt happened to be walking outside. Her silk wrapper was more highly colored than her complexion, which was very pale, as befit her delicate condition. "May I offer you dinner at our table, Mr. Jefferson? Our cook is not the equal of my sister-in-law's Sylvia, but she does tolerably well."

"Thank you, Mrs. Bracewell, but I expect Mrs. Vobe has already prepared my usual dish of vegetables." Tom rose to his feet. "I was complimenting your husband on your singing, which was cut so lamentably short the night of Mr. Nicholas Bracewell's death."

"I was fortunate to have had the advantage of tutors in music and deportment in my youth." Anne inclined her head with grave propriety, but Tom did not imagine the edge of mockery in her voice.

He heard the echo of Eliza's words in Anne's. Yes, Anne's family was of a higher status in Virginia than Eliza's, a fact of which both women seemed only too aware.

Making his excuses, Tom found his way to the street. There he retrieved the basket and stood for a moment listening to a mockingbird singing in a nearby tree. Just now it seemed to be repeating no particular melody. He wondered whether he could teach one of the little creatures a song, an Irish or Scottish air, perhaps, even though its duplication could be but a counterfeit of the original.

Just as the support Peter Bracewell had given Eliza at her husband's funeral was counterfeit, or perhaps as Peter's indignation or Eliza's excuses were counterfeit. The bird, though, did not purpose to deceive with its mimicry.

After stopping to speak with several other citizens, Tom returned to his lodgings and amazed his landlady by asking to purchase one of the chickens that occupied a pen behind her kitchen. "An old one will do, one destined soon for the pot," he explained.

"Well, then," replied Mrs. Vobe, "have that old cockerel in the far corner, the one's grown weary of his life and is pondering dumplings and gravy."

This chicken would not follow its relatives into dumplings and gravy or even into de Sequera's exotic sauce. The good doctor might be content to experiment upon himself, but Tom intended to take a safer course. He isolated the chicken in a small pen and set before it a dish of corn laced liberally with a draught from Nicholas's wine bottle. Leaving the animal pecking away at the food, he sat down to his own dinner, a splendid *potage à pois.*

He had had little need to inquire of the Bracewells' neighbors whether they heard the music of harpsichord and voice the night of Nicholas's death. With the windows standing open, he had heard both himself. He did, though, ascertain that Peter had recently, if reluctantly, turned his hand to Nicholas's business, and that the relations between the brothers had not always been so cordial as Peter would have Tom think, as the issue of his own debts caused a constant friction.

Mrs. Randolph had assured Tom as to the whereabouts of Eliza's Sylvia at the fatal hour. And Josiah Greenhow, who'd readily testified to Eliza's acquisition of the infamous bottle of wine soon before her husband's death, asserted that its cork had been fixed and whole when it left his hands.

Nothing, then, that Tom learned from the citizens of the town led him to believe either Bracewell a liar and therefore a murderer.

He returned to Mrs. Vobe's yard to discover the chicken in its death throes. Before he could do it a mercy by wringing its neck, it expired in a shuddering heap of feathers. Tom poked and prodded its lifeless body, but unlike a Roman haruspex of old declined to inspect its internal organs. He'd proved that the poison, probably arsenicum, had been introduced into the bottle of wine in the brief interval between its arrival at the house and Nicholas's pouring it out.

There should be some way of formulating a more exact test, to indicate not only the presence of poison but its specific sort. Then no uncertainties would remain on the mind, all would be demonstration and satisfaction. . . . No. Science could not illuminate the shadows of the human heart. It could identify the poison but not who placed it in the bottle. The question, as always, was *cui bono:* who benefited from the crime?

Peter might well have killed his brother to gain enough income to pay his debts and to live in the style to which he had accustomed himself. He, though, could not have been playing his harpsichord and poisoning the wine at the same instant.

Eliza might have killed her husband to prevent her own income from being diminished, as oftentimes widows found themselves obliged to take in lodgers or depend upon the kindness of relations, which, considering the demeanor of Eliza's relations, was not an alternative. But then, if Eliza had made good with her first marriage, why not make better with her second, especially with her first husband's estate as bait?

A squawk made Tom glance around. Mrs. Vobe's cat was crouching in the door of the kitchen, its fur forming a bristling ridge down its back. A mockingbird stood only a few feet away, wings half extended, cawing its contempt at its nemesis. No wonder it was named a "mocking" bird, when it not only copied but teased.

If the season had been spring, Tom would have thought the bird intended to draw the cat away from its nest. Such was always the maternal imperative, to protect the child even at the forfeit of one's own life. But the season was autumn. Perhaps the bird fancied the cat encroached upon its territory, which passion was also a human trait.

Tom considered that Nicholas's child was as much a motive in his death as his territory, his possessions. Eliza and Peter would each benefit from the other's demise, as Nicholas's property would go to his son, and the surviving adult, whether mother or uncle, would have control over its use.

But both Peter's and Eliza's accounts rang true. Neither countenance displayed any guilt or sly regard. Indeed, both seemed quite sincere. And yet one of them must be false. Tom needed more evidence, evidence that could be demonstrated to everyone's satisfaction.

The cat leaped forward. The bird launched itself into the air and flew away, evading the extended claws by inches. A thin dust swirled lazily into the air and then drifted back to earth. The cat slinked back into the kitchen, admitting to no defeat. Its paws left a spoor in the dust.

Frowning, Tom strolled closer to the site of the momentary battle. Had he not seen it for himself, still he could have reconstructed the affray from the marks in the dusk, the spiky prints of the bird's feet, the pugmarks of the cat, and the twin furrows where the bird's wings had brushed the earth upon its abrupt departure.

Tom's eye then turned to the wine bottle, still sitting where he'd laid it, on a shelf inside the chicken coop. A fine layer of dust and chaff shrouded its gleam. He remembered Mrs. Vobe, at the very moment poor Nicholas was hastening toward his mortality, entering Tom's room wiping another bottle with her apron. No doubt Greenhow had done the same, cleaning the bottle Eliza purchased of dust and dirt. . . .

If his mind could stretch itself to invent a new collective noun, it could also invent a new scientific test. One that could identify the hand that had poured the poison. Taking great care to lift the bottle by its lip, Tom held it up to the light and squinted at its smooth glass sides.

Tom waited politely as George Wythe seated his guests around the green baize-covered table in his office. Mrs. Nicholas Bracewell twitched her skirts away from Peter Bracewell's buckled shoes, while Mrs. Peter Bracewell folded her hands in her lap and looked about with little expression. Her husband and sister-in-law bent upon each other expressions of distrust and disdain, each complexion colored as pinkly as though Mr. Wythe's fire burned with much greater heat.

"Mr. Jefferson," said Wythe, seating himself in the remaining chair.

Stepping forward, Tom placed a clear pane of glass on the table between Eliza and Peter. "Would you each be so kind as to press your thumbs and fingertips firmly against this glass?"

"I beg your pardon?" demanded Peter.

Eliza said haughtily, "An exceedingly strange request, Mr. Jefferson."

"If you please," Wythe said, "indulge my young friend's scientific endeavors. He has explained his reasoning to me, and it rings true in every respect."

With indignant murmurings, first Eliza and then Peter did as he requested, even suffering Tom to apologetically roll their thumbs back and forth against the glass. He carried the pane closer to Wythe's lamp, scattered it with the fine dust he'd collected in Mrs. Vobe's yard, and blew the excess into the fireplace. He then inspected the resulting smudges through his refractive lens. "It seems as though the oils inherent in human flesh leave marks upon all they touch, in a process not dissimilar to the way marks are made upon paper by the metal type and ink of a printing press. These marks can be readily distinguished on such a hard, smooth surface as glass, be it this pane of glass I borrowed from Mr. Geddy's workshop, or the glass of a wine bottle, which must be grasped firmly lest it fall and break."

Not the least murmur or rustle of fabric came from any of the gathered souls.

Tom turned to the sheet of paper resting upon the corner of Wythe's desk. He'd employed the afternoon sunlight in scrutinizing each print upon the bottle and painstakingly sketching its patterns, so that now he had before him a gallery of whorling designs like miniature labyrinths. "I theorize," he continued, "that each human fingerprint is as distinct, albeit subtly, as each leaf upon a tree, or each snowflake falling from the sky in winter."

There, yes, one pattern matched those made by Eliza's fingers. Another matched the set he'd taken from himself, and a third matched that of Josiah Greenhow, who'd agreed with good humor to the test. Wythe himself had provided a wax seal pressed by Nicholas Bracewell's thumb, from which Tom had been obliged to extrapolate the rest of the dead man's grasp. But nowhere upon his paper was a copy of the pattern Peter had just this moment impressed upon the glass.

So, then. The presence of Eliza's prints proved nothing, as she'd already admitted touching the bottle. The absence of Peter's prints, though, proved that he'd never touched it at all, and was therefore innocent of pouring the arsenicum into its narrow mouth.

Tom might perhaps have settled then and there upon Eliza as the perpetrator, except he had yet one set of designs upon his paper for which he could make no attribution. Was it possible that Eliza and Peter were both telling the truth, and the murderer was someone else?

He could hardly test the fingertips of every citizen of Williamsburg who'd passed by the Bracewells' house during the fatal hour. But no. *Cui bono,* he reminded himself, and turned toward the group of people seated around the table. The disgruntlement of heirs.

From the chill twilight beyond the windows came the chirrup of a mockingbird, so gentle he would have found it hard to believe the same bird capable of the harsh squawks he'd heard this afternoon had he not heard them for himself. . . .

The answer winged into his mind like a mimicry of mockingbirds winging among the trees. He himself, not to mention the neighbors, had heard a woman's voice singing while Peter played the harpsichord. All had leaped to the assumption, as the cat had leaped toward the bird, that the voice belonged to Anne. But, as the cat had missed the bird, so assumption had missed fact.

Eliza had been practicing a song at that same hour. Without study, who could tell the song of one mockingbird from another? Who could tell Eliza's song from Anne's, particularly as Eliza had been endeavoring to copy Anne? That Anne had been privileged to possess tutors in music and deportment was a fact with which each woman mocked the other.

Tom considered Anne Bracewell's lacy cap, which was presented to his gaze as her own gaze was directed to her lap. From modesty or from guilt?

Any mother, avian or human, would put her child's welfare above her own. She would be compelled to defend any encroachment into her territory, even though such defense meant the risk of her own life. Eliza might have killed her husband to provide for her son, but Anne, too, had a child who wanted provision. As a *femme coverte,* her property might belong to her husband but his belonged to her. And to their child.

Anne had remarked upon Sylvia's purchase of arsenicum. Anne would have known Nicholas's and Eliza's habits as well as Peter. Anne, going about her lethal errand, might have deliberately started singing every time Eliza paused, so that music accompanied her trip through the dusk from house to house and back again as though in a tragic opera. It would have been the work of only seconds for her to steal the arsenicum from the kitchen on her way into the house and to dispose of its packaging in the privy on her way back.

Tom set his pane of glass on the table in front of her. "If you please, Mrs. Bracewell, might I have the impressions of your fingers as well?"

"What is the meaning of this?" Peter demanded, and again Wythe remonstrated.

Slowly Anne raised her hand and set it against the glass, so limp and feeble that Tom had to push her fingertips down with his own. A moment later he had ascertained that the remaining marks upon the poisoned bottle were indeed those of her hands. Glancing up, he met Wythe's solemn eyes, and received a nod of encouragement.

"Facts are stubborn things," Tom said. "The fact of who poured arsenicum in Nicholas's wine is now revealed. Mrs. Peter Bracewell left the marks of her fingers upon the bottle. Her husband, intent upon his music, was never sensible of his wife's brief absence from the room. Mrs. Nicholas Bracewell, intent upon hers, was never sensible of her sister-in-law's brief presence in her house."

Eliza's eyes darted to Anne's bowed head, and her countenance suffused with understanding. Peter's countenance went red. "You accuse my wife of murder?"

"I do, yes," said Tom. "Mrs. Bracewell no doubt intended Nicholas's death to be thought a natural one. And so would it have been, had you and Mrs. Nicholas Bracewell not chosen to contest the estate. In time Mrs. Anne would have discovered an opportunity to destroy the dregs of the poisoned wine, and no one would ever have been the wiser."

"But, but," stammered Peter. "Why?"

"For the child." Anne rose unsteadily to her feet, her complexion as pale as ash. Her hands rested upon the swelling of her belly. "I could not bear our child being born to less than the income he deserved, an income that his uncle permitted his own child but denied to ours. Now it is the child that I shall plead before the court. . . ." She fell as a curtain falls when the hooks are torn away, folding to the floor.

Eliza knelt over Anne and cradled her lolling head even as disgust wrote its lines across her features. Peter stared from Wythe to Tom and back again, as though they were capable of changing the situation in which he found himself.

"I shall send for the sheriff and his constable," said Wythe, his sober mien becoming grim. "I see no need, however, to conduct Mrs. Bracewell to the jail. She may stay in her own home until after the trial. Until after the delivery of the child."

Tom turned toward the window. Yes, all had been demonstrated. But he found little satisfaction in his demonstration. And yet his failure to solve the problem would have caused a different set of uncertainties to remain upon his mind.

Against the darkness he could see only his own shape reflected imperfectly in the glass. He could still hear, though, the song of the mockingbird outside. So men, he said to himself, often imitate the finer sentiments, but defectively and with less pleasure to those nearby than the mockingbird mimics music.

Tom threw open his window upon the bright, soft spring day. There were his little friends, perched among the new leaves of the tree just outside. Tom sang a few lines of "Barbara Allen" and first one, then the other mockingbird repeated them, heads tilted to the side, throats swelling, eyes shining like obsidian beads. When he completed his property at Monticello, Tom intended to populate it with mockingbirds in the most comfortable cages he could devise.

He considered also that his new house was in need of a mistress. Indeed, he had only this morning copied into his commonplace book Milton's lines celebrating the felicities of marriage, which, along with the joys of books, friends, and music, gave the lie to old Cicero and his dissatisfaction with living. Death came soon enough. Life was meant to be embraced.

As was Mrs. Martha Skelton. . . . But it was a truth universally acknowledged that a widow in possession of a good fortune might not necessarily be in want of a new husband.

He meant to convince Martha that he wanted her not for her fortune or her social position but for herself, just as he enjoyed the mockingbirds for themselves, and not because he intended to submit them to gravy or de Sequera's delectable tomato sauce. He scattered a few dried berries on the windowsill, and laid out several long red hairs from his own head.

In such a context he could not help but remember the Bracewells.

Anne had come to trial and been found guilty of murder, but the sentence of the court had not been carried out by human hands. Just past the new year she'd died as so many women died, bringing new life into the world.

Now Peter was courting another widow, this one with both children and fortune, who had expressed herself glad of Anne's daughter. Eliza, on the other hand, had settled down with her middling income and declared her intentions never to remarry.

One bird lit softly upon the sill and picked up a berry. The other seized upon the hair and flew away to build its nest, the task set before it by natural law. That same natural law that gave men the free will to covet and to murder. Or to do neither.

Was it not simply reason that no one ought to harm another in his life, health, liberty, or possessions? Was it not simply reason that all men were created equal, and that a government existed for men, not men for government? It went against the law of nature that the laws for the citizens of Britain should be the just laws, and those for the citizens of the American colonies only imitations, more imperfect in equity and justice than any song repeated by a mockingbird.

Tom leaned against the frame of the window and watched the mockingbirds weaving the long red strand among the twigs of their nest, building for the future.

Brad Reynolds

The Twin

As usual, the stories in our year's end collection span a gamut of styles, historical periods, and, most especially, settings. One of the locales explored was the wilderness of our forty-ninth state—Alaska—long the background for Dana Stabenow's mystery series. In *The Mysterious North,* she invited several fellow mystery authors to play in her backyard, and two of those stories are gracing our pages this year, the first by Jesuit Father BRAD REYNOLDS, a writer and photographer living in Portland, Oregon. His work has appeared in magazines and newspapers all over the nation, including *National Geographic, America Magazine, American Scholar, The Seattle Times*, and the *Anchorage Daily News*. More than 250 of his articles, stories, and poems have been published, as well as more than six hundred photos. He is also the author of the Mark Townsend mystery novels. His work displays his deep understanding of the Eskimo culture and its relevance to other societies throughout the world. He manages to make lively reading out of what could be, in lesser hands, dry and arcane material. In his story "The Twin," what begins as a simple trade in the back-country turns into something much more sinister in the span of just a few seconds.

The Twin

Brad Reynolds

Nothing can be said about Coal Porter to make him out as much of a man. But the way he went shouldn't happen to a dog. Porter was a bootlegger and he had a place outside of Bethel that was little more than a shack and was practically hanging over the bank of the Kuskokwim. When he put it up he was probably twenty or thirty feet back, but the river keeps eating the land in big bites and all of a sudden his place was perched right on the edge. So if Coal had stayed around he was going to have to move anyway. And that would have been a major problem because Coal Porter kept his liquor and drugs hidden in a cache beneath the cabin. He had a trapdoor built in the floorboards, and as often as the troopers checked the place out, they never found Coal's stuff. He was real slick that way.

He sold to anyone who had the money. He sold a lot of stuff. To the natives mostly, but there were plenty of white folks in Bethel who knew the shortest way to Coal Porter's place. And if someone was a little short on cash, old Coal was always willing to barter. He'd take your sno-go, your shotgun, or your hat if it was fur, didn't smell, and you offered it in a nice way. He'd trade for just about anything, but what he liked most of all was the Eskimo stuff. That homemade crafted stuff was always good at Coal Porter's. He made a wad of money hauling it into Anchorage and selling it to galleries and tourist stores. There's plenty of folks with shelves of pretty gewgaws that came out from underneath Coal Porter's floor. Lots of natives traded an ivory carving or a grass basket for a quart of cheap booze or a couple of joints, only to spot it in an Anchorage store window three months later, selling for three or four hundred bucks. The one word you never used in Coal's presence was credit. He ran a strictly cash-and-carry business and everyone knew it. But a desperate few prayed he might see the error in his ways and they would occasionally ask for credit. The bootlegger would give a little chuckle and then sic his rottweiler. Coal Porter was a mean weasel and no one liked him much although they sure did like what he had to sell.

Bobby Lincoln and Joe Moses were cousins, both from the same small village: a windblown, fly-specked, mosquito-ridden tundra town about sixty miles downriver from Bethel. The name of the place isn't important for you to know. There's good people still living there who had nothing to do with any of this. Both guys were in their early twenties—old enough to know better. Or at least you'd think. Neither was very big, but Bobby was the taller of the two. He wore his hair in a ponytail and he had long, yellow teeth and that hungry wolf look, which usually means trouble. Joe had short hair and a small, wiry frame. One of his upper front teeth had a chip missing and when he smiled it made other people smile too.

Bobby was definitely the meanest. He'd been on his own since he was about fourteen, doing pretty much what he wanted, when he wanted, to whomever he wanted. He stayed alone in an old cabin at the edge of the village. No one seems to know much about his folks. There's some who claim they're living in Fairbanks and some who say they're in jail. One guy from that same village claims Bobby ate them both when he was thirteen. He could have. He had the teeth for it.

Joe wasn't much better, but he did have family. He lived at the other end of the village with his twin sister, Alice, and his grandmother, one of the old-time Yupiks. The old woman took the two kids when their parents drowned coming back from Bethel one spring. She raised them as best she could, which didn't seem to be all that great. Joe wasn't too bad unless he was hanging around with his cousin, Bobby. Unfortunately, he was hanging around Bobby a lot.

And Bobby was hanging around Alice. A whole lot. He covered that girl like snow. Never mind that they were cousins and weren't supposed to be doing the things they were doing. The old grandmother was deaf as a stone and could sleep through a war, so Bobby and Alice used to wait until she pulled the cloth curtain across her end of the cabin, then they did the nasty while Alice's twin brother put on headphones and kept his eyes fixed mostly on video games. Yes, ma'am, there were mighty cozy times in that cabin. If Grandma wondered why her thin curtain kept fluttering in and out like the bellows on a pump organ, she never asked. She was no fan of Bobby Lincoln's, though. Whenever he came in the cabin she never offered tea or served him any kind of meal. As best she could she tried to ignore him. She kept all her old stuff in boxes at her end of the cabin and never would let Bobby Lincoln anywhere near them. She might have been deaf, but she wasn't blind and she wasn't stupid, either. They say her old man was a shaman—what the people called *angalkuk*—and there are some in the village who claim this woman had twice the smarts and three times the magic her husband ever did. That's one of those stories hard to prove either way. But the point is that everyone knew about Bobby and Alice and everyone knew they were cousins. When you live in a village of less than two hundred, people tend to get a little nervous about cousins getting familiar. You don't want your young folks pissing in the gene pool. But no one was about to tell Bobby Lincoln to keep away from Alice. Not if he ate his parents when he was only thirteen.

Alaska in early March isn't your finest time of year. It's been cold and dark about long enough and by then most of the snow is either black or yellow. Mold on the dry herring is the greenest thing in the village and folks are getting pretty sick of last summer's salmon. To say tempers get a little short is like saying Alaska gets a little cold. If you're going to be stuck in a village anytime in March, you're going to want to be unconscious as much of the time as possible. That's when a guy like Coal Porter becomes the best friend you've ever had. That's also when Coal Porter jacked up his prices about 150 percent. In March, best friends can get pretty expensive. The first eight days of that particular month were about as miserable a time as you can get. It was like Alaska was in reverse, heading back to the Ice Age. There was a hard snow falling straight down, blowing sideways, and coming right up out of the ground. And there was that kind of cold that gets inside your blood and starts to crystallize. Your teeth ache for no reason and your toes curl into hard little knots. March ninth got a little warmer and the tenth was a little better yet. On the eleventh, a few brave souls poked their heads outdoors to see if any mastodons were still around. By the twelfth it got up to minus-ten and folks were out in T-shirts, putting up beach umbrellas. In the Moses cabin, Grandma stayed behind her curtain for four days, and Alice was suffering a bad case of mattressback.

That's when Bobby Lincoln decided to ride into Bethel and visit Coal Porter, and he kept slugging Joe in the stomach until he agreed to go along. The trouble was, neither boy had any money. So Bobby came up with this great idea. First he picked a fight with Alice—something about the way she smelled—and then he stormed out of there, leaving just the twins and the old woman in the cabin. He wasn't gone five minutes before Grandma whipped back her curtain and stuck her head around, checking to make sure Bobby was really gone. She grabbed her bar of soap, her shampoo and towel and headed toward the steamhouse. That long in a cabin without running water, in that kind of cold, makes a long, hot steam feel about as good as two weeks in Hawaii. Bobby Lincoln was probably right about Alice's smell, but how could he tell over everybody else's? The girl, still miffed at her boyfriend, grabbed her own towel and followed her grandmother. Once the place cleared out, Joe put the other part of Bobby's plan into action. He went behind his grandmother's curtain and started rooting around in her boxes. That part of the cabin was fairly dark, there was only one window and it was above Grandma's bed. Most of her cardboard boxes were stacked against the wall. The top ones were filled with clothes. He found her yellow, calico *quspeq* lined with squirrel fur but kept digging. He uncovered an old pair of sealskin mukluks, but they had a gamey smell and weren't all that great so he set them aside. Joe opened another box and things started getting interesting. This was his dead grandfather's stuff. There was his sealskin hat and a pair of fur mittens; both had possibilities. Then he found a knife with a bone handle. He hit pay dirt with the next box, digging into old stuff the shaman used when he made magic in the *qasegiq*, the men's lodge. Joe felt a little nervous digging through that kind of stuff, so he didn't look too deep. Near the top of the box there was something wrapped in dark red corduroy and he lifted it out and unwrapped the cloth.

It was a mask. An old Eskimo mask. Joe carried it over to his grandmother's bed and examined it in the thin light coming through the window. It was carved from wood, oblong in shape, and would cover a man's whole face. Stuck in the forehead were three bent and ruffled white feathers, flecked with brown. Joe thought they might be owl. In the center of the mask, two holes were cut for nostrils, and above them, two for eyes. The mouth was a savage, leering gash with an opening big enough to stick your tongue through. The *angalkuk* had carved sharp and jagged teeth out of yellowed ivory and stuck them all around the mouth's opening. He had painted the mask ocher, but time and use had softened it to the color of faded brick. There was a band of black that stretched across both eyes, making the face look sort of like a raccoon's. Or a bandit's. In the back there was a leather strap to hold the mask in place.

Shamans were before his time and Joe didn't know a lot about them. But he knew a good *angalkuk* was supposed to have helpers who came out of the spirit world. His grandmother had told him that much. She said a *tuunraq* could either be the spirit of an animal or a human that came back to help the shaman do his work. And she said they could change their appearance, sometimes looking like the bodies of dead people. Her stories used to scare the bejesus out of Joe when he was little. He never knew his grandfather, and after hearing his grandmother's stories, he was kind of glad.

He wrapped the mask back in the corduroy and laid it on the bed, then started cramming the other stuff back into the boxes, restacking them against the wall. He laid the old knife with the bone handle next to the mask. The boxes of clothes he made sure went back on top, the way he found them.

His grandmother and Alice were still in their steam when he left the cabin. Smoke was curling out of the stovepipe poking through the steamhouse roof and he could see the plywood door to the cooling room was pushed half open.

His Arctic Cat was an old one and even in the best of conditions it took some work to start it. After days of sitting out in sub-zero temperatures, the battered snowmachine was acting like it never wanted to run again. But he kept choking and begging and swearing and finally the old thing kicked in. He let it run a minute, then jumped on and headed to Bobby's cabin. He had the knife tucked in his brown coveralls and the mask zipped inside his heavy black parka.

Bobby Lincoln thought his plan was one of the smartest things he ever made up right out of his head. And he figured they could use it over and over. All they had to do was wait for Grandma to leave, then Joe could rummage through her stuff. There were enough cardboard boxes piled in back of that cabin to last them a long, long time. They could probably trade for Coal Porter's whole cache if they wanted. The two boys wasted no time getting out of the village, and their tracks headed in a straight line to Bethel. Bobby let Joe carry the mask, but took the knife for himself. Those boys were thirsty and they ran their engines full out, racing across the frozen tundra like reindeer in heat. They made it to Coal Porter's place in a little over two hours. Both of them and their machines were coated in a sheet of frozen snow and ice. Bobby and Joe were slow getting off; their knees were frozen in position and ice was crusting their eyelids. It took a couple of minutes just to work out the frozen kinks in their bodies. And to finalize their plan. Since Joe had the mask, Bobby decided his cousin should go in and deal with Coal Porter alone. But hold out for the good stuff, Bobby warned him, don't give it away. Like he was a little kid or something.

Joe Moses pushed open the outer door to the cabin but before he went through the second one he unzipped his parka and lifted out the mask. Then he went inside to see the man.

Coal Porter was straddling a broken-backed kitchen chair, his big belly pushing against the table, slurping peaches out of a can. There was a puddle of the sweet, thick syrup on the table below him and rivulets of the same stuff were in his beard and running over his fingers. Coal was not a delicate eater. He had a two-year-old issue of *Playboy* spread out in front of him and he wasn't reading it for the articles. Sitting in the chair across from Coal was the rottweiler, its head bent over the table, licking the last morsels out of a can of Spam. There were no spills beneath the dog. They both looked up when Joe Moses stumbled in. The dog eyed the young man while Coal Porter fished the last two peaches out of the can. He was still chewing when he finally stood up. Joe unwrapped the mask and held it out in front of him and asked Coal what he could get for it.

Porter looked at the mask in Joe's hand like it might have been something the dog made. But before he reached for it he politely wiped his sticky hands on his jeans. Then he took the mask and hefted it, as if its value was based on its weight. He scowled down at the visage and observed as how it was an ugly old thing. Joe told him his grandfather made it and Coal Porter raised his eyebrows like that impressed him all to heck. He flipped it over and tested the leather strap, then pulled it over his own face, turned around to his dog, and let out a sudden whoop. The rottweiler jumped off its chair and scrambled headfirst under Coal's bed. Only its tail stump showed, and that was squirming a mile a minute. Coal Porter laughed and pulled the mask off his head and said he thought it was probably worth a pint of Jack Daniel's or a fifth of something like vodka. Unless the boy wanted some buds, then he could probably afford a dime bag.

Joe Moses scratched at the side of his hairless chin while he considered Porter's offers. He asked if Coal didn't think he couldn't offer just a little more. Maybe the pint *and* the buds, for instance. Porter didn't think he could. You sure? Joe asked. He was pretty sure, Coal said.

Joe shifted to his other foot and told Porter he'd have to go outside and talk to his cousin. Coal gave him a condescending smile, handed back the mask, and said, You do that. But when you leave the room, he warned, the offer might just have to drop a little lower. He looked around his cabin like there were forty, fifty other people standing in a line. My stuff is going fast, he told the boy.

Bobby Lincoln was not happy standing outside in minus-ten degrees. He went around the side and peed against the cabin wall while he waited. When Joe came out and told him what the offer was, he got even less happy. And when his cousin told him the offer might have even dropped lower after he left the cabin, Bobby Lincoln got downright upset. He didn't come racing sixty miles across the tundra to have some fat *gussak* gyp him out of what was rightfully his. That mask was worth a whole case of Jack Daniel's. The longer Bobby stood out there and railed about the white man inside the cabin, the madder he got. Until finally he grabbed the mask out of Joe's hands. Never mind; he said, I'll get it myself. And he pushed against the first door.

Then Bobby Lincoln did a funny thing. Before he charged through that second door he pulled the mask over his face, just like Porter had done. And as he went in, he let out a whoop, just about like Porter's.

Now the thing about a *tuunraq* is that you can't predict what it's going to do unless you're the *angalkuk* and used to dealing with things in the spirit world. Even then, shamans have got to keep a tight rein or the power can get out of hand. Which might account for what happened next in that cabin.

Coal Porter kept a twelve-gauge next to his table. But when Bobby Lincoln came in whooping, Coal was on his knees, his front half under the bed, trying to drag his dog out. His butt wiggled when he heard Bobby barging in, but he couldn't get out from under the bed in time. Lincoln had the shaman's old knife out. He hopped right onto the fat man's back and plunged the blade in as deep as it would go. He heard a groan come from underneath the bed and he pulled the knife out and then stabbed again. When Coal Porter's knees buckled beneath him, Bobby jumped off, grabbed the man's legs, and started pulling him out from under the bed. He left the knife still quivering in the man's lower back.

Joe Moses heard the noise and got into the cabin just as Bobby finished pulling Porter from under the bed. He froze in the middle of the floor, his mouth wide open, his eyes about as big as plates. He stood there as his cousin pulled out the knife and struggled to roll the fat man onto his back. Porter was burbling as bright blood started oozing out his mouth and Bobby kicked him in the side of his head. Then he reached down, grabbed a handful of Porter's greasy gray hair and went to work on his throat.

There wasn't anything about Coal Porter to make him much of a man, but the way he went shouldn't happen to a dog. Which may be what that rottweiler was thinking. Or it could have just been the smell of Coal Porter's blood. But that beast suddenly came tearing out from under the bed, not making a sound, and in one leap was across the room and onto Joe Moses, chomping at his throat and doing a pretty good job of what Bobby was just finishing on Coal Porter.

Joe was down on the floor, his hands grabbing at the dog, trying to pull it away from his throat, but the rottweiler was locked on and grinding away like a glacier on rock. Only a lot faster. And that same bright blood started flecking the stunned and terrorized face of Joe Moses. Bobby left Porter twitching in his own blood and went to help Joe. He kicked at the dog and landed a good one on its ribs, but the rottweiler just scooted away from Bobby, dragging poor Joe like he was a bloody rag doll.

Bobby kicked again but missed. By this time Joe's eyes were rolled to the back of his head and his tongue was lolled out but he was still breathing. Bobby Lincoln tried a couple more kicks but that rottweiler just kept moving away. He finally threw himself onto the dog, slashing it with that bloody knife of his. And then the dog let go of Joe, only it was too late. Bobby slashed and stabbed and beat on that animal until it was lying dead in a pool of blood and fur. The inside of that cabin was a sight.

He could see Joe's chest lifting and falling as he knelt beside him. His cousin's eyes were still back someplace where they didn't belong and his face was drained white. Joe's throat was ripped wide open, and the sounds that were coming out were like winds in a terrible storm. Bobby Lincoln knelt there and watched as his cousin died.

He didn't find Porter's cache, but he didn't look too hard, either. With three bodies and all that blood, Bobby Lincoln was anxious to be somewhere else. The *tuunraq* mask was lying next to Coal Porter and he carried it over and laid it just above Joe's head. He pushed the knife deep into the dog's side, then wiped his own bloody prints off it and lifted Joe's hand, wrapping his fingers around the bone handle and pressing hard. He did his best to keep his feet out of the pools of blood. When he left, he closed both doors behind him.

Bobby drove his snowmachine into Bethel, losing his trail in the town's streets. When he doubled back he purposely rode over his own tracks going in the other direction. By the time the boy got home, it was dark and he went directly to his own cabin and parked his machine around the side. Once inside, he called the Moses house and when Alice answered he asked to talk to Joe. When Alice said she thought her brother was with him, Bobby said no, he hadn't seen him since that morning. Then Bobby apologized for saying those rude things about the way she smelled. Alice was quiet a minute and then said that was okay because she did, but she and her grandmother had taken a steam and now she smelled pretty good.

Maybe Bobby would like to come over and smell her himself and he said maybe he would.

The twins' grandmother was sitting in front of the TV when Bobby Lincoln walked in but when she saw who it was she made a sour face and silently got up and went back to her part of the cabin, closing the thin cloth curtain behind her. Alice grinned and shrugged her shoulders. Bobby asked where was Joe and she said he still wasn't home. Maybe he went hunting, she guessed. It was Bobby's turn to shrug. Alice smelled pretty good and that night Bobby spent a lot of time checking her out. And in the morning, Joe still wasn't home.

The troopers came in about ten o'clock. Bobby and Alice were still under the blankets so they asked the two men in uniform to please step back outside until they were decent. When they came back in, the grandmother emerged from behind her curtain and they all sat down and heard the bad news. The troopers said they were still investigating at Porter's cabin, but it looked like Joe and Coal got into it and then the dog, too. They had found the trapdoor to Coal's cache from the blood that seeped into the floor's seams and they thought Joe was probably bartering for some of Coal's stuff. Joe had a mask he was trying to trade, the troopers explained. The grandmother's eyes clouded over and she shrunk down inside her *quspeq* and didn't lift her head up after that.

Alice was crying hard because this was her twin brother and now she and her grandmother were alone, and Bobby Lincoln wrapped his arm protectively around her shoulders and assured her he was there for her. The troopers told Alice they would keep her informed and then they left. She cried some more and Bobby held her tight. The grandmother got off her chair and went to the back of the cabin and pulled her curtain closed. Bobby did his best to comfort Alice and he never went far from her side the rest of the day.

That night they were watching *Wheel of Fortune* when Bobby Lincoln felt the hairs on the back of his neck rise straight up and begin to twitch. He looked back over his shoulder toward the curtain, thinking Grandma might be sneaking up on him with an axe, but her curtain was still pulled and there was no sign of the old woman. When he turned back around he caught some movement from the window in the kitchen and when he looked, there was Joe Moses, wearing the mask, looking in at him. Bobby let loose an awful yell, scaring poor Alice so bad she slid to the floor. He leaped off the couch and out the front door, racing around to the side of the house. Only Joe wasn't there. He went clear around until he reached the front door, then circled the house again, just to make sure. Joe wasn't there. A badly shaken Bobby Lincoln went back inside. Alice was off the floor by now, demanding an explanation, so Bobby told her he thought he saw someone at the window, only he didn't say he thought it was her twin. He kept that part to himself.

Watching television with Alice Moses was not quite as relaxing after that. Bobby kept squirming around, looking back at the window and finally Alice said fine, if he wasn't going to sit still, she was going to bed. She went back to check on her grandmother and say good night, then she crawled into her bed. Bobby watched as she undressed and then he joined her.

A wind blew up sometime around midnight and whistled around the cabin walls. Bobby woke up when it first started but recognizing the sound, rolled over and went back to sleep. Along around two A.M. there was a light tapping, as if a tree limb was knocking against one of the windowpanes. But in the Yukon-Kuskokwim Delta there are no trees, so this was an unusual sound and Bobby Lincoln woke a second time. When he looked for what was making the noise, there was Joe Moses in that mask again, looking right at him through the window, tapping his finger on the glass. They stared at each other for a few seconds, then Joe disappeared and Bobby got out of Alice's bed and went over to the window. There was nothing out there that he could see and if he wasn't naked he might have gone out to look. He was already shivering pretty bad and it wasn't from the cold. He got dressed and sat on the couch, waiting, but Joe never came back.

The next morning Alice's grandmother came out from behind her curtain, even though Bobby was still in the house. The laws of nature were stronger than her dislike for the boy, and nature was demanding she use the honey bucket. They kept it in a little porch off the side of the house, where the odor wouldn't drift back inside. Alice fixed her tea and toast while Grandma was gone and had it waiting on the table when she came back. The old woman looked over at Bobby, still sitting on the couch, and walked right past the table and into the back of the cabin, pulling the curtain firmly closed behind her. Alice picked up the tea and toast and followed her behind the curtain. There was no use arguing with the old girl so Alice sat on the bed next to her grandmother while she ate, then carried the empty cup and dirty plate back out to the sink.

You need to move down to my place, Bobby told her when she finished washing the breakfast dishes. But Alice said no, her grandmother needed her and she was staying there. Bobby left then and didn't come back until dinnertime.

The two of them sat at the table and ate caribou stew while they listened to Alice's grandmother eating hers on the bed behind the curtain. They could hear the old woman's spoon as it scraped against the bottom of her bowl and then Alice went back and carried the empty dish out to the sink. They watched TV again, but Bobby was waiting for Joe to reappear and neither one of them ever got too relaxed. About eleven o'clock, Alice went to bed and Bobby went to use the honey bucket. He was sitting out there in the dark, with his pants around his ankles, when the door suddenly flew back, slamming hard against the side. Joe Moses had on a thick, black snowsuit zipped up to his neck and he was still wearing that damn mask. This time he had a hatchet in his right hand and as Bobby started to lean down to grab his pants, Joe swung hard and buried the blade in the floor, right between Bobby's feet. If that boy could have squeezed down the honey bucket, he would have dived right in. He let loose a loud, high-pitched scream, which brought Alice running from the house wearing only a parka over her flannel nightgown. But by the time she got there her twin had already disappeared and all she saw was her boyfriend sitting there with his pants down, blubbering like a baby. And he kept crying as she helped him back into the house. They were both shivering when they came in and Alice's grandmother had her head poked around the curtain, watching as they shuffled over to the couch. Alice fixed him tea while Bobby sat there, still shaking. Then she cuddled up beside him and made him tell what happened.

First he told her about seeing Joe in the window the night before, and how he came back and tapped on the glass in the middle of the night. Alice put her hand to her mouth and her eyes grew large and round but she kept quiet and let him finish. Then he told her about sitting on the honey bucket and Joe yanking open the door and swinging at him with the hatchet. He said he could see Joe's eyes through the mask and they were shining like two red-hot coals. He thought he might have heard him let out a ghostly groan, too. When he was done, Alice asked why her brother would have swung at him with a hatchet. Bobby took a moment to think about that and then said he didn't really know. He and Joe were pretty good friends, he thought, but now that he was a ghost it was a little hard to figure out what his cousin might be thinking. Bobby didn't say anything about his participation in the events at Coal Porter's. He could see Alice was already upset about her twin being a ghost and he thought it best not to upset her any more than she already was. But then he did remind her that a *tuunraq* mask was supposed to have a lot of powers, and maybe it was making Joe's ghost do creepy things.

In all the time Alice lived with her grandmother, she had never asked much about her grandfather being a shaman. That seemed to be something her grandmother did not want to talk about about. Shamans were part of the old ways, and most of those were gone and long forgotten. There was still plenty that was magical in the village, but now it was television with movie channels and Internet connections and microwaved popcorn. Magic doesn't necessarily go away, it just changes its appearance. Sort of like a *tuunraq*. But if Joe's ghost was upset, they were going to have to find some way to calm it down. Maybe, Alice said thoughtfully, things might get better once they buried his body. Bobby said he wasn't sure he could wait that long, especially if Joe was going to keep doing things with a hatchet. Tapping on a window was one thing, but attacking a man when his pants were down was something else. He intended no offense to Alice, he said, but her twin had already killed Coal Porter for no reason anyone knew about. Now it looked like he was coming after his best friend.

Alice did take some offense to that. When someone has just called your twin brother a murderer, it's hard to keep feeling warm and cozy toward him. She looked over at Bobby Lincoln a moment and then suggested maybe he would feel safer if he stayed in his own house for a while. Maybe the reason her brother was upset was because Bobby seemed to be around all the time, eating their food and sleeping in her bed and not really doing much of anything to help out around the place. And Grandma was forced to take up permanent residence behind the curtain now, and maybe Joe was upset about that, too. Alice said that Joe might feel better about things if Bobby Lincoln slept in his own bed for a change. That cabin started feeling real chilly all of a sudden, as if the outside door had been left wide open or Joe's cold ghost was suddenly inside. Bobby's eyes narrowed into two small slits. He stood up from the couch and said yeah, maybe that wasn't such a bad idea Alice had. He always knew she cared more about that old woman than she did about him. And sleeping in her bed wasn't all that much fun right now. Maybe you're right, he said, tightening both his hands into fists. He started to step toward her when there was a loud knock from the side of the cabin. Bobby swung on his heel and ran to the window, peering out at the darkness. But if Joe was out there, he never saw him. Alice had stood up and moved over by the kitchen table and when Bobby turned back around he just looked at her standing there. Then he picked up his parka and pulled it on and stomped out the door, not even bothering to pull it shut behind him. Alice waited until she heard his snowmachine drive off, then she closed the door and locked it, climbed back into her bed, and cried herself to sleep.

The next morning, when Alice awoke, the curtain was pulled back and her grandmother was sitting at the kitchen table, sipping tea and watching her as she stirred in her bed. The old woman smiled softly and quietly wished her good morning. Alice smiled back.

The two women spent that day together, cleaning out the cabin and putting Joe's things off to one side. Alice came across a pair of Bobby Lincoln's boxer shorts and one of his sweatshirts and she folded them into a paper bag and set it next to the door. In the afternoon Alice and her grandmother baked bread and when one of them knocked the flour sack onto the floor they both giggled like little girls. Bobby did not come around, but neither did Joe or his ghost. There was bingo in the community hall that night and they both went and Alice won twenty dollars. Bobby Lincoln was not at bingo either.

He was still brooding about his argument with Alice. He had just about convinced himself that Joe Moses really was responsible for Coal Porter's death, and he was feeling righteously abused by Joe's ghost. And also a little scared. So going up to Alice's was not much of a temptation and he never even thought about going to bingo. Once it got dark, Bobby hung clothes over his windows and tried to ignore all the little night noises that he ordinarily never heard. He waited until after midnight to go to bed and he had a hard time falling to sleep.

Shortly after he did, he was awakened. The clothing he hung so carefully over his windows was on the floor and his small cabin was filled with moonlight. He could see someone moving in the far corner and then Joe Moses crossed the room and stood over his bed, looking down at him. Bobby could not cry out or move or do anything but stare up at the masked figure hovering over him.

He was blinded by the blood. He never saw Joe throw it, but there must have been about a cupful and suddenly his face was drenched in blood and his nostrils filled with the sharp, earthy stench. He grabbed blindly for his sheet, swiping at his eyes, trying to clear them. By the time he could see again, Joe was gone and there was moonlight pouring in through the open door. Bobby jumped out of bed and dressed himself, pulling on his parka and boots. He grabbed his mittens and raced out the door, climbed onto his snowmachine and tore out of town. In the stillness of the village you could hear his engine over a mile away as Bobby streaked across the tundra.

The next afternoon he was found by two hunters about thirty miles due west of the village, curled into a tight ball, lying in a snowdrift on the frozen tundra. He was wearing only one of his mittens and there was still some blood on his face, although it was frozen now. The hunters lifted his body onto their sled and followed Bobby's tracks back to his snowmachine, about four miles farther west. Why he took off like that, in the middle of the night, without first filling his gas tank, was a puzzle.

After the days of mourning, that village buried both boys at the same time, side by side. As was the custom, there was a potlatch in the school gym afterward.

Alice ended up burning the paper sack with the boxers and sweatshirt, and she gave most of her twin's things to the men and boys in the village. A few days after the burial, with her grandmother's help, she took down the curtain that divided the cabin. With just the two of them, there was no need for it. They pushed the dresser that used to be Joe's next to grandmother's bed, and Alice helped her unpack the clothes folded into the cardboard boxes. In the third box she opened, Alice found an oblong mask with yellowed ivory teeth set around the mouth hole and a band of black painted across the eyes. She carried it over to the window above her grandmother's bed and studied it in the light. The old woman watched her. When Alice turned toward her and held out the mask, Grandma lifted her eyebrows. Your grandfather made that, she told her. He made two exactly alike and he used them in the men's lodge sometimes. After you twins were born, Grandma said, he put them away. He did not know all the power in those twin masks and he wanted to wait until you and Joe were grown up. Grandma nodded to the mask in Alice's hands. You can have that one, she said. Your brother took the twin.

Edward D. Hoch

The Vampire Theme

EDWARD D. HOCH is the author of more than 750 short stories, and is believed by many to be the foremost author of short mystery fiction. Nick Velvet, a thief who—for a substantial fee—steals only items of no intrinsic value, appears in many of these stories. Other recurring characters are Dr. Sam Hawthorne, an elderly general practitioner, and the unusual Simon Ark, who claims to be a two-thousand-year-old Coptic priest.

Hoch has also served as president of the Mystery Writers of America, and received that organization's Grand Master award in 2001. He has not only written every type of mystery story, he's also invented a few along the way. "The Vampire Theme," his contribution to this year's collection, which first appeared in *Ellery Queen's Mystery Magazine,* shows him in fine form, as usual.

The Vampire Theme

Edward D. Hoch

Michael Vlado was always pleased to see his old friend Segar, though the former police captain rarely visited the Gypsy village since his promotion to a top security post in the Romanian government.

"I like to come here," he told Michael on this late-summer's day when the sky was a clear blue dotted only with a few lazy clouds. They were walking back to the corral where some of the foals were frisking with the mares. "It is only that I find too few excuses to venture into the mountains from Bucharest. It is a vast modern city now. You should visit us."

Michael smiled at him. "Perhaps I will. But what excuse did you find today, old friend?"

"I am driving across the Carpathians to the town of Sighisoara. Have you ever been there?"

"I have passed through it. Your maps will tell you my farm is about the halfway point. But there is nothing in Sighisoara to interest state security."

"Would you believe me if I told you the good people there are building a theme park to compete for tourist money by luring busloads of visitors there?"

"Surely not a Transylvanian Disneyland."

Segar chuckled. "You are not far off. It is to be a vampire theme park costing the equivalent of thirty million American dollars, most of it locally financed. If an agreement can be reached with Universal Pictures, the company that controls the rights to the film interpretation of Count Dracula, he will be celebrated with a roller coaster and haunted house. If they can't get the Dracula rights, they plan to use Vlad the Impaler, from medieval history."

"Perhaps he was a relative of mine," Michael Vlado said with a chuckle. "I can sell them the rights. But what does this have to do with security?"

"Anything that might bring thousands of tourists a year into the country has to do with security, Michael. Do you want to come along?"

"Stay over tonight for one of Rosanna's fine dinners," he decided. "In the morning I will drive to Sighisoara with you."

Michael's village of Gravita was in the foothills on the southern side of the Transylvanian Alps. In order to reach Sighisoara on the northern side they had to drive through the mountain pass that led through Brasov. It was a lonely journey with only occasional sightings of other cars. Michael could understand why Segar had desired companionship, and yet he had a suspicion that something else was involved. Surely Romania's security police must have small planes at their disposal for a 150-mile journey over the mountains. Segar would not have driven through Gravita unless he wanted Michael to accompany him.

"Are there any Roms involved in this theme park?" he asked Segar casually as they were driving through Brasov. They'd left his village at daybreak, around five o'clock, in hopes of reaching their destination well before noon. The mountain roads were not conducive to speeding.

"One of the chief backers is Saxon Medias. Do you know him?"

"Only by name. I wouldn't call him a true Rom. He has denied his Gypsy blood on more than one occasion when it suits his business interests."

"That may be a wise move on his part," Segar suggested. "Feeling is running against Gypsies in many countries these days."

"Mainly because they move around and cross national boundaries. The Roms who live in my foothill villages are not nomadic. We have been content there for generations. That is true of most Romanian Gypsies, as you know."

"Medias considers himself a businessman of the modern world. He spends much of his time in Vienna. To be associated with the legendary trickery and dishonesty of Gypsies would be fatal to his image."

Michael gazed out at the passing scene, where farmland was beginning to replace the rocky mountain crags. "What part does he play in this business?"

"He owns the land and will be a partner in the enterprise. Construction has already begun, and Medias maintains an office and home there. Most townspeople are in favor of the plan, but it was felt that the central government should have a voice in it, too. You know the Gypsy mind better than anyone I know, Michael. I'd like your opinion of him."

Soon they were in sight of the houses and buildings of Sighisoara, and Segar drove past fields of corn and occasional grape arbors. A vast area of farmland was being excavated for the project. "They hope to have it open by next year," he said. A sign by the road, flanking a field of sunflowers, read in quaint antique lettering: FUTURE HOME OF VAMPIRE LAND! KEEPING OUR HERITAGE ALIVE FOR THE NEXT GENERATION!

Michael shook his head. "Are they serious about this?"

"As serious as thirty million American dollars."

"I'm surprised they haven't been laughed out of the country! Somehow the idea of a vampire roller coaster in the middle of Romania seems—" He broke off as they rounded a corner and came upon a car wreck at the side of the road. A police car and an ambulance were already on the scene. It appeared the car had gone into a ditch.

"I'd better stop," Segar decided.

He showed the police officer his identity card and asked what had happened. "Car went off the road, sir," the officer responded, respectful of Segar's position. "The driver's dead. We haven't removed the body yet."

Michael peered in the window of the car. There was broken glass from one of the side windows on the seat, and the body of a short middle-aged man had a number of facial lacerations as well as a gash in his throat. Oddly, there was no blood visible in the car. "Something's wrong here," he said quietly to Segar.

"What's that?"

"Look for yourself. No blood."

Segar frowned. "What does that mean?"

"They'd better examine the body. Either he was killed somewhere else, or the vampire has come early to Sighisoara."

The dead man's name was Otto Critsaller. He was an Austrian developer who'd come from Vienna for meetings regarding the theme park. He'd been in Sighisoara for two days and apparently was on his way home at the time of the accident. Except that it wasn't an accident. Men with no blood in their bodies don't drive cars.

No one had seen the car go off the road and into the ditch. A passing farmer noticed it shortly before eight o'clock and notified the police. They learned this much when Segar telephoned the local authorities shortly before their afternoon meeting with Saxon Medias. They also confirmed Michael's suspicion that the body had very little blood remaining in it. "That didn't happen at the scene," Michael insisted. "Someone stopped him on his way home, killed him, drained his blood, and drove the car off the road."

"His wallet and money were still on him. There was no luggage in the trunk, only a cooler with a little water in it. That doesn't look as if he was headed home. But why would anyone do that? To publicize their vampire theme park?"

"Perhaps Saxon Medias can tell us when we see him," Michael suggested.

They met him at his makeshift office in the town hall, surrounded by plans and models for Vampire Land. Medias was a large man with piercing brown eyes and a bald head that seemed to be polished. He looked more like a wrestler than a business entrepreneur, but then Michael noticed a gold earring that matched his own and decided he was trying to be a Gypsy after all. When Segar introduced Michael as a Gypsy king, the large man smiled. "I knew you were one of us. Where are your people?"

"In Gravita, in the foothills north of Bucharest."

He nodded sagely, lighting a long Russian cigarette as he spoke. "Is vampire lore prevalent in your area?"

Michael told him, "I know of no one in our village who would cross the mountains to ride on a Dracula roller coaster."

"No, no!" Saxon Medias assured him. "That is for the tourists. I mean the real vampire lore. Have your people been visited in the nighttime?"

"Only by an occasional owl." Michael thought it wise not to mention the bats that sometimes hovered over his horse barn at dusk.

The man's brown eyes seemed to drill into him. "Then you are not a believer?"

"In many things, but not in vampires."

"I wasn't, either, in my younger days. Are you aware that a man was found dead here this very morning with most of the blood drained from his body?"

"We came upon the scene while driving in this morning," Segar told him. "Did you know him?"

Medias nodded. "Otto Critsaller from Vienna. I met with him yesterday. He was one of several contractors bidding on construction of our theme park. The site preparation and foundation work are already under way, but the main contractor has yet to be chosen."

"You mention the lack of blood," Segar remarked, reverting to his former days as a police investigator. "Do you really believe he was killed by a bloodsucking vampire?"

The Gypsy entrepreneur hesitated before he answered. "As a businessman I welcome the publicity. I would like nothing better than to have newspapers all over Europe report the story. What better way to publicize Vampire Land?" He allowed himself a slight smile. "But as a practical man I believe poor Critsaller was beaten and robbed somewhere else. He simply bled to death and the body was placed in his car to make it look like an unfortunate accident."

"His money wasn't taken," Segar said. "It doesn't look like robbery. Did you know him well?"

"I met him in Vienna and he'd been here three or four times before, discussing the project. A fascinating man, claimed to be an illegitimate descendant of Queen Victoria through a liaison her son Leopold had with a French girl in Paris in 1882. He really wanted the job, but there's a Romanian company and a Russian one who are also bidding."

He led them over to a table in one corner of the office where an elaborate scale model of the planned theme park was displayed. "We saw the land being cleared on our way in," Michael told him. "Do you really expect to have this built and open to the public by next year?"

"Not for the summer tourist season, I fear. The construction bids won't be in for another month. It depends upon the severity of the winter, but more likely it will be late next year at the very best."

"Will Critsaller's murder delay things?"

"It shouldn't. His firm was never more than an outside possibility."

A young dark-haired woman with a sturdy frame and thick legs entered the office with some papers. "The local police wish to speak to you when you're free," she told him.

"Thank you, Hilda." He turned back to them with a sigh. "I can see very little will be accomplished today. Just what was it that brought you here, Mr. Segar?"

"Security concerns. That is my job. As I understand it, you plan to bring a great many tourists into the country on bus tours."

"We hope to. A hotel chain has already expressed interest in building lodgings, although in its first stage the park will be compact enough to be experienced in a single day."

Segar made some notes. "There would not be any overnight visitors?"

"It's doubtful, until we put in more rides and attractions. To start, we will have the roller coaster, the haunted house, a golf course, and a small zoo. Something for the tourists, and for the local people as well." He pointed to the model. "In this area we'll have a medieval Main Street for shopping and entertainment events."

"There can't be many golfers in town."

The large man waved away the objection. "More people are taking it up. The new government has changed the way we live. Romania has entered the twenty-first century. I envision this town becoming a busy city someday."

Segar pondered that. "There's a feeling in Bucharest that you may be blurring the line between Transylvanian history and fiction."

"Some of our people are upset with the plans," Medias admitted. "Dr. Warsaw, a local physician, is leading a campaign against the theme park. However, I feel this is a way of honoring our heritage. I am not talking of the Dracula movies from Hollywood but rather our entire medieval history back to Vlad the Impaler."

"I think small children would find Dracula less scary than Vlad," Michael told him. "And I say that as one who bears a form of his name."

They talked for some time while Segar made occasional notes. Finally, when they parted, Medias shook hands with Michael and said, "Perhaps I can visit your village one day soon. Now I must excuse myself and go talk to the police."

"One thing," Segar said as they were leaving. "Critsaller had been here two days. Where was he staying?"

"We have only two hotels at present, and the Carpathian is the better of them. There are others closer to the ski slopes."

"Is that where he stayed? The Carpathian?"

"I believe so. He was there on his earlier visits." He called his secretary back in. "Hilda, was Critsaller at the Carpathian this time?"

"That's where he asked me to make the reservation. He preferred it because they have little refrigerators in the rooms, just like in the big cities."

Back in the car, Segar suggested they stop at the Carpathian. "He must have had a small suitcase or overnight bag with him. Would a thief have killed him for that?"

"Anything is possible," Michael replied.

But when they reached the Carpathian, a modest two-story hotel on the other side of town, a surprise awaited them. Otto Critsaller had not checked out. He was still registered in room 17. While Segar showed his credentials in an attempt to gain access to the room, Michael glanced around the small lobby. The place had no restaurant or bar, but a cooler with sliding-glass doors was available for guests to purchase beer and soft drinks for their room. A hotel bulletin board already displayed a sign proclaiming the advent of Vampire Land.

"All right," Segar said at last. "The manager will show us his room."

It was on the first floor near the back. He unlocked the door to let them in, then stood silently watching them. Segar went first to the closet door, opening it to reveal a dark blue garment bag. Inside were a change of clothes and a few toilet articles including an electric razor.

"He didn't check out," Michael said. "And he left his clothes here."

"Odd."

He left Segar to examine the garment bag while he toured the room. The bed was made and nothing seemed out of place. But then he remembered the little refrigerator under the television set. He opened it and found a plastic jug filled with a thick dark-red liquid. "What's this?"

Segar stared at it. "Blood?"

Michael opened the top and tried to pour a little out. "It's too thick for blood."

"Some sort of narcotic? Did he come here to buy it?"

"I don't know," Michael admitted. "We'd better leave it here for now."

When they were outside, Segar shook his head. "I don't know what we're getting ourselves into here. Do you have any suggestions?"

"Just one. Medias mentioned a local physician, Dr. Warsaw, who is opposed to the theme park. I wonder if his opposition might be so strong that he would kill off any would-be contractors."

The doctor was easy to locate, in his office at the town's clinic. He was a bald and bearded man with thick glasses. "I know nothing of this," he told them after Segar had explained the reason for their visit. "If I wanted to kill anyone it would be that damned Gypsy Saxon Medias, not some builder from Vienna."

"Do you have some prejudice against Gypsies?" Segar asked.

"No more so than anyone else. I would oppose Vampire Land no matter who proposed it." He had come around from behind his desk and now he removed his glasses to run a hand over his weary eyes. Michael thought it best to leave the questioning to Segar, and he took the opportunity to browse through some of Dr. Warsaw's medical texts. There was nothing on vampirism, of course. It wasn't even in the index.

Segar tried a different tactic. "Is there anyone in the town who might use violence to frustrate plans for Vampire Land?"

"Several people, some of whom are less charitable toward Gypsies than I am."

"Name one."

"Constello Alba. He's one of the workmen on the project, but he is quite outspoken against it."

There was nothing more to be learned from Dr. Warsaw, and they departed soon after. "What now?" Michael asked his friend.

"This Alba might be worth a visit. Let us drive out to the construction site."

Michael smiled. "You can't get away from police work, can you? Suppose you tell me the real reason you came here, and why you brought me along."

Segar headed the car back toward the construction site they'd observed on their way into town. "There have been threats," he answered reluctantly.

"What sort of threats?"

"My office has received three anonymous letters, apparently from the same person, warning of violence unless the Vampire Land project was halted. The tone of the letters seemed especially threatening toward Gypsies, and Saxon Medias was mentioned by name. I contacted the local authorities, but they treated the letters as some sort of hoax and wanted no government interference in their local affairs. The northern towns often treat the mountains as more than a geographic dividing line. They view it as a political one, too, and want nothing to do with Bucharest."

"But you came anyway."

"Because it is my job, Michael."

Segar turned the car into the bumpy dirt road past the Vampire Land sign. Perhaps a hundred workmen with heavy equipment were busy digging foundations for the theme-park structures. It took them awhile to locate Constello Alba. He was bare-chested and muscular, working in one of the holes while he directed the pouring of concrete. When he climbed up the ladder to meet them his expression was uncertain and a bit wary.

"You wanted me?"

Segar showed his credentials. "I understand you've been opposed to this project."

"Just opposed to Gypsies taking the jobs that belong to honest men."

"Are there Gypsies working here?"

For the first time Alba let his gaze shift to Michael, taking in the red tunic and the earring. "You're one of them, aren't you?"

"I am a Gypsy king from Gravita, across the mountains. Mr. Segar requested that I accompany him."

Alba spat on the ground before him. "I don't talk to Gypsies."

"Did you send the government some letters about this project?" Segar asked.

"I don't know what you're talking about."

"If you have a complaint, you should take it to your town government. We will not allow any sort of violent protest here. One man has already been killed this morning under suspicious circumstances."

"Ask the Gypsy about that. Ask Saxon Medias."

"Do you know anything about it?"

"No."

Michael asked, "Is this just a theme park, or do you believe there are real vampires roaming the land?"

Alba's expression turned just a bit sly. "They tell me that body this morning had been drained of blood. Is that true?"

"We're still investigating," Segar replied.

"Then it was either a vampire or some Gypsy trying to get publicity for his theme park."

"Can you believe Saxon Medias would kill someone just for publicity?"

He spat again. "I'd believe just about anything of a Gypsy."

"All right." Segar dismissed him with a wave. "Get back in your hole."

It was late afternoon by that time, and Michael knew they would be staying overnight. They took a room at the Carpathian and he telephoned home to tell Rosanna of their plans. Then Segar phoned Saxon Medias to tell him where they'd be.

It was just after midnight when the phone in their room rang. They'd just gone to bed and neither was asleep. Segar's bed was closest and he answered, speaking with growing alarm. "We'll be right there," he said, and hung up.

"What is it?" Michael asked.

"Get dressed! Someone just tried to kill Medias and his secretary. They threw firebombs at his house and her apartment."

The bombs were Molotov cocktails of the crudest sort, bottles of gasoline with flaming wicks in the neck. Medias had been lucky. The bomb missed his window and landed on the porch. The one at his secretary's ground-floor apartment had done more damage, smashing a window and setting fire to her living room carpet before it could be extinguished. They drove directly there and found Medias trying to comfort her.

"You're alive, Hilda," he said, holding her gently as she sobbed. "That's the important thing."

She was standing in the apartment doorway, unable to speak, wearing a robe over her nightgown. Firemen were pulling up the remains of the carpet and removing it, along with a coffee table that had been badly singed. The rest of the room had been spared, and even a clear glass vase crammed with too many sunflowers sat untouched atop the television set. "I was still up," she managed to tell them. "I was watching television when that flaming bottle came crashing through the window. My God, I thought I was going to die!"

"We saw a fellow named Constello Alba this afternoon," Segar told

Medias. "He seemed to have a great hatred of Gypsies in general and your theme park in particular."

Medias nodded. "He's been nothing but trouble. I'll ask the contractor to fire him in the morning."

"Do you think he could have done this?"

"If he didn't, he knows who did."

"Were both attacks at the same time?" Michael asked.

"Mine was first," Medias said. "I heard the bottle hit the porch about twenty minutes before midnight. I never thought to call Hilda and warn her."

"They hit me about ten minutes later," she told them. "I called the fire department and tried to throw water on it. When the firemen arrived I phoned Mr. Medias."

Michael stepped carefully over the soggy floor to the broken window. Glass crunched underfoot and he saw green pieces from the gasoline bomb. He picked a clear curved piece out of his rubber-soled shoe. He leaned through the broken window and glanced left and right along the straight lines of the building. More glass glittered in the grass below. "Did you see anyone at all out here?" he asked Hilda.

"No one. I thought I heard a car drive away but I couldn't be sure."

Segar took Michael aside. "Do you think this could be connected to Critsaller's killing?"

"I've never heard of a vampire throwing a Molotov cocktail. This seems more Alba's style. Yet would he be foolish enough to try this right after we'd questioned him?"

There was no answer to be found that night. One person was dead and two others had been attacked, yet the crimes hardly seemed related. Back at their hotel Michael went to sleep puzzling over it and remembering something else, something he'd read while looking through one of Dr. Warsaw's medical books.

In the morning Segar decided they should head back. "I can't help feeling that our presence yesterday somehow triggered those firebombs last night. I'm sorry I brought you into this, Michael. We seem to have stirred up more prejudice against Gypsies without really accomplishing anything else."

"We had nothing to do with anything that happened," Michael tried to assure him. "After breakfast we'll go back to Saxon's office and I'll try to explain it all."

"You know who killed Critsaller? And who firebombed Medias and his secretary?"

Michael nodded while he finished dressing. "It came to me when I woke up this morning, clear as day."

"Is this a matter for the local militia?"

"I'll let you be the judge of that."

"Certainly a vampire—"

"There was no vampire."

"—or someone pretending to be one—"

"Wait until we talk to Saxon Medias."

He was at his office when they arrived, nervously smoking one of his Russian cigarettes. "I've been up all night," he told them. "I took Hilda to my house and had her sleep in my bed. I planned to sleep on the sofa, but I stayed up instead, going over every letter and threat we received since our first announcement of Vampire Land."

"Did you find many leads?" Segar asked.

"Too many." He patted the pile of papers on his desk. "But once construction is complete and tourists begin arriving, the townsfolk will realize this is a boon and not a blunder. Even the news of this vampire killing could help us."

"Michael says there is no vampire," Segar told him.

The bald Gypsy frowned. "No vampire? Not a supernatural one, perhaps, but anyone who sucks the blood from a body could be considered a vampire."

Michael glanced around. "I'll tell you exactly what happened. Perhaps you'd want Hilda to join us and take notes."

"Certainly." He called her in from the next room and she joined them with her pad.

"You see," Michael began, "there was one fact none of you knew about Otto Critsaller. He was a hemophiliac."

"What?" Saxon Medias asked.

"A bleeder. Someone who suffers from a rare blood disease that prevents the blood from coagulating. It leads to excessive bleeding even from minor injuries, and can be fatal."

"How do you know that Critsaller suffered from this?"

Michael held up a finger. "You told me he claimed to be an illegitimate descendant of Queen Victoria's son Leopold. In glancing through one of Dr. Warsaw's medical texts I learned a great deal about hemophilia. Leopold was one of many royal personages in Europe afflicted with the disease. It's hereditary. Leopold's sons would have been free of it, but any daughters would have become carriers, passing it on to their own sons in fifty percent of the cases. It came down like that through perhaps three generations before Critsaller's mother would have passed it on to him."

"You said it happens only half the time," Segar pointed out.

"But it happened to Critsaller. We know because there was a cooler in his car with melted ice inside. He brought something with him that had to be kept cold. That's why he needed a hotel with a refrigerator in the room. On a trip like this, to a small Romanian town without modern medical facilities, he could take no chances. He brought along a blood concentrate called cryoprecipitate, prepared from the blood of a single donor of his blood type. It could be mixed with distilled water and given to him in a transfusion if necessary. Once I thought about it, I knew that had to be the answer. If someone had pumped or sucked the blood out of him, it would have been completely gone. The autopsy report told us some blood remained in the body, because the bleeding would have ceased once he died."

"Did Dr. Warsaw's book tell you who murdered him, too?"

"I didn't need that." Michael turned to Saxon Medias's secretary. "Hilda, suppose you tell us why you threw that vase at Otto Critsaller and killed him with it."

"It's all right," Segar announced, bending over the fallen woman. "She's only fainted."

Medias brought her a glass of water and soon she was sitting up, shaking her head. "This is unreal," she told Michael. "How could you have known?"

"There were too many sunflowers in your remaining vase. When I stepped on a piece of clear glass I assumed it was from your window, but then I noticed it was curved. You had two clear glass vases, and you threw one at Critsaller. It cut his neck and he bled to death on your living room carpet while you watched, helpless to do anything."

"He kept telling me to get the blood from the refrigerator. It didn't make sense."

"You look strong and he was a small man. After he died you managed to carry or drag him out to his car and drove it off the road where it was found later. Then you walked back home before it was fully daylight. But there was no way you could clean all that blood from your carpet. So you devised a plan with the Molotov cocktails. You threw one at your employer's porch to make it seem like a protest against the theme park. Then you drove quickly home and smashed your window from inside the house. The glass all went outside, but you didn't worry because the glass from the vase was still on the carpet inside. You didn't think about its being curved. And it was a bad idea to stuff all those sunflowers in one vase before you smashed the bottle of gasoline and set fire to your carpet."

Hilda shook her head. "I think I was in shock all day. He'd stopped by my apartment before, on his other trips, and behaved like a gentleman. This time was different. When I told him I wouldn't sleep with him he came at me. I picked up the vase to protect myself and he ran right into it. When I saw all the blood I just went to pieces. Somehow I had to get rid of the body and protect myself."

"You should have told me," Medias said. "I could have helped you. Perhaps I still can."

"All this must be reported to the local police," Segar told them.

"Of course."

He studied them for a moment and then said, "I leave that to you. Michael and I must be starting back."

Medias walked them to the car. "You have been very helpful in this matter. Come back when Vampire Land is open and I can give you free passes."

"We will do that," Segar promised, and Michael had the feeling he meant it.

Ralph McInerny

The Devil That Walks at Noonday

RALPH McINERNY is a professor of philosophy at the University of Notre Dame and the author of several series, including those starring Father Dowling, Andrew Broom, and Sister Mary Teresa, as well as his mysteries set at Notre Dame itself. He has also written several wonderful nonseries mystery novels, including *As Good as Dead, Slattery,* and *The Ablative Case.* Noted for his strong and colorful characters, as well as an enlightened approach to spiritual matters, McInerny's novels have been a staple for mystery readers since 1977. First published in *Ellery Queen's Mystery Magazine,* "The Devil That Walks at Noonday" does not feature any of Ralph's series characters, but instead is a self-contained short story that examines a familiar theme of his—the weight of human nature and conscience.

The Devil That Walks at Noonday

Ralph McInerny

After they had pumped his stomach in Emergency a rumpled, whiskery figure pushed aside the curtain and came into the alcove. Earl Green looked at him with the expression of one who had just come back from the dead. The man smelled of cigarettes and needed a shower.

"Mr. Green."

He nodded. The man opened and closed his wallet. "Rankin. You're lucky to be alive."

"Who isn't?"

"Why did you take poison?"

"Poison? It must have been something I ate."

"Like an arsenic sandwich?"

"Arsenic!"

Rankin nodded. "How did you get to the hospital?"

"I was having lunch. I collapsed. Someone must have made a call."

"Where were you having lunch?"

The memories might have been ancient, not just hours ago. Earl recalled the prelude to his being rushed to the hospital by paramedics but it all seemed so long ago.

"They start working on you in the ambulance?"

"I guess so."

"That's why you got here alive."

"You're not serious about the arsenic, are you?"

Rankin nodded and the smell of cigarettes and sweat was strong.

"That's why I'm here. There are two possibilities. Either you tried to commit suicide and thought better of it. Or someone wants to get rid of you."

"But I have no enemies."

"So it was suicide."

"No." Earl hesitated. "It's against my religion."

"It's against the law, too, but people do it all the time."

"I didn't commit suicide and no one wants to kill me."

"Tell me about lunch again."

Earl belonged to the brown-bag set at the office where he worked, occupying a middle position and perfectly content with it. He did not want anyone reporting to him and he felt no resentment when young people clambered past him up the corporate ladder. Every year there was a fresh supply of ambitious young people, the women as ambitious as the men, and Earl watched their single-minded drive to excel, be noticed, be promoted. In a year or two they disappeared from sight and he sometimes wondered what happened to them. There were lateral moves, of course, and a very few rose to real authority, but by and large they were used up and let go, burned out or urged to look elsewhere. Loyalty was nonexistent since every year there was another platoon of new employees in their dark suits and expensive ties and hungry looks. Earl's initial decision to resign from the rat race had not been philosophical. He had been influenced by two coworkers, Pence as an example, Martha as a confidante.

Pence was an older man whose serenity was noteworthy in the fast-paced firm. He had a corner office, he worked minimally but efficiently at his job, and lived for retirement. At first Earl was repelled by such deliberate mediocrity, then he became fascinated. One day he brought his lunch in a brown bag and looked into Pence's office at noon.

"Mind if I join you?"

"Pull up a pew," Pence said, closing his book.

"If you'd rather read . . ."

"Books are always waiting for us when we want them."

Earl tried to read the title of the book and Pence noticed. He held it up. "Henry James. *The American*. Do you know it?"

Earl felt almost ashamed when he said he did not.

"Then a great pleasure lies ahead of you."

Martha joined them, sitting primly on a straight-back chair with her open plastic lunch bucket on her lap. Pence assumed they knew each other, which they did not, but neither corrected the older man. Pence was talking about Henry James in a conversational tone, not a lecture, just speaking of an author he obviously loved and knew well. Earl's thoughts went back to high school assignments, but reading was obviously not a chore to Pence. But what most struck Earl Green was the fact that Pence had carved out a place for himself, more or less defined his own relationship to the firm, and was allowed to exist there on his own terms. At first it seemed lack of ambition; then it seemed the steady pursuit of a goal that had little to do with the boring tasks of the office.

"Is he married?" he asked Martha.

"Oh, yes. But his children are grown. He likes to say that they make far more money than he does."

Gradually Earl and Martha realized that they, too, wished to live as Pence did. Earl decided that it was merely a matter of having a different

ambition, not having none at all. Those who seemed to be giving everything to the firm were really only working for themselves, so maybe his
was not all that different an ambition after all. Pence's notion that his employment did not require that he deliver himself over body and soul to the
work that occupied him during the day seemed more sensible as time passed
and Earl watched with a distant air the young hotshots enslave themselves
to the routine of their work, seemingly thinking of nothing else but onward
and upward. He had learned a secret that they would never discover. Not
that he wasn't an excellent accountant, but he acquired the knack of re-
sisting the suggestion that he should aspire to rise above the comfortable
level on which he was. And Martha, too, was happy to be on a plateau.
With her he could discuss in veiled terms the bargain they had struck with
themselves. Of course, he never explained to Helen why major promotions
never came his way.

"Maybe you should talk to a headhunter and see what other possibilities there are."

"All jobs are pretty much the same for an accountant."

"But how can you know if you don't look?"

The trick was never to argue about it, to nod and seem to agree and
go on as before.

"Earl, sometimes I think you have no ambition at all."

"That's not true, Helen."

"Well, you could have fooled me."

"I would never try to fool you."

The one ambition he and Helen shared—to have a family—was denied
them, but Helen did not become resigned. She became more than ever
determined that Earl should rise in the company.

"I'm an accountant, Helen. I don't want to be promoted out of that."

"But young Jackson is now head of the department."

And so he was. Phil Jackson was a whirlwind, a great success, but
success brought ulcers, not a sense of achievement. And he developed an
interest in Martha. Earl observed the progress, or lack of it, of this office
romance. Martha told Jackson that she had no desire to quit working and
settle down.

"Oh, you should go on working. Marriage needn't interfere with your
job."

"It won't," Martha said, and eventually Jackson got her meaning. Earl
found that he was relieved when Jackson grudgingly gave up his pursuit of
Martha. Jackson needed someone who shared his attitude toward his job.

Eventually Pence retired, doing so at the earliest possible age, so he
could devote himself to cultivated leisure. "Our main task is to become a
real human being," he said in what Earl came to think of as Pence's farewell
address. "A job is only a means to that end."

Such heresy was not for the ears of such as Jackson, nor for Helen's,
either. Their domestic conversations turned constantly on Earl's status in

the firm. He found that he could win this argument only when he told Martha of it later.

"Has she ever thought of getting a job?"

Was that the solution? The problem was that Earl's developing understanding of himself excluded a working wife. He liked the thought of his wife at home, queen of all she surveyed, busy at her gardening, supported by him. But it was the degree of the support that became Helen's constant theme.

"There is nothing we need that we don't have."

"All you want is your books."

For he had come to imitate Pence in this as well. His mentor had had only a modest collection of books. "The public library, Earl, supplies me all I need."

That made sense to Earl. Each week he brought home an armload of books and each week when Helen saw them she groaned. Earl weathered the storm, mastering the impulse to instruct Helen on the meaning of life. Over the years, his wife became a bitter and discontented woman.

"If she were really discontent, she would leave you," Martha said.

"She would never do that."

"You're very sure of yourself."

"No, I am very sure of her. For all her complaints, she knows we have a comfortable life."

"Does she read?"

"She prefers television."

Silence. He appreciated the fact that Martha never criticized Helen. The two women met from time to time, at the annual office picnic, but Helen had no idea how important Martha was to his peace of mind at work. And at home, too. Listening patiently to Helen complain, Earl would imagine telling Martha of it. Martha would listen, nod, understand, but never say anything against Helen.

Earl was given Pence's office after the older man's retirement, and it was there, every workday at noon, that he and Martha had their lunches and talked. Martha had become enthralled with the novels of Willa Cather and it was a pleasure to listen to her speak of them. Her favorite was *Lucy Gayheart*. Earl's current enthusiasm was Trollope, but he would rather listen to Martha than speak.

Martha had struck him at first as plain, but with the passage of time he had come to think that hers was a rare beauty, as much of the mind as of the face, and she was aglow as she spoke of Cather's heroine. She was still speaking enthusiastically when the time came for her to return to her desk. Earl rose and accompanied her to the door. They reached for the knob simultaneously and his hand closed over hers. He did not withdraw it immediately. Martha avoided his eyes. When she was gone and the door again closed, he sat at his desk and stared at his hand. He could still feel the warmth of Martha's.

The following day, he left the door open as they had their lunch. Martha was silent, wanting him to speak. And he did, of Lady Glencora. Martha's face as she listened was a kaleidoscope of emotions. Earl fell silent. From the outer office came the murmur of voices. He found himself resenting the presence of others. The noon hour was his own, and Martha's. He got up and closed the door. When he turned, she looked at him, her face still soft with the emotion with which she had been listening to him. He crossed the room and stood before her. She dropped her eyes. After a moment, he bent and kissed the top of her head. Immediately she looked up and then his lips were on hers and he took her in his arms and held her close. Neither of them said anything. It was as if the years of their acquaintance had been moving toward this moment. He continued to hold her in his arms but after some minutes she moved away from him. Their silence was more eloquent than anything they had ever spoken. When he was alone, Earl realized that things would never be the same again.

There are men who can love two women, but Earl felt that he had never loved anyone but Martha. From that time on, evenings with Helen were an exquisite torture, the penalty he paid for being with Martha during the day. He began to leave earlier for the office and this was applauded by Helen, who took it for the belated birth of ambition. Martha noticed that he was coming in earlier and this became her practice as well. Now they had nearly an hour before the others arrived, as well as lunch together. As soon as Earl closed the door of his office on them Martha came wordlessly into his arms. For weeks he dwelt in a dream world until, in the nature of things, he found his furtive trysts with Martha insufficient. He imagined them planning to steal a weekend together, but he could never bring himself to make such a proposal to Martha. Their love participated in the literary loves of which they spoke with such enthusiasm. There was only one solution. He must free himself of Helen.

But how? He had been so acquiescent in her discontent that he could hardly tell her that he no longer loved her and wanted his freedom. For all her complaining, Helen had never shown any inclination to leave him. He began to imagine other ways in which he could be free of her. In the greenhouse off the garage, where Helen puttered with her plants, his eye fell on a little container of arsenic. He read up on the poison and imagined ways in which he could administer it to his wife. But his blood ran cold at the thought. The time came when he even thought of taking it himself, thereby finding a solution to his dilemma. And suddenly the plan formed in his mind.

There was no question of involving Martha in his plan. He knew her well enough to predict the horror with which she would react to such an idea. But he would need her unwitting help in order to bring it off. And everything worked as he had planned.

One noon hour, he suddenly stopped talking and rose to his feet.

"What's the matter?" Martha asked.

"I feel ill." He began to breathe with difficulty and then fell back in his chair. She rushed to his side and he managed to whisper, "Call nine-one-one."

It was when the ambulance was pulling into Emergency that he bit into the half-sandwich he had in his pocket. He knew panic when he saw how crowded it was in Emergency. He needed immediate treatment or he would die. Slumping to the floor got him the attention he needed and soon his stomach was pumped and he was safe.

Rankin said, "Are you married?"

"Yes. My wife should be notified!"

"Does she make your lunch?"

"Oh, come on. We're happily married."

Rankin loosened his tie. "It's hot in here." He might have been explaining the ripe odor that emanated from him. "Do you have arsenic around the house?"

"Of course not."

"What's your home number?"

He gave it to Rankin and the detective left. He was gone fifteen minutes and when he came back he smelled anew of cigarettes.

"She's on her way."

Earl said nothing. He wished that he felt more confidence in Rankin. Everything depended on the efficiency of the police, and now that seemed a slender reed to lean upon. All they had to do was put two and two together. But would they? For a fleeting moment Earl almost wished they wouldn't. His plan had seemed abstract before, but now Helen would play the role he had cast her for. His claim that he had a happy marriage would not hold up under scrutiny. Perhaps Martha would say something when she realized that Helen was under suspicion.

"You work at Bennington and Pryor?"

"For fifteen years." He looked at Rankin. "How did you know that?"

"I asked your wife."

Surely they would go there and find the other half of the peanut butter and jelly sandwich sprinkled with arsenic. Earl tried to relax in the confidence that everything would transpire as he planned. The thought of Martha brought back his resolve. Whatever happened, even if Helen was not formally accused, it would be an excuse to ask out of his marriage. The cloud of suspicion would suffice.

Rankin was still there when Helen came. The curtain was pulled aside and she just stood there staring at him.

"I'm all right," Earl said, and then he noticed the roses in Helen's hand.

She rushed in and stood beside him and burst into tears. Rankin took the flowers.

"You grow these yourself?" Rankin asked when Helen subsided.

"Helen has a green thumb," Earl said. He was upset by Helen's tears. She had the look of a distraught and loving wife whose husband had been restored to her.

Rankin was called to the phone and while he was gone Earl was moved to a room, Helen following along beside the stretcher like the widow of Naim.

"What on earth happened?"

Earl shrugged. "I felt sick and they brought me here."

"They said they pumped your stomach."

"It's not an experience I would recommend."

And then they arrived at the room and he was transferred to the bed. Helen had called Wilson, their doctor, and he had ordered the hospital stay. Helen had retrieved the roses from Rankin and now she fussed with them, asking a nurse to bring her a vase. Then she took up her vigil beside the bed. "I wish Dr. Wilson would get here."

"Helen, I'm all right."

"It couldn't have been food poisoning. I made your lunch. There was nothing that could possibly . . ."

"Of course not."

Wilson eventually came, checked the chart, hummed while he pressed his stethoscope to various parts of Earl's anatomy. They had put him in a hospital gown and he felt exposed with the covers thrown back.

"I want you to stay here at least tonight."

"I'll stay, too," Helen said.

"Helen, there's no need to do that. All I want to do is sleep."

"You poor darling. Of course you do."

Earl closed his eyes but knew that sleep would not come. Helen whispered with Wilson for some minutes and then the doctor left. Helen pulled a chair beside the bed and sat. When Rankin came back, Earl pretended to be asleep. The detective talked with Helen about her gardening.

"Do you ever use arsenic?"

"Why do you ask?"

"That's what they pumped out of your husband."

"Oh, my God. I didn't think he was that despondent."

"Was he despondent?"

"He wasn't happy at work. He was always passed over for promotion."

"He took it that hard?"

"Of course. It was all we talked of. But I can't believe . . ."

Earl managed not to smile. Everything was going to be all right. And then sleep came.

Helen was not there when he awoke. She had gone off with Rankin. The detective would want to see the greenhouse. He would find the arsenic. He would trace Helen's purchase of it. She would tell him that she had fixed his lunch as always.

Some hours later, she came in with Rankin, her face ashen. She tried to tell Earl what was happening. They thought she had poisoned his lunch!

Earl impressed himself with the indignation he showed, rising up in bed and threatening Rankin if he pursued that line of inquiry.

"Someone fed you arsenic, Mr. Green."

Helen began to wail, and then Rankin took her away. Ten minutes later Martha came into the room.

"They've arrested Helen," Earl said.

"How I hate her."

"Don't. She would never . . ."

"Oh, don't be a fool." And she bent over him and kissed him. Their new life together was about to begin.

"I'll get her the best lawyer."

"It won't matter."

"I can't go home to an empty house."

"You couldn't go back to a house with her in it."

He took her hand, remembering the first time his hand had closed over hers. There was really no need to say anything.

Helen was arraigned and held on suspicion of attempted murder. Martha had no compunction about telling the police about Earl's marriage and how unhappy he was with his harping wife.

"She is very loyal to you," Rankin observed.

"We've worked together for years."

Rankin nodded. He seemed to have taken a shower, but he still smelled of cigarettes. "The two of you always had lunch together?"

"She brought her lunch, too."

"You ate in your office?"

"Yes."

"There was arsenic in your sandwich."

"My God."

"What has Phil Jackson got against you?"

"Jackson? Nothing." But he remembered the younger man's interest in Martha. Had he told Rankin of that? How would his relations with Martha have been described by those in the office? It seemed to Earl that they had not bothered about being discreet. If Rankin had talked with Phil Jackson, he would have been given reason to wonder about Earl's inseparability from Martha.

"Your wife denies everything," Rankin said.

"I still don't believe she would do such a thing."

"Neither do I."

"What do you mean?"

"You should have worn gloves."

Earl just stared at the imperfectly shaven detective.

Rankin went on. "I got a set of your prints from a glass you used here. They match those on the arsenic container. Yours are the only prints on it."

"That's absurd."

"Maybe. But it's a fact. So we're back to the other alternative. You poisoned yourself."

"I would never do that."

"There is another possibility."

"What?"

"Martha."

"No!"

"So what's it going to be? Who did it?"

But of course no case could be made against Martha.

"I'm releasing your wife."

"And then?"

"Suicide is against the law. But it would be a waste of time prosecuting you." Rankin shook his head. "You are a bastard, Green. How could you do such a thing to your wife?"

Wilson ordered his release, but Martha came before he left the hospital room. She refused to let him take her hand and stared coldly at him.

"What a terrible thing to do."

"Has Rankin convinced you?"

"He didn't have to. You're a monster."

Earl left the hospital alone. He had lost both Martha and Helen. It was a clear, sunlit day but there were traces of cloud in the sky, white wisps of prelapsarian innocence. "I'm free," Earl told himself. "Free." And it was all he could do not to cry.

Doug Allyn

The Murder Ballads

Former musician, songwriter, and singer, DOUG ALLYN is the author of two successful mystery series set in Michigan—one featuring Latino Detroit policeman Lupe Garcia, and the other deep-sea diver, bar owner, and single mother Michelle Mitchell. Allyn has published many short stories and is a six-time recipient of the Ellery Queen Readers award. The Midwest is his domain and he has made it his own with sometimes wry, sometimes dark tales of the land and its people. Although the setting of "The Murder Ballads," also featured in *Ellery Queen's Mystery Magazine,* may seem to be medieval, it is a thoroughly modern tale from the first page to the last, blending renaissance music, electronic theft, and murder, each aspect with that ring of authenticity that Allyn always makes look so easy.

The Murder Ballads

Doug Allyn

Strumming his lute softly, Geoffry the Minstrel sauntered to the center of the great hall. And waited.

A striking figure of a man, he was tall and slender with a neatly trimmed blond beard. His tunic was raw silk, blood scarlet, trimmed with gold.

At the far end of the room his small band of musicians were in place, instruments tuned, watching for his signal. Still, Geoff made no move to begin. Waiting for his audience to notice him.

It took awhile. The revelers were happily hacking away at the carcass of the banquet's main course, a monstrous roast pig basted in beer with an apple in its mouth. The swine's carcass was scarcely recognizable now, and the drunken diners were equally disheveled, their fine clothing spattered with grease, spotted with wine.

At last, the host noticed the singer and shouted for silence. After waiting a moment longer for the din to settle, the minstrel struck a ringing chord on his lute.

"Good evening, milords, miladies, and those of you who fall somewhere in between. On behalf of our honored host, the Earl of McMahon"—he paused for a round of applause and slurred *Hear! Hear!*s—"my fellow players and I bid you welcome to this glorious feast of St. Falstaff, patron saint of beer, beer, and more beer. And, of course, lusty, busty ladies. Of which we have a bouncy abundance tonight."

Again he paused for hooting and applause. One reveler dribbled wine down his wife's bosom and earned a clout upside the head for his troubles. Much laughter.

"But I see you grow impatient for a song," Geoff continued dryly. "Since lust is obviously in the air, we'll sing a song of spring, the season when men's thoughts turn to what the ladies have been hoping for all winter. . . ." He scratched the lowest string of his lute with his thumbnail, imitating a woman's sensual moaning. More laughter and nudging.

"And so, let's think spring. Spring! The season of fertility and pheromones. Nature's very own . . . Viagra!"

The punchline drew a huge laugh. It always did. Mostly in sheer relief that despite his medieval garb and lute, Geoff's show wouldn't be a boring PBS riff on Greatest Hits of the Middle Ages.

With his audience primed and loosened up, Geoffry and his musicians broke into "Pastime with Good Company," a sprightly melody attributed to Henry VIII, though it might have been written by Henry Ford for all this lot cared.

Still, Geoff sang it with passion, caressing the lyrics with his clear tenor, startling the audience with the power and purity of his voice.

The roar of applause was genuine this time, true appreciation of the singer's art. But Geoff knew better than to milk it. Instead he called on Tiffany Miller to croon a bawdy Elizabethan ballad, "My Thing Is My Own."

Tiff's stunning high-fashion looks and low-cut Renaissance gown restored the mood of lusty revelry that made Geoff's group, Pearls B-4 Swine, minor stars on the corporate convention circuit.

Live the Legend. Dress up in Renaissance duds, get sloppy drunk, and grope your wives and girlfriends. To fat-cat yuppie business types, carousing in period costumes has both sex and snob appeal, a combination their fathers' Kiwanis Clubs can't match.

Bouncing the mood from lusty medieval to wry comic commentary, Geoffry the Minstrel and Pearls B-4 Swine kept the half-blasted Silicon Valley moguls in stitches for forty-plus minutes, no easy feat considering the condition of the crowd.

Late in the show, a drunken junior tycoon lurched toward the band, grabbing at Tiffany. As Tiff danced out of his grasp, Kirk Ohanian, the bearded, bear-sized drummer, took her place.

Waltzing the interloper back to his table, Kirk deftly parked him where he belonged, then gave him a stage kiss full on the mouth that brought a roar of laughter and applause as he capered back to the stage.

Geoff closed the show with Thomas Ravenscroft's "We Be Soldiers Three," urging the audience to join in on the chorus of "With never a penny of money . . . ," which the crowd found doubly hilarious since most of them had Bill Gates–type bucks.

With a dramatic bow, Geoffry the Minstrel politely thanked the sodden lords and ladies, then stalked out of the ballroom as boldly as he'd come.

Outside, he broke into a run, sprinting down the carpeted corridor to the hotel bar, banging through the double doors. The lounge was jammed, Saturday night singles hustling one another. College boys hitting on shopgirls, salesmen trying tired lines on hard-eyed divorcées.

"Cognac, no ice," Geoff ordered. "Do it twice."

"In a tankard or a ram's horn, milord?" the bartender asked, eyeing Geoff's jerkin and tights.

"Just gimme two snifters, pal." Geoff sighed. "And skip the comedy. I've had all the jokers I can handle for one night."

Reading Geoff's face, the bartender swallowed his next wisecrack. Even in costume, the minstrel's lanky frame looked crowbar-hard and his cool stare showed no humor at all.

Scanning the lounge, Geoff spotted an empty table in the corner and carried his drinks to it. By the time the other Pearls B-4 Swine players joined him, his first cognac was gone and the second was falling fast.

"Slow down, *amigo,*" Kirk Ohanian growled, lowering his bulk onto the chair beside Geoff. "Leave some hooch for the rest of us." Kirk, burly, dark, and heavyset, had a swooping Armenian moustache and a curly mop halfway to an Afro. He kicked out chairs for Tiffany Miller, the angelic blond vocalist, and Naomi Abrams, who played the Renaissance rebec, a pear-shaped fiddle.

A bit pear-shaped herself, with olive skin and a thick, raven-black mane, Naomi could have passed as Kirk's older sister. Or perhaps his brother in drag.

Tiffany was Naomi's opposite, slender as a willow and pale as buttermilk, with flowing, ash-blond tresses that tumbled like a waterfall to her narrow waist.

Neil Jannsen, the Pearls' agent, bustled in, spotted the group, and trotted to their table. In his tweed jacket, loafers, and sandy hair, Neil looked like a surfer who'd stumbled into the wrong century.

"Nice job, kids, management's ecstatic. Unfortunately, they paid us with a check so I won't have bucks until the banks open Monday. Anybody need a draw?"

"Can you front me a hundred?" Kirk asked. "I saw a neat bodhran in a pawnshop downtown."

"A lowdown what?" Neil said, slipping two fifties out of his money clip.

"A bodhran, not a lowdown, you friggin' Philistine." Kirk grinned, snatching the bills. "A traditional Irish drum."

"Buy an Irish drummer while you're at it," Tiffany griped. "You were dragging the tempo on my first solo, Kirk. Again."

"You mean you were rushing it again," Kirk shot back.

"Lighten up!" Geoff barked. "You're both wrong. I rushed the damned song. Wanted to get the hell out of there before they finished the pig and started on us."

"No way," Neil protested, "they loved you guys."

"They loved the pig, too, and look what happened to him," Geoff said, rising. "I'm going for a run to clear my head. I've got an early flight back to Motown."

"Are we rehearsing this week?" Tiffany asked.

Geoff nodded. "Wednesday, my place." He raised his last cognac, grimaced at the aroma, and lowered it again, untasted. "We'll polish up the tape I gave you last week, 'My Lady Doth Favor Love.' "

"Do you really need me for that?" Kirk asked. "My part ain't dick."

"Pearls B-4 Swine will be rehearsing Wednesday," Geoff said icily. "Last time I checked, you weren't an ex-Pearl. Yet."

Kirk grinned. "Like I said, I'll be there with bells on."

"I'd pay good cash money to see that." Naomi chortled. "Where you gonna hang 'em, big fella?"

"Hey, you guys are the band, right? The Pearls of . . . whatever the hell it is?" The swaying, sodden dancer from the banquet hall had followed them into the bar. Wearing a wine-stained caftan the size of a tent, he was clearly near his limit of booze, cholesterol, or both.

"They're the Pearls, I'm the manager," Neil said, rising to intercept the drunk. "Can I help you?"

"Came for the lady," Caftan said, leering at Tiffany as he slumped into Neil's chair, pushing him aside. "Brought cash with me."

"I'm always happy to discuss bookings for the *group*," Neil said pointedly, handing Caftan a card. "Call my office during business hours and—"

"Nah, I want her tonight," Caftan insisted. "You know, to play a private party."

"You heard the man," Kirk said, smiling dangerously. "Call him Monday."

"Nobody's talking to you, faggot," Caftan mumbled. "I already danced with you. I want a girl now. Hell, I'll take 'em both. Ten grand apiece, ladies, and all you gotta do—hey!"

Reaching across the table, Geoff hoisted the drunk up by his greasy collar. "Come on, sport, we're leaving. I'll walk you out."

"Is everything all right over there?" the bartender called.

"Just ducky," Geoff growled, marching the drunk toward the lounge door. "Wednesday," he yelled back to the group. "My place. And try being on time for a change!"

"What's eating him?" Tiffany asked.

"Not much." Kirk sniffed Geoff's cognac, then knocked it back in a single swallow. "His whole freakin' life, is all."

Sergeant Rosalia Morales eased the unmarked patrol car to a halt in front of the abandoned warehouse. Buzz Gillette glanced at her, arching his bushy eyebrows. "You sure this is the right address?"

"Geoff Prince leases the upper floor," she said, climbing out. "The block's scheduled for renovation next year. He's just ahead of the curve."

"Makes a helluva hideout," Gillette said, eyeing the rundown factories and storefronts as he eased his bulk out of the car.

They made an odd couple. Rosie, petite but sturdy, her ebony hair cut boyishly short in a Prince Val. Even her clothes were gender-neutral— dark slacks, blouse, and jacket. Black combat boots. Not designer boots. The real thing.

A hundred pounds heavier and a head taller, Buzz Gillette was linebacker-size. A star athlete in college, he was a bit soft around the middle now, reddish hair thinning out on top.

His face was equally red, with a drinker's permanent windburn. Sears sport coat, button-down shirt, clip-on tie.

Rosie rang the buzzer beside the battered freight door.

"Yeah?" A metallic voice echoed from the small speaker above the door.

"Police, Mr. Prince. We need to talk to you."

"About what?"

"About five minutes, sir. Unless you'd rather talk at the station for five hours. Your choice."

A moment's hesitation, then the door buzzed open. "Come on up."

They rode a rattletrap freight elevator to a landing that hadn't seen paint since the Depression. Rosie held her badge up to the peephole in the metal door. Geoff Prince, the minstrel, swung it open.

Her first impression? Grad student. Trim blond beard, tousled hair, blue-gray eyes that matched his U of Detroit sweatpants and T-shirt. Barefoot.

"I'm Sergeant Morales, Mr. Prince, fifteenth squad, Detroit Metro Homicide out of Murphy Hall. Sergeant Gillette here's from Atlanta, Georgia. We understand you were in Atlanta recently?"

"We played there this past weekend and probably a dozen times before that. Why?"

"It's a bit complicated. Can we talk inside?"

"Mi casa, su casa," Geoff said, standing aside, waving them in. Rosie scanned his face for sarcasm, didn't see any. Or much of anything else. Wary eyes. Guarded.

His apartment was the opposite. Wide open. Candle sconces flickering high on the brick walls gave the cavernous loft an oddly medieval air. The only modern touch was floor-to-ceiling windows offering a spectacular view of the Detroit skyline across an abandoned railroad yard.

Furnishings? Ultra-basic. A futon couch, mix-and-match chairs, oaken bookshelves, and a cast-iron Franklin stove. And yet the barren room felt surprisingly cozy. A haven.

Candlelight reflected from polished hardwood floors, flickering across a row of guitars displayed above the bookcase.

"What can I do for you?" Geoff asked.

"You might be doing life if we don't like your answers," Gillette said, moving closer to Geoff, crowding him. "You have a record for assaulting a police officer, Prince. Why is that? Don't you like cops?"

"I've got no problem with cops," Geoff said, holding his ground. "Especially pretty ones. Jerks bother me, though."

"Tell us about the assault charge," Rosie said, waving at Gillette to back off.

"It was in Tijuana, maybe five years ago. Took a swing at a *federale*. Spent two years in a Mexican jail thinking it over."

"And you liked jail so much you're in a hurry to go back?" Gillette prodded.

"Nope. But I learned a few things there. About my rights and the games cops play. We're done dancin', Sergeant. Tell me what you want or hit the door."

"Do you know any of these men?" Rosie said, handing Prince three snapshots.

Frowning, he looked them over. "Not offhand, but I meet a lot of people. This one needs vitamins. Bad."

"It's a morgue photo, wise-ass," Gillette said. "He's dead. And don't pretend you don't know these guys. We've got witnesses who place you with them."

"Maybe with this one," Geoff admitted, tapping the morgue snapshot. "Looks like a guy I met in the hotel bar in Atlanta Saturday night. He was healthier then."

"Why did you lie about knowing him?" Rosie asked.

"I don't *know* him, lady. From this picture, I can't even be sure it's the same guy. If it is, I bumped into him for about thirty seconds. Never caught his name. What did he die of?"

"You tell us," Gillette prodded. "You left the hotel bar with him around midnight. People saw you."

"I didn't leave with him." Geoff sighed. "I just walked him out the door. He went his way, I went mine."

"Which way was that?"

"I don't know where he went. I changed clothes and went for a run."

"Kind of late, wasn't it?" Rosie asked.

"I always run after a show. Helps blow off steam."

"Where did you run to?"

Geoff shook his head slowly. "You're gonna love this. I don't know."

"It was only three days ago." Gillette snorted. "Is your memory that bad?"

"My memory's okay, I just don't know Atlanta very well. When I left the hotel I think I headed west. I remember running along a river for a while, if that's any help."

"Which river?" Gillette prompted. "Peachtree? Proctor?"

"Don't have a clue. Maybe I could retrace the route for you, but at the time I really wasn't paying attention, you know?"

"I know you're digging yourself a hole, sport," Gillette said. "If this is your idea of an alibi—"

"Why would I need an alibi?" Prince flared. "What's this about?"

"Our witness said there was trouble between you and Cavanaugh," Rosie put in. "An argument. Tell us about that."

"Who's Cavanaugh?"

"Don't play dumb," Gillette snapped. "He's the guy in the picture."

"I told you I never got his name. And there was no argument. He was just drunk. He hassled us a little during the show, then followed us into the lounge."

"What did Cavanaugh hassle you about?"

"He apparently thought the girls in my band were for rent. They aren't."

"A drunk insulting your girlfriend must have made you pretty angry," Gillette said. "No wonder you popped him one in the mouth. Is that how it started?"

"Tiff and Naomi aren't girlfriends, they're musicians I work with. And I didn't pop Cavanaugh in the mouth or anyplace else. I just walked him out of the bar, end of story. In my business, handling drunks comes with the territory."

"What about the other two guys we showed you? Were they drunks, too?"

"I wouldn't know. Never saw either of them before."

"Wrong answer," Gillette said. "You saw one in Chicago last month and the other here in Detroit two months back. All three attended your show, then disappeared. The first two are still missing. Cavanaugh's body turned up because a farmer noticed his hogs acting strange."

Prince blinked. "Hogs?"

"Sure. The way hogs stink, you probably figured nobody'd notice a corpse turning ripe. But these were Georgia hogs, Prince. They rooted up the body. Shoulda buried him deeper."

"Let me get this straight. You figure I know something about this just because these guys were in the audience someplace I played? You've got to be kidding."

"Do these pictures look like we're joking, Mr. Prince?" Rosie asked.

"No, but just because people catch my show doesn't mean I know them. They're just faces in the crowd."

"Small crowds, though," Gillette said. "You play business conventions, right? Doing folk music for—"

"Renaissance music," Geoff corrected.

"Whatever. You play these little dinner gigs, guys get loaded and hit on your women. Must be frustrating."

"Compared to what? Conventions pay a lot better than coffeehouses. And what's that got to do with the three dead guys?"

"We didn't say the other two were dead," Gillette noted.

"Come on, you obviously think they are. What I don't see is why I'm a suspect. Because I talked to what's-his-name in a bar?"

"You were the last one to see Cavanaugh alive, Mr. Prince," Rosie said patiently. "Are you sure you never met the other two?"

"I don't party with these people, lady, I just sing for 'em. I showed Cavanaugh the door and that was it. Nothing else happened."

"Something must have," Morales said quietly. "You deposited thirty thousand in your investment account yesterday, Mr. Prince."

"I don't know what you're talking about. I deposited my paycheck yesterday, but it was a long way from thirty grand."

"You also wired thirty thousand from First National of Atlanta into your investment account, Mr. Prince. Did you think wire deposits weren't traceable? Where did that money come from?"

"Ma'am, I've only got one bank account. It's got something like fifty grand in it and it's taken me four years to save that. Where do you get off nosing around in my bank account anyway? Don't you need a warrant for that?"

"We had one. With three missing millionaires, judges tend to be very cooperative. How do you explain that second account?"

"The only money I know about was my paycheck, lady."

"And how much was that?"

"The Pearls get ten grand for a dinner show, Neil takes fifteen percent off the top for booking us, the three players get fifteen hundred apiece, I get the rest. I deposited thirty-eight, kept two hundred back for walk-around money. Want to count it?"

"Ten grand for a few tunes?" Gillette snorted. "I played guitar a little in high school, probably still remember 'Louie Louie.' Here, I'll show you." He reached for one of the instruments on the wall.

"Leave the guitars alone!" Geoff snapped.

"Relax, sport, I know what I'm doing—"

"Touch that guitar and I'll break you in half, Gillette, cop or no cop."

"Whoa," Gillette said, his eyes lighting up, "you don't talk to police officers like that, boy. You shoulda learned that down in Mexico."

"Everybody chill out," Rosie said, stepping between them. "What's all the fuss over an old guitar, Mr. Prince?"

"It's not a guitar, it's an eighteenth-century *vihuela* in original condition. There aren't a dozen like it in the world."

"Looks like a junker to me." Gillette snorted. "Considerin' your reaction, maybe I should search it for contraband."

"Let it alone, Sergeant," Rosie ordered. "We aren't here to play guitars. I'm still waiting, Mr. Prince. Where did the thirty-thousand-dollar deposit come from?"

"I have no idea. It's not mine. Look, I'm sorry this Cavanaugh character got himself killed, but I don't know doodley about it and I'm due at a recording session in twenty minutes."

"Cancel it," Gillette growled. "You're coming with us."

"No, I'm not," Geoff said, backing away. "I've told you everything I know, which is exactly nothing. We're done."

Prince wasn't bluffing. Rosie could see it in his eyes. And for a moment she was in the alley behind the party store, yelling at the two punks to halt and drop their weapons. Knowing they wouldn't . . . She shook her head.

"We're not going to arrest you, Mr. Prince," Rosie said. "Not today, anyway."

"Wait a minute," Gillette protested.

"I hate to be rude, but I have an appointment," Geoff said, opening the door. "Have a nice night. And the next time you want to see me? Try buying a ticket."

"We've got our man," Gillette said, easing down in the metal office chair. They were in Captain Cordell Bennett's office in the Frank Murphy Hall of Justice, Detroit P.D.'s Homicide/Interstate Crimes division.

"Prince has a record for violence, his alibi's a joke, he's holding part of the money, and he got jumpy as a cat when we questioned him," Gillette continued. "I wanted to haul him in and sweat him a little, but Sergeant Morales had other ideas."

"What's your take on him, Rosie?" Bennett asked, eyeing her over the bridge of his granny glasses. The spectacles and his shaved head gave Bennett a benign Buddha look that was deceptive. He'd risen through the ranks during Detroit's Murder City years. His stocky frame was cement-block solid. And his easy smile never reached his eyes.

"Buzz may be right," Rosie conceded. "Prince might be our guy. But he's also a street-smart ex-con with money. If we bust him now, he'll lawyer up and make bail before we finish processing his paperwork."

"Give me twenty minutes in a cage with him, I guarantee he'll be singin' like a bird," Gillette said quietly.

"It's a bit early in the game for that." Bennett shrugged. "How did Prince explain the thirty grand in his new account?"

"He couldn't," Gillette said. "Not without confessing."

"There's a lot more than thirty grand missing," Rosie countered. "The numbers aren't in on Cavanaugh yet, but Chicago tells me their victim was hit for nearly half a million and our vic lost about three hundred thousand, all done electronically, no tracks, no prints. The victims' PDAs are missing and—"

"PDA?" Gillette echoed.

"Personal Digital Assistant," Bennett explained. "Palm Pilots or whatever. Whoever did this probably used data from them to hack into the victims' bank accounts. He's either one hell of a computer ace or knows someone who is."

"I didn't see a computer at Prince's loft," Rosie said. "Some stereo gear, but no computer, no TV. The guy practically lives in the Dark Ages."

"We didn't search," Gillette said. "It could have been in another room."

"What room?" Rosie asked. "The place was wide open and the kind of electronic theft we're talking about would take state-of-the-art equipment."

Bennett sighed. "He must have it someplace. His new bank account was opened electronically, too. No signature, just a password. It looks like Prince opened it, but we can't link it directly to him."

"With fifty grand on hand, why would he bother to open a second account at all?" Rosie asked.

"I make Prince as a showboat," Gillette said. "He probably transferred the big bucks overseas, then plunked the thirty in his own account to rub our noses in it."

"I don't think so," Rosie said.

"Excuse me, were we at the same interview, Sergeant?" Gillette snapped. "Are you saying Prince is clean?"

"Nope," Rosie said, "but he's no fool, either. There was a moment . . . When you mentioned Cavanaugh's body being found on a farm, Prince reacted. Whether he's our guy or not, he knows something about this."

"Then why didn't he say so?"

"He's an ex-con, Gillette. He doesn't like cops. Or maybe he just doesn't like you. You tried to muscle him and it didn't fly. I want to try him again, Captain. On my own."

Bennett swiveled to face Gillette. "Any objection, Sergeant?"

Gillette had plenty of objections. But he swallowed them. He was a long way from Atlanta. "No problem, Captain. Your jurisdiction, your rules. Sergeant Morales and Prince did seem to . . . hit it off."

Bennett nodded. "Fair enough. If you think you can flip the guy, go for it, Morales. Just keep me posted."

"Yes, sir."

After Rosie left, Gillette realized Bennett was eyeing him. Smiling.

"What?"

"You think Sergeant Morales is a lightweight, don't you, Buzz? Some kind of affirmative-action bimbo?"

"No, I—"

"Don't blow smoke at me, Sergeant," Bennett said, waving off Gillette's objections. "It's a natural assumption for guys in our line of work. Good-looking minority female, must be boinkin' somebody to make promotion, right? Know how she got her shield?"

"No."

"She nailed two stickup guys in an alley off Dequinder. Warned 'em to drop their weapons, they didn't, she popped 'em. Two rounds apiece, right in the ticker. Both dead before they hit the ground. Cleanest shoot I've ever seen."

"Why tell me?"

"Word to the wise and all that."

"Maybe you should tell Geoff Prince."

"No need. If he crosses Rosie, he'll find out soon enough."

Papa Doc's Cajun Bar-B-Q. Best baby-back ribs in East Detroit. Rosie stepped inside, scanning the diner. Fifties decor, chrome stools along a Formica counter, pink leatherette booths. Geoff Prince and Pearls B-4 Swine were easy to spot. Papa's was nearly full, and they were the only white faces in the place.

In person, Tiffany looked even lovelier than she did on the poster Rosie'd bought in a local head shop. Kirk and Naomi were laughing about something. Rosie didn't recognize the stranger at the table, a balding, older man in a business suit.

The next victim, perhaps?

Prince spotted Rosie, but if he was annoyed he hid it well. He stood, waving her over.

"Miss Morales, nice to see you. I take it you've got some follow-up questions for your . . . interview?"

Rosie nodded. "One or two."

"No problem, we're about done here. Kirk, why don't you guys take Mr. Cox back to the studio and show him around? I'll be along as soon as I can."

"You're a reporter?" Naomi asked. "Which magazine?"

"She's a freelancer," Geoff said hastily, "but I promised her the time, so . . . ? Get going, give us some privacy, okay?"

"An interview, right," Tiff snorted, winking at Rosie as she sidled past. "Watch yourself, sister. Geoff's a ladykiller."

"I'll keep it in mind."

"Keep me in mind, too, *amiga,*" Kirk added, grinning. "Remember, drummers do it with rhythm."

"Out!" Geoff ordered. And then they were gone.

Leaving Rosie facing Geoff Prince. They eyed each other a moment in silence. Sizing up.

Wearing a gray Armani jacket over a Pistons T-shirt, Geoff looked semicivilized, Rosie thought. A guy you could take home to Mother. Assuming Mom's life insurance was paid up.

Dark woman, Geoff thought. Dark hair, dark jacket and slacks. Dark, unreadable eyes. A mystery.

"Thanks for not frisking everybody," Geoff said as Rosie took a seat facing him. "The bald guy is Warren Cox from Cable Music. We're trying to cut a deal for a Renaissance music channel. Could mean airplay and some semiserious bucks for the band. Assuming you don't hang me first. Can I order you something?"

"This isn't a social call, Mr. Prince."

"Pity." Geoff sighed. "I was hoping . . . never mind. What's up, Sergeant?"

"You are. My partner thinks you killed Cavanaugh and the other two as well. He's looking to bury you."

"But you're not?"

"Not yet," Rosie said. "Do you mind?" She filched a French fry from his plate. "I missed lunch."

"Do you always steal food from guys you're trying to burn?"

"Only when I'm hungry. And I'm not trying to burn you, Mr. Prince. But I do think you know something about these killings."

"You're wrong."

"Am I? When Gillette mentioned that Cavanaugh's body was found on a farm, you winced. Why was that?"

Surprisingly, he smiled. A good smile. It erased years from his eyes. "Not just any farm," he said. "A hog farm."

"That's right, it was a hog farm. So what?"

"It doesn't have anything to do with your case."

"Tell me about it anyway."

"It's in a song," he said, watching her face.

"A dead body turning up on a hog farm is in a song?"

He nodded. " 'The Ballad of Belle Gunness.' It's a murder ballad."

"A what?"

"A murder ballad. Do you know anything about the history of the minstrelsy, troubadours, any of that?"

"Just bits and pieces from a humanities class. Fill me in."

"Minstrels have been around since ancient times. Probably prehistoric. Homer, the guy who wrote the *Iliad?* He was a minstrel."

"What's Homer got to do with hog farms?"

"I'm getting to that. In olden days, troubadours did more than just entertain people. They were like singing reporters, carrying the news from place to place. Some songs were about politics or battles. Some were about murders. With names and places as factual as any news story. They're called murder ballads."

"And one of these . . . murder ballads? Is about a hog farm?"

"The Ballad of Belle Gunness," he said. "Belle was the most successful murderess in American history. La Porte, Indiana, 1908. Belle ran ads in Chicago and Indianapolis papers: 'Woman of property desires to meet man of means. Object: matrimony.' She'd write hot love letters to the poor saps who answered and arranged for a get-acquainted visit. At Belle's hog farm."

"What happened?"

"Her pen pals brought cash to prove their honorable intentions. And they disappeared. We aren't even certain how many men Belle killed. Somewhere between twenty and forty-five."

"That's quite a gap. If they found the bodies—"

"But they didn't. Not exactly. Belle apparently got tired of burying stiffs, so she started feeding the bodies to her hogs. Forensic medicine in 1908 was pretty crude. The coroner's best guess was . . ." He spread his hands.

"Between twenty and forty-five?" Rosie whistled. "My God. What about the local law? Didn't they tumble to what was going on?"

"According to the ballad, Belle and the county sheriff were lovers. Maybe it's true. He resigned after she split."

"What happened to Belle?"

"Nothing. She got away clean. Probably lived happily ever after."

"No kidding? And there's a song about all this?"

"Accurate to the last detail. Just like the songs about Jesse James, Claude Dallas, and a hundred other killers you've never heard of. Murder ballads. I cut an album of them a few years ago."

"Really? And was the song about the lady with the hog farm on it?"

Geoff hesitated, then shrugged. "Yeah," he admitted, his eyes locking on hers. "As a matter of fact, it was."

"Are you nuts?" Bennett growled when Rosie phoned in. "Do you know how many hog farms there are around Chicago? Not to mention Detroit."

"We won't have to check them all, Captain," Rosie countered, "just the ones within easy driving distance. How many can that be?"

Thirty-six, as it happened. But they only had to check a dozen or so. The two missing bodies turned up early in the search. Captain Bennett was impressed. So was Buzz Gillette.

"You nailed him." Gillette grinned, pounding his fist into his palm. "The guy pointed us at the two missing victims. It's as good as a confession."

Rosie sighed. "I wish it were that simple. Prince didn't tell us about the hog farms, remember? We told him. And he didn't point us anywhere. The murder ballad did."

"But it's Prince's song!"

"No, it's not, he just recorded it. The ballad was actually written in 1910. Pearls B-4 Swine released it on a CD five years ago. Thousands of people have heard it."

"Whoa up," Gillette said. "A guy sings about bodies buried on hog farms, argues with a guy who turns up dead on a hog farm, and you think it's all a coincidence?"

"I don't know what it is or what *he* is," Rosie snapped. "All we really know is that he gave us a break in this case and we're far from finished. We don't have the money yet—"

"Prince deposited thirty grand after the last killing!"

"Chump change," Bennett interjected. "The victims' accounts were hacked for nearly a million. Sergeant Morales is right. We can't connect Prince to the missing money or the first two victims. We don't have enough yet."

"We know they were in his audience," Gillette pleaded. "And he had a beef with Cavanaugh."

"There were five people at Prince's table that night," Rosie said. "All of them know the murder ballad. Not to mention the people who own the CD."

"Seems to me you're working overtime to prove the guy's innocent, Morales," Gillette observed.

"Somebody has to. You decided he was guilty the second he told you to take your paws off his guitar."

"Hold it, you two," Bennett interjected. "We're all on the same side here. Do you still consider Prince a suspect, Sergeant Morales?"

"Absolutely. Top of the list."

"Then keep working him. He tipped us about the bodies, maybe he knows more."

"Damn straight he does," Gillette groused. "He knows every freakin' detail firsthand."

"If he does, I'll nail him," Rosie snapped. "Right now I'm more interested in the song. Prince says murder ballads are factual and it's proved out so far."

"So?" Bennett asked.

"So maybe Gillette's right and it's not a coincidence. Maybe we're dealing with a copycat here. Someone who's using the murder ballad, or the crime that inspired it, for a model."

"Like the guy who sang it, for instance?" Gillette said.

"Possibly, but not necessarily. I looked up the original case. Belle Gunness really did murder at least two dozen victims and probably a lot more, and made a bundle doing it. If some psycho wanted a role model, Belle would make a beaut."

"Seems like a long shot," Bennett mused, "but it's worth a look. If our guy is following the Gunness woman's blueprint, he should be easy to nail."

"Maybe not," Rosie said. "Belle never served a day in jail. And before she skipped, she planted evidence on one of her farmhands. She almost got him hanged."

"You sound like you admire her," Gillette commented.

"A woman feeding mail-order boyfriends to the hogs? What's not to like?" Rosie quipped. "I just hope we're better than the cops in 1908. I'm going to see Prince, thank him for his help, and see what else he knows. I'll be in touch."

"Know what I'm wonderin', Captain?" Gillette said after she'd gone.

"What's that?"

"If Prince is crooning her any tunes besides this so-called murder ballad. Like love songs, for instance."

"You think Morales is falling for the guy? No way."

"You didn't see 'em together. It was like—electricity between them. You saying it's not possible?"

"No," Bennett said, thoughtfully cleaning his granny glasses. "I didn't say that."

"It's Sergeant Morales, Mr. Prince," Rosie said to the speaker over the warehouse door. "Can we talk a minute?"

"Do I need a lawyer?"

"Not today. This is more of a social call. A news update."

The street door buzzed open. Rosie found Geoff's apartment door ajar when she reached the landing after the rattletrap freight elevator ride. She could hear music from within, an ancient melody played on guitar. She started to knock, then didn't, unwilling to interrupt the song. Instead, she pushed the door open with her fingertips and tiptoed in.

Geoff Prince was sitting cross-legged on a cushion, cradling an antique guitar on his lap, his fingers caressing its strings as tenderly as a lover.

He didn't look up when she eased down on the divan across from him, and she didn't speak. She just listened. Let the melody wash over her, clearing her mind, carrying her back to gentler times.

When the song ended she was sorry. Neither of them spoke for a moment, lost in the spell of the melody.

"That was lovely," Rosie said at last. "What was it?"

"A Scottish border ballad, 'Song of the Outlaw Murray.' Seventeenth century. Or late fifteenth, depending on which historian you believe."

"A two-hundred-year difference?"

"With old anonymous songs you have to play detective, look for clues in the lyrics about who wrote it and when. There were two outlaws named Murray roughly a century apart. No one knows which of them the song's about. Maybe both."

"History repeating itself? Like the Ballad of Belle Gunness?"

"There was only one Belle Gunness."

"We're wondering if there's a brand-new one. We found the two missing victims, Mr. Prince. You were right, their bodies were buried on hog farms."

"I wasn't right, the ballad was. But I'm off the hook now, right?"

Rosie didn't reply, which was an answer of sorts.

"Damn," Geoff said softly. "I knew you were trouble the first time I saw you."

"You told us where to look for the bodies, Mr. Prince. The obvious inference is that you put them there or you know who did."

"If I'm involved, why would I tell you about the song?"

"People incriminate themselves every day, Mr. Prince. Don't you watch *Law & Order?*"

"I don't watch much TV. Broke the habit down in Mexico. What do you want from me, Morales?"

"For openers I'd like to hear your version of that murder ballad. Local record stores don't have the CD."

"It's out of print now. I should have a copy of it, though." Laying his guitar carefully aside, he padded to the bookshelf music system. Riffled through a row of CDs, pulled one out, frowning as he eyed the jacket.

"Is something wrong?" Rosie asked, rising, going to him.

"Time," he said, showing her the CD. "We cut this when we were first starting out, playing frat parties and coffeehouses. Seems like a lifetime ago. I was still writing songs then. One of them's on the album, 'The Ballad of Charles Manson.' "

"Of the Manson family? Why did you write about him?"

"Charlie's a songwriter, too, did you know that? He seemed made to order for an album of murder ballads."

"And was the song a hit?"

"Not really. The only people who liked it were Goth kids and psychotics. Our next album sold better, bawdy Renaissance love ballads. College kids flipped for it. Moved forty thousand copies the first month. Not much by pop standards, but for a folk album it's hot stuff. That's what we were celebrating when we got jammed up down in Mexico."

"What actually happened down there?"

"Pure punk-ass stupidity. We played a show in L.A., went down to Tijuana afterward with some guys from the record company. All of us drunk as skunks, actin' up in some bar. The law came in, a cop grabbed my arm. I tried to pull free, he slapped me, and I swung . . ."

Geoff shook his head slowly, remembering. "And in that instant my life changed. Forever. I'll never be the kid who sang on this CD again. That must sound crazy to you."

"No," Rosie said, remembering the alley, the wild eyes of the two punks. "Sometimes terrible things can happen in a heartbeat." Without thinking, she reached up and cupped his cheek with her palm. Their eyes met and held. And she felt her breathing go shallow. "What happened after you hit the cop?"

"They busted us. Leo was holding coke, and—"

"Leo?"

"Leo Neimi, my percussionist at the time. The trial took about ten minutes. We both went inside. And I'd really rather not talk about it."

"Then maybe you'd better play the song for me," she said, taking a deep breath and turning away.

He slipped the disk into the slot, programmed the player, then stalked off to the kitchen.

Rosie picked up the CD case. In the jacket photo, Geoff looked strikingly different, smiling, boyish, green as grass.

He looked harder now. Seasoned. Still handsome, but with a dangerous edge. Honed by hard times.

Tiffany looked about twelve, Naomi's bouffant hairstyle was even wider than her bottom. Kirk Ohanian wasn't in the photo at all. A tall, pigtailed Viking holding a leather drum was scowling at the camera instead. Leo Neimi?

A hillbilly fiddle opened the ballad at a peppy pace before Geoff's voice came in.

"Belle Gunness was a hefty gal down Indiana way, weighed nigh as much as any hog, so the Hoosiers say. . . ."

Geoff returned from the kitchen with two tulip glasses of white wine. Rosie accepted one, nodding her thanks, concentrating on the lyrics.

"What do you think?" he asked when it ended. "Top-forty stuff?"

"I expected it to be dark and grim. You played it for laughs."

"I played it the way it was written. Come on, a three-hundred-pound babe lures poor schmucks to her farm, steals their money, and feeds them to her pigs? In a weird way, it *is* funny."

"Not when you've seen the bodies," she said, sipping the wine. Tart and surprisingly good. "Nothing's funny about murder."

"Maybe it depends on who gets killed. In Mexico, my cellmate killed another con defending me. Beat him to death with a pipe. Maybe that was murder. Didn't seem like it at the time."

"It must have been tough for you down there."

"A skinny *gringo* kid with all those badass *hombres?* Yeah, it was hard. I made it through but I paid a pretty steep price."

"What price?"

"Everything," he said quietly. "In a place like that you shut your soul down. All I had was music. Sang songs to myself over and over again. They were my escape to other places, other times."

"Songs like the murder ballads?"

"Sometimes," Geoff admitted. "My cellmate liked them. I preferred Renaissance songs."

"Why?"

"Life was simpler then. We've got more gadgets now, but I'm not sure our lives are any better. Unless you think gangsta rap is a giant leap over Mozart."

"Maybe not." She smiled. "So you . . . try to live in the past?" She gestured at his barren loft.

"Nope, I live in the present like everybody else. I just try to keep it as simple as I can."

"No Internet connections?" she asked innocently.

"Neil, our manager, handles the Internet biz, I'm not on-line—damn. That was slick. For a minute I forgot why you came. That question was about the bank deposit, wasn't it?"

"You have thirty grand you can't explain, Mr. Prince."

"You're dead right. I can't. Because I don't know a damned thing about it!" The doorbell buzzed. Geoff stormed to the intercom and punched the talk button. "What!"

"Hey, it's me," Kirk Ohanian said, surprised at Prince's tone. "We're rehearsing tonight, right?"

"Yeah. Sorry, I forgot. Come on up." He buzzed the street door open. "You'll have to go," he said to Rosie. "No outsiders at rehearsals. And do me a favor. Keep up the reporter front, okay? With this royalties deal in the wind, the last thing I need is police trouble."

"You've got police trouble, like it or not, Mr. Prince."

"Not if you do your job right, lady. I'm no choirboy, but I haven't killed any millionaires lately."

"Okay, let's say I buy that. You're pure as the driven snow. Have you considered the implications?"

"What implications?"

"The evidence pointing toward you is no coincidence. Somebody knows enough about you to open a bank account in your name. Who? Who hates you enough to set you up?"

"Nobody, I hope," he said slowly. "There are articles about me and the band in fanzines and on the Internet. Maybe somebody collected the personal information there."

"I'm guessing it's someone closer. Give me some names, Geoff. Let me check them out. If you guess wrong, no harm, no foul."

"Damn," he said softly. "As much as I'd like to get myself out of this jackpot, I can't do that."

"But if they're innocent—"

"Come on, Rose, I don't run with angels. Turn anyone's life inside out, who knows what you'd find? Innocent people could get burned and it'd be my fault. Sorry, no sale."

"Have you got a death wish, Prince? Do you realize how much trouble you're in?"

"Sure. But Belle tried to frame her handyman, too. It all worked out in the end."

"You can't count on a happy ending just because the song has one."

"I'm not," he said simply. "I'm counting on you, Morales. I think in your heart you know I didn't do this."

They were very close now, too close for safety. And this time she didn't back away. His eyes were a lucent, icy blue, while hers were as dark as deep water. He gently touched her shoulders—there was a knock at the door.

"Open up," Kirk called.

"Gotta go. I'll be in touch," Rosie said.

"I look forward to it. I hope." Geoff sighed, unlatching the door.

"Yo, the little reporter *chica* from Papa Doc's," Kirk boomed with a huge grin. "You doing up close and personal interviews now? I'm your guy."

"Actually, I was just leaving," Rosie said. "Nice to see you again, Mr.—"

"Ohanian. Kirk. Call me Cap'n Kirk if you like. C'mon, I'll see you down to your car."

"There's no need—"

"Sure there is, this is a bad neighborhood. If I'm not back in an hour, start without me," he yelled at Geoff as he yanked open the freight elevator's safety gate. "Just kidding," he added to Rosie, waving her into the cage. "Go ahead, Miss Reporter, ask me anything."

"Have you known Geoff long?"

Kirk nodded. "Forever. He's like my little brother."

"But I noticed you didn't play on the band's first CD."

The Murder Ballads? No, that was the Pearl's original percussionist, Leo Neimi. Nice guy, but a major screwup. Oops, don't quote me on that, okay?"

"No problem. What happened to Leo Neimi?"

"Cocaine happened," Kirk said mildly. "After Leo and Geoff . . ." Kirk hesitated.

"It's all right, I already know about Mexico."

"Really? Geoff must like you a lot. He doesn't talk about that much," Kirk said, eyeing her curiously. "Anyway, by the time they got out, Leo was a total burnout, couldn't play at all. Geoff had to bag him. Funny thing, though . . ."

"What is?"

"I've been seeing Leo lately, some of the places we've played."

"Which places?"

"Atlanta, and a couple more before that. Chicago, maybe. Thing is, he didn't say hello. Just kinda stared at us. Like a freakin' zombie, which he pretty much is now. Ground floor, everybody out." He opened the lift gate with a flourish. "Watch your step, ladies and gents. On our left we have one of the meanest streets in Motown, while on our right we have . . . the same funky street. Where's your car, miss?"

"Just up the block," Rosie said. "I'm fine, really."

"You are indeed," Kirk agreed, offering his arm, "which is all the more reason I should walk you to your wheels."

As they approached the black Chevy with city plates, Kirk slowed, glancing from the car to Rosie.

"Whoa up, lady. That's not a press car, it's an unmarked patrol car, isn't it? What's going on? Is Geoff in some kind of trouble?"

"Should he be?"

"No way," Kirk said positively. "He's one of the straightest dudes I've ever known. What's going on?"

"I can't really talk about it, but maybe you can clear a few things up for me."

"Like what?"

"Does Geoff have any enemies? This Leo Neimi, for instance. Was he angry about being fired?"

Kirk nodded. "Mad as hell. Made some heavy threats about getting even, but he's so fried none of us took him seriously. Why? Is somebody threatening Geoff?"

"Something like that, yes."

"Could be Leo, or maybe the Goths. We've got a few looney fans, mostly Goth types. They're nuts about the *Murder Ballads* CD, especially the song Geoff wrote about Charles Manson. It's like an anthem for 'em. If the whole bunch of 'em wound up on the six o'clock news for whacking out movie stars and blaming it on the Beatles it wouldn't surprise me a bit."

"Which ones are the worst? Can you give me names?"

"I can do better than that," Kirk said, brightening. "We're playing the Scarborough Renaissance Fair this weekend outside Troy. The Goths will be there; maybe Leo will show, too. If I introduce you as a reporter doing an article about the band, Darth might talk to you."

"Darth?"

"The Goth head honcho. Mr. Personality."

"And you can arrange this?"

"Anything to help Geoff out. I'd be careful around Leo, though. He thinks Goths are plotting to steal his brain, and in that black outfit you could almost pass for a Goth yourself. Might want to add a couple tattoos, maybe get your nose pierced. I know a biker who works cheap. Want me to set you up?"

Rosie glanced up so sharply that Kirk burst out laughing.

"Gotcha," he chortled, shooting her with his forefinger. Kirk was still chuckling as she pulled away.

At the first stoplight Rosie tilted the rearview mirror to check her face. Could she really pass for a Goth? No way. Might be overdoing the hardcase career chick look a little, though. Or maybe not.

Geoff Prince liked her looks. She'd read it in his eyes. And that could be a problem.

Rosie often used her looks and personality to mellow out suspects, con them into cooperating. It was her edge.

Male detectives can bully perps. Rosie was too small to intimidate thugs, so she played them instead. Made nice, made them like her. Listened sympathetically while they bragged themselves into jail.

Prince was different, though. For the first time she wasn't sure who was playing whom. And she wasn't sure the game had anything to do with murdered businessmen.

According to the old ballad, Belle and the local sheriff had been lovers. Belle played him like a fish and left him twisting in the wind when she split. And that was the one thing Rosie was absolutely sure of. Nobody was going to hang her out to dry. Nobody.

Leaving their unmarked car in the lot with five thousand others, Rosie and Gillette paid their admission at the gate and followed the stream of tourists into the Scarborough Renaissance Fair. A gateway to the past. Sort of.

The entire municipal campground, which sprawled over fifty acres, had been temporarily converted into a reasonably realistic medieval village. Music and the shouts of barkers competed in a continual din. The very air had a sensual feel, flowers, incense, and exotic perfumes blending with the delicious aroma of roasting venison, turkey drumsticks, and the woodsmoke from a hundred open grills.

Artfully designed kiosks lined the unpaved streets, with vendors in Renaissance or medieval dress hawking everything from quarterstaffs to calligraphy.

A pudgy, red-robed cardinal in sandals was offering indulgences for three bucks a pop while twin witches in a nearby booth promised to brighten your future and curse your enemies for a fiver.

Screams erupted somewhere ahead in the crush of sightseers. People were shouting and shoving, trying to get out of the way. Gillette dropped into a crouch, sweeping his coat back, reaching for his weapon. . . .

The mob parted and a clown in a red Renaissance gown came sprinting past, shouting for help. His wig and dress were soaking wet and he was being chased by a jester on a Shetland pony laden with water buckets.

As the clown passed, the jester hurled a bucket of water in his general direction. Tourists screamed, ducking and dodging, then exploding into laughter. Confetti. They'd just been doused with a pail of confetti.

"Jesus H. Christ," Gillette growled, straightening his sport coat, "what kind of a nuthouse is this?"

"A profitable one, judging from this mob," Rosie said, grinning with relief. She'd dressed like a tourist today, blue peasant blouse, faded jeans, and sandals. Even a touch of lipstick.

Gillette was tieless, but in his navy blazer and brogans he might as well have been in uniform.

He'd noticed Rosie's softened image but made no comment. Working with women was risky business. No way to tell what'd tick 'em off. He'd been raised to stand up when a lady enters the room and call any female over twenty-one "ma'am." But a minority female who could shoot? The less said, the better.

She wouldn't be shooting anybody today. For her role as a reporter she was armed with a mini tape recorder and a notebook. No weapons, no need. Not with Gillette along for backup.

"How are we supposed to find Prince in this crush?" Gillette asked.

"The Pearls are performing on the . . . Verdant Stage," she said, checking her guidebook. "It's apparently halfway through the park. Just follow the crowd."

Easier said than done. In addition to the swarming sightseers, street performers constantly slowed their progress as tourists stopped to gawk and applaud. Jugglers, acrobats, a fire-eater. Eight royal guardsmen armed with pikes came marching past, followed by a towering, black-hooded executioner toting a five-foot broadsword. Dressed to kill.

The Verdant Stage was well named. The low platform was lavishly decorated with flowers and ferns, and even the roof was a floral tarpaulin stretched between two giant maples, giving the scene a marvelous woodland ambience.

Pearls B-4 Swine were in mid-performance, Tiff Miller singing "My Thing Is My Own" in her clarion soprano while Kirk capered about the stage, miming a rejected lover's disappointment.

"There's an alehouse with an observation deck just ahead," Gillette pointed out. "I can keep an eye on you from there without . . . cramping your style."

Rosie wondered if he was being sarcastic. Couldn't be sure, and didn't really care. "Go for it," she agreed, relieved to have Gillette out from underfoot. "No reason this has to be a grind. Have a cold one on me."

"Best advice I've heard since I got here. You take care now, little lady."

The big Georgian disappeared into the crush and Rosie did the same, worming her way through the audience to an empty wooden bench near the stage just as Tiff and Kirk finished their duet to rousing applause.

Bantering back and forth with some Canadian tourists, Kirk spotted

Rosie first and waved a hello. And then Geoff glanced her way. Only for a moment. Just long enough for Rosie to realize she was in deep trouble.

She wasn't a rookie. She'd had flings, a couple of heavy-duty affairs, and she'd even fallen seriously in love once. And yet, seeing Geoff Prince onstage, hearing his voice . . . she felt her heart lifting. Like a goo-goo-eyed teenager.

Damn it! This could not happen! No way. Angrily, she kicked her emotions back into line. The rules were set in stone. Never get emotionally involved with suspects. It wrecks justice, warps your judgment, and it can get you killed quicker than a high dive off a skyscraper.

Her mental discipline worked. Almost. Halfway through the song she was her cool, collected self again. Angry and observant.

Most of the Pearls' audience here were tourists—luau shirts, baggy shorts, sunburns. A few others were obviously fans or groupies, togged out in Renaissance garb that mimicked the band's outfits, singing along with every song. By heart.

But there was also a rougher element clustered in one corner. Teens and twenty-somethings tattooed to the max, wearing black Levis and vests or trenchcoats, spiked hair, spiked dog collars, spiky attitudes. Pale as the vampires in *The Lost Boys.*

Goths. New Age dropouts, descended from eighties punk rockers and millennium metal-heads. Hells Angels minus the motorcycles.

Most Goth kids are just making a style statement, like bellbottoms or letter sweaters. Others are serious trouble. Several high-school shooters were known Goths. Rosie's best guess about this bunch? Heavy-duty thugs. The real deal.

A towering Aryan type with an iron-pumper build, wearing a leather vest and kamikaze headband, was at the center of the Goth group. Lord of all he surveyed.

Familiar. Rosie was sure she'd seen him somewhere. Mug shots? A lineup? No, she would have remembered him from a lineup. The guy was nearly seven feet tall. Still, something about him seemed familiar. . . . It would come to her.

Fully in control now, her mood focused and fierce, she turned her attention back to the stage as the song was winding down. Forced herself to see Geoff Prince as just another skell. A suspect or a snitch.

It almost worked. Until the song slipped past her shields into a quiet corner of her heart. It was an ancient air about lost love, sung with such passion and longing that Rosie knew instinctively it was one of the melodies he'd repeated endlessly in prison. A love song. Not a murder ballad.

But the next tune was. Geoff and Tiffany sang "The Ballad of Belle Gunness" while Naomi fiddled and Kirk coaxed the crowd to join in on the chorus, turning a century-old serial killer into a sing-along joke.

The audience responded with glee, especially the Goths, and Rosie was glad Geoff had played the song. It reminded her that he was, after all, a performer. A showman. And murder was the reason she was here.

After the concert, Kirk sought her out while Geoff and the other Pearls chatted with the audience in the front row, signing autographs, selling CDs.

"Hey, if it isn't my favorite lady reporter. And looking especially fine, *chica*. How'd you like the show?"

"Very much," she said honestly.

"That last cryin' song got to you, didn't it?" Kirk grinned. " 'For My Olden Love.' Geoff always devastates the ladies with that one. Wish I could sing like that. All I can do is tap a drum and hope it matches somebody's heartbeat. Ready to meet the Goths?"

"That's why I'm here."

"Word to the wise, then. These guys are pushy. Might give you some guff, but they never heard a compliment they didn't believe. How do you want me to introduce you? Rosie the reporter?"

"That's me. I even brought a notebook."

"Good. What rag?"

"Rag?"

"You know, what magazine? Better make it *Reader's Digest*. The Goths won't know it. They're so wired to the Web I doubt they read anything on paper bigger than a ticket stub."

"They don't look much like computer geeks."

"Dungeons and Dragons," Kirk said, darkening. "They play it on the Internet twenty-four/seven. It's like a religion with 'em. Darth, the tall guy in the center? He's got a computer setup NASA would kill for. Ask him about it. It'll break the ice. Darth, my man!" Kirk boomed, holding Rosie's hand, threading her through the circle of Goths around the giant. "How you doin'?"

"Anybody I can," the Goth leader said, tapping the drummer's fist with his own. The two men were a striking contrast in style—Kirk an amiable, bearded bear, dressed in the jerkin and leggings of a feudal serf, while Darth was a towering study in studded leather, his hair a spiked Mohawk, wearing a vest that displayed his heavily tattooed arms, studded wristbands, and fingerless gloves with studded knuckles.

"This is Rosie the reporter," Kirk said. "She's doin' a piece on us. Be nice, okay? We need the ink."

"No problem. What do you want to know?" Darth asked, looking her up and down. Like a side of beef. His eyes had an odd gleam, and it suddenly struck her that she didn't know him at all. Only his eyes seemed familiar. Charles Manson had eyes like Darth's. So did Hitler. Glittering. Messianic.

"Captain Kirk tells me you're fans of the murder ballads," she said, keeping her tone light and breathy.

"Absolutely." Darth nodded. "Best stuff Prince ever did. This medieval crap's better'n rap, but the old blood ballads, they had something real to say."

"Like what?" Rosie prompted. "What do the murder ballads say to you?"

"That life's tough and the strong eat the weak. That song they did at the end of their set, 'Belle Gunness'? That chick knew how to live."

"Is that song a particular favorite of yours?"

"Nah. The Charles Manson tune's more my style, but Charlie wound up in slam city. Belle slammed everybody else. Gotta love that. Maybe you and me should try some slammin', babe."

"Not today," Rosie said evenly. "Kirk mentioned that you and your friends are into Dungeons and Dragons—"

"They're not friends. I'm an alpha male, they're my family," Darth said, moving closer. "Hell, I won most of 'em."

"Won them?"

"In the Dungeons. You play with us, you play for real. Lose and you gotta give it up."

"Give what up?"

"Your body, babe. You belong to whoever wins you. I won a chick from Tokyo a few days ago. She's flyin' in Tuesday. For the next month she's all mine."

"Wow, no kidding? You play internationally? You must be a whiz with computers."

"Damn straight," Darth said smugly.

"But doesn't it take a lot of equipment?"

"I got all the equipment you need right here—"

"I meant the computers. What kind of rig do you use?"

"Pentium 4 CPU with a 256-meg RAM, a 20-gig hard disk . . ." He hesitated, blinking. "Whoa up. What do computers and Dungeons have to do with the Pearls? Are you checking them out? Or me and mine? What magazine did you say you were with?"

"*Reader's Digest,*" Kirk put in hastily. "Gotta go. I promised Rosie I'd hook her up with Tiffany. Maybe later, big fella."

"Definitely." Darth stared after them as Kirk led Rosie away through the crowd. "Later. Definitely."

"Thanks," Rosie said, once they were clear of the Goth circle. "You really didn't have to do that. I was okay."

"I didn't do it for you, hon," Kirk said. "The Goths play rough and I'll be the one taking the heat if Darth makes you for a cop. Besides, while you were chatting him up I spotted Leo Neimi in the crowd doin' his Lurch imitation. Still want to talk to him?"

"You bet. Where is he?"

"He was at the back of the tent," Kirk said, looking around. "I don't see him now. Must've cleared out while I was saving your young butt."

"You didn't—"

"Yeah, right, I saved mine. Yours just happened to be along for the ride. Either way, Leo's in the wind. Shouldn't be hard to find, though. Do you know what he looks like?"

"Only from his picture on the CD jacket."

"That's Leo, big guy, hippie hairdo, eyes like pinwheels. Can't miss him," Kirk said. "You check the main drag, I'll scout behind the shops. If you spot him, better come get me to referee for you. Leo's more'n a little strange nowadays."

After Kirk disappeared into the crowd, Rosie scanned the tavern's observation deck, trying to signal Gillette that she was moving on. Couldn't see him clearly, the sun was in her eyes. But he waved back so she began drifting with the crowd, searching their faces for a cocaine-shattered ghost from Geoff's past.

It was a tough go. Sidling through the sea of milling tourists, Rosie figured her chances of finding Leo Neimi and Elvis were roughly equal. Too many faces, too much territory.

She glanced back to see if Gillette was following. Didn't spot him. But caught a glimpse of someone else. A tall figure in black leather, moving through the crowd toward her.

Darth? She didn't wait to find out. Picking up her pace, she threaded through the tourists. If she could put enough people between them—but it wasn't working. He was gaining on her, sightseers jumping out of his way. She stopped.

Hell, it wasn't Darth the alpha Goth at all. It was the hooded executioner she and Gillette had seen earlier, the giant with the five-foot sword. That's why the crowds were parting for him. He was one of the entertainers.

Shaking her head at her own fears, she scanned the mob for Gillette. Didn't see him. Odd. He should have caught up with her by now. . . .

The executioner was picking up speed, trotting. Heading directly for her. And for a fleeting instant she glimpsed his eyes through the eyeholes of the black leather hood. Caught the crazed gleam—

Sweet Jesus, it was Darth! Wearing a leather executioner's hood, cursing the crowd, roaring at them to stand aside. And raising his broadsword.

Was it just for show? Hell, no! The only things medieval about Darth were his weapon and the hood. The rest of him was strictly Goth. Two of his crew were with him, bulling through the crowd. Coming for her.

Instinctively she reached for her gun. Didn't have one. No sign of Gillette—damn!

Rosie bolted. Pushing her way through the crush, yelling for people to get out of the way. For a moment she thought she might get clear. Then somebody grabbed her arm.

A grinning tourist, holding her for the king's executioner. The idiot thought it was all a gag!

Twisting free, Rosie stiff-armed the dimwit in the throat, vaulting over him as he stumbled to his knees, gagging. But she'd lost precious seconds. They were almost on her.

Bouncing off a hefty matron's sunburned shoulder, Rosie sprinted into a shop. Renaissance clothing, capes, gowns. She dodged between the displays, looking for a back door. And then the executioner was there, blocking her path, swinging his great broadsword!

Any doubts she had about Darth's intent vanished in that instant. As Rosie dove beneath a rack of cloaks the sword whistled past her head, missing her by inches, ripping into the row of period costumes.

Scrambling beneath the displays, Rosie tumbled out the entrance while Darth was freeing his blade. One of his goons was waiting for her, arms outstretched. The street was an arena now, tourists and gawkers forming a circle around the store to watch the performance.

The Goth blocking her path wasn't as big as Darth, but close enough. Six feet tall, barechested to show off his tattoos and buffed-up build. But he was no fighter, just a goon.

He grabbed at Rosie, a big mistake in hand-to-hand combat. Ducking under his reach, Rosie kicked his kneecap loose, slamming her elbow into the bridge of his nose as he fell, leaving him dazed and writhing in the square.

And the crowd applauded. Cheering her!

"Way cool," a teenybopper said. "That almost looked for real."

"It *is* real, you morons!" she roared. "This isn't an act! I'm a police officer, these men are trying to kill me! Get out of here and get help. Somebody call nine-one-one!"

But they only clapped louder, laughing and cheering.

"Nine-one-one." A bald guy chuckled, nudging his wife. "That's a good one. Hey, look out, lady, here they come!"

Darth the executioner and the other goon burst out of the shop as Rosie whirled to face them.

The second Goth was smaller than the first, wiry, with a purple cobra tattoo encircling his throat, its fanged mouth gaping on his shaved head. He even moved a bit like a cobra, edging warily away from Rosie. He'd seen what happened to his pal, wouldn't make the same mistake.

Basic combat strategy. They'd rush in from two sides. Cobra would grapple with her, keeping her busy long enough for Darth to take her out.

Licking her lips, Rosie estimated the distance to Cobra. If she could mix it up with him first, Darth wouldn't be able to swing—but Cobra obviously knew something about martial arts. He stayed just out of range. Waiting for Darth's signal.

"For God's sake," Rosie shouted. "This is no show! Somebody help me!"

"Hey, no fair," the bald guy yelled. "She ain't got no sword! Somebody give the girl a sword."

"Booo! No fair!" The call echoed through the crowd. "Give her a sword. Give her a sword."

And incredibly, someone did. A dandy in Shakespearean tights stepped out of the crowd and gallantly tossed her his blade! A gleaming fencing foil.

Leaping high, Rosie snatched it out of the air before Darth could react. Plastic! The damned sword was a plastic replica! A freaking toy!

But maybe Darth and his pal didn't realize it yet.

Screaming like a banshee, Rosie charged the smaller Goth, slashing wildly at him with her plastic foil. He panicked, backing away, turning to run. But the cheering crowd wouldn't let him. They joined hands, blocking his path.

As Rosie lunged at Cobra, trying to kick him down, someone in the crowd shoved him back into the circle, slamming him into her. Reeling, she stumbled backward, struggling desperately to pull free, Cobra clawing at the sword as they went down.

And then Darth was standing over her, his sword raised—

"Drop it!" Gillette roared. "Right freakin' now! Do it!"

Too late! The blade whistled down as Gillette fired, grabbing Cobra's vest. Rosie had wrestled him around, using him as a shield.

Cobra screamed as the huge blade bit into his shoulder, and then he and Rosie went down under the pile as Darth toppled over on them.

Swinging her fists and elbows, Rosie fought to free herself from the bloody jumble. The terrified crowd stampeded, trampling one another, fleeing the gunfire and the play that had just exploded into reality.

A hand seized Rosie's shoulder but she squirmed away, hammering a backfist into—

Gillette's face! Groaning, he stumbled to his knees beside her, holding his nose with his free hand.

"Damn it! Chill out, Morales! I think you broke my freakin' nose. Get the hell out of the way, will ya?"

"I'm trying," Rosie panted, scooting backward on her butt, kicking her way clear of the muddle. "Where the hell were you?"

"Playin' tourist," Gillette snapped. "I lost you in the crowd, wound up tailing somebody in a blouse like yours. Didn't realize what was up until I heard you yelling. And you're welcome."

"Yeah, right," Rosie panted. "Thanks for saving my life, Gillette."

"No charge, Morales. Thanks for breaking my nose."

"You're welcome." And suddenly they were both grinning like idiots, shaking their heads. A close call. Very close.

"Help me," the Goth groaned, struggling to roll Darth's dead weight off him. "Somebody help me."

"Quit whinin', junior," Gillette growled. "I've cut myself worse shavin'. Is the other one dead?"

"Oh, yeah," Rosie nodded, swallowing. She pressed a fingertip against Darth's carotid artery but there was really no need. The executioner's hood had a third bloody eyehole punched between the original two. "Dead. Definitely."

"Is he our guy?"

"I sure as hell hope so," she said.

"Congratulations, you two." Captain Bennett beamed. "While you were getting patched together in the emergency room, a search team turned over Darth Steiner's apartment. They found PDAs belonging to all three victims, along with doctored nude photos of Tiff Miller promising a wild night. Notes on his desk indicate that he used his monster computer rig to raid their bank accounts."

"What about Geoff Prince?" Rosie asked. "Did Darth plant that second bank account on him?"

"Don't know yet. The nerd squad tells me it may take a month to sort out the guy's hard drives. He customized most of his software and protected the data with high-tech firewalls. They don't know where he transferred the money yet, or how he set Prince up. Apparently Steiner's a computer genius. Or was, I should say. That was a hell of a shot you made, Sergeant Gillette. A bit risky, though, with so many people around."

"Some," Gillette admitted. "But Steiner was taller than most and I knelt to fire. If I'd missed, the bullet would have landed in Lake St. Clair. I hope."

"And I'd be minus my head," Rosie added.

"That'd be a shame," Gillette said, getting serious. "You've got a good head for police work, Morales. You were right. I wanted to bust Prince that first day because he ticked me off. But you figured he was innocent for . . . whatever reason. And you played the thing out. You saved me from making a dumb-ass mistake and I appreciate it."

"Before you two get all mushy on me, I need to walk Sergeant Gillette through his statement a few times before he meets with the shooting board," Bennett said. "It's just a formality, but you know the drill."

"Been there, done that," Rosie said, rising. "Can I grab a shower and change clothes before I talk to the board?"

"Go ahead," Bennett said, "I won't need you for a few hours. Oh, by the way, I canceled that APB you put on Leo Neimi."

"Why? He may have information we can use."

"You'd need a medium to get it. Neimi's dead."

"Dead?" Rosie echoed. "How? When?"

"Drug overdose, eighteen months ago. Are you okay, Morales? You look a little pale."

Rosie didn't ring the buzzer at Prince's building. After stopping at her flat to pick up her weapon and a jacket, she climbed the fire escape, jimmied a window of the vacant loft next door, and let herself out into Prince's hallway.

The door was open. Music was playing within, a medieval melody. Live or a recording? She couldn't tell.

Flattening herself against the wall, she drew her weapon and peered around the doorframe. Couldn't see anything at first. Dusk was falling and no lights were on.

As her eyes adjusted she spotted Prince, sitting cross-legged in front of his huge bay window, battered guitar cradled in his lap. Staring out into the twilight as he played.

Stepping quietly inside, Rosie covered him, scanning the room.

"You're too late," Geoff said quietly. "He's gone. You don't need the gun. Unless you're going to shoot me."

"I might. I didn't know what I'd find here. Whether you'd be gone. Or maybe dead."

"If Kirk wanted to hurt me he would have done it a long time ago. He was my cellmate down in Mexico. The only two *gringos* in the place. With all those *hombres.*"

"You and Kirk. Not you and Leo?"

"Leo was holding coke the night we got busted. Went to a different prison. I never said he was my cellmate."

"You never warned me about Kirk, either. And you knew what he was. All along."

"No. I . . . wondered. But I didn't know and I still can't believe how far he went. I would have warned you if I'd known."

"Damn it, I asked you for names—"

"It wasn't that simple. I couldn't rat Kirk out on the off chance he might be guilty. I owe him my life."

"Because he killed somebody defending you in prison? What about the lives of the three businessmen he murdered?"

"I didn't *know* he was involved."

"You didn't want to know!"

"Maybe that's true," he admitted, glancing up at her. "Maybe I didn't want to believe it because I owed him. Big-time. And because he's my friend."

"If he was such a great friend, why did he plant that money on you?"

"I don't think he did. It was a mistake he wouldn't have made. Belle didn't set up a fall guy until she was ready to bail out. Are you sure Kirk made those deposits?"

"No," she admitted. "It could have been Darth. Probably was, in fact. And what about Darth? When did he and Kirk hook up?"

"I . . . knew they were friendly but didn't think much about it. Everybody likes Kirk. He's a charmer. Or didn't you notice?"

"I noticed. And you're right, he's a very likable guy. Which is one more reason you should have warned me."

"Yeah, I should have. I see that now. I'm sorry I didn't. I guess that doesn't matter much now, does it?"

She didn't answer. Which was an answer of sorts.

"So," he said. "What now? Am I still a suspect?"

"I don't know what you are. You definitely have some questions to answer."

"I don't know where he is. I'd tell you if I did."

"It's not my problem anymore. I'm going to ask to be transferred off this case."

"Why?"

"Don't be an idiot. You know why."

"Because of me, you mean?"

"No, because of me," she snapped. "I need to sort some things out about myself and this job. And maybe about you. But however it turns out, I doubt very much we'll be pals afterward. Or anything else."

"Maybe we'll be colleagues," Geoff said.

"Colleagues? What are you talking about?"

"I think we'll be talking again. About Kirk."

"But you said—"

"I don't know where he is, truly. But we'll be hearing from him again."

"How do you mean?"

"You met Kirk. He's bright and funny and glib. And an egomaniac. A natural-born performer. But being a sideman wasn't enough. The world is his stage now. And he's a big star. Putting on the ultimate show."

"My God," she said. Getting it. Finally getting it. "The murder ballads. It's not a game. It's a performance."

"In that cell, music was my escape, it kept me sane. I think it did the opposite to Kirk. The murder ballads are five centuries of master plans for him. Who did what, how they got caught or got away with it. Belle is just one ballad. He'll use a different one next time."

"But . . . won't you be able to recognize it?"

"I don't know. We were in that cage a long time, Rose. We sang a lot of songs."

"How many?" She swallowed. "How many murder ballads are there?"

"Hundreds," Geoff said quietly. "He knows hundreds of them."

Sharyn McCrumb

The Vale of the White Horse

SHARYN MCCRUMB, an award-winning Appalachian writer, is best known for her Ballad novels, set in the North Carolina/Tennessee mountains. The latest of these, *Ghost Riders* (Dutton, July 2003), chronicles the Civil War in the North Carolina mountains and its echoes in the region today. Her novels include the *New York Times* bestsellers *She Walks These Hills* and *The Rosewood Casket,* which deal with the issue of the vanishing wilderness. Other Ballad novels include the *New York Times* Notable Books *If Ever I Return Pretty Peggy-O, The Hangman's Beautiful Daughter,* as well as the national bestsellers *The Ballad of Frankie Silver* and *The Song Catcher.* Her works, published in more than ten languages, are studied in both the United States and abroad, and she was the first writer-in-residence at King College in Tennessee. She has spoken on her work at the Smithsonian, Oxford University, the University of Bonn, and in 2001 she served as fiction writer-in-residence at the WICE Conference in Paris.

About "The Vale of the White Horse," which appeared in *Murder, My Dear Watson,* she writes, "I think the connection between the character of Grisel Rountree in 'The Vale of the White Horse' and Nora Bonesteel, the wise woman in the Ballad novels, is the fact that they are both part of an ancient British folk tradition, which reached the Appalachians during the eighteenth-century frontier settlement of the southern mountains. Those mountains are, by the way, part of the same chain as the mountains that pass through Ireland, Cornwall, Wales, and Scotland. All these mountains used to be one contiguous orogeny, but with plate tectonics and sea-floor spreading, the Atlantic divided the mountains beginning 250 million years ago. But they are the same mountains. So the Anglo-Scottish settlers of the Appalachians are to their U.K. counterparts, just as their respective mountains are kin geologically."

The Vale of the White Horse

Sharyn McCrumb

Grisel Rountree was the first to see that something was strange about the white chalk horse.

As she stood on the summit of the high down, in the ruins of the hill fort that overlooked the dry chalk valley, she squinted at the white shape on the hillside below, wondering for a moment or two what was altered. Carved into the steep slope across the valley, the primitive outline of a white horse shone in the sunshine of a June morning. Although Grisel Rountree had lived in the valley all seven decades of her life, she never tired of the sight of the ancient symbol, large as a hayfield, shining like polished ivory in the long grass of early summer.

The white horse had been old two thousand years ago when the Romans arrived in Britain and the people in the valley had long ago forgotten the reason for its existence, but there were stories about its magic. Some said that King Arthur had fought his last battle on that hill, and others claimed that the horse was the symbol for the nearby Wayland smithy, the local name for a stone chamber where folks said that a pagan god had been condemned to shoe the horses of mortals for all eternity.

Whatever the truth of its origins, the village took a quiet pride in its proximity to the great horse. Every year when the weather broke, folks would make an excursion up the slope to clean the chalk form of the great beast, and to pull any encroaching weeds that threatened to blur the symmetry of its outline. They made a day of it, taking picnic lunches and bottles of ale, and the children played tag in the long grass while their elders worked. When Grisel was a young girl, her father had told her that the chalk figure was a dragon whose imprint had been burned into the hill where it had been killed by St. George himself. When she became old enough to go to the village dances, the laughing young men had insisted that the white beast was a unicorn, and that if a virgin should let herself be kissed within the eye of the chalk figure, the unicorn would come to life and gallop away. It was a great jest to invite the unmarried lasses up to the hill "to make the unicorn run," though of course it never did.

Nowadays everyone simply said the creature was a horse, though they did allow that whoever drew it hadn't made much of a job of it. It was too stretched and skinny to look like a proper horse, but given its enormous size, perhaps the marvel was that the figure looked like anything at all.

The hill fort provided the best view of the great white horse. Anyone standing beside the chalk ramparts of the ancient ruins could look down across the valley and see the entire figure of the horse sprawled out below like the scribble of some infant giant. Grisel Rountree did not believe in giants, but she did believe in tansy leaves, which was why she was up at the hill fort so early that morning. A few leaves of tansy put in each shoe prevented the wearer from coming down with ague. Although she seldom had the ague, Grisel Rountree considered it prudent to stock up on the remedy as a precaution anyhow. Besides, half the village came to her at one time or another to cure their aches and pains, and it was just as well to be ready with a good supply before winter set in.

She had got up at first light, fed the hens and did the morning chores around her cottage, and then set off with a clean feed sack to gather herbs for her remedies and potions. She had been up at the ruins when the clouds broke, and a shaft of sunlight seemed to shine right down on the chalk horse. She had stopped looking for plants then, and when she stood up to admire the sight, she noticed it.

The eye of the great white horse was red.

"Now, there's a thing," she said to herself.

She shaded her eyes from the sun and squinted to get a clearer image of the patch of red but she still couldn't make it out. The eye did not appear to have been painted. It was more like something red had been put more or less in the space where the horse's eye ought to be, but at this distance, she couldn't quite make out what it was. She picked up the basket of herbs and made her way down the slope. No use hurrying—it would take her at least half an hour to cross the valley and climb the hill to the eye of the white horse. Besides, since whatever-it-was in the eye was not moving, it would probably be there whenever she reached it.

"It'll be goings-on, I'll warrant," she muttered to herself, picturing a courting couple fallen asleep in their trysting place. Grisel Rountree did not hold with "goings-on," certainly not in broad daylight at the top of a great hill before God and everybody. She tried to think of who in the village might be up to such shenanigans these days, but no likely couple came to mind. They were all either past the point of outdoor courting or still working up to it.

Out of ideas, she plodded on. "Knowing is better than guessing," she muttered, resolving to ignore the twinge of rheumatism that bedeviled her joints with every step she took. The walk would do her good, she thought, and if it didn't, there was always some willow tea back in the cottage waiting to be brewed.

Half an hour later, the old woman had crossed the valley and reached the summit where the chalk horse lay. Now that she was nearer she could see that the splash of red she had spotted from afar was a bit of cloth, but it wasn't lying flat against the ground like a proper cape or blanket should. She felt a shiver of cold along her backbone, knowing what she was to find.

In the eye of the white horse, Grisel knelt beside the scarlet cloak spread open on the ground. She wore a look of grim determination, but she would not be shocked. She had been midwife to the village these forty years, and she laid out the dead as well, so she'd seen the worst, taken all around. She lifted the edge of the blanket and found herself staring into the sightless eyes of a stranger. A moment's examination told her that the man was a gentleman—the cut of his bloodstained clothes would have told her that, but besides his wardrobe, the man had the smooth hand and the well-kept look of one who has been waited on all his life. She noted this without any resentment of the differences in their stations: such things just were.

The man was alive, but only just.

"Can you tell me who did this to you?" she said, knowing that this was all the help he could be given, and that if there were time for only one question, it should be that. The rest could be found out later, one way or another.

The man's eyes seemed to focus on her for a moment, and in a calm, wondering voice he said clearly, *"Not a maiden . . ."*

And then he died. Grisel Rountree did not stay to examine him further, because the short blade sticking out of the dead man's stomach told her that this was not a matter for the layer-out of the dead but for the village constable.

"Rest in peace, my lad," said the old woman, laying the blanket back into place. "I'll bring back someone directly to fetch you down."

"Missus Rountree!" Young Tom Cowper stood under the apple tree beside the old woman's cottage, gasping for breath from his run from the village, but too big with news to wait for composure. "They're bringing a gentleman down from London on account of the murder!"

Grisel Rountree swirled the wooden paddle around the sides of the steaming black kettle, fishing a bit of bedsheet out of the froth and examining it for dirt. Not clean yet. "From London?" she grunted. "I shouldn't wonder. Our P.C. Waller is out of his depth, and so I told him when I took him up to the white horse."

"Yes'm," said Tom, mindful of the sixpence he had been given to deliver the message. "The London gentleman—he's staying at the White Horse, him and a friend—at the inn, I mean."

Grisel snorted. "I didn't suppose you meant the white horse on the hill, lad."

"No. Well, he's asking to see you, missus. On account of you finding the body. They say I'm to take you to the village."

The old woman stopped stirring the wash pot and fixed the boy with a baleful eye. "Oh, I'm to come to the village, am I? Look here, Tom Cowper, you go back to the inn and tell the gentleman that anybody can tell him the way to my cottage, and if he wants a word with me, here I'll be."

"But, missus—"

"Go!"

For a moment Tom gaped at the tall white-haired figure, pointing imperiously at him. People roundabouts said she were a witch, and of course he didn't hold with such foolishness, but there was a limit to what sixpence would buy a gentleman in the way of his services as a messenger. Choosing the better part of valor, he turned and ran.

"Who is this London fellow?" Grisel called after the boy.

Without breaking stride Tom called back to her, "Mis-terr Sher-lock Holmes!"

Grisel Rountree finished her washing, swept the cottage again, and set to work making a batch of scones in case the gentleman from London should arrive at tea time, which, if he had any sense, he would, because anybody hereabouts could tell him that Grisel Rountree's baking was far better than the alternately scorched and floury efforts of the cook at the village inn.

The old woman was not surprised that London had taken an interest in the case, considering that the dead man had turned out to be from London himself, and a society doctor to boot. James Dacre, his name was, and he was one of the Hampshire Dacres, and the brother of the young earl over at Ramsmeade. The wonder of it was that the doctor should be visiting here, for he had never done so before, though they saw his brother the baronet often enough.

A few months back, the young baronet had been a guest of the local hunt, and during the course of the visit he had met Miss Evelyn Ambry, the daughter of the local squire and the beauty of the county. She was a tall, spirited young woman, much more beautiful than her sisters and by far the best rider. People said she was as fearless as she was flawless, but among the villagers there was a hint of reserve in their voices when they spoke of her. There was a local tradition about the Ambrys—people didn't speak of it in these enlightened times, but they never quite forgot it either. Miss Evelyn was one of the Ambry Changelings, right enough. There was one along in nearly every generation.

By all accounts Miss Evelyn Ambry had made a conquest of the noble guest, and the baronet's visits to the district became so frequent that people began to talk of a match being made between the pair of them. Some folk said they would have been betrothed already if Miss Evelyn's aunt had not suddenly taken ill and died two weeks back, so that Miss Evelyn had to observe mourning for the next several months. And now there was more mourning to keep them apart—his lordship's own brother.

Grisel was sorry about the about the young man's untimely death, but it's an ill wind that blows nobody good, she told herself, and if the doctor's passing kept his brother from wedding the Ambry Changeling, it might be a blessing after all. Whenever a silly woman sighed at the prospect of a wedding between Miss Evelyn and the baronet, Grisel always held her peace on the subject, but she'd not be drinking the health of the handsome couple if the wedding day ever came. It boded ill for the bridegroom, she thought. It always had done when a besotted suitor wed an Ambry Changeling, and so Grisel had been expecting a tragedy in the offing—but not this particular tragedy. The baronet's younger brother dying in the eye of the white horse. She didn't know what it meant, and that worried her. And his last words— "Not a maiden"—put her in mind of the village lads' old jest about the unicorn, but how could a gentleman doctor from London know about that? It was a puzzle, right enough, and she could not see the sense of it yet, but one thing she did know for certain: death comes in threes.

She was just dusting the top of the oak cupboard for the second time when she heard voices in the garden.

"Do let me handle this, Holmes," came the voice of a London gentleman. "You may frighten the poor old creature out of her wits with your abrupt ways."

"Nonsense!" said a sharper voice. "I am the soul of tact, always!"

She had flung open the cottage door before they could knock. "Good afternoon, good sirs," she said, addressing her remarks to the tall, saturnine gentleman in the cape and the deerstalker hat. Just from the look of him, you could tell that he was the one in charge.

The short, sandy-haired fellow with the bushy mustache and kind eyes gave her a reassuring smile. "It's Mistress Rountree, is it not? I am Dr. John Watson. Allow me to introduce my companion, Mr. Sherlock Holmes, the eminent detective from London. We are indeed hoping for a word with you. May we come in?"

She nodded and stepped aside to let them pass. "You're wanting to talk about young Dacre's death," she said. "It was me that found him. But you needn't be afraid of upsetting me, young man. I may not have seen the horrors you did with the army in Afghanistan, but I'll warrant I've seen my share in forty years of birthing and burying folk in these parts."

The sandy-haired man took a step backward and stared at her. "But how did you know that I had been in Afghanistan?"

"Really, Watson!" said his companion. "Will you never cease to be amazed by parlor tricks? Shall I tell you how the good lady ferreted out your secret? I did it myself at our first meeting, you may recall."

"Yes, yes," said Watson with a nervous laugh. "I remember. I was a bit startled because the innkeeper said that Mistress Rountree had a bit of reputation hereabouts as a witch. I thought this might be a sample of it."

"I expect it is," said Holmes. "People are always spinning tales to explain that which they do not understand. No doubt they'll be coming out with some outlandish nonsense about the body of Mr. Dacre being found in the eye of the white horse. I believe you found him, madam?"

Grisel Rountree motioned for them to sit down. "I've laid the tea on, and there are scones on the table. You can be getting on with that while I'm telling you." In a few words she gave the visitors a concise account of her actions on the morning of James Dacre's murder.

"You'll be in the employ of his lordship the baronet," she said, giving Holmes an appraising look.

He nodded. "Indeed, that gentleman is most anxious to discover the circumstances surrounding his brother's murder. And you tell me that Dr. Dacre was in fact alive when you found him?"

"Only just, sir. He had been stabbed in the stomach, and he had bled like a stuck pig. Must have lay there a good hour or more, judging by all the blood on the grass thereabouts."

"And you saw no one? There are very few trees on those downs. Did you scan the distance for a retreating figure?"

She nodded. "Even before I knew what had happened, I looked. I was on the opposite hill, mind, when I first noticed the red on the horse's eye, so I could see for miles, and there were nothing moving, not so much as a cow, sir, much less a man."

"No. You'd have told the constable if it had been otherwise. And the poor man's final words to you were—"

"Just like I told you. He opened his eyes and said clear as day. *Not a maiden.* Then he lay back and died."

"*Not a maiden.* He was not addressing you, I take it?"

"He were not," snapped the old woman. "And he would have been wrong if he had been."

"Did the phrase convey anything to you at the time?"

"Only the old tale about the white horse. The village lads used to say that if anyone were to kiss a proper maiden standing upon the chalk horse, the beast would get up and walk away. So perhaps he had been kissing a lady? But that's not what I thought. The poor man was stabbed with a woman's weapon—a seam ripper, it were, from a lady's sewing kit—and I think he was saying that the one who used it was not a woman, despite the look of it."

Holmes nodded. "Let's leave that for a bit. I find it curious that the doctor was walking on the downs at such an odd hour. In fact, why was he here at all? The family estate, Ramsmeade, is some distance from here."

"The doctor's brother is engaged to a squire's daughter hereabouts," said the old woman.

"So I am told. I believe the Dacres had come to attend a funeral at the Hall."

"T'were the squire's younger sister. Christabel, her name was. Fanciful name for a flighty sort of woman, if you ask me. Ill for a long while, she was, and her not thirty-five yet, even. Young Dacre were a doctor, you know. So when the squire's sister took sick, the family asked Dr. Dacre to do what he could for the poor lady, on account of the family connection, you see. The doctor's brother affianced to the niece of the sick woman."

"Ah! Mr. Dacre often visited here to treat his patient, then?"

"Not he. He has a fine clinic up in London. She went up there to be looked after. Out of her head with worry, she was, poor lamb. Even came here once to see if I had any kind of a tonic that might set her to rights. *Now, Mistress Rountree,* she says to me, *I've got such a pain in my tummy that I don't care if I live or die, only I must make it stop. Is there anything you can give me for it?* But I told her there were nought I could do for her, excepting to pray. There never has been for such as she. An Ambry Changeling, she was. Know it to look at her, though I kept still about that. So up she went to London, and died upon the operating table up at the Dacre clinic."

"It was not, by any chance, a childbirth?" said Watson.

Grisel gave him a scornful look. "Childbirth? Not she! I told you: an Ambry Changeling she was. Not that I believe all the tales that are bandied hereabouts, but call it what you will, there is a mark on that family."

"Now that is interesting," said Holmes. He had left off eating scones now, and was pacing the length of the cottage while he listened. "What do people say about the Ambrys? A family curse?"

"Not a curse. That could be lifted, maybe. This is in the blood and there's no getting away from it. The Ambrys are an old family. They've been living at the Hall since the time of the Crusades, that I do know. Churchyard will tell you that much. But folk in these parts say that one of the Ambry lords, a long time back, married one of the fair folk. . . ." She hesitated, choosing her words carefully. "One of the lords and ladies . . ."

"He married into the nobility, you mean?" asked Watson.

"Stranger than that, I think," said Holmes, still pacing. "I think Mistress Rountree is using the countryman's polite—and wary—circumlocution to tell us that an Ambry ancestor took a bride from among the Shining Folk. In short, a fairy wife."

The old woman nodded. "Just so. They do say that she stayed for all of twenty years and twenty days with her mortal husband, and she bore him children, but then she slipped away in the night and went back to her own people. She was never seen again, but her bloodline carries on in the Ambrys to this day. Their union was blessed with five children—or blessed with four, perhaps. The fifth one took after the mother. And ever since that time there has been in nearly every generation that one daughter who takes after the fairy side of the family—a changeling."

"Fascinating," said Holmes.

"But hardly germane to an ordinary stabbing death," said Watson.

"One never knows, Watson. Let us hear a bit more. By what signs do you know that an Ambry boy or girl is the family changeling?"

"It's always a girl," said the old woman. "The prettiest one of the bunch, for one thing. Tall and slender, with beautiful dark hair and what some might call an elf face—big eyes and sharp cheekbones—not your chocolate box pretty girl, but a beauty all the same."

"A lovely girl in every generation?" Dr. Watson laughed. "That sounds like the sort of curse any family would envy."

"But that's not the whole of it," said Grisel. "That's only the good part."

"I suppose they were high-tempered ladies," Watson said, smiling. "The pretty ones often are, I find. Still, I hardly think that fairy stories would deter a modern gentleman."

"There is a good deal of sense wrapped in country fables," said Holmes. "He might do well to heed them. However, I don't quite see its connection to the death of the good doctor. Was the Ambry family angry that Christabel Ambry had died in the doctor's care?"

"No. She were in a bad way, and they knew there was little hope for her. They didn't suppose anybody could have done any more than what he did."

"I wonder what was the matter with her?" mused Watson.

"That is your province, Watson," said Holmes. "You might call in at the clinic and ask. I shall pursue my present line of inquiry. We know that Dacre arrived here on the Friday. The funeral, then, was on Saturday, and he was found dying within the white horse in the early hours of Sunday morning. He had been stabbed with a silver seam ripper from a sewing kit, but his last words—presumably on the subject of his murderer—were: *Not a maiden.*"

"Is there a tailor in these parts?"

"Watson, I hardly think that James Dacre would be taking an evening stroll across the downs with the village tailor."

"Nor do I," said Grisel Rountree. "Anyhow, we don't have one. So you do think the person up on the hill was a lady after all?"

"We must not theorize ahead of the facts," said Holmes. "This seems to be a country of riddles, and the meaning of the doctor's words is still not clear."

A few days later Sir Henry Dacre, Bart., received his distinguished London visitors in his oak-paneled study at Ramsmeade. He was an amiable young man with watery blue eyes and a diffident smile. At his side was a dark-haired woman whose imperious nature made her seem more the aristocrat than he. She was nearly as tall as Sir Henry, and her sharp features and glowing white skin were accentuated by the black of her mourning clothes.

"Good morning, Mr. Holmes, Dr. Watson," Sir Henry said. "May I present my fiancée, Miss Evelyn Ambry. My dear, these are the gentlemen I told you about. They are looking into the circumstances surrounding the death of poor James."

She inclined her head regally toward them. "Do sit down, gentlemen. We are so anxious to hear of your progress."

Dr. Watson raised his eyebrows, glancing first at Holmes and then at their host. "The matters we have to discuss are somewhat delicate for a lady's ears," he said. "Perhaps Miss Ambry would prefer not to be present."

Evelyn Ambry gave him a cool stare. "If the matter concerns my family, I shall insist on being present."

Sir Henry gave them a tentative smile. "There you have it, gentlemen. She will have her way. If Miss Ambry wishes to be present, I'm sure she has every right to do so."

With a curt nod, Sherlock Holmes settled himself in an armchair near the fire. "As you wish," he said. "I have never been squeamish about medical matters myself. By all means let us proceed. As to the physical facts concerning the death of your late brother, we have done little more than confirm what was already known: that he died in the early hours of twelve June as the result of a stab wound inflicted in his upper abdomen. The weapon was a seam ripper, but it was not of the professional grade used by tailors. Rather it seemed more appropriate to the sewing of a woman."

"I have not the patience for sewing," said Miss Ambry. "Such an idle pastime. Grouse shooting is rather more in my line."

"Yet the instrument was of silver, which seems to preclude the villagers from ownership. Does anyone in your household possess such an item?"

She shrugged. "Not to my knowledge. Did you ask the household staff?"

"Yes. They could not be certain either way. Leaving that aside, we know that the doctor came to the village to attend the funeral of his patient, Christabel Ambry, that he stayed at the inn, and after seven in the evening, when he had a pint in the residents' lounge, he was not seen until the next morning, when his body was found in the vale of the White Horse. This much we knew. So we turned out attention to London."

Sir Henry nodded. "You think some enemy may have followed my brother down from London and quarreled with him?"

"I thought it most unlikely," Holmes replied. "In any event we were unable to discover any enemies."

"No, indeed," said Watson. "Dr. Dacre was highly esteemed in the medical profession. His colleagues liked him, and his patients are quite distressed that he has been taken from them."

"He was the clever one of the family," said Sir Henry. "But a dear fellow all the same."

"Are you quite sure that James had no enemies?" asked Evelyn Ambry. "Surely you did not interview every one of his patients? What about the relatives of the deceased ones?"

"Indeed we have not yet spoken with you," said Holmes. "I believe you would be included in the latter category. Had your family any resentment toward Dr. Dacre as a physician?"

"Certainly not!" Her cheeks reddened and she pursed her lips in annoyance. "Christabel was very ill. We had long feared the worst. I never go to doctors myself, but I thought James was an exceptional physician. He was tireless on Christabel's behalf. He fought even after we all had given up hope."

"Had the doctor ever mentioned any unhappy patients?" asked Watson, addressing Sir Henry.

"Never," said Sir Henry. "He seemed quite content in his relations with mankind, taken all round."

"Which brings us to *womankind*," murmured Holmes. "I am thinking of the doctor's final words: *Not a maiden*. Had your brother any romantic attachments, Sir Henry?"

"Yes. James was engaged to an American heiress. She was in New York at the time of his death, and as she was unable to return for the funeral, she has remained in America with her family. She is quite distraught. They were devoted to each other."

"I see. So there is no question, then, of a dalliance with a village maiden?" He glanced at Miss Ambry to see if the question called for an apology, but she had managed a taut smile.

"James was not at all that sort of man," she said. "Anyone can tell you that. He lived for his work, and he was quite happy to allocate the rest of his attention to Anne. She is a charming girl."

Dr. Watson cleared his throat. "I have been examining the medical records of Dr. Dacre's patients. They all seem straightforward enough. He specialized in cancer—a sad duty most of the time. I did wonder about your aunt, though, Miss Ambry. The records on her case were missing. There was only an empty folder with her name on it, and a scribbled note: *'No hope! Orchids?'* "

"Do you know what Christabel Ambry died of?'

"Cancer, of course," said Evelyn. "We knew that. I'm afraid we did not press for details. Christabel seemed not to want inquiry on the subject."

"In that case, why did Dacre destroy the records?" said Watson. "He seems to have discussed the case with no one. And what of the notation on the folder?"

"Orchids? Well, perhaps he was thinking of sending flowers for the funeral," Sir Henry suggested.

"Orchids would be most unsuitable, Henry," said his fiancée.

"Well, I suppose they would be. At any rate I know he sent a wreath, but I'm dashed if I know what it was. White flowers, I think. I confess it is all Greek to me, gentlemen."

Sherlock Holmes stared. "I wonder if . . ." He stood up and began pacing before the hearth. After a few more moments of muttering, during which he ignored their questions, Holmes held up his hand for silence. "Well, we must know. Watson, again your medical skills will be called upon. Let us go and see the squire. I fear that we must discover a buried secret."

"I will not give you a love potion, Millie Hopgood, and that's *final*," said Grisel Rountree to the rabbit of a girl in her cottage door. "That young man of yours is a Wilberforce, and everybody knows the Wilberforces are mortally shy. He's the undertaker's boy, and he don't know how to talk to live people, I reckon."

"Yes, but—"

"All he wants is a bit of plain speaking from you, and if you won't make up your mind to that, all the potions in the world won't help you."

"Oh, I couldn't, I'm sure, Missus Rountree!" gasped the girl. "But as you'll be seeing him up to the Hall today, I was thinking you might have a word with him yourself."

"Me going to the Hall? First I've heard of it."

The girl pulled an envelope out of her apron pocket, holding it out to the old woman so that she could see the wax seal crest of the Ambrys sealing the flap. "I'm just bringing it now. The two gentlemen from London are back, and they'd like a word with you."

"Well? And what has your young Wilberforce to do with it?"

"Please, missus, they're going into the vault—after Miss Christabel."

"I am coming, then," said the old woman. "See you tell Miss Evelyn that I am coming straightaway."

Grisel Rountree found Sherlock Holmes walking in the grounds of Old Hall within sight of the Ambry family vault. It was a warm June afternoon, but she felt a chill on seeing him pacing the lawn, oblivious to the riot of colors in the flowerbeds or the beauty of the ancient oaks. As single-minded as Death, he was. And as inevitable.

"So you've gone and dug up Miss Christabel, then?" she said. "Well, I don't suppose dug up is the right term, as she were in a vault."

He nodded. "It all seemed to come down to that. Dr. Watson is in the scullery there, performing an autopsy, but I think we both know what he will find."

"The lady died of cancer," said Grisel Rountree, looking away.

"Christabel Ambry died of cancer, yes," said Holmes.

"Ah," said the old woman. "So you do know something about it."

"I fancy I do, yes." He turned in response to a shout from the door of the scullery. "Here he is now. Shall we hear his report or will you speak now?"

"Does Miss Evelyn know what you are doing?"

"She has gone out with a shooting party," said Holmes. "We are quite alone, except for the undertaker's boy."

"Wilberforce," she said with a dismissive sigh. "He hasn't the sense to grasp what to gossip about, so that's safe. Let the doctor tell you what he makes of it."

Watson reached them then, rolling down his sleeves, his forearms still damp from washing up after the procedure. "Well, it's done, Holmes," he said. "Shall I tell you in private?"

Holmes shook his head. "Miss Rountree here is a midwife and local herbalist. I rather fancy that makes her a colleague of yours. In any case she has always known what you have just been at pains to discover. Do tell us, Watson. Of what did Christabel Ambry die?"

Watson reddened. "Cancer, right enough," he said gruffly. "Testicular cancer."

"You must have been surprised."

"I've heard of such cases," said Watson. "They are mercifully rare. It is a defect in the development of the fetus before birth, apparently. When I opened up the abdomen, I found that the deceased had the . . . er . . . the reproductive organs of a male. The testes, which had become cancerous, were inside the abdomen, and there was no womb. The deceased's vagina, only a few inches long, ended at nothing. I must conclude that the patient was—technically—male."

"An Ambry Changeling," said Holmes.

"But how did you know, Holmes?"

"It was only a guess, but I knew, you see, that *orchis* is the Greek word for testis, and I was still thinking about the changeling story. It was an old country attempt to describe a real occurrence, is it not so, madam?"

Grisel Rountree nodded. "We midwives never knew what their insides were like, of course, but the thing about the Ambry Changelings is that they were barren. Always. Oh, they might marry, right enough, especially to an outsider who didn't know the story about the Ambrys, but there was never a child born to one of them. Some of them were good wives, and some were bad, and more than a few died young, like Christabel Ambry, rest her soul, but there was never an Ambry changeling that bore a child. That could be curse enough to a landed family with the property entailed, don't you reckon?"

"Indeed," said Holmes. "And the doctor knew of this?"

"He did not," said Grisel Rountree. "None of us were like to tell him—no business of his, anyhow. And when Miss Christabel came to see me, she said she might be going up to London to the clinic. *But I'll not be airing the family linen for Dr. Dacre, Grisel,* she says to me. *Not with Evelyn engaged to his brother.* Miss Christabel put off going to a doctor for the longest time, afraid he'd find out too much as it was."

"And Miss Evelyn stated that she never consults physicians."

Watson gasped. "Holmes! You don't suppose that Evelyn Ambry is . . . is . . . well, a man?"

"I suppose so, in the strictest sense of the definition, but the salient thing here, Watson, is that Evelyn Ambry cannot bear children. Since she is engaged to the possessor of an entailed estate, that is surely a matter of concern. I fear that when Dr. James Dacre discovered the truth of the matter, he conveyed his concerns to Evelyn Ambry—probably at the funeral. They arranged to meet that night to discuss the matter."

"Why did he not tell his brother straightaway?"

"Out of some concern for the feelings of both parties, I should think," said Holmes. "Far better to allow the lady—let us call her a lady still; it is too confusing to do otherwise—to allow the lady to end it on some pretext."

Grisel Rountree nodded. "He mistook his . . . person," she said. "Miss

Evelyn was not one to give up anything without a fight. I'll warrant she took that weapon with her in case the worse came to the worst."

"Not a maiden," murmured Watson. "Well, that is true enough, I fear. But the scandal will be ruinous! Not just the murder, but the cause . . . Poor Sir Henry! What happens now?"

From the downs above the Old Hall the sound of a single shot rang out, echoing in the clear summer air.

"It has already happened," said Grisel Rountree, turning to go. "It's best if I see to the laying out myself."

"Now there's a thing," said Sherlock Holmes.

Stanley Cohen

A Girl Named Charlie

STANLEY COHEN maintains both engineering and writing careers simultaneously, and has won awards in both areas. In addition to five novels, he has contributed short stories to mystery magazines; many of his stories have been anthologized as well. He has also written extensively for professional journals. He works in a voice that has been developed slowly but successfully over several decades, his material growing in stature each time out. His specialty is putting ordinary characters into a situation where they do something that isn't quite ordinary for them—and then bearing the usually terrible consequences that happen afterward. "A Girl Named Charlie," which first appeared in *Murder in the Family,* is no different.

A Girl Named Charlie

Stanley Cohen

W ait!" Harry Waller said. "Stop! Just stop! Put your clothes back on. I've changed my mind."

"You what?"

"I've changed my mind. So just put your clothes back on. Okay?"

She stopped disrobing, and she didn't say anything, but she was clearly annoyed.

He watched her get back into her things, a bizarre collection of tacky, youthful clothing. His earlier impression of her had been dead wrong. She was no adult! He refused to believe that she could be nineteen. Or even eighteen. She might not yet be seventeen! A kid who might've been coming home from high school, in a plaid miniskirt, a blouse getting a little threadbare, and a worn, rope-knit sweater. But a beautiful kid, with virtually no makeup. Beautiful! She had to be younger than his own two daughters in college, either of whom would have envied her perfect, light auburn hair that fell straight from the crown of her head down around her shoulders.

Now that he looked at them for the first time, her shoes gave some things away. Street-worn wooden platforms with what looked like six-inch heels, the uppers attached to the blocky platforms by brassy nails, a few of the nails missing here and there. Without the shoes, she was *really* tiny. He glanced at her coat, lying across a chair, that had to keep out the bitter winds of the city's winter, and it was a ratty little thing of nondescript fake fur.

He was glad he'd stopped her before she finished removing everything. And he felt queasy as he shook his head and wondered: How in God's name had he ever allowed himself to come to be in that grubby little room with her? She was definitely not an adult! And even if she were . . . But when she'd first approached him on the street, she was a beautiful young woman with a smile that would easily capture any man's fantasies, and he rationalized that he was away from home, in another part of the country, where no one knew him, and it had been such a long time. . . .

"Listen," she said, and she wasn't smiling anymore, "even if we don't do nothing, if that's the way you want it, I still have to have my fifty. If we come up here to this room, I have to get my money."

"I'll give you your money. Don't sweat it. Okay?" Anything to just get himself out of there, and try to forget that he'd ever set foot in the place. But then, on a sudden impulse, he asked her, "Tell me something. How much of that fifty dollars do you get to keep?"

"Who wants to know?" Her facial expression had become rock-hard.

He hated seeing her face change that way. Where was that totally disarming smile he'd seen back on the street when she first approached him? That had been really something. "I do," he answered.

"What do you wanna know for?"

"I don't know. Just curious. I'm not asking for any particular reason."

"You a cop?"

He chuckled. "No," he answered as benignly as he could, "I am *not* a cop."

She studied him. "You older ones always ask the same damn questions."

It served him right. She'd probably heard more than a few reformers' diatribes from her customers. Her "johns." But afterward, most probably. After they'd allow her to ply her chosen trade. He was not about to become one of her johns. But he really did want to know. "Look. I changed my mind because . . . I really just don't feel too hot. Okay?" Then he quickly added, "Listen, I'm sure you'd've been great. Something really special. I'm real sure you'd've made my trip to New York something to remember. Okay?"

This made her smile, and once again he saw the face that had so completely captured his attention when she first approached him on Eighth Avenue, standing in the entryway to an adult books, videos, and specialties shop. "You don't know what you missed," she said with a confident smile as she finished getting back into her clothes. "I'll tell you that. And now, if you don't mind, give me my fifty dollars. I've got to get back down on the street."

"Wait!"

"What for?"

"I really want to know."

"Know what?"

"How much of that money you get to keep."

"You're a cop!"

"Oh, come on. I'm not a cop. I don't even live around here. I'm from Ohio, as a matter of fact. Just another visitor to this big city of yours. But I like knowing about things. How much of this money do you get to keep for yourself?"

"Look, I've got to get back on down there. If I don't make my quota, sometimes it gets a little rough."

He saw a trace of fear in those clear blue eyes of hers and it almost made him flinch. Did this kind of story still exist in the world? Wasn't it ancient history? He took out his money clip and peeled off three twenties. "Here's your fifty and an extra ten. Now you don't have to be in such a hurry. Okay?"

She eagerly reached for the money. "Thanks." A windfall. It brought back her smile.

"Now, I really want to know. How much of this sixty dollars do you get to keep?"

"Why do you older guys always wanna ask a bunch of crazy questions?" Then she said, "Okay, if you wanna know so bad, I'll tell ya. I don't keep any of it."

"Not even the extra ten?"

"I don't keep *any* of it."

"Who gets it?"

"I give it all to my man."

"Your pimp."

"If you don't mind, I'd rather you don't call him by that word. Okay?"

"Just one big happy family? Right?"

"Matter fact, yeah."

"What do *you* call him?"

"I call him Cecil. His name is Cecil."

"Cecil?"

"That's what I said. That's his name."

"And you're telling me you just hand over every nickel you take in? You don't get to keep anything for yourself? No percentage? Absolutely nothing?"

Defiantly she said, "That's right!"

"What's in it for you? What do you do if you need something? A drink. Something to eat. Some clothes or whatever."

"He *gives* me money. Whatever I happen to need, he takes care of."

Well, of course! He could easily tell that by looking at her lovely, stylish clothes. He shook his head. "What about the extra ten I just gave you? Are you maybe going to at least keep that for yourself?"

A trace of a smile and a devilish gleam in her eye. Like she was going to be getting away with some big-time larceny. "Yeah, I might keep that."

"Where do you live, sweetheart?"

She shrugged. "Right here, mostly. Once in a while, Cecil takes me out to his place." Her face brightened. "God, you should see his pad! Really fancy place. He's got this great view of Central Park! . . . And he took me to this really fancy restaurant once. French."

He looked around the grubby room. A bed and not much else. A small three-drawer dresser and a couple of wooden chairs. And a tiny bathroom with fixtures that belonged in a junk heap somewhere. He glanced into the bathroom and saw a filthy shower curtain and a couple of unclean-looking towels hanging from hooks. And the room was one flight up a littered stairwell above an adult books and videos shop. He looked back at her. "Why the hell are you . . . If you were at least a smart little operator, quietly building yourself a small fortune, then *maybe* . . . maybe I could understand. . . ."

"I'm doing all right," she snapped with all that defiance.

"I can almost tell." He shook his head. "Look, if this is what you want to do, it's your business, but it seems to me you should at least be getting a little something for yourself out of what you're doing here."

"Mister, if you don't mind, I'd like to go back downstairs. You came up here because you wanted to. Right? Nobody forced ya. You coulda gotten what you paid for. Right? Now, if you don't mind, let's go!"

"Hold it a minute!" he said, almost shouting. "I'm paying for your time. Right? I even gave you more than you asked for. Remember?"

She recoiled from the abrupt change in his raised voice. She was suddenly a child being scolded by her father.

"How many men a day do you, uh, bring up here?" And as he asked the question, he was thinking, for his own amusement, "up here, to this lovely super-palazzo of sensuous pleasure."

She shrugged. "I don't know. Different numbers. Six. Seven. Eight, sometimes. The best I ever did was, I think it was . . . I think it was ten. Boy, was I hustling that day! Cecil doesn't like it if I don't get at least four."

"And you give all the money to him?"

"I already told you that."

"And it's fifty every time?"

"Once or twice I got talked into going for less and Cecil wasn't too happy about it." That little shadow of fear crept back over her eyes.

"Do you ever get more than fifty?"

"Sometimes. Listen, I'm good. You don't know what you're missing."

"And you give all the money, every single bit of it, to Cecil?"

"I already told you that."

"How often does he come and check up on you?"

"Usually once a day. Sometimes twice, but not often. And then at the end of the night."

"I suppose he's got other girls working for him as well. Right?"

"That's right."

"How many, all together? Do you know?"

With a shake of her head, she said, "Matter fact, no. I really don't know."

"You girls ever get together and compare notes?"

"Oh, Cecil don't allow that."

He shook his head. "What's to stop you from keeping some of what you take in? Keeping it for yourself?"

"He *definitely* don't allow that."

"How would he know?"

"He just comes and takes it all."

"Hide some of it, then."

"I can't do that." Once again that little specter of fear moved across her face.

"Now listen to me for a minute," he said. "And listen carefully. Suppose you kept what you got from just one man each day and put it in the bank. Just one. And otherwise went right on, business as usual. Come on. It seems to me that you're certainly entitled to do that. And he'd have no way of knowing you were doing it if he only comes around once a day. Now *think* about this. At fifty dollars a day, do you realize you could put away over a thousand dollars a month?"

"But I already told you, I can't do that."

"The hell you can't! You can!"

"No, I can't!"

"Yes, you can. And I'm going to set it up for you. I'm going to open you a savings account in the closest bank around here. And every day you go and take your little passbook and deposit what you get from just one man. Just one. And give the rest to Cecil like you've been doing. Before you know it, you'll have a lot of money. Do you understand?" He studied her fragile, clear-skinned face as she looked away in deep thought. How in God's name had she gotten to where she was? . . . And how often, during a day's work, had she probably had to endure some kind of terrible abuse at the hands of some who-knows-what kind of john?

"I better not try it," she said, finally. "I don't need it. He takes care of everything."

"The passbook is small. You can keep it someplace." He looked at the cavernous shoulder bag she carried. "You could hide it somewhere down in that. What about in the lining? Or you could hide it here in the room. He won't find it. You said he only comes around once or twice a day. Why is it you don't want some money of your own?"

She looked away again. Her mind was finally dealing with the possible treasure he was setting before her. The wheels were turning. "I don't know. . . . You really think over a thousand dollars in a month? That's a lotta money."

"I'll set the whole thing up. You won't have to do a thing. I'll bring you the passbook tomorrow. I'll meet you here in front of the shop downstairs at noon tomorrow. Okay? Tomorrow, twelve noon, sharp. Incidentally, I guess I need to know your name."

She hesitated a moment. "You have to know that?"

This amused him. "How can I open the account in your name if I don't know your name?"

A trace apprehensively, she said, "It's Charlie."

"Charlie?"

"That's what I said."

"Is that short for . . . uh, what . . . Charlene or something like that?"

"It's Charlie. Just plain Charlie."

"How'd you happen to get a name like that?"

"My daddy wanted a boy." A look of severe pain darkened her face.

"Then change it! A name's a name. You can have any name you want. . . . I don't suppose your daddy's anywhere around to object. Am I right?"

"Hell, *I* don't know where he is. I don't even know if he's still alive."

"I might have guessed as much. And your mother, too, probably. Right?"

"I'm not exactly sure where she is, either. And I'm not looking for her. Not with the man she's with now."

"That's too bad." But not all that surprising. "Where do you live, Charlie?"

"Right here. I told you that."

"Oh, right. You did." He looked around the room again and shook his head. "Okay, so we'll stick with Charlie for now. Charlie what? What's your last name?"

"Sweeney."

"And I'll probably need your address. What's your address, Charlie Sweeney?"

She thought a moment and then shook her head. "I don't know what it is. I never looked. We'll have to get it off the door downstairs. If there is a number . . . Hey! Why do you want to go to all this trouble, anyway?"

It was time for *him* to think a minute. He smiled. "Don't worry about it. I really don't think you'd understand. . . . C'mon. Let's go."

As they walked out of the room, he said, "Listen. Why don't you give me back my fifty and I'll use that to open the account for you? And keep the ten, in case something comes to mind that you need for yourself."

She looked sharply at him, her expression tough once again.

He laughed and shook his head. "Forget it, forget it, I'll use another fifty to open the account for you. And don't worry about it. I can afford it."

He spotted Charlie in front of the same shop, her hands in the pockets of the ratty coat, her voluminous bag slung over her shoulder. She was walking back and forth, doing her thing, approaching one man after another with her disarming, absolutely unforgettable smile. Her long hair shone in the brilliant winter sun.

As he was about to cross the street, she spotted him. She immediately turned and reversed her direction, quickening her steps as she did.

He had to hustle to catch her, dodging the heavy traffic as he made his way across the street. "Charlie!"

When he finally caught up with her and touched her shoulder, she stopped and spun around, defiant again, her eyes blazing.

"What the hell's the matter with you?" he said. "I'm bringing you the bank passbook just as I said I would."

"I don't want it. I told you I didn't want it, and I *do not* want it."

"Don't be a fool! I want you to have it. Now listen to me. I've gone to a lot of trouble and expense for you to have this. Okay?"

"I said I don't want it!"

362 | S T A N L E Y   C O H E N

"Well, want it or not, you've got it." He took out an envelope, removed the passbook, and showed her the deposit notation. "See right here? Fifty bucks for a start. You're all set up. One deposit a day and you'll have a thousand dollars in less than a month. In fact, in a little over three weeks."

"*You* keep the book," she said.

"It's for you. Don't you understand?" He looked helplessly around. He had a plane to catch. "Here. Take it." He stuffed the envelope into her bag.

She reached into her bag, found it, took it out, and threw it down onto the sidewalk.

He quickly picked it up and grabbed her arm and stuffed the envelop back into her bag. "Charlie, listen to me! You keep this!" He looked around him, wondering if anybody was watching this bizarre little scene.

She shrugged, finally, and then turned and started walking away from him, the passbook still in her bag.

"Wait a minute. I've got to tell you a couple of things. It's the bank right down there on the corner." He pointed at it. "There are two signature cards in there with it. Sign them by the red *X* and take them to the bank. That gets the account started. Okay? Ask for Mrs. Walsh. That's *Walsh*. W-a-l-s-h. I wrote her name on a little slip of paper and it's in there, too. She'll take care of you. Okay? Charlie, you're gonna be rich!"

She studied him for a moment and, finally, the defiance slowly disappeared from her face. She smiled her smile. "Thanks."

He made a mental note to remember that smile. It was a great smile. "Good luck, Charlie."

The flight attendant handed him two little miniatures of good scotch and he poured them over ice. He took a sip and shook his head. Charlie Sweeney. A young girl named Charlie Sweeney. Sixty and then fifty more. A hundred and ten dollars! But what the hell! It'll have been well spent if it helps her. Before coming to New York on this trip, he wouldn't have considered himself capable of going anywhere near any part of the Charlie business. But that was only until he got a look at that captivating smile in the dark light of evening.

"Look out for Sin City, Harry. And all those ladies of the night. They'll see you coming and pick you like a Christmas goose! And you won't have your wife to keep you out of trouble this time."

He'd heard all of the usual, silly locker-room-style banter before leaving for New York, and found it amusing but inconsequential. Yes, he'd often taken Martha with him when possible, on trips of this kind, but, regrettably, they'd been separated for almost a year. But still, he was no candidate for any contact with the ladies of the night. He never had been and, even without Martha, wasn't about to ever start.

He'd worked in New York for a couple of years before his work took him to the Midwest, and during those early years, while still single, he'd had good relationships with a couple of rather nice women, but none of them led to marriage. But even when he wasn't involved in one of those affairs, the thought of going anywhere near one of the play-for-pay ladies, on the stroll, as they were called, had never so much as entered his mind. And on subsequent trips back, his total disinterest had been exactly the same.

His four days in New York had gone well. He'd been tied up with business contacts the first three nights. A lot of good food, and even more satisfying, good business results, and to add to the pleasure of the trip, a chance to enjoy some real theater for a change, by taking clients, something he'd missed since moving to the Midwest. So, finding himself totally un-involved and bored his last evening, he gave in to the silly urge to just take a walk and behave like a tourist and wander over to have a quick tourist's look at some of the seamy underside of the world's greatest city.

After an early dinner alone in a good restaurant near his hotel, he walked out of the hotel on Lexington, up to Park Avenue, south on Park, through the newly renovated Grand Central (he'd been told *not* to miss that), onto Forty-second Street, and west on Forty-second. When he reached the Times Square area, it wasn't the glitter in the glitter capital of the universe that impressed him (he knew it would still be there), as it was just the quantity of it, the absolute glut. No other place in the world was anything like it.

He continued walking west on Forty-second, and this block had def-initely changed for the better since his last visit. Two large, newly renovated and reopened Broadway theaters. In fact, he'd even taken his clients to one of them the previous night, where he thoroughly enjoyed actually getting to see the spectacular, tough-ticket Disney production of *The Lion King*.

He reached Eighth Avenue, looked north, and to his surprise, most of what he remembered seeing there over the years was gone. This particular strip of Sin City, for the most part, had been cleaned out. The marquees of all the porno theaters he vaguely recalled along there, hyping double and triple features in lurid titles, were dark. And since it was not yet eight o'clock, patrons of the many legitimate theaters in the area were scurrying around to make their curtains.

He decided to walk up Eighth and take a closer look. He headed up the street, did notice the bright lights of one place that called itself a sex club, and also saw a couple of shops offering adult books, videos, and other merchandise. He stopped for a moment in front of one of the more pro-vocative shops, and suddenly found himself face-to-face with a girl named Charlie Sweeney.

"Hi." Her smile had been simply beautiful.

"Hello," he'd responded, with his own smile. How could he not do so to a person with that face?

"Wanna go out?"

"Want to do what?" He understood perfectly but asked the dumb question anyway.

"Would'ja like some company? . . . You know."

. . .

He sipped his drink and gazed out the plane window at the horizon. Flying had a pacifying quality about it. Rationalizations came easier, especially with a double scotch in hand. On the first moment he saw her, he considered it virtually impossible that *her* face could exist against the backdrop of those surroundings. But since it had been almost a year, and he was miles away from home, it was easy to convince himself that he had been possessed by the moment.

The hundred and ten dollars helped ease the guilt he felt for that brief moment of lunacy. As things turned out, he didn't let it happen. And besides that, he'd done something *for* her. Something worthwhile. Maybe he'd changed her life, turned it around, helped her go from there to, hopefully, someplace better. . . . He'd be back in New York again in a couple of months. He'd have to wander back over to her territory and check up on her. See if she was still around there. See if she was getting rich.

He drained his glass. The liquor helped a lot.

Back in the Big Apple with a couple of midday hours to waste before his flight home, and consumed by curiosity, he headed straight for Eighth Avenue. He walked up and down the street looking for her, but didn't see her anywhere. He considered forgetting about the whole business, just leaving well enough alone, but his curiosity got the best of him.

He entered the sex shop uncertainly and looked around the place. The proprietor was the only person there.

Feeling like an idiot but determined to go ahead with it and check up on his one-hundred-and-ten-dollar investment, he said, "Uh, I'm looking for . . . Uh, would you happen to know the whereabouts of a young woman named Charlie Sweeney?"

The man studied him for a couple of seconds. "Just a minute." Then he walked through a door behind a wall of paperbacks. He picked up a phone and dialed a number.

The heat of extreme uneasiness crept over him as he waited for the proprietor to return. He considered just walking out and not risking any further embarrassment. But, what the hell! He was from out of town, so to speak. And he really wanted to know about Charlie. He glanced around him at all the book covers and videocassettes and other items on display. He heard the man's low voice as he talked into the phone, but couldn't make out anything the man said.

When the man reappeared, he asked the man, "Is she around here somewhere, do you know? Will she be very long? I really don't have a lot of time. I, uh, have to catch a plane."

"Just a couple minutes." The man's expression was somewhat cryptic.

He suddenly wished he hadn't come back to the shop. It wasn't all that important, all that big a deal. Curiosity. Maybe a chance to see that face and beautiful smile again. Just see how she was doing . . . After all, he'd invested money. Right? . . . He decided that he hoped she *wouldn't* be anywhere around, and he considered just dashing the hell out of there, but the proprietor's reaction to his inquiry had him intrigued. And, as he stood there, feeling like some kind of idiot, fidgeting as the minutes ticked by, he admitted to himself that, yes, he was *really* curious to see her again.

After some ten or fifteen minutes, a man in a rumpled jacket and tie entered the shop. "Are you the man looking for Charlie Sweeney?"

"Uh, not exactly, I, uh . . ."

The man drew a gold detective's shield from his jacket pocket. "I'd like to ask you to come over to precinct headquarters and fill out a statement for us."

"There must be some mistake, I, uh . . ."

"You asked about Charlie Sweeney. Right?"

He felt like an idiot. Why did he ever come back to this place?

"Look," the cop said. "It's just a routine thing. There's no charges involved. . . . Hey! Take it easy! I told you there's no charges. We won't do *anything* that would cause you any kind of embarrassment. Okay?"

"Uh, I really don't have any time for that sort of thing. I have to get to the airport to catch a plane."

"We'll give you a ride to the airport." The cop smiled. "In an unmarked car."

"I have to go back to my hotel first and pick up my stuff. I don't want to miss my flight. I really don't have enough time, if you don't mind."

"What time's your flight?"

He hesitated, and then blurted out the truth. "It's at three-ten."

"Where's your hotel?"

"On Lex."

"We've got plenty of time. We'll be glad to take you by your hotel and then give you a lift to the airport. Okay?" The cop smiled again. "And like I said, I'm in an unmarked car. Okay?"

"Then, can you at least give me some idea of what this is all about?"

"You came in here and asked for Charlie Sweeney. Right?"

Reluctantly, he admitted, "Yes."

"Well, she's dead. And we're working on the case."

He gasped. "Dead! Of what?"

"Her pimp beat her to death. But we think we've got a pretty tight case on him, and anything you can add could turn out to be a big help. And, like I said, everything'll be held in strictest confidence. We won't do *anything* to cause you any embarrassment. Okay?"

"I'd still rather not be involved in all this."

"I'm afraid we're not going to give you that option. I'm going to have to insist that you come to the station with me. But the whole thing won't take but a few minutes. And like I said, we'll be more than glad to take you by your hotel and then get you out to the airport in plenty of time for your three-ten flight."

He sat in front of a desk, the detective who'd picked him up sat in a chair next to him, and another detective behind the desk sat with his hands on the keyboard of a typewriter, asking the questions and typing in his answers.

"And you did go up to her room with her?"

"Yes, but we didn't do anything. Really. I absolutely did not touch her."

"Something made you change your mind? I assume that when you went up with her, you'd planned to"—a trace of a smile—"avail yourself of her services."

"This is very embarrassing. . . ."

"As we've assured you, we'll protect your privacy. We're just trying to get all the stuff we can get our hands on to nail this bastard. Cecil Brown is a lowlife of the first order, and we want him bad. And I think we've got him on this one. Anyway, go on. What happened when you went to her room?"

"Nothing. I suddenly realized how young she was, and felt like a complete idiot, and that was that. I felt really terrible about the whole thing. I still can't believe I'd gone up there with her."

"You give her any money?"

"Oh, she insisted. Whether we *did* anything or not."

"Even though you didn't do anything?"

"That's what she said. And she was, how shall I say it, pretty emphatic about that."

"How much did you give her?"

"She said I had to give her fifty. Which, incidentally, she told me was all going to Cecil, as she referred to him. Well, what I had handy was a bunch of twenties, and I was feeling sorry for her, so I gave her three twenties. Sixty dollars. I figured maybe she'd at least keep the ten."

"And then you both just returned to the street? That's it?"

"That's it. . . . Tell me something. Why'd he kill her? She gave me the impression she was making a lot of money and giving every penny to him."

"Well, it was apparently because she was holding out some of her take. And the Cecil types don't go along with that. But we think we've got a pretty tight case on him. She'd been squirreling some money away in a bank over in the neighborhood she worked, and when we brought the son of a bitch in, we found her passbook in his briefcase." A snicker. "Can you imagine an animal like him with a briefcase? Alligator leather, no less."

He felt a little sick. "Just out of curiosity, do you think I might see the passbook?"

The cop thought a minute. "Sure. I don't see any reason why not." He went to a file cabinet and returned with a large envelope. He reached into it and fished around until he found the little book. "This is it. One thing I can't fathom is why he kept it. But those guys aren't too smart, fortunately."

Harry recognized the soiled and bent but familiar little passbook the cop handed him, and opened it. . . . The book still contained only one entry, a deposit of fifty dollars.

Jon L. Breen

The Adventure of the Mooning Sentry

JON L. BREEN, who supplies our erudite and thorough year's end wrapup of the mystery field, has been a reference librarian and former sportscaster, but is much better known as the author of several first-rate novels and even more first-rate short stories. He has also been acclaimed for his skills as an editor and scholar. He is the winner of two Edgar awards for nonfiction books about the mystery field. His novels reflect his love of horseracing, baseball, and the world of books. Now that he has retired at a youthful age, his many readers are looking forward to new Breen novels and stories, and we're happy to supply them with one here. "The Adventure of the Mooning Sentry," another story featuring the inimitable Sherlock Holmes, first appeared in *Murder, My Dear Watson,* and combines two of Jon's passions—mystery and movies.

The Adventure of the Mooning Sentry

Jon L. Breen

Despite the implied finality of "His Last Bow," and the elegiac note that concluded that tale, few of my readers have been willing to believe that Sherlock Holmes, with his mental powers and patriotic enthusiasm at their peak, would retreat into permanent retirement at his country's darkest hour. When that east wind blew across England, he did not wither before its blast. Indeed, he undertook several more investigations in his country's service before the world war had finished energizing, glorifying, decimating, and mutilating a generation of young men.

Early in the autumn of 1917, I received a surprising invitation to a weekend house party at the country holding of Sir Eldridge Masters, a wealthy baronet best known as an amateur historian—or, less politely, a dilettante. The gathering was to be in honor of a visiting American cinematograph director, and would include a special showing of one of the fellow's films. It all sounded very jolly, to be sure. However, not feeling particularly festive in those dark days, and finding weekend house parties a somewhat frivolous activity with the country at war, I was about to decline. But a second message in the next day's post changed my mind: "My dear Watson, / Do please join me in accepting Sir Eldridge's hospitality. Come alone, bring your sidearm, and withhold recognition of an old friend. Your country needs you, and so do I. / Holmes." Loyalty to friend and to king made a negative response unthinkable.

Everything about the Masters estate, from the long winding carriageway lined with lime trees to the venerable oaks framing the great ivy-covered house itself, bespoke wealth and tradition. When I arrived by pony cart from the station that evening in early October, the other guests had already assembled. From my room, I was shown to what the butler characterized as the "small ballroom," a chamber quite large enough for most purposes in which a score of men in white ties and women in stunning gowns posed in the light of a crystal chandelier with a grand staircase behind them. Spirits flowed freely, with only the lack of young male servants to suggest the country was at war. I was immediately greeted and taken aside by my host, an erect man of around sixty with an impressive gray moustache and a hesitant manner of speech that contrasted with his military bearing.

"Dr. Watson, isn't it? So good of you to come, so, ah, very good of you." With a hand on my sleeve, he lowered his voice conspiratorially. "Now, ah, when we come upon our mutual friend, you know, ah, that is, you have been apprised . . ."

"Certainly, Sir Eldridge. I understand fully." In truth, I understood nothing, except that our host was aware of Holmes's mission, whatever it was, and that I was to take the cue for my behavior from Holmes.

A young woman of about thirty approached us from across the ballroom. She was ethereally lovely, but the grandness of her gown only served to accentuate her frailty and fragility. She had the air of someone doggedly performing an unavoidable duty. A spinster daughter of the house, I concluded, but my surmise proved incorrect.

"My dear," Sir Eldridge said, "may I present Dr. Watson. Doctor, my wife, Lady Miranda Masters."

"Welcome, Dr. Watson," she said, her voice little more than a whisper. Sir Eldridge watched her with a keen eye and obvious concern as we exchanged the traditional comments of hostess and guest. Her words were perfect, but her manner nervous and distracted. Even as we spoke her eyes, looking troubled, even haunted, darted about as if searching corners of the room for someone or something. Looking at her lovely face, I was certain I had seen her before.

Courtesy forbids questioning a man about his wife's past, but as Lady Miranda moved on to mingle with other guests, Sir Eldridge seemed to read my mind. "My wife was on the, ah, stage before our marriage, Dr. Watson. She enjoyed, ah, quite a popular following before consenting to, shall we say, cast her lot with me. She was known then as Miranda Delacorte."

I did not comment on my difficulty in believing this wispy wraith could command a stage, but again my expression apparently made the comment for me.

"My wife has, ah, not been well, I fear. Her health is a matter of grave concern to me. Grave concern, indeed."

I feared I was on the brink of being consulted in my professional capacity, but the subject was closed by the weaving approach of a portly man who had clearly been imbibing copiously of his host's generosity.

"Sir Eldridge, my congratulations on your book. A superb overview of the Etruscans in all their merry malefaction and malfeasance, eh?"

"Ah, thank you, Mr. Barrows. I, of course, value your opinion most highly indeed. Do you, ah, know Dr. Watson? This is Mr. Conrad Barrows, someone rather in your line."

"Oh? Medical man?" I ventured.

"More your, ah, literary line. Mr. Barrows is a book critic, who was, ah, most kind to my rather amateurish tome on the Etruscans. A hobbyist's scribbling, I fear."

"You are much too modest, Sir Eldridge," Barrows protested. "You made those mad Italians come to life more vividly than a battalion of professors!" He turned to me. "And what sort of writing do you do, Dr. Watson?"

Our host looked rather embarrassed. "Surely you're aware of Dr. Watson's accounts of his cases with Mr. Sherlock Holmes."

"Oh, *that* Dr. Watson. But you see, I never review fiction."

I suspected the fellow was being deliberately offensive, but I did not rise to the bait, merely muttering something polite. In truth, I'd been accused before of writing fiction—by Holmes himself, in fact!

"Well, now, Sir Eldridge," Barrows went on, "when will we be so honored that we may give honor to our guest of honor, eh?"

"Mr. Griffith has been, ah, resting in his room. His schedule has been, ah, rather taxing of his energies, I fear. You see, he, ah, only recently returned from filming at the front in France. But, ah, he will be down to introduce the showing of his film for us, and after that he will be pleased to, ah, mingle with all the guests."

Barrows looked around the room with comic exaggeration. "Well, the poor fellow. You know what he wants, Sir Eldridge. Money. Investors for his next project, whatever it is. My understanding is that his latest production, *Intolerance,* has done disappointing business in the States."

"Really? But, ah, I believe it has attracted large audiences here—"

"Certainly. Where it had the good fortune of opening at the Drury Lane on the very next day after President Wilson announced America's entry into the War. But now the chap once again needs money. And when he descends from his cloister, makes his dramatic entrance, what will he find? A room full of actors and society ladies who long to pose for the cinematographs, eh?"

Sir Eldridge seemed flustered. "Well, ah, really, I hardly think—"

A tall, saturnine figure with a commanding presence, which was only intensified by the stunningly beautiful woman on his arm, came to our host's rescue. "You malign Sir Eldridge, Mr. Barrows," the newcomer intoned, in a rich theatrical voice. "I do believe that I, apart from our distinguished hostess who has retired from the stage, am the only professional thespian in the room. My companion, Lady Veronica Travers, surely has the beauty to shine on the cinema screen but has to my knowledge no such ambitions."

The humorous sidelong glance the magnificent Lady Veronica gave her companion suggested ambitions beyond his knowledge.

"And these guests," the actor went on, his rolling delivery now commanding the attention of the entire room, "are here neither to flaunt their wealth nor to seek immortality on film but rather to appreciate the greatest artistic advance of our young century. For *The Birth of a Nation* has revolutionized the cinema, raising a commercial novelty to the stature of an art that may stand beside painting, sculpture, and drama in the pantheon of human aesthetic endeavor. And any viewing of great art is enhanced by the presence of the artist. Thus, I long to sit at the feet of Mr. David Wark Griffith, not for any employment he might afford this poor and aging player but for the enlightenment that can come from any association, however brief, with a genius." He paused for a moment, possibly allowing an opportunity for applause. "But I must apologize for my rudeness in interrupting your conversation, gentlemen."

"Not at all, Hope, ah, not at all," Sir Eldridge said. After formally presenting us to Lady Veronica, he introduced the actor as Sherrington Hope, but I knew him by another name. On some past occasions, my friend had so transformed himself with wigs and false whiskers as to fool even me. This time, however, the disguise was more one of speech and manner. I had known from first glance that this preening, posing ham was none other than Sherlock Holmes.

Another guest joined our circle then, a tall and well-built American, with a sensitive, long-jawed face, but loud and brash as his countrymen so often are. Sir Eldridge introduced him merely as Ernest Wheeler.

"Say, Dr. Watson, this is a pleasure. We're in this thing with you now, and about time, too. We'll take care of the kaiser for you."

"Yanks come to crown or kill the kaiser," Barrows slurred, having armed himself with another glass from a servant's passing tray. "Jolly big of you, big of you indeed. We're probably in for some dreadful American films about the war now, eh?"

"Isn't that exactly why Mr. Griffith has come to our shores?" Lady Veronica, speaking for the first time, revealed a melodious voice that complemented her visual beauty. "I understand he's been asked by the government to make a film to aid the war effort."

"It won't be dreadful, though, I can assure you of that," Holmes said.

"As I heard it," Barrows said, "the whole idea was to convince the Yanks to come in with us." Addressing the American, he added, "And now that you lot are in with all your colonial superiority, the war won't last past Tuesday, so who needs the film?"

"Well, I guess morale is still important," Wheeler replied, choosing as I had to ignore the critic's offensiveness.

"Some of us," Lady Veronica went on pointedly, "appreciate your country's entry on the side of righteousness, Mr. Wheeler, even if our friend Mr. Barrows takes it as an opportunity for derision."

Barrows seemed instantly abashed, saying with inebriated dignity, "I do apologize to one and all for my flippantly habitual manner, that is to say, my habitually—well, you take my meaning, I'm sure. We should all be grateful, as Lady Veronica so rightly asserts, to our colonial allies. I abase myself, Mr. Wheeler."

"No apology necessary," the American replied briskly.

"But, Mr. Wheeler, we don't see many American travelers these days," the critic went on. "Are you by chance of Mr. Griffith's battlefield-touring troupe of cinematographic artistes?"

"Oh, no, no, indeed. Rarely even attend the flickers, to tell you the truth. I owe my presence here to an interest in common with Sir Eldridge, whose hospitality I have been enjoying for nearly a week. I'm a professor of Etruscan literature, you see, at the University of California."

"A rare speciality, sir," Holmes remarked.

"A criminally undervalued body of literature, Mr. Hope. I have done my best to give it the serious study it deserves."

"Well, then, you and Sir Eldridge will have a lot to talk about, won't you?" I said, doing my bit to soothe the uneasy atmosphere. I was relieved when Wheeler drifted away. He seemed a pleasant enough fellow, but Americans can be wearing at times.

A group of unobtrusive servants—mostly women even for this technically demanding job—had begun to prepare an area of the "small ballroom" for the film viewing, hanging a screen on one wall, carrying in a projector, arranging the seating. The chairs looked to be antiques, and it struck me as ironic we would be sitting on such venerable objects while enjoying such modern entertainment. A half dozen musicians, apparently employed to accompany the film, were unveiling their instruments and setting up their stands.

It was at this point that the guest of honor, the celebrated D. W. Griffith, made his entrance down the staircase at the other end of the room. He was a tall and commanding figure, his most prominent features a hawkish nose and a receding hairline. My impulse, in common with the other guests, was to draw toward the guest of honor, but Holmes took the opportunity to pull me aside for a quiet word.

"I must be quick, old fellow. We are here at the behest of my brother Mycroft. Put simply, Griffith is to make a film to help the war effort, and a German spy is believed to be among our fellow guests, possibly with the intent of assassinating Griffith. We must not let that happen." He laughed loudly, as if I had made some great joke, then added, "Lady Miranda has reported seeing a sinister stranger, both in the garden and in the house, oddly dressed and able to vanish as suddenly as he appears. No one else has seen this person, however, and Sir Eldridge fears she may be unbalanced, losing her reason."

"And is she?"

"It's too soon to say. We must be alert to anything," To this point, Holmes had spoken quietly and almost without moving his lips. Now he raised his voice for the benefit of those guests nearest us. "Come, Doctor. Let us hear what the great man has to say."

But in fact, as we approached the circle around Griffith, another guest was doing most of the talking. It was the American, Ernest Wheeler, who apparently had chosen to provide an excessively complete answer to a polite question about his academic specialty.

"You know, Mr. Griffith, the Etruscans were a happy, fun-loving people, much more so than the Romans who eventually overran them. Though they were a religious people, they had liberal attitudes to merrymaking and, shall we say, romance."

"My sort of people," the director murmured humorously.

"Yes, indeed your sort. I often think it would be enjoyable to be an Etruscan. But then I remember that not all Etruscans had a life of pleasure, that many of their celebrations included the beating of their slaves. Slavery is an ugly stain on human history. I am embarrassed that our country was so slow to rid itself of that deplorable institution."

"But so we did, sir, and painfully."

"Some of our countrymen who have seen *The Birth of a Nation* believe you regret the abolition of slavery."

Griffith drew himself up, but his tone remained civil. "That is a gross and I think deliberate misunderstanding of my film. I am a Southerner, through and through, but I am no champion of slavery. The themes of my film were the effects of war on the individual and the human hunger for power and exploitation, not a brief for the subjugation of one race by another."

The tension in the air was palpable, and Sir Eldridge looked speechless with embarrassment at seeing one American guest insulting another. Though controlling his emotions, the courtly Griffith appeared old-fashioned enough to demand satisfaction at dawn. Once again, it was Lady Veronica who came forward to calm the waters.

"Surely, Mr. Wheeler, we needn't refight the American Civil War here in Sir Eldridge's ballroom, when shortly we can watch it unfold most vividly and brilliantly on the screen."

As Griffith smiled her way, I imagined a degree of lust mingled with the gratitude in his regard. If Lady Veronica does long to pose for cinematographs, I reflected, she might get her chance.

"You are very kind, m'lady," Griffith said. "But I must offer one small correction. In my part of the world, we prefer to call it the War Between the States."

"I understand some of your actors and technicians accompanied you to our shores, Mr. Griffith," Lady Veronica went on. "Will none of them be joining us this weekend?"

Griffith smiled. "I fear I have been keeping them much too busy for that, m'lady, but they have found their stay as memorable as I. Miss Lillian Gish, a most brave lady, accompanied me to the front. We were, I hasten to assure you, well chaperoned by others of my company. And Miss Dorothy Gish made her contribution to the war effort during her crossing by coaching General Pershing for his newsreel appearances—but perhaps I am telling secrets."

"Ah, ladies and gentleman," said our host, finding his voice at last, "if you will kindly take your seats, Mr. Griffith has agreed to say a few words to us before we view his wonderful and, ah, might I say, historic film."

As the guests moved to the other end of the room, Holmes attached himself to Griffith, very convincingly suggesting an actor seeking a role. But the director, understandably, appeared more intrigued by Lady Veronica on his other arm.

I took a seat in the back row, where I could observe the entire gathering. To my surprise, the American professor sat down next to me, looking rather more pleased with himself than embarrassed at the tension he had caused.

"Don't think I'm too popular at the moment, Dr. Watson," he said. "The way some of these folks were looking at me, I could figure in one of your stories before the night is out. 'The Adventure of the Murdered Professor,' eh? But where I come from, that war isn't really over yet, and I don't know if it ever will be. Have you seen this film before?"

"Can't say that I have. Don't get out to the cinema much. Busy practice, you know."

"Certainly. Mr. Griffith's presentation of American history purports to be scholarly—he even provides occasional pretentious footnotes. But his memory is selective, owing to his background, I guess. When they stop to change reels, I'll try to give you a more truthful view of the facts."

"That will be splendid," I replied, with an utter lack of sincerity.

When we all were seated, D. W. Griffith, standing in front of the white screen, assured us how welcome he had been made in England, how enthusiastically he and President Wilson supported our great cause, and how he chose to let his film speak for itself. Then he proceeded to orate at such length, I began to doubt we'd see the film at all. He praised Lord Beaverbrook, the head of the government's cinematograph office who had invited him to Britain, and Minister of Munitions Winston Churchill, who had suggested to him many promising ideas for scenarios. He spoke of being under fire during his time at the front in France. He movingly described the impact of observing the war firsthand on this side of the channel. He and his company were staying at the Savoy, and from their rooms they could watch the German airplanes flying up the Thames to their targets. He remarked on his British ancestry, his Kentucky boyhood, his father's heroism in the War Between the States, his family poverty, his early films for a company called Biograph, and finally some details on the making of the film that would soon speak for itself. He made no reference to the controversy that apparently had attended its release in the States, but my American companion whispered in my ear accounts of the negative reaction of Negroes to their depiction (sometimes inflammatory, other times merely patronizing) by white actors in the film, and of the story's origin in a vicious novel championing white supremacy, Thomas Dixon's *The Clansman*.

At last, the lights were dimmed and the film itself began. All thought of political issues and questions of historical accuracy were banished. *The Birth of a Nation* proved as extraordinary as had been promised. The period leading to the war was depicted in historical tableaux. A prosperous Southern family, the Camerons, and their Northern visitors, the Stonemans, were introduced. The ties of friendship and romance forged among the younger generation would soon be tested. The acting in these scenes, particularly by the young women of the two families, was remarkably subtle and natural, free of exaggerated gestures and excessive emotions.

The attention of the audience was rapt throughout these early scenes. Then, about one hour into the film, came one of its few humorous moments. In a Northern hospital, the magnificent Lillian Gish, in the role of Elsie Stoneman, the daughter of Northern abolitionist Austin Stoneman, has been working as a nurse, serenading on the banjo the Southern hero, Benjamin Cameron, played by Henry B. Walthall. At one point, Miss Stoneman passes a Union sentry, leaning on his rifle, who sighs and looks longingly at this beautiful woman. It was a memorable human moment, but its effect was broken by a loud scream.

Someone turned on the electric lights, and all the assembled guests turned to see Lady Miranda, on her feet with her fists to her cheeks, sobbing uncontrollably, a terror-stricken look in her eyes. Sir Eldridge reached out to support her. The projector stopped.

"My dear, ah, my dear," was all the baronet could say.

"It's him! It's him! He's the one! He's the one, I tell you."

"Come, my dear," Sir Eldridge said, and with the help of Holmes and Lady Veronica, he guided her out of the room. As the only medical man present, I followed to give what aid I could.

"My wife is, ah, somewhat upset," Sir Eldridge said. "Can you, ah, give her something to help her rest?"

Before I could suggest a sedative, Holmes gently asked the stricken woman, "Whom did you see, Lady Miranda?"

"He's a murderer, I know it. The man on the screen. The man who looks at her in that terrible way."

"He's an actor," Lady Veronica said reasonably. "He's admiring her beauty and daydreaming. It's only a play."

Lady Miranda tried to take this in, her features troubled. "An actor? But I never played with him. Have you, Mr. Hope?"

Holmes shook his head. "But he's an American actor, Lady Miranda. One of Mr. Griffith's company. Where had you seen him before?"

"In the garden. Three nights ago. He appeared out of the shadows, looking at me, just as in the film. And then he was gone, as suddenly as he had come." She turned to Sir Eldridge, imploring him. "I told you to look for him, dear."

"I did look, my dear," said Sir Eldridge sadly and gently. "I looked, and all the servants looked. We looked everywhere. There was no one."

"Then last night. I saw him again. In my bedroom. He was there, and then he wasn't. He might have murdered me. He might have murdered us all. I told you I saw him, dear. I told you. But you said there was no one."

"And there was no one, my dear."

"But there was. You thought I imagined him. I knew I had seen him, but I came to believe he was a ghost, one only I could see. Yet there he was on the screen tonight, so that proves he exists, doesn't it? If I imagined him or if he was a ghost, he couldn't appear in Mr. Griffith's film, could he? He's here to do some evil, I know it, I can feel it."

Sir Eldridge shook his head sadly. With a nod from Holmes, I carried out my professional duty and administered a sedative. Lady Miranda was delivered to the charge of her lady's maid, and the rest of us returned to the small ballroom, where D. W. Griffith was again speaking to the other guests, noting that while his film had been controversial, audiences had usually found that particular scene more amusing than disturbing. When he saw the four of us return, he fell silent and looked inquiringly at our host. Sir Eldridge, with a halting reference to his wife's delicate health, insisted the screening continue.

As the film went on, even the genius of Griffith and the amazingly natural performances of his actors could not keep at bay the many thoughts that passed through my mind. Among them was the question of whether Holmes's masquerade was in danger of exposure. Some of the guests had looked at him suspiciously, and I could imagine what they might be thinking. It was natural that Sir Eldridge, her husband, or Lady Veronica, another woman, or I, a doctor, should have attended to the stricken lady. But why this flamboyant actor?

When the screening had finished and the assembled guests retired, Holmes and I visited the great cinematograph director in his bedroom. Immediately, Holmes dropped the Sherrington Hope masquerade and revealed to Griffith his true identity.

"It is an honor, sir, to meet someone so preeminent in his chosen profession," the director declaimed.

"No more so than you are in yours," Holmes replied handsomely, but somewhat impatiently, eager to move past the customary civilities. "Mr. Griffith, what was the name of the actor who played the mooning sentry that so frightened Lady Miranda?"

"Many have asked me, but I have to confess I don't know," Griffith replied. "He was a day player, an extra. We employed hundreds of them on that picture. Quite often, I would pick one out of the crowd and give him a bit of business to do. That particular idea proved a great success, but of course, we didn't know that at the time. At the end of the day, the fellow presumably picked up his wages and we never saw him again. Miss Gish might recall his name, I suppose, but I cannot."

"So," I ventured, "this fellow was not among the actors who came with you here or went with you to France?"

"Certainly not. I only brought a few of my most important players."

"Might he have sailed here on his own?"

"I should think that very unlikely, Watson," Holmes said, before Griffith could answer.

"Quite so," I said. "You are probably quite right to believe that Lady Miranda was imagining things. She is certainly in a perilous state of mental health and could be subject to hallucinations."

"No. In fact, I believe the mooning sentry that appeared to her was quite real and of sinister origin. But it need not have been the same man who portrayed the sentry in the film. All it would take was the blue cap and jacket, belt and sword of a Union Army sentry, plus a long face, a mustache, a tilt of the head, and a comical expression of longing. In her emotional state, Lady Miranda would be unlikely to notice subtle differences in the face of the person on the screen."

"But why?" I demanded.

"Mr. Griffith, did any of the costumes from your film accompany you to England?"

"No," the director answered. "Why would they, unless it were for a museum exhibit of some sort?"

"Still, the sentry uniform would be easy enough to copy," Holmes mused.

"But why?" I asked again.

Ignoring me, Holmes told the director, "We shall be outside your door throughout the night, Mr. Griffith. We are armed and prepared for any eventuality. If anything unusual occurs, call on us."

"Yes, certainly," the puzzled American said.

And so we remained. After two hours, at about the point I had decided our efforts were unnecessary, we heard sounds of a struggle in Griffith's room. I drew my pistol as we burst through the door. Outlined in the moonlight from the window, we saw a figure in a Union sentry uniform, arms outstretched, hands encircling the throat of D. W. Griffith, who gripped his assailant's wrists in desperate defense.

"Raise your hands!" Holmes shouted.

The attacker emitted a mad growl and continued his assault. I fired, striking the attacker in the shoulder. With a howl of pain, he released Griffith's throat and surged toward the open window by which he had undoubtedly entered the room. For only an instant I saw his maddened, ravaged face, just long enough to recognize the American professor, Ernest Wheeler. As he climbed through the window, his wounded arm betrayed him; he lost his grip and fell with an anguished cry.

"Quick, Watson!" Holmes cried. "He must not escape." Holmes could still move quickly when the occasion demanded it. I followed my friend's reckless descent of the stairs, barely conscious of doors opening, lights going on, and querulous voices.

When I bent over the body of the man who had called himself Ernest Wheeler, lying where he fell under Griffith's second story window, I quickly saw there was nothing I could do for him. The broken ivy clutched in his hand told the tale. He had been fatally injured, his neck broken in his fall.

We heard Sir Eldridge's voice imploring his guests not to leave the house. Then the baronet, in his dressing gown, rushed to join us under the window.

"What has happened? My God, what has happened?" he demanded, looking down at the body. I quickly recounted the attack and its dramatic conclusion.

"He must have climbed from his window to enter Griffith's," the baronet said, looking upward. "They aren't far apart, and there are, ah, sufficient hand- and footholds to give purchase. Still, it would have required considerable, ah, agility and indifference to danger."

"And a touch of madness, if you ask me," I said.

Sir Eldridge shook his head disbelievingly. "So that's the end of it. And he can never tell his tale. But, ah, I would say it's better this way."

"I daresay you would," Holmes replied.

"Well, that is to say, your brother's information was that a German spy was among my guests, and, ah, there he is, isn't he?"

"There he is indeed. In his Union sentry's uniform from the American Civil War. Not standard issue for German spies, I shouldn't think."

"I believe he was a bit of a lunatic," I offered. "He certainly appeared to have a genuine hostility toward Griffith, even when they were introduced in the ballroom. Perhaps that was why he was given the job, eh?"

"But that leaves unexplained the ghostly appearances by which Wheeler terrorized your wife, Sir Eldridge."

"Oh, yes, I see," the baronet nodded. "Now at last I see. She really did see someone in the garden and in her room, and I was convinced it was, ah, part of her illness. I never suspected Wheeler."

"I suspected him at once," Holmes said. "Why do you suppose it became part of this assassin's mission to drive your wife mad?"

Sir Eldridge shook his head sadly. "I cannot think. She has, ah, suffered so much, my poor dear, and I have done her an injustice. Perhaps now things will become brighter for her."

"So they may if she gets away from here as quickly as possible," Holmes said sharply.

"Sir, ah, what are you suggesting?"

"Why is it, Sir Eldridge, you haven't even inquired how I came to suspect Ernest Wheeler, how I knew he was an impostor? I am accustomed to imprecations to explain my deductions. My vanity is wounded by your indifference."

The baronet essayed an unconvincing laugh. "Ah, Mr. Holmes, I do apologize for my failure. Tell us now, if you please."

"Wheeler claimed to be a professor of Etruscan literature. You know as well as I, Sir Eldridge, that there is no Etruscan literature to profess. Unlike the writings of the Greeks and Romans, whatever literature your Etruscans produced failed to survive their civilization. The average uninformed person might take Wheeler's claim at face value. But he could never have fooled an Etruscan expert like you with that absurd story. Could he?"

"And so I told the fool when he had already adopted it," Sir Eldridge said softly. "Go on, then. What else do you have to say?"

"The rest is surmise, but with a foundation of logic. The assassin stayed under your roof. You knew he was an impostor, so you must have been in league with him. You, sir, are the German agent my brother warned me about. Either your wife had begun to suspect your activities, or information she had been exposed to made you believe she might come to know the truth. You feared she might use this weekend event to expose you. You had for some time isolated her and essayed to ruin her health, physical and mental. The physical part of it, through what poisons I do not know, but the mental part consisted in ghostly appearances by Wheeler during the past week in his disguise as the mooning sentry. You hoped, as proved the case, that your wife would react hysterically to the sight of the mooning sentry on the screen, that whatever babbling she might do to me or to any other guest would be ignored in view of her obvious madness. Can you deny this, sir?"

Sir Eldridge's vague manner had disappeared. When he dropped the mask, his cultured accent was the same, but his clipped tones sounded subtly Germanic. I gripped my revolver warily.

"You were right, Dr. Watson. Wheeler was quite mad. He is actually an American as he claimed, an assassin for hire to the highest bidder. He had an ancestor who performed such services for the Union Army, and he had an unbalanced hatred of the American South and, for whatever reason, of D. W. Griffith. When he appeared here with that ridiculous Union Army uniform and his litany of grievances against Griffith and the Confederacy, I could have cursed my superiors for their administrative failures, but instead I chose to use what they had provided me in as creative a manner as I could." The baronet's body tensed subtly, and a look in his eye suggested he was poised for action, but he went on speaking in the same even, clipped tones. "If you had not been here, Holmes, I might have succeeded. How many of my guests had any idea if the Etruscans had a literature or not?"

With that he sprang at Holmes, a dagger clutched in his hand. Before my friend could test his joints with a defensive move, my pistol spoke for me. The wound to Sir Eldridge Masters was enough to stop him, but he would live to stand trial for treason.

The next day, as Holmes and I shared a pony cart to the railway station, I remarked, "I ought to have known that Wheeler chap was up to no good when he suggested that dreadful title, 'The Adventure of the Murdered Professor.' Deplorable taste. I wouldn't dream of putting a tale before the public with an unpleasant word like murder or death in the title. My literary agent would never approve."

"I do recall you made one exception to that rule, Watson, or nearly. Wasn't there a story called 'The Dying Detective'?"

"Yes, yes, so there was. But you'll never die, Holmes."

"You'll never let me, my dear fellow."

John Lutz

Second Story Sunlight

The epitome of the professional mystery writer, JOHN LUTZ has written more than thirty novels, after beginning his writing career with short stories. Fred Carver, a former policeman who solves a series of dark crimes in the Florida Keys, is the protagonist in several of his books. Lutz's novels are noted for tight plotting and well-rounded and believable characters. He has been awarded an Edgar, two Shamus awards, and the Shamus Award for lifetime achievement. His most recent novel, *The Night Watcher,* was hailed as "an instant classic of ominous urban crime" by *Mystery Scene* magazine. His other series character, hapless detective Alo Nudger, he of the tissue-paper constitution and eternally upset stomach, appears in "Second Story Sunlight," which was first published in *Most Wanted,* a collection of stories by past presidents of the Private Eye Writers of America, a position Lutz has also held.

Second Story Sunlight

John Lutz

Nudger didn't so much mind that he always found himself in the longest line, but he wondered why there was never anyone behind him. That was how it was now, while he waited to deposit the check he'd received for recovering a lost deer. The animal had been one of many removed from a wooded area in one of St. Louis's wealthier suburbs. The residents there resisted any effort to trap or shoot the animals, though they were problematic and a traffic hazard. So with the best of intentions and at great expense, they'd had scores of the deer tranquilized and transferred to various wilderness areas, where most of them died from the shock of relocation or were killed by hunters.

A problem arose when one of the community's leading families had looked on one of the transported deer as a family pet. They had fed it, named it Beamer, set out a salt lick, and the animal had begun hanging around and the children had become fond of it. The family missed the deer and had hired Nudger to get it back. Armed with a photograph of Beamer wearing a frivolous hat at an outdoor birthday party, Nudger had flown to Fargo, North Dakota, paid most of his promised fee to a scout and trapper, and had actually located the animal and had it transported back to St. Louis County, where it was struck by a car.

Now here was Nudger standing in line before a teller's cage in Maplewood Bank. He had to get the Beamer check deposited so it would clear and he could mail his alimony check to his horrendous former wife, Eileen. She and her lover-lawyer, Henry Mercato, were threatening to take Nudger to court again in an attempt to raise his monthly payments. How they could do this, since Eileen, at the apex of one of those barely legal home-product pyramid schemes, earned more money than he did, was beyond Nudger. But then, he was always last in line with no one behind him. He loathed the idea of going back into court to do battle with Eileen and Mercato. He was afraid of the whole business and wanted nothing to do with it.

Eileen had left another message on his answering machine referring to him as "the turnip that would bleed." She and Mercato were a bad influence on each other. Matchmakers say there is someone for everyone, but it was amazing that those two had found each other.

Ah! Nudger was finally at the teller's window. As the man ahead of him moved to the side and left, the woman behind the marble counter moved the hands of a small mock clock to read 2:00. Beside the artificial clock was a sign declaring that deposits after that time wouldn't be posted until the next day's date. Nudger glanced at his wristwatch. Two o'clock.

"But I've been standing in line twenty minutes," he told the woman.

"I'm sorry, sir," she said with a sad shake of her head. "I can't make an exception. It's all done by computer now, you know."

Nudger knew. He made his deposit anyway. Eileen's check would be a day late and there would probably be another turnip message on his machine. There sure wasn't going to be much left of his Beamer fee, he thought, gazing at the deposit slip as he walked from the bank. Money wasn't going very far these days, especially since the area where his office was located was becoming gentrified.

Nudger still didn't know quite what to make of this gentrification, but it was undeniable and as insidious as floodwater. First it had been a trendy Creole restaurant opening down the street, then several antique shops had appeared. So it continued, along with an article in the newspaper about how Maplewood real estate was appreciating so rapidly. Then along came a coffee shop, a café, a music shop, a health food store. The B&L Diner, where Nudger sometimes used to have lunch or breakfast, he noticed was now called Tiffany's. Probably the food had improved, like a lot of other things in the area, but Nudger missed his old down-at-the-heels neighborhood.

His office hadn't moved or improved, its old window air conditioner protruding from a second-floor window over Danny's Donuts. And at least Danny's was still there. Though Danny had made a concession to the march of progress by featuring a "donut du jour" every week.

As Nudger entered the aromatic donut shop, he saw that this week's spotlighted confection was the same as last week's, something called the Plowman's Feast that had cheese and vegetable bits imbedded in the dough. Nudger had been appalled when he'd first seen one of the things, but Danny had assured him that the "artsy types" who'd moved into the neighborhood saw them as brunch food and were buying them as fast as they could be deep-fried. Nudger wasn't sure Danny was being completely honest, as there seemed to be the usual dearth of customers whenever he was in the shop.

"Hey, Nudge!" said the basset-hound-featured Danny, as he stood behind the counter wiping his hands on the gray towel always tucked in his belt. "You had lunch?"

"Just awhile ago," Nudger said quickly. The thought of Danny's dark and turgid coffee, along with what he invariably offered Nudger, the always featured and unpopular Dunker Delite, made Nudger's delicate stomach kick and turn. Nudger swallowed and got up on a stool at the counter. "I'll take a glass of ice water, though."

Danny shoveled some crushed ice in a glass, then ran tap water. He set the glass on a square white paper napkin in front of Nudger. "You notice my mural, Nudge?" He motioned toward a side wall. "An artist fella just moved in a few blocks from here painted it for me in exchange for a gross of Plowman's Feasts last week."

Nudger hadn't noticed any mural. He turned on his stool to look. A mural, all right, covering most of the east wall, an undersea scene of whales swimming among smaller fish above exotic sea growth on the ocean floor. It wasn't half bad. "Beautiful," Nudger said. "And environmentally correct."

Danny was grinning. "You notice something?"

Nudger looked again. "Whales, mostly."

"You look close and you can see the other fish are just fish, but the whales ain't just whales. They're shaped like Dunker Delites."

"Um," Nudger said, turning away and sipping some water while his mind absorbed this. "Painter's a talented guy."

"Sure is. And generous, considering all the other work he's doing."

"He's got a job other than painting?" No surprise there.

"None as I know of, but he and his new bride are fixing up a house on Emler Avenue, one of them old Victrolians. That's what the Plowman's Feasts were for, their wedding. I went to it. They got married over in the park wearing clothes made completely out of leaves and stuff. Everything natural."

"Romantic," Nudger said, thinking maybe it was.

The door opened and Nudger and Danny were surprised to see the bulk of St. Louis Police Lieutenant Jack Hammersmith enter the donut shop. It was almost ninety degrees outside, but Hammersmith, as usual, appeared cool as a scoop of vanilla mint. He was wearing blue uniform pants and no cap. His sleek gray hair was unmussed by summer breezes, and his smooth pink chin and jowls bulged over a white shirt collar. Visible in his shirt pocket were two of the putrid greenish cigars that he loved to smoke when he wanted to be alone.

He said hello to Nudger and Danny, then stared at the new mural.

"What the hell are Dunker Delites doing with fins?"

"They're supposed to be whales," Danny said in an injured tone.

"Sort of a combination of each," Nudger said, trying to protect Danny's feelings.

"You're kinda out of your jurisdiction," Danny said, knowing Hammersmith was a city cop and this was the municipality of Maplewood.

"Got a Major Case Squad crime," Hammersmith said, easing his way up on a stool two over from Nudger so there'd be plenty of room. The Major Case Squad was made up of city and county cops and called into action whenever a serious crime was committed in the area. That way there

would be less territorial squabbling, and the facilities of the largest departments were available.

"You want a Dunker Delite?" Danny asked.

Hammersmith looked at him suspiciously. "Yesterday's unsolds?"

Danny blushed. Odd in a man in his fifties.

"Just some water like Nudger's," Hammersmith said.

As he placed the glass of ice water on the counter before Hammersmith, Danny asked the question Nudger was considering. "So what kinda
crime brought the Major Case Squad to Maplewood?"

"Homicide," Hammersmith said, sipping water, then using his paper
napkin to dab at his lips with the peculiar delicacy of the obese and graceful.
"Guy named Lichtenberg, over on Emler Avenue."

Danny released his grip on his gray towel, letting it flop back over his
crotch. "Huh? That's the artist did my mural!"

"I know he is," Hammersmith said. "That's how come I knew those
whales were Dunker Delites."

For Danny it was a slam dunk. After Hammersmith had gone back out into
the summer heat, Danny had easily talked Nudger into trying to find out
who killed Lou Lichtenberg. That it was an open homicide case didn't
dissuade Danny; being Nudger's ersatz receptionist and sometimes helper,
he knew Nudger's occasional disregard for rules. And of course Nudger
was breaking one of his rules he least liked to disregard. He tried never to
get involved in homicides. Already one person was dead, so was it all that
unlikely another would wind up in that state? And with his luck . . .

"Just report to me whenever you want, Nudge," Danny was saying as
Nudger waved a limp good-bye and pushed out through the grease-stained
glass door into the heat.

Later that day in his hotbox office, Nudger phoned Hammersmith and
got the basics: Lou Lichtenberg and his bride, Linda, had bought an old
Victorian house on Emler a couple of months ago and had been living in
it while they fixed it up. Like many rehabbers, they couldn't afford to stay
in their own digs and be eaten up by rent money along with the funds they
were pouring into the project house.

Last night, while they were stripping paint from an old wooden banister, Linda had taken a break and driven to Mr. Wizard to buy them a
couple of chocolate strawberry concretes. She'd returned to find her husband sprawled at the base of the stairs. At first she assumed he'd accidentally
fallen and was unconscious. The paramedics who responded to her 911 call
saw immediately that he was dead. At St. Mary's Hospital emergency, it
didn't take long for a nurse to notice the bullet hole behind his ear.

So, murder without a doubt.

"Any hint of motive?" Nudger asked.

Hammersmith chuckled on the other end of the connection. "Hear
tell, everybody liked the dead guy. He was one of those free spirits, and a
talented painter, according to his friends. Since he'd just turned forty, he

decided to settle down, become a husband and home owner."

"What about the wife?"

"Linda. Skinny, pretty, distraught. She isn't faking it, Nudge; she really is grieving over hubby. Course, I could be fooled."

Nudger doubted it.

"She and the painter lived together the past five years, dated a couple of years before that. She's a photographer, but her stuff doesn't sell."

"Did her husband's paintings sell?"

"Yeah, but not for much."

"Should I ask if you found the murder weapon?"

"All we know about it," Hammersmith said, "is it was a twenty-two caliber."

"Could it have been a professional hit, Jack?"

"Crossed my mind—small caliber weapon, one shot behind the right ear, soft bullet that spread and tumbled inside the skull. I don't guess we can rule it out. Or maybe the killer's somebody who saw a movie about a professional hit man."

Nudger hoped the latter was the case. The idea of crossing paths with a pro made his sensitive stomach twitch. He didn't like playing in somebody else's backyard, especially if the somebody was the sort of person who might bury him there.

"Nudge," Hammersmith said, "tell me you aren't going to be mucking around in this case."

"Can't do that, Jack."

"Danny hire you?"

"He was fond of the dead guy," Nudger said. "Went to his wedding, supplied Plowman's Feasts in exchange for the guy painting those Dunker Delite whales. Dead guy was a regular customer of Danny's, and how many of those are there?"

Hammersmith knew the last was a rhetorical question. He didn't give Nudger the usual stern warning about overstepping the line in an active case. Merely hung up without saying good-bye. Nudger wasn't surprised by this abruptness. Hammersmith insisted on being the one to terminate phone conversations, and he often acted suddenly so as not to lose the opportunity. Had a thing about it. Nudger didn't mind. Almost everybody had a thing.

After replacing the receiver on his desk phone, he sat in his tiny, stifling office above the donut shop and gazed out the window at pigeons roosting on a ledge of the building across Manchester. The pigeons seemed to sense his attention and gazed back at him. He had never liked the way pigeons looked at him, as if they took for granted something about him that he maybe didn't even know himself.

He turned away from the window, wincing as his swivel chair squealed like an enraged soprano. Bile lay bitter beneath his tongue. Something square and on fire seemed to be lodged low in his throat. The cloying scent of baked sugar from the shop below was making him nauseated. His stomach hurt. Really hurt.

Wrong business, he told himself for the thousandth time, and reached for the roll of antacid tablets on his desk. I'm in the wrong business. Wrong world, maybe.

He barely chewed several antacid tablets and almost choked swallowing the jagged pieces.

Lou Lichtenberg's obituary in the paper the next morning said that he would be cremated, his ashes spread over the Mississippi that he loved to paint, and that there would be a memorial service at a later date.

Nudger put down the *Post-Dispatch* and used the number Danny had given him to phone the widow. When he mentioned Danny, she agreed to talk with him.

Linda Lichtenberg was twenty pounds too thin to be healthy and had a long, wan face out of a Renaissance painting. Telling her how considerate she was to agree to see him at such a time in her life, Nudger thought she looked born to grieve.

They were in the spacious living room of the old house on Emler. It was a mess, with an attached living and dining room, rough hardwood floors, yellowed enameled woodwork partly stripped to its original oak, and bare plaster walls too rough for paint or paper. Beyond where Linda sat on a threadbare sofa was the stairway with the long wooden banister she and her husband had been stripping. The upper part was paint-streaked bare wood, the lower the same yellowed white of the rest of the unstripped woodwork. A worn gray carpet ran up the stairs, the sort of thing easy to trip over.

"If Danny says you're okay, I want to talk to you," Linda said. Her pink-rimmed eyes were pale blue and bloodshot from crying. "I never thought I'd say this, but I'm beginning to believe in the death penalty. I gotta be honest—I want revenge. I want to see the bastard that killed Lou roasted alive!" Strong words from such a frail-looking woman.

With Nudger gently urging her along, she related the simple story told to and by Hammersmith. She and Lou had been stripping paint from the banister. She'd gone out to get ice cream. When she returned, she found Lou at the base of the stairs. She thought he'd fallen and was unconscious, so she called 911. It was the paramedics who discovered he was dead.

When she was finished talking, Nudger glanced around the partly rehabbed living and dining rooms.

"I know it doesn't look like much now," Linda said, "but Lou and I had plans."

"I don't see any of his paintings. I mean the kind you do on canvas."

"His temporary studio was going to be upstairs. Some of his work is up there, if you want to see it."

Nudger told her that he did, then followed her up the steep flight of steps and along a hall to a large second-floor room that was part of an addition to the house. There were skylights set in the slanted ceiling.

"It would have been a good place to work," Linda said sadly. "Lou didn't even have a chance to get properly set up."

Nudger walked over to where two canvases leaned against a wooden railing at the top of the steps. "Mind if I look?"

Linda shrugged. "It's why we came."

Nudger examined each painting. One was an unremarkable woodsy landscape. The other was of a slender nude woman standing near a window and bathed in golden sunlight. Her head was bowed and her long arms hung languidly at her sides.

"Lou's *Woman in the Light*," Linda said. "His last painting. He did it here because of the skylights."

"You?"

She bit her lower lip. "Me."

"It's beautiful." Nudger meant it.

Linda turned away. "Lou was so talented. His death is such a damned shame."

"What made him paint the whale mural in Danny's?" Nudger asked, thinking it was a long way from the elegant, glowing woman on the canvas before him.

"Donuts. He did it in exchange for donuts for our wedding. It isn't that good, and he knows it."

"Danny likes it."

"Danny is sweet."

"From all those donuts," Nudger said. Got him a smile. "Can you think of anybody your husband might have angered lately, anyone who might have wanted to get even with him?"

"No. I told the police no, too. Lou was an artist; he didn't have any real enemies. Hell, he didn't even live in this world."

Nudger told her he understood, but he wasn't sure if he did.

He found his own way out, leaving her with her grief and the canvas image of herself in sunlight that no longer existed.

Nudger met with a woman he knew named Roseanne. She was slim, attractive, and the director of a small, privately funded museum near Grand Avenue. She wasn't from New York, but she had been there and often dressed in black. He regarded her as his art expert.

"Lou Lichtenberg," he said, standing near a lifesize bronze Apollo in the museum. It made him feel inadequate.

"Dead," Roseanne said. She was a woman who got to the point.

"Did he have talent?"

"Yes."

"Was he going to make it as an artist?"

"Who knows? He didn't understand or accept the marriage of art and commerce."

"Meaning?"

"Look around you, Nudger."

He did, and saw several ordinary objects—a clock, a chunk of concrete with steel rods protruding from it, a toaster, a suitcase, a small refrigerator. Next to each object was an X-ray view of its insides.

"The museum has an exhibit running this week of work done by the Anti-Christo."

"Isn't Christo the guy who wraps unlikely things in cloth—I mean, like coastlines or whole buildings?"

"The same. But the Anti-Christo displays solid objects, along with their fluoroscopic images or X rays. The idea is he shows them *un*wrapped, bare of any surface or subterfuge. His work sells for a fortune."

"Is it art?"

"The market says it is. Is he as talented as Lou Lichtenberg was? Not on your life! Is he more successful as an artist? Yes."

"I don't like your business," Nudger said. "It's full of phonies."

Roseanne smiled. "Yours isn't?"

Hammersmith had told Nudger the Lichtenbergs bought their aged Victorian lady from Norton Anston, the last of a family that had lived in the house for almost a hundred years. Once wealthy from the timber business, they'd fallen on hard times during the Depression and never gotten up. Norton Anston had been reared in comparative poverty that he'd managed to raise only to bare sustenance through a struggling antiques shop. He'd jumped at the Lichtenbergs' offer for the old house. The closing brought him the most liquidity he'd ever experienced.

Anston now lived in an expensive condo in West County, where he agreed to talk with Nudger.

"To tell you the truth," he said, "it was a relief to get rid of the old family house. It had become a costly and troublesome relic. Better somebody young battle the termites and mold than a man my age."

That remark kind of bothered Nudger, because Anston seemed to be in his late forties, Nudger's age. Though he looked older, Nudger assured himself; assessing Anston's thin hair, double chin, thickened waist, crow's feet. Nudger's hair wasn't all that thin. Except on top: bald spot the size of a half dollar—quarter or maybe nickel.

"I understand you sold the house yourself," he said to Anston, "rather than go through a Realtor."

Anston smiled with a kind of toothy avarice, reminding Nudger of someone he couldn't quite place. "Sure. Why pay a commission?"

Why indeed? Nudger thought.

"In my business—buying and selling antiques—there's not much profit margin. I've learned to squeeze a dollar till it bleeds, and I don't apologize."

This guy talked disturbingly like Eileen. "Were the Lichtenbergs satisfied with the deal?"

"They wouldn't have made it if they weren't," Anston said. "Matter of fact, I'd say they were overjoyed. You know, young people, first-time home owners. Kind of touching."

Nudger remembered when he and Eileen, as man and wife, had bought a subdivision house, how for a while it had seemed like a castle. Then a dungeon.

"They had big plans for the place," Anston said. "Talked of turning it into a bed and breakfast."

"Really?" That was the first Nudger had heard of a B and B plan.

Anston glanced at his wristwatch. "I hate to rush this," he said, "but I'm supposed to meet someone at the Gypsy Caravan."

Nudger raised an eyebrow.

"Big antiques show comes to town every year. Dealers from all over the country. Nothing to do with real Gypsies."

Nudger chuckled in a way that should let Anston know he wasn't that naïve, then thanked him for his time.

Nudger had parked in the shade, but as usual, starting his old Honda was a struggle in the heat. When he finally was able to get the balky little engine running, he saw Anston pull from the condo driveway in an even older car, a rusty Ford station wagon. It was the proceeds from the sale of the family home, Nudger decided, that had enabled Anston to afford such a nice condo, and maybe with cash left over. He probably hadn't gotten around to buying a new car yet.

Nudger's phone was ringing as he entered his apartment on Sutton, noticing how shabby it looked after Anston's condo. As he picked up the receiver, he reached out with his free hand and switched on the window air conditioner.

Hammersmith was on the phone. Nudger moved as far away from the humming, rattling window unit as the cord would allow so he could hear.

"What I hear," Hammersmith said, "is that you've been nosing around the Lichtenberg case like a pig digging for truffles." Hammersmith would know about truffles. Food. "What have you discovered, Nudge?"

"Facts or truffles?" Nudger asked. "I'll trade either or both."

"Make it both," Hammersmith said. "That way you might stay out of trouble."

"Facts: Lichtenberg was a genuinely talented painter. If he had any enemies, I haven't uncovered them. He and his wife were happy with their new home. And they were considering turning it into a B and B."

"Breaking and entering?"

"B and B. Bed and breakfast."

"Oh. And your truffles?"

"The house's previous owner, Norton Anston, needed the money when he sold the place. The wife, Linda, is genuinely grief-stricken, and my guess is she had nothing to do with her husband's death. And it seems to me that there aren't many Lichtenberg paintings lying around the place, considering what a dedicated artist he was. Of course, all truffles are subjective."

"Sometimes when a painter dies, his work suddenly is in demand and the price goes up," Hammersmith said.

"You thinking somebody with lots of Lichtenberg paintings might have killed him?"

"I admit it's only a truffle," Hammersmith said. "Here's another one: a real estate agent says Anston took advantage of the young, artistic, and naïve couple and sold the house for more than it was worth. Only opinion, of course."

"What about your facts?"

"Official cause of death was what you'd expect, Nudge—bullet to the brain, massive damage. No powder burns on the victim's hands, though he was shot from close range. So no chance of suicide. And whoever killed him was probably a smoker."

"Huh?"

"Fresh burn spot on the stairway carpet where the gunman must have stood, from a cigarette or cigar ember."

"Lou and Linda were stripping the banister. Maybe they burned off some of the old paint and singed the carpet," Nudger suggested.

"A possibility," Hammersmith said grudgingly. "I'll check with the wife, who incidentally ran into some friends while buying ice cream at Mr. Wizard's at the time hubby was being shot. Not to mention the kid who waited on her. He lives across the street from the Lichtenberg house and remembered her being there. So her alibi checks out strong."

"Maybe she shot Lou before she left the house," Nudger said. "Or right after returning."

"Not according to people who heard the shot. Though they didn't know at the time that was what they heard. Also, there was no gunpowder residue on her hands."

"You still considering a hit man?" Nudger asked.

"Yeah, but one thing doesn't ring true. We got a misshapen twenty-two bullet like a pro might have left in a victim, only it's more misshapen than it oughta be, considering the soft tissue it went through once it entered the skull. There's no way we can ID the make of gun, or even match the bullet in ballistics tests."

"Did the killer leave a shell casing?"

"Nope. That sounds like a pro. Unless it was an amateur using a revolver and the casing stayed in the cylinder. The way the bullet doesn't provide a lead, or any potential court evidence through ballistics, it mighta been a pro with some new kind of gun that makes his job safer."

"Have you noticed how everything's become a battle with technology?" Nudger asked.

"Tell me about it, Nudge. I'm recording this conversation, gonna convert it into print, then scan it into my electronic murder file. Might write a book someday."

"Is that legal, Jack?"

But Hammersmith had hung up.

• • •

"I heard you and your husband were going to convert the house into a B and B," Nudger said, standing on the Victorian home's wide gallery porch and enjoying a glass of lemonade Linda Lichtenberg had just handed him.

"Not right away," Linda said. "But, yes, that was the plan. Eventually, we were going to convert the garage to Lou's studio and put in another garage under the house at basement level. He could work out there in peace and quiet while I was dealing with guests." She slumped down in an old wood glider hung on rusty chains, as if her energy had just left her in a rush, and was obviously trying not to cry. "It's awful, how everything can change in an instant. Now, without Lou's income, I won't even be able to afford to stay here."

"Will you sell the house?"

She shook her head no. "We owe so much it wouldn't make sense. I'm going to let the bank take it. People like me, like Lou, I think we just weren't born to be property owners, to live normal lives."

"What about your husband's paintings? Can't you sell some of them?"

"There aren't any left except the two upstairs. I won't part with *Woman in the Light,* and the landscape is old work and practically worthless. We sold Lou's backlog of work in order to make a down payment and pay closing costs on this place."

"Who bought Lou's paintings?"

"I couldn't tell you. You'd have to check with the Plato Gallery. That's who sold most of Lou's work. When it sold."

Standing on the porch and looking at the dejected figure in the glider, Nudger felt his eyes tear up. He turned away and swiped at them with a knuckle, then talked with Linda Lichtenberg about anything other than her dead husband until the lemonade glass was empty.

The Plato Gallery was in the wealthy suburb of Clayton and displayed antiques as well as artwork. A gaunt man with a white Vandyke beard approached Nudger just inside the door and asked if he could be of help. He was dressed in black except for a white handkerchief that flowered from his blazer pocket.

"Do you have any Lou Lichtenbergs?" Nudger asked.

The man smiled sadly and shook his head. "I wish we did. The artist died recently, you know, and the value of his work has risen. But we sold the last of his paintings over a month ago, cheaper than we should have even then because he needed the money."

"For his Victorian house," Nudger said.

The man's dark eyes brightened. "Oh, you knew Lou?"

"No," Nudger said, and explained.

The man in black turned out to be Plato Zorbak, the owner and manager of the gallery, and when Nudger was finished talking he said with surprising fervor, "I hope they catch the evil swine who shot Lou. He doesn't deserve any mercy."

"Who bought his paintings?" Nudger asked.

"Most of them sold to a dealer in New Orleans—he buys for a number of clients."

A well-dressed man and woman entered the gallery, and before Zorbak excused himself to wait on them, Nudger asked a final question: "About how much have Lou Lichtenberg paintings appreciated since his death?"

"As of now," Zorbak said, "about three hundred percent. And climbing, because Lou was a bona fide talent." He backed away, eager to greet his clientele and escape Nudger, who was obviously no art buyer. "Please feel free to look around before you leave," Zorbak said politely.

Nudger thanked him and did stay for a few minutes. Something had caught his eye.

When he returned to his office, he stopped in Danny's for a cup of coffee to go. After climbing the steps in the stifling stairwell to his office door, he went inside, walked to the tiny half-bath, and poured the horrible brew down the washbasin drain slowly so Danny wouldn't hear pipes gurgling below.

Then Nudger switched on the air conditioner and sat down behind his desk. There was a message on his machine. Eileen's voice: "Nudger, if you call the bank you'll see that your measly checking account has been frozen. If you don't—"

Quickly he pressed DELETE.

He slid the desk phone over and called Maplewood Bank, but he didn't ask about his account. He talked to someone he knew in the loan department and asked what would happen when the bank repossessed Lou and Linda Lichtenberg's house.

"Banks don't really want to foreclose on anyone's house," he was assured. "We're not in the real estate business and don't want to be. The house will be sold on the courthouse steps to the highest bidder."

Nudger said thank you, depressed the phone's cradle button for a dial tone, then called Hammersmith at the Third District.

"Nudge," Hammersmith said, "I don't have time for you. Crime in our fair city demands my constant attention."

"If you promise not to hang up on me," Nudger said, "I'll tell you who killed Lou Lichtenberg."

Now and then life provided a sweet moment outside the donut shop.

The next morning, Nudger sat at the counter in Danny's Donuts. Before him were two free Dunker Delites and a large foam cup of coffee. He was trying to figure a way not to consume any of it without bruising Danny's feelings. Next to Nudger sat Hammersmith. He'd devoured three Plowman's Feasts and was determinedly working on a fourth, drinking only ice water, pretending everything was delicious. Showing his human side, Nudger thought.

"So how'd you figure it out?" Danny asked Nudger.

"By putting together facts and truffles."

Hammersmith glared at him while chewing a mouthful of donut.

"Property values in Maplewood are skyrocketing. The Lichtenbergs were going to open a B and B and build a new garage at basement level. With Lou's death, the house will be foreclosed on and sold on the courthouse steps. A straw party from New Orleans bought up Lou's paintings at the Plato Gallery. Seeing the antique guns at the Plato Gallery was the final tip-off."

"Yeah?" Danny asked, looking at Nudger like a curious basset hound.

"Shnot nishe to toy with people, Nudge," Hammersmith said around a large bite of featured pastry.

"I asked myself questions," Nudger said. "Who might have been surprised by increasing property values and want to buy the Lichtenberg house at auction? Who would know enough to buy Lou's paintings through a straw party as an investment if they planned on murdering him? Who dealt in antiques and had access to an antique flintlock gun that might shoot a chunk of lead pried from a twenty-two cartridge, leave a burned spot on the carpet from powder dropping from the gun's flash pan, and leave a deliberately mutilated slug impossible to trace or match with modern weapons? Who might have left behind one of Lou's best and most valuable paintings because he'd know the subject was the painter's wife and having possession of it might draw suspicion to him? And who might have something to hide if the cellar in the old family home were dug up to accommodate a basement garage?"

"The answer's pretty simple when you stop to think about it," Danny said.

"And the proof came," Hammersmith said, "when we dug beneath the house and found the bones of antiques dealer Norton Anston's wife, who was supposed to have run away to Las Vegas twenty-five years ago."

"Poor woman didn't get any farther than the basement," Danny said.

"She's gotten even with Anston now. He's confessed to her murder, and to Lou Lichtenberg's. And he says he'd like to murder Nudger."

"Make sure he's locked up tight," Danny said.

Nudger didn't feel he had to second that. He gathered his complimentary Dunker Delites and coffee, along with a paper napkin, and slid off his stool.

"Where you going, Nudge?" Danny asked.

"Gonna eat breakfast upstairs," Nudger said. "Lots of paperwork to do, and I'm expecting a phone call."

"Lemme know if you're still hungry later," Danny said.

Hammersmith was grinning at Nudger as he went out.

Nudger hadn't mentioned the real reason he'd begun to suspect Anston of Lou Lichtenberg's murder. One of the barracudas swimming among the Dunker Delite whales in the mural Lou had painted for Danny looked amazingly like Norton Anston.

To Nudger, anyway.

Lawrence Block

A Moment of Wrong Thinking

LAWRENCE BLOCK has won the Nero Wolfe award, four Shamus awards, five Edgars, two Japanese Maltese Falcon awards, and an Anthony, in addition to being named a Grand Master of the Mystery Writers of America. His more than forty novels include leading characters Matthew Scudder, a former New York City detective turned private investigator, and Bernie Rhodenbarr, a used-book dealer who supports himself as a burglar on the side. Mr. Block has also published numerous volumes of short stories, including a recent collection of all his short fiction, *Enough Rope,* as well as several excellent books on the craft of writing. His most recent novel, *Small Town,* takes a startling and unforgettable look at the reality of life in post-9/11 New York City, and struck a chord with readers across the nation, who sent it onto the *New York Times* bestseller list. "A Moment of Wrong Thinking" brings together Matt Scudder and what isn't a crime at all. But its mention sends Scudder down memory lane, to a case that wasn't so easy. This story first appeared in the anthology called *Murder in the Family.*

A Moment of Wrong Thinking

Lawrence Block

Monica said, "What kind of a gun? A man shoots himself in his living room, surrounded by his nearest and dearest, and you want to know what kind of a gun he used?"

"I just wondered," I said.

Monica rolled her eyes. She's one of Elaine's oldest friends. They were in high school together, in Rego Park, and they never lost touch over the years. Elaine spent a lot of years as a call girl, and Monica, who was never in the life herself, seemed to have no difficulty accepting that. Elaine, for her part, had no judgment on Monica's predilection for dating married men.

She was with the current one that evening. The four of us had gone to a revival of *Allegro,* the Rogers and Hammerstein show that hadn't been a big hit the first time around. From there we went to Paris Green for a late supper. We talked about the show and speculated on reasons for its limited success. The songs were good, we agreed, and I was old enough to remember hearing "A Fellow Needs a Girl" on the radio. Elaine said she had a Lisa Kirk LP, and one of the cuts was "The Gentleman Is a Dope." That number, she said, had stopped the show during its initial run, and launched Lisa Kirk.

Monica said she'd love to hear it some time. Elaine said all she had to do was find the record and then find something to play it on. Monica said she still had a turntable for LPs.

Monica's guy didn't say anything, and I had the feeling he didn't know who Lisa Kirk was, or why he had to go through all this just to get laid. His name was Doug Halley—like the comet, he'd said—and he did something on Wall Street. Whatever it was, he did well enough at it to keep his second wife and their kids in a house in Pound Ridge, in Westchester County, while he was putting the kids from his first marriage through college. He had a boy at Bowdoin, we'd learned, and a girl who'd just started at Colgate.

We got as much conversational mileage as we could out of Lisa Kirk, and the drinks came—Perrier for me, cranberry juice for Elaine and Monica, and a Stolichnaya martini for Halley. He'd hesitated for a beat before ordering it—Monica would surely have told him I was a sober alcoholic, and even if she hadn't he'd have noted that he was the only one drinking—and I could almost hear him think it through and decide the hell with it. I was just as glad he'd ordered the drink. He looked as though he needed it, and when it came he drank deep.

It was about then that Monica mentioned the fellow who'd shot himself. It had happened the night before, too late to make the morning papers, and Monica had seen the coverage that afternoon on New York One. A man in Inwood, in the course of a social evening at his own home, with friends and family members present, had drawn a gun, ranted about his financial situation and everything that was wrong with the world, and then stuck the gun in his mouth and blew his brains out.

"What kind of a gun," Monica said again. "It's a guy thing, isn't it? There's not a woman in the world who would ask that question."

"A woman would ask what he was wearing," Halley said.

"No," Elaine said. "Who cares what he was wearing? A woman would ask what his wife was wearing."

"A look of horror would be my guess," Monica said. "Can you imagine? You're having a nice evening with friends and your husband shoots himself in front of everybody?"

"They didn't show it, did they?"

"They didn't interview her on camera, but they did talk with some man who was there and saw the whole thing."

Halley said that it would have been a bigger story if they'd had the wife on camera, and we started talking about the media and how intrusive they'd become. And we stayed with that until they brought us our food.

When we got home Elaine said, "The man who shot himself. When you asked if they showed it, you didn't mean an interview with the wife. You wanted to know if they showed him doing it."

"These days," I said, "somebody's almost always got a camcorder running. But I didn't really think anybody had the act on tape."

"Because it would have been a bigger story."

"That's right. The play a story gets depends on what they've got to show you. It would have been a little bigger than it was if they'd managed to interview the wife, but it would have been everybody's lead story all day long if they could have actually shown him doing it."

"Still, you asked."

"Idly," I said. "Making conversation."

"Yeah, right. And you want to know what kind of gun he used. Just being a guy, and talking guy talk. Because you liked Doug so much, and wanted to bond with him."

"Oh, I was crazy about him. Where does she find them?"

"I don't know," she said, "but I think she's got radar. If there's a jerk out there, and if he's married, she homes in on him. What did you care what kind of gun it was?"

"What I was wondering," I said, "was whether it was a revolver or an automatic."

She thought about it. "And if they showed him doing it, you could look at the film and know what kind of a gun it was."

"Anybody could."

"I couldn't," she said. "Anyway, what difference does it make?"

"Probably none."

"Oh?"

"It reminded me of a case we had," I said. "Ages ago."

"Back when you were a cop, and I was a cop's girlfriend."

I shook my head. "Only the first half. I was on the force, but you and I hadn't met yet. I was still wearing a uniform, and it would be awhile before I got my gold shield. And we hadn't moved to Long Island yet, we were still living in Brooklyn."

"You and Anita and the boys."

"Was Andy even born yet? No, he couldn't have been, because she was pregnant with him when we bought the house in Syosset. We probably had Mike by then, but what difference does it make? It wasn't about them. It was about the poor sonofabitch in Park Slope who shot himself."

"And did he use a revolver or an automatic?"

"An automatic. He was a World War Two vet, and this was the gun he'd brought home with him. It must have been a forty-five."

"And he stuck it in his mouth and—"

"Put it to his temple. Putting it in your mouth, I think it was cops who made that popular."

"Popular?"

"You know what I mean. The expression caught on, 'eating your gun,' and you started seeing more civilian suicides who took that route." I fell silent, remembering. "I was partnered with Vince Mahaffey. I've told you about him."

"He smoked those little cigars."

"Guinea-stinkers, he called them. DeNobilis was the brand name, and they were these nasty little things that looked as though they'd passed through the digestive system of a cat. I don't think they could have smelled any worse if they had. Vince smoked them all day long, and he ate like a pig and drank like a fish."

"The perfect role model."

"Vince was all right," I said. "I learned a hell of a lot from Vince."

"Are you gonna tell me the story?"

"You want to hear it?"

She got comfortable on the couch. "Sure," she said. "I like it when you tell me stories."

• • •

It was a weeknight, I remembered, and the moon was full. It seems to me it was in the spring, but I could be wrong about that part.

Mahaffey and I were in a radio car. I was driving when the call came in, and he rang in and said we'd take this one. It was in the Slope. I don't remember the address, but wherever it was we weren't far from it, and I drove there and we went in.

Park Slope's a very desirable area now, but this was before the gentrification process got underway, and the Slope was still a working-class neighborhood, and predominantly Irish. The house we were directed to was one of a row of identical brownstone houses, four stories tall, two apartments to a floor. The vestibule was a half-flight up from street level, and a man was standing in the doorway, waiting for us.

"You want the Conways," he said. "Two flights up and on your left."

"You're a neighbor?"

"Downstairs of them," he said. "It was me called it in. My wife's with her now, the poor woman. He was a bastard, that husband of hers."

"You didn't get along?"

"Why would you say that? He was a good neighbor."

"Then how did he get to be a bastard?"

"To do what he did," the man said darkly. "You want to kill yourself, Jesus, it's an unforgivable sin, but it's a man's own business, isn't it?" He shook his head. "But do it in private, for God's sake. Not with your wife looking on. As long as the poor woman lives, that's her last memory of her husband."

We climbed the stairs. The building was in good repair, but drab, and the stairwell smelled of cabbage and of mice. The cooking smells in tenements have changed over the years, with the ethnic makeup of their occupants. Cabbage was what you used to smell in Irish neighborhoods. I suppose it's still much in evidence in Greenpoint and Brighton Beach, where new arrivals from Poland and Russia reside. And I'm sure the smells are very different in the stairwells of buildings housing immigrants from Asia and Africa and Latin America, but I suspect the mouse smell is there, too.

Halfway up the second flight of stairs, we met a woman on her way down. "Mary Frances!" she called upstairs. "It's the police!" She turned to us. "She's in the back," she said, "with her kids, the poor darlings. It's just at the top of the stairs, on your left. You can walk right in."

The door of the Conway apartment was ajar. Mahaffey knocked on it, then pushed it open when the knock went unanswered. We walked in and there he was, a middle-aged man in dark blue trousers and a white cotton tank-top undershirt. He'd nicked himself shaving that morning, but that was the least of his problems.

He was sprawled in an easy chair facing the television set. He'd fallen over on his left side, and there was a large hole in his right temple, the skin scorched around the entry wound. His right hand lay in his lap, the fingers still holding the gun he'd brought back from the war.

"Jesus," Mahaffey said.

There was a picture of Jesus on the wall over the fireplace, and, similarly framed, another of John F. Kennedy. Other photos and holy pictures reposed here and there in the room—on tabletops, on walls, on top of the television set. I was looking at a small framed photo of a smiling young man in an army uniform and just beginning to realize it was a younger version of the dead man when his wife came into the room.

"I'm sorry," she said, "I never heard you come in. I was with the children. They're in a state, as you can imagine."

"You're Mrs. Conway?"

"Mrs. James Conway." She glanced at her late husband, but her eyes didn't stay on him for long. "He was talking and laughing," she said. "He was making jokes. And then he shot himself. Why would he do such a thing?"

"Had he been drinking, Mrs. Conway?"

"He'd had a drink or two," she said. "He liked his drink. But he wasn't drunk."

"Where'd the bottle go?"

She put her hands together. She was a small woman, with a pinched face and pale blue eyes, and she wore a cotton housedress with a floral pattern. "I put it away," she said. "I shouldn't have done that, should I?"

"Did you move anything else, ma'am?"

"Only the bottle," she said. "The bottle and the glass. I didn't want people saying he was drunk when he did it, because how would that be for the children?" Her face clouded. "Or is it better thinking it was the drink that made him do it? I don't know which is worse. What do you men think?"

"I think we could all use a drink," he said. "Yourself not least of all, ma'am."

She crossed the room and got a bottle of Schenley's from a mahogany cabinet. She brought it, along with three small glasses of cut crystal. Mahaffey poured drinks for all three of us and held his to the light. She took a tentative sip of hers while Mahaffey and I drank ours down. It was an ordinary blended whiskey, an honest workingman's drink. Nothing fancy about it, but it did the job.

Mahaffey raised his glass again and looked at the bare-bulb ceiling fixture through it. "These are fine glasses," he said.

"Waterford," she said. "There were eight, they were my mother's, and these three are all that's left." She glanced at the dead man. "He had his from a jelly glass. We don't use the Waterford for every day."

"Well, I'd call this a special occasion," Mahaffey said. "Drink that yourself, will you? It's good for you."

She braced herself, drank the whiskey down, shuddered slightly, then drew a deep breath. "Thank you," she said. "It *is* good for me, I'd have to say. No, no more for me. But have another for yourselves."

I passed. Vince poured himself a short one. He went over her story with her, jotting down notes from time to time in his notebook. At one point she began to calculate how she'd manage without poor Jim. He'd been out of work lately, but he was in the building trades, and when he worked he made decent money. And there'd be something from the Veterans Administration, wouldn't there? And Social Security?

"I'm sure there'll be something," Vince told her. "And insurance? Did he have insurance?"

There was a policy, she said. Twenty-five thousand dollars, he'd taken it out when the first child was born, and she'd seen to it that the premium was paid each month. But he'd killed himself, and wouldn't that keep them from paying?

"That's what everybody thinks," he told her, "but it's rarely the case. There's generally a clause, no payment for suicide during the first six months, the first year, maybe even the first two years. To keep you from taking out the policy on Monday and doing away with yourself on Tuesday. But you've had this for more than two years, haven't you?"

She was nodding eagerly. "How old is Patrick? Almost nine, and it was taken out just around the time he was born."

"Then I'd say you're in the clear," he said. "And it's only fair, if you think about it. The company's been taking a man's premiums all these years, why should a moment of wrong thinking get them off the hook?"

"I had the same notion myself," she said, "but I thought there was no hope. I thought that was just the way it was."

"Well," he said, "it's not."

"What did you call it? A moment of wrong thinking? But isn't that all it takes to keep him out of heaven? It's the sin of despair, you know." She addressed this last to me, guessing that Mahaffey was more aware of the theology of it than I. "And is that fair?" she demanded, turning to Mahaffey again. "Better to cheat a widow out of the money than to cheat James Conway into hell."

"Maybe the Lord's able to take a longer view of things."

"That's not what the fathers say."

"If he wasn't in his right mind at the time . . ."

"His right mind!" She stepped back, pressed her hand to her breast. "Who in his right mind ever did such a thing?"

"Well . . ."

"He was joking," she said. "And he put the gun to his head, and even then I wasn't frightened, because he seemed his usual self and there was nothing frightening about it. Except I had the thought that the gun might go off by accident, and I said as much."

"What did he say to that?"

"That we'd all be better off if it did, himself included. And I said not to say such a thing, that it was horrid and sinful, and he said it was only the truth, and then he looked at me, he *looked* at me."

"What kind of a look?"

"Like, See what I'm doing? Like, Are you watching me, Mary Frances? And then he shot himself."

"Maybe it was an accident," I suggested.

"I saw his face. I saw his finger tighten on the trigger. It was as if he did it to spite me. But he wasn't angry at me. For the love of God, why would he . . ."

Mahaffey clapped me on the shoulder. "Take Mrs. Conway into the other room," he said. "Let her freshen up her face and drink a glass of water, and make sure the kids are all right." I looked at him, and he gave my shoulder a squeeze. "Something I want to check," he said.

I went into the kitchen, where Mrs. Conway wet a dishtowel and dabbed tentatively at her face, then filled a jelly glass with water and drank it down in a series of small sips. Then we went to check on the children, a boy of eight and a girl a couple of years younger. They were just sitting there, hands folded in their laps, as if someone had told them not to move.

Mrs. Conway fussed over them and assured them everything was going to be fine and told them to get ready for bed. We left them as we found them, sitting side by side, their hands still folded in their laps. I suppose they were in shock, and it seemed to me they had the right.

I brought the woman back to the living room, where Mahaffey was bent over the body of her husband. He straightened up as we entered the room. "Mrs. Conway," he said, "I have something important to tell you."

She waited to hear what it was.

"Your husband didn't kill himself," he announced.

Her eyes widened, and she looked at Mahaffey as if he'd gone suddenly mad. "But I saw him do it," she said.

He frowned, nodded. "Forgive me," he said. "I misspoke. What I meant to say was that the poor man did not commit suicide. He did kill himself, of course he killed himself—"

"I saw him do it."

"—and of course you did, and what a terrible thing for you, what a cruel thing. But it was not his intention, ma'am. It was an accident!"

"An accident."

"Yes."

"To put a gun to your head and pull the trigger. An accident?"

Mahaffey had a handkerchief in his hand. He turned his hand palm-up to show what he was holding with it. It was the cartridge clip from the pistol.

"An accident," Mahaffey said. "You said he was joking, and that's what it was, a joke that went bad. Do you know what this is?"

"Something to do with the gun?"

"It's the clip, ma'am. Or the magazine, they call it that as well. It holds the cartridges."

"The bullets?"

"The bullets, yes. And do you know where I found it?"

"In the gun?"

"That's where I would have expected to find it," he said, "and that's where I looked for it, but it wasn't there. And then I patted his pants pockets, and there it was." And, still using the handkerchief to hold it, he tucked the cartridge clip into the man's right-hand pocket.

"You don't understand," he told the woman. "How about you, Matt? You see what happened?"

"I think so."

"He was playing a joke on you, ma'am. He took the clip out of the gun and put it in his pocket. Then he was going to hold the unloaded gun to his head and give you a scare. He'd give the trigger a squeeze, and there'd be that instant before the hammer clicked on an empty chamber, that instant where you'd think he'd really shot himself, and he'd get to see your reaction."

"But he did shoot himself," she said.

"Because the gun still had a round in the chamber. Once you've chambered a round, removing the clip won't unload the gun. He forgot about the round in the chamber, he thought he had an unloaded weapon in his hand, and when he squeezed the trigger he didn't even have time to be surprised."

"Christ have mercy," she said.

"Amen to that," Mahaffey said. "It's a horrible thing, ma'am, but it's not suicide. Your husband never meant to kill himself. It's a tragedy, a terrible tragedy, but it was an accident." He drew a breath. "It might cost him a bit of time in purgatory, playing a joke like that, but he's spared hellfire, and that's something, isn't it? And now I'll want to use your phone, ma'am, and call this in."

"That's why you wanted to know if it was a revolver or an automatic," Elaine said. "One has a clip and one doesn't."

"An automatic has a clip. A revolver has a cylinder."

"If he'd had a revolver he could have played Russian roulette. That's when you spin the cylinder, isn't it?"

"So I understand."

"How does it work? All but one chamber is empty? Or all but one chamber has a bullet in it?"

"I guess it depends what kind of odds you like."

She thought about it, shrugged. "These poor people in Brooklyn," she said. "What made Mahaffey think of looking for the clip?"

"Something felt off about the whole thing," I said, "and he remembered a case of a man who'd shot a friend with what he was sure was an unloaded gun, because he'd removed the clip. That was the defense at trial, he told me, and it hadn't gotten the guy anywhere, but it stayed in Mahaffey's mind. And as soon as he took a close look at the gun he saw the clip was missing, so it was just a matter of finding it."

"In the dead man's pocket."

"Right."

"Thus saving James Conway from an eternity in hell," she said. "Except he'd be off the hook with or without Mahaffey, wouldn't he? I mean, wouldn't God know where to send him without having some cop hold up a cartridge clip?"

"Don't ask me, honey. I'm not even Catholic."

"Goyim is goyim," she said. "You're supposed to know these things. Never mind, I get the point. It may not make a difference to God or to Conway, but it makes a real difference to Mary Frances. She can bury her husband in holy ground and know he'll be waiting for her when she gets to heaven her own self."

"Right."

"It's a terrible story, isn't it? I mean, it's a good story as a story, but it's terrible, the idea of a man killing himself that way. And his wife and kids witnessing it, and having to live with it."

"Terrible," I agreed.

"But there's more to it. Isn't there?"

"More?"

"Come on," she said. "You left something out."

"You know me too well."

"Damn right I do."

"So what's the part I didn't get to?"

She thought about it. "Drinking a glass of water," she said.

"How's that?"

"He sent you both out of the room," she said, "before he looked to see if the clip was there or not. So it was just Mahaffey, finding the clip all by himself."

"She was beside herself, and he figured it would do her good to splash a little water on her face. And we hadn't heard a peep out of those kids, and it made sense to have her check on them."

"And she had to have you along so she didn't get lost on the way to the bedroom."

I nodded. "It's convenient," I allowed, "making the discovery with no one around. He had plenty of time to pick up the gun, remove the clip, put the gun back in Conway's hand, and slip the clip into the man's pocket. That way he could do his good deed for the day, turning a suicide into an accidental death. It might not fool God, but it would be more than enough to fool the parish priest. Conway's body could be buried in holy ground, regardless of his soul's ultimate destination."

"And you think that's what he did?"

"It's certainly possible. But suppose you're Mahaffey, and you check the gun and the clip's still in it, and you do what we just said. Would you stand there with the clip in your hand waiting to tell the widow and your partner what you learned?"

"Why not?" she said, and then answered her own question. "No, of course not," she said. "If I'm going to make a discovery like that I'm going to do so in the presence of witnesses. What I do, I get the clip, I take it out, I slip it in his pocket, I put the gun back in his hand, and then I wait for the two of you to come back. And *then* I get a bright idea, and we examine the gun and find the clip missing, and one of us finds it in his pocket, where I know it is because that's where I stashed it a minute ago."

"A lot more convincing than his word on what he found when no one was around to see him find it."

"On the other hand," she said, "wouldn't he do that either way? Say I look at the gun and see the clip's missing. Why don't I wait until you come back before I even look for the clip?"

"Your curiosity's too great."

"So I can't wait a minute? But even so, suppose I look and I find the clip in his pocket. Why take it out?"

"To make sure it's what you think it is."

"And why not put it back?"

"Maybe it never occurs to you that anybody would doubt your word," I suggested. "Or maybe, wherever Mahaffey found the clip, in the gun or in Conway's pocket where he said he found it, maybe he would have put it back if he'd had enough time. But we came back in, and there he was with the clip in his hand."

"In his handkerchief, you said. On account of fingerprints?"

"Sure. You don't want to disturb existing prints or leave prints of your own. Not that the lab would have spent any time on this one. They might nowadays, but back in the early sixties? A man shoots himself in front of witnesses?"

She was silent for a long moment. Then she said, "So what happened?"

"What happened?"

"Yeah, your best guess. What really happened?"

"No reason it couldn't have been just the way he reconstructed it. Accidental death. A dumb accident, but an accident all the same."

"But?"

"But Vince had a soft heart," I said. "Houseful of holy pictures like that, he's got to figure it's important to the woman that her husband's got a shot at heaven. If he could fix that up, he wouldn't care a lot about the objective reality of it all."

"And he wouldn't mind tampering with evidence?"

"He wouldn't lose sleep over it. God knows I never did."

"Anybody you ever framed," she said, "was guilty."

"Of something," I agreed. "You want my best guess, it's that there's no way of telling. As soon as the gimmick occurred to Vince, that the clip might be missing, the whole scenario was set. Either Conway had removed the clip and we were going to find it, or he hadn't and we were going to remove it for him, and *then* find it."

" 'The Lady or the Tiger.' Except not really, because either way it comes out the same. It goes in the books as an accident, whether that's what it was or not."

"That's the idea."

"So it doesn't make any difference one way or the other."

"I suppose not," I said, "but I always hoped it was the way Mahaffey said it was."

"Because you wouldn't want to think ill of him? No, that's not it. You already said he was capable of tampering with evidence, and you wouldn't think ill of him for it, anyway. I give up. Why? Because you don't want Mr. Conway to be in hell?"

"I never met the man," I said, "and it would be presumptuous of me to care where he winds up. But I'd prefer it if the clip was in his pocket where Mahaffey said it was, because of what it would prove."

"That he hadn't meant to kill himself? I thought we just said . . ."

I shook my head. "That she didn't do it."

"Who? The wife?"

"Uh-huh."

"That she didn't do what? Kill him? You think *she* killed him?"

"It's possible."

"But he shot himself," she said. "In front of witnesses. Or did I miss something?"

"That's almost certainly what happened," I said, "but she was one of the witnesses, and the kids were the other witnesses, and who knows what they saw, or if they saw anything at all? Say he's on the couch, and they're all watching TV, and she takes his old war souvenir and puts one in his head, and she starts screaming. 'Ohmigod, look what your father has done! Oh, Jesus Mary and Joseph, Daddy has killed himself!' They were looking at the set, they didn't see dick, but they'll think they did by the time she stops carrying on."

"And they never said what they did or didn't see."

"They never said a word, because we didn't ask them anything. Look, I don't think she did it. The possibility didn't even occur to me until some time later, and by then we'd closed the case, so what was the point? I never even mentioned the idea to Vince."

"And if you had?"

"He'd have said she wasn't the type for it, and he'd have been right. But you never know. If she didn't do it, he gave her peace of mind. If she did do it, she must have wondered how the cartridge clip migrated from the gun butt to her husband's pocket."

"She'd have realized Mahaffey put it there."

"Uh-huh. And she'd have had twenty-five thousand reasons to thank him for it."

"Huh?"

"The insurance," I said.

"But you said they'd have to pay anyway."

"Double indemnity," I said. "They'd have had to pay the face amount of the policy, but if it's an accident they'd have had to pay double. That's if there was a double-indemnity clause in the policy, and I have no way of knowing whether or not there was. But most policies sold around then, especially relatively small policies, had the clause. The companies liked to write them that way, and the policy holders usually went for them. A fraction more in premiums and twice the payoff? Why not go for it?"

We kicked it around a little. Then she asked about the current case, the one that had started the whole thing. I'd wondered about the gun, I explained, purely out of curiosity. If it was in fact an automatic, and if the clip was in fact in his pocket and not in the gun where you'd expect to find it, surely some cop would have determined as much by now, and it would all come out in the wash.

"That's some story," she said. "And it happened when, thirty-five years ago? And you never mentioned it before?"

"I never thought of it," I said, "not as a story worth telling. Because it's unresolved. There's no way to know what really happened."

"That's all right," she said. "It's still a good story."

The guy in Inwood, it turned out, had used a .38-caliber revolver, and he'd cleaned it and loaded it earlier that same day. No chance it was an accident.

And if I'd never told the story over the years, that's not to say it hadn't come occasionally to mind. Vince Mahaffey and I never really talked about the incident, and I've sometimes wished we had. It would have been nice to know what really happened.

Assuming that's possible, and I'm not sure it is. He had, after all, sent me out of the room before doing whatever it was he did. That suggested he hadn't wanted me to know, so why should I think he'd be quick to tell me after the fact?

No way of knowing. And, as the years pass, I find I like it better that way. I couldn't tell you why, but I do.

Marcia Talley

Too Many Cooks

Few writers have made as large a splash on the mystery scene as
MARCIA TALLEY has recently. Her first Hannah Ives novel, *Sing
It to Her Bones,* won the Malice Domestic Grant in 1998 and was
nominated for an Agatha Award as Best First Novel of 1999.
Unbreathed Memories, the second in the series, was a Romantic
Times Reviewer's Choice nominee for Best Contemporary Mystery of 2000. Hannah's third adventure, *Occasion of Revenge,* was
released in August 2001. Marcia is also the editor of a collaborative
serial novel, *Naked Came the Phoenix,* where she joined twelve
bestselling women authors to pen a tongue-in-cheek mystery
about murder in an exclusive health spa. Her short stories have
appeared in magazines and collections, including "With Love,
Marjorie Ann," which received an Agatha Award nomination for
Best Short Story of 1999. She lives in Annapolis, Maryland, with
her husband, Barry, a professor at the U.S. Naval Academy. Her
Agatha–nominated story "Too Many Cooks," first published in
Much Ado About Murder, takes a humorous look at the three
witches of *Macbeth,* and how perhaps they weren't quite as sinister
as they appeared.

Too Many Cooks

Marcia Talley

History is not what you thought. It's what you can remember.
—W. C. Seller and R. J. Yeatman, *1066 and All That*

Merab wrapped her fingers tightly around the neck of the burlap sack and, with her free hand, gathered up the skirts of her gown and scrambled over the stile. Once over the wall, she relaxed against the smooth stones, grateful for their warmth as it penetrated the light fabric of her cloak. She closed her eyes, turned her face toward the sky, and inhaled deeply, delighting in the sweet smell of new-mown hay baking in the afternoon sun. A blissful moment later, she glanced back the way she had come, the hint of a smile on her lips. It had been only a small incantation, after all, but powerful enough to topple that ruffian, to send him sprawling with a satisfying *splat,* facedown into a puddle of mud that hadn't been there only seconds before.

A pity she hadn't been able to remember the spell before that other rogue had hurled an egg at her. She picked at the yolk spots on her plain gray gown. She shrugged—a small matter. They would hardly be noticed among the other stains—brown and tan and iridescent green—that speckled the panels of her skirt.

Dragging the sack and stepping high, Merab crossed the field. A soft breeze lifted her hair, sending the dark, tightly coiled strands dancing about her shoulders and drifting lazily across her cheeks. Overhead, a sparrow circled leisurely. "Later," she sang to the bird with a friendly wave of her hand. "Zipporah's expecting me and it doesn't do to keep Zipporah waiting."

The field ended at a dirt track deeply rutted by the wheels of the King's wagons. Merab followed the track for half a mile, then veered left at the three-trunked birch tree that marked the path through the wood to the cottage she shared with her sisters. "Cottage" was perhaps too grand a word for the elaborate lean-to of lashed timbers that made a shallow vestibule just outside the entrance to their true living quarters: a deep natural stone cave. In a sunny clearing to the left lay the garden, stoutly fenced to discourage the deer, and just beyond it, the hives.

As she emerged from the trees, Merab noticed white smoke drifting lazily from the roof hole and she feared she would be late for dinner. She slipped through the door and leaned, slightly breathless, against the jamb.

"There you are!" Zipporah set aside the mortar and pestle with which she had been grinding herbs for the stew, now cheerfully bubbling in an iron pot hanging from a spit over the grate. She wiped her hands on her apron. "I was beginning to think I'd have to send Little Miss Feckless out to find you." She nodded toward the hearth where Merab's younger sister, Dymphna, sat on a stool busily shelling peas into her skirt. "As much good as that would have done."

Merab flinched as Zipporah snatched the sack from her hand and snapped, "Let's see what you've brought us today, sister." Holding the sack by the bottom corners, she upended it, sending a cascade of small parcels, wrapped in brown cloth and tied with rough string, spilling over the tabletop. Zipporah felt along the edges of the sack, then shook it vigorously until the last packet, a small leather pouch, dropped out. She began sorting through them. "Dried whelk, laver, lizard's toe, shark's tongue, wolf teeth . . ." She looked up. "Where's the pepper?"

Merab picked up a twist of cloth, sniffed it, then placed it next to a small loaf of sugar. It wasn't always easy to separate the items they used for cooking from those they would need for spells. She sneezed.

"Bless you!" Zipporah muttered, barely pausing in her inventory. "Tiger gut, eye of new . . ."

Merab froze as Zipporah untied the packet and fingered the small dried pellets it contained. Newt eyes had grown so expensive that Merab had substituted toads' eyes for their slightly smaller and scarcer cousins. The bat wool she'd scraped from the inside of her own cloak, and although she couldn't say for sure, the Turk's nose the old leech had sold her that morning bore a remarkable resemblance to the nether end of a chicken. The pennies Merab had been able to save weighed heavily in her pocket, but oh! how she wanted a new gown. And how else to afford the fine wool, soft as eiderdown and blue as the Highland skies, that she'd been admiring each week at the market?

While Zipporah refolded the packet of toads' eyes and continued sorting, Merab inched toward Dymphna, whose head was bowed, her face nearly invisibly in the smoky room. She'd been oddly silent.

"Dymphna?"

Dymphna shuddered, and when she looked up, it was with red and swollen eyes. To Merab's utter astonishment, the girl's cheeks and chin were covered with a straggly beard the same cinnamon color as her hair.

"Dymphna!"

Her sister's face was a hirsute mask of misery. "It was the baldness remedy," she whimpered.

Zipporah's voice sliced through the haze like a scythe. "Silly hen got too close to the cauldron."

"You asked me to stir it!" Dymphna wailed.

Zipporah turned, hands on broad hips; eyes like currents in a plump Easter bun. "At least we know it works!" She threw back her head and roared with laughter, sending the chickens scurrying from under the table and into the yard.

Merab fished a small knife from her pocket. "Here. Let me cut it off."

"No!" Dymphna raised both hands. "I tried. It just comes back all the thicker."

Merab thought back to the big leather book the leech kept chained to his wall. She'd read something about this. "Southernwood boiled in barleymeal?"

"That's for pimples," Zipporah snorted. She shuffled across the room and loomed over the dejected Dymphna. "So much ado! It'll probably be gone by morning. In the meantime . . ." She pointed toward a small table set in a corner near the cottage's only window. "There's the book and there's the quill. Write down the recipe before you forget."

Holding her skirt out before her, Dymphna struggled to her feet. She dumped the peas, bouncing and pattering, into a wooden bowl, then, dragging her stool along with her, crossed to the table and sat down. She turned the book to a fresh page and smoothed it out carefully with the flat of her hand. After a thoughtful moment, she dipped the quill into a flask of ink and wrote "Receipt for Baldness" in a precise, round hand.

Truth to tell, there weren't many recipes in the book. In the year since Squire and Mistress Weird had perished in a tragic encounter with a wild boar, leaving their three daughters with nothing save two gold coins and this rude cottage, the women had struggled to support themselves with spell craft, conjuring, dowsing, and the occasional exorcism. Hecate dropped in from time to time to offer advice, but Zipporah had little patience for the hag's old-fashioned ways.

"Surely, to be profitable, magic must be put to more practical use," Zipporah was fond of saying. "Moon drops!" she had sniffed after Hecate's last visit. "If I listened to her, we'd soon be dancing around our cauldrons like fairies in a ring!"

Under their older sister's guidance, then, they'd turned their eyes toward practicalities. Six months ago Merab had witched a well for Lord Lennox, and the news of her success had quickly spread. They'd had a recent commission from Lady Macbeth, and the baldness potion had been for King Duncan himself. "A royal charter!" Zipporah had enthused, rubbing her work-roughened hands together. Thinking about Dymphna, Merab hoped King Duncan wouldn't mind looking like a monkey.

Her musing was interrupted by the hollow pounding of hooves and the barking of dogs. The cat napping on the sill near Dymphna's scribbling hand arched its brindled back and hissed at something outside the glass. Zipporah was halfway to the door when the knocking began.

"Mistress! Open up!"

Merab's fingers curled tightly around the knife she still held while Zipporah reached for the broom, then cautiously lifted the latch. She eased the door open and with one piercing black eye, peered through the crack. "Oh! It's you." Her shoulders relaxed and she threw the door wide to a young man Merab recognized by the badge on his tunic as a messenger from Inverness. "Come in." Zipporah held up a hand. "But wipe your feet first. I've just laid clean straw."

The messenger balanced unsteadily on their threshold, first on one foot and then the other, using the edge of his dagger to scrape layers of mud from his boots. "The Lady Macbeth sends her compliments." He wheezed. "She is riding this way and begs that you speak with her."

"We await her pleasure," said Zipporah.

Merab and Dymphna exchanged worried glances. Perhaps the potion hadn't worked. Soon they might be practicing their art from the bottom of the loch.

At Merab's invitation, the messenger dipped his drinking horn into a cask of barley water and drank deeply. Meanwhile, Dymphna threw another log on the fire and busied herself with the bellows.

But even before the messenger could drain his horn, Lady Macbeth stood tall in the doorway before them. She wore a blue robe, trimmed with pearls, and an overskirt embroidered with fine silver thread. A silver fillet held a square of pale gauze in place over her hair, which Merab could see was the color of burnished gold. "Greetings, Weird Sisters." The hand Lady Macbeth raised in salute was milky white, the fingers almost too narrow and delicate for the heavy rings they wore. "I've ridden all the way from Inverness to thank you."

Zipporah whisked a stool from under the table and bid their visitor sit. Lady Macbeth complied, settling her skirts prettily around her. Then she leaned forward, her voice low. "On Candlemas Eve, while my husband's servants were occupied preparing their master for bed, I slipped the potion you concocted into my husband's wine. Later when I crept into his chamber . . ." Astonishment sparkled in her violet eyes. "Never was there such a marvel! A veritable tent pole beneath the sheets!"

Lady Macbeth snapped her fingers and the messenger, who had been lounging negligently against the door frame, sprang to attention. "See to the dogs," she ordered. The youth scurried away. After he had gone, the lady continued. "As my lord is so fond of saying, 'Drink provokes the desire but takes away the performance.' But not that night. Saints, no! I think he was nearly as astonished as I."

Her eyes alight with joy, Lady Macbeth laid a hand on Zipporah's arm. "And now, I am with child, Mistress Weird!" She stroked her belly. "And I desire that this child shall be King of Scotland!"

"But, Lady!" Merab exclaimed. "Your husband is Thane of Glamis. The Thane of Cawdor stands between him and the kingdom, and both the Thane of Cawdor and King Duncan still live!"

Lady Macbeth's lips drew back in a smile, her teeth flashing white in the gathering dusk. "Exactly."

Merab's hand flew to her mouth, stifling a gasp.

Lady Macbeth drew her cloak more closely around her. "There must be some incantation, some potion to aid in our noble purpose."

Zipporah aimed a silencing glance at Merab, then bowed to the Lady. "Your wish is our command, dear Madam."

Lady Macbeth's gaze fell on each of the sisters in turn, then she winked. "My husband will be abroad tomorrow, hunting with his nobles on the heath." She rose from her stool and glided to the door as if she wore wheels rather than boots. Zipporah followed, bobbing up and down like a cork.

At the door, Lady Macbeth turned. From beneath her cloak she withdrew a small leather purse, shook it so the gold coins it contained clinked dully together, then placed the purse on Zipporah's upturned palm. "See to it, then." She smiled. "I can be very, very grateful." Waving a beringed hand, she caroled, "Farewell, my lovelies!" and in a miasma of sweet Arabian perfume, she was gone.

Zipporah latched the door and fell back upon it, both hands, still holding the purse, pressed over her heart. "What a triumph!" Suddenly her eyes narrowed. "Dymphna! Where are you?"

Dymphna emerged from the shadow of the wardrobe. Zipporah skewered the hapless girl with her eyes. "You did write it down, didn't you? The impotence cure? Tell me you wrote it down."

Dymphna's shaggy chin dipped to her chest. "The quill needed sharpening."

"You didn't write it down?" Zipporah's face grew dangerously red.

Dymphna shook her head. "But I'm sure I can remember!" she added brightly. "I have an excellent memory." She closed her eyes for a moment, then began speaking, as if reading the formula off the inside of her eyelids. "Mandrake root ground with seed of lemon, a pinch of St. John's wort, blue salts from the pools in the Sildenafil Hills . . ."

Zipporah's eyes grew hard. "How much salt?"

"I don't remember."

"A handful," Merab offered.

"And honey," Dymphna concluded. "That's all."

Zipporah sighed. "I pray you are right, sister. If not, it could take another one thousand years to recreate that formula!"

The next morning, two hours after the sun had gently nudged aside the moon, the Weird Sisters sat around their table amid a jumble of parchment scrolls and leather-bound volumes. Dymphna glanced up from the *Herbarium of Apuleius* she was perusing. "No poisons, Zipporah."

Merab nodded, her ebony curls bobbing vigorously. "I agree. No killing. I draw the line at killing."

Zipporah rested her chin on one hand. With the other she tapped her long fingernails on the tabletop.

"Maybe we can drive King Duncan away," Merab suggested. "Far, far away."

"But where?" Zipporah's nails clicked annoyingly against the wood.

"To England. I hear his son, Malcolm, is already there, petitioning King Edward for support."

"So?" Dymphna wanted to know.

"Macbeth is King Duncan's half-brother," Merab explained. "With both Duncan and Malcolm out of the country, Macbeth might well be declared King."

Dymphna stared at her sister, her eyes wide. "But Lady Macbeth expects us to meet her husband on the heath. Today!"

"We can still meet him. . . ." Zipporah said.

"With no ready spell? No incantation? No potion?"

Zipporah smiled. "Remember when you fell into the loch and I gave you that bolus for leg cramps?"

Dymphna nodded.

"Sugar."

Dymphna's eyebrows disappeared under an untidy fringe of hair. "Sugar, you say? But it worked! It cured my cramps!"

"The sugar cured nothing more than your mind, dear sister. So, until we can brew the proper potion, let us play with his mind."

"But will he believe whatever nonsense we tell him?" Merab watched as her older sister crossed to the cupboard, opened a carved wooden casket, and withdrew a leather pouch and a looking glass that had once belonged to their mother.

Zipporah propped the mirror against a candlestick, spread the contents of the pouch on the table in front of her, then began fastening rounded pellets of sap to her forehead and chin, smoothing out the edges and blending them seamlessly into her skin. She reserved a particularly large and misshapen pellet for the tip of her nose. "He will, dear sisters, if we dress the part."

Zipporah turned and Merab fell over backward, laughing, at her sister's transformation into a crone.

Zipporah's eyes darted appraisingly from Dymphna to Merab and back again. "Dymphna, you'll do as is."

Dymphna, whose beard had grown another two inches overnight, burst into tears.

"As for you, sweet Merab, you're far too comely for a midnight hag." Zipporah stuck her head into the wardrobe, rummaged about, and emerged in triumph a few moments later holding a tattered cloth of graying gauze. Holding it by the corners, she tossed it over Merab's head and watched as it settled lightly around her shoulders and hips, until its ragged edges just dusted the floor.

"You look like a plinth," Dymphna snuffled, dragging a frayed sleeve across her nose. "A cobweb-covered plinth."

Zipporah studied Merab's costume critically, the corners of her mouth turned down. "Don't just stand there, Merab. Wave your arms!"

Merab flapped her arms like a wounded stork.

"Now, moan."

The wounded stork keened and howled, as if near death.

Zipporah chortled. "That will have to do."

Merab dropped her weary arms and staggered about the room in a tight circle. "I can't see very well."

With a guiding hand on her back, Zipporah pushed Merab toward the door. "Never mind. You won't have to. Just follow my lead." She glanced over her shoulder at Dymphna, still sulking by the hearth. "Snap out of it. Dymphna! Come, now! It's show time!"

"Show?" Dymphna squeaked.

"Show!" cried her older sister.

"Show! Show! Show!" flapped the stork.

As the women had planned, Macbeth and his party stumbled upon the Weird Sisters on the banks of a rocky, babbling stream. Dymphna had coaxed some kindling and a pile of short logs into a hot fire and had set a small, three-legged cauldron, filled with water, over it to boil. When the steam began to rise, Zipporah tossed in a handful of greenish-yellow pellets. Singing "The Poor Soul Sat Sighing by a Sycamore Tree" in her reedy soprano, she circled the cauldron, around and around, until smoke boiled from it, spilled over the sides, and billowed across the brown furze thick as a winter's fog, licking hungrily at their ankles. The hunting party, with trumpets blaring and dogs braying, thundered to a halt a few hundred yards away, their banners fluttering in the mild breeze. While their steeds snorted and stamped, rattling their bridles, two men dismounted and approached warily.

"Banquo and Macbeth," Zipporah whispered. "I recognize them from the organized horse-battles last spring."

Dymphna pouted. "You'd think they'd be polite enough to remove their hats!" she complained.

Zipporah touched her sister's cheek. "Sweet Dymphna. Have you taken a good look at yourself?"

Dymphna's lower lip began to quiver dangerously under its new growth of beard. Zipporah held up a finger to silence her. "Shhhhhh. Here comes Banquo."

A tall man, wearing a rust-colored tunic with ties up the front and a cloak thrown over his broad shoulders, stopped twenty paces away, his left hand toying nervously with the hilt of his sword. "Who are you?" he demanded. His eyes narrowed. "At first I thought you were women, but then . . ." He squinted at Dymphna. "You are bearded!"

Dymphna stuck her chin out defiantly, but Merab could see that her sister's fingernails were digging deeply into her palms.

Merab felt Zipporah's elbow sharp against her ribs. "Whooo, whooo, whooo," she moaned.

Banquo staggered backward. "Are you not of this world?"

His companion raised a cautionary hand, then advanced with long, confident strides. Slightly shorter than his friend, Macbeth wore a Saxon tunic with a wide, embroidered hem and loose oversleeves. A belt, inlaid with precious stones, was buckled at his waist; he wore fine leather boots. "Speak!" Macbeth commanded.

Zipporah spread her arms wide. "All hail, Macbeth. Hail to you, Thane of Glamis!"

"All hail, Macbeth. Hail to you, Thane of Cawdor!" cried Dymphna, quickly catching on.

"All hail, Macbeth, who will be King hereafter!" finished Zipporah with another flourish of her arms.

Macbeth's eyes widened with astonishment. "But how can this be? The Thane of Cawdor still lives!"

"Eeyow, eeyow, eeyow!" Merab shrieked, completely ignoring the question.

"Wait a minute!" Banquo interjected, his face alight. "You've given my noble friend here a happy fortune. If you can really see into the future, what do you see in it for me?"

"Hail!" cried Merab.

"Hail!" croaked Dymphna.

"Hail!" shouted Zipporah. She leaned in Banquo's direction and whispered, "More is less and less is more."

Banquo's brow knit in puzzlement. "What is that supposed to mean?"

"Thou shall get kings though thou be none," chanted Zipporah.

Merab felt the sting of Zipporah's elbow again. She spun in a tight circle, arms pinwheeling. "Banquo and Macbeth, all hail!" she chanted. "Banquo and Macbeth, all hail!" until Zipporah touched her arm, signaling it was time for them to depart. The women turned their backs to the men and their faces toward the river.

"Wait a minute! Tell me more!" demanded Macbeth.

But Zipporah said nothing. With a theatrical gesture, she tossed another handful of pellets into the steaming cauldron. A choking mist arose, enveloping them all. "Come, sisters," she hissed into the fog. "Let us fly!"

Leaving the two men to stumble blindly back to their horses, the Weird Sisters scurried away, following the bank of the stream until they found themselves once again in the safety of the wood.

"Why did we run?" panted Dymphna, doubled over with her hands resting on her knees.

Merab had stripped off her shroud and was leaning against a tree. "Yes, why?"

"Always," Zipporah grinned toothily, "leave them wanting more." She peeled a wart off her cheek and laughed.

Two days later, the rising sun found the sisters gathered once more around their table. "It's a message from Lady Macbeth," Zipporah said as she spread the parchment out on the table in front of her. "Do you want the good news first, sisters, or the bad news?"

Merab circled the table, ladling pease porridge into their trenchers. "What does the message say?"

"The Thane of Cawdor has been executed for treason."

The ladle clattered against the pot. "That means . . ."

"Exactly," said Zipporah. "And King Duncan is coming to Castle Inverness *tonight."*

"But we haven't had time to prepare the potion with the power of persuasion," worried Dymphna, her face once again clear and pink owing to the belated application of a paste made of lentils, blue-green algae, and flaxseed.

Zipporah shoved her porridge to one side. "I know. And the lady requires more of the sleeping potion, as well." She rose from her chair and crossed to the shelf, where she rummaged through the clutter of flasks, vials, and bottles assembled there. One by one, she lifted the stoppers and sniffed. "Ah, here it is." She set the flask aside. "Now," she said, "we've no time to lose! Quickly, Dymphna! Where did you put the recipe?"

In less time than it took to churn butter, the Weird sisters stood, once again, around a bubbling cauldron. "Double Bubble, spoil the hubble . . ." Zipporah read from the parchment Dymphna had produced.

Merab peered cautiously into the cauldron. "It's pink," she said in a worried voice. She dipped in an experimental finger. "And sticky."

Zipporah shook her head. "That's not right. It should be brown." She squinted suspiciously at the parchment, its edges brown and curling, the writing dense and crabbed. She held the parchment close to her nose, then at arm's length before sending an accusing glance in Dymphna's direction. "Are you sure this is the potion with the power of persuasion, sister?"

Dymphna nodded. "Would you like *me* to read it?"

Zipporah blinked twice, shrugged, then thrust the parchment toward Dymphna. "Very well. You read. I'll stir." She grasped the wooden paddle with both hands and began stirring, her whole body swaying rhythmically with each turn of the paddle.

> *Double, double, toil and trouble,*
> *Fire burn and cauldron bubble,*

read Dymphna.

> *Fillet of a fenny snake,*
> *In the cauldron boil and bake.*

Dymphna nodded at Merab, who selected a serpentine object from the ingredients laid out on the table in front of her and tossed it into the pot.

As the snake sank, Merab studied the pink mixture with rising panic. Surely it wouldn't make any difference? What could it matter that she'd collected that snake from the woods and not from the fen?

"Merab!" She was suddenly aware that Zipporah was shouting at her.

Merab returned her attention to her task. As Zipporah stirred and Dymphna chanted, Merab tossed the ingredients, as Dymphna called for them, one by one into the pot.

Eye of newt . . .

Merab's heart began to hammer against her ribs.

> *And toe of frog.*
> *Wool of bat,*
> *And tongue of dog.*

Merab was breathing so rapidly she felt light-headed. Tongue of dog! O gods and goddesses! She hadn't been able to bring herself to do it. The mongrel had been brown and white, its tail wagging joyously, its nose wet and black against her cheek. Merab reached for a shriveled strip of dried venison and tossed it into the pot instead.

Zipporah stirred more vigorously, her heels rising in and out of her shoes. "Now!" she cried.

> *Double, double, toil and trouble,*
> *Fire burn and cauldron bubble,*

the three sisters chanted in unison.

> *Scale of dragon, tooth of wolf,*

Dymphna continued.

> *Witches mummy, maw and gulf*
> *Of the ravin'd salt-sea shark,*
> *Root of hemlock digg'd i' the dark . . .*

Swift as raindrops flying before the wind, the magic words tumbled from Dymphna's mouth, and just as quickly, Merab tossed the ingredients, one after the other, into the pot. The mixture boiled thick and slimy— bubbles formed, swelled, and erupted on the surface of the sludge like breakfast porridge. As Merab watched, the porridge in her own stomach churning, the mixture gradually changed from pink to lavender, from lavender to gray, from gray to a dull brown. The storm raging in her stomach began to subside.

Zipporah blessed the mixture with a final counterclockwise stir. A pale finger of bluish smoke drifted toward the ceiling and swirled around the tied bundles of herbs drying in the rafters. "There! That should do it."

Merab stepped back from the cauldron with relief. "I'm curious about something, Zipporah. Back there on the heath. Why did you talk in riddles? Why didn't you tell Macbeth straight out that he'd be king?"

Using a wooden spoon, Zipporah ladled the potion into an earthenware jar that the Queen's messenger would soon take to the castle kitchens. "Men like conundrums," she explained. "It gives them something to puzzle over. If Lord Macbeth didn't have to figure some of it out for himself, no one could convince him we'd given him his money's worth."

It was quiet in the woodland cottage for the next several weeks. While Zipporah tended the garden—plucking weeds, loosening the dirt around the roots of the parsnips and carrots, picking bugs off the leaves of the lettuce plants—Merab brewed up a batch of comfrey for the butcher's bronchitis and a love potion for the tavern-keeper, whose wife had run away with the handsome, young ironmonger. Dymphna studiously copied recipes into her book.

On the second day of the third week, the sisters had just settled down for a dinner of roast capon and peas, when a sudden commotion on the roof of the cottage made them lay down their knives and look up at one another in alarm. A clatter like hail erupted from the hearth and smoke blew backward down the chimney, scattering ashes in every direction.

Suddenly Hecate stood solid as a tree before them. From neck to ankles, the Mistress of the Moon was swathed in diaphanous silver robes; a cape spun of cobwebs shimmered from her shoulders. In contrast, her face was flushed with rage and her mouth worked up and down soundlessly.

Merab sprang to her feet, gingerly brushing a glowing cinder from her skirt. "Hecate! Why do you look so angry?"

Hecate shrugged out of her cape, letting it drift to the floor, where it settled in a glistening pool at her feet. "Haven't I good reason, you brazen hussies?" she hissed.

Zipporah rose from her chair, elbowed Merab out of her way, and stood before the enraged goddess. "I'm sure we don't have the slightest idea what you're talking about, Madam."

Hecate leaned forward, sputtering hellfire. "How *dare* you work spells on behalf of that man without consulting me?" Her eyes, cold as winter ice, locked with Zipporah's. "Amateurs! Bumbling amateurs! Do you know what you've done?"

Merab shook her head, eyes downcast, as Hecate's icy gaze settled on her.

"Do you?" Hecate shouted at Dymphna.

Dymphna recoiled.

Hecate jabbed a long, crooked finger in the direction of Dymphna's upturned nose. "What on earth did you tell the man? What did you tell Macbeth?"

"Please, Madam. Sit." With the toe of her shoe, Zipporah pushed a stool cautiously in Hecate's direction. Hecate considered it for a moment, then, reining in her temper like a team of wild horses, she swallowed her anger and sat down with a flump.

"We told him he'd be King," Zipporah confessed. "We thought we'd give him something to think about until we had time to prepare the potion that would actually make it happen."

Hecate's voice dripped with sarcasm. "Apparently the man and his lady wife were unwilling to wait."

"What?" Merab's hands flew to her cheeks, her mouth yawning wide.

Hecate nodded gravely. "Macbeth murdered King Duncan that very night."

Dymphna collapsed heavily on the hearth, her hands pressed between her knees. "Surely you're mistaken! Lord Macbeth a murderer? But he seemed so good-natured!"

"No mistake," said Hecate. "And they wasted little time moving their house hold from Inverness to the royal castle at Dunsinane."

"But what about King Duncan's bodyguards?" Merab wondered.

"Suspicion fell on them at first, of course," Hecate explained, "especially when they were found smeared with blood, sleeping with a bloody dagger between them."

"Sleeping?" Merab cried. "That makes no sense at all. Why wouldn't they have flown after committing so vile a deed?"

"They were locked—all unknowing—in Morpheus's arms." Hecate reached inside her purse and withdrew a familiar, pear-shaped object. "I discovered this flask near their cots."

Merab plucked the familiar flask from Hecate's hands, removed the cork, stared at the milky residue coating the bottom, and sniffed. She turned toward Zipporah, one eyebrow raised in surprise. "This is the sleeping draught we prepared for Lady Macbeth!"

Hecate leaned forward. "I rather thought so."

"So the Lady drugged the guards and murdered the King while they slept?"

"Not the Lady. Lord Macbeth himself."

Dymphna sprang to her feet. She had found her tongue at last. "But what of the other potion we prepared for the Lady?"

Hecate's eyebrows knit in puzzlement. "What other potion?"

"Our plan was bloodless, Madam, and twofold. Lady Macbeth was to introduce the potion into the mussel broth to be served at the banquet. It would bewitch King Duncan with an overwhelming desire to join his son in England. Then the nobles, equally enchanted and twice as fickle, would declare Macbeth King."

Zipporah groaned. "We sent complete instructions! Oh, why didn't

Lady Macbeth use the potion? Why didn't she give it a chance to work?"

Hecate's words were blunt. "Maybe she did. Perhaps the fault lay in the potion."

Thinking about her secret economies, Merab felt herself shrinking inside her skin. Soon she would be as tiny as the field mouse that sometimes winked at her from the darkened corner near the hearth. If only she hadn't been so selfish! If she had it to do all over again, she'd pay whatever it cost for the newt eyes, she'd even sail to Constantinople and slice the nose off Sultan Ala-ud-din-Kaidobad himself.

"But we followed the formula," Dymphna protested. "Exactly."

Hecate's voice softened. "Yet something went quite wrong at the banquet, I fear. Lord Macbeth had a fever on the brain. He had visions of bloody heads. He saw Banquo's ghost. On and on he raved, until Lady Macbeth sent the guests home and hustled her husband, raving still, to his bedchamber."

"Perhaps he was drunk," Merab suggested.

"Besides," Zipporah added, "Banquo's not dead. We saw him ourselves not long ago. With Lord Macbeth. On the heath."

"Oh, Banquo's quite, quite dead." Hecate cast her eyes heavenward. "I passed his blameless soul as it soared over the moon, heading toward the stars."

"Who . . . ?" Dymphna's eyes grew wide.

"Three thugs, his spirit told me. Hired by Macbeth."

Zipporah bowed her head. "Macbeth is obsessed, 'tis certain, twisted by ambition. Even now, with the kingship firmly in his grasp, he rages on." She looked up. "Oh, Hecate! Does his lust know no bounds?"

"I must lay that responsibility at your feet, Zipporah. What did you put into that potion? Insane root?"

Merab stepped between Hecate and her older sister. "No potion's to blame, Madam. We told Banquo he would beget kings."

"And for that, he died," Dymphna whimpered.

Zipporah straightened. "Where's Macbeth now?"

"Pursuing Macduff," Hecate informed them.

"But surely I heard that Macduff is safely away with Malcolm in England?"

Hecate looked grave. "No one, I fear, is safe from Macbeth's evil designs and enterprises. But rest easy," she continued. "I believe I've found the solution. Remember the old sow's blood charm?" She grinned. "I used it to conjured up some apparitions for our impatient King. First a talking head. Then a bloody child. 'None of woman born shall harm Macbeth,' I bid the child say." She cackled, her mouth wide, revealing black and pointed teeth. "I'm particularly proud of that riddle."

"*All* men are born of woman," Dymphna insisted.

Hecate looked amused. "So it would seem."

Dymphna stared at the rafters for a moment, then shrugged and pointed at her sister. "Zipporah's good at riddles."

Hecate considered this information with a satisfied expression on her face. "Try this one, then: 'Macbeth shall never vanquished be until Great Birnamwood to high Dunsinane hill shall come against him.' "

The furrows deepened in Dymphna's brow. "How could a wood remove to the top of a hill?"

Zipporah spoke at last. "It can't, of course. That's what makes it so brilliant. With Macbeth secure in his kingship, the carnage should cease."

Dymphna clapped her hands. "Moon and stars be praised! What you said about Macduff troubled me greatly for it's not only he who's endangered, but his wife and precious children, too."

Hecate smiled modestly, then waved an impatient hand. "Speaking of danger, why didn't you answer my question? What *did* you put into that potion?"

Dymphna plucked the parchment from an earthenware pot where she had stored it, unrolled the document, and recited the ingredients, one by one, as her finger traced a path down the page. "Adder's fork, blind-worm's sting, lizard's let, howlet's wing, goat gall, yew . . ." When she had finished, she turned to Hecate. "Well?"

"It sounds right." Hecate sat in silence for a moment, thinking. "But in truth, I'm puzzled, because the insanity didn't stop with the King. Now it's Lady Macbeth who's gone stark-staring mad. Everybody's talking about it. The torches are always lit in the castle. She walks in her sleep. And lately I've heard reports of compulsive hand-washing." Hecate slid off the stool and hovered before them, her feet floating a hand's breadth above the floor. "I don't know what went wrong, but it's up to me, as usual, to set things right." Her eyes blazed. "Do you have any of that potion left?"

Zipporah nodded. "In the cupboard. In the large crock."

Hecate picked up the crock with both hands, crossed to the hearth, and emptied its contents into the cauldron. She glared at Merab. "Now, mistress, the rest of your stores!"

"Oh, no!" Merab wailed.

Hecate was firm. "It's the only way." While she stood to one side, heckling and prodding, the sisters reluctantly emptied all their potions, tonics, elixirs, tinctures, and physics, each bolus and pill, every ointment, syrup, and lotion, into the iron cauldron. Once, Hecate caught Dymphna's hand just as it disappeared into her pocket with a vial of syrup extracted from eastern poppies. "I said *everything!*" and Dymphna watched, long-faced, as the pain remedy joined its brethren in the pot, soon swirling with a malignant, purplish-green sludge.

Zipporah's eyes lingered on her jars, flasks, flagons, bottles, boxes, and bowls, all empty, lined up on the tabletop. "I think your measures excessive, Madam."

Hecate gathered up her gossamer cloak and, with a flourish, settled the shimmering fabric over her shoulders. She floated toward the door. "Next time perhaps you'll consult me before going off with your bows half-strung.

Now," she commanded, pointing to the cauldron, "dump it—*all* of it—into the loch."

"Loch Ashie?" The mixture stared up at Merab like a malevolent blob and she vowed she'd never bathe in the clear, cool waters of Loch Ashie again.

"No, fool. Loch Ness." And with a final stab of her finger, Hecate vanished.

"Come!" Zipporah ordered. "Let's get this over with before that wretched hag returns. Dymphna, you fetch the wheelbarrow."

Merab already had her arms around the belly of the cauldron at its widest part. "Umph!" she grunted. "I can't do this by myself."

Zipporah helped Merab inch the cauldron across the floor of beaten earth toward the waiting wheelbarrow. "When I count to three, lift," Zipporah instructed. She adjusted her grip, took a deep breath—*one, two, three!*

"Oh!" shouted Merab, staggering under the sudden weight. She watched helplessly as the liquid swirled dangerously, reared over the lip of the cauldron with tentacle-like fingers, and sloshed, wet and slightly warm, all over her clothing. "Oh, dear," she exclaimed, but she was too busy to do anything but ignore it. Swearing and grunting, the women muscled the cauldron into the wheelbarrow, then stepped back, arms tingling with fatigue, to catch their breath.

Zipporah suddenly gasped. "Look, Merab! Look at your gown!"

Merab stared. Where once she had worn plain, gray homespun, scorched with pinholes and decorated with flecks of soil and food, her gown was now fine and white, spotless as a field of high mountain snow. "My spots!" she whooped. "They're gone!"

Dymphna smiled at Zipporah slyly. "I suppose you'll be wanting me to write this formula down, won't you, sister?" With her thumb and index finger, she penned an imaginary note against the cloudless blue sky. "Receipt for Spot Remover."

"What I want," Zipporah grumbled, "is to consign every drop of this loathsome liquid to the bottom of Loch Ness. Then, I plan to take up something safe, like midwifery, and forget we ever heard of the King and Queen of Dunsinane."

Merab's brow knit in puzzlement. "But I don't understand. If Macbeth . . ."

Zipporah pressed a finger, hard, against her sister's lips. "It's bad luck to say his name! I forbid it. From henceforth whenever we refer to that man, if we refer to him at all, it will be as 'that Scottish King.' "

She bent her knees, lifted the handles of the wheelbarrow, and with Dymphna straggling behind, rolled it down the path, through the garden, past the hives and into the wood. With the cat weaving about her ankles, Merab watched until Zipporah's silver head and Dymphna's copper one were lost among the shimmer of the early summer leaves. Merab gazed down in wonder at the pristine landscape of her gown. "Too bad it isn't blue," she said to the cat. And she went inside to consult the *Herbarium* to see what she could do about that.

Robert Barnard

The Path to the Shroud

ROBERT BARNARD was born in 1936 in Essex, England, and has served as lecturer and professor at universities in Australia and Norway. His innovative novels are well-plotted solutions of murders, but are also noteworthy for their wit, social satire, and the author's depiction of human nature at its best, worst, and everything in-between. Besides his more than thirty novels, Barnard is also the author of nonfiction works about Agatha Christie and Charles Dickens, as well as *A Short History of English Literature*. He is one of those writers who has never written the same book twice, finding new ways of turning old forms into contemporary crime fiction of the highest rank. The story chosen for inclusion in this year's volume, "The Path to the Shroud," which first appeared in *Ellery Queen's Mystery Magazine,* is a fine example of a mystery master at the top of his game.

The Path to the Shroud

Robert Barnard

Violetta knew she had made a mistake almost as soon as she got into the shop. She had come in because she noticed a sign saying "English Books" in the window. English newspapers had been easy to obtain in Parma, books less so. Now that she was inside the shop, she realized just from casting her eyes around the covers of books on display that she was in a religious bookshop. Not at all what she needed. She was in Italy for experiences, but not for religious ones, or not Christian ones. She dawdled around the pokey interior only to avoid the ungraciousness of walking straight out again.

The face hit her before she even found the section of English books. The sepia image of a bearded man, infinitely kind, unendingly forgiving: the picture of a man (Violetta thought) who grieved for the sufferings and forgave the transgressions of his fellow men—strong, loving, understanding. Who was he? She struggled with the title of the book: *Il Sudario di Torino*. She frowned.

Torino she knew. It was one of the places she had put among the possibilities on her itinerary: Turin. Then "sudario"—but of course! She didn't even need to scrabble in her bag for her pocket dictionary: This must be the face of the man on the Turin Shroud.

She looked again, concentrating on the face. The man seemed to look back, equally intent on her. Again she felt that the eyes of the man *saw*, saw *into*, understood. It was as if her whole life, her rackety, unstructured, uncertain journey through this and that enthusiasm or commitment, was in this man's brain as he gazed at her, and as if his insight gave the whole messy cycle a meaning and a purpose.

"Do you have this book in English?" Violetta asked the woman behind the counter. She shook her head slowly, but went over to the two or three shelves of English books to check. Then she shook her head more decidedly.

"Is not 'ere in Eenglish. In Torino maybe you find."

"I'm going to Turin," said Violetta, suddenly definite.

"Turin, yes. You find there per'aps. We 'ave phamplet in four languages. Maybe you like, so you read a little first?"

Violetta took the proffered "phamplet," and immediately decided to pay the four thousand lire demanded for it. The face was on the front page, and English was one of the four languages, along with French, Spanish, and German. She went out into the morning sunlight with a strange feeling of lightness, almost of happiness. She couldn't remember the last time she had felt almost happy.

She didn't look at the pamphlet when she got back to her hotel room. She saved it up. She showered, made herself up as if going to a party, then went back into town and made for the great square in front of the cathedral and baptistery. She walked purposefully across its cobbled expanse to the Angiol d'Oro nestling in the corner. She had been saving up one of the few remaining good restaurants of Parma, and tonight was certainly the night. She had no need of a book to console her loneliness. She watched the other customers, relished the food slowly, and dreamed of the bearded face that had somehow—miraculously?—been preserved on the shroud. She ended with the best Gorgonzola she had ever had in her life, relished the last of the wine, then headed back to her hotel.

The pamphlet was still nestling in the big, shabby old bag she always took with her on these exploratory holidays. She took it out, then sat on her bed feeling replete, contented, and above all full of anticipation.

She read the text of the pamphlet first. It was aimed at the faithful—and Violetta had never been that, in any sense. However, it did not shrink from the findings of modern research. Scientists were of the opinion (they did avoid the word "proved") that the shroud was in fact of thirteenth or fourteenth century provenance, just the period when mentions of this wonderful relic of Christ's death began to be recorded. The image of the man was not made by any conventional paint, stain, or other artist's material. Indeed, it seemed that science was unable to suggest what the image consisted of at all, other than with such (unscientific, surely?) images as "a burst of radiant energy." That conjecture tickled Violetta's interest almost as much as the face itself. She looked back at the cover.

Violetta was a great frequenter of art galleries—hence, Italy, hence the Italian cities slightly off the usual tourist trail. Her interest in art was amateur but intense. And she could swear that the image of the man on the shroud was like no image of a man in any thirteenth or fourteenth century painting. It was too realistic, not stylized enough. This was a man you could touch, imagine embracing. It was like an old sepia photograph of one's great-grandfather as a young or youngish man. Even if the image were of paint, Violetta could not have believed it was made in the thirteenth century.

As it was, it was not of paint, it was made by some substance or process unknown even to modern science, and it was an image startlingly modern in its realism.

Violetta got up and poured herself a whiskey from the liter bottle she had had to trail around Parma to find. She had been devastated to discover at Heathrow that duty-free bottles were no longer available to travelers within Europe.

"Bugger the Common Market!" she had shouted at the girl behind the till. Still, she had at last found a supply in Parma, and would get more before moving on, just in case.

Walking around her hotel room, whiskey-and-water in hand, Violetta decided that she was rather pleased the shroud was of medieval material. It removed the religious trappings, which roused no resonances in her own mind.

It left, though, the image of a medieval man, and the mystery of an image of him projected onto his shroud by no known means. That was exciting.

Violetta had always felt she had a gift for the paranormal, just as she had had a series of flirtations with alternative therapies and folk medicines. Karmas and Eastern thought systems and even simple hypnotism were things that fascinated her, and she had been "into" many of them with great thoroughness before passing on to the next enthusiasm. She had no problem with an image, whether of Christ or of some medieval man, projected after death onto the shroud in which his body was wrapped. She definitely preferred the idea of its being a man of the thirteenth or fourteenth century. Christ was a known factor: Both the worshiper and the skeptic had a picture of him based on things he did, things he said—or was supposed to have done and said. But the medieval man had mystery: The nature of this figure who lived life so intensely that his image projected itself after death onto his shroud was no problem to absorb for one who had taken spirit manifestations and advice from the great beyond in her stride. Its attraction was that *she* could create him from his image. From the fact, that body, she could mold a figure in whom she could believe.

"A man of Turin," she said out loud. "Perhaps the ancestor of a man, even many men, living in Turin today."

Two whiskeys later, as she drifted off into sleep, the image of the man was gaining substance. A man who filled every minute with vitality, experience, passion; one who "loaded every rift with ore" because he sensed that his life would be short. A man who lived and understood life so completely and intensely would be one who understood others, saw through to their essence, knew and forgave them because life was not for the saints and the mystics and the hermits. It was a messy business for all the rest—people who tried to engage with it totally.

The next day Violetta took the train to Turin. Coming out of the magnificent station, she saw the Grand Palace Hotel. Somewhere a little bit grander than she was used to. Somewhere where she might entertain people . . . someone. She walked across, found they had a room vacant, and took it.

That evening she did no more than prowl around the environs of the hotel and station, dropping into a little restaurant for pasta and then swordfish. She read the Terry Pratchett she had brought with her. It would be ostentatious to read about the shroud in Turin itself.

The next day she really set out to explore the city. She walked and walked, her eyes darting everywhere as she fluttered from wide street into spacious square.

Eventually, she knew, she would go and see the shroud. The real thing was on exhibition for millennium year. Normally only a copy was shown, even to the faithful. But the shroud could wait. She skirted the great squares of the old Piedmontese capital, sometimes glancing at the expensive shops, but usually trailing her eyes restlessly from face to face, from besuited business executives to overalled plumbers and builders, from waiters and bus drivers to tourists in shorts and loud skirts. After an hour or more she sat down at a table in an outdoor café on the Piazza Castello.

"Una spremuta di arancia, per favore," she told the waiter, after subjecting him to a prolonged but unsatisfactory scrutiny.

Restlessly she resumed her inspection of the townsmen from afar. Absentmindedly she stirred sugar into her *spremuta.* Tasted it—delicious. She sat back in her chair.

Then, suddenly, she saw him. She would have said to the end of her life, if she had lived long, that an emanation from him came across the huge square from the royal palace at the far side and seized her. Perhaps the truth was that he was standing in the middle, and matched from afar the specifications of what she was seeking. Tall, bearded—and even from a distance, she felt sure, magnetic. She slapped notes down on the table and left the café, crossing the road, then into the main body of the Piazza Castello. Now she could see him from a distance of twenty yards or so, still looking in her direction. Suddenly he turned and walked in the direction of the royal palace. There was no question what Violetta would do. She had already marked it down as one of her sort of places. Now it moved to being a top priority.

She strode ahead, almost running in her eagerness not to lose sight of him—past tourists feeding the birds, past a newsstand with a placard reading: ANCORA UNA DONNA UCCISA. She gained the entrance to the palace and saw him coming out of the ticket office–cum–bookshop. Breathless by now, she ran in and again slapped money down. The woman behind the grille told her that a tour started in five minutes. Trying to get her breath back, she stood for a moment outside, under the dark arches that bordered the central courtyard. There was a little knot of people to her left, and cautiously she went over and mingled with them. Almost all seemed to be tourists. But there, among them, he was: tall, solidly built, with the bushy beard and long hair of the shroud giving him the air of a young patriarch. He was half turned away from her so she could not see his eyes. Then a small woman came along to herd them together, apologizing for her poor English but explaining that in every room there was a notice in three languages explaining the room's contents and purpose. Violetta wondered whether the Man of the Shroud spoke English.

Once they got past the magnificent staircase, it was easy to keep close to him. Sometimes she darted up to the notices and ostentatiously read the English text. It was in the third room, the Queen's Reception Room, that he came up behind her and spoke to her.

"You like palaces and such things?"

His voice was soft but urgent, his English heavily accented but seductive. Seductive on a high intellectual and spiritual plane, Violetta decided.

"Very much," she answered, smiling up at him. Now she could see his eyes, which had a piercing intensity. "This one is very fine, if maybe a little musty."

"Musty? What is musty? You hexplain?"

"Musty—well, it's old, a bit shabby, decaying a little."

"Ah, I understand. But it is old. Nothing 'as been done to it for years. The kings of Savoy, they became kings of Hitaly, then kings of nowhere at all. You see?"

"Very well. You speak beautiful English."

"Not at all. I need a good teacher. So you see, no one 'as lived 'ere for years, for a century and a 'alf. So it become a bit musty, like you say. But full of 'istory."

"Yes, it's certainly that. Was this king who became King of Italy the one called Victor Emmanuel, or was that later?"

"Italy have two kings called Vittorio Emanuelle, two called Umberto. The wife of the first King Umberto, Queen Margherita, she 'ave a pizza named after her."

"Oh, of course."

"The second Umberto, 'e die in exile, and 'e give the shroud to the Cathedral."

"*Really?* The shroud! . . . Has anyone ever told you that you look like the man in the shroud?"

The man—still she did not know his name—shrugged.

"Some."

"Plenty of women, I should think."

"Some. Men and women." He said it distinctly, as if offended.

"I'm sorry. I didn't mean to suggest you were a ladykiller."

She did not notice his faint start.

"What is that—a lady-what?"

"Ladykiller. It's another word for a Don Juan or a Casanova."

"Ah—a Casanova. Maybe all Italian men have a little bit of a Casanova in them."

"Maybe they do. . . . Do you live in Turin?"

"Yes—I have a little flat."

She nearly asked him what a native of Turin was doing going on a conducted tour of one of its monuments with a party of tourists, but she bit the question back.

"It must be a wonderful city to live in."

"It is very hexciting. It suits me. I live my life fully and eagerly."

"I'm sure you do!" She said it not flirtatiously but seriously. "I felt that, too, about the man in the shroud."

"You did?"

"Scientists who have carbon-dated it say it's not two thousand years old, just six hundred or so. I had the idea, the image of a man of the Middle Ages or the Renaissance who had lived life to the full, with such energy, such zest. . . . Eagerly, like you said."

"Maybe you are right. Maybe he was my many-greats-grandfather."

They looked at each other and laughed. If she had not been under the spell of the shroud, she might have seen that his eyes were cold, that they belied his laugh.

The tour of the royal apartments was coming to an end. They emerged into the courtyard of the palace, then through an arch back to the Piazza Castello. Violetta could see her man for the first time in the sunlight. How strong the mouth was, how bright the eyes! He was even more exciting than she had thought.

"I've been so glad of your company. Could I buy you coffee? Or lunch—it's not far off lunchtime."

"Alas—I have to go back to my flat, my studio. I am a poor artist. I must get images from the palace into my sketchbook—mere stuff for the tourist trade, you understand, but my living. This hevening. What about dinner this hevening?"

"What a good idea!" said Violetta, at last giving way to her girlish flirtatiousness. "Why don't you come to my hotel? I believe the Grand's dining room is excellent. Or we could go out to a restaurant."

The man shook his head.

"I am not a person to call at a respectable hotel. I would not compromise a fine lady like yourself—me, a poor, dirty artist. You come to my flat. I cook you a fine meal, authentic, something handed down in my family for generations."

"How exciting!"

"I promise you, exciting! Here is my card. You come at eight?"

"Eight o'clock," she said, looking at the card, "Mario Pertusi."

"But you can call me Casanova. The ladykiller."

They both laughed again. She wished she could kiss him her *arrivederci,* but she just said it and raised her hand, walking away across the square, past the newsstand with its shrieking headline, past the cafés and the banks and the tourist office. Before plunging into the small streets leading to the cathedral she looked around, but her poor eyesight did not allow her to see Mario Pertusi still watching her from the entrance to the Palazzo Madama, his eyes cold and searing, his thin-lipped mouth open in anticipation.

And while Pertusi went back to his studio flat, with its crude drawings of women in notebook after notebook, its worse-than-amateur attempts at oil paintings of screaming red mouths, bulging eyes, slashed breasts, which he now turned with practiced hand to the wall, Violetta went to the cathedral and the line to see the shroud, under skies that were clouding over fast. She was told that you had to buy a ticket to see it, and that the ticket office (of course) was elsewhere, back in the Piazza Castello. When she had bought it and taken it back to the cathedral, she was told that the ticket was for admittance at a certain time—at seven o'clock that evening, in fact.

"Are you trying to keep the damned thing secret?" she yelled at the scandalized priest on the door, then turned and ran out into the heavy rain that had now been pouring for five minutes. She looked around at the sodden nuns, at the priests with little groups from their villages, the women's groups that bore an awful resemblance to British Women's Institutes. She screwed up her ticket and dropped it on the cathedral steps.

"I don't need to see him," she said. "I've seen him."

She made her way, absurdly happy and at peace, back to the Grand Hotel. She didn't need lunch—couldn't face anything so mundane. In her room she bathed, then lay on her bed dreaming, *seeing* him—the all-forgiving eyes, the air of vast and varied experience, the presence of a man who took on his shoulders the whole burden of sinning humanity.

Soon she sank into a light doze. Then she got up, put on her best and silkiest underclothes, her smartest dress. She emptied her bag to find his card and looked at his address. That was easy enough: a tiny street off the Via dell' Accademia. She could hardly wait, but forced herself to. To drink whiskey would be like some kind of profanation. She must have all her senses alert, alive. At last it was time. She skirted the Piazza Carlo Felice till she found the Street of the Academy. At last she found Mario's little road, and number twelve. It was an old house, shabby, dirtied by a million Fiats, by the dust and grime of passing humanity. There were no bells on the outside, but plenty of light inside. He had put them on for her. Third floor, it had said on the card. She went inside and walked up the stairs, hardly able to contain her excitement. There were two flats on the third floor, one seemingly empty. On the other was the name: MARIO PERTUSI. She waited for one delicious moment.

Then she rang the bell to begin her assignation with her shroud.

Jerry Sykes

Closer to the Flame

JERRY SYKES's short stories have appeared in a number of magazines and anthologies. He is also the editor of the anthology *Mean Time: New Crime for a New Millennium*. His fiction is stamped with a British working-class melancholy that reminds many readers of the Angry Young Man era of Britain back in the late 1950s and early 1960s, when such important authors as John Osborne, Colin Wilson, and Alan Sillitoe were emerging. Although many American writers set books and stories in the United Kingdom, it is rare to see an author from the other side of the pond set a story in the United States. We are very pleased to present a fine example of the latter, "Closer to the Flame," first published in the British anthology *Crime in the City*.

Closer to the Flame

Jerry Sykes

In the distance the surface of the Colorado River shimmered like snakeskin in the late afternoon sun. Small tufts of mist broke on the pebble shores and lifted into the air like tender smoke. On the near bank, the interstate rose out of the mosaic of motels and office blocks at the foot of the Convention Center, stalked across the river and disappeared into the emerald ripples of land that bordered the city to the south.

Dennis Lane stared out across the hill country where it seemed he had spent his entire childhood alone and afraid, waiting for his father to return home with the latest form of discipline he had discovered to help him in his responsibility as a sole parent. His mother had died when Dennis was three and his father had struggled to look after him on his own. A willing student, he had listened to everyone for advice—from the school principal and the local doctor to his unmarried sister down in Galveston and his friends on the bowling team. Not that it made any difference. In the end he had always fallen back on his hands, and Dennis had soon come to resent the people who had made his father feel such a failure: his father probably would have fared much better if left to his own devices and free from secondhand expectations, and Dennis himself would have been much happier. He closed his eyes for a moment and shook the memories from his head and then turned away from the hills.

Reflected in the side of the Convention Center he could see the dome of the state capitol, an Austin landmark for over a hundred years. Built from pink granite quarried at nearby Marble Falls, the building had once been the seventh largest in the world, and it still drew an impressive number of visitors each year—but still nowhere near as many visitors as the building on which he himself now stood.

The sun broke free from the shade of the thunderheads that had started to bunch overhead, and he blinked at the sudden shock to his pupils. He dropped his head to look out across the clipped spread of lawn at the foot of the tower. School had been out a couple of months but a number of students still decorated the area. In the far corner of the lawn a man dressed in purple track pants practiced tai chi, calm and deliberate in his actions. To his left, a couple of jocks in UT colors hurled a football back and forth to the annoyance of a plump girl in red jeans trying to read a fat paperback. Beneath the shade of a cedar tree a couple of female students chatted quietly. All of a sudden one of them tossed back her head and fell flat on her back. She spread her arms in a sudden burst of emotion and stretched her thin limbs into the shape of a star. Dennis felt a chill run up his spine.

On the first day of August 1966, a former marine named Charles Whitman climbed into the observation deck of the University of Texas Tower and, armed with an assortment of weapons, started to snipe at unwary students and teachers on the campus. In what was then the largest simultaneous mass murder in American history, Whitman managed to shoot forty-five people, killing fourteen of them, before a pair of Austin police officers stormed the deck and killed the sniper himself.

Dennis recalled his father telling him how he had listened to the incident live on KTBC, a cub reporter crouched behind the mobile news vehicle out on Guadalupe telling people to keep away from the UT Tower. Later in the broadcast, the reporter had read out a list of the victims to the anchorman in the studio. The anchor had listened in silence for a moment and then broke in and said: "Read that list again, please. I think you have my grandson on that list."

Dennis could tell from his tone that his father had been impressed with the man's dedication to his job, his professionalism, but to Dennis the cold-bloodedness of the anchor's words struck a far greater chill in his young heart than the fatal actions of the killer himself. And it was a feeling that had stayed with him across the years. He took a deep breath and stepped back, reached out and ran his hand across the memorial plaque attached to the inside of the stone balcony. It had taken the people of Austin a long time to come to terms with the tragedy of that day over thirty years ago. And now another mass killer had struck at the heart of their city.

BONNIE LANE: FORMER WIFE

He used to feel my period pains. Every month he'd get these cramps in his stomach at the same time that I started my period. And he always knew when it was going to happen. The same every month, as if he could sense what my body was going through. And I'm not one of those women that're that regular, y'know, so it's not like he could work it out or anything like that. I wouldn't have to tell him, and I never turned into some kind of monster with PMS so that it'd be obvious. It was as if he just knew. I mean, I never heard of that before, y'know. You hear about groups of women that live together—nuns, you hear about nuns—you hear about groups of women that live together falling into the same cycle. But guys and sympathetic pains? Uh uh. But Dennis was different. Oh, he suffered nothing serious, but a couple of times I remember that he couldn't eat anything for a day or so. And sometimes, sometimes he used to smoke pot to help ease the pain. He said it was as good as any painkillers you could buy in the drugstore. He used to bring home some of the stuff he'd confiscated from kids out on the street. Skim a little off the top, nothing too real, nothing too noticeable. Personal use, y'know. He tried to turn me on to it, but I . . . The only time I tried it I got sick and I never tried it again.

GRIFFIN CLARK, AUSTIN PD: PARTNER, HOMICIDE DIVISION

I remember driving back to the station with Dennis one night, sometime around the start of the hunt for the Smiler. It had just turned one and the radio announced that another body'd been found. I don't know, it must've been the second or third, I don't recall. No, that's right, it was the third. Anyhow, it was that time that the press came up with the name—Smiler. The press thought that it might focus the public and help us out, or at least make people more wary: the guy was still out there, no doubt about that. A couple of lovebirds'd stumbled across the body in a picnic area out in McKinley Falls State Park, hidden behind some cherry trees. Hancock, Blake Hancock. He was a teacher at the junior high on the other side of the park. His neck had been cut from ear to ear, "like some horrific kind of weird smile," the kids'd said. And Dennis? Man, I've never seen him so juiced up. When he heard that the guy'd been a teacher he just started in on this shit about how he understood—that's the very word he used: "understood"—about how he understood what was goin' on in this guy's mind, the Smiler. What was in his head, why he was doin' what he was doin' and how he was now goin' to catch the guy.

MARC LOURIS, AUSTIN PD: CLASSMATE, POLICE ACADEMY

Dennis was never the brightest of guys, bookwise—he seemed to float around average the whole time we were in the academy—but he was always the first to pick up on the practical side of things: dismantling weapons, surveillance techniques, all that kind of stuff. Most times, he just had to watch the instructor once and that was it— he had it.

ETHAN ROBINSON, AUSTIN PD: FORMER PARTNER, ROBBERY DIVISION

I wouldn't call him a kleptomaniac—that's not fair and it wouldn't be true. But whenever we worked a burglary together, particularly if it was at someone's home, most times he'd end up taking something from the scene. He told me once that it was a way of getting inside the perp's head, turning on the same vibes that'd stirred him up in the first place. Made him commit the crime. Oh, nothing major—a photograph or a lighter, something small that he could slip into his pocket. Personal stuff. But it's not as if he was the first. No, sir, I've worked with guys that'd steal the cash from a dead man's wallet, pocket his credit cards and sell 'em on the street. All kinds of shit like that. But with Dennis it was always personal stuff. And it seemed to work 'cause he always got his man. Dennis was a good cop.

• • •

The unmarked police car pulled to a halt in front of the condo on San Jacinto and Dennis Lane climbed out and stretched his arms in the air. He nodded at the uniform in front of the place and then looked up and down the street. The sun had started to set behind the hotels lined up on the shores of nearby Town Lake and the area was bathed in a sulphurous sheen. On the corner a man in a lilac polo shirt and headphones fiddled with a broken sprinkler on his lawn, and across the street a couple of kids in bulky shorts jumped in the heat and rattled the roof of the family car with a basketball.

Ethan Robinson opened his door and flipped his smoke onto the hot tarmac, climbed out of the car and followed Lane into the cool of the condo's lobby. The door to an apartment on the third floor stood open a fraction. A slice of sun on the carpet sat outside the apartment, like a sundial snapshot of the time of the break-in. Robinson pushed the door open a little farther and a sheet of hot air curled around his torso. He felt a catch in his throat.

"Jesus Christ," he said. "We should be able to lock this guy up just for havin' no aircon, man, victim or not. S'like a fuckin' desert in here."

In the far corner of the room a man in a rumpled T-shirt and blue shorts sat on a chair in front of the window, staring out into the street. At the sound of Robinson's voice he turned and looked at the pair of cops with flat eyes.

"This your apartment?" said Robinson.

The man stood and stepped closer to Robinson. "That's right," he said, a touch of defiance in his voice. "This is my home."

"And you are?"

"Michael Usher."

"You live here alone, Mr. Usher? There's no . . . You're not married?"

The man shook his head. "Just me."

Robinson looked into the shade that buffeted the walls, the rubble of broken china and furniture that littered the floor. "You know what happened, Mr. Usher?"

Usher hiked his shoulders, pursed his lips. "No," he said. "I just came home and found the place like this."

"Kids," said Lane. "Most likely kids after a quick score."

Robinson looked across at his partner and let out a short breath, rubbed the heel of his hand across the perspiration on his forehead. He took a notebook and a pencil out of his pocket. "You know what's been taken?"

"The TV, for a start," said the man, and pointed to a dusty space in the corner.

"I'll check out the rest of the apartment," said Dennis, and disappeared into the dark stretch of hall that led to the rooms at the rear. He padded into the bedroom, picked up scattered clothes and at once dropped them in the same place. He lifted a slat on the blinds and peered out into the street behind the condo. Heat and dusk had cleared most of the area and all he could see was a Hispanic kid in yellow trunks rolling a watermelon on the sidewalk.

He picked up a photo frame from the sill: a blond boy of about three or four squinted into the sun, a stretch of sunkissed beach behind him. He had the same flat forehead as the man in the front room: father and son, Dennis reckoned, and slipped the frame into the inside pocket of his jacket.

A couple of hours later, Dennis took a detour on his trip home and headed out past the condo. He pulled to the curb across the street and peered up at the dark and silent front of the apartment: the man in the T-shirt and shorts had headed out to his local bar to bitch to his buddies about the fall of the area, the invasion of treacherous kids.

Dennis jumped out of the car, lifted a holdall from the backseat, and headed into the condo. He took the stairs at a run, and on the third floor took a pocketknife from his coat and popped the lock on the door in less than a minute, then slipped into the apartment and left the door ajar.

He stood in the center of the front room and looked around. The tenant had attempted to clean up the place a little, but it still looked like the local kids had bounced a basketball around. Dennis scoped each aspect of the room in turn and then crossed to a bookcase and dropped a silver Buddha statue into the holdall. He ran his hand across a line of CDs on another shelf, pulled out ones that he knew, and dropped them in the holdall with the Buddha. He crossed to the bureau and rifled the compartments, scattering papers and documents across the floor. He came across a passport and a driver's licence and bundled them into the holdall; a pack of un-opened photos still in the store's envelope and a pocket calculator landed on top of the passport and the driver's licence.

In the bedroom he added a couple of Ralph Lauren shirts and a pair of faded Levi's to the haul; a pair of battered loafers and a fresh pair of white Reeboks trailed the clothes. He hitched the holdall across his shoulder and left the apartment, left the front door open and tilted to ten o'clock, the time of his escape.

HARVEY CARTER, LAWYER: RACQUETBALL PARTNER

No matter how busy we were, we always used to try and meet up about once a week to play racquetball. I work for a law firm downtown and I use the sport to ease a lot of the stress that builds up in the job. I think Dennis felt the same about being a cop, that he needed some kind of release. I remember one time the game had gotten pretty competitive, more competitive than usual, and as I went for a low backhand I slipped and fell and sprained my wrist. Dennis took me down to the emergency room and then drove me home. But then just before we were due to meet the following week, I had this call from his wife, Bonnie. She said that Dennis still had some pain in his wrist and that he couldn't make it. I didn't know what to say, I didn't understand what she was talking about. I mean, it was me that'd sprained my wrist, right?

GRIFFIN CLARK, AUSTIN PD: PARTNER, HOMICIDE DIVISION

I remember the time Dennis first told me his theories about the Smiler, about the reason he cut people's throats from ear to ear. He told me that it was because. . . . Dennis had this idea that the guy had been abused as a kid and that all he could remember was this smile on his abusers' faces as they . . . y'know, you understand what I'm tellin' you? The smile that told him that it was over? That they were done with him? You do? Good. I don't know where that theory came from, it was never raised in the nine months I worked the case and it was not an idea that made it into the paperwork.

KENT BURKE: CRIME REPORTER, *AUSTIN STAR*

There was a dark side to Dennis that he kept hidden from most people. It was something that you could maybe catch a glimpse of if you caught him off guard. Fifteen months ago, a friend of mine, his daughter was raped one night after a trip to the movies, right on campus. Nineteen, straight-A student, heading to be a doctor. Pretty, sweet and pretty just like her mother. She was badly beaten and a couple of bones in her left hand had been broken. I don't know, maybe she put up a fight, but she'd also been hit around the head and suffered a fractured skull. Terrible. Couple of nights later I ran into Dennis out at that cops' bar down near the river, the Lantern. I used to hang out there quite a lot, meet up with a couple of guys who'd tipped me stories in the past. On this particular night someone pointed me in his direction, told me that he was the primary on the case and that maybe I should introduce myself, buy him a beer. Well, I never met this guy before, and he was friendly enough, but there was something about him that made me take a step back. I asked him about the rape case, asked him what had happened and how the investigation was going. I never told him that I was a friend of the family, I didn't want him to feel that he couldn't tell me the truth. I don't know, maybe it was because he was half drunk—he had this kind of dull stare and his breath stank of Jack Black—but the way he talked about the girl, about her breasts and stuff, made me think that maybe his sympathies lay elsewhere.

Dennis took a pull of cold Bud, put the bottle back on the bar, and then looked across at the woman in the Ryan Adams T-shirt. She had been clocking him for the last hour. She was kind of pretty in a raw way, with thick black hair that fell like a stream at dusk across her shoulders, but her face held a sadness that hinted at a lifetime of mistakes and missed opportunities. Dennis had spotted it the moment he saw her and he had felt no inclination to add to her woes, but after three or four drinks his defenses slipped and he shot her a lopsided smile and nodded at the vacant stool beside him. The woman smiled and looked into the faces of her friends for a second, then snaked around the far end of the bar and hitched herself up on the stool beside Dennis.

"Hey," said Dennis. "Get you a drink?"

"Yeah, thanks," she said, and shuffled around on the stool a little.

"Cold Bud okay?"

"Sure, what else you gonna drink when it's as hot as this?" she said, and blew a jet of air up over her brow, flapped her hand in front of her face. She smiled and her teeth reflected neon sparks from the mirror behind the bar.

Dennis turned and raised his hand to the bartender, ordered a couple of bottles of Bud and then spun back around on his stool.

The woman held out her hand to him and said, "Marnie. Marnie Stead."

"Ethan," said Dennis, and took her hand and kissed it.

Dennis followed Marnie up the path that led from the street to a staircase at the rear of the house, his footsteps dull echoes in the moonlit silence. She lived in a studio apartment on the fourth floor, and had invited him up for coffee after he'd treated her to takeout steak burritos from the Little City Café on the ride home. They had eaten in the car and afterward she had kissed him and tasted chili and bourbon on his lips: She'd rubbed the band of soft white skin on the third finger of his left hand to let him know that she wasn't after commitment beyond the next few hours.

Sodium lamps cast a pale ocher sheen across the main street, but the foot path faded into darkness behind the house and he could just make out her outline ten feet ahead of him, the softness of her ankles and the easy hitch of her buttocks. To his left, knotted rosebushes lined the back wall of a car parts warehouse, the path itself patched in dusted oil and littered in flattened soda and beer cans. Brilliant stars sparked from a hot clear sky and the moon looked like a chipped blue marble.

Marnie reached the end of the path, spun on her toes, and tossed Dennis a smile just as a security light came on above her head that turned her face the color of burnt copper. It seemed to hover in the air for a moment, and then she disappeared around the corner and he heard her feet hit an iron staircase.

Dennis broke into a run, felt his blood rise in his heart and in his limbs and start to thump in his ears. He chased after Marnie, and at the foot of the staircase he reached up and snatched hold of her hair and yanked her back down onto the path.

Marnie let out a startled cry and her limbs bucked in a spastic attempt to hold on to the iron rail, but her efforts were in vain. Her hands clutched at thin air as the back of her head hit the path with a hard and sickening thump. Before she could climb to her feet, Dennis straddled her at the hips, pinned her to the concrete, and punched her in the face. Her head hit the path once more and then seemed to shake for a brief second before it slumped to the side; a trickle of blood curled out of her nose and pooled in the hollow of her shoulder, and her eyes rolled up in her head.

Dennis took hold of her ankles and pulled her into the darkness at the rear of the house, shot a look out to the street in both directions. He dropped to his haunches and took hold of the front of her jeans and snatched at the buttons, tore the T-shirt from her chest. He ripped the pair of battered Nikes from her feet and tossed them farther into the darkness; slid jeans and panties from hips that felt both hot and cold in his hands and dropped them on the path. His breath came in harsh rasps and he paused for a second. Then he fell back on his heels and peered out once more at the street for a shift in the atmosphere, potential witnesses to the attack. He looked into the four corners of darkness around him and then, satisfied that he acted in isolation, dropped his hands onto the path and stared into the woman's face. Tortured, bloodied, pained, and silent. He lifted a thick bunch of her hair and spread it across her eyes with tenderness, closed her mouth with the palm of his hand.

GRIFFIN CLARK, AUSTIN PD: PARTNER, HOMICIDE DIVISION

Dennis had this idea that the places where the Smiler had picked up his victims held some kind of significance for him, something that reminded him of his childhood. But most of the places were not the kinds of place that you'd normally associate with kids, like playgrounds, schools, swimming pools, those kinds of places. No, Dennis believed that the killer'd been lonely and abused as a kid and that the places he picked his victims from were the kinds of places that a lonely and abused kid'd hang out—libraries, bookstores, the airport—places where there were loads of other people around, loads of adults, loads of parents. I mean, like he said, why else would the Smiler pick up his victims in places where sometimes there would literally be hundreds of witnesses? I had the impression that the reason Dennis believed this was because he himself had been a lonely child and that these were the kinds of places that he'd hung out in.

BONNIE LANE: FORMER WIFE

Another thing he used to do—and this'd just drive me crazy—was copy me when we were talking. At home in the den watching TV, having a meal in a restaurant or a drink in a bar, even at my mother's, for God's sake. Gestures, hand movements, the way I sipped a cup of coffee or smoked a cigarette—everything. If I crossed my ankles, he'd cross his ankles; if I scratched my head, he'd scratch his head. It was like looking in a mirror, one of those creepy mirrors that you find at old-fashioned amusement parks. I don't think he knew that he was doing it but it used to drive me crazy.

GRIFFIN CLARK, AUSTIN PD: PARTNER, HOMICIDE DIVISION

After we found the third victim—Blake Hancock, the teacher—and we knew that we had a serial killer on our hands, Dennis became obsessed with the Smiler and spent all his waking hours on the case. In addition to the official reports, he started to keep this scrapbook of all the newspaper clippings that he could find—not just from the local papers but from the New York Times *and the* Washington Post *as well. And every so often he'd tell me about one of the little theories that he'd come up with about the Smiler. Like the fact that all his victims were—and I think this is what he said, but don't quote me—"figures of assumed authority," although I've no idea what he meant by that. I even heard that he'd turned a room at home into some kind of command center with crime scene photos and all that kind of shit pinned to the wall. He never mentioned it to me, so it could just have been a rumor, but it wouldn't have surprised me. I do know that he had this map of the city pinned above his desk in the squadroom, with little colored pins in it where he reckoned the Smiler would strike next.*

Dennis rolled the napkin into a ball and tossed it into the trash can on the sidewalk. He rubbed his hands on his pants and then lifted a pack of Camels from the dash and put a match to one, snapped the flame out of the match and dropped it out on the tarmac. He took a pull on the Camel and behind the smoke he could taste the barbecue smoke that drifted from one of the concession stands on the banks of Town Lake.

Ten minutes earlier he had heard the applause for the final act of the annual Aquafest rise and fall, and people now started to drift from the site. The moon lit the mass of communal bonhomie that bubbled into the street and split it into smaller and smaller packs until faces started to form out of the darkness. Dennis let his eyes drift across the faces that appeared for a minute or so and then stopped on a couple as they halted to let a fifties Oldsmobile pull out from the curb in a crescendo of noise and fumes and Buddy Holly.

The pair seemed familiar. It took Dennis a moment to identify them as the couple that he had come across outside the Continental Club a month or so earlier. He had responded to a disturbance call only to arrive at the bar to find a paramedic bunched over the woman and the kid already cuffed and in the back of a cruiser. The woman had a fresh bruise on the side of her face that matched the shape of the knuckles on the kid's right hand, but even after Dennis had spoken to her she had still refused to press charges and he had had no choice but to turn the kid loose. The woman had been a trainee parole officer and he remembered wondering at the time if it had been part of her training to date a jerk.

The couple walked down the street to an old blue Honda. The kid unlocked the car and then took hold of the woman's arms and tried to push her inside, but she held her arms stiff at her sides and refused to move, her mouth a firm line of defiance. The kid's mouth opened in a shout lost in the pack and his face turned crimson.

Dennis fired up the car, tapped the pedal and eased across the street, pulled up behind the Honda. He climbed out of the car and walked around to the front of the Honda, rested his hand on the roof as if he intended to hold it back if the kid tried to drive away.

CLOSER TO THE FLAME | 443

"Hey, haven't I seen this movie before?" said Dennis.

The kid turned to look at him, bunched his face into a question.

"Hey, Detective Lane," said the woman after a moment, a clear and hopeful smile on her face. He noticed that fear colored her pupils black. "Been enjoying the music?"

Dennis felt his head turn from her in embarrassment and he understood at once that he had not misinterpreted the scene. "You remember what we talked about the last time we spoke?" he said to the kid.

The kid shot a look across the street at the audience that had started to pool on the curb, and turned back to Lane. He opened his mouth to speak, but then he seemed to pull back into himself and he snapped his lips shut.

"This is not—" started the woman, but Dennis cut her off with a raised palm.

"Look," he said, and pointed at her upper arm where bruises had started to rise in the skin. "You may not think that you deserve better than this little piece of shit—"

"Hey," interrupted the kid, but the woman punched him on the arm and he fell quiet.

Dennis smiled and took a step closer to the woman. "Connie?" he said, and she nodded.

"Look, Connie, you've got a kind face, you look like the kind of person that'd give someone a second chance. But I reckon that this here piece of shit's had just about all the second chances that he could take. That so, kid?"

The kid looked into the cop's face, hit steel, and his mouth crumpled into a sneer.

"Smells like you've had a few drinks, too," said Dennis.

"Couple of beers or so," replied the kid.

"And the rest," said Dennis. "Still, what the hell do I care if you still want to jump behind the wheel—it's too much like bullshit to write up a DIU on a night like this. But there's no way I'm going to let you drive this lady home. C'mon," he added, and pointed into the Honda, "climb in the car and get the fuck out of here before I change my mind."

The kid reached out to the woman but she stepped aside and his hand snatched at air.

"Travis, no," she said, and turned her back on him. Her shoulders seemed to have lifted a couple of inches and her voice had a clarity and strength that hadn't been there a moment earlier.

The kid snarled at her and then climbed into his car, stoked up the motor, and laid rubber on the tarmac as he shot out from the curb and headed toward the interstate.

Dennis trailed him with his eyes until he disappeared and then turned back to the woman and said, "That was very brave of you, Connie. But the way you treated him'll prey on his mind, so you'd be wise to bear that in mind the next few days." He took a pack of Camels from his pocket and offered her one. She declined his offer and he put the pack back in his pocket. "You need me to call you a cab?" he said.

She looked at his face, turned aside. "That's okay," she said. "I think I saw one of my girlfriends back there. I can catch a ride from her."

Dennis looked at the tailenders coming out of the park, the dark spaces behind them. "You sure she's still here?" he said. "Looks like most folks've already upped and left. You want me to give you a ride home? It's the least I could do in the circumstances."

The traffic on Barton Springs Road was thick in the heat of the summer. The tarmac shimmered in front of them like an oasis, and the air that hit his face felt like it had been shot from the tailpipe of one of the semis that roared in the blind distance. Kids in more open top autos from the fifties cruised the street, and at the junction of Bouldin Dennis saw a man cross the intersection with a red-faced toddler asleep in the front seat beside him. The man looked like he hadn't slept in a month, ashen and drawn.

For a couple of miles, Dennis chatted about the kind of music he liked to listen to, the fresh bands that had come up in Austin of late, the old-timers he had seen rise and fall and rise once more. Connie listened in silence for a time, but then he noticed that she had started to squirm a little in her seat. "Hey, don't let the kid rattle you."

"I just ran into him at the Aquafest," she said. "I had no idea he was still in Austin. Last time I spoke to him—after . . . after that time at the Continental Club, I told him I didn't want to see him anymore—he told me that he'd been offered a job down in Corpus Christi and he planned to move down there."

He turned and offered her a smile, noticed a tear on her cheek. "You want to stop and talk about it? There's a quiet bar . . ."

"I'm in no fit state to be out in public," she said.

"Okay, how about Barton Springs?" said Dennis, his tone loose and casual. "Couple of tins of cool beer from the liquor store before I drop you back home."

Connie looked at him in surprise—she never expected to be hit on by a cop, even one that had just pulled her out of a difficult situation. She still felt a little jumpy from the encounter with Travis, but as she looked at the cop once more she felt a kind of loyalty come upon her. He's only trying to be kind, she told herself. "Sure, that'd be nice."

Dennis purchased some beers at a store near the entrance to Zilker Park and then took the car to a spot that overlooked Barton Springs, the natural swimming pool in the park. Three or four people still bobbed in the water on the far side of the lake, brilliant specks under a fresh moon. He parked the car a hundred feet from the only other car in the lot, then popped one of the beers and handed it to Connie. He turned to pull out another beer from the paper sack on the backseat and took the chance to look around the dirt lot and the rest of the immediate area.

Connie picked up on his actions and said, "What're you looking for? You expecting someone?"

"No, but you can never be too careful with the Smiler still out there."

Shock filled her features. "Hey, you're not using me as some kind of bait, are you? Is that why you brought me out here?"

"Hey, c'mon," said Dennis. "You know that's not true. You know why we came out here."

Connie shuffled in her seat, uncomfortable in the car all of a sudden. She looked out across the lot to where a bunch of people climbed up the hill from the side of the water, towels draped across their shoulders. She took a sip of beer and put the can on the dash. "Well, thanks for the beer but I really should be getting back."

"Okay," said Dennis, and touched her on the forearm. "Let's not talk about the Smiler no more."

Connie pointed at a young couple beside a blue sedan. "Hey, look, there's Reba Ball," she said, a quiver in her voice once more. "She lives just across the street from me. That must be her new boyfriend. I heard they were staying with her folks for a couple days."

"Let's just finish our beer and then I'll take you home," said Dennis.

Connie opened the door and dropped a foot onto the dirt lot. "I'll just go ask if I can get a ride home," she said, and quickly stepped out of the car and started to walk in the direction of the blue sedan.

"Hey, hold on a minute," cried Dennis, and snapped open the door and hurried around to the other side of the car. He felt his heart thump deep in his chest, and his breath came in hard bursts.

"C'mon, I'm sorry, okay?"

But Connie had started to run, and in a moment pulled up in front of the young couple.

Dennis could tell at once from their curious faces that they had never seen her before. She started to speak and after a couple of seconds the man peered across her shoulder at him, a look of deep concern on his face. The woman continued to stare into Connie's face, and then she reached out and took Connie's hand and helped her into the backseat of the car and then climbed in beside her. The man shut the door behind them and then slid into the driver's seat. He stoked up the motor and pulled out of the lot in a cloud of dust. Connie did not look back, did not offer him a smile of thanks.

Dennis stood and stared after the car until the red taillight sheen faded from the pecan tress that surrounded the lot, then shook his head and turned to look out across the lake. The people on the far shore had packed up and left and he found himself alone under the moon. Raccoons and rabbits bundled around in the brittle shrubs beneath the pecan trees, and in the distance he could hear the mournful cries of a bluebird. He strolled around the hill a short distance and tossed some pebbles into the lake and smoked a couple of Camels, kicked at the hard earth in frustration and then headed back up to the car.

He had just put his hand on the door handle when he felt his head jerk back and a coldness prick the skin beneath his left ear. On instinct he tried to turn, but before he could shift his feet or lift his hands to his head the coldness had spread across to his other ear and he felt his throat start to burn. Intense pain spread across his chest and out into his arms, shot across his torso, and in seconds he dropped to his knees and then fell flat on his face in the earth. Darkness filled his head and drained across his face, blacking out his vision. His other senses started to fail, one at a time, and his last sensation was of the smell of pecans returning to the earth.

BONNIE LANE: FORMER WIFE

Do I think that Dennis was the Smiler? No, of course not. Oh, I know that the murders stopped once that Dennis himself had been murdered, but there's not one shred of physical evidence to prove that Dennis had had anything to do with any of the murders.

ETHAN ROBINSON, AUSTIN PD: FORMER PARTNER, ROBBERY DIVISION

No.

GRIFFIN CLARK, AUSTIN PD: PARTNER, HOMICIDE DIVISION.

You're asking me if I think that another cop found out that Dennis was the Smiler and took him out? What kind of ridiculous question is that? Dennis just had a hair up his ass on this one and ended up too close to the flame, that's all. End of story.

John Vermeulen

Chalele

Belgian author JOHN VERMEULEN published his first novel (juvenile science fiction) at the age of sixteen, and became a full-
time professional writer in 1979. Since then, he has written more
than thirty books of science fiction, juvenile fiction, several thrillers, historicals, and erotic novels. He has won several prizes, and
his work has been translated into German, Japanese, and French.
Two of his historical novels reached the bestseller lists in Germany
and Switzerland. He has also written many short stories for magazines such as the Dutch editions of *Playboy, Penthouse,* and *Chez.*
A sailing addict, he worked for a long time as a water sports
journalist and for a decade was editor-in-chief of the Belgian
sailing magazine, *Yachting.* His story, "Chalele," first appeared in
the Belgian anthology *Dodelijke Paringsdans (Deadly Mating Dance),*
and has a twist ending you'll have to read to believe.

Chalele

John Vermeulen

Sultry Arusha was a very long way from home, and I had been sleeping in lonely, muggy hotel rooms for far too long. The view of the overly praised Kilimanjaro was not really comforting. So I hardly hesitated when I walked through the swing doors of the club and saw the gorgeous mulatto sitting at the left end of the bar. I had always been led to believe that mulattos combined the best of two worlds when it came to bed techniques, and I was looking for a chance to experience this personally.

"Am I allowed to talk to you, or do you want to be left alone?" I had always found this a handy opening phrase. It enabled them to get rid of you without being too unfriendly and without you losing face.

At close quarters the mulatto looked even better than from afar. But she was not at all friendly. She did not even look up. "Leave me alone," she said in a low guttural voice.

She had talked with her face away from me and I hoped I had misunderstood her. Pointing at her empty glass, I tried again: "Can I offer you . . . ?"

She slid down from her stool so brusquely that it fell over, glanced furiously at me with her big dark eyes, and then stormed out with angry steps into the burning sun.

Bewildered I looked at the black bartender, who was nodding as if he found these sorts of scenes normal. Fortunately he did not grin as well. I hate it when these blacks jeer at you. "Wrong stuff," he said seriously.

I ordered rum. "What is wrong with that lady?"

"The fact that she is a mister . . ." Mozazu still kept his big and overly white teeth covered.

Aversion ousted the bewilderment. "A guy? That dish?"

"Sad story," Mozazu said in his somewhat shaky French. With the shot glass he was cleaning he pointed at a not-so-young white man with ginger hair who sat alone at a table reading a book. "Mister Maarssen can tell you all about it. Sad story," he repeated.

At first Maarssen did not seem inclined to satisfy my sudden curiosity, but when I had assured him that I was not a journalist—I am a good liar—and after three glasses of straight rum, he began to come around. "No one believes it, and that is one of the reasons I do not like to tell the story," he explained.

"Strange stories do not surprise me anymore," I answered truthfully. "I come to Africa more often, you know." I briefly glanced at the bartender behind his deserted bar, staring into space with sad eyes. I wondered what such a man thought about during his empty moments. Still disbelieving, I asked: "Was that gorgeous dish really a man?"

"Has been," Maarssen answered. "My brother witnessed it all from close by. He is a doctor, you know."

"So, just a transsexual, then?" I felt some disappointment.

"You could call it that, yes. . . ." Maarssen looked as serious as Mozazu, and with the same sad eyes. "If you leave the 'just' out of it . . ." He, too, glanced at the bartender. "The poor soul has been *ensorceré*, bewitched. . . ." He tossed down the last of his third glass of rum. "At least that is my opinion."

For a moment I had the impression that evil creatures were grinning at me from the many dark corners of the scarcely lit bar, and I sensed the beginning of a shiver. The word "bewitched" had a totally different meaning under the dense foliage of the Tanzanian jungle than it had a few thousand miles to the north. Only the ignorant tourists laughed about it, at least as long as they stayed within the relative safety of their hotel or their photo safari bus.

I signaled to Mozazu with my glass. "I would really like to hear the whole story," I said to Maarssen.

"Yes, I bet you do. . . ." He was silent until the bartender had filled our glasses again. Then he asked somberly: "Are you sure you are not a journalist?"

I felt ill at ease under the look from his watery, yellow eyes. A little impatient, I asked: "What difference does it make?" The entire jungle buzzed with tall stories.

Maarssen looked away. "It is just. . . ." He took his glass and sipped as if to taste that it was the same rum as before. "Each time I get the feeling I really should not be telling it, that I should not even know it."

"Does your brother feel the same?"

"My brother is dead. . . ."

The evil monsters in their dark corners leered at me. "I'm sorry," I said.

"Ah, well, Frank was an old bastard, maybe he was worn out. Many people die of a heart attack, especially in this rotten climate. And doctors stuff themselves and booze all the time, just like anybody else."

I got the idea that Maarssen did not think much of his late brother.

"Well, all right, then, here is the story of Chalele, the Mau-Maru sorceress," Maarssen said resignedly. He pushed aside the book he had been reading. It was a well-thumbed pocket edition of *The Reincarnation of Peter Proust*. "A certain Freddy—I do not even know his surname—was taking a hiking trip through the jungle with a couple of other rich good-for-nothings. Organized by one of those tour operators who get rich because of such clowns. Sleeping in single tents, washing when you happened to find a puddle, daytrips in the steaming heat, being eaten by vermin, no contact with the civilized world—that kind of fun. That gives them prestige with their friends at home who do not have as much guts, or who are not so stupid. Well, after a couple of days their two native guides got lost. Of course, they were city boys who had put on a loincloth in order to earn a few bob and had as much notion of the jungle as those white idiots. Our heroes imagined it would help if they knocked their guides senseless, after which those guys immediately took off. The blacks are not what they used to be. . . ."

Maarssen looked diapprovingly at him and took a sip of his rum. His fingers compulsively caressed the cover of the book on the table.

"After they had wandered around without their guides for a couple of days, they reached a village more dead than alive. Pure luck, because there are not as many villages out there as you might think." Maarssen gestured vaguely in the direction of the door to show what he meant by "out there." "The villagers were friendly and our brave expedition were met with a warm welcome, even though the chieftain was the only one who understood three words in French. They were the Mau-Marus, reasonably nice people without much interest in the rest of the world. Some of their habits are not so nice. For instance, they expect their women to kill themselves if their husband leaves them. Somewhere at the outskirts of their village there is a gantry with a machete attached to it. The blade is razor-sharp and adjustable to the height of the throat. The victim must try to decapitate herself by running into it at great speed. If she succeeds she will be reunited with her husband in a new and better life. . . ." Maarssen's look traveled to the book on the table. "So the Mau-Marus believe in a kind of reincarnation, even though they have never heard of the word. This book is a fake, a sort of a whodunit. . . ." He took a long draught from his rum. "A neck is tougher than you think, and according to Frank it was as good as impossible for a Mau-Maru woman to decapitate herself, however hard she ran. The problem would be the vertebra, which . . ."

I put my hand up to stop him. "Never mind," I said hastily. I had enough when they slit their own throat.

Maarssen shrugged indifferently. "Still, to get on with my story: Hospitable as they were, those blacks made sure that all the needs of their white guests were met." For a moment he looked at me without saying a word to make sure I had caught his drift. "All the needs," he stressed needlessly. "And that is where trouble started for Freddy. He had the misfortune of getting a girl with too much temperament. Maybe they set her at him deliberately. I suppose those people want to have fun sometimes. On top of that those children drink themselves stoned with some love potion before they start, so they go totally crazy. Anyway, in the middle of the night the village is startled by an awful yelling. Everybody stormed out thinking someone was being attacked by a wild animal or something. . . ." Maarssen paused to nip his drink.

"Well?" I asked impatiently.

"Freddy lay on the ground by the fire twisting and screaming. He had no clothes on and the others saw that he was all covered in blood from the waist down. . . ."

Maarssen paused again, but I remained silent, feeling slightly sick because of what my imagination had put into my mind.

"That hot devil had almost bitten it off," Maarssen continued. "The blood squirted out. . . ." He glanced at me with a look that said "you asked for it." "And then Chalele came on. Chalele was the tribe's sorceress. . . ."

I tried to guess the further course of events, how Freddy got totally castrated and so on, but something was not right. Insecurely, I asked: "Was Freddy a mulatto, then?"

Maarssen shook his head, a bit impatiently as if he thought that was a stupid question. "Some of those witch doctors know their stuff and Chalele was one of them. Freddy recovered almost miraculously, and after a couple of days he was cured enough to notice the remarkable beauty of his sorceress. . . ." Maarssen looked dreamy. "Some of these black women are real beauties. . . ."

I thought of the gorgeous mulatto at the bar a while ago, and tried again to make the connection. But I failed.

"Chalele had everything to get a weak character like Freddy really hot, and he did. But she remained indifferent to his advances, and what does a bastard who is used to getting everything he wants do then?"

"He raped her," I stated.

Maarssen nodded. "He was probably too stupid to comprehend that a village sorceress is quite different from a girl they let you use. But, as I said, the Mau-Marus are nice people, and they only drove their white guests out of their village instead of making soup of their intestines. They even showed them the direction of Arusha."

Maarssen emptied his glass and I beckoned the bartender while I waited for the rest of the story. I had given up trying to anticipate what was to come.

"The idiots had more luck than they deserved, and they got out of the jungle alive, after which they took the first plane to Europe. The only one that was not on the flight was Freddy. He had had too much time to think, and thinking is not good for a guy like him. He had come to the conclusion that he had not just lusted after Chalele's ebony thighs, but that he was genuinely in love with her. That his life had no purpose without her and all the other nonsense your glands make you believe in such a situation. He got it so bad that he was even prepared to live with the Mau-Marus. Ah, well, for someone who has had everything else, having nothing but a clay roof over your head can have its charms."

"Crazier things have been done for the favors of a woman," I remarked.

Maarssen shrugged his shoulders so as to indicate that he was above that.

"Well, he hired a real guide and marched into the jungle to the Mau-Marus again. However, he did not meet as warm a welcome as the first time. They did not even let him into the village. They made him wait at the outskirts of the village for twenty-four hours, before the chieftain came to tell him that Chalele was dead. Shortly after Freddy had left, she had fallen ill and had not been able to cure herself. According to Frank, Freddy had given her a virus she was not immune to. This happens often during such contacts."

"Poor Chalele," I said. Freddy's feelings left me cold. I disliked rapists.

Maarssen seemed to hold another view. "Poor Freddy," he said. "And then the chieftain said something strange. He said that Chalele had known that Freddy would return to the village, and she had made a concoction with which he could free himself of his love for her. He had to drink part of it, and part of it he had to rub onto his genitals. The Mau-Marus seem to know that love is governed by an organ other than the heart."

For a moment I had a vision of boxes of chocolates on Valentine's Day in the shape of a penis. All in all, a living heart was more repulsive. Our culture was strange.

Maarssen continued: "Deeply affected, Freddy took the medicine home. A normal guy would have turned to the bottle, but Freddy was far gone enough to try the concoction of the one he adored."

The hairs on my neck stood on end. The little monsters in the dark corners seemed to hold their breath in excited anticipation. "Poison?" I asked. "Excruciating pains?"

Maarssen shook his head, slightly impatient. "The jungle does not solve its problems that easily. Frank has tried to get a drop of the stuff analyzed, but the lab here in Arusha is too primitive for the finer work. They only found traces of the poison from the bufo marinus—a sort of giant toad—from seeds from the tchatcha tree, and from the skin of a tree frog. Furthermore, it contained a lot of bacteria that are mainly found in the human vagina, plus a whole lot of chemically inert substances that the lab did not know. The analyst said that the stuff reminded him of something that had been scraped out of a four-year-old grave."

"And Freddy poured it down his throat?" I already knew I would not be eating that night.

Maarssen looked at me with his watery eyes. "You said it yourself a while ago: some idiots do the strangest things because of a woman."

I sank back in my chair and breathed out. "Continue," I asked him.

"Freddy had been back in Arusha for a week when Frank first got involved. They had found Freddy unconscious in his bathroom and called for a doctor. . . ."

Maarssen apparently waited until I got impatient, but I was not to be caught out.

"It was horrible," Maarssen said, and his voice conveyed real horror. "When Frank told me the story I immediately felt sick—and I can take a lot. Freddy had used Chalele's concoction as he had been told. At first he did not see any effects, but after two days he got trouble with going to the loo. Afterward, he told Frank it had been 'as if they were squeezing it.' Only by pressing really hard had he been able to empty his bladder. And then, after about a week, it happened. . . ." Maarssen was silent and looked at me, but I did not flinch. "Freddy pressed and pressed, and then . . ." He scratched behind his right ear and put on a horrified expression. "Then his genitals just fell apart. The entire thing perished to dust and pieces, as if it had been made of clay. Of course, Freddy fainted. You would for less."

I swallowed and breathed as deeply as possible. I had been taught you could sometimes suppress the urge to vomit this way.

"In the hospital Frank discovered to his bewilderment that underneath Freddy's 'withered' penis, as he called it, was a rudimentary vagina. Freddy was in the process of becoming a woman down there, for the full hundred percent."

My stomach kept playing up. It never occurred to me that this whole story might be a tasteless joke.

"And it was not over yet," Maarssen continued mercilessly. "Freddy developed breasts at high speed, his body hair disappeared, and his beard stopped growing. The final phase of the metamorphosis took a little longer. It took weeks before his skin got dark and he developed the features of a negroid woman."

I made a weak attempt at mockery: "And then he got pregnant, I suppose?"

Maarssen appeared or pretended not to have heard me. "Chalele had taken her revenge," he said into space. "The revenge of a witch doctor. . . ."

I tried to take no notice of the demons in their dark niches who were now mocking me openly and making obscene gestures. "Was there really no other explanation possible? I mean, there are more men walking around in an attractive woman's body. . . ." I shut up when I realized where I was, at two paces from the green madness of the jungle, where rational explanations tended to sound absurd.

Maarssen said: "When you get older you realize that you had better accept things as they are, instead of looking for an explanation." He emptied his sixth or seventh glass of rum. I had lost count. "Nobody around here has ever seen this Chalele, at least not the real one. . . ."

My gaze was drawn to the book on the table. "Reincarnation?"

Maarssen shrugged once more. "Certainly not in the sense the Shiites see it. You should just stick to witchcraft, that is the most simple."

"That is not an explanation!"

"Exactly," Maarssen said, a little self-satisfied.

Shivery, I said: "I spoke to her!"

"I would not worry about it," Maarssen advised me. "Go home and write a short piece about it for the silly season, it does not always have to be UFOs." There was not a trace of ridicule in his eyes.

For the time being I did not write a short piece about it. And I kept worrying, until I met Maarssen a few weeks later in the club.

He was sitting at his usual table reading a book, and Mozazu stood in his usual place behind the bar staring into space. The devils in the dark corners were probably still there, but lying low for the moment.

I ordered two glasses of rum and joined Maarssen. He was still reading *Peter Proust,* I noticed. Maybe he was learning the book by heart. He accepted the glass of rum, closed the book, and looked at me expectantly.

"I am going home shortly," I announced. "And I thought I would come to say good-bye."

"Someone who treats is always welcome," Maarssen answered.

I took a surreptitious look at the left-hand corner of the bar. "Have you seen Chalele . . . Freddy at all?"

Maarssen looked surprised. "Have you not heard? Everyone in Arusha is talking about it!"

Suddenly the unpleasant itch of the hairs on my neck was there again. "I have just returned from Mombasa, I am not up to date with the local gossip." I looked tensely at Maarssen. "What happened?"

"Freddy is dead."

"Oh!" was all I could think of to say.

"He killed himself. Maybe there were forces at work that made him do it, who can tell?" As usual, Maarssen did not seem interested in guessing an explanation.

The itch on my neck grew into a real shiver. Suddenly the monsters were back and they were grinning diabolically. "How did it happen?" I stared at Maarssen in frightened anticipation.

"He did it with a stolen motorbike. . . ." Maarssen emptied his glass completely before he went on. "He tied a steel cable between two trees, at the height of his throat. . . ." The empty glass banged onto the wooden table and I jumped to my feet. "If what the Mau-Marus believe is right, he will have started a new and better life with his beloved. . . ."

Just a story, I thought the next day while the jet engines of the plane toiled to snatch their load away from the eternal pull of the African continent. I stared through the scratched window to the fading dark jungle.

"Do you want a drink, sir?"

The voice of the stewardess had the same color as the jungle. The young woman was black, her eyes were mysterious pools, and her teeth were white and smiling temptingly.

Forcefully I suppressed the suddenly emerging lust. "Just give me something," I said. "Anything will do, as long as it is not rum. . . ."

When she bent forward to place the glass on my table, I saw the fine horizontal scar on her throat.

"Are you not feeling well, sir?" The black goddess looked worried.

I tore my gaze away from hers. "I am all right," I mumbled.

I already knew I would have one more nightmare in the weeks to come.

Bill Pronzini

Wrong Place, Wrong Time

BILL PRONZINI has written more than fifty mystery, science fiction, horror, and western novels, including the Nameless Detective series. A former newspaper reporter, Pronzini began his writing career with the 1971 publication of *The Stalker.* He has also written more than three-hundred short stories and articles, and several of his books have been adapted for film. His work as an anthologist is also varied, with more than ninety short-story anthologies edited that cover a wide variety of genres and subjects. As has been said in these anthologies before, his Nameless books form a vital and important chronicle of one of crime fiction's most credible and human private detectives ever written. In the top-of-the-line story "Wrong Place, Wrong Time," which was first published in *Most Wanted,* Nameless's humanity and his sleuthing instincts are on full display in only a few thousand words.

Wrong Place, Wrong Time

Bill Pronzini

Sometimes it happens like this. No warning, no way to guard against it. And through no fault of your own. You're just in the wrong place at the wrong time.

Eleven P.M., drizzly, low ceiling and poor visibility. On my way back from four long days on a case in Fresno and eager to get home to San Francisco. Highway 152, the quickest route from 99 west through hills and valleys to 101. Roadside service station and convenience store, a lighted sign that said OPEN UNTIL MIDNIGHT. Older model car parked in the shadows alongside the rest rooms, newish Buick drawn in at the gas pumps. People visible inside the store, indistinct images behind damp-streaked and sign-plastered glass.

I didn't need gas, but I did need some hot coffee to keep me awake. And something to fill the hollow under my breastbone: I hadn't taken the time to eat anything before leaving Fresno. So I swung off into the lot, parked next to the older car. Yawned and stretched and walked past the Buick to the store. Walked right into it.

Even before I saw the little guy with the gun, I knew something was wrong. It was in the air, a heaviness, a crackling quality, like the atmosphere before a big storm. The hair crawled on the back of my scalp. But I was two paces inside by then and it was too late to back out.

He was standing next to a rack of potato chips, holding the weapon in close to his body with both hands. The other two men stood ten feet away at the counter, one in front and one behind. The gun, a long-barreled target pistol, was centered on the man in front; it stayed that way even though the little guy's head was half turned in my direction. I stopped and stayed still with my arms down tight against my sides.

Time freeze. The four of us staring, nobody moving. Light rain on the roof; some kind of machine making thin wheezing noises—no other sound.

The one with the gun coughed suddenly, a dry, consumptive hacking that broke the silence but added to the tension. He was thin and runty, mid-thirties, going bald on top, his face drawn to a drum tautness. Close-set brown eyes burned with outrage and hatred. The clerk behind the counter, twenty-something, long hair tied in a ponytail, kept licking his lips and swallowing hard; his eyes flicked here and there, settled, flicked, settled like a pair of nervous flies. Scared, but in control of himself. The handsome, fortyish man in front was a different story. He couldn't take his eyes off the pistol, as if it had a hypnotic effect on him. Sweat slicked his bloodless face, rolled down off his chin in little drops. His fear was a tangible thing, sick and rank and consuming; you could see it moving under the sweat, under the skin, the way maggots move inside a slab of bad meat.

"Harry," he said in a voice that crawled and cringed. "Harry, for God's sake . . ."

"Shut up. Don't call me Harry."

"Listen . . . it wasn't me, it was Noreen. . . ."

"Shut up shut up shut up." High-pitched, with a brittle, cracking edge. "You," he said to me. "Come over here where I can see you better."

I went closer to the counter, doing it slow. This wasn't what I'd first taken it to be. Not a holdup—something personal between the little guy and the handsome one, something that had come to a crisis point in here only a short time ago. Wrong place, wrong time for the young clerk, too.

I said, "What's this all about?"

"I'm going to kill this son of a bitch," the little guy said, "that's what it's all about."

"Why do you want to do that?"

"My wife and my savings, every cent I had in the world. He took them both away from me and now he's going to pay for it."

"Harry, please, you've got to—"

"Didn't I tell you to shut up? Didn't I tell you not to call me Harry?"

Handsome shook his head, a meaningless flopping like a broken bulb on a white stalk.

"Where is she, Barlow?" the little guy demanded.

"Noreen?"

"My bitch wife Noreen. Where is she?"

"I don't know. . . ."

"She's not at your place. The house was dark when you left. Noreen wouldn't sit in a dark house alone. She doesn't like the dark."

"You . . . saw me at the house?"

"That's right. I saw you and I followed you twenty miles to this place. Did you think I just materialized out of thin air?"

"Spying on me? Looking through windows? Jesus."

"I got there just as you were leaving," the little guy said. "Perfect timing. You didn't think I'd find out your name or where you lived, did you? You thought you were safe, didn't you? Stupid old Harry Chalfont, the cuckold, the sucker—no threat at all."

Another head flop. This one made beads of sweat fly off.

"But I did find out," the little guy said. "Took me two months, but I found you and now I'm going to kill you."

"Stop saying that! You won't, you can't. . . ."

"Go ahead, beg. Beg me not to do it."

Barlow moaned and leaned back hard against the counter. Mortal terror unmans some people; he was as crippled by it as anybody I'd ever seen. Before long he would beg, down on his knees.

"Where's Noreen?"

"I swear I don't know, Harry . . . Mr. Chalfont. She . . . walked out on me . . . a few days ago. Took all the money with her."

"You mean there's still some of the ten thousand left? I figured it'd all be gone by now. But it doesn't matter. I don't care about the money anymore. All I care about is paying you back. You and then Noreen. Both of you getting just what you deserve."

Chalfont ached to pay them back, all right, yearned to see them dead. But wishing something and making it happen are two different things. He had the pistol cocked and ready and he'd worked himself into an overheated emotional state, but he wasn't really a killer. You can look into a man's eyes in a situation like this, as I had too many times, and tell whether or not he's capable of cold-blooded murder. There's a fire, a kind of deathlight, unmistakable and immutable, in the eyes of those who can, and it wasn't there in Harry Chalfont's eyes.

Not that its absence made him any less dangerous. He was wired to the max and filled with hate, and his finger was close to white on the pistol's trigger. Reflex could jerk off a round, even two, at any time. And if that happened, the slugs could go anywhere—into Barlow, into the young clerk, into me.

"She was all I ever had," he said. "My job, my savings, my life . . . none of it meant anything until I met her. Little, ugly, lonely . . . that's all I was. But she loved me once, at least enough to marry me. And then you came along and destroyed it all."

"I didn't, I tell you, it was all her idea. . . ."

"Shut up. It was you, Barlow, you turned her head, you corrupted her. Goddamn traveling salesman, goddamn cliché, you must've had other women. Why couldn't you leave her alone?"

Working himself up even more. Nerving himself to pull that trigger. I thought about jumping him, but that wasn't much of an option. Too much distance between us, too much risk of the pistol going off. One other option. And I'd damn well better make it work.

I said quietly, evenly, "Give me the gun, Mr. Chalfont."

The words didn't register until I repeated them. Then he blinked, shifted his gaze to me without moving his head. "What did you say?"

"Give me the gun. Put an end to this before it's too late."

"No. Shut up."

"You don't want to kill anybody. You know it and I know it."

"He's going to pay. They're both going to pay."

"Fine, make them pay. Press theft charges against them. Send them to prison."

"That's not enough punishment for what they did."

"If you don't think so, then you've never seen the inside of a prison."

"What do you know about it? Who are you?"

A half truth was more forceful than the whole truth. I said, "I'm a police officer."

Barlow and the clerk both jerked looks at me. The kid's had hope in it, but not Handsome's; his fear remained unchecked, undiluted.

"You're lying," Chalfont said.

"Why would I lie?"

He coughed again, hawked deep in his throat. "It doesn't make any difference. You can't stop me."

"That's right, I can't stop you from shooting Barlow. But I can stop you from shooting your wife. I'm off duty but I'm still armed." Calculated lie. "If you kill him, then I'll have to kill you. The instant your gun goes off, out comes mine and you're also a dead man. You don't want that."

"I don't care."

"You care, all right. I can see it in your face. You don't want to die tonight, Mr. Chalfont."

That was right: he didn't. The deathlight wasn't there for himself, either.

"I have to make them pay," he said.

"You're already made Barlow pay. Just look at him—he's paying right now. Why put him out of his misery?"

For a little time Chalfont stood rigid, the pistol drawn in tight under his breastbone. Then his tongue poked out between his lips and stayed there, the way a cat's will. It made him look cross-eyed, and for the first time, uncertain.

"You don't want to die," I said again. "Admit it. You don't want to die."

"I don't want to die," he said.

"And you don't want the clerk or me to die, right? That could happen if shooting starts. Innocent blood on your hands."

"No," he said. "No, I don't want that."

I'd already taken two slow, careful steps toward him; I tried another, longer one. The pistol's muzzle stayed centered on Barlow's chest. I watched Chalfont's index finger. It seemed to have relaxed on the trigger. His two-handed grip on the weapon appeared looser, too.

"Let me have the gun, Mr. Chalfont."

He didn't say anything, didn't move.

Another step, slow, slow, with my hand extended.

"Give me the gun. You don't want to die tonight, nobody has to die tonight. Let me have the gun."

One more step. And all at once the outrage, the hate, the lust for revenge, went out of his eyes, like a slate wiped suddenly clean, and he brought the pistol away from his chest one-handed and held it out without looking at me. I took it gently, dropped it into my coat pocket.

Situation diffused. Just like that.

The clerk let out an explosive breath, and said, "Oh, man!" almost reverently. Barlow slumped against the counter, whimpered, and then called Chalfont a couple of obscene names. But he was too wrapped up in himself and his relief to work up much anger at the little guy. He wouldn't look at me, either.

I took Chalfont's arm, steered him around behind the counter, and sat him down on a stool back there. He wore a glazed look now, and his tongue was back out between his lips. Docile, disoriented. Broken.

"Call the law," I said to the clerk. "Local or county, whichever'll get here the quickest."

"County," he said. He picked up the phone.

"Tell them to bring a paramedic unit with them."

"Yessir." Then he said, "Hey! Hey, that other guy's leaving."

I swung around. Barlow had slipped over to the door; it was just closing behind him. I snapped at the kid to watch Chalfont and ran outside after Barlow.

He was getting into the Buick parked at the gas pumps. He slammed the door, but I got there fast enough to yank it open before he could lock it.

"You're not gong anywhere, Barlow."

"You can't keep me here—"

"The hell I can't."

I ducked my head and leaned inside. He tried to fight me. I jammed him back against the seat with my forearm, reached over with the other hand and pulled the keys out of the ignition. No more struggle then. I released him, backed clear.

"Get out of the car."

He came out in loose, shaky segments. Leaned against the open door, looking at me with fear-soaked eyes.

"Why the hurry to leave? Why so afraid of me?"

"I'm not afraid of you. . . ."

"Sure you are. As much as you were of Chalfont and his gun. Maybe more. It was in your face when I said I was a cop; it's there now. And you're still sweating like a pig. Why?"

That floppy headshake again. He still wasn't making eye contact.

"Why'd you come here tonight? This particular place?"

"I needed gas."

"Chalfont said he followed you for twenty miles. There must be an open service station closer to your house than this one. Late at night, rainy—why drive this far?"

Headshake.

"Must be you didn't realize you were almost out of gas until you got on the road," I said. "Too distracted, maybe. Other things on your mind. Like something that happened tonight at your house, something you were afraid Chalfont might have seen if he'd been spying through windows."

I opened the Buick's back door. Seat and floor were both empty. Around to the rear, then, where I slid one of his keys into the trunk lock.

"No!" Barlow came stumbling back there, pawed at me, tried to push me away. I shouldered him aside instead, got the key turned and the trunk lid up.

The body stuffed inside was wrapped in a plastic sheet. One pale arm lay exposed, the fingers bent and hooked. I pulled some of the sheet away, just enough for a brief look at the dead woman's face. Mottled, the tongue protruding and blackened. Strangled.

"Noreen Chalfont," I said. "Where were you taking her, Barlow? Some remote spot in the mountains for burial?"

He made a keening, hurt-animal sound. "Oh, God, I didn't mean to kill her. . . . We had an argument about the money and I lost my head. I didn't know what I was doing. . . . I didn't mean to kill her. . . ."

His legs quit supporting him; he sat down hard on the pavement with legs splayed out and head down. He didn't move after that, except for the heaving of his chest. His face was wetter than ever, a mingling now of sweat and drizzle and tears.

I looked over at the misted store window. That poor bastard in there, I thought. He wanted to make his wife pay for what she did, but he'll go to pieces when he finds out Barlow did the job for him.

I closed the trunk lid and stood there in the cold, waiting for the law.

Sometimes it happens like this, too.

You're in the wrong place at the wrong time, and still things work out all right. For some of the people involved, anyway.

Bob Mendes

Fleeting Fashion

In 1984, Dutch author BOB MENDES started his literary career with the publication of a collection of poems, *Met rook geschreven (Written with Smoke)*, followed by *Alfa en Omega (Alpha and Omega)*. His breakthrough as a novelist came in 1988 with *Een dag van schaamte (A Day of Shame)*, a factual thriller concerning the Heysel European Cup soccer game disaster. Since then he has published eleven thrillers, several short stories, and two plays. Some of his books have been published in Germany, France, and the United States. His magnum opus, *The Power of Fire*, is being filmed in English by an American/Belgian joint-venture, Ciné3. He returns to the pages of *The World's Finest* with "Fleeting Fashion," which was first published in his native Netherlands in *The Best Mystery Stories of Flandern*, translated into English by Donna de Vries.

Fleeting Fashion

Bob Mendes

"Open sesame," I murmured, and the automatic revolving door obeyed. Not missing a beat, I strode across the rust-red carpet with its Ambassador logo and into the lobby of the hotel. I was here to reserve a room for a friend from South Africa, soon to arrive in Antwerp for a well-earned vacation.

Two uniformed receptionists behind the counter wore the same rusty shade as the carpet. Across the lobby I saw a porter next to a trolley, a pinstriped suit with a briefcase, two breathtaking models sporting designer gear from Wild & Lethal Trash, and a hunk of well-built stud material— Roman features and a skintight New Wave outfit—with a bulging portfolio at his side. Towering above this cluster of humanity bobbed the shaved skull and wire-haired beard of Wally Berendrecht, celebrated fashion designer and artistic director of LANDED: MODE2001, a stunning event that had recently blasted Antwerp onto the fashion map of the world. And, for that matter, a guy I counted among my former clients. All eight people had one thing in common: hands folded on top of their heads, they looked scared to death.

The ninth person in the room was about six feet tall, an individual with the demeanor of a cat. Although his back was to me. I got the impression of an electrician called in to make a repair. Dressed in overalls and a knit cap, he waved a soldering iron in the general direction of his frightened audience.

Still behind the electrician, I gestured to Berendrecht. "Hi, Wally," I said, breaking the silence. "What's up? The fuses blown?"

The electrician turned his head. What I had seen as a knit cap was a balaclava—essentially a mask that exposed only his eyes and nose—and the soldering iron was a pistol, now aimed straight at my heart.

"Hands up, stupid bitch!"

Obediently, I folded my hands on my head. "You're obviously at the wrong address, pal," I said, trying to sound helpful. "This looks like a meeting of fashion designers to me. Plenty of ideas, but no money. Get the picture?" As I talked, I edged forward a step. He had the bright green eyes of a bad-tempered tomcat. I waited for him to shift his glance, knowing it was impossible for him to keep an eye on all sides of the lobby at once.

Suddenly Berendrecht broke into a coughing spell. The man in the balaclava swiveled his head instinctively, just long enough for me to raise my leg and aim the toe of my boot at man's most vulnerable spot. Unfortunately, I wasn't the only one to take advantage of the distraction. The young man with the Roman features had shoved the models aside and was charging toward the entrance with the speed of a cheetah.

Balaclava darted into his path, intending to stop him. Just as quickly, the guy on the run changed direction, managing to evade the enemy but failing to see that I—balancing on one leg at this point—was in the way. He collided with me at full speed, and together we crashed to the floor in a tangle of arms and legs. As I fell to the ground, the back of my head hit the edge of a low stone table. No sooner had a bolt of lightning pierced my skull than my world turned pitch black.

Regaining consciousness, I heard the nearby wail of a siren, not realizing at first that the ambulance making all the racket was transporting me. With a groan, I tried to sit up, but a paramedic gently pushed me back into a prone position. "If I were you, I'd move as little as possible," he advised. "You don't want to end up with a splitting headache."

I already had a splitting headache. Who was this guy—a bloody mind reader?

Succumbing to the pain, I closed my eyes.

Stitched up and still a tad shaky the next day, I hightailed it to Wally Berendrecht's fashion house. Arriving at his immense showroom on Saint Antonius Street—picture a runway complete with the barely visible fins of two jumbo jets descending into the clouds and an enormous spaceship about to land—I spotted Wally on center stage, so to speak, at a desk the size of a postage stamp. The interior landscape surrounding him was nothing less than a colorful and dynamic piece of theater.

Wally himself looked less than dynamic. Neither his eccentric denim suit nor the four flashy rings on his right hand could hide his dismal state of mind. I asked him for a full version of the facts. The newspapers had simply reported a holdup thwarted by the heroic intervention of Sam Keizer, Antwerp's top female private detective, who had stumbled onto the scene by accident. Journalists do tend to exaggerate, but I was delighted to see that my name was spelled correctly, which isn't always the case.

A somber Wally stared into space. "We didn't see him come in. Suddenly this guy was screaming, 'Hands up. Everybody against the wall.' When Mario told him to fuck off, the guy got so furious I was sure he'd start shooting. That's when you walked in. You probably saved Mario's life."

"Who's Mario?"

"Mario Becha, my friend. We're also business partners."

"Is he the guy who knocked me over?"

"Yes. But he didn't get hurt. He scrambled to his feet and was out of there like a flash. The robber was so rattled by the incident that he shoved the gun in his overalls and took off after Mario."

"And then?"

"And then nothing. Nobody saw the thug leave the building. Nobody saw him get into a car. The police took our statements, and that's it."

"If that's the whole story, then why do you need a private detective?"

Berendrecht toyed with the topaz ring on his middle finger. "According to the police, the holdup man was interested in nothing but the hotel safe and our wallets," he said, almost in a whisper. "But there was more to it."

"What makes you think that?"

"This."

He handed me a folded sheet of paper. "Someone dropped this through my mail slot this morning."

I unfolded the paper and read: *We Have Portafoglio 2003. Now You Pay Money. Presto! No Police! We Have Him To. We Cut Both To Pieces If No Pagare.*

The letter was signed: *Sangue!*

I shook my head. "What kind of nonsense is this? Whose wallet are they talking about? And why do you have to pay for something they already have?"

"Portafoglio 2003 is the collection I've designed for spring 2003."

"So we're talking blackmail. Somebody's stolen the designs and is threatening to shred them if you don't pay."

"That's about it."

"What does Becha have to say about this?"

Lower lip quivering, eyes brimming with tears, he replied, "Mario's vanished without a trace. Since his spectacular exit, no one has seen him."

"Oh. So that explains the reference to 'We Have Him To'?"

"Yes. And it also explains why the letter threatens to cut 'both' to pieces."

"Any idea who *Sangue* is?"

"No. Unless it means that blood will flow. *Sangue* is 'blood' in Italian. Whoever wrote the message used a combination of broken English and Italian."

"Hmm. I assume you have copies of the designs."

"Of course. They don't call this the Computer Age for nothing. My digital designs are on hard disk, and I have backups as well."

"Have you checked to see that everything's intact?"

His deep blue eyes widened in concern. "No. Keizer, you don't think that . . ." As he leaned forward on both hands, the desk nearly collapsed under his weight. A moment later, Berendrecht managed to pull himself together. "Impossible. The computer is accessible only if you know the code, and my backups are in the safe."

"Codes and safes can be cracked."

"Not these. They're protected with a silent alarm. Fool around with my computer and the cops will have you handcuffed before the screen lights up."

Five minutes later I faced a totally crushed man. The files in question had been erased, and the door to the safe was wide open. The backup CD-ROMs had disappeared.

"Who else had the code?"

Again his lip trembled, and for a second I thought he'd burst into tears. Finally controlling his emotions, he said, "Only Mario."

"Could Mario be in cahoots with the blackmailers?"

"For God's sake, Keizer. Is nothing sacred? He's my partner, the only person I can count on in a crisis." He clenched his fists in impotent rage. "Just get me that son of a bitch, and I'll throttle him with my own hands."

I believed him. "How much is the collection worth?"

He paced up and down the room. "Worth? How much is a flash of inspiration worth? How much are revolutionary ideas worth? My collection would have left the entire world of fashion gasping for breath. Major fashion houses were fighting for my designs, without having seen the sketches. I've promised a number of designs to each of the big names. I've received advances on the royalties. They've spent an absolute fortune on preparations for the promotion campaign." He threw his hands up in despair and dropped them, crestfallen. "If I don't have the collection ready on time, it's the end of us all—me, Yves Saint Laurent, Gucci, Kawakubo, the whole kit and caboodle."

His doom-and-gloom pronouncement sounded like a gross exaggeration to me. The fashion houses he mentioned were my idea of big business. Companies able to survive a catastrophe. "Can't you reproduce the sketches? Surely the ideas are still in your head."

A look of utter shock passed over his face—the expression of a priest unjustly accused of pedophilia. "A true artist never copies his own work," was the haughty reply.

I glanced at the door to his private quarters. "Have you checked out Mario's room?"

"Mario doesn't live here. He has a waterfront apartment on the Vlaamse Kaai."

"Shall we go take a look?"

"I can't leave right now. I'm expecting Tom Ford in a few minutes— the creative director at Gucci. He's coming to see the design of a watch that I promised to give him for Gucci Timepieces." He ran a hand over his smooth pate in obvious desperation. "Good Lord, what am I going to do?"

Wally's distress was so palpable that my own eyes almost filled with tears.

The sound of his cell phone ended the dramatic break in our conversation. Excusing himself, he walked a discreet distance away before taking the call.

On the desk was a small tray of labeled keys. Out of Berendrecht's line of vision, I rifled through them until I found one tagged "Mario." I slipped the key into my pocket and sauntered over to a salesgirl. "Wally's asked me to go to Mario's on the Vlaamse Kaai," I lied. "Do you have the address?"

She shook her head. "All I know is that he lives above an Italian restaurant called Al Dente."

With the phone still pressed to his ear, Berendrecht turned in my direction. Waving good-bye, I departed the fashion emporium.

The front door wasn't locked. Without ringing the bell, I entered the building and walked upstairs. From the stairway I had of clear view of Al Dente's kitchen—gleaming stoves arrayed with steaming pots and pans—but not a glimpse of the cook or his assistants. The door to the apartment was open as well. My loud "Hello!" drew no response, so I let myself in.

It didn't take a trained eye to see that something was wrong. The place looked more like a charity shop than like the home of a man romantically involved with Wally Berendrecht, famed fashion designer and international trendsetter. Gays in such circles are more likely than not to be meticulous, artistically talented people. This apartment, however—an overgrown garden of kitsch furniture and gaudy colors—was a prime example of bad taste. The couch was stacked with cartons of boxes and cans labeled spaghetti, macaroni, pomodoro, and calamaro. A dozen wicker-basket bottles of Chianti were parked in one corner, and the distinct aroma of garlic, hanging in clusters on the wall, penetrated the room. Just as I realized that this was no apartment, but a storage place for the restaurant downstairs, I heard the sound of footsteps approaching. I glanced over my shoulder. Blocking the doorway was a man in a tall white hat. Mid-fifties, broad-shouldered, he had a remarkable gut jutting out over his belt. Spotting the carving knife in his hand, I scuttled back a few steps.

The cook's sneer was sinister. "Trapped, *signora*. Your looting days are over."

I returned his insult with a polite smile. "Oh, dear. I guess you weren't holding open house today after all."

"Not for you." He conjured up a cell phone and tried punching in a number while keeping the point of the knife aimed in my general direction.

"Don't call the police just yet," I said. "I'm a private detective. I'm looking for Mario Becha. He does live here, doesn't he? Or am I mistaken?"

"Save your excuses for the cops."

"No, really." I held out my plasticized ID card, complete with photo, license number, and the seal of the Ministry of the Interior.

He looked at the card, still doubting my story. "What are you doing here?"

"Just what I said. I'm looking for Mario Becha. Do you know him?"

He lowered the knife. "*Si*. Nice guy. One of our regular customers. He lives next door, in the loft of the old tobacco warehouse."

We walked downstairs, single file. The cook apologized for having jumped to conclusions. The neighborhood had been experiencing a frustrating series of robberies and nighttime break-ins. Even though it was doing its best, the Antwerp Police Department had come up with absolutely nothing. The business community had begun operating its own security force.

Outside the restaurant, he pointed to the converted harbor warehouse where Becha lived. Before I had a chance to question him further, he made a beeline for his kitchen.

Though I didn't expect Becha to be at home, I rang the bell anyway. Only after getting no response did I fish the key out of my pocket. A rather rickety elevator transported me to the top floor. Becha's loft was impressive. The expansive space mimicked the project Wally Berendrecht and his Antwerp Six had created to convince fashion aficionados that the city is a serious player in the game of haute couture. A flowing labyrinth of rooms echoed the themes featured in last year's exhibitions: influencing the living area were concepts that Wally had labeled "Mutilate" and "Radicals," while "Emotions" and "2Women" had obviously been a source of inspiration for the bedroom. Each room displayed a thematic color and made an individual statement. Carefully positioned photos and items of clothing completed each picture.

I looked for signs that Becha had spent the night here, but found nothing relevant. No eye-opening scent of espresso or *uova strapazzate,* no sultry odor of warm bodies in the bedroom. With the exception of several open bedroom closets and empty hangers scattered on the floor, the place was immaculate.

I walked back to the living area, a ballroom-sized space that opened onto a roof garden. This part of the loft was decorated with quirky silhouettes and pictures of outrageous fashion statements that illustrated, like a journey through time, alternating aesthetic ideals and trends in fashion. In one corner, which served as office space, a table accommodating the usual computer equipment had a desklike projection heaped with documents. I turned on the computer and checked the files for anything resembling Portafoglio 2003.

Nothing.

I moved to the desk. Not knowing where to begin, I stared at the piles of letters, bills, memos, and notes indicating various appointments with fashion houses and models. Lying to one side were a couple of open envelopes—perhaps mail received the previous day. One held an invoice from Pegasus, a travel agency specializing in golf vacations in exotic countries.

Running my eyes down the itemized list, I felt my heart skip a beat. At the same time, I heard a noise behind me. I spun around in the chair.

A woman entered the room through the door to the roof garden. Nearly six feet tall, this gal was built like a professional boxer.

"Wally?" Obviously confused, she fell silent. Her glance took in the space behind me, as though she were expecting someone else. Her emerald-green eyes were familiar. "Who are you? What do you want?" she asked, her voice fraught with suspicion.

For the second time that day I felt like a thief caught red-handed. "I'm Sam Keizer," I blurted out. "I was sent here by Wally Berendrecht. He's worried about Mario Becha's disappearance. I'm a private detective."

"Fat chance. I'm Ann Demeester, Mario's assistant. If you were working for Wally, I would have been informed." Her eyes took in the flickering computer screen. "This looks more like a case of industrial espionage to me." Her aggressive approach left no doubt in my mind. This amazon was ready to charge.

"Take it easy," I said. "Let's not get physical." I reached into my pocket for my ID. She evidently thought I was going for a weapon and grabbed my arm. "Take your hands off me," I warned. "This is the way accidents happen."

When she paid no attention to my warning, I caught her wrist and twisted hard. A split second later I was flat on my back halfway across the room, wondering what had hit me. Shaking my head to clear my senses, I saw Ann move into position beside me.

"Now do you want to tell me who you're working for, or do you need more convincing?" She bent over, grasped my elbow, and helped me to my feet.

"Damn it, Ann. Didn't I tell you to keep your hands to yourself?" I shoved her away—obviously not gently enough to suit her—and went flying for a second time, landing on the carpet some distance behind me. Still reeling from the first attack, I watched Ann's sturdy shoes approach. I was livid.

As she lifted her right leg to kick me in the stomach, I grabbed her foot with both hands, simultaneously pushing up on her heel and twisting her toes in the opposite direction. Rotating her torso in an attempt to keep her balance, Ann fell facedown with a thud. In a flash I was on top of her, immobilizing her with a simple wrist grip. Hearing her whimper, I had second thoughts. After all, the wrist is a relatively fragile joint and one prone to injury. She tapped the floor twice with her free hand, but I ignored the karate signal for surrender and increased the pressure on her wrist. "Well, Ann. Looks like it's your turn to talk. How did you suddenly appear on the patio?"

"I live in the loft next door. I heard you walking around in here." She swiveled her head to meet my eyes. Despite the hard muscles of her athletic body, she was helpless in my grip. Her eyes sparkled with fury and pain. "Let me go."

Suddenly I realized where I had seen her before. "Your eyes betray you, sister," I said. "What were you doing at the Ambassador yesterday—with a balaclava over your head?"

"You're out of your mind."

"Whatever. Shall I call the police?"

Her body went slack. "Okay. I'll tell you what I know. Just let me go. Please."

I released her. She got up with a groan, massaging her wrist and re-arranging her clothing. She took a thin cigarette from Mario's desk and lit it. She had the kind of boyish body that made me think of a good-looking guy in girly garb—or maybe an attractive lesbian decked out as a man? "I did it for Mario. It was supposed to be a publicity stunt."

"Are you talking about the theft of Portafoglio 2003?"

She exhaled a plume of smoke. "That's right. Stealing the designs was meant to put the new collection on the front page. Thanks to your un-expected interference, Mario panicked and made a run for it."

"You mean he crashed into me deliberately?"

"He couldn't risk having my identity exposed."

"Hmm. But he did take the designs along, didn't he?"

She nodded. "And I had no option but to take off after him."

"Where is he now?"

She shrugged. "Beats me. I haven't seen him since. When I heard you moving around in here, I thought maybe Mario was back."

"Did Wally know what you guys were up to?"

"No. I don't think so."

"And the ransom note? Was that part of the stunt?"

"What ransom note?" She seemed genuinely surprised.

I described what Wally had showed me. I asked if she thought Mario was capable of leaving his lover in the lurch. Only Mario, I reminded her, had access to the codes that opened the files and to the safe containing the backups. She refused to believe he would play dirty. Then I suggested that Mario had *really* been kidnapped, that rival fashion houses had called in the Mafia, and that gangsters had forced Mario to blackmail his partner. The very idea apparently shocked her so badly that I nearly accepted her total faith in Mario. But part of me resisted.

Later, on the sidewalk outside the loft, I spotted the Italian cook in the door of the restaurant, catching a breath of fresh air. I asked when he'd last seen Mario.

"Last night," he replied. "Right before we started serving dinner. He got into a taxi carrying a case—looked like some kind of big tube."

"A golf bag?"

"Might have been."

"Was he alone?"

"Yes. First time in a while I've seen him without a female companion."

"Female? But I thought he was gay."

"Becha? If Becha's gay, then I'm the Virgin Mary!"

"He's not Wally Berendrecht's boyfriend?" I asked, stunned.

The cook laughed. "Those two are the wildest womanizers I know."

I thanked him and walked to my car, which was parked on Zuider-dokken, an old canal filled in and converted into a lovely Flemish avenue. With still a block to go, I called Pegasus on my cell phone. I'd used the agency to book a golf vacation for myself not long ago, and the number was still in the electronic phonebook of my Nokia. When an agent answered, I asked her to reserve a room for me at the same hotel where my golf partner, Mario Becha, was staying during the Mauritius Open.

"I'm sorry to disappoint you," she said, "but Mr. Becha canceled his trip to Mauritius yesterday."

"Really? Did he say why?"

"No. But he did seem quite upset. Maybe it had something to do with the holdup at the Ambassador Hotel."

"Possibly. Are you sure it was Mr. Becha you talked to?"

"I can't be positive. I haven't spoken to him that often. Will you be reserving a room anyway?"

"No, thanks. I need to get in touch with him first."

By now I'd reached my car. Before driving off, I weighed the possibilities. Had someone kidnapped Mario Becha, or had he orchestrated the abduction himself? If the latter were true, was his motive based on media attention for the new collection, or was he out to blackmail his partner? And what part did Ann Demeester play in the scheme? When she caught me rummaging around in Becha's loft, she initially thought I was Wally Berendrecht. Why? Was she expecting Wally? And why had she let me go on believing that Becha and Berendrecht were lovers? Clearly, my next step was to interrogate Ms. Demeester in depth. I pulled my mini disc recorder from my bag, attached the microphone, and stuffed the device in my pocket.

Sneaking into somebody's apartment, even with a key, is illegal. If caught, I could lose my license. But in terms of sheer adrenaline, it beats the most potent ecstasy pill and is a lot less damaging to the body. The lurking threat of Mario's androgynous assistant and her lethal hip throw served to fuel the excitement.

My entrance was anything but thrilling, however, particularly since I'm not turned on by sensual photos of Coco Chanel and Rei Kawakubo. I moved as stealthily as possible. The door to the roof garden was still open. Stepping outside, I noted that the corresponding door to Demeester's loft was also ajar. Sounds were coming from the living room. I recognized the voice of Ann Demeester obviously giving someone a piece of her mind. A man's voice fired off monosyllabic replies. Curious, I stepped over the low wall separating the patios and peeked inside.

Ann stood by the fireplace, facing a man in an armchair. From my position, only the back of his head was visible. Plainly at odds with Ann's point of view, he shook his head, more than once, and snorted in contempt. As he rose from the chair, I recognized the person I had seen only once before. Mario Becha.

Was I surprised? Not really. I might have expected to find him there. By now my body was a live nerve ending, coiled to spring. I wasn't sure what to do. Burst into the room and scare the living hell out of them? Demand an explanation? Or make a quiet departure, call Berendrecht, and let him decide how to proceed? I was still considering my options when the sound of a phone interrupted their conversation.

Ann picked up the receiver. "Yes?" She frowned. "You're too late. Keizer's already been here." And a moment later, "No, she doesn't know that Mario's with me." Another pause. "I still think involving her was stupid. That was only asking for trouble." After listening to the caller's reply, she handed the receiver to Becha, with these words, "Incredible. He's just discovered that Keizer took the key."

As Becha started talking, I switched the recorder on. This could prove to be interesting.

Back at Berendrecht's place of business, a fashion show was in full swing. Though the girls showing the collection didn't have the supermodel status of a Claudia Schiffer or a Naomi Campbell, they were slender and elegant enough to mesmerize a gaggle of gaping Japanese clients at the end of the catwalk.

Berendrecht saw me come in and, like a battleship barreling toward its target, headed straight in my direction. "Where have you been?" he growled.

I gave him my sweetest smile. "I was having tea with Ann Demeester. You run into the most interesting people when you're with Ann."

His look expressed nothing but boredom. "Come with me." He made an abrupt turn and led me to an office at the rear of the building. Inside the room, he turned to face me. "What kind of interesting people?" he barked, unable to hide a slight tremor in his voice.

"How about Mario Becha?"

"You found him?"

"That wasn't so hard. He was at home—that is, if he and Ann Demeester have adjoining lofts."

He swallowed. "And the *portafoglio*? Did you find that, too?"

"Give me a break, pal," I replied, my voice like ice. "There is no portfolio."

A deep red flush darkened his face and neck. "What do you mean, no *portafoglio*? I worked two goddamn years on those designs. Day and night. You yourself saw Mario take off with them under his arm. He had no choice. He was running for his life. The competition was scared shitless that I'd wipe them right off the market. Their only solution was to zap the entire collection."

"Cut the crap, Wally. There was no new collection. You'd run out of inspiration. And the contract stipulated the return of all advances and the payment of a hefty fine if you didn't come up with the designs, and pronto. You were forced to resort to gutter tactics. So you staged a phony holdup with the help of Becha and Demeester, and you hired me to give your dirty scheme the stamp of authenticity."

His reaction bordered on hysteria. "Wrong!" he screamed. "My designs are absolutely sensational. Mario and Ann will back me all the way. I swear that . . ."

I had switched on my recording of the phone call, damming his torrent of words in midstream. As he listened, all hope drained from his face.

"Well?"

It took him a moment to regain his composure. "I really do have a new collection for 2003," he said, eyes pleading for understanding. "But the designs are so radical, so off the wall, that the fashion houses insist on waiting at least a year before launching the collection. I thought a fake robbery would be a great way to package the delay."

"I doubt the authorities will buy that."

He flopped down on a chair. "Okay, Sam Keizer. You win. Name your price. How much to destroy that tape and forget the whole disaster?"

I stared through the doorway at the model on the catwalk. Draped around that young body was the kind of haute couture I couldn't afford in a hundred years.

The look in my eyes was one Wally had seen before. "Berendrecht fashions for the next two years," he mumbled. "Anything you want."

My father's wise voice echoed through my brain: "Sam, adorn your soul with the ornament of honesty." Good advice—but powerful enough to outweigh the irresistible temptation of Wally's offer?

Piet Teigeler

Flying Fast

Currently living in Spain, PIET TEIGELER found that when he retired from journalism after thirty years, he had more questions than answers on his mind. He decided to write ten crime novels to try and answer those questions, and the result includes *Dead Lady on Saint-Anna, Elvis Dead in Deurne,* and *Three Dead Masters.* His novels feature the Belgian police officer, Commissaris Carpentier, and his aide, Chief Inspector Dewit, but he claims his antagonists are his real heroes. His story selected for inclusion this year, "Flying Fast," is a mind-bending tale of duty, courage, and time travel. Just read on, and you'll see what we mean. This story first appeared in the anthology *Salamander-DAS.*

Flying Fast

Piet Teigeler

We departed from Langley at sixteen hundred, midnight in Baghdad. Everything about the flight was classified: the plane, its cargo, and especially its mission. The precision bombing of Saddam's bunker with a tactical warhead, and the landing of two hundred Iraqi exiles, who would take over the government immediately, was not going to take place, officially.

My copilot, Jeremiah Manning, and I flew Harriers since the Falklands, so we know all there is to know about vertical takeoff, which was probably the main reason why British pilots were chosen for this mission. Although there must have been some political afterthoughts: nobody has dropped an atom bomb on a live enemy since World War II, and even if our baby only yields eighteen kilotons, Washington must have hesitated to use it, without the consent of its allies.

"Forty mil!" announced Jerry, and I braced myself for the building pressure of re-entry into the atmosphere. At the exit point, roughly forty kilometers above the earth's surface, I had cut the engines and we had coasted up to a high point of around sixty kilometers before beginning to fall back down to around thirty-five kilometers. As it descends into denser air, our plane is pushed up by the increased aerodynamic lift. At this point we briefly fire our engines, propelling ourselves back into space. The whole process is repeated every two minutes, the aircraft skipping off the top layer of the atmosphere, like a pebble skittering in slow motion across the surface of a pond.

"They're puking," said Jerry. "Every single one of them!"

I glanced at one of the monitors surveying the cabin. At Langley our passengers had been issued traditional air sickness bags. Weightlessness renders those useless, but nobody seemed to have thought of that. The XY-Zoroaster was an experimental aircraft after all, and theoretically the sensation of slowly transiting, from weightlessness to about one-point-five gravity, should not be more burdening than using a swing in a children's playground.

"Let them suffer a bit," I said, shrugging it off.

"You'll go down in history as a callous bastard, Joey!" my copilot said, indicating the battery of recording equipment our principals had installed in the cockpit.

"Our body is God's temple," I answered. "Those politicians back there should have shown more respect for their bodies!"

At forty-seven years of age, I am top-fit and, like all workout buffs, I tend to look down on people who neglect their physique.

"You know," I said, grinning, "that one of those sorry sacks of shit actually asked to be seated in the smoking zone?"

Jerry didn't answer. He doesn't share my enthusiasm for exercise. He is about my age and there is some gray at his temples, but he is one of those skinny types who, time and again, seem to pass their physical effortlessly, no matter the amount of abuse they inflict on their body.

After that we had no more time for banter. The distance between Langley and our target was 10.001 kilometers, a trip that would involve about eighteen skips. From the time we set our bearings to 45.4 degrees northeast, the flight would take us just over seventy-two minutes.

Even if there had been secret tests with hypersonic flight for years, our mission was a historic one for sure. Not only were we the first passenger flight to cruise at an average speed of Mach 10, we were also turning a new page in military history.

My mind must have been wandering for a moment, for the knife was already at my throat before I could react to Jerry, crying out in surprise.

"Don't move!"

The fellow, whose swarthy face was reflected in the instrument panel before me, didn't have to repeat that order. I have a healthy respect for eleven centimeters of honed carbon steel, pressed against my jugular vein.

"Take it easy," I croaked. "We can work it out!"

My eyes darted over the instrument panel. The cabin monitor showed rows of motionless passengers, sagging in their seats. It seemed that death threats and skyjacking were not the only crimes the swarthy pirate was committing.

"What did you do?" asked Jerry. "Poison them?"

"Never mind," said the hijacker. "Just obey orders, and we'll all survive!"

"You are a U.N. soldier," said Jerry, glancing over his shoulder. "You're supposed to keep the peace. This is mutiny, they'll hang you!"

The vague image, reflected by the instrument panel, showed shoulder patches and a sky-blue beret. The man's dark complexion and short, bristly beard would cause alarm bells to go off in any aircraft security personnel. Except that this guy was our security chief himself, the captain in command of a heavily armed platoon, the existence of which all governments on the planet would deny.

"You go here," the man said.

He pushed a piece of paper in my hand. I read: *31°47" N, 35°13" E.*

"Okay," I said, "no sweat, mate!"

While I punched in the new coordinates, I repeated them out loud.

"Jerusalem!" Jerry said.

This guy is incredible, I bet he can work out geographic coordinates much faster in his head than you and I could key them into a computer.

"So you want to nuke the oldest civilization in the West!" I said. "Why?"

"He's nuts," said Jerry, who is known in the force as an atheist radical. "These guys have been crazy for more than four thousand years!"

The hijacker said nothing. He stood behind me and the blade of his K-Bar knife tickled my throat.

"Sorry," I said, "I have to bend over for this."

"For what?"

"Every two minutes," I replied, "we dip into the earth's atmosphere. At that time, I have to fire the engines in order to go back into space. Alternatively we can plunge to the surface; it would take us just under a full minute to crash."

The knife did not leave my throat and nothing happened for about twenty seconds.

"You better decide now," Jerry said. "Once we are on a dive, it will be too late!"

That was, of course, nonsense. The XY-Zoroaster is the most fuel-effective airplane ever built, and even if we were to lose several kilometers of height, we should not have any problems getting back into space, using our special air-breathing combined-cycle engines. But soldier boy didn't know that and Jerry's lie signaled me that he knew what I was up to.

"Ten seconds from now," I said.

I bent over, grasping the joystick. The hand with the knife yielded and I started counting down. Then I pushed the throttle to full.

The hijacker flew backward and was knocked unconscious against one of the steel beams that separated the cockpit from the cabin. By the time we reached Mach 15, Jerry hollered that I should slow down. I was struggling to get out of the upper layers. Not because of our unheard-of acceleration. Jerry and I were wearing G-suits and the poor bastards in the cabin were not my immediate concern. For all I knew, they were all dead, before I even began my maneuvre.

"It's stuck!" I shouted.

Nobody had ever reached this kind of speed within the earth's atmosphere, and the plane reacted sluggishly, whereas the throttle resisted our combined efforts to force it back.

Now heat was our problem. Any object speeding through the atmosphere will compress and heat the air in front of it. Hypersonic aircraft that fly along strictly atmospheric trajectories can only get rid of this heat by dumping it into their fuel and then burning the fuel in the engines. That is why earlier hypersonic aircraft were inefficient: the faster you fly the more fuel you must carry as a heat sink. In the end, the first hypersonic planes were carrying more fuel than payload. By hopping in and out of space, the XY-Z was able to radiate the excess heat. Which is to say that we did not have any conventional heat protection.

Seconds before we burned to a crisp, the pointed nose of our magnificent aircraft pierced the last layer of the exosphere. The sensation of weightlessness felt like a fresh shower on a hot day.

Jerry got out of his chair and used olive-green cord from our survival kit to truss up our knocked-over pirate.

"Any damage?" he yelled.

There was. At first I even thought that all systems were off. Not that it affected our flight. Now that our speed was down to a more conventional Mach 10, the XY-Z reacted lightly to the joystick and the throttle was as functional as ever. The instruments were the problem. Not the simple ones, like the compass or the altimeter—they worked fine, all right. But almost everything else had failed.

Jerry was fiddling with the GHFS.

"Don't!" I said. "Strict radio silence!"

"Except in an emergency," Jerry argued. "What do you think this is?"

I shrugged. What did we have to lose? The mission had to be aborted anyway. Or, rather, it had aborted itself. How are you going to precision bomb without instruments?

Or tell your principals, without a radio, that you'd like to come home? The Global High Frequency System only emitted static today.

"Have you tried Sigonella?" I asked.

"And Incirlik," Jerry said. "Both ground stations are stone dead!"

"And there is no transmission from the GPS-satellites either," I worried.

"There are no satellites!" Jerry concluded.

He was staring into the void beyond the porthole, where the familiar constellations blinked their reassuring lights. It was a moonless night, but you could work out the position of earth's guardian by the absence of starlight in that location. But none of the luminous dots were visible that should have given away the presence of orbiting satellites, not one.

"Let's go down right here," Jerry said.

I nodded. We had to look after the passengers and, considering our cargo, Jerusalem was the only safe place to land for hundreds of miles around.

But the eternal city was not where it should have been. When XY-Z thundered out of the clouds, we did not see any light at all. When we came closer, tilting to commence our vertical landing, our landing lights revealed only stony desert and heavily wooded hills.

"Take the highest point!" Jerry advised.

With his eyes riveted to the monitors of the tail videos, he talked me in, centimeter after centimeter.

When I cut the engines and an unworldly silence was invading the cockpit, Jerry was busy with his pocket calculator.

"I don't believe it myself," he said, "but we are right on top of the Temple Mount!"

The casualties were heavy. The G-forces had provoked massive heart attacks in more than a hundred weak or elderly politicians. The stuff that the hijacker had used to sedate them had killed at least another twenty passengers.

Even one of the commandos of the security platoon had succumbed to the drug cocktail in his coffee. We were no more than fifty now.

Jerry and I didn't take any more chances: we had taken all the soldiers' weapons while they were still unconscious. Now my copilot and I were the only ones who were armed to the teeth.

"Where are we?" asked the young woman with the sergeant's stripes, who was very efficient in organizing the evacuation of the dead and the wounded.

"Jerusalem," said Jerry.

"Oh, yeah?" said the girl. "My name is Sarah Levi. Take it from an Israeli: Jerusalem does not look like this at all!"

"Not in our time," I said.

While I watched the realization dawning on the horror-stricken face of the young woman, I went over the whole equation again, but there was no other explanation: we had crossed the time-barrier.

Since Einstein, mankind had known about the relation between time, space, and speed, but nobody had ever experienced it beyond the schoolboy-experiment of walking inside a moving train.

Another first! But Colonel Joey Marsh would not be remembered for commanding the first hypersonic passenger flight, nor for dropping the first atom bomb since Nagasaki. Not even for being the first to cross the time barrier. I would be remembered for disappearing from the radar screens. With my two hundred passengers and my live warhead, I would overshadow the bloody Bermuda Triangle itself!

Using a pneumatic shovel from our cargo bay, we had buried our dead. An elderly man with a white beard had mumbled something in a foreign tongue, signing crosses in the air. A younger man had spoken in another language, bowing to the east, kneeling and touching his forehead to the ground.

Now we were together in the cabin, having breakfast. We had enough water and emergency rations to last us a couple of weeks. We also had fuel enough to try and reverse the maneuvre that had brought us here, but we wanted to rest first and calculate everything that was calculable. At least now our batteries were still charged.

"Company!" Jerry warned, raising his P90. He had taken the first watch, scanning our surroundings from the safety of the cockpit.

I followed his pointing finger to one of the screens. A very old man and a boy, guiding him by the hand, stood out there. They were dressed in the manner of desert people: long robes and pieces of cloth to cover their heads.

Both men fell to their knees. I could almost understand why. After we had buried the dead, I had lingered outside. XY-Zoroaster, a black triangle of steel and epoxy, standing on its tailfins, thirty-five meters high, was an awesome sight, even to me, a sophisticated citizen of the twenty-first century. No wonder that two prehistoric shepherds thought that they were in the presence of the Most High.

The old man was crying and speaking in some guttural language.

"Aramaic," said Sarah Levi, who was looking on over my shoulder. "He is asking for mercy!"

I must have gaped at her, for she added in an irritated tone of voice: "What? So I am a scholar, as well as a soldier! How else are we going to decipher the Dead Sea Scrolls?"

"Ask their names," I said.

The two poor souls outside flattened themselves as our hailing system boomed over their heads.

I could make out "Abraham" when the old man answered, but the second name was lost to me.

Sarah was shouting what sounded like a string of abuse. The old man looked up at our cathedral of black steel, worlds of sorrow in his eyes.

"What is going on?" I asked. "Tell me, for Pete's sake!"

"The young guy is Ishmail," Sarah spat. "It is now years before the birth of Isaac, who shall become the ancestor of the Jewish people. This first son of Abraham is the progenitor of the Arab race, so let's strike at the root of the evil!"

I watched in horror as the old man was binding his son's hands behind his back and laying him, facedown, on a flat rock. When Abraham's dagger flashed in the early sunlight, I was running down the ladder and shouting "No!"

Was it an act of God that, at this very moment, I saw a ram with its horns entangled in a bush?

We made it back, thanks to Jerry. Our calculations might have been a fatal millimeter off, but my copilot's uncanny sense of direction pointed us smack in the middle of the black hole that almost ripped us apart and which finally transported us back to our own universe.

The digital clock on the instrument panel announced August 1, 2002, 1:32 A.M. We had lost one half hour, not much for a trip to Old Testament times. Our disappearance and subsequent reappearance were not on any newscast and all seemed to be as it was before. Until I caught a newsflash about a single casualty from an event called Palestine Festival. A young boy seemed to have been stabbed to death by an inebriated sailor. The newscaster spoke about "unheard-of violence" and announced a week of mourning throughout the Holy Land. The boy's burial was to take place today; the rites would be celebrated by an ecumenical team of officials from all world religions.

While we headed home, I left Jerry in command. Not so much because he had saved our lives, although that played a certain role. But I needed the hour from here to Langley to rehearse my explanation of the events.

Why and how had I lost one hundred and fifty passengers, why was I bringing my warhead back, and above all why did I embark on my mission in the first place? I was sure of it: the politicians would find it utterly incomprehensible that I had intended to nuke Baghdad—and who had ever heard of a gentleman named Saddam Hussein?

Maybe I could tell them the truth: I had saved the life of a prehistoric shepherd, and that was all there was to tell. I did not want to be accused of jumping to conclusions!

After the old man and the boy had sacrificed the ram and we had eaten some chops that tasted remarkably gamy, we sat around the fire.

"Abraham," the old man said, beating his chest.

Ishmail did the same, so I, too, pointed to myself and said my name was Joey.

The old man just looked stunned, but Ishmail kissed the leather of my boots, before he spoke my name, pronouncing it carefully:

"Jahweh!"

Ina Coelen

The Best Time for Planting

The capacity for crime lurks in everyone's heart, from the most hardened criminal to the most innocent and pure. German author INA COELEN knows this better than most people, and her story, "The Best Time for Planting," shows it. This story was first published in *The Many Deaths of Mr. S.*

The Best Time for Planting

Ina Coelen

"I can't just sit back and do nothing," gasped the gardener, wiping the sweat from his forehead with his sleeve. "I've got to do something about it!" He determinedly dug out another piece of earth with the spade and threw it so that it landed exactly on top of the rest of the pile. He was standing up to his hips in the hole he had been digging for a few hours. "This pen-pusher turns up here and I am expected to get out of the way. No, not me! Not Herbert Baumgartner!" He threw the spade away and jumped up out of the hole. He inspected his work critically. "It's fine, except it needs to be deeper," he decided.

He unscrewed the lid of his thermos flask and poured what was left of his coffee into his mug. He longingly looked across to the large detached house, whose garden he was working in. From inside he could hear happy voices. Every now and then Alvine's light laughter reached him outside.

"Oh, Alvine . . ." Herbert sighed. About an hour ago she and her sister, Marga, had brought a drink out to him. They had laughed and flirted with him and just as Alvine playfully kissed him on the cheek Mr. S. had come strolling over the lawn. The mood had been spoiled.

Mr. S.'s land neighbored that of the Bausch sisters. Through a garden door, the lock of which Mr. S. had repaired, he gained entrance to Alvine and Marga's garden. They didn't seem to mind. Mr. S. had only recently moved here, and apart from a few rumors Herbert didn't know much about him. Mr. S. was in his early fifties, gray hair, gray suit, of average build, not really a ladies' man. His manners were perfect, though, and that's what won them over, Herbert sadly realized. Mr. S. impressed the ladies with his good manners and intellectual behavior and made himself indispensable with small favors.

From the start Mr. S. had been ready with gardening tips and lectured that the best time for planting was up until the end of October. Herbert Baumgartner seethed inside as this imposing know-it-all gave his lecture.

He, who had worked here since being an apprentice, was expected to take advice from this "clever clogs" who spent half the day shifting files in his office in the town hall.

Just as Herbert had been about to get really angry, the sisters had ushered Mr. S. into the conservatory.

Up until a few weeks ago, the gardener had been the cook of the roost. Marga had baked for him several times and both women had showered him with kindness and attention. Herbert had been sure that he stood a chance with the girls. Then Mr. S. arrived on the scene. Alvine was led to believe he was a poor widower. Herbert had heard from rumors, however, that his wife and children left him after it was known that he has connected with a bank robbery.

Sullenly, Herbert slid back into the hole. He wanted to complete the digging today. Tomorrow he would dig up the nut tree and replant it here. It was a thorn in his chest that for quite a while Mr. S. had enamored himself with the women of the area.

"I'm not going to have my nose pushed out by him," mumbled Herbert, digging himself into a rage. Quickly the hole became deeper and wider.

He had always been easily excited, and angered very quickly. Even more so since Mia had gone. They hadn't been married—Herbert hadn't thought it was necessary—but he had been dumbfounded when she wanted to leave him. After he found out that she had cheated on him with the baker, he first beat up the baker and then Mia. Afterward, he had stood in the bakery, enraged. Everything was either white from the flour or red from the blood. Herbert had screamed, "Come home!" Mia didn't come home, though. At some time she had secretly taken her things and left the flat keys on the hall table. He had lived alone since then. Here and there he had had a fling but nothing serious. Fortunately, he wasn't at home much. Instead he spent his time working in the most beautiful gardens in the town or in the cemetery. The fresh air was good for him, he could get rid of his frustrations through physical labor. Now that he was getting on sixty, he was starting to feel the first aches and pains of his age, and wished that he had someone waiting at home for him. Herbert thought he looked okay. His hair was sun-bleached, his silver sideburns and moustache resembled those of Clark Gable.

He had really pursued pretty Evelyne until he discovered that she wasn't just single, but was a single parent. He retreated quickly and had then not only tended the plump widow Wohlgemuth's garden but tended her as well. She had often invited him around for a meal. He had been pleased, as the way to a man's heart is through his stomach.

Then out of nowhere Mr. S. appeared. He had purchased a flat in the same building and Widow Wohlgemuth had let herself be beguiled straightaway by this charming and articulate phony. Herbert had retreated in a huff, although, as it turned out, it had worked out quite well—for in the meantime he had hooked the Bausch sisters, both in their early fifties, with a zest for life, still quite attractive, and inheritors of the famous paper factory Bausch and Bogen. They owned one of the largest properties in the area, with a splendid garden and a huge house. Herbert dreamed of ending his days here. The signs had looked good until Mr. S. started visiting the sisters.

What sounded like a gunshot brought an abrupt end to his thoughts, but then he realized that it must have been the popping of a cork. Herbert threw his spade down. That would be just the thing, a duel at dawn. "I'm not giving in so easily!" he grunted, and imagined the scene in front of him: himself and Mr. S.; back to back; their pistols at the ready. Herbert had no experience with guns and feared that Mr. S., as a suspected bank robber, would probably be at an advantage. "I'm not a coward!" he shouted out into the starting twilight. He reckoned he'd stand a better chance in a one-to-one fight, man to man, as he had with the baker. "I'll get you!" he yelled out of his hole in the ground. But then again Mr. S. was nearly ten years younger than him; the risk of a defeat suddenly seemed too high for Herbert. He spat contemptuously on the topsoil and only then noticed how deep the hole was. He found himself at eye-level with the turf. "I'm not going to be booted out by you!" he hissed, while trying, to no avail, to crawl out of the hole. The earth was damp and smooth and only after several attempts did he finally end up on his stomach on the lawn. From the house he could hear lively laughing and the clinking of glasses.

"I am going to poison you! I am going to make a brew of poison and garden herbs and then we'll drink a toast." Herbert searchingly looked around. Even if it had been a bit lighter, he would have found neither lily of the valley nor laburnum, not to mention oleander or meadow saffron. He tried to brush the worst of the mud off his trousers and looked down into the nearly two-meter-deep hole. "Oh, damn! I am going to have to fill up half of it again," he swore, took a few large stones and threw them into the hole. He walked slowly toward the veranda, where he heard Marga tipsily trill, "Cheers, Willi! You can call me Marg." She giggled devilishly. Herbert tightened his fist. He then picked up the twenty-kilo stone, which had been lying next to the veranda steps. He dragged it to the hole and threw it in as though he wanted to kill his adversary with it. Then he went home moodily, without saying good-bye.

He was sleeping restlessly and dreamlessly when he was woken by the merciless ringing of his telephone. "Oh, Herbert!" murmured Alvina. "Could you come really quickly?"

Irritated, he looked at his alarm clock. "It's four o'clock in the morning!"

"You could say it's an emergency!" Marga interjected. "And it would be better if you were to use the side entrance."

"Oh!" replied Herbert, and didn't want to ask any questions.

"We'll explain everything when you get here. Please hurry," Marga finished.

Without wasting any time Herbert got dressed, got on his bike, and rode to the sisters' house. He felt good, he was needed again. The side door was slightly ajar and he slipped in without being seen. He went through the hall to the living room. He didn't know what he had expected but it wasn't what he saw. Alvine and Marga were leaning over a case that was full to the brim. They were giggling like teenagers and sorting bank notes according to size and color. Both of them were wearing dark tracksuits and had their hair tied tightly at their necks.

"There you are already," beamed Alvine, she jumped up and pulled him farther into the room.

"Have you ever seen so much money? I bet it's a million. Just look at it! The bore had this hidden in his flat and hadn't dared to spend it. The idiot, he didn't deserve any better!"

Marga threw her sister a look. "Now don't talk like that, you shouldn't speak ill of the dead." She quickly put her hand to her mouth. "Whatever will Herbert think of us?"

"Oh, he couldn't stand him, either. Isn't that right, Herbert?"

Alvine took him by the arm and held a bundle of money under his nose.

"What do you think? Shall we all go on a cruise? We haven't been on holiday for years. We put every last penny into the house and the factory. Now it's time to enjoy life."

"All of the money is from Mr. S.?" Herbert heard himself saying.

"Yes, just imagine!" Marga beamed. "He robbed a bank but he was so frightened of being caught that he didn't spend the money."

"You know a lot," replied Herbert, just to hear the sound of his own voice. He wasn't sure whether he was dreaming or not.

"Willi," Alvine said, giggling, "couldn't take his alcohol. As soon as he'd had a drop to drink, he started talking."

"Exactly," Marga interrupted her. "He could confide in us. Always having to keep a secret, it's enough to make anybody strange." She winked slyly at her sister.

"Yesterday evening he told us where he had hidden his suitcase full of money," explained Alvine. "Marga went over to his flat and, taking precautions, took the suitcase. Now it looks as though Mr. S. has gone on a journey—and that's true in a way." She beamed at Herbert.

"Gone on a journey," Herbert repeated.

"On his last journey, so to speak." Marga was getting impatient.

"And how is Willi, Mr. S. . . . I mean . . ." Herbert struggled for words.

Marga threw him a conspiratorial look. "He couldn't take alcohol and particularly not what we mixed into it."

"And now," Marga added, wide-eyed, "he's at the bottom of the hole with his suitcase. You've got to replant the nut tree quickly. The cycle of the moon means that now is the best time for planting."

Martin Spiegelberg

The Money to Feed Them

Another German author of note is MARTIN SPIEGELBERG, who is quickly gaining a reputation in his native land for quick, clever thriller and mystery stories, like the one we've included here. "The Money to Feed Them" first appeared in the anthology *Death on the Waters and Other Criminal Stories,* and is a tale of cross and double-cross, where the only winners are the sharks.

The Money to Feed Them

Martin Spiegelberg

"How about going to the dining room for breakfast?" Helmholtz asked his wife.

"Too strenuous, and it's much more romantic in bed."

Helmholtz was a bit surprised at her answer, because over the years all romance had disappeared from their marriage. And if Sabina had any romantic feelings while having breakfast in bed, they certainly weren't about him, but about Christopher Lambert, or one of the other male models whose films she consumed by the dozen.

Only on video, of course, because the idea of going to the movies was always turned down with the comment "Too strenuous."

Sabina had the telephone receiver in her hand. *"Due* breakfast, but *subito* and *avanti,"* she said. Helmholtz rolled his eyes and sighed. She was not too good at foreign languages. He was proud of his fluent Spanish, which he had learned during his time in South America. Oh, the old days. He sighed again. There was a knock on the door. He opened it and Manolo, the waiter, came in with the breakfast tray. He winked at Helmholtz and said something about the feeding of the pachyderms in quick Spanish because the señora would have understood the word "elephant." Helmholtz grinned at him, gave him a five-hundred-peseta bill, and answered with the classic line of all Iberian *machos: "Hay que ser hombre."*

The remark that one has to be a man seemed a bit ridiculous, coming from his mouth. A lot smaller than his wife, not even half her weight, and totally dependent on her and her parents' goodwill. That was all that was left of him. He had not even kept his own name because Sabina's father had insisted on him adopting her last name. She was the only child, and the name of the Düsseldorf family of steel tycoons was not to be allowed to die.

Good Lord, that woman can eat, he thought for the umpteenth time, as he watched her wolfing her breakfast. He felt slightly nauseous.

"Don't you want to eat, Karli?" Sabina called from the bed. There was still a bit of egg yolk sticking to her chin as she spread honey—lots of it— on a sweet bread roll.

"I'll be back soon, sweetie. I'll just shave first," he answered, hoping that she would have eaten up the breakfast for two before he had finished his morning toilet.

When he came out of the bathroom a bit later, shaven, showered, and with freshly brushed teeth, she had indeed left only a slice of toast, a bit of cheese, and a cup of coffee.

"It's your own fault, why do you always have to take so long in the bath?" she said. The egg yolk on her chin had dried, and she rolled out of bed to get dressed. He turned around, ate the toast with the cheese, and drank the coffee.

When he had first met Sabina, the cheerful blond girl from the Rhine, twenty years ago, one could have called her "not really skinny." Later on, the specifications could have gone from "pudgy" through "fat" to "monstrous." He could think of no word to describe her present physical state. Recently, he had begun to answer the question, whether he and Sabina had children, with the question: "Do we look like circus artists?"

Sabina would then giggle and say: "Oh, my Karli, always ready with a joke."

He had lost his sense of humor a long time ago.

"Don't forget, you have to get the cabriolet," Helmholtz said.

"Can't you get it, Karli? It's such a long way to the car hire office, and the heat is terrible, and I don't speak Spanish."

"It was your idea to hire the cabriolet, and the office is just a few meters from the hotel. All the clerks speak fluent German and the doctor has told you to get a bit of exercise," Helmholtz said. It was important that she should fetch the car.

"You always leave everything to me," Sabina complained. "I never wanted to go to this stupid island in the first place. I'd rather have gone on a cruise. And now you won't even get that car. And it's so hot outside."

"Don't forget your driver's license and your credit card, sweetie," Helmholtz said relentlessly. Sometimes you have to be tough—*hay que ser hombre*.

She put on a flower-patterned dress. In the early days, she had bought her dresses in boutiques. Later on, she had had to go to special shops for oversize women. Then she had had to have her clothes tailor-made; what she was wearing now looked like it had been created by Omar the tentmaker.

"Well, all right," said Sabina, and stomped out of the door.

Helmholtz took his most beautiful silken scarf from a drawer; today was a special day, after all. He stood in front of the small mirror and tied it artistically. It took almost five minutes before he was satisfied. Then he went to the large mirror and inspected himself carefully. The slender body, the sun-tanned skin, the meticulously trimmed little mustache; he looked damn good for a man in his mid-forties. That was Suzy's opinion, as well. And Manuela's. And Yukiko's. He could still have a lot of fun, the time of lies and secrets would soon be over—after an appropriate period of mourning, of course. He had already selected the black suit. He smiled thoughtfully, admiring his perfect white teeth. Then he took the navy-blue jacket from the wardrobe—it looked good with his white linen trousers—and put on the sailor's cap that Sabina had bought him. He fetched a few things from the top compartment of the wardrobe—he had chosen a hiding place that lazy Sabina would never find—put them in a small bag, and sauntered out of the room to the hotel bar. It would take ages until Sabina had made her way to the car hire office and filled in all the forms. She always made things like this unnecessarily complicated. Enough time for a little refreshment. Recently, he had developed the habit of having a brandy after breakfast.

"Morning, Paco," he said to the bartender. "Give me a *Lepanto,* please."

He had quickly made friends with many of the employees because there were not many tourists who spoke Spanish.

"A *Lepanto,* very well, señor. Is it your birthday today?"

"Life, my dear Paco," Helmholtz said, "is too short to drink bad brandy, to read bad books, or to hang around with boring people." Before Helmholtz had married into the steel family, he had not been able to tell good brandy from bad. The people he hung around with were all pretty boring, and he had never read books. Except Sabina's savings books, perhaps.

Paco laughed dutifully and filled the glass generously.

Helmholtz drank his brandy quickly but with pleasure. Then he said: "Give me a last-but-one." He never ordered a last one because in Spain that meant bad luck.

"*Un penultimo,* señor, very well." This time, he filled the glass even more generously.

Helmholtz saw the bright red cabriolet stop in front of the hotel, with Sabina in the driver's seat. He finished his drink, paid, leaving a good tip, as always, and went to the door.

"Thank you very much, señor. And have a nice day!" Paco called after him. I will indeed have a very nice day, Helmholtz thought, and walked toward the car and Sabina. He enjoyed the admiring glances of four pale British ladies, who were sitting around a table, drinking tea and playing bridge.

"Where have you been? I've been waiting all this time," Sabina complained, as he took his place beside her.

"I had a little conversation with the bartender. Poor guy has so few people to talk to."

"Sometimes I think you enjoy talking to those primitive Spanish farmboys more than you enjoy talking to me."

This might be true, my dear, because these farmboys sometimes say really clever things, and they are on a level of intelligence that you will never reach.

These people were the descendants of the *conquistadores,* who had subjugated half the world. He felt more affinity with them than with his compatriots. And, in actual fact, he did look more like a Spaniard than a Teuton.

"Oh, no, sweetie," he said. "It's just fun to practice my Spanish before I lose it completely."

"Then why don't you take care of Daddy's Spanish business associates? But you'd never think of working, would you?"

That's what *you'd* like, he thought, for me to be your high-handed father's dog. I'd rather do nothing.

"But you'd rather do nothing and have others pay the bills," she said, as though she had read his mind.

In a very short time, I'll do nothing even more intensely than now, he thought with a smirk. He transformed the smirk into his usual charming smile, and said: "You know how it is, sweetie. In the firm I would only cause trouble and irritation. Daddy said so himself. So I keep my hands off the family business."

"You're a good-for-nothing, and you always will be. But a nice one," she added, producing the caricature of a sweet smile.

She took the next bend at high speed, at which his stomach heaved and the large brandies caused a revolution in his brain.

"Exactly," he said, "why should we argue? It's a wonderful day and we've been looking forward to the trip."

"What's in your bag?" Sabina asked.

"Bathing stuff. I thought maybe we'd go to the beach in San Vicente."

"You don't want to step into that mud puddle, do you? It's teeming with all kinds of germs, and there's oil and jellyfish, too."

She never went to the beach; there was no bathing costume big enough anyway, and she must have had the remnants of a sense of shame, because she refused to have one made. No, she hadn't done any swimming in ten years, and any other kinds of exercise, like aerobics, cross-country skiing, or cycling, had been put into the drawer marked TOO STRENUOUS after a very short time.

"We don't have to," he said.

"You can go for a swim tomorrow. But today you're on a trip with me."

And you walk next to me on a short leash, without barking or biting, he completed the sentence in his mind.

A short time later they arrived at San Vicente. Sabina parked the car in front of the medieval church, which was one of the island's points of interest.

"Come on, let's have a look at the church. It's sure to be a bit cooler inside," Helmholtz said.

From Sabina came the inevitable "Too strenuous," this time with an added: "And it's cool in the café, as well."

Helmoltz slowly walked to the church, which was, as almost every building here, painted in white lime. Inside it was so cold that he started to shiver. The walls were meters thick. The church had also served as a refuge from all kinds of conquerors who had infested the island over the centuries.

Helmholtz looked at everything mentioned in the guidebook and then went back to the village square. Apart from Sabina, there were just a few locals sitting on the café's shady terrace. But even in among a hundred tourists, she would have stuck out like a sore thumb. She busily worked her way through assorted cakes, pies, tarts, and other sweets, which occupied the whole table. The grown-ups watched her surreptitiously; the children stared at her as though she were some strange animal in the zoo. These people, whose ancestors had had all kinds of experiences for two thousand years, had never seen anything like this.

It was rather embarrassing, but Helmholtz had long since got used to this feeling. The waiter came and eyed him with a pitiful expression. He ordered a coffee and a brandy, and when he finished them, Sabina had finished her second breakfast, too.

"What else do we have to do?" she asked when they were back in the car. It sounded as though they'd had a long day's sightseeing tour behind them.

"The marine aquarium might be interesting. It's not far away, and there is a well-known seafood restaurant right nearby," Helmholtz said.

"Seafood restaurant sounds tempting, but that aquarium sounds like strenuous walking."

"No, it isn't," Helmholtz said, opening the guide book. "The book says that on request you'll be driven around in an electric car. And *Los Tiburónes* possesses the longest underwater tunnel in Spain."

"That puts a different character to it, not having to walk. And that tunnel might be nice. What's the meaning of *Los Ti . . . ?*"

"*Tiburónes,*" Helmholtz completed. "It means 'The Sharks.' According to the book they've also got the biggest collection of sharks in Spain."

"Probably the only one," Sabina said.

A quarter of an hour later they parked in front of a large sign saying AQUA PARK LOS TIBURÓNES. JOSÉ MARIA VARGAS. The paint was peeling off the sign and the whole thing made a rather decayed impression. There were only two other cars and a cross-country motorbike in the parking lot.

"Looks like it's closed," Sabina said.

"Impossible. The book says it's open daily from ten A.M. until eight P.M."

They left the car and walked the few steps to the cash desk. The tickets were cheap and there was a videocassette and a book of photos for sale, both made by someone called Juan Vargas. Behind the desk sat a fat-bellied, heavily sweating man who wore old jeans, a yellow T-shirt, and had a three-day old beard. He took the money, handed over the tickets, and had a short look at the visitors. He raised his eyebrows, looked again, and his sullen face suddenly lit up.

"Eso es increíble! Señora Helmholtz!"

"How do you know me?" Sabina asked incredulously.

"How could I not know you, señora? I worked for your papa for fifteen years. In Düsseldorf."

The man spoke German with a hardly noticeable accent. He jumped from his chair and left the ticket office. He smiled from ear to ear, exposing a large gold tooth. Funny, thought Helmholtz, in southern countries even fat people move with a certain elegance.

The cashier shook Sabina's hand heartily. To Helmholtz it looked as though he would never let go of it.

"With your permission, my name is José Maria Vargas, I am the owner of this humble enterprise. But please call me Pepe, like my friends do."

It was hard to believe, but Sabina had blushed like a fourteen-year-old girl. Wrong. Helmholtz corrected himself, nowadays even fourteen-year-old girls don't blush anymore.

"Er . . . Nice to meet you, Herr . . ."

"Pepe!" said the man.

"Herr . . . Pepe. This is my husband, Karl Heinz," Sabina said, clumsily pointing at Helmholtz.

The Spaniard briefly shook Helmholtz's hand and said, "Good morning," without even looking at him.

"When señora Helmholtz gives me the honor of her visit, it is my pleasure to show you around, personally. You are invited, of course."

He bounced back to the cash desk like a rubber ball, came back with the few peseta bills, gave them to Sabina, and said: "At the end of your visit, you will receive the video of our park, made by my brother Juan, as a gift."

He shouted something in quick Spanish, at which a skinny old man appeared through a door and took the place behind the cash desk.

"Just in case there will be other guests arriving. But probably the tw— three of us will be on our own. Business is rather lean at the moment. Please wait a minute, I'll be back with the electric car."

"He's really falling over himself. . . ." Helmholtz said. "Must have good memories of his years in Germany."

"I'm sure he felt fine in our firm. Our treatment of our people was always exemplary."

I know, I know, Helmholtz almost said, but he managed to bite his tongue.

"This guy is too obtrusive for my liking," he said. "He can hardly keep his hands off you. Probably expecting a good tip."

Sabina eyed him as though he came from Mars. "Is this jealousy? Good

God, good old Karli is turning into a raving Othello." She started to giggle, her face turned red, and she had to sit on a bench, otherwise she might have fainted.

That would be an even more elegant solution, Helmholtz thought, for her to collapse right here and now and die of a heart attack. Would save me a lot of money.

Her face was its normal color again, but she was still giggling quietly when Pepe returned with the electric car. "I am glad señora, to see you in such a happy mood," the Spaniard said, as he elegantly jumped from the car. With grandeur he offered Sabina his arm. She stood up, put her arm in Pepe's, and allowed herself to be led to the car. Even with a kind of grace, Helmholtz thought to his surprise.

"Would you please take a seat, too, señor," Pepe said. Helmholtz trotted behind them and sat on the backseat. Sabina had placed herself next to Pepe, of course.

They drove—endlessly, it seemed to Helmholtz—through the park. It didn't offer too much. A few touseled parrots, a pool in which two fungus-covered dolphins unenthusiastically performed their poor tricks, a couple of sad-looking chimpanzees in a hedge, that was all. Pepe chattered without a pause and a fascinated Sabina hung on his every word. Eventually Pepe said: "And now, señores, Pepe Vargas will present you the Aqua Park's absolute climax: The Shark Tunnel."

They drove down a ramp, and suddenly they seemed to be in complete darkness. Their eyes quickly adjusted to the dim light and finally they could see everything. The tunnel was about two meters wide, so the car could pass easily. Pepe stopped and lectured on the different kinds of sharks swimming about in the pool. It was a horrid sight. The fishes passed by noiselessly and elegantly, showing their teeth and watching their watchers with small cold eyes.

"Tell me, Herr . . . er, Pepe, you don't have too awfully many customers," Sabina said.

That was more than understatement; they were the only visitors in the park.

"How can you afford to feed them?"

Typical, Helmholtz thought, that's all she can think of, but he had not considered Pepe's creativity and talent for improvisation.

"Can you keep a secret señora?" he asked in a hushed voice and with a conjurer's expression. He moved closer to Sabina and tried in vain to put his arm around her shoulders. She nodded eagerly and blushed again.

"The fishes are not real," he whispered. Good golly, this guy Pepe was a genius. He had exaggerated his Latin-lover routine a little bit, but now she herself had given him a reason to take her away.

"Whaddyamean, not real?" she asked.

"You are perfectly right, señora, we could never afford to feed twenty sharks of this size. That is why we use electric mockups."

At that moment a hammer shark swam by, magnified by the glass.

Sabina was nonplussed. "And how do they work?" she asked excitedly.

"We have a central terminal, with one of our men moving them about by remote control. And at night we pull them out to recharge their batteries."

"Unbelievable!" Sabina saw a five-meter-long dangerous-looking fish swim by. "Herr . . . Pepe, I believe everything you say except that."

She has swallowed the bait, Helmholtz thought, and inwardly shouted for joy.

"I give you my word, madam." Oh, Lord, he has progressed from "señora" to "madam" now. He indeed exaggerated a tiny bit, but she fell for it, and that was the important thing.

"And if you don't believe me, it will be my pride and my pleasure to show you the terminal. Let nobody say that Pepe Vargas lies to his guests. There is just one condition."

"And that is?" Sabina asked.

"You must never in your life ever tell anybody about what you are going to see right now. And this goes for the señor as well."

"You can rely on me," Helmholtz said. "But I don't feel like going with you. I'm not feeling too well."

"Oh, come on, Karli," Sabina said. "You'll never get to see anything like this again."

"No, really, I'd prefer to have another look at the fishes, or, rather, the technical miracles."

"I am not going to abduct your wife for too long," Pepe said, offering his arm again and leading her toward a door. Hopefully not, Helmholtz thought. Make it short, I don't want her to suffer for too long. In actual fact, she was quite nice. He was astonished that he was already thinking of her in the past tense.

Helmholtz returned to the exit. Not too fast, but not too slowly, either. Without looking at anyone directly, but also without avoiding their looks. He reached the car and searched his pockets for the key. Suddenly he remembered that Sabina had kept the keys in her handbag. He smirked. In the Buenos Aires underworld they had called him *serpiente,* the snake. Because of his alertness, and because of his relentlessness. There are things, he thought, that you don't ever lose, not even after years of boring marriage. Three minutes later he was off in a northerly direction.

He had considered closing the car roof, but he decided against it. The model he drove was so common over here, that nobody would remember him, and a closed cabriolet would be more conspicuous in weather like this. He carefully observed the vehicles behind him, and for some time he thought he was being followed by a motorcycle. But it turned off onto a dirt track shortly before La Siesta, and Helmholtz muttered under his breath, as if someone could have heard him: "Now don't get paranoid, old man, nothing can happen to you."

• • •

In the north of the island there was the famous coastal road. Famous for its grand views and dangerous bends. The narrowest bend with the grandest view was called, for obvious reasons, *curva del diablo,* because the devil took his toll now and again. Every year some tourists died because they tried to cope with the bend and enjoy the view at the same time. Most of these tourists drove cabriolets. There was a *mirador,* a bay for looking and taking pictures, with a parking lot, on which Helmholtz parked the car. He could watch the coastal road in both directions, to make sure there were no witnesses. He had to wait for ten minutes, but he had even thought of bringing a camera along, so the passersby only saw a tourist taking pictures and forgot him immediately. Finally the road was clear. Helmholtz took his bag from the trunk, sat in the car, started the engine, and drove onto the road. Fortunately, Sabina had chosen a car with an automatic gearbox, but that was obvious, because the handling of a gearshift was "too strenuous" for her. Helmholtz had already equipped himself with a long stick. He released the handbrake and set the gear lever to "forward." As the car slowly started to roll, he got out and jammed the stick hard against the accelerator. The car jumped forward and disappeared forever. The cliff was five hundred meters high. Helmholtz heard a quiet "splash," as the car fell into the sea.

Pity, it was almost new, he thought. But why? The company is insured, and when I have Sabina's money, I'll never drive a shabby thing like that again. Nothing less than Ferrari. Everybody knew that Sabina never put on a seatbelt. Quite logical, the seatbelt to fit her had still to be invented. He had read that the tidal current was particularly strong here, so it would not be a surprise that her body was never found.

He heard an approaching car and hid behind a bush. Then he undressed and put on the rough cotton trousers, the dirty shirt, and the worn–out jacket, the things that he had brought with him in the bag. An old straw hat completed the impression of a local farmer. He thought about taking a snapshot of himself, using the self–timer, because this certainly was a rare sight: *Serpiente,* the most elegant gangster of Buenos Aires, or Handsome Carlos, as he was called in the Düsseldorf scene, dressed up as a Spanish peasant. Blockhead, he thought to himself, creating the evidence yourself.

The stick he had used to shove the car over the cliff now served him well as a walking stick, and he reached the next village an hour later. He had stored the fashionable clothes in his bag. He took the bus to the island capital and found a public toilet, which he entered as a poor farmer and left as an elegant tourist.

There was enough time to bathe and change before dinner. He washed very thoroughly, because in a way he felt dirty, even though he had not killed her himself. That had always been his weak spot: he couldn't stand physical violence and preferred to leave the dirty work to others. So he had an accomplice, but that was unavoidable. Pepe had the reputation of being extremely discreet, and he was being well paid.

Helmholtz put on his evening suit, had a dry sherry at the bar, and went to the dining room. Each of the tables was set for four people, and the Knesebeck couple, with whom they shared the table, were already there.

"Good evening, Herr Helmholtz," said Frau Knesebeck. "Where have you hidden your wife?"

"She should arrive any minute. You know, we took a trip in a cabriolet today, and she insisted on seeing the coastal road in the north. I didn't join her because, with all those bends, I easily get carsick."

"Dangerous, that road," Knesebeck said. He was a retired general, and still spoke in a short, sharp, military way. "Three men copped it already this year, I hear."

"Albert!" exclaimed his wife. "Don't frighten Herr Helmholtz."

"My wife is a very good and careful driver," Helmholtz said. "And the rented car is practically new and in a very good state. Maybe she has taken a little snack and will be a bit late."

"Yes, maybe," Frau Knesebeck said, and had that pitying look that everybody had when Sabina's appearance was alluded to.

"Never agreed with giving driver's licenses to women," Knesebeck snarled. "They drive either like snails or like bleeding pigs."

"Albert!" Mrs. Knesebeck said.

"True, isn't it?" was his answer. Without a uniform and a monocle he just didn't seem complete.

"What did you look at, Herr Helmholtz," Frau Knesebeck asked, to distract his attention from her husband's foulmouthed talk.

"We were in San Vicente first and had a look at the church. Then we went to the Aqua Park."

"Bad reputation, that place," Knesebeck said. "Owner s'posed to be the top mobster back in Germany."

"But really, Albert, that's all rumors. But they say that the park is in a rather miserable state."

"Well," said Helmholtz, "apart from the shark tunnel it's nothing to write home about."

"C'lossal chaps, those sharks. Eat anything gets in their way. Wonder where the dough comes from."

"Yes, I've heard that the park is always close to bankruptcy," Frau Knesebeck said.

Helmholtz loathed this typical Teutonic habit of saying the worst things about other people and then softening it with a casual "they say" or "I've heard." Everywhere else this was called slander; among people like the Knesebecks it was supposed to be conversation.

"When we were there, we were indeed the only customers. How do they afford to feed all those animals, when business is so slow?"

"Hashish!" the General trumpeted. "Big drug dealer, that guy Vargas. Impossible under Franco!"

"Yes, the word goes around that the park is just camouflage for a flourishing hashish business," said his wife.

The Knesebecks spent half their time over here, and usually they were up to date with the island gossip. But this time they were not quite fully informed, because Pepe did not only sell hash. From machine guns to heroine, one could buy anything one's heart desired at the Aqua Park.

"Gone over the cliffs, your spouse, I guess," Knesebeck said, when the dessert was served.

"She is a bit flighty, sometimes," Helmholtz said. "She has probably changed her mind and had dinner somewhere else."

"Always had a rather different idea of flightiness, hahaha."

Helmholtz preferred to take his digestive in better company—his own—and politely wished the Knesebecks a good night. He took a short walk through the town, had brandies in several bars, and talked to the bartenders. Now that it was over, he was so happy that even the unbearable Knesebecks could not spoil his mood. He had finally gotten rid of that stupid cow, and the money was his. As her husband, he was the solitary heir, of course.

Deep in thought about where to go to with all the dough—Acapulco, Rio, or perhaps Bali?—he went back to the hotel, slightly tipsy from happiness and brandy.

"Good evening, Rosita," he greeted the receptionist.

"Good evening, señor," she answered. "The señora is upstairs already."

"The what?"

"She just picked up the key five minutes ago," said Rosita.

"This must be . . . You sure it was my wife?" Perspiration covered his entire body. He paled.

"I don't think I would mistake her for someone else," Rosita said with the well-known pitying look.

His pulse rate had doubled. He was unable to think clearly.

"Aren't you well? You're very pale. Do you want me to call a doctor?" Rosita asked.

"Nonono, I'm fine," Helmholtz said, as he turned round and stumbled to the stairs. He went up slowly, step by step. Something had gone terribly wrong. But what? His brain started to work again. He was *serpiente,* the gangster, after all, and he was master of all situations. He would find an explanation for his sudden disappearance. And what a hard time he was going to give old Pepe when he got his hands on him. He could overcome his dislike of violence, if it was absolutely necessary. He reached the door and knocked.

"Come in, Karli, it's open!" Sabina called. I'm sure I'll invent a story that this dummy believes, he thought as he went in.

Sabina sat in an armchair pointing a little revolver at him. In her hand the piece looked like a toy—but still dangerous enough.

"Surprise!" she said in that sweetish voice that he had always hated. "Freeze, Karli. Or you're dead."

He stood very still.

With her left hand she picked up the receiver. Her right hand never moved and her eyes never left him. In fluent, almost perfect Spanish, she told the receptionist that she had caught a burglar, and could she please call the police. She replaced the receiver.

"But, Sabina," he said, confused, "where did you learn Spanish?"

"Pepe tought me. For the future boss of the *Aqua Park Los Tiburónes,* it is appropriate to speak the local language. Apart from that, Pepe likes to speak to his *querída* in his native tongue."

Helmholtz couldn't believe it.

"By the way, Karli, the chain of evidence is complete. We didn't know exactly what you were going to do with the car, so Juanito followed you on his motorbike. When you drove up toward the coastal road, everything was clear. Juanito knows every dirt track on the island, and when you arrived at the *curva del diablo,* he was already there with his videocamera. The car's unfortunate end has been filmed in best quality."

Of course, the video and the book of photos by Juan Vargas. Pepe's brother.

"That proves nothing," he said. "It's only of interest to the insurance agents. The cops won't bother."

"Juanito also filmed you giving the fifty-thousand mark advance payment to Pepe. And he has recorded the conversation with a special microphone."

Finito, Helmholtz thought. That's enough for a life-long sentence.

Somebody hammered on the door. *"Abrir la puerta! Policía!"*

"Un momento!" Sabina called.

"But . . . why?" asked Helmholtz.

"Don't you know, Karli? It's a big mistake to think that sex is only for young and sporty people. Don't you know the song 'Animal Crackers,' by Melanie?"

He only knew Elvis and the Beatles, and at that moment, he could not have cared less.

"In that song there is a line that goes:

> *. . . so I'll be a fatty for all my life.*
> *But some people think that fatties are nice."*

It was incredible.

"You and Pepe?"

"Yes, me and Pepe. And if that's what you mean: No, Pepe Vargas is not a circus artist, but for a man of his volume he is quite agile."

The hammering on the door got louder. Still pointing the gun at Helmholtz, Sabina rolled out of the armchair to open it.

"You and Pepe. How long?" he asked.

"Five years." She opened the door. "Where do you think he found the money in the first place—to feed all the animals?"

Raymond Steiber

Mexican Gatsby

Last year one of the lights in the mystery field went out with the passing of RAYMOND STEIBER, who was a frequent contributor to *Ellery Queen* and *Alfred Hitchcock*. He also had written one novel, *The High Castle,* but was known for his short fiction, which combined elements of high adventure, espionage, and mystery, often in a tidy package that left readers breathless. "Mexican Gatsby," from *Ellery Queen Mystery Magazine,* is just such a story, and was nominated for the Mystery Writers Association Edgar award for short fiction.

Mexican Gatsby

Raymond Steiber

O ld lovers often put new obligations on you, and that was why I found myself on the balcony of a hotel in Cabo San Mateo with a telephone in my hand, pulling my final weight for Dinah Turney.

Cabo San Mateo was divided into two distinct parts, and I could see both of them from where I was sitting. The new town with its glass-fronted hotels and well-groomed beaches and the old town with its crowded-together fishing boats and tile-roofed houses, the two of them separated by a broad Pacific bay.

There was a third town up in the hills above the cape, a place where there were wide puddles in the mud streets after any rain and always a smell of garbage in the air.

It provided the town with its cleaning ladies and waiters and pool attendants and lawn boys. Its petty thieves and prostitutes as well. Cabo San Mateo needed all of them in order to operate.

The man on the other end of the telephone didn't want to talk to me. But then why should some narco-gangster's flunky want to talk to somebody from the States who might turn out to be a DEA agent? So I played my trump card and told him what I was and the buzzer went off as it always does—in big city bars; in small towns, wherever people like me find themselves in the course of business, people who are plugged in to the great Dream Machine and can deliver some part of what it has to offer.

He told me to hold on and went off to confer with someone. Then he came back and asked for credentials.

I gave him the names of some people he could call in L.A. Then I added the titles of some pictures. *Nightmare City, Gangster, Hurry the Night.*

It was *Gangster* that turned the trick and got me in to see Felipe Cruz. He'd seen that one. But then what would you expect of some narco-gangster's gofer?

· · ·

Cruz's villa was located out toward the end of the cape. There were a lot of big houses out there; fitted this way and that into the natural contours in order to provide maximum privacy on a minimum of land.

A couple of guards with pockmarked faces stopped my cab at the wrought-iron gate. They wore black pants and tailless shirts that hung outside their trousers. The shirts were meant to conceal the pistols they carried, but the material was so thin that you could see them anyway.

The short brick drive curved through a dense growth of flowering plants and delivered me to a modern white villa with a red tile roof. I paid off the driver, and a young girl took me through the cool, sparsely furnished interior to the pool out back.

It was nicely set against the greenery there, a transparent jewel with the villa on one side of it and a gently sloping hill on the other. There was another Shirt out there with his barely concealed weapon and a fat guy stretched out on a lounger, and finally Cruz himself—or a man I took to be Cruz: a young barechested hoodlum sitting in the shade of an umbrella.

The girl took me over, and I introduced myself.

"I'm Mike Bergman," I said.

For a moment he eyed me morosely, then he gave a nod. "Sit down."

He was decently built with a smooth, hairless chest. There was nothing special about the face except the eyes, which were somewhat feminine. Or maybe feline would be a better word. There were a dozen *mestizos* just like him in every village between here and San Diego, and yet there was something that marked him out, too. In my business it's called presence, and if you've got it, you can go a long way.

He watched me impassively.

"So what do you want me for? A movie?"

The fat guy laughed sneeringly without raising his head.

"I flew down here to see Kristel Turney."

"Maybe he wants her for a movie," the fat guy said.

"Shut up, Justo."

His eyes turned back to me. I wondered if I was supposed to be afraid of him. I didn't feel afraid, but maybe it was the setting.

"I'm a friend of Kristel's mother," I said. "She passed away at Cedars of Lebanon last week. Her last request was that I come down here and see that her daughter was all right."

"Don't you expect her to be?"

"I don't expect anything. I'm here to carry out a mission for a dear friend. When it's done, I go back where I came from. Haven't you ever had obligations like that?"

He seemed to think it over.

After a moment he said: "She's upstairs taking a siesta."

"I can wait. Or I can come back later."

"Or you can just stay away, movie man," Fat Boy said.

Cruz motioned for the girl, then sent her to wake Kristel.

"This is a nice place," I said to make conversation.

"Money buys you anything," Cruz said.

"Sure. But it doesn't have to buy you things that are any good."

"I needed a place, and it was on the market. What does a movie producer do?"

"He's the guy who makes the picture happen in spite of the best efforts of the actors, the director, and the moneymen to see that it doesn't."

"That's what I do, too. I make things happen, even when people don't want it that way." A twenty-five, twenty-six-year-old with that sure undercurrent of menace someone that age can have. Yes, I guess he did make things happen.

"Jorge saw this movie of yours. *Gangster.*"

It had been a story about an inner-city gang facing off against the Mob. We'd used a rap star for the lead, and he'd been so intimidated by the responsibility that he'd tried to bluster his way through the part instead of giving a performance. The director and I had had to stay on him every minute, but even so he'd half-ruined the picture. I looked at the rough cut and thought how good it could've been if he'd just relaxed and played himself. Still, it'd had enough shootouts and explosions to make money, and certainly enough to satisfy some dimwit Third World narco-crook.

"How do you make a movie like that?"

"What do you mean?"

"How do you set it up?"

That was the thing all right, particularly if you were an independent like me. Basically you found a property and costed it out and then shopped it around. It routinely took months, even years, to get something off the ground. And even then it could all fall apart on you. Interesting the young rapper and then signing him on had made the difference with *Gangster.* And then, of course, we were stuck with him.

I told Cruz about it. It was less simple than sticking a gun in somebody's face, but the object was about the same. Get the thing done.

About the time I finished, Kristel showed up.

She was the archetypical California blonde and nothing like her mother, who'd been dark and voluptuous. Long legs, long hair, and just enough curves to make her interesting without robbing her of her nymphet quality. She was twenty and so American-looking that you'd never take her for anything else. You could see why Cruz had been drawn to her. She was the babe he'd been seeing all his young life in the movies and on TV and who a kid like him would never have a chance at. But then the narco-money had started pouring in, and like a fancy car or this villa, she'd suddenly become available to him.

And as for her—a young hoodlum like him exuding equal amounts of danger and sex appeal—well, write your own scenario. I'd certainly had a hand in enough like that.

I got her off around the other side of the pool where I could talk with her privately. She wore a tank top and cutoffs and sandals. Here and there her perfect skin was marred by strings of mosquito bites.

I said: "You know your mother's gone."

She played with a strand of hair. "I heard about it," she said indifferently.

They hadn't been close for three or four years, and then with all her health problems Dinah had just given up on Kristel. And as for her father, he'd faded out of the picture so long ago that nobody even remembered what he'd looked like.

"Before she passed, she asked me to come down here and see how you were doing. She was worried about you."

"You're not going to give me a big lecture, are you? Because I'm too old for that crap now."

"No. But maybe you ought to stop a moment and look where you're going."

"I'm not going anywhere."

"I mean, think, Kristel. These are gangsters you're mixed up with."

"So what about the sharks you swim with in your business? What about you? How're any of you any better?"

"Maybe we're not, ethically speaking. But nobody I know's ever cut anybody's liver out over a movie deal gone bad. There's a difference between being a hustler and a killer."

"I don't see any difference."

That was the way it went. She'd drifted down here and got mixed up with Cruz and that was how it would go on—for now, anyway—until she got bored with it and moved on. Or, more likely, Cruz grew bored with her. And as for me, I was too old to matter. For God's sake, I'd been around so long I'd actually slept with her *mother*. What did I know about anything?

I pushed it far enough to feel I'd met my obligation, then let it go.

"It's your life, Kristel. But look—if you're ever in a jam, call me and I'll be there for you."

I wrote my unlisted number on the back of a business card and tucked it in a pocket of her cutoffs. Then I walked around the pool to take my leave of Cruz.

I asked about calling a cab.

"No problem. Jorge will drive you. Hey, we're eating in town tonight. You come along with us. This place we're going is good."

Well, why not? I'd made enough movies about gangsters. I might as well break bread with one. I nodded my assent, and Jorge, who was one of the Shirts, drove me back to town. The vehicle was a black Grand Cherokee with tinted glass all around—which in Mexico is as much a mark of the narco-gangster as his cold eyes or his MAC-10 machine pistol.

I took a cab to the restaurant. It was a new place that sat out over the water, and the weather was just right for us to sit on a covered terrace while overhead fans stirred the breeze.

Kristel was there in a white dress that flowed off her left shoulder and across her young breasts and showed off her perfect tan. She sat next to

Cruz, which meant that I had to sit next to Fat Boy, who, it turned out, was Cruz's cousin. The rest of the party was made up of Shirts.

Cruz and Fat Boy were wearing so many rings and medallions that when they picked up a fork you expected them to clank. But I'd seen as bad in movie people. The difference was that in these guys it was a display of power, not wealth, and a dangerous power at that. Rattlers came in bright colors and so did Latin American hoodlums.

The seafood menu was good, the talk mainly stupid and boring, about fifty notches below what you'd hear in your average sports bar. That was something the movies, including my own, always got wrong. We have smart writers put clever lines in the mouths of men who in real life are only brutal and banal. Then the hoodlums ape the lines back to us because it's cool and that's the way they think they ought to talk. Sometimes you wonder if that's all they ape. How many real-life killings go down because that's the way the Corleones would do it or those guys in *Goodfellas*.

Kristel said virtually nothing. This was the boys' table and she was just there for decoration—to show off that Cruz was important enough to have somebody like her. If it bothered her, she didn't let on, and I wondered just what sort of story was playing in her head. Not the one that was going on around her, that was for sure.

The food got cleared away, and Cruz said: "If I wanted to make a movie, here in Mexico, what would it cost?"

"It would depend on the script. Also what sort of production values you went for and the type of cast. And where you intended to distribute it, Latin America or U.S.A. and the world."

"But it'd be cheaper here—right?"

"Maybe."

"I want to make a movie. I want to make the movie of my life. Like this *Gangster* of yours."

I didn't blink an eye. Everybody you met wanted to make a movie. Every shoe clerk and postal worker and waitress had a script tucked away somewhere. And they all seemed to buttonhole me.

"I got money I could put up," Cruz said. "And I got friends who could put up more."

I shook my head. "Don't get mad, but no U.S. producer would touch your money. The Feds'd make it look like money laundering and seize all his assets and the next thing he knew he'd be in bankruptcy court. You could maybe find some Latin American producer."

"I want it in English. I want it Hollywood."

Like the fancy car. Like the California blonde. That was how you validated yourself. That was how you proved you'd made the big time.

"We'll talk about this some more," Cruz said. "You come out on my boat tomorrow. Catch some fish. See what you think when I tell you some things."

So I agreed to do that. In the end I agreed to a lot of things.

• • •

He had a pretty good story to tell the next afternoon on his boat, and he continued it that evening over food and drinks at the villa. You had to fish for the details because he didn't understand any of that, how it was the little stuff that made a movie work, Alec Guinness's walk in those le Carré things, which he picked up from watching real-life spymaster Maurice Oldfield, the business about the blueberries in *Casino*. But the stuff was there, all right. The frightened birdlike look in Fernando Gomez's eyes when his luck had finally run out. The way the young hoodlum had burst into tears when they came to kill him, and how later his brother had begged Cruz to lie and tell everybody he'd gone out like a man. The *loco* Jimenez brothers who were so ruthlessly violent that they eliminated entire families, and how in the end, for everybody's mutual safety, they'd had to be exterminated themselves.

I began to see the shape of a possible screenplay and the larger-than-life characters who would inhabit it. It got me a little excited—which is what you need if you're ever going to get a picture off the ground. But where would I find somebody to play Cruz? Today's young actors were all soft at the center. They couldn't project believable levels of toughness like the actors of an earlier generation could—Cagney, for instance, who'd been raised on the meaner streets of New York, or Lee Marvin, who'd been hardened in the crucible of war. And they didn't have the acting skills of a De Niro or an Al Pacino.

It had been Fat Boy—Justo—who'd plucked Cruz off a village street and got him on with the Gomez organization. Gomez was a mid-level narco-gangster who owed allegiance to the Jimenez brothers, who ran everything up north.

They owned cops, parts of the military, government officials, even some U.S. customs agents. Anybody who got in their way ended up in the Tijuana city dump where the wild dogs of the place feasted on their bodies. They ruled by terror and were virtually untouchable.

Cruz had a reputation as a tough, and had been hired as an enforcer. His first kill had been the boy who'd cried, and in my mind I saw how it would play on the screen—as if it were only fodder for a movie and not something that had really happened.

Then, a year later, he'd been given the job of killing Gomez himself as part of a power play against the Jimenez brothers—his boss, his own *patron*. I fit that into the arch of the screenplay as well, matching it with the first killing.

Eventually, as the war with the Jimenez brothers had continued, he'd taken Gomez's place. The finish had come at an abandoned mine when the brothers had been shot down and pitched, still breathing, into the depths. Cruz hadn't been in on that—that had been strictly a Tijuana affair—but in my movie he would be.

And now he was almost respectable—a big-time narco-gangster who no longer dirtied his hands with actual killings and seldom had to order one. And in five years, in seven years, he'd be more respectable still—a man known for his investments and real estate holdings and a colorful past.

Except that he wouldn't. He was just a killer who'd got lucky and someday would get unlucky and didn't have, as others might have, that part in him that would avoid it. And that was grist for my movie, too.

In the end we came to an agreement. He'd supply the details and I'd put together a project based on his life story. But there'd be no money involvement. I'd raise the cash the way I always did, by begging it from moneymen who wouldn't know a good movie if it came up and bit them on the knee.

We shook hands on it, and afterward Fat Boy walked me to the door.

"You know who he wants for the lead in the movie."

"Tell me."

"Himself."

I thought about the troubles I'd had with the rap artist. "I don't think so, Justo."

"He'll do it if he wants to. And you'll like it, too, movie man."

Then he laughed in that sneering fashion of his and left me there in the dark.

I brought in Brian Singer to do the treatment. He was an old pro. He'd know how to shape the thing. We set up shop in my hotel in Cabo San Mateo and spent four or five evenings or afternoons a week out at the villa. Singer asked Cruz a lot of to-the-point questions about Gomez and the Jimenez brothers. Cruz had, in fact, never met them in the flesh but he knew plenty about them. Cruz didn't like Singer until Brian began showing him how certain scenes would play on the screen. Then he began seeing him as a necessary evil.

One night on the way back to the hotel Brian said: "You're going to have trouble with this guy when he sees the final draft of the treatment. He'll start acting like the worst pampered star you ever ran into, except that a star can only get you fired off the picture whereas this guy can kill you."

"I already thought about that. That's why there're going to be two treatments. One he likes and one we actually go to bat with. Don't worry. I'll do the dog work on the treatment he sees."

"What happens when he sees the movie?"

"I'll be in Los Angeles and he'll be here and I'll write him a note lamenting all the changes the distributors forced on us."

"The other thing we need is a finish for this thing, and right now I can't think of anything with any punch."

"We'll get to it. One thing, I don't want your standard machine-gun gangster climax."

"That's what the distributorship want. And remember, Mike, you still got to bring a director in on this thing. I mean, this isn't the nineteen forties. You aren't Daryl F. Zanuck with absolute control over what gets shot."

"Too goddam bad, too," I said.

. . .

Spending a lot of time with Cruz also meant spending time with Kristel. Not that we got any closer. She was more inclined to hang out with the Shirts, the Mexican guys, than with Brian and me. But then they were her age, they were inclined to indulge in the same sort of horseplay around the pool. Although sometimes I wondered if that horseplay didn't have an element of playacting about it, if it wasn't just a way of drawing a line, with Brian and me on one side of it and her on the other.

Once, when Brian and I were waiting outside, we heard her and Cruz arguing in the villa. What surprised me was that it was her voice that dominated. That was unexpected—it suggested things about her that I hadn't yet noticed. Abruptly the argument ceased, and a few minutes later Cruz came striding out of the villa and we started our session. Then, about halfway through it, Kristel appeared. She had finger marks on her throat and a swollen nose.

Cruz gazed at me through half-closed eyes. Fat Boy watched, too, with a smirk on his face. He was waiting to see which way I'd go. Whether I'd play the coward and ignore Kristel's condition or try to take her aside and find out what had happened. Either way I'd lose, and that was what Fat Boy particularly wanted to see. It would make his day.

But Kristel spoiled it for him by coming over and leaning on Cruz's chair and allowing him to slide his arm around her hip. All the while she stared at me with her gray California eyes and dared me to interfere. But I wasn't playing that game. I'd only help her if she asked for help.

Little by little, and mostly thanks to Jorge, we found out what the fight had been about. There were a pair of sisters Cruz kept in an apartment in the old part of town, and once or twice a week he'd spend an afternoon, an evening, or an entire night with them, sometimes taking Fat Boy along.

He had a brothel he liked to visit, too. Tia Anita's. He and Justo and the Shirts would descend on it *en masse* and party with the whores till dawn. When he returned to the villa, it was usually to find his fancy shirts cut up with a pair of scissors and his handmade shoes floating around in the pool. Then, from what we heard, he'd smack Kristel around and throw her in the pool with the shoes and keep her there half the morning, shoving his bare foot in her face every time she tried to climb out.

And yet, despite the violence, there was apparently something theatrical about it, too—as if each of them was playing a role for the benefit of the Shirts and enjoying it immensely even as they screamed and threatened and sobbed.

"This is great stuff," Brian said. "You can't *buy* this kind of stuff. It'll play big on the screen."

But, remembering Dinah, I wasn't sure I wanted to use Kristel in that way. Then I thought: She'll probably like it. And once he calms down, Cruz'll probably like it, too.

. . .

Finally Brian had his treatment, and I had my Trojan Horse treatment as well. We went out to the villa to lay it at the feet of Cruz.

I explained to him what a treatment was.

"It's a super-detailed outline with most of the big scenes sketched in. It's sort of like a rough blueprint for the picture."

I'd had a local bind it for me in leather covers, and now I handed it to Cruz. We were in the living room for a change, and the afternoon light came softly through the broad windows.

I expected Cruz to open the treatment and begin paging through it. But he just sat there staring at me malevolently as if I'd deliberately shamed or insulted him. Then I realized what it was. The bastard was an illiterate.

He said: "Justo, come over and read this aloud to us."

"I'll do it if you want," I said.

"No. Justo does it. Justo has a fine voice."

So Fat Boy picked up the treatment and spent the next hour stumbling through it in fractured English, and all the while Cruz stared at Brian and me across the coffee table. He was waiting for us to begin sniggering at Justo's reading—which also would have been to snigger at him. Hoping, almost, that we'd do it so he could call in the Shirts and show us who was master here—and never mind who could read and write. Never mind who was able to operate in the larger world where words counted for more than pistols.

Justo finished, and Cruz just sat there.

Seething. I thought.

Then he gave a signal.

"Take these two back to their hotel."

In the back of the car, Brian said: "I don't think he liked your treatment, Mike."

"I tried to make it too much like a real one. And then he was mad as hell because we figured out he can't read. It's like we spit on him."

Just after dark, Justo showed up at the hotel. He smelled of booze and had a sheaf of scrawled notes in his hand.

After we'd left, Cruz had gone into a rage, punching the walls and kicking furniture around. Then he'd calmed down, outwardly at any rate, and gathered up everybody but Kristel and headed for that brothel he liked. But while they all partied, he'd sat and brooded. Finally he'd grabbed Justo and taken him to one side and begun dictating to him. They'll put this in the movie and that, and they'll show me in this way. And you'll go tell them to do it.

The notes didn't make any sense, even when I had Justo read them aloud.

"I'm going back to Tia Anita's."

"No, you're not, Justo. You're going to sit right here and the two of us are going to work these notes out and put together just what Felipe wants."

"You going to make me, movie man?"

"You're goddam right I'm going to make you. Unless you want to have a falling out with that cousin of yours."

He told me several obscene things he'd like to do with my mother, but he stayed anyway and we worked on it till past midnight. When he left, he had a funny look in his eyes—as if he'd never seen me before. What he'd really never seen was a producer dragging out the heavy artillery to save a film project.

I banged out a new Trojan Horse treatment. It was stupid and illiterate and utterly unfilmable, but it would hold Cruz until Brian and I could get out of town, and that was all I wanted.

I called the villa and told the Shirt who answered that we'd be out that evening to show Cruz the new material. The Shirt sounded hungover. If that was all he took away from the type of place I imagined Tia Anita's to be, he could count himself lucky.

As we rode out, Brian read the juicier parts of the treatment and laughed.

"You got no shame, Mike."

"I'm in the movie business. What do you expect?"

Cruz was waiting for us at poolside. He wore a pale yellow blazer and a dark blue shirt open at the neck and pants to match. He looked un-shaven—or maybe partially shaven would be more accurate—as if he'd taken the best shot at it he could manage. I noticed that there were a couple of broken windows on the second floor of the villa—Kristel's reaction, presumably, to last night's binge at Tia Anita's.

"I'll read it," I said. "It'll save time."

Cruz eyed me morosely. He was prepared to like this treatment as little as he'd liked the last. What he'd do about it probably depended on how hungover he still was.

I'd pitched dozens of film ideas. I'd pitched them to moneymen and studio production chiefs and A-list movie stars. You gauged your audience and presented your material accordingly, dumb or smart, using every trick at your command. You wanted that yes, that green light, even if it was only a temporary green light, the head nod that kept the project alive and moved it along to the next step.

I gave Cruz all of it. All the purples and reds. I pumped up the lead role because that pumped him up, too. I made a narco-gangster's wet dream out of it, full of power and cruelty and greed and self-love. It was like a parody of everything Cruz was in reality, but all he'd see would be the bright colors and himself as a kind of movie god.

It was the most cynical performance I've ever given in my life—and I'm a guy who'd set new records in that department. Every once in a while I'd catch a glimpse of Brian out of the corner of my eye and see that he had a frozen smile on his face. I knew what he was thinking. No way this guy's going to swallow this. He'll have his buddies beat the hell out of us.

But I knew better than that. I knew that I had Cruz—that he was eating it up. Toward the end, he couldn't even sit still anymore. He was up on his feet, strutting around with excitement.

When I finished, he rushed over and gave me a bear hug.

His eyes were bright.

"You know there is only one man who can be in this movie, Mike."

"Sure. But that's going to be a tough sell to the moneymen. They'll want somebody like Pacino."

"Pacino's too old. And who can play Felipe Cruz like Felipe Cruz can play him?"

"I think you'd be good, Felipe. I think it'd be something special."

"Then you must make it happen, Mike."

"Brian and I are flying out early tomorrow morning. Don't expect any news for a while. It takes time to get these things off the ground. Months, maybe a year or more."

"With this thing you read me? Are these people stupid? Maybe I should come and talk to them."

But he wouldn't. The minute he crossed the border, the DEA would bring him down like a jacklighted deer. He wasn't protected in the U.S., he didn't have a wall of *mordida* around him like he had here.

Cruz was still dancing with excitement. "Justo, get some drinks out here. We'll all get smashed again."

Brian sidled up to me. "Let's get out of here before this guy wakes up on us."

"One drink to make it look good, then we'll split. That's why I had the cab wait."

A drinks cart was pushed out on the apron of the pool.

I had a Campari and soda. Brian took a glass of whiskey that I knew he'd leave somewhere untouched.

Then Kristel showed up. She wore the white gown that swept off one shoulder across her breasts. It looked torn and dirty, and her bare feet were dirty, too. She had a split lip, and there were bruise marks on her arms and shoulders. Her right eye was just about swollen shut, and her blond hair was as wild as Medea's.

She stood there at the edge of the darkness beyond the pool. Her eyes went first to this one, then to that, finally fixing on Cruz. She came forward then, almost gliding on her bare feet.

"Lover," she whispered.

Cruz didn't hear her, hadn't even seen her.

"Mi esposo."

Then he did see her and at once there was a small automatic pistol in her hand and it belched flame.

The first shot hit him in the chest. He staggered back, eyes wide with terror. He who had killed so many—was this girl-woman now going to kill him?

The second shot caught him in the throat. It was horrible to see. Bloody as the movies were, they couldn't match this.

He turned then, voluntarily or involuntarily, so that the third shot caught him high in the back and threw him into the pool.

Kristel smiled then. It was a small smile and just for herself—satisfaction with what she'd done. The way she'd arranged it and carried it out. Her star turn in a vehicle that was supposed to belong to somebody else.

Cruz hung there in the crystal-blue water. He was lit from beneath by the pool lights. Blood trailed out behind him like purple smoke. The best lighting man in Hollywood couldn't have set it up better.

Brian gripped my arm. "Here's the finish we've been looking for, Mike."

The beautifully lit corpse in the water. The long-legged California blonde on the apron with a pistol in her hand—Lana Turner, Lizabeth Scott, Kim Basinger.

"We'll need some lines," I said tightly. "Somebody has to say something."

"Wait—Fat Boy'll give them to us."

We gazed across the apron at Justo. He was down on one knee with a shocked look on his face and no idea what to do next. And he stayed there, speechless, for more time than we could ever allow the scene to play.

Joan Waites

Three Killings and a Favor

JOAN WAITES is a pseudonym for a mainstream fiction author who pens mystery fiction when she gets a chance. "Three Killings and a Favor" is her latest short story, and it's a killer, both figuratively and literally. This story first appeared in the anthology, *Murder on Sunset Boulevard*, and one hopes to see more from her, no matter what name she chooses to write under.

Three Killings and a Favor

Joan Waites

Romeo Carlos de Jesus is not a man you meet on the way up, understand? He's blown up cars and burned down houses, shot people in the face, stabbed, beaten, and poisoned traitorous men, unfaithful women, and annoying pets. So when he comes sauntering up to me while I'm sitting in the park, fear slams through me like an eighteen-wheeler. It constricts my breath, brings heat to my face and makes my fingertips tingle, like when you're driving and realize that you're about to smash into something. I figure this is it, I'm going down, *all the way down,* to be tortured for eternity and made to crave ice water.

I could scramble over the bench and up the hill into the shrubs, but he'd shoot me in the back. I could dodge him and run forward, dive into the lake, but he'd follow me and drown me there. I could leap upon him and scratch at his eyes, bite his nose like they showed us way back when in self-defense class, but he'd mace me with my own pepper spray and stab me in the gut. So I sit. Rub my sweaty hands against my pale blue skirt. And I wait, endlessly it seems, while he lopes across the green, green grass and finally slows to a stop in front of me.

"I understand, *guera,* that you are in some trouble, no?" His voice is rich and calm and throaty. His accent is pronounced. He rolls his *R*s and speaks slowly.

I slit my eyes at him. My throat is too dry to respond even if I had something to say.

"The Cabrera brothers, they tell me you have seen a thing not meant for your eyes. Some guns. In a barrel you thought would contain hazardous waste. No?"

He is close enough that I can smell him, not cologne or aftershave but the scent of Romeo himself, an earthy, promising scent. It is everything I can do to keep from shaking. The strain of keeping still leaves me unable to stop the tears.

Romeo closes his eyes and shakes his head, smiling. "No, no, no, señorita. No need for tears. When it comes, it will be painless. That was what the brothers requested."

He pulls a Kool menthol cigarette from the pack rolled up in his sleeve, replaces the pack. I notice his jeans. They fit him in that impossible way jeans do in the ads, tight in the ass and crumpled, but not baggy, everywhere else. These are over black work boots. He pulls a lighter from these incredible jeans and lights the cigarette, then slides the lighter back into his pocket.

He is a handsome man, this Romeo de Jesus. But he is a killer. He is not much past my twenty-three years, just thirty, I think. I know him, or rather know *of* him, from the waste treatment plant I work at. He comes in and has conversations with the Cabrera brothers. They speak in Spanish. I understand little of this exotic language and I'm glad for it. Certain things are not disguised by a language barrier, and I don't want to hear specifics.

Romeo takes a luxurious drag from his menthol, blows the smoke in a stream that reminds me of a dragon. He assesses me. I swallow. He pulls the cigarette from his mouth and offers it to me. I smoked only briefly, in college, but I appreciate the gesture and accept.

Romeo lights another for himself, then sits down close to me on the bench. We sit like that for a long while, smoking in silence like old friends and staring out over Silver Lake. Then he says, "Tell me your name, señorita."

"They didn't tell you?"

"Of course, they did. But I want to hear you say it. It's different when a woman speaks her own name than when a man repeats it." He smiles.

"Sarah. Sarah Bradstone."

"And your middle name?"

"Ramona."

"Well, Señorita Sarah Ramona Bradstone, I am telling you that I am not generally in the business of killing little girls for making mistakes at work." He grins. "First thing, the Cabrera brothers tell me: the man who carelessly included such a drum with a regular legitimate shipment, kill him. I check and I find that this man has repeatedly been warned about just this very offense many times, and also evidence that he is a snitch. So I kill him."

He grins again. It starts me shaking and this time I can't control it. Any minute I'm expecting his gun to my temple, cool and deadly. He carries it tucked in his waistband in the back. His T-shirt is loose over the top of it, but you can see it if you look.

He sets a hand on my back and I jump. He shakes his head like before. "Let me finish."

I nod, finishing my cigarette and rubbing it out against the wood of the park bench.

"Here is what they tell me next," Romeo says. "They tell me a girl has seen their trade, their guns, and they don't know what to do. I tell them: Pretend it's not yours! No, they say. Too late. Kill her. So I check and I find that this girl's first job from college is working with these Cabrera brothers. These are bad men, and she is greener than the unripe jalapeño, this little Sarah Ramona Bradstone."

His dark eyes hold my gaze. My mouth opens but I say nothing.

His voice is low and velvety. "I tell them I will not take this job. They do not like that answer. They threaten me and make black promises against me."

Romeo sits back against the bench and crosses his feet at the ankles. He clasps his hands behind his head and looks up at the sky. It's a big, blue, cloudless sky and he sighs, contentedly.

"Dying men tell the truth. I am telling you to go home and pack a bag, and we will put you on a plane."

"Is this you?" Romeo holds a framed photograph of a curvy blonde in a green dress.

"No, that's Madeline, my sister."

"Are you sure? She looks just like you." He laughs gently. "If I came and she were here, I would kill her and think I'd killed you."

I cringe at this, but more because I'm expected to by polite society than because it really bothers me. It *should* bother me. But it doesn't. Like his not needing directions from Silver Lake to my place in Hollywood should have bothered me and didn't. He drove me right down Sunset in his sexy black Porsche, oblivious to the envious stares of people on the sidewalks. He knew what street to turn on. And he got lucky, found parking just two blocks away.

Thinking of parking reminds me. "Madeline is stopping by for coffee today!"

"At what time?"

"After her shop closes. Usually around six."

"You should not say good-bye. But probably you must. Just do not tell her where you are going. Otherwise, I have wasted my favor on you." He smiles. It is a fond and trusting smile.

I return to ransacking my closet, trying to decide what I should bring to wear for the rest of my life in New York. Romeo is on my cordless telephone, ordering a ticket and using a credit card, *his* credit card, to pay. He meanders here and there through my sunny little one-bedroom apartment, examining everything in a way that reminds me of a cat. Every time he moves toward me I'm expecting his gun. I'm not convinced he's even on the phone. I think he's just holding it to his ear as a prop, trying to calm me down so he can sneak up from behind. Panic keeps rising in my chest and I breathe, breathe, breathe to fight it back.

I stuff a black dress into the single remaining corner of my duffel. I am wrestling it closed when Romeo gets off the phone and helps. "Tonight, at eleven-fifty, your plane takes off," he tells me.

I glance at my Bettie Page clock. Her little pitchfork's on the four and her long devil's tail is just past the six. "Lotta time between now and then."

"Do not worry, we will spend it. And we will be home at seven so you can have coffee with your sister. Are you hungry? I am hungry. What would you like to eat?"

Last Supper, is what I'm thinking but I keep this to myself. "There's a Cajun place up the street a ways. We could walk there."

He nods approval and we set off, up my street to La Cienega, then up the hill to Sunset.

A place appears different once you know you are about to leave it. I stand waiting for the light to change and gaze down this street I have lived on or near since I came here five years ago to go to UCLA. It suddenly looks to me as it did the first time I saw it, fantastic and impossible with its billboards and television screens, larger-than-life images and naked, gender-ambiguous models. Have I really lived here five years? Is there actually a man standing next to me who should and might murder me before the day is up? A shudder runs through me.

Romeo has a way of keeping near me, like a possessive boyfriend. There was no question of who would drive from Silver Lake; my Honda is abandoned there. And there was his pacing in the apartment. I never would have made it past him out my door. Now he stands close behind me, propped against the light pole with one lean, muscular arm, so that he'd easily block me if I were to try to run.

We say almost nothing in the fifteen minutes it takes to get to the restaurant, the Cajun Bistro. Romeo's keys are clipped to his belt loop and jangle rhythmically as he walks. Once there, we sit on the patio and watch the people go past. He sits next to me rather than across the table, and I can smell the heat coming off him. I order a glass of wine. I think I can use it. Romeo asks for iced tea. We both get the shrimp jambalaya.

I am still very much afraid of Romeo. I am still convinced he will put a bullet in my head before the end of the day. Maybe on the way to the airport. *Probably,* I've decided. But something—the wine perhaps? the calmness of the man and his promise of no pain?—something has made me distance myself from this grim reality of imminent death. I'm relaxed and at peace. New York or hell, it's all the same.

The sun is beginning to drop and the sky is spread with deep tones of evening. It has been a mild spring day, the kind that breeds both restlessness and complacency, often in the same soul. We both gaze skyward for a long while.

"It's nice to be out," I say.

Romeo nods. "Not such a bad day to die."

This is it. Panic runs through me in a hot streak, despite my momentary acceptance. I flinch and pull away.

But from nothing. There is no weapon, only Romeo's easy smile. "The señorita misunderstands me," he says in his velvet voice, *R*s rolling.

He waits for me to compose myself. As I do so I see him differently. There is a veiled sadness apparent in his face, and a strange, new urgency in his eyes.

He peers down Sunset Boulevard. "I told you that a dying man tells the truth. Let me tell someone my tale, as well. I used to be a factory worker. I was happy, I worked hard during the week and on weekends had a lady friend to keep me busy."

He shifts his gaze to me. "Then something happened," he says. "Somebody in my family was killed, assassinated. Not for anything they did, but because someone told untrue stories about this person. Falsehoods told to the wrong people will do that, will get a man killed. I had to avenge that death. That is how it began, Sarah."

I look at him quizzically.

"When people know you have killed a man," he explains, "they seek you out. They say please. Help me. You tell them you only committed this act out of vengeance, to avenge the murder of an innocent man. They say, '¡Si señor, yo tambien!' I want this man dead because he raped my wife. This man I want killed for trying to murder my grandfather.

"You will believe them," Romeo tells me. He leans close to me and his eyes stare into mine, searching. "You will believe them because you are green and angry. Still filled with heat in spite of your revenge. Looking for a place to put this anger. So you believe them because you *believe* them. Later, you believe them because it suits you to do so. Eventually, you don't believe them at all, not even the few who are not lying. You don't care. You travel and trade in bad people. These are all bad people. Why should you not line your pockets with their lives?"

He sits up straight, sips his tea. Shaking his head, he says, "But you are not bad people. Nothing I can tell myself will make me believe this time. So now you know it all, señorita. Why I kill for money and why I'm not killing you. You know how it began, and how it continues."

I find I can't look at him. I gaze out over his head to the sky above him, now a stunning purple and red. "How will it end?"

Romeo's voice holds gentle laughter. "Someone will assassinate me."

"The Cabrera brothers?"

"Yes. Someone they hire. Today, tomorrow? These could be my last minutes to enjoy."

Now I do look at him. I shake my head, disbelieving. "Why would you do that? Why would you risk your life for me?"

He gazes at me pointedly.

I put my hands up, surrendering. "Just curious."

Romeo considers me, seems to make a decision. "Many years ago, someone did me a favor. I have owed this favor for a long time, but I always was assured that God would tell me when the time had come to repay it." He nods in my direction. "It has come today."

We sit in silence for a long while and I ponder this strange man next to me, this man who has his own code and keeps strictly to it. He takes another drink from his tea, then stretches out the way he did on the park bench, with his ankles crossed and his hands behind his head. His eyes are closed now. He appears asleep.

There is a small group of birds behind us. Tiny, nervous birds, chattering and flitting about, looking for crumbs. I take a piece of bread from the basket they brought us with our drinks, then twist my chair around so my back is to the table. I pull small pieces off the bread and watch the birds struggle with one another over the morsels. They are very fluffy, with bright orange beaks, and very bold, coming within inches of my fingers.

"Romeo?"

"Hmm?"

I lean way over, to try to get one of the little birds to eat from my hand. "Do you believe in heaven?"

Pop!

Crimson splashes bright against Romeo's white shirt. And everything stands still for a split second.

Instinct scrambles me from my chair. I crouch down behind the table, and from here I catch a glimpse of a man in jeans and a black T-shirt. He wears thick black gloves. He is not six feet from us, gun still raised. How did we not see him? Romeo, how?

The women at the table nearest ours scream. I'm thinking: *I'm next!* I leap from the table and shove the women out of my way, hurdle over the little white picket fence. My feet slap! slap! against the pavement. My breath goes ragged and my heart pounds in my ears. I peer over my shoulder. No one. I stop. Not smart, maybe, but I do it anyway and run back the block I've come. Maybe he wasn't shot, maybe I made a mistake, maybe . . .

A crowd has gathered, hysterical. A woman is pointing down the alleyway and screaming, "He went that way, he's there!"

I ease thorugh the ring of people. No one stops me or seems to recognize that I just ran off. I look closely at my hitman-turned-gaurdian. His eyes are still closed.

"Romeo?"

No response. There is a hole in his chest and I see that the back of the chair is spattered with blood.

I put two fingers against his strong, lean neck. Nothing.

A tear runs down my face. For this monstrous man who spared my life, I am crying. One tear, then another.

Romeo is still smiling.

The distant whine of sirens pulls me from my reverie. If the cops take me in, I'm dead for sure. The Cabrera brothers will kill me on the way to the stationhouse.

I jerk Romeo's Porsche keys from his belt loop and push back through the crowd again, my hand to my face. People ask me did I know him? Am I all right? I just nod. Once I break free from them, I cross Sunset and run again, all the way down La Cienega's steep hill, not stopping until I get to my street. I slow to a walk halfway up the block from my place. My chest and throat are burning, my calf muscles ache, I swear I'm on fire. But the farther I walk, the better I feel. Soon my breathing is normal, even though my throat still stings. My mouth is parched, and I am dreaming of a huge glass of cool water when I see Madeline's new yellow Beetle outside my building.

Fear crashes through me again. Only this time the fear is for someone else. I start running, but my body forbids it. Pain slams me harder, stomps most of the fear into a cold dread.

My front door is still open. Collapsed face down in my kitchen is my sister, who looks just like me. There is a small wound in her temple and just a trickle of blood. Quick and painless, like Romeo promised. And I understand now that he hadn't been guessing, he *knew*, knew they were coming for him and for me, knew that Madeline would be mistaken for me if I wasn't there.

Only Madeline didn't *do* anything. She didn't do anything! And who are these people to kill a girl for their mistakes anyway?

There is something new in me now, not the sadness I expected, but something ferocious. The rage and howl of the need for vengeance. Sure, I'm green like Romeo said, but I'm not stupid. I know it's easier to get a gun in Hollywood than it is to make a phone call. I know that there are advantages to people believing that you're dead. And I know a whole hell of a lot about chemistry, more than enough to kill somebody. Or three somebodies: the man who pulled the trigger and the brothers who hired him to do it.

I heave my stuffed duffel bag over my shoulder and make my way down the stairs and out to the black Porsche. *My* black Porsche.

Mike Doogan

War Can Be Murder

The other mystery story set in the frozen tundra of Alaska is MIKE DOOGAN's "War Can Be Murder." Born and raised in Alaska, he has traveled to the ends of the forty-ninth state, and has kept his sanity through it all to report on what he has seen and done. Mike's been everywhere and done just about everything. In the interim, he's managed to write a regular opinion column for the *Anchorage Daily News,* as well as a number of magazine articles, a number of books about Alaska, and enjoys the wonder of it all. His story, first published in *The Mysterious North,* also won the Robert L. Fish award for best first mystery short story of 2002.

War Can Be Murder

Mike Doogan

Two men got out of the Jeep and walked toward the building. Their fleece-lined leather boots squeaked on the snow. One of the men was young, stocky, and black. The other was old, thin, and white. Both men wore olive drab wool pants, duffel coats, and knit wool caps. The black man rolled forward onto his toes with each step, like he was about to leap into space. The white man's gait was something between a saunter and a stagger. Their breath escaped in white puffs. Their heads were burrowed down into their collars and their hands were jammed into the pockets of their coats.

"Kee-rist, it's cold," the black man said.

Their Jeep ticked loudly as it cooled. The building they approached was part log cabin and part Quonset hut with a shacky plywood porch tacked onto the front. Yellow light leaked from three small windows. Smoke plumed from a metal pipe punched through its tin roof. A sign beside the door showed a black cat sitting on a white crescent, the words CAROLINA MOON lettered beneath.

"You sure we want to go in here?" the black man asked.

"Have to," the white man said. "I've got an investment to protect."

They hurried through the door and shut it quickly behind them. They were standing in a fair-sized room that held a half-dozen tables and a big bar. They were the only ones in the room. The room smelled of cigarette smoke, stale beer, and desperation. The white man led the way past the bar and through a door, turned left, and walked down a dark hallway toward the light spilling from another open door.

The light came from a small room that held a big bed and four people not looking at the corpse on the floor. One, a big, red-haired guy, was dressed in olive drab with a black band around one bicep that read "MP" in white letters. The other man was short, plump, and fair-haired, dressed in brown. Both wore guns on their hips. One of the women was small and temporarily blond, wearing a red robe that didn't hide much. The other woman was tall, black, and regal as Cleopatra meeting Caesar.

"I tole you, he give me a couple of bucks and said I should go get some supper at Leroy's," the temporary blond was saying.

" 'Lo, Zulu," the thin man said, nodding to the black woman.

"Mister Sam," she replied.

"What the hell are you doing here, soldier?" the MP barked.

"That's *Sergeant,*" the thin man said cheerfully. He nodded to the plump man. "Marshal Olson," he said. "Damn cold night to be dragged out into, isn't it?"

"So it is, Sergeant Hammett," the plump man said. "So it is." He shrugged toward the corpse on the floor. "Even colder where he is, you betcha."

"Look, you," the MP said, "I'm ordering you to leave. And take that dinge with you. This here's a military investigation, and if you upstuck it, I'll throw you in the stockade."

"If I what it?" Hammett asked.

"Upstuck," the MP grated.

"Upstuck?" Hammett asked. "Anybody got any idea what he's talking about?"

"I think he means 'obstruct,' " the black man said.

"Why, thank you, Clarence," Hammett said. He pointed to the black man. "My companion is Clarence Jefferson Delight. You might know him better as Little Sugar Delight. Fought Tony Zale to a draw just before the war. Had twenty-seven—that's right, isn't it Clarence?—twenty-seven professional fights without a loss. Not bad for a dinge, eh?" To the plump man, he said, "It's been awhile since I was involved in this sort of thing, Oscar, but I believe that as the U.S. Marshal you're the one with jurisdiction here." To the MP, he said, "Which means you can take your order and stick it where the sun don't shine."

The MP started forward. Hammett waited for him with arms hanging loosely at his sides. The marshal stepped forward and put a hand on the MP's chest.

"Maybe you'd better go cool off, fella," he said. "Maybe go radio headquarters for instructions while I talk to these folks here."

The MP hesitated, relaxed, said, "Right you are, Marshal," and left the room.

"Maybe we should all go into the other room," the marshal said. The others began to file out. Hammett crouched next to the corpse, which lay on its back, arms outflung, completely naked. He was a young slim, sandy-haired fellow with blue eyes and full lips. His head lay over on his shoulder, the neck bent much farther than it should have been. Hammett laid a hand on the corpse's chest.

"Give me a hand, Oscar, and we'll roll him over," he said.

The two men rolled the corpse onto its stomach. Hammett looked it up and down, grunted, and they rolled it back over.

"You might want to make sure a doctor examines that corpse," he said as the two men walked toward the barroom. "I think you'll find he was here to receive rather than give."

The temporary blonde told a simple story. A soldier had come into her room, given her two dollars and told her to get something to eat.

"He said don't come back for an hour," she said.

She'd gone out the back door, she said, shooting a nervous look at the black woman, so she wouldn't have to answer any questions. When she returned she'd found the soldier naked and dead.

"She told me," the black woman said to the marshal, "and I sent someone for you."

"What did you have to eat?" Hammett asked the temporary blonde.

"Leroy said it was beefsteak, but I think it was part of one of them moose," she said. "And some mushy canned peas and a piece of chocolate cake. I think it give me the heartburn. That or the body."

"That's a story that should be easy enough to check out," Hammett said.

"And what about you, Zulu?" the marshal asked.

"I was in the office or behind the bar all night, Mister Olson," the black woman said. "That gentleman came in, had a drink, paid the usual fee, and asked for a girl. When I asked him which one, he said it didn't matter. So I sent him back to Daphne."

"Seen him before?" the marshal asked.

"Lots of men come through here," Zulu said. "But I think he'd been here before."

"He done the same thing with me maybe three, four times before," the temporary blonde said. "With some a the other girls, too." She shot another nervous look at the black woman. "We talk sometimes, ya know."

"Notice anybody in particular in here tonight?" the marshal said.

"Quite a few people in here tonight," Zulu said. "Some for the music, some for other things. Maybe thirty people in here when the body was found. I think maybe one of them is on the city council. And there was that banker . . ."

"That's enough of that," the marshal said.

"And he could have let anybody in through the back door," Zulu said.

The red-haired MP came back into the barroom, chased by a blast of cold air.

"The major wants me to bring the whore in to the base," he said to the marshal.

"I don't think Daphne wants to go anywhere with you, young man," Zulu said.

"I don't care what a whore thinks," the MP said.

Zulu leaned across the bar and very deliberately slapped the MP across the face. He lunged for her. Hammett stuck a shoulder into his chest and the marshal grabbed his arm.

"You probably don't remember me, Tobin," Hammett said, leaning into the MP, "but I remember when you were just a kid on the black-and-blue squad in San Francisco. I heard you did something that got you thrown out of the cops just before the war. I don't remember what. What was it you did to get tossed off the force?"

"Fuck you," the MP said. "How do you know so much, anyway?"

"I was with the Pinks for a while," Hammett said. "I know some people."

"You can relax now, son," the marshal said to the MP. "Nobody roughs up Zulu when I'm around. You go tell your major that if he wants to be involved in this investigation he should speak to me directly. Now beat it."

"I'm too old for this nonsense," Hammett said after the MP left, "but you can't have people beating up your partner. It's bad for business."

"There ain't going to be any business for a while," the marshal said. "Until we get to the bottom of this, you're closed, Zulu. I'll roust somebody out and have 'em collect the body. Otherwise, keep people out of that room until I tell you different."

With that, he left.

"I believe I'll have a drink now, Zulu," Hammett said.

"You heard the marshal," the black woman said. "We're closed."

"But I'm your partner," Hammett said, grinning.

"Silent partner," she said. "I guess you forgot the silent part."

"Now there's gratitude for you, Clarence," Hammett said. "She begs me for money to open this place and now that she has my money she doesn't want anything to do with me. Think what I'm risking. Why, if my friends in Hollywood knew I was part owner of a cathouse . . ."

"They'd all be lining up three-deep for free booze and free nooky," Zulu said. "Now you two skedaddle. I've got to get Daphne moved to another room, and I'll have big, clumsy white folk tracking in and out of here all night. I'll be speaking to you later, Mister Sam."

The two men went back out into the cold.

"Little Sugar Delight?" the black man said. "Tony Zale? Why do you want to be telling such stories?"

"Why, Clarence," Hammett said, "think how boring life would be if we didn't all make up stories."

The black man slid behind the wheel and punched the starter. The engine whirred and whined and exploded into life.

"You can drop me back at the Lido Gardens," Hammett said. "I have a weekend pass and I believe there's a nurse who's just about drunk enough by now."

Hammett awoke the next morning alone, sprawled fully clothed on the bed of a small, spare hotel room. One boot lay on its side on the floor. The other was still on his left foot. He raised himself slowly to a sitting position. The steam radiator hissed and somewhere outside the frosted-over window a horn honked. Hammett groaned loudly as he bent down to remove his boot. He pulled off both socks, then took two steps across the bare, cold floor to a small table, poured himself a glass of water from a pitcher, and drank it. Then another. He took the empty glass over to where his coat dangled from the back of a chair and rummaged around in the pockets until he came up with a small bottle of whiskey. He poured some into the glass, drank it, and shuddered.

"The beginning of another perfect day," he said aloud.

He walked to the washstand and peered into the mirror. The face that looked back was pale and narrow, topped by crew-cut gray hair. He had baggy, hound-dog brown eyes and a full, salt-and-pepper mustache trimmed at the corners of a wide mouth. He took off his shirt and regarded his pipe-stem arms and sunken chest.

"Look out, Tojo," he said.

He walked to the other side of the bed, opened a small leather valise, and took out a musette bag. Back at the washstand, he reached into his mouth and removed a full set of false teeth. His cheeks, already sunken, collapsed completely. He brushed the false teeth vigorously and replaced them in his mouth. He shaved. Then he took clean underwear from the valise, left the room, and walked down the hall toward the bathroom. About halfway down the hall, a small, dark-haired man lay snoring on the floor. He smelled of alcohol and vomit. Hammett stepped over him and continued to the bathroom.

After bathing, Hammett returned to his room, put on a clean shirt, and walked down a flight of stairs to the lobby. He went through a door marked CAFÉ and sat at the counter. A clock next to the cash register read 11:45. A hard-faced woman put a thick cup down in front of him and filled it with coffee. Hammett took a pair of eyeglasses out of his shirt pocket and consulted the gravy-stained menu.

"Breakfast or lunch?" he asked the hard-faced woman.

"Suit yourself," she said.

"I'll have the sourdough pancakes, a couple of eggs over easy, and orange juice," Hammett said. "Coffee, too."

"Hey, are these real eggs?" asked a well-dressed, middle-aged man sitting a few stools down. The left arm of his suit coat was empty and pinned to his lapel.

The hard-faced women blew air through her lips.

"Cheechakos," she said. "A course they're real eggs. Real butter, too. This here's a war zone, you know."

She yelled Hammett's order through a serving hatch to the Indian cook.

"Can't get this food back home?" Hammett asked the one-armed man.

"Ration cards," the man replied. "Or the black market."

"Much money in the black market?" Hammett asked.

The one-armed man made a sour face.

"Guess so," he said. "You can get most anything off the back of a truck, most of it with military markings. And they say the high society parties are all catered by Uncle Sam. But I wouldn't know for certain." He flicked his empty sleeve. "Got this at Midway. I'm not buying at no god-damn black market."

A boy selling newspapers came in off the street. Hammett gave him a dime and took a newspaper, which was cold to the touch.

"Budapest Surrenders!" the headline proclaimed.

A small article said the previous night's temperature had reached twenty-eight below zero, the coldest of the winter. In the lower, right-hand corner of the front page was a table headed "Road to Berlin." It showed that allied troops were 32 miles away at Zellin on the eastern front, 304 miles away at Kleve on the western front, and 504 miles away at the Reno River on the Italian front.

The hard-faced woman put a plate of pancakes and eggs in front of Hammett. As he ate them he read that the Ice Carnival had donated $1,100 in proceeds to the Infantile Paralysis Fund, the Pribilof Five—two guitars, a banjo, an accordion, and a fiddle—had played at the USO log cabin, and Jimmy Foxx had re-signed with the Phillies. He finished his meal, put a fifty-cent piece next to his plate, and stood up.

"Where do you think you are, mister?" the hard-faced woman said. "Seattle? That'll be one dollar."

"Whew!" the one-armed man said.

Hammett dug out a dollar, handed it to the woman, and left the fifty-cent piece on the counter.

"Wait'll you have a drink," he said to the one-armed man.

Hammett walked across the lobby to the hotel desk and asked the clerk for the telephone. He consulted the slim telephone book, dialed, identified himself, and waited.

"Oscar," he said. "Sam Hammett. Has the doctor looked at that corpse from last night? Uh-huh. Uh-huh. Was I right about him? I see. You found out his name yet and where he was assigned? A sergeant? That kid was a sergeant? What's this man's army coming to? And he was in supply? Nope, I don't know anybody over there. But if you want, I can have a word with General Johnson. Okay. How about the Carolina Moon? Can Zulu open up again? Come on, Oscar. Be reasonable. They didn't have anything to do with the killing. All right, then. I guess we'd better hope you find the killer soon. See you, Oscar. Bye."

Hammett returned to his room, put on his overcoat, and went out of the hotel. The air was warmer than it had been the night before, but not warm. He walked several blocks along the street, moving slowly over the hard-packed snow. He passed mostly one or two-story wooden buildings, many of them hotels, bars, and cafés. He counted seven buildings under construction. A few automobiles of prewar vintage passed him, along with several Jeeps and a new, olive drab staff car. He passed many people on foot, most of them men in work clothes or uniforms. When his cheeks began to get numb, he turned left, then left again, and walked back toward the hotel. A couple of blocks short of his destination, he turned left again, crossed the street and went into a small shop with BOOK CACHE painted on its window. He browsed among the tables of books, picked one up, and walked to the counter.

"Whatya got there?" the woman behind the counter asked. Her hair as nearly as gray as Hammett's. *"Theoretical Principles of Marxism* by V. I. Lenin." She smiled. "That sounds like a thriller. Buy or rent?"

"Rent," Hammett said.

"Probably won't get much call for this," the woman said. "How about ten cents for a week?"

"Better make it two weeks," Hammett said, handing her a quarter. "This isn't easy reading."

The woman wrote the book's title, Hammett's name and barracks number, and the rental period down in a register, gave him a nickel back, and smiled again.

"Aren't you a little old to be a soldier?" she asked.

"I was twenty-one when I enlisted," he said, grinning. "War ages a man."

When it came time to turn for his hotel, Hammett walked on. Two blocks later he was at a small wooden building with a sign over the door that read MILITARY POLICE.

"I'm looking for the duty officer," he told the MP on the desk. A young lieutenant came out of an office in the back.

"Sam Hammett of General Johnson's staff," Hammett said. "I'm working on a piece for *Army Up North* about military policing and I need some information."

"Don't you salute officers on General Johnson's staff?" the lieutenant snapped.

"Not when we're off duty and out of uniform, sir," Hammett said. "As I'm certain they taught you in OCS, sir."

The two men looked at each other for a minute, then the lieutenant blinked and said, "What can I do for you, Sergeant?"

"I need some information on staffing levels, sir," Hammett said. "For instance, how many men did you have on duty here in Anchorage last night, sir?"

Each successive "sir" seemed to make the lieutenant more at ease.

"I'm not sure," he said. "But if you'd like to step back into the office, we can look at the duty roster."

Hammett looked at the roster. Tobin's name wasn't on it. He took a notebook out of his coat pocket and wrote in it.

"Thank you, sir," he said. "Now I'll need your name and hometown. For the article."

Back at the hotel, Hammett removed his coat and boots. He poured some whiskey into the glass, filled it with water, lay down on the bed, and began writing a letter.

"Dear Lillian," it began. "I am back in Anchorage and have probably seen the end of my posting to the Aleutians."

When he'd finished the letter, he made himself another drink and picked up his book. Within five minutes he was snoring.

He dreamed he was working for the Pinkerton National Detective Agency again, paired with a big Irish kid named Michael Carey on the Fatty Arbuckle case. He dreamed he was at the Stork Club, arguing with Hemingway about the Spanish Civil War. He dreamed he was in a watering hole on Lombard with an older Carey, who pointed out red-haired Billy Tobin and said something Hammett couldn't make out. He dreamed he was locked in his room on Post Street, drinking and writing *The Big Knock-over*. His wife, Josie, was pounding on the door, asking for more money for herself and his daughters.

"Hey mister, wake up." It was the desk clerk's voice. He pounded on the door again. "Wake up, mister."

"What do you want?" Hammett called.

"You got a visitor downstairs. A shine."

Hammett got up from the bed and pulled the door open.

"Go get my visitor and bring him up," he said.

The desk clerk returned with the black man right behind him.

"Clarence, this is the desk clerk," Hammett said. "What's your name?"

"Joe," the desk clerk said.

"Joe," Hammett said, "this is Clarence 'Big Stick' LeBeau. Until the war came along he played third base for the Birmingham Black Barons of the Negro league. Hit thirty home runs or more in seven—it was seven, wasn't it, Clarence?—straight seasons. If it weren't for the color line, he'd have been playing for the Yankees. Not bad for a shine, huh?"

"I didn't mean nothing by that, mister," the desk clerk said. "You neither, Clarence." His eyes darted this way and that. "I got to get back to the desk," he said, and scurried off.

"Welcome to my castle," Hammett said, stepping aside to let the black man in. "What brings you here?"

"I've got to get started to Florida for spring training," the black man said. "The things you come up with. I didn't know white folk knew anything about the Birmingham Black Barons. And why do you keep calling me Clarence?"

"It suits you better than Don Miller," Hammett said. "And it keeps everybody guessing. Confusion to the enemy."

"You been drinking?" Miller said.

"A little," Hammett said. "You want a nip?" Miller shook his head. "But I've been sleeping more. The old need their sleep. What brings you here?"

"I was at the magazine office working on the illustrations for that frostbite article when I was called into the presence of Major General Davenport Johnson himself. He said you'd promised to go to a party tonight at some banker's house, and since he knew what an irresponsible S.O.B. you were—those were his words—he was ordering me to make sure you got there. Party starts in half an hour, so you'd better get cleaned up."

"I'm not going to any goddamn party at any goddamn banker's house," Hammett said. "I'm going to the Lido Gardens and the South Seas and maybe the Owl Club."

"This is Little Sugar Delight you're talking to, remember," Miller said. "You're going to the party if I have to carry you. General's orders."

"General's orders," Hammett said, and laughed. "That'll teach me to be famous." He took off his shirt, washed his face and hands, put the shirt back on, knotted a tie around his neck, put on his uniform jacket and a pair of glistening black shoes that he took from the valise, and picked up his overcoat.

"All right, Little Sugar," he said, "let's go entertain the cream of Anchorage society."

Hammett got out of the Jeep in front of a two-story wooden house. Light spilled from all the windows and the cold air carried the muffled murmur of voices.

"You can go on about your business," he told Miller. "I'll walk back to town."

"It must be twenty below, Sam," Miller said.

"Nearer thirty, I expect," Hammett said. "But it's only a half-dozen blocks and I like to walk."

Indoors, the temperature was 110 degrees warmer. Men in suits and uniforms stood around drinking, talking, and sweating. Among them was a sprinkling of overdressed women with carefully done-up hair. A horse-faced woman wearing what might have been real diamonds and showing a lot of cleavage walked up to Hammett.

"Aren't you Dashiell Hammett, the writer?" she asked.

Hammett stared down the front of her dress.

"Actually, I'm Samuel Hammett, the drunkard," he said after several seconds. "Where might I find a drink?"

Hammett quickly downed a drink and picked up another. The woman led him to where a large group, all wearing civilian clothes, was talking about the war.

"I tell you," a big, bluff man with dark, wavy hair was saying, "we are winning this war because we believe in freedom and democracy."

Everyone nodded.

"And free enterprise, whatever Roosevelt might think," said another man.

Everyone nodded again.

"What do you think, Dashiell?" the woman asked.

Hammett finished his drink. His eyes were bright and he had a little smile on his lips.

"I think I need another drink," he said.

"No," the woman said, "about the war."

"Oh, that," Hammett said. "First of all, we're not winning the war. Not by ourselves. We've got a lot of help. The Soviets, for example, have done much of the dying for us. Second, the part of the war we are winning we're winning because we can make more tanks and airplanes and bombs than the Germans and the Japs can. We're not winning because our ideas are better than theirs. We're winning because we're drowning the sonsabitches in metal."

When he stopped talking, the entire room was quiet.

"That was quite a speech," the woman said, her voice much less friendly than it had been.

"You'd have been better off just giving me another drink," Hammett said. "But don't worry. I can get it myself."

He was looking at a painting of a moose when a slim, curly-haired fellow who couldn't have been more than thirty walked up to him. He had a major's oak leaves on his shoulders.

"That was quite a speech, soldier," the major said. "What's an NCO doing at this party, anyway?"

"Ask the general," Hammett said.

"Oh, that's right, you're Hammett, the hero of the morale tour." The major took a drink from the glass he was holding. "You must be something on a morale tour with speeches like that." When Hammett said nothing, the major went on, "I hear you're involved in the murder of one of my sergeants."

Hammett laughed. "I don't know about involved," he said, "but I've got a fair idea who did it."

The major moved closer to Hammett.

"I think you'll find that in the army, it's safer to mind your own business," he said. "Much safer."

Hammett thrust his face into the major's face and opened his mouth to speak, but was interrupted by another voice.

"Ah, Sergeant Hammett," the voice said, "I see you've met Major Allen. The major's the head of supply out at the fort."

"Thanks for clearing that up, General," Hammett said. "I thought maybe he was somebody's kid and these were his pajamas."

The major's face reddened and his mouth opened.

"Sergeant!" the general barked. "Do you know the punishment for insubordination?"

"Sorry, General, Major," Hammett said. "This whiskey just plays hob with my ordinarily high regard for military discipline."

The major stomped off.

"That mouth of yours will get you into trouble one day, Sergeant," the general said. He sounded as if he were trying hard not to laugh.

"Yes, sir," Hammett said. "But he is a jumped-up little turd."

"Yes, he is that," the general said. "Regular army. His father was regular army, too. Chief of supply at the Presidio. Did very well for himself. Retired to a very nice home on Nob Hill. This one's following in the family footsteps. All polish and connections. There, see? See how politely he takes his leave of the hostess. Now you behave yourself." The general looked at the picture of the moose. "Damned odd animal, isn't it?" he said, and moved off.

The general left the party a half hour later and Hammett a few minutes after that. He made his way down the short, icy walkway and, as he turned left, his feet flew out from under him. As he fell he heard three loud explosions. Something whirred past his ear. He twisted so that he landed on his side and rolled behind a car parked at the curb. He heard people boil out of the house behind him.

"What was that?" they called. And, "Are you all right?"

Hammett got slowly to his feet. There were no more shots.

"I'm fine," he called. "But I could use a lift downtown, if anyone is headed that way."

It was nearly midnight when Hammett walked into the smoke and noise of the Lido Gardens. A four-piece band was making a racket in one corner, and a table full of WACs was getting a big play from about twice as many men in the other. Hammett navigated his way across the room to the bar and ordered a whiskey.

"Not bad for a drunk," he said to himself and turned to survey the room. His elbow hit the shoulder of the man next to him. The man spilled some of his beer on the bar.

"Hey, watch it, you old bastard," the man growled, looking up. A broad smile split his face. "Well, if it isn't Dash Hammett, the worst man on a stakeout I ever saw. What are you doing here at the end of the earth?"

"Dispensing propaganda and nursemaiding Hollywood stars," Hammett said. "Isn't that why every man goes to war? And what about you, Carey? The Pinks finally figure out how worthless you are and let you go?"

The two men shook hands.

"No, it's a sad tale," the other man said. "A man of my years should have been able to spend the war behind a desk, in civilian clothes. But then the army figured out that a lot of money was rolling around because of the war and that money might make people do some bad things." Both men laughed. "So they drafted me. Me, with my bad knees and failing eyesight. Said I had special qualifications. And here I am, back out in the field, chasing crooks. For even less money than the agency paid me."

"War is indeed hell," Hammett said. "Let me buy you a drink to ease the pain." He signaled to the bartender. When, both men had fresh drinks, he asked, "What brings you to Alaska?"

"Well, you'll get a good laugh out of this," Carey said. "You'll never guess who we found as a supply sergeant at Fort Lewis. Bennie the Grab. And he had Spanish Pete Gomez and Fingers Malone as his corporals."

"Mother of God," Hammett said. "It's a surprise there was anything left worth stealing at that place."

"You know it, brother," Carey said. "So you can imagine how we felt when all of the paperwork checked out. Bennie and the boys wouldn't have gotten much more than a year in the brig for false swearing when they joined up if it hadn't been for some smart young pencil pusher. He figured out they were sending a lot of food and not much of anything else to the 332nd here at Fort Richardson."

"Don't tell me," Hammett said. "There is no 332nd."

"That's right," Carey said. "The trucks were leaving the warehouses, but the goods for the 332nd weren't making it to the ships. There wasn't a restaurant or diner or private dinner party in the entire Pacific Northwest that didn't feature U.S. Army butter and beef. We scooped up Bennie and the others, a couple of captains, a major, and a full-bird colonel. All the requisitions were signed by a Sergeant Prevo, and I drew the short straw and got sent up here to arrest him and roll things up at this end."

"It seems you got here just a bit late, Michael," Hammett said. "Because unless there are two supply sergeants named Prevo, your man got his neck broken in a gin mill last night. My gin mill, if it matters."

"This damned army," Carey said. "We didn't tell anybody at this end, because we didn't know who might be involved. And it looks like we'll never find out now, either."

"I don't know about that," Hammett said. "I need to know two things. Were the men running the supply operation at Fort Lewis regular army? And what was it a kid named Billy Tobin got kicked off the force in 'Frisco for? If you can answer those questions, I might be able to help you."

Before Hammett went down the hall to the bathroom the next morning, he took a small pistol from his valise and slipped it into the pocket of his pants. He left it there when he went downstairs for bacon and eggs. As he ate, he read an authoritative newspaper story about the Jap Army using babies as bayonet practice targets in Manila. He spent the rest of the day in his room, reading and dozing, leaving the room to take one telephone call. He ate no lunch. He looked carefully up and down the hallway before his visit to the bathroom. When his watch read 7:30, he got fully dressed, packed his valise, and sat on the bed. Just at 9 P.M., there was a knock on his door.

"Mister," the desk clerk called. "You got a visitor. The same fella."

Hammett walked downstairs and settled his bill with the clerk. He and Miller went out and got into a Jeep. Neither man said anything. The joints on the far side of the city limits were doing big business as they drove past. The Carolina Moon was the only dark building. As they pulled up in front of it, Hammett said, "You might want to find yourself a quiet spot to watch the proceedings."

"What you doing this for?" Miller asked. "Solving murders isn't your business."

"This one is my business," Hammett said. "Zulu's got to eat, and I want a return on my investment. Nobody's making any money with the Moon closed."

"You and Miss Zulu more than just business partners?" Miller asked.

"A gentleman wouldn't ask such a question," Hammett said, "and a gentleman certainly won't answer it."

Hammett hurried into the building. He had trouble making out the people in the dimly lit barroom. Zulu was there, and the temporary blonde. The marshal. The MP. Carey, a couple of tough-looking gents Hammett didn't know, and the major from the party. The MP was standing at the bar, looking at himself in a piece of mirror that hung behind it. Everyone else was sitting. Hammett went around behind the bar, took off his coat, and laid it on the bar. He poured himself a drink and drank it off. The MP wandered over to stand next to the door to the hallway.

"I see you've got everyone assembled," Hammett said to Carey.

The investigator nodded. "The major came to me," he said. "Said as it was his sergeant that was killed, he wanted to be in on this."

"That's one of the things that bothered me about this," Hammett said. "Major Allen seems to know things he shouldn't. For instance, Major, how did you know I was involved in this affair?"

The major was silent for a moment, then said, "I'm certain my friend Major Haynes of the military police must have mentioned your name to me."

"We'll leave that," Hammett said. "Because the other thing that bothered me came first. Oscar, did you call the MPs the night of the killing?"

The marshal shook his head.

"Then what was the sergeant doing here?"

"Said he was in the neighborhood," the marshal said.

"But, Oscar," Hammett said, "don't the MPs always patrol in pairs on this side of the city limits?"

"They certainly do," the marshal said. "What about that, young fella?"

The MP looked at the marshal, then at Hammett.

"My partner got sick," he said. "I had to go it alone. Then I saw all them soldiers leaving here and came to see what was what."

"Michael?" Hammett said.

"Like you said, the duty roster said the sergeant wasn't even on duty that night," the investigator said.

Everyone was looking at the MP now. He didn't say anything.

"This is your case, Oscar," Hammett said, "so let me tell you a story.

"There's a ring of thieves operating out of Fort Lewis, pretending to send food to a phony outfit up here, then selling it on the black market. The ones doing the work were crooks from San Francisco. Tobin here would have known them from his time with the police there.

"Their man on this end, the fellow who was killed the other night, didn't seem to have any connection with them. Michael told me on the telephone today that he was from the Midwest and had never been arrested. He seemed to be just a harmless pansy who used the Moon to meet his boyfriend."

"That's disgusting," the major said.

"That's what happens when the army makes a place the dumping ground for all of its undesirables Major," Hammett said. "What did you do to get sent here?"

"I volunteered," the major grated.

"I'll bet you did," Hammett said. "Anyway, last night Michael reminded me that Tobin here had been run off the San Francisco force for beating up a dancer at Finocchio's. He claimed the guy made a pass at him, but the inside story was that it was a lover's quarrel."

"That's a goddamn lie!" the MP shouted.

"It's just one coincidence too many," Hammett said, his voice as hard as granite. "You know the San Francisco mob. They're stealing from the government. Prevo was in on the scheme. He was queer. You're queer. You're sewn up tight. What happened? He get cold feet and you had to kill him?"

The MP looked from one face to another in the room. Then he looked at Hammett.

"I didn't kill the guy," the MP said. "It was him." He pointed to the major.

Everyone looked at the major, then back at the MP. He was holding his automatic in his hand.

"That's not going to do you any good, young man," the marshal said. "This is Alaska. Where you going to run?"

The MP seemed not to hear him.

"I ain't no queer!" he shouted at Hammett. "I hate queers. I beat that guy up 'cause he made a pass at me, just like I said. I'd have killed him if I thought I'd get away with it. Here, I was just giving the major a little cover in case anything happened. Like the place got raided or something. Then the other day he told me some pal of his had warned him that they'd knocked over the Fort Lewis end of the deal and we were going to have to do something about his boyfriend. 'Jerry will talk,' he said. 'I know he will.' I told him I wasn't killing anybody. The stockade was better than the firing squad. So he comes out the back door of this place the other night and says he killed the pansy himself."

"That's a goddamn lie," the major shouted, leaping to his feet. "I don't even know this man. I've got a wife and baby at home. I'm no fairy."

"You're in for it, Tobin," Hammett said to the MP. "He doesn't leave anything to chance. Why, he tried to shoot me last night just on the off chance I might know something. I'll bet he does have a wife and child. And I'll bet there's nothing to connect him to either you or the corpse. And there's the love letters Michael found in your footlocker."

"Love letters?" the MP said. "What love letters?" He looked at Hammett, then at the major. Understanding flooded his face.

"You set me up!" he screamed at the major. "You set me up as a fairy!"

The automatic barked. The slug seemed to pick the major up and hurl him backward. The temporary blonde screamed. All over the room, men were taking guns from holsters and pockets. They seemed to be moving in slow motion. The MP swung the gun toward Hammett.

"You should have kept your nose out of this," the MP said, leveling the automatic. His finger closed on the trigger.

Don Miller stepped out of the hallway behind the MP and laid a sap on the back of his head. The MP collapsed like he was filled with sawdust.

Miller and Hammett looked at each other for a long moment. Hammett took his hand off the pistol in the pocket of his coat.

"I think that calls for a drink," he said, pouring himself one.

The marshal was putting cuffs on the MP. Carey looked up from where the major lay and shook his head.

"I guess this means you'll be able to open up again, Zulu," Hammett said.

The following afternoon Miller found Hammett lying on a table in the cramped offices of the magazine *Army Up North*, reading Lenin.

"I've got some errands to run in town," he told Hammett.

"Fine by me," Hammett said, sitting up. "I've been thinking I'll put in my papers. The war can't last much longer and this looks like as close as I'll get to any action."

"You'd have been just as dead if that MP shot you as you would if it'd been a Jap bullet," Miller said.

"I suppose," Hammett said. "This morning the general told me that they were going to show Major Allen as killed in the line of duty. They'll give Tobin a quick trial and life in the stockade. The whole thing's being hushed up. The brass don't want to embarrass the major's father, and they don't want the scandal getting back to the president and Congress. This is the country I enlisted to protect?"

Miller shrugged. "I got to be going," he said.

"Right you are," Hammett said. "And, by the way, thanks for stepping in last night. I didn't want to shoot that kid and I didn't want to get shot myself."

Miller turned to leave.

"I suppose I'll just give the Moon to Zulu if I go," Hammett said.

"That'd be real nice," Miller said over his shoulder.

He went out, got into a Jeep, drove downtown, and parked. He walked into the federal building, climbed a set of stairs, walked down a hallway, and went through an unmarked door without knocking. He sat in a chair and told the whole story to a man on the other side of the desk.

"That's all very interesting," the man said, "but did the subject say anything to you or anyone else about Marx, Lenin, or communism?"

"Is that all you care about?" Miller asked. "I keep telling you, I've never heard him say anything about communism."

"You've got to understand," the man said. "This other matter just isn't important. The director says we are already fighting the next war, the war against communism. This war is a triumph of truth, justice, and the American way. And it's over."

Miller said nothing.

"You can let yourself out," the man said. Then he turned to his typewriter, rolled a form into it, and began to type.

Daniel Stashower

The Adventure of the Agitated Actress

DANIEL STASHOWER is the author of five mystery novels and two biographies. His most recent book is *The Boy Genius and the Mogul: The Untold Story of Television,* and he won the MWA Edgar award for best biographical/critical work for *Teller of Tales: The Life of Arthur Conan Doyle.* Stashower is also a part recipient of the Raymond Chandler Fulbright Fellowship in Detective and Crime Fiction Writing. A freelance journalist since 1986, his articles have appeared in *The New York Times, The Washington Post, Smithsonian Magazine, National Geographic Traveller,* and *American History.* He lives near Washington, D.C., with his wife, Alison, and son, Sam. His story, "The Adventure of the Agitated Actress," lets him combine his knowledge and passion for Sherlock Holmes with a very clever mystery. This story first appeared in *Murder, My Dear Watson.*

The Adventure of the Agitated Actress

Daniel Stashower

W e've all heard stories of your wonderful methods, Mr. Holmes,"
said James Larrabee, drawing a cigarette from a silver box on the table.
"There have been countless tales of your marvelous insight, your ingenuity
in picking up and following clues, and the astonishing manner in which
you gain information from the most trifling details. You and I have never
met before today, but I dare say that in this brief moment or two you've
discovered any number of things about me."

Sherlock Holmes set down the newspaper he had been reading and
gazed languidly at the ceiling. "Nothing of consequence, Mr. Larrabee,"
he said. "I have scarcely more than asked myself why you rushed off and
sent a telegram in such a frightened hurry, what possible excuse you could
have had for gulping down a tumbler of raw brandy at the 'Lion's Head'
on the way back, why your friend with the auburn hair left so suddenly
by the terrace window, and what there can possibly be about the safe in the
lower part of that desk to cause you such painful anxiety." The detective
took up the newspaper and idly turned the pages. "Beyond that," he said,
"I know nothing."

"Holmes!" I cried. "This is uncanny! How could you have possibly
deduced all of that? We arrived in this room not more than five minutes
ago!"

My companion glanced at me with an air of strained abstraction, as
though he had never seen me before. For a moment he seemed to hesitate,
apparently wavering between competing impulses. Then he rose from his
chair and crossed down to a row of blazing footlights. "I'm sorry, Frohman," he called. "This isn't working out as I'd hoped. We really don't need
Watson in this scene after all."

"Gillette!" came a shout from the darkened space across the bright line
of lights. "I do wish you'd make up your mind! Need I remind you that
we open tomorrow night?" We heard a brief clatter of footsteps as Charles

Frohman—a short, solidly built gentleman in the casual attire of a country squire—came scrambling up the side access stairs. As he crossed the forward lip of the stage, Frohman brandished a printed handbill. It read: "William Gillette in His Smash Play! Sherlock Holmes! Fresh from a Triumphant New York Run!"

"He throws off the balance of the scene," Gillette was saying. "The situation doesn't call for an admiring Watson." He turned to me. "No offense, my dear Lyndal. You have clearly immersed yourself in the role. That gesture of yours—with your arm at the side—it suggests a man favoring an old wound. Splendid!"

I pressed my lips together and let my hand fall to my side. "Actually, Gillette," I said, "I am endeavoring to keep my trousers from falling down."

"Pardon?"

I opened my jacket and gathered up a fold of loose fabric around my waist. "There hasn't been time for my final costume fitting," I explained.

"I'm afraid I'm having the same difficulty," said Arthur Creeson, who had been engaged to play the villainous James Larrabee. "If I'm not careful, I'll find my trousers down at my ankles."

Gillette gave a heavy sigh. "Quinn!" he called.

Young Henry Quinn, the boy playing the role of Billy, the Baker Street page, appeared from the wings. "Yes, Mr. Gillette?"

"Would you be so good as to fetch the wardrobe mistress? Or at least bring us some extra straight pins?" The boy nodded and darted backstage.

Charles Frohman, whose harried expression and lined forehead told of the rigors of his role as Gillette's producer, folded the handbill and replaced it in his pocket. "I don't see why you feel the need to tinker with the script at this late stage," he insisted. "The play was an enormous success in New York. As far as America is concerned, you *are* Sherlock Holmes. Surely the London audiences will look on the play with equal favor?"

Gillette threw himself down in a chair and reached for his prompt book. "The London audience bears little relation to its American counterpart," he said, flipping rapidly through the pages. "British tastes have been refined over centuries of Shakespeare and Marlowe. America has only lately weaned itself off of *Uncle Tom's Cabin.*"

"Gillette," said Frohman heavily, "you are being ridiculous."

The actor reached for a pen and began scrawling over a page of script. "I am an American actor essaying an English part. I must take every precaution, and make every possible refinement before submitting myself to the fine raking fire of the London critics. They will seize on a single false note as an excuse to send us packing." He turned back to Arthur Creeson. "Now, then. Let us continue from the point at which Larrabee is endeavoring to cover his deception. Instead of Watson's expression of incredulity, we shall restore Larrabee's evasions. Do you recall the speech, Creeson?

The actor nodded.

"Excellent. Let us resume."

I withdrew to the wings as Gillette and Creeson took their places. A mask of impassive self-possession slipped over Gillette's features as he stepped back into the character of Sherlock Holmes. "Why your friend with the auburn hair left so suddenly by the terrace window," he said, picking up the dialogue in midsentence, "and what there can possibly be about the safe in the lower part of that desk to cause you such painful anxiety."

"Ha! Very good!" cried Creeson, taking up his role as the devious James Larrabee. "Very good indeed! If those things were only true, I'd be wonderfully impressed. It would be absolutely marvelous!"

Gillette regarded him with an expression of weary impatience. "It won't do, sir," said he. "I have come to see Miss Alice Faulkner and will not leave until I have done so. I have reason to believe that the young lady is being held against her will. You shall have to give way, sir, or face the consequences."

Creeson's hands flew to his chest. "Against her will? This is outrageous! I will not tolerate—"

A high, trilling scream from backstage interrupted the line. Creeson held his expression and attempted to continue. "I will not tolerate such an accusation in my own—"

A second scream issued from backstage. Gillette gave a heavy sigh and rose from his chair as he reached for the prompt book. "Will that woman never learn her cue?" Shielding his eyes against the glare of the footlights, he stepped again to the lip of the stage and sought out Frohman. "This is what comes of engaging the company locally," he said in an exasperated tone. "We have a mob of players in ill-fitting costumes who don't know their scripts. We should have brought the New York company across, hang the expense." He turned to the wings. "Quinn!"

The young actor stepped forward. "Yes, sir?"

"Will you kindly inform—"

Gillette's instructions were cut short by the sudden appearance of Miss Maude Fenton, the actress playing the role of Alice Faulkner, who rushed from the wings in a state of obvious agitation. Her chestnut hair fell loosely about her shoulders and her velvet shirtwaist was imperfectly buttoned. "Gone!" she cried. "Missing! Taken from me!"

Gillette drummed his fingers across the prompt book. "My dear Miss Fenton," he said, "you have dropped approximately seventeen pages from the script."

"Hang the script!" she wailed. "I'm not playing a role! My brooch is missing! My beautiful, beautiful brooch! Oh, for heaven's sake, Mr. Gillette, someone must have stolen it!"

Selma Kendall, the kindly, auburn-haired actress who had been engaged to play Madge Larrabee, hurried to Miss Fenton's side. "It can't be!" she cried. "He only just gave it—that is to say, you've only just acquired it! Are you certain you haven't simply mislaid it?"

Miss Fenton accepted the linen pocket square I offered and dabbed at her streaming eyes. "I couldn't possibly have mislaid it," she said between sobs. "One doesn't mislay something of that sort! How could such a thing have happened?"

Gillette, who had cast an impatient glance at his pocketwatch during this exchange, now stepped forward to take command of the situation. "There, there, Miss Fenton," he said, in the cautious, faltering tone of a man not used to dealing with female emotions. "I'm sure this is all very distressing. As soon as we have completed our run-through, we will conduct a most thorough search of the dressing areas. I'm sure your missing bauble will be discovered presently."

"Gillette!" I cried. "You don't mean to continue with the rehearsal? Can't you see that Miss Fenton is too distraught to carry on?"

"But she must," the actor declared. "As Mr. Frohman has been at pains to remind us, our little play has its London opening tomorrow evening. We shall complete the rehearsal, and then—after I have given a few notes—we shall locate the missing brooch. Miss Fenton is a fine actress, and I have every confidence in her ability to conceal her distress in the interim." He patted the weeping actress on the back of her hand. "Will that do, my dear?"

At this, Miss Fenton's distress appeared to gather momentum by steady degrees. First her lips began to tremble, then her shoulders commenced heaving, and lastly a strange caterwauling sound emerged from behind the handkerchief. After a moment or two of this, she threw herself into Gillette's arms and began sobbing lustily upon his shoulder.

"Gillette," called Frohman, straining to make himself heard above the lamentations, "perhaps it would be best to take a short pause."

Gillette, seemingly unnerved by the wailing figure in his arms, gave a strained assent. "Very well. We shall repair to the dressing area. No doubt the missing object has simply slipped between the cushions of a settee."

With Mr. Frohman in the lead, our small party made its way through the wings and along the backstage corridors to the ladies' dressing area. As we wound past the scenery flats and crated property trunks, I found myself reflecting on how little I knew of the other members of our troupe. Although Gillette's play had been a great success in America, only a handful of actors and crewmen had transferred to the London production. A great many members of the cast and technical staff, myself included, had been engaged locally after a brief open call. Up to this point, the rehearsals and staging had been a rushed affair, allowing for little of the easy camaraderie that usually develops among actors during the rehearsal period.

As a result, I knew little about my fellow players apart from the usual backstage gossip. Miss Fenton, in the role of the young heroine Alice Faulkner, was considered to be a promising ingenue. Reviewers frequently commented on her striking beauty, if not her talent. Selma Kendall, in the role of the conniving Madge Larrabee, had established herself in the provinces as a dependable support player, and was regarded as something of a mother hen by the younger actresses. Arthur Creeson, as the wicked James Larrabee, had been a promising romantic lead in his day, but excessive drink and gambling had marred his looks and scotched his reputation. William All-erford, whose high, domed forehead and startling white hair helped to make him so effective as the nefarious Professor Moriarty, was in fact the most gentle of men, with a great passion for tending the rose bushes at his cottage in Hove. As for myself, I had set out to become an opera singer in my younger days, but my talent had not matched my ambition, and over time I had evolved into a reliable, if unremarkable, second lead.

"Here we are," Frohman was saying as we arrived at the end of a long corridor. "We shall make a thorough search." After knocking on the un-marked door, he led us inside.

As was the custom of the day, the female members of the cast shared a communal dressing area in a narrow, sparsely appointed chamber illumi-nated by a long row of electrical lights. Along one wall was a long mirror with a row of wooden makeup tables before it. A random cluster of coat racks, reclining sofas, and well-worn armchairs was arrayed along the wall opposite. Needless to say, I had never been in a ladies' dressing room before, and I admit that I felt my cheeks redden at the sight of so many underthings and delicates thrown carelessly over the furniture. I turned to avert my eyes from a cambric corset cover thrown across a ladderback chair, only to find myself gazing upon a startling assortment of hosiery and lace-trimmed drawers laid out upon a nearby ottoman.

"Gracious, Mr. Lyndal," said Miss Kendall, taking a certain delight in my discomfiture. "One would almost think you'd never seen linens before."

"Well, I—perhaps not so many at once," I admitted, gathering my composure. "Dr. Watson is said to have an experience of women that ex-tends over many nations and three separate continents. My own experience, I regret to say, extends no farther than Hatton Cross."

Gillette, it appeared, did not share my sense of consternation. No sooner had we entered the dressing area than he began making an energetic and somewhat indiscriminate examination of the premises, darting from one side of the room to the other, opening drawers and tossing aside cushions and pillows with careless abandon.

"Well," he announced, after five minutes' effort, "I cannot find your brooch. However, in the interests of returning to our rehearsals as quickly as possible, I am prepared to buy you a new one."

Miss Fenton stared at the actor with an expression of disbelief. "I'm afraid you don't understand, Mr. Gillette. This was not a common piece of rolled plate and crystalline. It was a large, flawless sapphire in a rose gold setting, with a circle of diamond accents."

Gillette's eyes widened. "Was it, indeed? May I know how you came by such an item?"

A flush spread across Miss Fenton's cheek. "It was—it was a gift from an admirer," she said, glancing away. "I would prefer to say no more."

"Be that as it may," I said, "this is no small matter. We must notify the police at once!"

Gillette pressed his fingers together. "I'm afraid I must agree. This is most inconvenient."

A look of panic flashed across Miss Fenton's eyes. "Please, Mr. Gillette! You must not involve the police! That wouldn't do at all!"

"But your sapphire—?"

She tugged at the lace trimming of her sleeve. "The gentleman in question—the man who presented me with the brooch—he is of a certain social standing, Mr. Gillette. He—that is to say, I—would prefer to keep the matter private. It would be most embarrassing for him if his—if his attentions to me should become generally known."

Frohman gave a sudden cough. "It is not unknown for young actresses to form attachments with certain of their gentlemen admirers," he said carefully. "Occasionally, however, when these matters become public knowledge, they are attended by a certain whiff of scandal. Especially if the gentleman concerned happens to be married." He glanced at Miss Fenton, who held his gaze for a moment and then looked away. "Indeed," said Frohman. "Well, we can't have those whispers about the production, Gillette. Not before we've even opened."

"Quite so," I ventured, "and there is Miss Fenton's reputation to consider. We must discover what happened to the brooch without involving the authorities. We shall have to mount a private investigation."

All eyes turned to Gillette as a mood of keen expectation fell across the room. The actor did not appear to notice. Having caught sight of himself in the long mirror behind the dressing tables, he was making a meticulous adjustment to his waistcoat. At length, he became aware that the rest of us were staring intently at him.

"What?" he said, turning away from the mirror. "Why is everyone looking at me?"

"I AM *not* Sherlock Holmes," Gillette said several moments later, as we settled ourselves in a pair of armchairs. "I am an actor *playing* Sherlock Holmes. There is a very considerable difference. If I did a turn as a pantomime horse, Lyndal, I trust you would not expect me to pull a dray wagon and dine on straw?"

"But you've studied Sherlock Holmes," I insisted. "You've examined his methods and turned them to your own purposes. Surely you might be able to do the same in this instance? Surely the author of such a fine detective play is not totally lacking in the powers of perception?"

Gillette gave me an appraising look. "Appealing to my vanity, Lyndal? Very shrewd."

We had been arguing back and forth in this vein for some moments, though by this time—detective or no—Gillette had reluctantly agreed to give his attention to the matter of the missing brooch. Frohman had made him see that an extended disruption would place their financial interests in the hazard, and that Gillette, as head of the company, was the logical choice to take command of the situation. Toward that end, it was arranged that Gillette would question each member of the company individually, beginning with myself.

Gillette's stage manager, catching wind of the situation, thought it would be a jolly lark to replace the standing set of James Larrabee's drawing room with the lodgings of Sherlock Holmes at Baker Street, so that Gillette might have an appropriate setting in which to carry out his investigation. If Gillette noticed, he gave no sign. Stretching his arm toward a side table, he took up an outsize calabash pipe and began filling the meerschaum bowl.

"Why do you insist on smoking that ungainly thing?" I asked. "There's no record whatsoever of Sherlock Holmes having ever touched a calabash. Dr. Watson tells us that he favors an oily black clay pipe as the companion of his deepest meditations, but is wont to replace it with his cherrywood when in a disputatious frame of mind."

Gillette shook his head sadly. "I am *not* Sherlock Holmes," he said again. "I am an actor *playing* Sherlock Holmes."

"Still," I insisted, "it does no harm to be as faithful to the original as possible."

Gillette touched a flame to the tobacco and took several long draws to be certain the bowl was properly ignited. For a moment, his eyes were unfocused and dreamy, and I could not be certain that he had heard me. His eyes were fixed upon the fly curtains when he spoke again. "Lyndal," he said, "turn and face downstage."

"What?"

"Humor me. Face downstage."

I rose and looked out across the forward edge of the stage.

"What do you see?" Gillette asked.

"Empty seats," I said.

"Precisely. It is my ambition to fill those seats. Now, cast your eyes to the rear of the house. I want you to look at the left-hand aisle seat in the very last row."

I stepped forward and narrowed my eyes. "Yes," I said. "What of it?"

"Can you read the number plate upon that seat?"

"No," I said. "Of course not."

"Nor can I. By the same token, the man or woman seated there will not be able to appreciate the difference between a cherrywood pipe and an oily black clay. This is theater, Lyndal. A real detective does not do his work before an audience. I do. Therefore I am obliged to make my movements, speech, and stage properties readily discernible." He held the calabash aloft. "This pipe will be visible from the back row, my friend. An actor must consider even the smallest object from every possible angle. That is the essence of theater."

I considered the point. "I merely thought, inasmuch as you are attempting to inhabit the role of Sherlock Holmes, that you should wish to strive for authenticity."

Gillette seemed to consider the point. "Well," he said, "let us see how far that takes us. Tell me, Lyndal. Where were you when the robbery occurred?"

"Me? But surely you don't think that I—"

"You are not the estimable Dr. Watson, my friend. You are merely an actor, like myself. Since Miss Fenton had her brooch with her when she arrived at the theater this morning, we must assume that the theft occurred shortly after first call. Can you account for your movements in that time?"

"Of course I can. You know perfectly well where I was. I was standing stage right, beside you, running through the first act."

"So you were. Strange, my revision of the play has given you a perfect alibi. Had the theft occurred this afternoon, after I had restored the original text of the play, you should have been high on the list of suspects. A narrow escape, my friend." He smiled and sent up a cloud of pipe smoke. "Since we have established your innocence, however, I wonder if I might trouble you to remain through the rest of the interviews?"

"Whatever for?"

"Perhaps I am striving for authenticity." He turned and spotted young Henry Quinn hovering in his accustomed spot in the wings near the scenery cleats. "Quinn!" he called.

The boy stepped forward. "Yes, sir?"

"Would you ask Miss Fenton if she would be so good as to join us?"

"Right away, sir."

I watched as the boy disappeared down the long corridor. "Gillette," I said, lowering my voice, "this Baker Street set is quite comfortable in its way, but do you not think a bit of privacy might be indicated? Holmes is accustomed to conducting his interviews in confidence. Anyone might hear what passes between us here at the center of the stage."

Gillette smiled. "I am *not* Sherlock Holmes," he repeated.

After a moment or two Quinn stepped from the wings with Miss Fenton trailing behind him. Miss Fenton's eyes and nose were red with weeping, and she was attended by Miss Kendall, who hovered protectively by her side. "May I remain, Mr. Gillette?" asked the older actress. "Miss Fenton is terribly upset by all of this."

"Of course," said Gillette in a soothing manner. "I shall try to dispense with the questioning as quickly as possible. Please be seated." He folded his hands and leaned forward in his chair. "Tell me, Miss Fenton, are you quite certain that the brooch was in your possession when you arrived at the theater this morning?"

"Of course," the actress replied. "I had no intention of letting it out of my sight. I placed the pin in my jewelry case as I changed into costume."

"And the jewelry case was on top of your dressing table?"

"Yes."

"In plain sight?"

"Yes, but I saw no harm in that. I was alone at the time. Besides, Miss Kendall is the only other woman in the company, and I trust her as I would my own sister." She reached across and took the older woman's hand.

"No doubt," said Gillette, "but do you mean to say that you intended to leave the gem in the dressing room during the rehearsal? Forgive me, but that seems a bit careless."

"That was not my intention at all, Mr. Gillette. Once in costume, I planned to pin the brooch to my stockings. I should like to have worn it in plain view, but James—that is to say, the gentleman who gave it to me— would not have approved. He does not want anyone—he does not approve of ostentation."

"In any case," I said, "Alice Faulkner would hardly be likely to own such a splendid jewel."

"Yes," said Miss Fenton. "Just so."

Gillette steepled his fingers. "How exactly did the jewel come to be stolen? It appears that it never left your sight."

"It was unforgivable of me," said Miss Fenton. "I arrived late to the theater this morning. In my haste, I overturned an entire pot of facial powder. I favor a particular type, Gervaise Graham's Satinette, and I wished to see if I could persuade someone to step out and purchase a fresh supply for me. I can only have been gone for a moment. I stepped into the hallway looking for one of the stagehands, but of course they were all in their places in anticipation of the scene three set change. When I found no one close by, I realized that I had better finish getting ready as best I could without the powder."

"So you returned to the dressing area?"

"Yes."

"How long would you say that you were out of the room?"

"Two or three minutes. No more."

"And when you returned the brooch was gone?"

She nodded. "That was when I screamed."

"Indeed." Gillette stood and clasped his hands behind his back. "Extraordinary," he said, pacing a short line before a scenery flat decorated to resemble a bookcase. "Miss Kendall?"

"Yes?"

"Has anything been stolen from you?" he asked.

"No," she answered. "Well, not this time."

Gillette raised an eyebrow. "Not this time?"

The actress hesitated. "I'm sure it's nothing," she said. "From time to time I have noticed that one or two small things have gone astray. Nothing of any value. A small mirror, perhaps, or a copper or two."

Miss Fenton nodded. "I've noticed that as well. I assumed that I'd simply misplaced the items. It was never anything to trouble over."

Gillette frowned. "Miss Fenton, a moment ago, when the theft became known, it was clear that Miss Kendall was already aware that you had the brooch in your possession. May I ask who else among the company knew of the sapphire?"

"No one," the actress said. "I only received the gift yesterday, but I would have been unlikely to flash it about, in any case. I couldn't resist showing it to Selma, however."

"No one else knew of it?"

"No one."

Gillette turned to Miss Kendall. "Did you mention it to anyone?"

"Certainly not, Mr. Gillette."

The actor resumed his pacing. "You're quite certain? It may have been a perfectly innocent remark."

"Maude asked me not to say anything to anyone," said Miss Kendall. "We women are rather good with secrets."

Gillette's mouth pulled up slightly at the corners. "So I gather, Miss Kendall. So I gather." He turned and studied the false book spines on the painted scenery flat. "Thank you for your time, ladies."

I watched as the two actresses departed. "Gillette," I said after a moment, "if Miss Kendall did not mention the sapphire to anyone, who else could have known that it existed?"

"No one," he answered.

"Are you suggesting—" I leaned forward and lowered my voice. "Are you suggesting that Miss Kendall is the thief? After all, if she was the only one who knew—"

"No, Lyndal. I do not believe Miss Kendall is the thief."

"Still," I said, "there is little reason to suppose that she kept her own counsel. A theatrical company is a hotbed of gossip and petty jealousies." I paused as a new thought struck me. "Miss Fenton seems most concerned with protecting the identify of her gentleman admirer, although this will not be possible if the police have to be summoned. Perhaps the theft was orchestrated to expose him." I considered the possibility for a moment. "Yes, perhaps the intended victim is really this unknown patron, whomever he might be. He is undoubtedly a man of great wealth and position. Who knows? Perhaps this sinister plot extends all the way to the—"

"I think not," said Gillette.

"No?"

"If the intention was nothing more than to expose a dalliance between a young actress and a man of position, one need not have resorted to theft. A word in the ear of certain society matrons would have the same effect, and far more swiftly." He threw himself back down in his chair. "No, I believe that this was a crime of opportunity, rather than design. Miss Kendall and Miss Fenton both reported having noticed one or two small things missing from their dressing area on previous occasions. It seems that we have a petty thief in our midst, and that this person happened across the sapphire during those few moments when it was left unattended in the dressing room."

"But who could it be? Most of us were either on stage or working behind the scenes, in plain view of at least one other person at all times."

"So it would seem, but I'm not entirely convinced that someone couldn't have slipped away for a moment or two without being noticed. The crew members are forever darting in and out. It would not have drawn any particular notice if one of them had slipped away for a moment or two."

"Then we shall have to question the suspects," I said. "We must expose this nefarious blackguard at once."

Gillette regarded me over the bowl of his pipe. "Boucicault?" he asked.

"Pardon?"

"That line you just quoted. I thought I recognized it from one of Mr. Boucicault's melodramas."

I flushed. "No," I said. "It was my own."

"Was it? How remarkably vivid." He turned to young Henry Quinn, who was awaiting his instructions in the wings. "Quinn," he called, "might I trouble you to run and fetch Mr. Allerford? I have a question or two I would like to put to him."

"Allerford," I said, as the boy disappeared into the wings. "So your suspicions have fallen upon the infamous Professor Moriarty, have they? There's a bit of Holmes in you, after all."

"Scarcely," said Gillette with a weary sigh. "I am proceeding in alphabetical order."

"Ah."

Young Quinn returned a moment later to conduct Allerford into our presence. The actor wore a long black frock coat for his impersonation of the evil professor, and his white hair was pomaded into a billowing cloud, exaggerating the size of his head and suggesting the heat of the character's mental processes.

"Do sit down, Allerford," Gillette said as the actor stepped onto the stage, "and allow me to apologize for subjecting you to this interview. It pains me to suggest that you may in any way have—"

The actor held up his hands to break off the apologies. "No need, Gillette. I would do the same in your position. I presume you will wish to know where I was while the rest of you were running through the first act?"

Gillette nodded. "If you would be so kind."

"I'm afraid the answer is far from satisfactory. I was in the gentlemen's dressing area."

"Alone?"

"I'm afraid so. All the others were on stage or in the costume shop for their fittings." He gathered up a handful of loose fabric from his waistcoat. "My fitting was delayed until this afternoon. So I imagine I would have to be counted as the principal suspect, Gillette." He allowed his features to shift and harden as he assumed the character of Professor Moriarty. "You'll never hang this on me, Mr. Sherlock Holmes," he hissed, as his head oscillated in a reptilian fashion. "I have an ironclad alibi! I was alone in my dressing room reading a magazine!" The actor broke character and held up his palms in a gesture of futility. "I'm afraid I can't offer you anything better, Gillette."

"I'm sure nothing more will be required, Allerford. Again, let me apologize for this intrusion."

"Not at all."

"One more thing," Gillette said as Allerford rose to take his leave.

"Yes?"

"The magazine you were reading. It wasn't *The Strand*, by any chance?"

"Why, yes. There was a copy lying about on the table."

"A Sherlock Holmes adventure, was it?"

Allerford's expression turned sheepish. "My tastes don't run in that direction, I'm afraid. There was an article on the sugar planters of the Yucatán. Quite intriguing, if I may say."

"I see." Gillette began refilling the bowl of his pipe. "Much obliged, Allerford."

"Gillette!" I said in an urgent whisper, as Allerford retreated into the wings. "What was that all about? Were you trying to catch him out?"

"What? No, I was just curious." The actor's expression grew unfocused as he touched a match to the tobacco. "Very curious." He sat quietly for some moments, sending clouds of smoke up into the fly curtains.

"Gillette," I said after a few moments, "shouldn't we continue? I believe Mr. Creeson is next."

"Creeson?"

"Yes. If we are to proceed alphabetically."

"Very good. Creeson. By all means. Quinn! Ask Mr. Creeson to join us, if you would."

With that, Gillette sank into his chair and remained there, scarcely moving, for the better part of two hours as a parade of actors, actresses, and stagehands passed before him. His questions and attitude were much the same as they had been with Allerford, but clearly his attention had wandered to some distant and inaccessible plateau. At times he appeared so preoccupied that I had to prod him to continue with the interviews. At one stage he drew his legs up to his chest and encircled them with his arms, looking for all the world like Sidney Paget's illustration of Sherlock Holmes in the grip of one of his three-pipe problems. Unlike the great detective, however, Gillette soon gave way to meditations of a different sort. By the time the last of our interviews was completed, a contented snoring could be heard from the actor's armchair.

"Gillette," I said, shaking him by the shoulder. "I believe we've spoken to everyone now."

"Have we? Very good." He rose from the chair and stretched his long limbs. "Is Mr. Frohman anywhere about?"

"Right here, Gillette," the producer called from the first row of seats. "I must say this appears to have been a colossal waste of time. I don't see how we can avoid going to the police now."

"I'm afraid I have to agree," I said. "We are no closer to resolving the matter than we were this morning." I glanced at Gillette, who was staring blankly into the footlights. "Gillette? Are you listening?"

"I think we may be able to keep the authorities out of the matter," he answered. "Frohman? Might I trouble you to assemble the company?"

"Whatever for?" I asked. "You've already spoken to—say! You don't mean to say that you know who stole Miss Fenton's brooch?"

"I didn't say that."

"But then why should you—?"

He turned and held a finger to his lips. "I'm afraid you'll have to wait for the final act."

The actor would say nothing more as the members of the cast and crew appeared from their various places and arrayed themselves in the first two rows of seats. Gillette, standing at the lip of the stage, looked over them with an expression of keen interest. "My friends," he said after a moment, "you have all been very patient during this unpleasantness. I appreciate your indulgence. I'm sure that Sherlock Holmes would have gotten to the bottom of the matter in just a few moments, but as I am not Sherlock Holmes, it has taken me rather longer."

"Mr. Gillette!" cried Miss Fenton. "Do you mean to say you've found my brooch?"

"No, dear lady," he said, "I haven't. But I trust that it will be back in your possession shortly."

"Gillette," said Frohman, "this is all very irregular. Where is the stone? Who is the thief?"

"The identity of the thief has been apparent from the beginning," Gillette said placidly. "What I did not understand was the motivation."

"But that's nonsense!" cried Arthur Creeson. "The sapphire is extraordinarily valuable! What other motivation could there be?"

"I can think of several," Gillette answered, "and our 'nefarious blackguard,' to borrow a colorful phrase, might have succumbed to any one of them."

"You're talking in circles, Gillette," said Frohman. "If you've known the identity of the thief from the first, why didn't you just say so?"

"I was anxious to resolve the matter quietly," the actor answered. "Now, sadly, that is no longer possible." Gillette stretched his long arms. Moving upstage, he took up his pipe and slowly filled the bowl with tobacco from a ragged Persian slipper. "It was my hope," he said, "that the villain would come to regret these actions—the rash decision of an instant— and make amends. If the sapphire had simply been replaced on Miss Fenton's dressing table, I should have put the incident behind and carried on as though I had never discerned the guilty party's identity. Now, distasteful as it may be, the villain must be unmasked, and I must lose a member of my company on the eve of our London opening. Regrettable, but it can't be helped."

The members of the company shifted uneasily in their seats. "It's one of us, then?" asked Mr. Allerford.

"Of course. That much should have been obvious to all of you." He struck a match and ran it over the bowl of his pipe, lingering rather longer than necessary over the process. "The tragedy of the matter is that none of this would have happened if Miss Fenton had not stepped from her dressing room and left the stone unattended."

The actress's hands flew to her throat. "But I told you, I had spilled a pot of facial powder."

"Precisely so. Gervaise Graham's Satinette. A very distinctive shade. And so the catalyst of the crime now becomes the instrument of its solution."

"How do you mean, Gillette?" I asked.

Gillette moved off to stand before the fireplace—or rather the canvas-and-wood strutting that had been arranged to resemble a fireplace. The actor spent a moment contemplating the plaster coals that rested upon a balsa grating. "Detective work," he intoned, "is founded upon the observation of trifles. When Miss Fenton overturned that facial powder she set in motion a chain of events that yielded a clue—a clue as transparent as that of a weaver's tooth or a compositor's thumb—and one that made it patently obvious who took the missing stone."

"Gillette!" cried Mr. Frohman. "No more theatrics! Who took Miss Fenton's sapphire?"

"The thief is here among us," he declared, his voice rising to a vibrant timbre. "And the traces of Satinette facial powder are clearly visible upon— wait! Stop him!"

All at once, the theater erupted into pandemonium as young Henry Quinn, who had been watching from his accustomed place in the wings, suddenly darted forward and raced toward the rear exit.

"Stop him!" Gillette called to a pair of burly stagehands. "Hendricks! O'Donnell! Don't let him pass!"

The fleeing boy veered away from the stagehands, upsetting a flimsy side table in his flight, and made headlong for the forward edge of the stage. Gathering speed, he attempted to vault over the orchestra pit, and would very likely have cleared the chasm, but for the fact that his ill-fitting trousers suddenly slipped to his ankles, entangling his legs and causing him to land in an awkward heap at the base of the pit.

"He's out cold, Mr. Gillette," came a voice from the pit. "Nasty bruise on his head."

"Very good, Hendricks. If you would be so good as to carry him into the lobby, we shall decide what to do with him later."

Miss Fenton pressed a linen handkerchief to her face as the unconscious figure was carried past. "I don't understand, Mr. Gillette. Henry took my sapphire? He's just a boy! I can't believe he would do such a thing!"

"Strange to say, I believe Quinn's intentions were relatively benign," said Gillette. "He presumed, when he came across the stone on your dressing table, that it was nothing more than a piece of costume jewelry. It was only later, after the alarm had been raised, that he realized its value. At that point, he became frightened and could not think of a means to return it without confessing his guilt."

"But what would a boy do with such a valuable stone?" Frohman asked.

"I have no idea," said Gillette. "Indeed, I do not believe that he had any interest whatsoever in the sapphire."

"No interest?" I said. "What other reason could he have had for taking it?"

"For the pin."

"What?"

Gillette gave a rueful smile. "You are all wearing costumes that are several sizes too large. Our rehearsals have been slowed for want of sewing pins to hold up the men's trousers and pin back the ladies' frocks. I myself dispatched Quinn to find a fastener for Mr. Lyndal."

"The essence of theater," I said, shaking my head with wonder.

"Pardon me, Lyndal?"

"As you were saying earlier. An actor must consider even the smallest object from every possible angle. We all assumed that the brooch had been taken for its valuable stone. Only you would have thought to consider it from the back as well as the front." I paused. "Well done, Gillette."

The actor gave a slight bow as the company burst into spontaneous applause. "That is most kind," he said, "but now, ladies and gentlemen, if there are no further distractions, I should like to continue with our rehearsal. Act one, scene four, I believe . . ."

It was several hours later when I knocked at the door to Gillette's dressing room. He bade me enter and made me welcome with a glass of excellent port. We settled ourselves on a pair of makeup stools and sat for a few moments in a companionable silence.

"I understand that Miss Fenton has elected not to pursue the matter of Quinn's theft with the authorities," I said, after a time.

"I thought not," Gillette said. "I doubt if her gentleman friend would appreciate seeing the matter aired in the press. However, we will not be able to keep young Quinn with the company. He has been dismissed. Frohman has been in touch with another young man I once considered for the role. Charles Chapman."

"Chaplin, I believe."

"That's it. I'm sure he'll pick it up soon enough."

"No doubt."

I took a sip of port. "Gillette," I said, "there is something about the affair that troubles me."

He smiled and reached for a pipe. "I thought there might be," he said.

"You claimed to have spotted Quinn's guilt by the traces of face powder on his costume."

"Indeed."

I lifted my arm. "There are traces of Miss Fenton's powder here on my sleeve as well. No doubt I acquired them when I was searching for the missing stone in the dressing area—after the theft had been discovered."

"No doubt," said Gillette.

"The others undoubtedly picked up traces of powder as well."

"That is likely."

"So Quinn himself might well have acquired his telltale dusting of powder *after* the theft had occurred, in which case it would not have been incriminating at all."

Gillette regarded me with keen amusement. "Perhaps I noticed the powder on Quinn's sleeve before we searched the dressing area," he offered.

"Did you?"

He sighed. "No."

"Then you were bluffing? That fine speech about the observation of trifles was nothing more than vain posturing?"

"It lured a confession out of Quinn, my friend, so it was not entirely in vain."

"But you had no idea who the guilty party was! Not until the moment he lost his nerve and ran!"

Gillette leaned back and sent a series of billowy smoke rings toward the ceiling. "That is so," he admitted, "but then, as I have been at some pains to remind you, I am *not* Sherlock Holmes."

Anke Gebert

Two in the Same Boat

Despite the precarious literary situation in Germany, the majority of our foreign stories have come from the Rhineland, and this year is no different. Next up is ANKE GEBERT's story of love, hate, and canoeing, "Two in the Same Boat." Born in 1960, she is a freelance author of novels, nonfiction, and illustrated books, and currently lives in Hamburg. For those wishing more information (and who can read German), her Web site can be found at www.ankegebert.de. Her story chosen for this year's volume first appeared in the anthology *Sport is Murder.* It was translated into English by Stephanie Schoebel.

Two in the Same Boat

Anke Gebert

Only her love for him made Ellen sit in that boat. Together with him—Jochen. And she had let herself be abused by him for the past two weeks. She actually hated canoe tours, camping holidays, or caravan outings. According to Ellen, these particular holiday categories had no style—they were for the primitives. Until she met him: Jochen. From him she took things she had never taken from any man before him. Ellen's acquaintances described this relationship as "love is blind" and refused to invite them to their parties. Ellen's best friend had asked her worriedly whether she might have a masochistic bent. Ellen punished her friend by breaking up with her. Since then half a year had passed.

Lately it occasionally happened that Ellen despised herself for letting Jochen humiliate her. And she got increasingly annoyed when he told people who were not interested the same stories over and over again with unbroken enthusiasm. Like the one about him being a geography teacher who had only stupid pupils in his classes. These days youngster did not even know where east or west were located, never mind where the sun rose. He had to drum the compass card into them by teaching them, like little idiots, silly nursery rhymes, playing on the first letters of north, east, south, and west. Ellen preferred to keep it to herself that she very well knew how a compass card looked on paper but most of the time could not make out north and south in the open air. Another story Jochen loved to tell was how he chose to buy this very blue canoe, in which they were sitting right now (one out of the stocks of the FDJ, the East German youth organization), in the former GDR, since it used to be cheaper there, much cheaper than in the West. How he had found one dumb East German who had been keen on exchanging his silly East German currency for the course 6:1 into Deutschmarks. Thus Jochen had paid only ninety dollars.

In this very canoe Ellen had been sitting for the past two weeks and had been paddling for her love, sometimes thinking she was paddling out of it.

When they had put the collapsible boat back into one of Hamburg's small harbors to let it into the water, Jochen had criticized her for not knowing where to place transom 23. When Ellen was about to climb in with her brand-new white sneakers, which she had bought especially for this tour, he yelled at her that she was dirtying his beautiful boat and whether she was not aware of the fact that even on the big yachts everybody took off his shoes. On their tour they were carrying the canoe around every lock because Jochen wanted to save the fees. Ellen had grown increasingly exhausted from the long paddling. At one point she lost grip of the bow when she had to carry it once more, including all their luggage. Her first impulse was to get down to her knees and ask Jochen for forgiveness, but then she had held herself back, for that was the moment when he had called her a "silly cow" for the first time.

By now they had reached the lake in Plaue, the third largest in the lake district of East German Mecklenburg. And as always it was up to Jochen to decide that the two of them would not choose one of the comfortable camping sites or even a picturesquely located youth hostel directly by the water, but would rather camp secluded and remote in their own little igloo tents. Otherwise, according to Jochen, one might as well go on a package tour, which was not his style at all and completely lacking in style anyway. Meanwhile, Ellen dreamed with every stroke her way back onto the five-star cruise, where she and her best girlfriend had once spent their holiday—all inclusive.

The couple paddled to a deserted spot. Thick brush grew there into the water. Jochen was still not willing to talk to Ellen because she had had the audacity to drop his wonderful canoe. He insinuated that she had done this on purpose, knowing very well that she had never liked his canoe in the first place. . . .

But Jochen's silence did not bother Ellen as much as usual. She told herself that with every stroke she would come closer to the destination— the end of this tour. She had to endure these tortures only a little while longer until Mueritz, the largest of the lakes in Mecklenburg—and then all the way back to Hamburg, of course. Ellen dispelled the idea of the luxury of a hot shower; the water of the lake was cold, so cold that Jochen, unlike her, had not been washing himself during the last few days.

Whenever Ellen had occasionally turned around unexpectedly at the beginning of the tour, she had caught Jochen taking a rest so that it was she alone who had been paddling for several kilometers. Naturally Ellen had not complained. At the moment Jochen was also paddling forcefully, presumably to avoid freezing to death, for the clothes he was wearing were as cold and damp as hers. For all those past two weeks they had been on tour, it had been raining almost nonstop.

Ellen took off her socks and rolled up her trousers to pull the canoe ashore together with Jochen and leave it at the slim and stony stretch. She fought her way through thick bushes, tick-infested fern, and two-meter-high stinging nettle to find a place for putting up their tent. Ellen was secretly gloating when she pictured how the mosquitoes would attack Jochen in huge swarms.

From early on Ellen had been spared by mosquitoes, or, to be more exact, from that day she had accompanied her father into the dense forest to dig up earthworms. It was her job back then to keep ready a tin filled with dark forest soil into which her father could then drop the dug-up worms. There must have been thousands of mosquitoes in that dark and cavelike forest, for the then seven-year-old Ellen did not know which one she should frighten away first. And she had to do it in secret because her father did not tolerate it when his daughter was fidgeting around. "Don't act so silly—just because of a few mosquitoes!" The buzzing around Ellen's small body sounded increasingly agitated as if these mosquito crowds could not believe how much blood had been handed to them on a silver platter. At some point the itching on Ellen's body became constant; minutes later it did not bother her anymore. Shortly afterward the child fainted. The tin with the earthworms fell with her to the ground. Only after the father had collected his fishing baits again did he carry his daughter out of the woods. In the daylight he realized that her body was heavily reddened and swollen.

Since that day mosquitoes avoided Ellen as if her blood had been contaminated by all those bites. Actually, that should have made her grateful to her father. . . .

Ellen and Jochen put up the tent on the black muddy forest soil. Ellen had a hunch as to how the cold would creep through the thin floor of the tent during the upcoming night—through the foam mattress and the sleeping bag right into their bodies. Even Jochen must have realized how uncomfortable this spot was, because he suggested to paddle off once more before lying down, to find a place where one could eat and drink among other people. That took Ellen by surprise, not only because he was talking to her again but also because Jochen declared that he would invite her for dinner—something he had never done before. Jochen and Ellen had separate accounts, which, as far as they were concerned, was the proper thing to do for a modern couple (this did not stop him from borrowing money from Ellen quite often, which he never paid back).

When Jochen drank, there were moments in which he could be charming. And so Ellen was in a hurry to get back into the canoe.

They were paddling for more than an hour when they found a village with a pub called the Anchor. The couple left their numb sweaters over the chairs to dry. Ellen ordered the cheapest dish, fried eggs with bread, so that Jochen would not think she wanted to take advantage of his invitation. Jochen drank one schnapps after another, accompanied by a big steak and a double helping of mushrooms and croquettes.

Two locals joined them at their table and bought several rounds of herbal schnapps. It did not take long and Jochen told his story about how clever he had acted fifteen years ago, when he struck that great deal with the avaricious East German, who yearned for Deutschmarks, making the purchase of the canoe so cheap. Discreetly Ellen kicked him on the shin from under the table, but Jochen did not seem to comprehend that right in the middle of East Germany one should not go on about how East Germans would never ever understand market economy. Jochen did not realize that one of the two local men, the one with the black mustache, brought his chair nearer to Ellen so that she could feel his thigh next to hers. Ellen let it happen and excitedly downed as many drinks as the man bought her. When the guy finally went to the toilet and turned to Ellen, looking invitingly at her, she did not follow him because the point was finally reached where the German-German reunification had ended for her.

After that man had returned to the table, the evening came to a rapid end. The two local men insisted on accompanying Ellen and Jochen to their canoe to say farewell. During the whole evening they had repeatedly told stories about how nasty the water of the lake in Plaue could be.

Up to thirty meters deep was the lake at some points, so deep that the story of a sunken city had been making the rounds for the last hundred years. Even today the fishermen's nets would get caught by the top of the sunken church tower. Much to Ellen's surprise Jochen did not object to the two men, although he had just lectured her that this was a legend that was originally told of the nearby lake in Ploetze but not of this one in Plaue. The men had also reported that sudden winds had already capsized many a boat and that the nights on the water got so dark that one could not recognize the person in front of you. Jochen did not consider these stories disturbing at all. He was from Hamburg and knew the waters because he paddled on the river Elbe regularly. That he was actually referring to one of the smaller canals at which the garden plot he had inherited from his mother was located—this detail he withheld.

At the shore the two locals pushed off Ellen and Jochen in their boat. Right then Ellen was sure that it was the wrong direction they were heading to. But Jochen would not hear a word against what the two "nice" locals had told him. He was the geography teacher here and therefore knew into which direction they had to paddle. Ellen was glad that she had her big sweater with her. It was not only very dark this night but also unusually cold. Jochen had left his sweater in the pub and asked Ellen whether he could have hers. Ellen heard herself answer "No." Only one hour later did Jochen agree that they would probably never get to their destination, their little tent in the remote forest, if they did not reorient themselves in the dark. He ordered to paddle back and away from the reed belt, farther onto the lake so that they got a glance of the shore from farther away and might recognize some spots that would make them find the position of their tent.

A strong wind sprang up. Like a cotton ball the collapsible boat drifted on the water. Naturally Jochen blamed Ellen—for the forgotten sweater, for the wrong direction, for the wind. And again he called her a silly cow.

Strong gusts of wind made the waves pound against the canoe. Water swept over the rail. While Ellen had been paddling for her love at the beginning of the tour, it now seemed to her that she was paddling for dear life. In the far distance she spotted the big camping site on which she had wanted to put up their tent hours ago. A campfire was dying out over there. Some points of light revealed that there were still flashlights or candles on in some of the tents. That meant Ellen and Jochen still had more than one hour to paddle to reach their tent in the remote forest cave.

When they had reached the reed belt again, the canoe was gliding calmly through the water as though through a black, leaden mass. Exhausted, Ellen turned to take a look at Jochen and noticed that again he was not paddling. She put her paddle across her knee and said, "It's your turn now! At least here at the reed you could do something."

Drunk as he was, Jochen was not able to move the canoe forward. They were going in circles as if they had entered a whirlpool. Ellen realized that she had rocked this man through the waters from Hamburg to Mecklenburg for the last fortnight. And now this, although Ellen was the one who hated canoe tours!

"Listen, honey," she heard Jochen beg in a flattering tone, "please be a sport and paddle again."

Ellen liked him begging for something and she intended to enjoy this awhile longer. She did not do anything. Only when the canoe had started to rock harder, she noticed that Jochen had began to undress behind her back—he was stark naked.

Jochen dropped heavily into the water. Ellen clung to the canoe in shock. Jochen surfaced again, panting because the cold was taking a lot out of his body.

"Then I'll pull the canoe—and you!" he called, and seemed to be happy with his idea. He moved hand over hand along the rail toward the bow and tore the rope into the water. For one moment Ellen was surprised, amused at what he came up with to please her. She had never seen Jochen that boisterous. The next minute she got into a panic, when she asked herself how he would manage to get back into the canoe.

Jochen wrapped the rope around his wrist and swam for a few meters, breathing heavily. After a few strokes his strength deserted him. He had never been much of a swimmer.

Without further notice he dragged himself into the canoe from the side so that it tilted.

"Are you out of your mind!" yelled Ellen.

Jochen jolted the canoe and ordered her to make an effort to keep the balance. But Ellen was far less heavy than him so that it was impossible for her to counter his weight. Jochen was not to be stopped from giving it further trials and kept lifting himself onto the slim rim of the canoe to get back to his seat.

It took Jochen only a second to capsize the canoe as he let out a single, brief scream.

Ellen toppled into the water and got stuck underneath the canoe with her feet between the luggage, which had slipped away from the bow from the capsizing. Jochen swam without making any progress, jerkily tearing the rope again and again to keep the canoe from sinking. Thus he made it impossible for Ellen to get rid of her shackles. At some point she was so exhausted that she gave up trying to free her feet under water and opened her eyes and mouth defenselessly. A bit later a part of the luggage slid out of the bow and spun to the lake's bottom. Ellen drifted upward on the rest of it.

The rope wrapped tight around his wrist, Jochen was still pulling the canoe, which continuously sank. He had not once dived for Ellen and was now yelling: "There you are, finally! Give me a hand here! The canoe is about to sink!"

Ellen started swimming. Toward the camping site. Her legs felt heavy in the water, she made only small progress. Suddenly her feet bumped into something. She remembered the sunken city that was supposed to be dwelling bagdeep down in the lake of Plaue. But it was Jochen's canoe that was resting almost two meters deep, still tied to the rope—with the bow still pointing upward—because Jochen would not let go of it. Ellen was tempted to kick against it but decided not to waste her energy. With a huge effort she took off her white sneakers and continued swimming.

Jochen called after her. "Where do you think you're going? You can't leave me alone just like that! Silly cow. You'll pay for that. My boat, my beautiful boat . . ."

All she needed was for him to tell one of his stories now, how he got that canoe from that East German fifteen years ago . . . Ellen was tempted to cover her ears but she needed her arms for swimming. Stroke by stroke— toward the light of the small, almost dying campfire on that still distant camping site.

Suddenly Jochen appeared behind her, clinging to Ellen's back. "I can't go on," he panted. "You have to save me."

His weight pressed her under water. The rope cut into Ellen's body. Jochen's nudity made her slip off whenever she tried to ward him off. He clung to her sweater. Slowly the canoe pulled the couple down with it, into the deep. It tore at Jochen more, however, since he could no longer stick both to Ellen and his beloved canoe at the same time. He had to make a decision and that was in favor of the canoe. When he let go of Ellen for a second, she reached the surface and started swimming. Stroke by stroke. Inch by inch. She could not even hear Jochen calling after her any longer. Jochen tried to pull his canoe back up. Instead he was taken down along with it—with every inch faster into the deep. Into the sunken city.

Ellen swam. She started to think about rather trivial matters then. About whether she should dare to knock on strange tents at night to ask for help for Jochen. And about how one would knock on a tent . . .

Ellen waited at the shore until morning. The last bit of the campfire's embers had warmed her and dried her sweater. When the sun rose, the water lay there silvery-gray. There were no men or boats to be seen on the whole lake. A swarm of seagulls sailed somewhere in the distance and dived down toward the water's surface with a sudden scream.

Ellen put on her sweater and walked a few meters into the lake. After she had taken a good look around, she went briefly under water. She ran to the first person who crept sleepily out of his tent to go fishing early in the morning. In a flustered manner she told him that she and her friend had capsized. She managed to cry. The angler, a friendly Saxon, gave Ellen some money for a telephone call. She phoned the police and hysterically shouted into the receiver that someone had to come and dive for her friend and his canoe urgently. She could not describe the exact spot since she had been swimming all night to stay alive. . . .

Shortly afterward Ellen called her best girlfriend, the one whom she had not spoken to for half a year, thanks to Jochen. Ellen told her that she needed a holiday desperately and asked whether her friend would accompany her—on a cruise starting from Hamburg harbor, all inclusive.

Jeremiah Healy

Aftermath

Former military policeman, attorney, and law professor JERE-MIAH HEALY is a nine-time Shamus award nominee, and his book, *The Staked Goat,* was honored with the award. His series character, John Francis Cuddy, is a former Army police lieutenant, a widower, and a private investigator in Boston, where Healy lives and works. He brings quiet literacy and social observation to his stories, turning contemporary issues of crime and punishment into work of lasting literary merit. "Aftermath" features his other series character, tennis instructor and detective Rory Calhoun, who lives and works in sunny Florida. Recently his creator began spending a few months out of the year there as well, so it's no small wonder that some of his stories also are set there. But although the climate is sunny, the crimes can be dark indeed, as shown by this story, which first appeared in *Most Wanted.*

Aftermath

Jeremiah Healy

I had just finished a grueling, three-set match against Max Limbeck, a terrific singles player from Austria, on one of those hundred-ten humidity, mid–October days that South Florida doesn't trumpet to potential tourists. Max and I were walking back to the Lauderdale Tennis Club's patio when a female voice from the tiki bar called out, "Rory?"

I turned, Max saying he had to go on the Internet for the book he was writing about his homeland's political history. The female voice belonged to Kathy Rifflard, one of the tennis center's administrators. She perched on a stool next to another woman I'd never seen before.

"Kathy," I said, moving toward her while using a hand towel from my racquet bag to mop my face.

She turned to the other woman. "This is Greer Ballantine. She'd like to talk with you. Professionally."

As Kathy returned to the center, I smiled at Ballantine, then used the towel to sweep down my sweat-soaked shirt and gesture over my shoulder toward the condo unit I rented. "Maybe after I take a shower?"

Ballantine looked as though she hadn't smiled in a while. "Mr. Calhoun, I've flown all the way from New York. How about we talk now instead?"

I moved us to one of the umbrellaed patio tables, mostly for privacy, partly to keep Greer Ballantine out of the sun. Like most of our Northeast snowbirds, she didn't have any summer tan left. Some of them had already arrived, many shaken by the terrorist attacks on September 11 the month before. They were people I knew, so I'd asked them, gently, if they and theirs had come through the tragedies safely. Given how somber Ballantine appeared, I didn't ask her the same question.

As we settled into the white resin chairs, I tried to gauge the woman.

Pushing fifty, Ballantine was matronly, with even features, brown hair, and piercing green eyes. She wore a light, daisy-print dress and sensible heels, which tempered rather stumpy calves. I couldn't see her teeth, less because she still hadn't smiled and more because her whole face seemed set in a frown as permanent as stone.

Ballantine laid her handbag on the table. "Want to know how I picked you as a private investigator?"

"My name?"

"That's right." She showed neither surprise nor satisfaction. "When I was a kid, the actor Rory Calhoun was in this TV series called *The Texan*. I had a crush on him, so when I saw your name in the Yellow Pages down here, it seemed kind of an omen."

My mother'd had similar feelings toward Calhoun, though at a later, more dangerous age, which led her not just to marry a guy with the same last name but also to give me that first one. However, I wasn't sure I got Ballantine's "omen" allusion, and said so.

She rolled her shoulders, some wisps of hair getting stuck to her forehead by the stultifying breeze. "Did you lose anyone to September eleventh?"

"I have some friends down here who lost friends, or former neighbors. Nobody I knew personally, though."

Ballantine nodded. "My husband, Ted, became an international insurance broker twelve years ago. He was attending a seminar in the World Trade Center that day."

From the tone of her voice, I didn't ask the next logical question. "Ms. Ballantine, I'm sorry."

"Would it be okay if . . . I've never done this kind of thing before. Do you have to call me 'Ms. Ballantine' because of some professional reason?"

A person who could think past her pain. "No. 'Rory' is fine with me if 'Greer' is fine for you."

Not exactly a smile, but maybe a little sidestep from the frown. "Ted and I were married twenty-three years ago. Our daughter, Lisa, is a junior in college, and our son, Kevin, graduates high school in June." From her handbag, she drew a family candid showing her two clean-cut kids and a man with reddish, curly hair, all four smiling. "My own family—Mom and Dad, I mean—were well off, and I was an only child, so money's not the problem, especially with the group-life policy from Ted's company."

I didn't see where Ballantine was going, but I figured to let her take me there.

"Ted and I have been . . ." Now a sigh. "Jesus, for over a month, I tried to stop doing that—talking like he was still alive? But now I don't . . ."

Her hand snaked back into the handbag like it was the most natural act one could perform. She came out with a packet of tissues and used one to dab at her eyes, twice on each side. "Sorry."

"No need to apologize, Greer. You just lost your husband."

Ballantine seemed to freeze, the tissue now fluttering in the breeze. "That's why I'm here, Rory. I'm not sure I have."

I came back to the table from the bar with a coffee for Ballantine and a Diet Dr. Pepper for me. "There's some reason to think your husband survived the attack?"

She nipped at the rim of the cup. "Ted hasn't been accounted for, which isn't conclusive, of course. However, several more people from his company are also missing, and we family members posted on the Web site the city set up as kind of an information-exchange bulletin board."

Not being into computers, I probably looked a little blank, because Ballantine added, "You know, 'This is my husband's name and description; have you seen him or talked to anyone who has?' "

"I understand."

A nod, and then more coffee. "Well, another broker, José Acosta, also attended the seminar. His wife, Carolina, contacted me, because her husband was among the missing, too. In fact, I'm staying at their place in Miami Beach." More coffee still. "Carolina says José called on his cellular after the plane . . . after the explosion to tell her he was going to try to go down the stairs and . . . and then some personal stuff." Ballantine used another tissue as efficiently as she had the first. "Carolina said José didn't mention Ted, though."

"And you thought that was odd?"

"No. No, given the . . . I'm not sure Ted would have mentioned José if the situation was reversed. I mean, they were friends, but given the distance between their offices, more from seeing each other at business things like the seminar." Another dab at her eyes. "It's just that I had no information about Ted, whether he got out or not." Her hand went again into the bag, this time withdrawing a folded paper. "Until this arrived."

Ballantine handed it to me. I opened what proved to be a credit-card statement. Lots of entries on it.

I glanced up at Ballantine, who without saying as much implied that I should read the thing more carefully.

I did. Dozens of entries pre–September 11, but none on that date or thereafter. Except for the last one, "TASTE OF CHINA FT LAUDERDALE FL," with both a "transaction date" and a "posting date" of the twenty-ninth.

Over two weeks after the terrorist attacks.

I stared up at Ballantine now.

She said, "See?"

"You didn't cancel the charge card?"

"No." A dismissive wave of her hand. "It just wasn't very high on my list of priorities. And besides, I never dreamed anyone could be such a . . . bastard as to take and use it."

I'd read about a "friend" of another victim actually stealing a charge card from the descedent's apartment in Brooklyn and running up a huge bill. "Have you contacted the police?"

Another sigh. "I figured they were pretty swamped, and even if I did, they'd still have to come down here to find anything out about this restaurant, assuming that's what Taste of China is. And no other money—ATM, checking, money markets—has been touched since the eleventh."

"Greer, you realize this could mean any one of several things."

A slight hardening of the features now. "I'm not stupid, Rory. In the week since that statement arrived, I haven't thought about much else. The restaurant could have made a mistake writing down somebody else's card number. Or that random bastard could have found Ted's card in the rubble somewhere, although I don't see a low-life traveling fifteen hundred miles *not* using it until he had a yen for Szechuan. Or . . . or Ted could be alive and staying down here."

"And you'd like me to find out which?"

Ballantine blinked a few times, but without tears now. "I've thought a lot about that, too. I'm not sure I really *want* to know, but I owe it to Lisa and Kevin to find out what actually happened to Ted."

As Greer Ballantine wrote me both a retainer check and the address of the Acosta home in Miami Beach, I wondered why she hadn't included herself in the "owe" part of that last sentence.

After showering in the condo I rented next door to Court 13, I checked the telephone book under "Taste of China" and found an entry for it on a boulevard near the Hollywood line south of downtown Fort Lauderdale. Then I changed into a clean T-shirt and shorts before climbing into my Chrysler Sebring convertible.

No one born in South Florida would ever mistake me for a native son. For one thing, I have a year-round tan while most people brought up down here try to avoid the sun as much as possible. For a second, I don't just own a convertible: I drive with the top down during the day, even in the withering heat and humidity of June onward, though I do run the air conditioner full blast. But then the "real" Floridians have never been through the kind of winters I used to face, playing mostly satellite tournaments in European and smaller American cities when tennis meant indoor facilities and erstwhile spectators who kept asking one another which one of us second-tier pros was Becker or Agassi or Sampras.

Like many restaurants in the area, Taste of China turned out to be tucked into a strip mall between two budget motels. I found a parking space a few doors down, then walked past the place once, T-shirt already plastered to my shoulder blades. Kind of a hole-in-the-wall, with a counter for takeout and a few tables for eating, a big WE DELIVER sign in red letters on the window. The sort of place a cost-conscious tourist might patronize for something to bring back to the room.

Retracing my steps, I went in, a string of brass balls tied to the door making an incongruous "jingle-bells" sound as I both opened and closed it. The short, plump man behind the counter was Asian and middle-aged, with a front tooth missing as he smiled and said, "Help you?"

"I hope so." I showed the man my identification. He took awhile to read it, and I noticed that the pale green order slips in front of him on the counter bore what I assumed were Chinese characters.

Then he said, "We have no troubles here."

"And I'm not trying to cause you any." I took out the charge-card statement Greer Ballantine had given me. "We think this last entry might be a fraudulent one, and I thought you could tell me why."

The man looked down at the paper, but not for nearly as long as he had my license. "You wait."

He disappeared through the swinging door into the chatter and clatter of a busy kitchen. When he came back out, a young Asian woman with his build but a suspicious cast to her eyes trailed behind him.

She said, "What do you want from us?"

No accent on her words. "As I told this gentleman, I'm a private investigator. My client has reason to believe this entry from your restaurant may be fraudulent, and I'd like to find out what you know about the person you served."

The young woman glanced down at the statement for even a shorter period than the man had. "We serve a hundred people every day. How would my father or me remember that?"

I showed her the candid of the Ballantine family. "Could it have been this man?"

I caught a flicker of emotion as the father glanced toward his daughter, though she might have been a poker player betting the mortgage, saying only, "I don't recognize him."

"Well, would your records show whether the person who used the card ate here, ordered takeout, or"—I pointed to the window sign—"had something delivered?"

"We don't have to show you any records without an order from the courts."

I was running into the Great Stonewall of China. But why? "If there is a fraud problem here, wouldn't you like it resolved without having to *involve* the courts. Or the police?"

She had all her front teeth, and now they nibbled on her lower lip.

I said, "Or the newspapers, and the resultant bad publicity."

More nibbling.

I leaned forward now, my elbows on their counter. "Or the Immigration and Naturalization Service?"

Now she leaned into me, nose-to-nose since I was bent at the waist. "My father became a citizen five years ago, and I was born here. You can't scare us, and you can't make us talk to you. So leave, or I will call the police myself."

Technically, she was right. I couldn't make them cooperate, so I left with what remained of my bluff intact for possible later use. And by the time I reached the Sebring, I'd thought of a question I should have asked Greer Ballantine.

Carolina Acosta lived in a neighborhood of beautiful homes with pastel stucco walls and orange-tiled roofs in Miami Beach about six blocks back from the ocean. When I pulled into the semicircular driveway, I saw a Mazda Miata convertible parked behind a Lexus sport ute. Ringing the doorbell brought a willowy, olive-skinned woman with long black hair and a stylish silk dress, yellow in a way that nearly matched her eyes. I pegged her as fortyish, careful about her appearance, a quiet resignation radiating from her face.

"Yes?"

"Ms. Acosta, my name's Rory Calhoun."

"Ah, Greer's private investigator."

"Yes. Is she here?"

"No. Greer said that after speaking with you, she just wanted to walk for awhile along the beach, so I took her in the Miata and will pick her up again in a few hours. But, please, come in."

I followed Acosta through a terra-cotta foyer, her sandals clicking off the fired clay like the shoes of a horse trotting along a paved street. We entered a living room decorated with oil paintings, the similar style and brush strokes depicting what I guessed to be Cuban street scenes.

"Do you paint?" I said, taking-a-seat-on a plush chair as Acosta settled into her couch.

"No, but my husband's father did in Havana, before the revolution. When the family ran from Castro, they couldn't bring his works with them. Everything you see on these walls he painted from memory. A way for him to deal with his . . . loss."

Acosta cleared her throat, no doubt reminded of her own.

I said, "Greer told me about your husband. I'm very sorry."

"Thank you. It's not been an easy time for any of us."

"I wonder if I could leave a message for her?"

"Certainly. Do you wish to tell me, or would you rather write one down for confidentiality purposes?"

Another woman who could think past her pain. I said, "Writing might be easier."

She reached over to a telephone on a small table, came back with a pad and pencil.

As I wrote my request for Ballantine to call her husband's credit-card company to see what signature the original receipt from Taste of China had on it, Acosta said, "In a way, I was luckier than most."

I looked up at her.

She drew in a breath. "José was able to call on his cellular before . . . before the tower he was in collapsed."

"Greer told me you'd had that chance to speak with him."

A sudden sniffle and a hard swallow, making me realize that the resignation covering Acosta's sadness was only a thin veneer. "Actually, no. I was out. A routine errand, nothing that couldn't have waited, but he therefore had to leave a message on our tape machine." She shook her head now. "José was such a gregarious man, always introducing people he knew and liked to one another at parties, kind of a . . . one-man welcome wagon." The tears began. "We always communicated so well with each other, too. But now, I have his last thoughts and words only on a scratchy, ninety-nine-cent audio cassette."

As Carolina Acosta began to cry, I thought that, even then, she'd come out ahead of Greer Ballantine.

"So, Rory, perhaps we shall play again tomorrow, yah?"

I'd just parked my car in one of the dedicated spaces for residents of the Wingfield building, and Max Limbeck was coming off Court 13, a smile on his ruddy face, the short, blond hair on his skull looking almost like acrylic fuzz on a stuffed animal.

"I hope so. How's the book coming along?"

"Slowly, but it comes. I made contact with an important source today on the Internet. A magical system, don't you think?"

"For some." Then I had an idea. "Max, could we visit a Web site using your computer?"

"But of course." A slight, courtly bow. "Come by in one half hour, and I will be ready to assist you."

"Rory, this is the Web site you wished." Max bowed his head. "Tragic, tragic, but perhaps a way for those hurt to find closure, yah?"

I looked over his shoulder. The screen seemed impossibly complicated to me. "Can you tell how it's organized?"

"I believe so." Max did something to make the images jump back and forth. "Families or friends post the names of those missing, with contact addresses or telephones. Then those who believe they have information communicate to the survivors."

I gave him the names I'd come across so far. Greer Ballantine and Carolina Acosta had indeed listed their husbands.

"Max, is there any way you can find out if other people from South Florida posted as well?"

"Some moments, and we shall see."

It did take awhile, but eventually he came up with many missing people posted with contact addresses in the area. Three names caught my eye, because each was connected to insurance as an industry.

"Do you wish anything further, Rory?"

"Maybe if you could print out the insurance ones we found?"

"The push of a button." Then a grim cast to Max Limbeck's eyes as he twisted his head my way. "If only it could be so easy to find them in real life, yah?"

• • •

Patrick Kelly worked at an Irish pub in Delray Beach. It didn't take very long to establish that the thirty-something with beefy forearms, receding hair, and seashell ears answered to that name.

Kelly had been using a wipe cloth like a squeegee on the mahogany bar. At two-thirty on a weekday afternoon, things were slow enough that he said he could talk with me over the Guinness I'd ordered. My guess was that, as soon as I mentioned my mission, Kelly would have found time to talk during happy hour on his saint's day.

"Have you any news at all about my Fiona?"

"I'm sorry, but none. You might be able to help me, though, with somebody else in the Towers that day."

Kelly's eyes had gone funny as soon as I'd replied in the negative, but he nodded his head abruptly. "I'm sure they'd do the same for me."

"How did your wife come to be in New York on the eleventh?"

"She did insurance brokering for a big outfit down here. I'm not certain I ever understood what all it involved. But I do know Fiona had to travel several times over the summer toward arranging something for one of her firm's real estate clients."

"Did she mention her attending a seminar in the World Trade Center that day?"

"A seminar? Do you mean for insurance lessons and so forth?"

"Yes."

Kelly weighed that. "No. No, and Fiona did go to one of those over in Fort Myers on the Gulf Coast six or seven months past. I'm sure she would have told me if she'd been doing the same this time around."

I asked about the Taste of China restaurant in Hollywood.

"Man, that would be forty miles or more to the south of us. Bit of a hop just to take away some egg rolls, eh?"

"Did your wife ever mention another insurance broker named Ted Ballantine?"

"Like the ale, you mean?"

"Yes."

More weighing. "No. Was he from the Big Apple?" A grunt that I realized constituted a small laugh. "That's what Fiona always called it, you know. 'The Big Apple.' Loved to get out of Delray in the heat of summer, even for more of the same up north. In fact, we talked the night before by telephone, herself telling me from the hotel bed that it was to be a grand fall day dawning the next morning."

As someone clamored for a Harp draft, Patrick Kelly ran the wipe cloth under his nose before slapping it over his shoulder. "Couldn't have been more wrong now, could she?"

The second person posting on the Web site lived in one of Boca Raton's many gated communities. I didn't think I'd get beyond the sentry box until I mentioned September 11 to the guard, who spoke into a telephone before putting a three-hour, dated pass on the dashboard of my Sebring and giving me left-right-left directions to wind through the maze of townhoused blocks. I ended up in front of a generic cluster, a woman already outside her front door despite the humidity. From fifty feet away, I underestimated her age by twenty years, but up close, the shiny skin and slightly popped eyes betrayed one facelift too many.

"You're the private investigator?"

"Yes, ma'am. Doris Steinberg?"

"I don't want to seem suspicious, but could I see some identification?"

"You bet."

She read my license quickly, then said, "We'll be a lot cooler inside."

The interior of the house was furnished starkly, but despite the fact that the decor was mostly lost on me, it seemed very upscale, as though I'd stumbled into a museum of modern art. Steinberg gracefully settled on a chrome-and-leather chair while I took its mate across from her. Then a skittering sound, and I turned to see a moppy mongrel the size of a toy poodle jump up into my lap.

"Oh, I'm so sorry. Sabra, get down from there."

The little thing looked up mournfully at me. "It's okay, Mrs. Steinberg. I like dogs."

"She's been like that, ever since . . . ever since Sam didn't come home last month." A pause, maybe Steinberg's way of holding it in, as I scratched my new best friend between the ears. " 'Sabra' means an Israeli-born girl. Sam saw her wandering a street in Jerusalem when we were visiting two years ago, and he resolved to bring her home. The paperwork? Don't ask. But Sabra imprinted on him as though she sensed he'd saved her."

"Mrs. Steinberg, I'm sorry to cause you to revisit September eleventh, only—"

"Mr. Calhoun, you're not the one 'causing me to revisit.' I've done it every day since, and right now I can't imagine not doing it every other day I'm on this earth." A second pause. "Do you . . . Is there anything about Sam I should know?"

Which is when it hit me. Doris Steinberg, and maybe Patrick Kelly as well, thought I might be the bearer of bad tidings, a definitive DNA match or something like that. "No, I'm afraid not. But you might have some information that could help me on another person caught in the Towers that day."

Steinberg's face indicated neither relief nor disappointment. "Go ahead."

"How did your husband come to be there on the eleventh?"

"Sam was trying to pave the way for his son-in-law."

I noted the "his" as opposed to "our," but when Steinberg didn't go on, I said, "Pave the way?"

"In the insurance brokerage business. Sam was seventy-two, and he'd retired six years ago to get out of the New York winters. We met down here thereafter. He'd lost his first wife to cancer nearly thirty-five years into their marriage, and I'm afraid their daughter didn't marry too . . . wisely. So Sam flew back up there from time to time, trying to get the boy a good job. They were both in the World Trade Center that morning, kind of the mentor tutoring his protégé through an interview with a friend in the business. Sam was like that, always trying to give back." Now a longer pause. "The son-in-law got out, by the way. Sam's friend was . . . He'd had polio as a child, and Sam lagged behind to help him. Giving back in a different way, I guess."

I was sorry I hadn't known him. "Did your husband ever mention a Ted Ballantine, also an insurance broker?"

Steinberg looked down at the floor. "No. No, I don't recall that name. But then, Sam finished in the business before he met me, and I think he believed that any reference by him to the 'old guys up north' might make me suspect that he was really missing his old life with his dead wife."

I thought it safest just to nod rather than mention the Chinese restaurant.

Steinberg said, "Now I'm learning in my own way what Sam might really have felt."

When this time she closed her eyes and brought a hand to her face, I quietly set Sabra back onto the floor and let myself out of Doris Steinberg's now even more museumlike town house.

Stepping across the threshold of the small single-family on a postage-stamp lot in Dania, I felt as if I were in a chapel. Religious icons sprouted all over the place, the most prominent an indoor shrine to the Blessed Virgin Mary, a miniature fountain burbling beneath her feet.

Mercedes Delgado, maybe sixty and dressed in a black veil and kerchief, ushered me toward the only chair in the living room. The man of comparable age sitting on the couch had to use a cane to lever himself up and shake my hand. I didn't suggest he stay seated, as it felt somehow wrong to excuse him from being polite.

Eduardo Delgado said, "Wine, beer, coffee?"

There was none showing on their little tables. "No, thank you. And I hope I won't have to take up much of your time."

"Time we have," from Mr. Delgado, settling back down. "And much to be grateful for."

Since his wife appeared dressed for a funeral, I was taken aback a bit. "How so?"

She said, "Our Azura is return to us from the Gates of Hell."

"Your daughter?"

"Yes," said the father. "Azura always is trying to improve herself, so she attends a 'seminar' in New York City."

Bingo. Maybe.

He went on. "She wishes to become a partner in her firm of insurance."

The mother put in, "Even before she marry."

Mr. Delgado shrugged. "It is the way here. We bring Azura over from Cuba in the Boatlift, the time of the Marielitos. She is just seven years old, and she sleeps in my arms the whole way. But we are able to raise her in our religion, because Florida is the United States, and we find freedom here for everything. The Muslim terrorists, they do not understand this any more than Fidel's communist ones."

Mrs. Delgado muttered something in Spanish that had the ring of a curse to it.

Fairly certain of where they stood on that issue, I said, "You mentioned 'seminar' before?"

"Yes," from the father. "Azura studies hard here, learns to speak English with no accent I can hear. But to advance, she must go to other places, like New York. Each month for almost one year."

"Did she ever mention a man named Ted Ballantine?"

The mother looked at the father, but he stayed on me, a little glassy-eyed now.

Mr. Delgado said, "Not that last name, but close. Teddy Ball, the man who saves our Azura from the Towers."

"God bless his soul," from his wife.

I turned to her. "He's . . . dead?"

The mother looked shocked. "Dead? *Muerto?* No. No!"

Some machine-gun Spanish from the husband, but in a soft voice. Then to me, "Mercedes does not understand English quite so good. She means Teddy should be blessed for all eternity, because he keeps our daughter from being kill when so many others are."

I tried to tread lightly. "Are they living up in New York City?"

The father said, "No. After the disaster, when Azura leaves the hospital there, they move into the house he buys for her in Hollywood."

"Before they marry," observed Mrs. Delgado, in English but using her curse tone.

I said, "Before . . . ?"

Her husband smiled in a worldly way. "Mercedes does not like that our daughter lives with a man before marriage. But they go to the church next month, more sooner than they plan for. And it is good, because Teddy can be with Azura more now."

The mother said, "A hero, is true. But he want no fame for it."

Somehow I wasn't surprised about that. "Since their names are so similar, maybe your Teddy might know the man I'm trying to help. Could you give me the Hollywood address?"

It turned out to be a nice starter home there, maybe ten blocks from the Taste of China's strip mall but set back into a residential neighborhood. Basketball hoops on the carports and bicycles in the drives, a perfect spot for prospective . . . newlyweds.

I parked the convertible on the street and walked up to the front door. Knocking, I heard an immediate "Coming" from a male voice, and moments later the man with reddish, curly hair in the Ballantine family candid opened the door.

"Can I help you?" he said.

I held up my license and the photo his wife had given me.

"Oh, no."

"If you let me in, this might be easier."

"Who is it?" called a female voice from the rear of the house.

Ballantine called back. "Just someone to see me about a . . . job reference."

I thought that was pretty cute.

Then he said, "Please, don't say anything to Azura."

"She's going to find out sooner or later."

"Maybe not," said Ballantine, though without even a hint of threat in the way he said it.

We went toward the other voice, now asking, "Teddy, maybe I should meet him?"

Ballantine ushered me into the Florida room, a glass–walled area that in cooler weather would give way to screens and a pleasant view of a gardened backyard.

A view that Azura Delgado couldn't appreciate.

The sunglasses were wraparounds, but just the way she stood from the swinging sofa and slightly misdirected her face told me the eyes behind them didn't know quite where I was. She extended a hand, also off-kilter. I stepped forward and took it, Delgado angling fifteen degrees to now face me squarely.

"Aren't you going to introduce yourself?" she said.

"Sorry. My name's Rory, Rory . . . Calvert. Pleasure to meet you."

"Believe this: It's a pleasure for me to meet *any*one." Then a bright, musical laugh, and I noticed a pair of Walkman headphones down around her collared blouse, almost like a necklace.

Ballantine said, "Mr. Calvert wants to talk with me alone."

"That's fine, Teddy. But, please, Mr. Calvert, stop by to say good-bye before you leave, okay?"

"I will."

Ballantine led me back into the living room. I let him sit first.

He waited, then said, "I'm pretty sure she'll have the headphones back on now."

I eased into a chair. "How bad is it?"

"The blindness? Permanent."

"Nothing the doctors can do?"

"Mr. Calhoun, it's not just her vision that's gone." Ballantine looked at his hands. "The dust storm took Azura's eyes themselves."

Jesus Christ.

He glanced over to me. "As an insurance broker, I used to be pretty good at making pitches. Let me try to make you understand."

"That might not be any of my business."

He began to wring his hands now. "Indulge me. Please?"

After a moment, I leaned back in my chair.

Ballantine canted his head toward the Florida room. "I hooked up with Azura last year, through a friend of mine from the trade named José Acosta."

"I've met his wife."

"You have?"

"Through yours."

Ballantine blanched, but drove on. "I was nuts about Azura from the get-go. Well, José didn't know her that well—she'd just interned with his office down here for a few months. And he didn't mention to her that I was married."

"And, conveniently, neither did you."

"No. No, I . . . Azura'd told me about her family, how they'd escaped Cuba over freedom of religion. I knew she, and her parents, would never go for it. So I told her a . . . white lie."

Or a dark gray one. "That you were a widower?"

"No. Divorced. That was okay with Azura, but wouldn't have been with her family, so we agreed to use a different last name for me—just with them—to keep 'Ted Ballantine' in the background afterward."

"Meaning after you skipped out on your wife and kids."

Ballantine gave me a fighting look, then stood down. "There wasn't anything left of that marriage, Mr. Calhoun. I was staying in the house, and on the job, just to see our younger—Kevin—through high school. I set some money aside over time, enough for this house, a car. Once Kevin graduated, I planned to move out. Start divorce proceedings against Greer in New York, fly down here, the works."

"But then comes September eleventh, and you see your big chance."

He flinched. "Azura and I met at the seminar, as we always tried to do whenever she came up to New York on business. We were about to get on the elevators when the first plane hit. Thank God we headed directly for the stairs and got a good ways down before the second. . . . I mean, I saw it later on the news, and I couldn't understand how even . . ."

Ballantine shook his head. "Anyway, we reached the plaza level, but it was chaos, and a lot of people were milling around, watching the flames pour out of both towers above us. Some people . . . some people trapped higher than the fire just jumped rather than be burned alive. It was horrible, like something out of Hieronymus Bosch, that medieval painter of hell?"

I sensed a deflection. "Sounds to me that you got a good enough start, you should have been clear of the danger zone."

"We would have been. But Azura insisted on staying behind to help people. She'd taken first-aid classes, and a lot of rescue-unit firefighters were blowing past the less injured to go up into the Towers after the ones more . . . Well, I stayed to help, too, and I'd just gotten an older man behind an ambulance when the first tower, the second to be hit, began coming down. It was . . . indescribable. Like a gray, swirling blizzard, but not just dust.

Shards and chips and . . . When the air cleared a little, I could see the ambulance was riddled like it'd been through a war. And people were on the ground everywhere, coughing and choking, writhing and moaning. And I started screaming for Azura, and she didn't answer and didn't answer, and then I heard her voice, and I had to push through a horde of terrified people covered in ash like . . . zombies, trampling over her, trying to just breathe. Azura could talk, barely, but her . . . her eyes, she must have turned into the dust storm, I don't know. I managed to get her to another ambulance, then waited for somebody to help us. I didn't know how to contact Azura's parents right away, and then I . . . I admit it. I started thinking."

"That you could just fade away with the thousands of others who didn't make it out."

Ballantine clasped his hands now. "Try to see it from my side, please? I'd have received something from a divorce, but basically Greer would have gotten the house, and the court would have ordered me to put both kids through college. Fine, I expected that. Only there'd always be the chance that somebody would say something, even José or his wife at our wedding, since Azura insisted on inviting them for his having introduced us. But then, with the terrorist attacks, I had a way out. Plenty of money for Greer, both from her parents' side and my life policy. More than enough to educate Lisa and Kevin, even for condos and cars of their own. And no pain of betrayal for Greer and our kids, or for Azura and her family."

"But then why use the charge card at Taste of China?"

"I didn't." A slow breath. "I'd established an account at another take-out place. But one day I was on a job interview in Miami, and when I called home, Azura said she'd order Chinese for us. Only our regular restaurant's delivery guy was out sick, and Azura didn't want to 'bother' me or have me drive out of my way to pick it up. So instead she called Directory Assistance, got the number of another nearby place that could deliver, and ordered from there instead."

"Taste of China."

A slump to his shoulders. "I'd kept one charge card from my 'old life,' just in case of some unmanageable emergency. The thing was in a dresser drawer here. Well, Azura somehow stumbled on it, maybe while learning to put clothes away. She had no cash on hand, so she used the card to pay for the delivery."

"And signed the receipt?"

"Yes, but I examined it that next morning, when she 'surprised' me by revealing what she'd done, and her signature was illegible."

Which meant that Greer Ballantine wouldn't find out anything by asking the charge-card company whose name was on their original.

"Azura was so . . . pleased." A note of pride crept into Ballantine's voice. "That she could accomplish even a simple task like that without her . . . her being able to see? But when I went to Taste of China—"

"—they'd already processed the transaction."

Just a nod. "I bribed them, saying that my wife was an illegal immigrant, and that I was afraid she'd be deported if the truth came out. The owner and his daughter seemed to . . . understand."

"All so neat and tidy."

Ballantine finally flared. "Look, Mr. Calhoun. I'm not blameless here, and I don't pretend to be. But I love Azura, and I owe her for what happened, especially since she really was at that seminar as a cover story toward seeing me. She needs a husband now more than my prior family does, and truly, Greer and the kids are better off both emotionally and financially with me 'dead.' How about sparing everybody any more heartache from the aftermath of this horror?"

I told Ted Ballantine I'd think about it, but by the time I'd stopped back in the Florida room and touched the bravely extended hand of the future Azura "Ball," I already knew I was going to be telling Greer Ballantine about the "random bastard" who must have fraudulently used her dead husband's credit card.

Peter Tremayne

Whispers of the Dead

PETER BERRESFORD ELLIS has been writing full-time since 1975, producing works of history, literary biography, historical novels, horror-fantasy novels, adventure-thrillers, and mysteries under three different names. Under the pseudonym of Peter Tremayne, he chronicles the investigations of seventh-century Irish nun Sister Fidelma, a highly educated authority on the complicated religious and legal codes of the Celtic culture. Ellis is considered one of the world's foremost experts on the ancient Celts, and his knowledge shows on every page of his story chosen for this year's volume. "Whispers of the Dead," first published in *Murder Most Catholic,* is a police procedural set in seventh-century Ireland, where the sleuthing sister brings to light a case of murder most foul.

Whispers of the Dead

Peter Tremayne

Abbot Laisran sat back in his chair, at the side of the crackling log fire, and gazed thoughtfully at his cup of mulled wine.

"You have achieved a formidable reputation, Fidelma," he observed, raising his cherublike features to his young protégée who sat on the other side of the fireplace, sipping her wine. "Some Brehons talk of you as they would the great female judges such as Brig or Dari. That is commendable in one so young."

Fidelma smiled thinly. She was not one given to vanity, for she knew her own weaknesses.

"I would not aspire to write legal texts as they did, nor, indeed, would I pretend to be more than a simple investigator of facts. I am a *dálaigh,* an advocate. I prefer to leave the judgment of others to the Brehons."

Abbot Laisran inclined his head slightly as if in acceptance of her statement.

"But that is the very thing on which your reputation has its foundation. You have had some outstanding successes with your investigations, observing things that are missed by others. Several times I have seen your ability firsthand. Does it ever worry you that you hold so much responsibility?"

"It worries me only that I observe all the facts and come to the right decision. However, I did not spend eight years under instruction with the Brehon Morann of Tara to no avail. I have come to accept the responsibility that goes with my office."

"Ah," sighed the abbot, " 'Unto whomsoever much is given, of him shall much be required.' That is from—"

"The Gospel of Luke," Fidelma interrupted with a mischievous smile. Abbot Laisran answered her smile.

"Does nothing escape your attention, Fidelma? Surely there must be cases when you are baffled? For instance, there must be many a murder over which it is impossible to attribute guilt."

"Perhaps I have been lucky," admitted Fidelma. "However, I do not believe that there is such a thing as a perfect crime."

"Come, now, that must be an overstatement?"

"Even when we examine a body with no evidence of who he, or she, was in life, or how and when he, or she, died, let alone by whose hand, a good observer will learn something. The dead always whisper to us. It is our task to listen to the whispers of the dead."

The abbot knew it was not in Fidelma's nature to boast of her prowess; however, his round features assumed a skeptical expression.

"I would like to make a wager with you," he suddenly announced.

Fidelma frowned. She knew that Abbot Laisran was a man who was quick to place wagers. Many was the time she had attended the great Aonach Life, the fair at the Curragh, for the horseracing, and watched Abbot Laisran losing as well as winning as he hazarded money on the contests.

"What manner of wager had you in mind, Laisran?" she asked cautiously.

"You have said that the dead whisper to us and we must have ears to listen. That in every circumstance the body of a person will eventually yield up the information necessary to identify him, and who, if anyone, is culpable for the death. Have I understood you correctly?"

Fidelma inclined her head in agreement.

"That has been my experience until now," she conceded.

"Well, then," continued Abbot Laisran, "will you take a wager with me on a demonstration of that claim?"

"In what circumstances?"

"Simple enough. By coincidence, this morning a young peasant woman was found dead not far from this abbey. There was no means of identification on her and inquiries in the adjacent village have failed to identify her. No one appears to be missing. She must have been a poor itinerant. One of our brothers, out of charity, brought the body to the abbey. Tomorrow, as is custom, we shall bury her in an unmarked grave." Abbot Laisran paused and glanced slyly at her. "If the dead truly whisper to you, Fidelma, perhaps you will be able to interpret those whispers and identify her?"

Fidelma considered for a moment.

"You say that she was a young woman? What was the cause of her death?"

"That is the mystery. There are no visible means of how she died. She was well nourished, according to our apothecary."

"No signs of violence?" asked Fidelma, slightly bemused.

"None. The matter is a total mystery. Hence I would place a wager with you, which is that if you can find some evidence, some cause of death, of something that will lead to the identification of the poor unfortunate, then I will accept that your claim is valid. So, what of the wager?"

Fidelma hesitated. She disliked challenges to her abilities but, on the other hand, some narcissistic voice called from within her.

"What is the specific wager?" she asked.

"A screpall for the offertory box of the abbey." Abbot Laisran smiled. "I will give a screpall for the poor if you can discover more about the poor woman than we have been able to. If you cannot, then you will pay a screpall to the offertory box."

A screpall was a silver coin valued to the fee charged by a *dálaigh* for a single consultation.

Fidelma hesitated a moment and then, urged on by her pride, said: "It is agreed."

She rose and set down her mulled wine, startling the abbot.

"Where are you going?" he demanded.

"Why, to view the body. There is only an hour or two of daylight left, and many important signs can vanish in artificial light."

Reluctantly, Abbot Laisran set down his wine and also rose.

"Very well." He sighed. "Come, I will show you the way to the apothecary."

A tall, thin religieux with a beak of a nose glanced up as Abbot Laisran entered the chamber where he was pounding leaves with a pestle. His eyes widened a little when he saw Sister Fidelma enter behind the abbot. Fidelma was well known to most of the religious of Abbey of Durrow.

"Brother Donngal, I have asked Sister Fidelma to examine our unknown corpse."

The abbey's apothecary immediately set aside his work and gazed at her with interest.

"Do you think that you know the poor woman, Sister?"

Fidelma smiled quickly.

"I am here as a *dálaigh,* Brother," she replied.

A slight frown crossed Brother Donngal's features.

"There is no sign of a violent death, Sister. Why would an advocate have an interest in this matter?"

Catching the irritable hardening of her expression, Abbot Laisran intervened quickly: "It is because I asked Sister Fidelma to give me her opinion on this matter."

Brother Donngal turned to a door.

"The body lies in our mortuary. I was shortly to prepare it for burial. Our carpenter has only just delivered the coffin."

The body lay under a linen sheet on a table in the center of the chamber that served as the abbey's mortuary, where bodies were prepared for burial.

Sister Fidelma moved toward it and was about to take a corner of the sheet in her hand when the apothecary coughed apologetically.

"I have removed her clothing for examination but have not dressed her for the coffin yet, Sister."

Fidelma's eyes twinkled at the man's embarrassment, but she made no reply.

The corpse was that of a young woman, perhaps no more than twenty years old. Fidelma had not entirely hardened herself to premature death.

"She is not long dead," was Fidelma's first remark.

Brother Donngal nodded.

"No more than a day and a night, I reckon. She was found this morning and I believe she died during the night."

"By whom was she found?"

"Brother Torcan," intervened Abbot Laisran, who was standing just inside the door observing them.

"Where was she found?"

"No more than a few hundred paces from the abbey walls."

"I meant, in what place, what were the conditions of her surroundings?"

"Oh, I see. She was found in a wood, in a small clearing almost covered with leaves."

Fidelma raised an eyebrow.

"What was this Brother Torcan doing there?"

"Gathering edible fungi. He works in the kitchens."

"And the clothes worn by the girl . . . where are they?" Fidelma asked.

The man gestured to a side table on which clothing was piled.

"She wore just the simple garb of a village girl. There is nothing to identify her there."

"I will examine them in a moment and likewise will wish to speak to this Brother Torcan."

She turned her gaze back to the body, bending forward to examine it with careful precision.

It was some time before she straightened from her task.

"Now, I shall examine the clothing."

Brother Donngal moved to a table and watched while Fidelma picked up the items. They consisted of a pair of sandals called *cuaran,* a single sole of untanned hide, stitched together with thongs cut from the same hide. They were almost worn through. The dress was a simple one of wool and linen, roughly woven and threadbare. It appeared to have been secured at the waist by a strip of linen. There was also a short cape with a hood, as affected by many country women. Again, it was obviously worn and fringed with rabbit fur.

Fidelma raised her head and glanced at the apothecary.

"Is this all that she was wearing?"

Brother Donngal nodded in affirmation.

"Was there no underclothing?"

The apothecary looked embarrassed.

"None," he confirmed.

"She did not have a *ciorbholg?*"

The *ciorbholg* was, literally, a comb-bag, but it contained all the articles of toilet, as well as combs, which women carried about with them no matter their rank or status. It served women in the manner of a purse and it was often tied at the waist by a belt.

Brother Donngal shook his head negatively once more.

"This is why we came to the conclusion that she was simply a poor itinerant," explained the abbot.

"So there was no toilet bag?" mused Fidelma. "And she had no brooches or other jewelry?"

Brother Donngal allowed a smile to play around his lips.

"Of course not."

"Why of course not?" demanded Fidelma sharply.

"Because it is clear from this clothing, Sister, that the girl was a very poor country girl. Such a girl would not be able to afford such finery."

"Even a poor country girl will seek out some ornaments, no matter how poor she is," replied Fidelma.

Abbot Laisran came forward with a sad smile.

"Nothing was found. So you see, Fidelma, this poor young woman cannot whisper to you from her place of death. A poor country girl and with nothing to identify her. Her whispers are silent ones. You should not have been so willing to accept my challenge."

Fidelma swung around on him to reveal the smile on her face. Her eyes twinkled with a dangerous fire.

"On the contrary, Laisran. There is much that this poor girl whispers; much she tells us, even in this pitiable state."

Brother Donngal exchanged a puzzled glance with the abbot.

"I don't understand you, Sister," he said. "What can you see? What have I missed?"

"Practically everything," Fidelma assured him calmly.

Abbot Laisran stifled a chuckle as he saw the mortified expression on the apothecary's face. But he turned to her with a reproving glance.

"Come, now, Fidelma," he chided, "don't be too sharp because you have been confronted with an insolvable riddle. Not even you can conjure facts out of nothing."

Abbot Laisran stirred uncomfortably as he saw the tiny green fire in her eyes intensify. However, when she addressed him, her tone was comparatively mild.

"You know better of me, Laisran. I am not given to vain boasting."

Brother Donngal moved forward and stared at the body of the girl as if trying to see what it was that Fidelma had observed.

"What have I missed?" he demanded again.

Fidelma turned to the apothecary.

"First, you say that this girl is a poor country girl. What makes you arrive at such a conclusion?"

Brother Donngal regarded her with an almost pitying look.

"That was easy. Look at her clothing—at her sandals. They are not the apparel of someone of high rank and status. The clothes show her humble origins."

Fidelma sighed softly.

"My mentor, the Brehon Moran, once said that the veil can disguise much; it is folly to accept the outside show for the inner quality of a person."

"I don't understand."

"This girl is not of humble rank, that much is obvious."

Abbot Laisran moved forward and peered at the body in curiosity.

"Come, Fidelma, now you are guessing."

Fidelma shook her head.

"I do not guess, Laisran. I have told you," she added impatiently, "listen to the whispers of the dead. If this is supposed to be a peasant girl, then regard the skin of her body—white and lacking color by wind and sun. Look at her hands, soft and cared for as are her nails. There is no dirt beneath them. Her hands are not callused by work. Look at her feet. Again, soft and well cared for. See the soles of the feet? This girl had not been trudging fields in those poor shoes that she was clad in, nor has she walked any great distance."

The abbot and the apothecary followed her instructions and examined the limbs she indicated.

"Now, examine her hair."

The girl's hair, a soft spun-gold color, was braided behind her head in a single long plait that reached almost to her waist.

"Nothing unusual in that," observed Laisran. Many women in the five kingdoms of Eireann considered very long hair as a mark of beauty and braided it in similar style.

"But it is exceptionally well tended. The braiding is the traditional *cuilfhionn* and surely you must know that it is affected only by women of rank. What this poor corpse whispers to me is that she is a woman of rank."

"Then why was she dressed as a peasant?" demanded the apothecary after a moment's silence.

Fidelma pursed her lips.

"We must continue to listen. Perhaps she will tell us. As she tells us other things."

"Such as?"

"She is married."

Abbot Laisran snorted with cynicism.

"How could you possibly know that?"

Fidelma simply pointed to the left hand of the corpse.

"There are marks around the third finger. They are faint, I grant you, but tiny marks nevertheless that show the recent removal of a ring that has been worn there. There is also some discoloration on her left arm. What do you make of that, Brother Donngal?"

The apothecary shrugged.

"Do you mean the marks of blue dye? It is of little importance."

"Why?"

"Because it is a common thing among the villages. Women dye clothes and materials. The blue is merely a dye caused by the extract of a cruciferous plant *glaisin*. Most people use it. It is not unusual in any way."

"It is not. But women of rank would hardly be involved in dyeing their own materials and this dye stain seems fairly recent."

"Is that important?" asked the abbot.

"Perhaps. It depends on how we view the most important of all the facts this poor corpse whispers to us."

"Which is?" demanded Brother Donngal.

"That this girl was murdered."

Abbot Laisran's eyebrows shot up.

"Come, come, now. Our apothecary has found no evidence of foul play—no wounds, no bruising, no abrasions. The face is relaxed as if she simply passed on in her sleep. Anyone can see that."

Fidelma moved forward and lifted the girl's head, bringing the single braid of hair forward in order to expose the nape of the neck. She had done this earlier during her examination as Brother Donngal and Abbot Laisran watched with faint curiosity.

"Come here and look, both of you. What, Brother Donngal, was your explanation of this?"

Brother Donngal looked slightly embarrassed as he peered forward.

"I did not examine her neck under the braid," he admitted.

"Well, now that you are examining it, what do you see?"

"There is a small discolored patch like a tiny bruise," replied the apothecary after a moment or two. "It is not more than a fingernail in width. There is a little blood spot in the center. It's rather like an insect bite that has drawn blood or as if someone has pricked the skin with a needle."

"Do you see it also, Laisran?" demanded Fidelma.

The abbot leaned forward and then nodded.

Fidelma gently lowered the girl's head back onto the table.

"I believe that this was a wound caused by an incision. You are right, Brother Donngal, in saying it is like a needle point. The incision was created by something long and thin, like a needle. It was inserted into the nape of the neck and pushed up hard so that it penetrated into the head. It was swift. Deadly. Evil. The girl probably died before she knew that she was being attacked."

Abbot Laisran was staring at Fidelma in bewilderment.

"Let me get this straight, Fidelma. Are you saying that the corpse found near this abbey this morning is a woman of rank who has been murdered? Is that right?"

"And, after her death, her clothes were taken from her and she was hurriedly dressed in poor peasant garb to disguise her origin. The murderer thought to remove all means of identification from her."

"Even if this is true," interrupted Brother Donngal, "how might we discover who she was and who perpetrated this crime?"

"The fact that she was not long dead when Brother Torcan found her makes our task more simple. She was killed in this vicinity. A woman of rank would surely be visiting a place of substance. She had not been walking any distance. Observe the soles of her feet. I would presume that she either rode or came in a carriage to her final destination."

"But what destination?" demanded Brother Donngal.

"If she came to Durrow, she would have come to the abbey," Laisran pointed out. "She did not."

"True enough. We are left with two types of places she might have gone. The house of a noble, a chieftain, or, perhaps, a *bruighean,* an inn. I believe that we will find the place where she met her death within five or six kilometers of this abbey."

"What makes you say that?"

"A deduction. The corpse newly dead and the murderer wanting to dispose of it as quickly as possible. Whoever killed her reclothed her body and transported it to the spot where it was found. They could not have traveled far."

Abbot Laisran rubbed his chin.

"Whoever it was, they took a risk in disposing of it in the woods so near this abbey."

"Perhaps not. If memory serves me right, those woods are the thickest stretch of forest in this area even though they are close to the abbey. Are they that frequented?"

Abbot Laisran shrugged.

"It is true that Brother Torcan does not often venture so far into the woods in search of fungi," he admitted. "He came on the corpse purely by chance."

"So the proximity of the abbey was not necessarily a caution to our murderer. Well, are there such places as I described within the distance I have estimated?"

"An inn or a chieftain's house? North of here is Ballacolla, where there is an inn. South of here is Ballyconra where the lord of Conra lives."

"Who is he? Describe him?"

"A young man, newly come to office there. I know little about him, although he came here to pay his respects to me when he took office. When I came to Durrow as abbot, the young man's father was lord of Ballyconra but his son was away serving in the army of the High King. He is a bachelor newly returned from the wars against the Ui Neill."

"Then we shall have to learn more," observed Fidelma dryly. She glanced through the window at the cloudy sky.

"There is still an hour before sunset," she reflected. "Have Brother Torcan meet me at the gates so that he may conduct me to the spot where he found the body."

"What use would that be?" demanded the abbot. "There was nothing in the clearing apart from the body."

Fidelma did not answer.

With a sigh, the abbot went off to find the religieux.

Half an hour later Brother Torcan was showing her the small clearing.

Behind her, Abbot Laisran fretted with impatience. Fidelma was looking at a pathway that led into it. It was just wide enough to take a small cart. She noticed some indentations of hooves and ruts, undoubtedly caused by the passage of wheels.

"Where does that track lead?" she asked, for they had entered the clearing by a different single path.

It was the abbot who answered.

"Eventually it would link to the main road south. South to Bally-conra," he added significantly.

The sky was darkening now and Fidelma sighed.

"In the morning I shall want to see this young lord of Conra. But it is pointless continuing on tonight. We'd best go back to the abbey."

The next morning, accompanied by the abbot, Fidelma rode south. Ballyconra itself was a large settlement. There were small farmsteads and a collection of dwellings for workers. In one nearby field, a root crop was being harvested and workers were loading the crop onto small carts pulled by single asses. The track twisted through the village and passed a stream where women were laying out clothes to dry on the banks while others stirred fabrics into a metal cauldron hanging over a fire. The pungent smell of dyes told Fidelma what process was taking place.

Some paused in their work and called a greeting to the abbot, seeking a blessing, as they rode by. They ascended the track through another field toward a large building. It was an isolated structure that was built upon what must once have been a hillfort. A young man came cantering toward them from its direction, sitting easily astride a sleek black mare.

"This is young Conri, lord of Conra," muttered Laisran as they halted and awaited the man to approach.

Fidelma saw that the young man was handsome and dark-featured. It was clear from his dress and his bearing that he was a man of rank and action. A scar across his forehead indicated he had followed a military profession. It seemed to add to his personality rather than detract from it.

"Good morning, Abbot." He greeted Laisran pleasantly before turning to Fidelma. "Good morning, Sister. What brings you to Ballyconra?"

Fidelma interrupted as Laisran was opening his mouth to explain.

"I am a dálaigh. You would appear to be expecting visitors, lord of Conra. I observed you watching our approach from the hill beyond the fortress before you rode swiftly down to meet us."

The young man's eyes widened a little and then he smiled sadly.

"You have a sharp eye, dálaigh. As a matter of fact, I have been expecting the arrival of my wife during these last few days. I saw only the shape of a woman on horseback and thought for a moment . . ."

"Your wife?" asked Fidelma quickly, glancing at Laisran.

"She is Segnat, daughter of the lord of Tir Bui," he said without disguising his pride.

"You say you have been expecting her?"

"Any day now. I thought you might have been her. We were married only three months ago in Tir Bui, but I had to return here immediately on matters pertaining to my people. Segnat was to come on after me but she has been delayed in starting out on her journey. I only had word a week ago that she was about to join me."

Fidelma looked at him thoughtfully.

"What has delayed her for so long?"

"Her father fell ill when we married and has only died recently. She was his only close kin and she stayed to nurse him."

"Can you describe her?"

The young man nodded, frowning.

"Why do you ask?"

"Indulge me for a moment, lord of Conra."

"Of twenty years, golden hair and blue eyes. What is the meaning of these questions?"

Fidelma did not reply directly.

"The road from Tir Bui would bring a traveler from the north through Ballacolla and around the abbey, wouldn't it?"

Conri looked surprised.

"It would," he agreed irritably. "I say again, why these questions?"

"I am a *dálaigh*," repeated Fidelma gravely. "It is my nature to ask questions. But the body of a young woman has been found in the woods near the abbey and we are trying to identify her."

Conri blinked rapidly.

"Are you saying that this might be Segnat?"

Fidelma's expression was sympathetic.

"We are merely making inquiries of the surrounding habitations to see if anything is known of a missing young woman."

Conri raised his jaw defiantly.

"Well, Segnat is not missing. I expect her arrival any time."

"But perhaps you would come to the abbey this afternoon and look at the body? This is merely a precaution to eliminate the possibility of it being Segnat."

The young man compressed his lips stubbornly.

"It could not possibly be Segnat."

"Regretfully, all things are possible. It is merely that some are more unlikely than others. We would appreciate your help. A negative identification is equally as helpful as a positive one."

Abbot Laisran finally broke in.

"The abbey would be grateful for your cooperation, lord of Conra."

The young man hesitated and then shrugged.

"This afternoon, you say? I shall be there."

He turned his horse sharply and cantered off.

Laisran exchanged a glance with Fidelma.

"Was this useful?" he asked.

"I think so," she replied. "We can now turn our attention to the inn, which you tell me is north of the abbey Ballacolla."

Laisran's face lightened.

"Ah, I see what you are about."

Fidelma smiled at him.

"You do?"

"It is as you said, a negative is equally as important as a positive. You have produced a negative with young Conri, so now we will seek the identity of the murdered one in the only possible place."

Fidelma continued to smile as they turned northward back toward the abbey and beyond to Ballacolla.

The inn stood at a crossroads, a sprawling dark building. They were turning into the yard when a muscular woman of middle age driving a small mule cart halted, almost blocking the entrance. The woman remained seated on her cart, glowering in displeasure at them.

"Religious!" She almost spat the word.

Fidelma regarded her with raised eyebrows.

"You sound as if you are not pleased to see us," she observed in amusement.

"It is the free hospitality provided by religious houses that takes away the business from poor people such as myself," grunted the woman.

"Well, we might be here to purchase some refreshment," placated Fidelma.

"If you can pay for it, you will find my husband inside. Let him know your wants."

Fidelma made no effort to move out of her way.

"I presume that you are the innkeeper?"

"And if I am?"

"I would like to ask you a few questions. Did a young woman pass this way two nights ago? A young woman who would have arrived along the northern road from Tir Bui."

The big woman's eyes narrowed suspiciously.

"What is that to you?"

"I am a *dálaigh* and my questions must be answered," replied Fidelma firmly. "What is your name, innkeeper?"

The woman blinked. She seemed ready to argue, but then she compressed her lips for a moment. To refuse to answer a *dálaigh*'s questions laid one open to fines for obstructing justice. A keeper of a public hostel had specific obligations before the law.

"My name is Corbnait," she conceded reluctantly.

"And the answer to my first question?"

Corbnait lifted her heavy shoulders and let them fall expressively.

"There was a woman who came here three nights ago. She merely wanted a meal and fodder for her horse. She was from Tir Bui."

"Did she tell you her name?"

"Not as I recall."

"Was she young, fair of skin with spun-gold hair in a single braid?"

The innkeeper nodded slowly.

"That was her." Suddenly an angry expression crossed the big woman's face. "Is she complaining about my inn or of the service that she received here? Is she?"

Fidelma shook her head.

"She is beyond complaining, Corbnait. She is dead."

The woman blinked again and then said sullenly: "She did not die of any food that was served on my premises. I keep a good house here."

"I did not specify the manner of her death." Fidelma paused. "I see you drive a small cart."

Corbnait looked surprised at the sudden switch of subject.

"So do many people. I have to collect my supplies from the outlaying farms. What is wrong with that?"

"Do you also dye clothes at your inn?"

"Dye clothes? What games are you playing with me, Sister?" Corbnait glanced from Abbot Laisran back to Fidelma as if she considered that she was dealing with dangerous lunatics. "Everyone dyes their own clothes unless they be a lord or lady."

"Please show me your hands and arms?" Fidelma pressed.

The woman glanced again from one to another of them but, seeing their impassive faces, she decided not to argue. She sighed and held out her burly forearms. There was no sign of any dye stains on them.

"Satisfied?" she snapped.

"You keep your hands well cared for," observed Fidelma.

The woman sniffed.

"What do I have a husband for if not to do the dirty work?"

"But I presume you served the girl with her meal?"

"That I did."

"Did she talk much?"

"A little. She told me she was on the way to join her husband. He lives some way to the south of the abbey."

"She didn't stay here for the night?"

"She was anxious to reach her husband. Young love!" The woman snorted in disgust. "It's a sickness you grow out of. The handsome prince you thought you married turns out to be a lazy good-for-nothing! Take my husband—"

"You had the impression that she was in love with her husband?" cut in Fidelma.

"Oh, yes."

"She mentioned no problems, no concerns?"

"None at all."

Fidelma paused, thinking hard.

"Was she alone during the time she was at the inn? No one else spoke to her? Were there any other guests?"

"There was only my husband and myself. My husband tended to her horse. She was particular about its welfare. The girl was obviously the daughter of a chieftain, for she had a valuable black mare and her clothes were of fine quality."

"What time did she leave here?"

"Immediately after her meal, just two hours to sunset. She said she could reach her destination before nightfall. What happened to her? Was she attacked by a highway robber?"

"That we have yet to discover," replied Fidelma. She did not mention that a highway robber could be discounted simply by the means of the poor girl's death. The manner of her death was, in fact, her most important clue. "I want to have a word with your husband now."

Corbnait frowned.

"Why do you want to speak with Echen? He can tell you nothing." Fidelma's brows drew together sternly.

"I will be the judge of that."

Corbnait opened her mouth, saw a look of steadfast determination on Fidelma's face, and then shrugged. She suddenly raised her voice in a shrill cry.

"Echen!"

It startled the patient ass and Fidelma's and Abbot Laisran's horses. They shied and were skittish for a few moments before they were brought under control.

A thin, ferret-faced man came scuttling out of the barn.

"You called, my dear?" he asked mildly. Then he saw Abbot Laisran, whom he obviously recognized, and bobbed servilely before him, rubbing his hands together. "You are welcome, noble Laisran," before turning to Fidelma and adding, "You are welcome, also, Sister. You bless our house by your presence. . . ."

"Peace, man!" snapped his burly wife. "The *dálaigh* wants to ask you some questions."

The little man's eyes widened.

"Dálaigh?"

"I am Fidelma of Cashel." Fidelma's gaze fell on his twisted hands. "I see that you have blue dye on your hands, Echen."

The man looked at his hands in bewilderment.

"I have just been mixing some dyes, Sister. I am trying to perfect a certain shade of blue from *glaisin* and *dubh-poill* . . . there is a sediment of intense blackness that is found in the bottom of pools in bogs, which I mix with the *glaisin* to produce a dark blue. . . ."

"Quiet! The sister does not want to listen to your prattling!" admonished Corbnait.

"On the contrary," snapped Fidelma, irritated by the bullying woman, "I would like to know if Echen was at his dye work when the young woman was here the other night."

Echen frowned.

"The young woman who stayed only for a meal and to fodder her horse," explained his wife. "The black mare."

The man's face cleared.

"I only started this work today. I remember the girl. She was anxious to press on to her destination."

"Did you speak to her?"

"Only to exchange words about her instructions for her horse, and then she went into the inn for a meal. She was there an hour or so, isn't that correct, dearest? Then she rode on."

"She rode away alone," added Corbnait, "just as I have told you."

Echen opened his mouth, caught his wife's eye, and then snapped it shut again.

Fidelma did not miss the action.

"Did you want to add something, Echen?" she prompted.

Echen hesitated.

"Come, if you have something to add, you must speak up!" Fidelma said sharply.

"It's just . . . well, the girl did not ride away entirely alone."

His wife turned with a scowl.

"There was no one else at the inn that night. What do you mean, man?"

"I helped her onto her horse and she left the inn but as she rode toward the south I saw someone driving a small donkey cart join her on the brow of the hill."

"Someone joined her? Male or female?" demanded Fidelma. "Did you see?"

"Male."

Abbot Laisran spoke for the first time.

"That must be our murderer, then," he said with a sigh. "A highway robber, after all. Now we shall never know who the culprit was."

"Highway robbers do not drive donkey carts," Fidelma pointed out.

"It was no highway robber," confirmed Echen.

They swung around on the little man in surprise.

"Then tell them who it was, you stupid man!" yelled Corbnait at her unfortunate spouse.

"It was young Finn," explained Echen, hurt by the rebuke he had received. "He herds sheep on Slieve Nuada, just a mile from here."

"Ah, a strange one that!" Corbnait said, as if all was explained to her satisfaction. "Both his parents died three years ago. He's been a recluse ever since. Unnatural, I call it."

Fidelma looked from Corbnait to Echen and then said, "I want one of you to ride to the abbey and look at the corpse so we can be absolutely sure that this was the girl who visited here. It is important that we are sure of her identity."

"Echen can do it. I am busy," grumbled Corbnait.

"Then I want directions to where this shepherd Finn dwells."

"Slieve Nuada is that large hill you can see from here," Abbot Laisran intervened. "I know the place, and I know the boy."

It was not long before they arrived at the shepherd's dwelling next to a traditional *lias cairach* or sheep's hut. The sheep milled about over the hill, indifferent to the arrival of strangers. Fidelma noticed that their white fleeces were marked with the blue-dyed circle that identified the flock and prevented them from mixing into neighboring flocks during common grazing.

Finn was weathered and bronzed—a handsome youth with a shock of red hair. He was kneeling on the grass astride a sheep whose stomach seemed vastly extended, almost as if it were pregnant but unnaturally so. As they rode up they saw the youth jab a long, thin, needlelike *biorracha* into a sheep's belly. There was a curious hiss of air and the swelling seemed to go down without harm to the sheep, which, when released, staggered away, bleating in irritation.

The youth look up and recognized Abbot Laisran. He put the *biorracha* aside and came forward with a smile of welcome.

"Abbot Laisran. I have not seen you since my father's funeral."

They dismounted and tethered their horses.

"You seem to have a problem on your hands," Abbot Laisran said, indicating the now transformed sheep.

"Some of them get to eating plants that they should not. It causes gas and makes the belly swell like a bag filled with air. You prick them with the needle and the gas escapes. It is simple and does not hurt the creature. Have you come to buy sheep for the abbey?"

"I am afraid we are here on sad business," Laisran said. "This is Sister Fidelma. She is a *dálaigh*."

The youth frowned.

"I do not understand."

"Two days ago you met a girl on the road from the inn at Ballacolla." Finn nodded immediately.

"That is true."

"What made you accost her?"

"Accost? I do not understand."

"You were driving in a donkey cart?"

"I was."

"She was on horseback?"

"She was. A black mare."

"So what made you speak to her?"

"It was Segnat from Tir Bui. I used to go to her father's fortress with my father, peace on his soul. I knew her."

Fidelma concealed her surprise.

"You knew her?"

"Her father was chieftain of Tir Bui."

"What was your father's business in Tir Bui? It is a long journey from here."

"My father used to raise the old horned variety of sheep that is now a dying breed. He was a *treudaighe* and proud of it. He kept a fine stock."

The *treudaighe* was a shepherd of rank.

"I see. So you knew Segnat?"

"I was surprised to see her on the road. She told me she was on her way to join her husband, Conri, the new lord of Ballyconra."

Finn's voice betrayed a curious emotion, which Fidelma picked up on.

"You do not like Conri?"

"I do not have the right to like or dislike such as he," admitted Finn. "I was merely surprised to hear that Segnat had married him, when he is living with a woman already."

"That is a choice for the individual," Fidelma reproved. "The New Faith has not entirely driven the old forms of polygyny from our people. A man can have more than one wife just as a woman can have more than one husband."

Abbot Laisran shook his head in annoyance.

"The Church opposes polygyny."

"True," agreed Fidelma. "But the judge who wrote the law tract of the Bretha Croilge said there is justification for the practice even in the ancient books of the faith, for it is argued that even the chosen people of God lived in a plurality of unions so that it is no easier to condemn it than to praise it."

She paused for a moment.

"That you disapproved of this meant you must have liked Segnat. Did you?"

"Why these questions?" countered the shepherd.

"Segnat has been murdered."

Finn stared at her for some time, then his face hardened.

"Conri did it! Segnat's husband. He only wanted her for the dowry she could bring into the marriage. Segnat could also bring more than that."

"How so?"

"She was a *banchomarba,* a female heir, for her father died without male issue and she became chieftainess of Tir Bui. She was rich. She told me so. Another reason Conri sought the union was because he had squandered much of his wealth on raising war bands to follow the High King in his wars against the northern Ui Neill. That is common gossip."

"Gossip is not necessarily fact," admonished Fidelma.

"But it usually has a basis of fact."

"You do not appear shocked at the news of Segnat's death," observed Laisran slyly.

"I have seen too many deaths recently, Abbot Laisran. Too many."

"I don't think we need detain you any longer, Finn," Fidelma said after a moment. Laisran glanced at her in astonishment.

"Mark my words, you'll find that Conri is the killer," called Finn as Fidelma moved away.

Abbot Laisran appeared to want to say something, but he meekly followed Fidelma to her horse and together they rode away from the shepherd's house. Almost as soon as they were out of earshot, Abbot Laisran leaned forward in excitement.

"There! We have found the killer. It was Finn. It all adds up."

Sister Fidelma turned and smiled at him.

"Does it?"

"The motive, the opportunity, the means, and the supporting evidence—it is all there. Finn must have killed her."

"You sound as if you have been reading law books, Laisran," she parried.

"I have followed your successes."

"Then, tell me, how did you work this out?"

"The *biorracha,* a long sharp needle of the type that you say must have caused the girl's mortal wound."

"Go on."

"He uses blue dye to identify his sheep. Hence the stain on the corpse."

"Go on."

"He also knew Segnat and was apparently jealous of her marriage to Conri. Jealousy is often the motive for murder."

"Anything else?"

"He met the girl on the road on the very night of her death. And he drives a small donkey cart to transport the body."

"He did not meet her at night," corrected Fidelma pedantically. "It was some hours before sunset."

Abbot Laisran made a cutting motion with his hand.

"It is as I say. Motive, opportunity, and means. Finn is the murderer."

"You are wrong, Laisran. You have not listened to the whispers of the dead. But Finn does know the murderer."

Abbot Laisran's eyes widened.

"I fail to understand. . . ."

"I told you that you must listen to the dead. Finn was right. It was Conri, lord of Ballyconra, who murdered his wife. I think the motive will be found to be even as Finn said . . . financial gain from his dead wife's estate. He probably knew that Segnat's father was dying when he married her. When we get back to the abbey, I will send for the local *bó-aire,* the magistrate, to take some warriors to search Conri's farmstead. With luck he will not have destroyed her clothing and personal belongings. I think we will also find that the very black mare he was riding was the same the poor girl rode on her fatal journey. Hopefully, Echen will be able to identify it."

Abbot Laisran stared at her blankly, bewildered by her calmness.

"How can you possibly know that? It must be guesswork. Finn could have just as easily killed her as Conri."

Fidelma shook her head.

"Consider the death wound. A needle inserted at the base of the neck under her braid."

"So?"

"Certainly, a long sharp needle, like a *biorracha,* could, and probably did, cause that wound. However, how could a perfect stranger, or even an acquaintance such as Finn, inflict such a wound? How could someone persuade the girl to relax unsuspecting while they lifted her braid and then, suddenly, insert that needle? Who but a lover? Someone she trusted. Someone whose intimate touch would arouse no suspicion. We are left with Segnat's lover—her husband."

Abbot Laisran heaved a sigh.

Fidelma added, "She arrived at Ballyconra expecting to find a loving husband, but found her murderer who had already planned her death to claim her inheritance."

"After he killed her, Conri stripped her of her clothes and jewels, dressed her in peasants' clothes and placed her in a cart that had been used by his workers to transport dyed clothing. Then he took her to the woods where he hoped the body would lay unseen until it rotted or, even if it was discovered, might never be identified."

"He forgot that the dead can still tell us many things," Fidelma agreed sadly. "They whisper to us and we must listen."

Brendan DuBois

An Empire's Reach

Former newspaper reporter and technical writer BRENDAN DUBOIS has published over fifty short stories, many of which have been extensively anthologized. "The Necessary Brother" received a Shamus award for best short story of the year, and his masterpiece, "The Dark Snow," was nominated for an Edgar. His series character is Lewis Cole, a magazine writer and former Department of Defense research analyst who investigates murders in DuBois's home state of New Hampshire. The fascinating and inventive novel, *Resurrection Day*—which takes place in an alternate 1972, ten years after the Cuban missile crisis erupted into nuclear war—is a tightly plotted thriller, and received the Sidewise Award for best alternative history novel of 1999. In "An Empire's Reach," first published in *Alfred Hitchcock's Mystery Magazine,* another of his signature characters—Turner, the hard-bitten ex-military man—is found for one last assignment.

An Empire's Reach

Brendan DuBois

It was a warm Thursday morning in June in Quebec City when Turner noticed the blond American woman watching him again, for the third day in a row.

He was set up on the Terrasse Dufferin, a wide wooden boardwalk just below the Château Frontenac, a hotel that looked like a castle that had been lifted from the Loire Valley in France and brought to this high point of land in the city, brick by brick, tower by tower, stone by stone. The boardwalk held dozens of green park benches and overlooked the St. Lawrence River and the lower part of Quebec City. However, since Turner was working, his back was to the river and he was facing the château with his sketch supplies. He was working on the one thousand twenty-first (or maybe the one thousand twenty-second—he had once lost count) sketch of the famed hotel, which had seen such noble guests over the years as Winston Churchill, Franklin Roosevelt, Queen Elizabeth II, and, during one flush month, himself.

Turner sold his sketches to the passing tourists who thronged the Terrasse Dufferin most every day, except for the cold winter months when the wind coming up the icy St. Lawrence can cut one right to the bone. There were a lot of other artists at work in different parts of the city doing straight portrait work or caricatures, so when he first arrived here, he knew he had to set himself up differently. His gimmick—arrived at after lots of thinking and observing the other street artists—was that he did up the sketch of the château, and then sketched in the customer, or the customer and her husband, or the customer and the entire family, walking in front of the historic building.

A nice gimmick, one that had given him a fairly comfortable career over the years. He enjoyed the give-and-take between himself and the customer, the dickering, the exchange of money for the painting. He'd never thought he would be interested in being a businessman, but over the years here, he had found a taste for it—though an unlikely career, no doubt about it.

But the blond woman, whom Turner had noticed right away three days ago, didn't seem very interested in his career.

She was in her early thirties, slim, and on all three days she wore tight black slacks and comfortable walking shoes. Each day she had on a different colored sweater; today's was a light peach. She carried a small black leather knapsack on her back every day, and her hair was pulled back in a simple ponytail. He would have taken her for any one of the many attractive women in Quebec City except that she was too intense-looking for the average Quebeçois—which made her an American—and she wasn't as stylishly dressed.

Today he finished the first sketch of the morning—save for the space where he inserted a paying customer—and saw her again, sitting on the nearest park bench, leafing through a Fodor's guidebook and looking up at the château, the six large cannon across the way, nearby Governor's park, the tall monument to Wolfe and Montcalm in the park, and the rows of three-story buildings that rose up on St. Genevieve that held a number of bed and breakfasts as well as the American consulate. She continued staring up toward the park until Turner spotted her glancing again toward him, and he caught her eye.

It was hot for June in Quebec, and Turner swallowed some bottled water that he had purchased earlier from the tiny Bar Laitier, which carried ice cream, beverages, and fruit. He scratched at the back of his neck, where a thin souvenir chain rubbed against his small ponytail. Time for a haircut pretty soon. Turner looked again at the woman and grinned and crooked a finger at her. Even at this distance, he could see her blush. She snapped shut the guidebook, accidentally dropped it on the boardwalk, picked it up, and put it in her knapsack. She then stood up and came over to him. He liked the way her legs moved in the slacks.

"Yes?" she asked, her voice quick, not at all sounding like someone who was on vacation.

"What can I do for you?" Turner asked.

"What do you mean?"

"What I mean is that you've been coming here for three days in a row, checking me out, and I'm curious why you're doing that."

A faint smile crossed her face. "And you think I'm checking you out. Why's that? Maybe I'm just interested in your art."

"Two wrong answers," Turner said, enjoying the little give and take. "This isn't art. It's just my livelihood. I'm not good enough to be an artist."

The smile grew just a bit as she sat down next to him. "And what was my second wrong answer?"

"Everyone who comes by here and talks to me, they look at my work for a while to see what I'm doing," he said. "From the first day, you didn't care what I was drawing. It could have been Elvis emerging from the Mother Ship, up on the Plains of Abraham. No, young lady, you've kept your eye on me from moment one. And why are you doing that?"

"Because we need your help, Major Turner."

In his shock he almost knocked over his sketchpad. It had been years since anyone had said that to him, and he didn't like it.

Turner sat still for a couple of minutes, then took another swig of water. He found his mouth had gotten quite dry, and he took a couple of more swallows. "Congratulations," he said finally. "You've gotten my attention."

"So far, so good."

"Let's start with the obvious," Turner said. "Who are you, and who are the 'we' that you mentioned?"

She reached into her knapsack, handed him a business card, and then flipped open a slim leather wallet. It had her picture and an official seal and lots of signatures and other information. "Ann Morse," she said. "Department of Defense." She put the wallet back into her knapsack.

He rubbed at the raised seal on her business card, then returned it to her. "It says here you work for the Defense Research Agency."

"I do."

"Well, goody for you," Turner said. "Do they have a nice dental plan?"

"I have no complaints," she said.

"You stick around long enough with the Department of Defense, you'll find you'll have more complaints than you know what to do with."

Morse put her small knapsack on her lap. "You're a hard person to find, Major Turner."

"The fact that you've found me means it couldn't have been that difficult."

Her hands were still on the knapsack. "Still, it took a long time. Your pension check arrives here in Quebec City after going through four different mail drops and mail forwarding companies, one of which is in the British Virgin Islands, which wasn't very cooperative with our inquiries. The cost of all that mail forwarding must take a healthy portion out of your monthly check."

"Just a cost of doing business, of protecting my privacy," Turner said, looking intently at this pretty young woman. He wondered how she had been chosen to come talk to him. Drafted or volunteered? A familiar choice from his generation, a few decades ago.

He added, "Plus, the American dollar goes very far in Canada. I can do much better here than anywhere else. For a while I thought of going to Paris. You know why?"

"No, I do not," she said.

"Traditional dumping ground for American exiles after a war. Look at Hemingway, Dos Passos, Stein. All of them ended up there. But I spent a couple of months in Paris and decided to come to Quebec City. The food is better here and the waiters have a friendlier attitude. Which raises a question—what brings you to Quebec City, Mrs. Morse?"

"Ms. Morse," she corrected. "What brings me to Quebec City is you, Major Turner."

"Mr. Turner, if you please," he said. "Go on, I'm flattered."

She looked away for a moment as a juggler, wearing a rainbow-colored top hat that was about five feet tall, went by on a unicycle. "What brings me here is your service in Vietnam, Maj—excuse me, Mr. Turner. I need to talk to you about it."

"Go right ahead," he said, feeling something queasy begin to roll around in his insides. They're here, a voice inside started murmuring, they finally found out what happened.

"You served with an artillery unit. You served honorably. Yet when you left Vietnam and returned to the United States, you retired early, in 1976. You could have had a fulfilling career in the army. Why did you leave?"

He looked over at his artist supplies, at the sketch of the Château Frontenac and the boardwalk. He picked up a pencil and went to work, filling in some of the background. "I tell you what, Ms. Morse. Do me a quick favor. Walk over to those large cannon over there, just beyond that little ice cream place. Look at those cannon and tell me what makes them unusual, then we'll talk. All right?"

Her face was expressionless which Turner found fascinating. She was good. She was very good. She just nodded and picked up her knapsack and guidebook and walked over to the six cannon each the size of a small telephone pole, set on metal carriages. A couple of kids were playing on top of the large black barrels, riding astride them like carousel horses. He liked the way she walked, like the way the black slacks hugged her.

When she came back, she sat down at the exact same spot. "Very interesting. Those cannon were once used for the defense of Quebec City. Four of them are British in origin; they still have the arrow mark and the seal of Queen Victoria. The other two are from Imperial Russia, and they bear the double-headed eagle symbol of the czars. They were captured by the British during the Crimean War, and were later brought here as part of the city's defenses."

Morse paused, pulled back a free strand of blond hair. "But you already knew that, Mr. Turner, didn't you? So what was the point of this little exercise?"

He pulled his pencil away from his sketching. "The point was to make sure you knew, Ms. Morse." He pointed to the six cannon with his pencil. "Don't you see it? British and Russian cannon, transported thousands of miles from Asia to defend territory in North America once controlled by the French. Three empires, clashing and coming together, here, on this little point of land. Empires have a very long reach, Ms. Morse. I can't think of a better example than these cannon, right here."

She kept on looking at him with those steady blue eyes. "And your tour in Vietnam. How does that connect with obsolete cannon, hundreds of years old?"

He smiled at her. "The reach of an empire, Ms. Morse. That was what was being displayed in Vietnam, now nearly four decades ago. The reach of an American empire, to come up against the reach of a Soviet empire, being fought over a place that was once controlled by the French empire. That's what was going on, the clash of empires. An old story, one that's still going on in other places of the world. Just like in Kosovo. Or East Timor. Or even Iraq. Which brings us back to my original question. Why are you and your people so interested in what an artillery officer did back then?"

She ignored the question, brought up one of her own. "And why are you so interested in empires, Mr. Turner?"

He sighed at all the old memories she was disturbing. "Because I find that all empires battle in public, while in private the businesses that support the empires are keeping an eager eye on developments. Because it all does come down to business. The trading companies that supported the French and British here in Canada. The transnationals that supported us in Iraq and Kosovo. Because I've seen what can happen when empires overextend their reach. You send men and material, thousands upon thousands of miles away from home, to implement plans and procedures that are drawn up in cool and safe meeting rooms in an office building. Plans and procedures developed by well-fed men who had never heard a shot fired in anger, had never burrowed their heads in the ground when mortar rounds went whistling overhead or spent the night near the wire, with a weapon in hand, shaking with fear, wondering if the little snap of a twig meant a burrowing animal or a sapper squad about ten seconds away from slitting your throat."

Turner looked over at her and then back at his sketchpad. "No, nobody had any of those frontline experiences when they drew up their plans, their little maps and rules of engagement in Vietnam. And have you read their biographies now, their self-serving stories? They knew early on it was a waste of time, that the whole effort wouldn't work. But did they stop? Did they resign? Did they protest against their own president? No, no, and no. And tens of thousands of us and millions of them died because of their pride, or their honor, or whatever. All because they were far away and didn't know a thing. Look. You ever have any contract work done in your home? Like a new roof or deck?"

"Excuse me?" she asked, looking confused.

"C'mon, you heard the question. Ever have any contract work done on your house? Or condo? Or wherever the hell you live, Ms. Ann Morse of the Defense Research Agency?"

"Yes," she admitted. "Had new kitchen cabinets installed last year."

"Really? Tell me, did you keep a close eye on the contractors? Was everything put in properly? Were there any problems?"

She shrugged her slim shoulders. "Oh, the usual. Missing parts. Days when the workers didn't show up. Another day when they drilled the wrong holes for the faucets on the sinks."

"Oh, I'm sure," Turner said. "Now imagine trying to do that same job from several thousand miles away, when the time zone is all different, when your noontime is their midnight, and you can only communicate by telephone or mail. How efficient a job would have happened? Not very efficient, right? Now, imagine trying to fight a war on those terms from so far away. Not like today, with the Internet and the satellite communications and all those high-tech goodies."

"Building a kitchen cabinet and conducting war can't be compared like that, Mr. Turner."

"Tough," Turner said. "I just did it. When the North finally overran the South in '75, you know what picture stuck in my mind the most?"

"Do tell me."

He wasn't sure if she was being sarcastic or not, but he still pressed on. "It was when the helicopters had left Saigon, carrying out the last of the Embassy staff and all of those desperate refugees. They then landed on aircraft carriers, out there in the China Sea, and when too many helicopters had landed on the flight deck, they ended up pushing the surplus helicopters into the ocean. Can you believe that? Flying machines worth millions of dollars, dunked into the drink. Didn't make a hell of a lot of sense, did it? All of that equipment, all of those supplies, dumped over the side or left behind. Millions of dollars worth. Hell, I heard some of our stuff is still being used by the Vietnamese, decades later."

There, he thought. Enough bantering around. Let's see if she would take the bait.

And she certainly did.

Morse cleared her throat. "That's why I'm here to talk to you, Mr. Turner. About some equipment that was left behind. Equipment that you were responsible for. In a place called Depot Four."

He closed his eyes, listening to the thumping noise of people walking by on the boardwalk, almost drowned out by the humming from the traffic on the highway at his back, that ran parallel to the St. Lawrence River. For a sudden moment he felt warm, sweltering warm, as if he were back there, back in the jungles, where it rained for months at a time and mud sometimes reached up to your knees, and everything was damp and moldy and filled with mildew. . . .

"Depot Four," Turner finally said. "What about Depot Four?"

"You were once one of the officers responsible for Depot Four," she said, her voice curiously flat, "You know what was contained in Depot Four. Mr. Turner, we have a problem. Some of the items stored in Depot Four are still there almost thirty years later. And we need your help in getting them out."

Even though he had guessed long ago what had really happened back there, hearing the truth from this pretty young lady made his hands shake. He put down his brushes and clasped his hands.

"Depot Four . . ." he said. "We had lots of ammunition depots scattered throughout that poor country. Concrete bunkers stuck out in the middle of nowhere, some in secret locations, containing everything from

5.56-millimeter cartridges to rockets to artillery shells. Everything you needed in prosecuting an empire's war. And when an empire moves into battle, everything battle-related, no matter how unlikely you might need it, moves with it. Including . . . special weapons. Contained in Depot Four." He suddenly turned to her and raised his voice in anger. "How in hell did this happen, that those weapons were left behind? We're not talking about helicopters and gas tanks, are we? My God, you mean we actually left behind tactical nuclear weapons, battlefield nukes, in Vietnam?"

"It would appear that way," Morse said, looking right at him, her voice still calm. "The Department of Defense is one of the largest bureaucracies in the world, Mr. Turner. I don't believe I'm telling you anything new. Paperwork gets shuffled, overlooked. Orders are given and months later are still not fulfilled. Certain items that should have been removed as part of our demobilization back then—like a number of 155-millimeter artillery shells with five kiloton warheads—were still there in 1975. When the North invaded, everyone was surprised at how quickly the South collapsed. A number of supplies, as you mentioned, were left behind, including those tactical nuclear weapons in Depot Four. Those responsible at the time managed to cover it up for a while by judicious shuffling of paperwork. It was only a few years ago that we learned the truth, that twenty of those artillery shells were still there in that bunker. Since then we've done some additional intelligence work. The bunker has been overgrown by jungle and remains undisturbed, and we can tell by remote-sensing that those warheads are still there."

The sense of warmth and humidity that had come to him earlier was gone. All he felt now was a cool breeze coming up from the river. He hunched forward some as a group of laughing tourists passed by, maps held high in their hands, looking for him, looking for some adventure, looking for some damn thing.

Turner cleared his throat. "So why are you here, Ms. Morse?"

She leaned in closer. "For several months prior to 1975, you were one of the last supervisors of Depot Four."

"So what. Lots of guys supervised Depot Four. Why bother to contact me?"

"Because of how you gained access, Mr. Turner. Let me refresh your memory. To gain access to Depot Four, two officers, each with a separate key, had to approach an interior door. Both keys had to be used to open the door. One key was code-named Alpha, the other, Omega. Today security systems are fully computerized, and the key system you were familiar with has been destroyed, which left us with a problem. Since we've determined what was left behind in Depot Four, we have secured an Alpha key from a retired officer, such as yourself, who managed to hold on to a key as a souvenir when he left service. But an Omega key remains missing. We know that you were issued one of those keys as part of your responsibilities. The paperwork on whether you returned your Omega key is, shall we say, incomplete."

He stared up at the monument to Wolfe and Montcalm that commemorated the deaths of a British general and a French general in 1759, in a battle that destroyed a French empire and helped create a British one, and that didn't even last an afternoon, up there on the Plains of Abraham.

Turner said, "And when you get both keys, what then? A little tour group with a couple of trucks rolls up to an abandoned bunker and merrily drives away to Thailand with its booty?"

"No," she said, "not quite. A covert force would have to go in to remove the warheads, which is why we need the other key. With the two keys in hand, a covert force could get in and out rather quickly. Without the key, they would need to blast their way in with explosives. And you know how those bunkers were designed, Mr. Turner. That would mean a lot of time, a lot of energy, and a lot of noise. None of which we can afford."

He rubbed his hands together. "Well, here's a thought for you, Ms. Morse. Why not the truth?"

He had a sense that he had shaken her up some. She sat back against the park bench, rubbed a hand against her ponytail. "Excuse me, Mr. Turner. What do you mean, the truth?"

Turner decided he liked seeing her confused. "Why not go to the Vietnamese, tell them the truth? Tell them what we did back then and ask permission to come in-country and remove the warheads. Perhaps pay a few million dollars in fees or fines or whatever. Wouldn't that work better than all that hi-tech Rambo stuff, sneaking in after dark with keys and guns blazing? Why not the truth?"

Morse paused for a moment. "Suppose we do that. And suppose they don't let us in?"

He shrugged. "The price you pay."

"Then you've just created another nuclear power in Southeast Asia," Morse said. "You know the problems and tensions between India and Pakistan. Does the region need another country with nuclear weapons? Does it?"

Turner suddenly laughed out loud, infuriating Morse, who snapped, "Is there something funny I said back there? Is there?"

He wiped at his eyes, still smiling. "I'm sorry, I'm just laughing at the irony of it all. All the money, blood, and treasure we spilled from the fifties to the seventies to prevent a Communist Vietnam from coming into being. And what happened? Not only does a Communist Vietnam exist, we actually helped arm it with the deadliest weapons on the planet. You have to admit, Ms. Morse, that's pretty funny, in a black way."

"I don't have to admit a thing," she said. "But I need to ask you, Mr. Turner. The Omega key. Do you have it?"

He said the carefully rehearsed words in a quiet tone. "I'm afraid I can't help you."

"You're not answering the question."

He said, "What's the price, then?"

Her eyes narrowed. "A hundred thousand dollars."

"Try ten million," he said. "If I have it, of course."

Her face reddened. "That's outrageous."

"Let's see, we leave behind nuclear weapons in a country that we tried to bomb back to the Stone Age, and you call me outrageous. I'm many things, Ms. Morse, but I don't think I'm being particularly outrageous. And don't try to appeal to my patriotism next. It won't work. I'm a businessman now, pure and simple. All of those empires fought and continue to fight for one thing and one thing only. Business. We fought in Iraq for oil. We fought in Kosovo to preserve stability in Europe so that our stock market wouldn't tumble. That's another reason why I left the Army. I decided it was better to be a businessman by myself than to be a sap fighting for one."

She slowly stood up, shaking her pretty head. "Is that it, then? A businessman seeking ten million dollars?"

He looked up at her. "Why not? It sure would be nice to move to a bigger apartment. The one I'm living in now doesn't give out much heat, and you won't believe how cold it can get here in January. Plus, with money in the bank like that, I won't have to spend as much time out here, waiting for tourists to stop by."

"You could be brought back to the United States for justice."

"You'll find the Canadians still aren't that helpful when it comes to returning Vietnam vets who claim to be oppressed. And what would you do if you got me back in the States? Torture me to locate the key? That's a stretch, even for you and your folks."

She handed over her business card, which he kept this time. "I'm afraid I'm out of time, Mr. Turner. If you ever decide to change your mind, our offer still remains. A hundred thousand dollars. That is, if you do have the key. If not, then we'll try something else."

He turned the card over and put it in his shirt pocket. "I'm sure you will. Good day, Ms. Morse."

"And to you, Mr. Turner."

Turner watched her walk down the boardwalk, until she disappeared in a mass of tourists standing around a large statue of Samuel de Champlain near the Château Frontenac. When he could not see her anymore, he picked up his brushes and pencils and went to work on the sketch before him. Within a half hour he was finished and he sat back to admire what he had done. In front of the château he had sketched a pretty blond woman in black slacks, with a knapsack slung across her back, walking away. Her face was obscured by her hair, but that didn't matter. He knew what she looked like, and that's what counted.

Later, when it was time for his lunch, he walked the several blocks to his apartment, a third-floor walk-up on rue Autueil. As he strolled along, he amused himself by noticing the people passing him by on the sidewalk, seeing how they were dressed and how they walked, and whispering to himself, "tourist, tourist, native, tourist . . ." He climbed the narrow stairs up to his apartment easily, having given up cigarettes years ago. When he unlocked the door and stepped inside, he paused for just a moment to take in his surroundings.

The apartment was a mess. Furniture had been rolled over, the coverings and cushions torn away. All of his books had been tossed in a heap, as well as a few framed sketches of his own. He slowly walked through the apartment, seeing how the searchers had gone to work. Everything and anything he owned had been examined, torn open, and tossed asunder. His clothing was all in a pile as well, the seams ripped apart. Even the toothpaste had been squeezed out into his bathroom sink, along with the contents of a couple of shampoo bottles, and the meager collection of food and drink in the tiny refrigerator had also been dumped in the sink.

"Well," he said, going into the bedroom, where the bedding and mattress and box springs were upended in a corner. He sat down by the wrecked remains of his nightstand, drew his knees up to his chin, and smiled despite all that he saw about him.

A ruse, that was all. Ann Morse of the Defense Research Agency had come to him and conversed for long minutes, letting him vent and go on and on, while her compatriots were busy at work here, tearing the place apart. No wonder she hadn't interrupted him while he had ranted. No wonder. She only wanted to allow as much time as necessary so that this place could be searched and when enough time had passed, she had brusquely dismissed him and had gone on her way. She hadn't been interested in a deal; she had only been interested in keeping him occupied during that time.

He reached over and picked up his satchel and removed the sketch of her walking in front of the château. He still had her business card, which gave a post office box address in Arlington, Virginia. Maybe he'd mail it to her someday. Maybe. But there were other things to do first, and right away.

From the mess of his bedroom he retrieved the telephone and a Bell Canada phone book. He put the phone in his lap and looked up two phone numbers, which he then carefully wrote down. The first phone number was for the American Consulate. And the second was for the Vietnamese Consulate.

Another smile. He reached under his ponytail and felt for the tiny chain, then bent his head forward, ducking some as the chain came free. A large key dangled from the end of the chain. He turned it over and examined it, just as he had examined it before, thousands of times. A simple brass key, with the Greek symbol for Omega in the center: Ω. Whaddya know. Back there in '75, before leaving the country, when papers were being burned and installations abandoned, he thought this would make a great souvenir, and he had certainly been right.

Once he had been a soldier, and now he was a businessman, and an old souvenir from his service was about to set him up in a sweet deal indeed.

He picked up the phone, noted the two phone numbers, and started dialing.

"Let the bidding begin," Turner said.

Jeffery Deaver

Surveillance

Former attorney JEFFERY DEAVER is perhaps best known for his books about Lincoln Rhyme, a quadriplegic who solves crimes using his computer and the able help of Amelia Sachs. Deaver is noted for his encyclopedic knowledge on a wide variety of subjects, as well as his use of various types of forensics, combining them both into plots with several twists and turns along the way. He has been an international bestseller for a decade and his audience increases in size and enthusiasm with each book. Under the pseudonym William Jeffries, he also writes a series featuring John Pellam, a location scout for movie studios. His short story, "Surveillance," published earlier this year in *Ellery Queen's Mystery Magazine,* is in the traditional Deaverian style—starring a protagonist who isn't what he seems. For that matter, no one in the story is exactly who he first seems to be. Read on and just try and guess how this one will turn out.

Surveillance

Jeffery Deaver

The knocking on the door not only woke Jake Muller from an afternoon nap but it told him immediately who his visitor was.

Not a polite single rap, not a friendly Morse code, but a repeated slamming of the brass knocker. Three times, four, six.

Oh, man, not again.

Rolling his solid body from the couch, Muller paused for a moment to slip into a slightly higher level of wakefulness. It was five P.M. and he'd been gardening all day—until about an hour ago when a Dutch beer and the warmth of a May afternoon had lulled him to sleep. He now flicked on the pole lamp and walked unsteadily to the door, pulled it open.

The slim man in a blue suit and sporting thick, well-crafted politician's hair brushed past Muller and strode into the living room. Behind him was an older, burlier man in tweedy brown.

"Detective," Muller muttered to the man in blue.

Lieutenant William Carnegie didn't reply. He sat on the couch as if he'd just stepped away from it for a trip to the bathroom.

"Who're you?" Muller asked the other one bluntly.

"Sergeant Hager."

"You don't need to see his ID, Jake, do you?" Carnegie said.

Muller yawned. He'd wanted the couch but the cop was sitting stiffly in the middle of it so he took the uncomfortable chair instead. Hager didn't sit down. He crossed his arms and looked around the dim room, then let his vision settle on Muller's faded blue jeans, dusty white socks, and a T-shirt advertising a local clam dive. His gardening clothes.

Yawning again and brushing his short, sandy hair into place, Muller asked, "You're not here to arrest me, right? Because you would've done that already. So, what do you want?"

Carnegie's trim hand disappeared into his trim suit jacket and returned with a notebook, which he consulted. "Just wanted to let you know, Jake—

we found out about your bank accounts at West Coast Federal in Portland."

"And how'd you do that? You have a court order?"

"You don't need a court order for some things."

Sitting back, Muller wondered if they'd put some kind of tap on his computer—that was how he'd set up the accounts last week. Annandale's Major Crimes Division, he'd learned, was very high-tech; he'd been under intense surveillance over the past several months.

Living in a fishbowl . . .

He noticed that the tweedy cop was surveying the inside of Muller's modest bungalow.

"No, Sergeant Haver—"

"Hager."

"—I don't look like I'm living in luxury, if that's what you were observing. Because I'm not. Tell me, did you work the Anco case?"

The sergeant didn't need the glance from his boss to know to keep mum.

Muller continued. "But you *do* know that the burglar netted five hundred thousand and change. Now if—like Detective Carnegie here thinks—I was the one who stole the money, wouldn't I be living in something a little nicer than this?"

"Not if you were smart," the sergeant muttered, and decided to sit down.

"Not if I were smart," Muller repeated, and laughed.

Detective Carnegie looked around the dim living room and added, "This, we figure, is sort of a safehouse. You probably have some real nice places overseas."

"I wish."

"Well, don't we all agree that you're not your typical Annandale resident?"

In fact, Jake Muller *was* a bit of an oddball in this wealthy Southern California town. He'd suddenly appeared here about six months ago to oversee some business deals in the area. He was single, traveled a lot, had a vague career (he owned companies that bought and sold other companies, was how he explained it). He made good money but had picked for his residence this modest house, which, as they'd just established, was nowhere close to luxurious.

So when Detective William Carnegie's clever police computer compiled a list of everyone who'd moved to town not long before the Anco Armored Delivery heist four months ago, Muller earned suspect status. And as the cop began to look more closely at Muller, the evidence got better and better. He had no alibi for the hours of the heist. The tire treads on the getaway car were similar to those on Muller's Lexus. Carnegie also found that Muller had a degree in electrical engineering; the burglar in the Anco case had dismantled a sophisticated alarm system to get into the cash storage room.

Even better, though, from Carnegie's point of view, was the fact that

Muller had a record: a juvenile conviction for grand theft auto and an arrest ten years ago on some complicated money-laundering scheme at a company he was doing business with. Though the charges against Muller were dropped, Carnegie believed he was let go only on a technicality. Oh, he knew in his heart that Muller was behind the Anco theft, and he went after the businessman zealously—with the same energy that had made him a celebrity among the citizens of Annandale. Since Carnegie had been appointed head of Major Crimes two years ago, robberies, drug sales, and gang activities had dropped by half. Annandale had the lowest crime rate of any town in the area. He was also well liked among prosecutors—he made airtight cases against his suspects.

But on the Anco case he stumbled. Just after he'd arrested Jake Muller last month a witness came forward and said the man seen leaving the Anco grounds just after the robbery didn't look at all like Muller. Carnegie asserted that a smart perp like Muller would use a disguise for the getaway. But a state's attorney decided there was no case against him and ordered the businessman released.

Carnegie fumed at the embarrassment and the blot on his record. So when no other leads panned out, the detective returned to Muller with renewed fervor. He kept digging into the businessman's life and slowly began shoring up the case with circumstantial evidence: Muller frequently played golf on a course next to Anco headquarters—the perfect place for staking out the company—and he owned an acetylene torch that was powerful enough to cut through the loading-dock door at Anco. The detective used this information to bully his captain into beefing up surveillance on Muller.

Hence, the interrupted nap today with the stop-the-presses information about Muller's accounts.

"So what about the Portland money, Jake?"

"What about it?"

"Where'd the money come from?"

"I stole the crown jewels. No, wait, it was the Great Northfield Train Robbery. Okay, I lied. I knocked over a casino in Vegas."

William Carnegie sighed and momentarily lowered his eyelids, which ended with perfect, delicate lashes.

The businessman asked, "What about that other suspect? The highway worker? You were going to check him out."

Around the time of the heist a man in a public-works jumpsuit was seen pulling a suitcase from some bushes near the Anco main gate. A passing driver thought this looked suspicious and noted the license plate of the public-works truck, relaying the information to the Highway Patrol. The truck, which had been stolen a week before in Bakersfield, was later found abandoned at Orange County's John Wayne airport.

Muller's lawyer had contended that this man was the robber and that Carnegie should pursue him.

"Didn't have any luck finding him," the Annandale detective said.

"You mean," Muller grumbled, "that it was a long shot, he's out of the jurisdiction, and it's a hell of a lot easier to roust me than it is to find the real thief." He snapped, "Goddamn it, Carnegie, the only thing I've ever done wrong in my life was listening to a couple of buddies I shouldn't have when I was seventeen. We borrowed—"

" 'Borrowed'?"

"—a car for two hours and we paid the price. I just don't get why you're riding me like this."

But in truth, Muller knew the answer to that perfectly well. In his long and varied career, he'd met a number of men and women like self-disciplined William Carnegie. They were machines powered by mindless ambition to take down whoever they believed was their competitor or enemy. They were different from people like Muller himself, who are ambitious, yes, but whose excitement comes from the game itself. The Carnegies of the world were ruled solely by their need to win; the process was nothing to them.

"Can you prove the funds came from a legitimate source?" the sergeant asked formally.

Muller looked at Carnegie. "What happened to your other assistant, Detective? What was his name? Carl? I liked him. He didn't last too long."

Carnegie had gone through two assistants in the time he'd been after Jake Muller. Muller supposed that though the citizenry and the reporters were impressed with the obsessive-compulsive cop, he'd make his coworkers' lives miserable.

"Okay," the detective said. "If you're not going to talk, that's just the way it is. Oh, but I should let you know: We've got some information we're looking at right now. It's very interesting."

"Ah, more of your surveillance?"

"Maybe."

"And what exactly did you find?"

"Let's just call it interesting."

Muller said, " 'Interesting.' You said that twice. Hey, you want a beer? You, Sergeant?"

Carnegie answered for both of them. "No."

Muller fetched a Heineken from the kitchen. He continued: "So what you're saying is that after you've gone over this interesting information, you'll have enough evidence to arrest me for real this time. But if I confess, it'll go a lot easier. Right?"

"Come on, Jake. Nobody was hurt at Anco. You'll do, what, five years. You're a young guy. It'd be a church social for you."

Muller nodded for a moment, drank a good bit of beer. Then said seriously, "But if I confessed, then I'd have to give the money back, right?"

Carnegie froze for a moment. Then he smiled. "I'm not going to stop until I nail you, Jake. You know that." He said to the sergeant, "Let's go. This's a waste of time."

"At last there's something we agree on," Muller offered, and closed the door after them.

The next day, William Carnegie, wearing a perfectly pressed gray suit, white shirt, and striped red tie, strode into the watch room of the Annandale police station, with Hager behind him.

He nodded at the eight officers sitting in the cheap fiberglass chairs. The men and women fell silent as the detective surveyed his troops.

Coffee was sipped, pencils tapped, pads doodled upon.

Watches glanced at.

"We're going to make a push on the case. I went to see Muller yesterday. I lit a fire under him and it had an effect: Last night I was monitoring his E-mail and he made a wire transfer of fifty thousand dollars from a bank in Portland to a bank in Lyon, France. I'm convinced he's getting ready to flee the jurisdiction."

Carnegie had managed to get level-two surveillance on Muller. This high-tech approach to investigations involved establishing real-time links to his on-line service provider and the computers at Muller's credit card companies, banks, cell phone service, and the like. Anytime Muller made a purchase, went on-line, made a call, withdrew cash, and so on, the officers on the Anco team would know almost instantly.

"Big Brother's going to be watching everything our boy's doing."

"Who?" asked one of the younger cops.

"1984?" Carnegie responded, astonished that the man hadn't heard of the novel. "The book?" he asked sarcastically. When the officer continued to stare blankly, he added, "Big Brother was the government. It watched everything the citizens did." He nodded at a nearby dusty computer terminal and then turned back to the officers. "You, me, and Big Brother—we're closing the net on Muller." Noting the stifled grins, he wished he'd been a bit less dramatic. But damn it, didn't they realize that Annandale had become the laughingstock of Southern California law enforcers for not closing the Anco case? The CHP, the LAPD, and even the cops in small towns nearby couldn't believe that the Annandale Police, despite having the biggest per capita budget of any town in Orange County, hadn't collared a single perp in the heist.

Carnegie divided the group into three teams and assigned them to shifts at the computer workstations, with orders to relay to him instantly everything that Muller did.

As he was walking back to his office to look further at Muller's wire transfer to France, he heard a voice. "Hey, Dad?"

He turned to see his son striding down the corridor toward him, dressed in his typical seventeen-year-old's uniform: earrings, shabby *Tomb Raider* T-shirt, and pants so baggy they looked like they'd fall off at any moment. And the hair: spiked up and dyed a garish yellow. Still, Billy was an above-average student and nothing like the troublemakers that Carnegie dealt with in an official capacity.

"What're you doing here?" he asked. It was early May. School should be in session, shouldn't it?

"It's parent-teacher day, remember? You and Mom're supposed to meet Mr. Gibson at ten. I came by to make sure you'd be there."

Damn . . . Carnegie'd forgotten about the meeting. And he was supposed to have a conference call with two investigators in France about Muller's wire transfer. That was set for nine forty-five. If he postponed it, the French policemen wouldn't be available later because of the time difference and the call would have to be delayed until tomorrow.

"I've got it on my calendar," the detective said absently; something had begun to nag at his thoughts. What was it? He added to his son, "I just might be a little late."

"Dad, it's important," Billy said.

"I'll be there."

Then the thought that had been buzzing around Carnegie's consciousness settled. "Billy, are you still taking French?"

His son blinked. "Yeah, you signed my report card, don't you remember?"

"Who's your teacher?"

"Mrs. Vandell."

"Is she at school now?"

"I guess. Yeah, probably. Why?"

"I need her to help me with a conference call. You go on home now. Tell your mother I'll be at the meeting as soon as I can."

Carnegie left the boy standing in the middle of the hallway and jogged to his office, so excited about the brainstorm of using the French teacher to help him translate that he nearly collided with a workman hunched over one of the potted plants in the corridor, trimming leaves.

"Sorry," he called, and hurried into his office. He phoned Billy's French teacher and when he told her how important the case was she reluctantly agreed to help him translate. The conference call went off as scheduled, and the woman's translation efforts were a huge help; without his brainstorm to use the woman he couldn't have communicated with the two officers at all. Still, the investigators in France reported that they'd found no impropriety in Muller's investments or financial dealings. He paid taxes and had never run into any trouble with the gendarmes.

Carnegie asked if they had tapped his phone and were monitoring his on-line and banking activities.

There was a pause and then one of the officers responded. Billy's French teacher translated, "They say, 'We are not so high-tech as you. We prefer to catch criminals the old-fashioned way.'" They did agree to alert their customs agents to check Muller's luggage carefully the next time he was in the country.

Carnegie thanked the two men and the teacher, then hung up.

We prefer to catch criminals the old-fashioned way. . . .

Which is why we'll get him and you won't, thought the detective, as he spun around in his chair and began staring intently at Big Brother's computer monitor once again.

Jake Muller stepped out of the department store in downtown Annandale, following the young man he'd noticed in the jewelry department.

The boy kept his head down and walked quickly away from the store.

When they were passing an alleyway Muller suddenly jogged forward, grabbed the skinny kid by the arm, and pulled him into the shadows.

"Jesus," he whispered in shock.

Muller pinned him up against the wall. "Don't think about running." A glance toward the boy's pockets. "And don't think about anything else."

"I don't—" the boy said with a quivering voice. "I don't have a gun or anything."

"What's your name?"

"I—"

"Name?" Muller barked.

"Sam. Sam Phillips. Like, whatta you want?"

"Give me the watch."

The boy sighed and rolled his eyes.

"Give it to me. You don't want me to have to take it off you." Muller outweighed the boy by fifty pounds.

The kid reached into his pocket and handed him the Seiko that Muller had seen him lift off the counter at the store. Muller took it.

"Who're you? Security? A cop?"

Muller eyed him carefully and then pocketed the watch. "You were clumsy. If the guard hadn't been taking a leak he would've caught you."

"What guard?"

"That's my point. The little guy in the ratty jacket and dirty jeans."

"He was a security guard?"

"Yeah."

"How'd you spot him?"

Muller said grimly, "Let's say I've had my share of run-ins with guys like that."

The boy looked up for a moment, examined Muller, then resumed his study of the asphalt in the alley. "How'd you spot *me?*"

"Wasn't hard. You were skulking around the store like you'd already been busted."

"You gonna shake me down or something?"

Muller looked up and down the street cautiously. Then he said, "I need somebody to help me with this thing I've got going tomorrow."

"Why me?" the boy asked.

"There're some people who'd like to set me up."

"Cops?"

"Just . . . some people." Muller nodded toward his pocket. "But since *I* spotted *you* boosting this, I know you're not working for anybody."

"Whatta I have to do?"

"It's easy. I need a driver. A half-hour's work."

Part scared, part excited. "Like, how much?"

"I'll pay you five hundred."

Another examination of the scenery. "For a half-hour?"

Muller nodded.

"Damn. Five hundred?"

"That's right."

"What're we doing?" he asked, a little cautious now. "I mean, exactly."

"I've got to . . . pick up a few things at this place—a house on Tremont. I need you to park in the alley behind the house while I go inside for a few minutes."

The kid grinned. "So, you going to jack some stuff? This's a heist, right?"

Muller shushed him. "Even if it was, you think I'd say it out loud?"

"Sorry. I wasn't thinking." The boy squinted, then said, "Hey, there's this friend of mine? And we've got a connection. He's getting us some good stuff. I mean, way sweet. We can turn it around in a week. You come in with a thousand or two, he'll give us a better discount. You can double your money. You interested?"

"Drugs?"

"Yeah."

"I don't ever go near 'em. And you shouldn't, either. They'll screw up your life. Remember that. . . . Meet me tomorrow, okay?"

"When?"

"Noon. The corner of Seventh and Maple. Starbucks."

"I guess."

"Don't guess. Be there." Muller started to walk away.

"If this works out, you think maybe there'd be some more work for me?"

"I might be away for a while. But, yeah, maybe. If you handle it right."

"I do a good job, mister. Hey, what's *your* name?"

"You don't need to know that."

The kid nodded. "That's cool. Sure . . . One other thing? What about the watch?"

"I'll dispose of the evidence for you."

After the kid was gone Muller walked slowly to the mouth of the alley and peeked out. No sign of Carnegie's surveillance team. He'd been careful to lose them, but they had this almost magical ability to appear from nowhere and nail him with their Big Ear mikes and telephoto lenses.

Pulling on his Oakland baseball cap and lowering his head, he stepped out of the alley and walked down the sidewalk fast, as if satellites were tracking his position from ten thousand miles in space.

The next morning William Carnegie was late coming into the office.

Since he'd screwed up by missing the parent-teacher meeting yesterday, he'd forced himself to have breakfast with his wife and Billy.

When he walked into the police station at nine-thirty Sergeant Hager told him, "Muller's been doing some shopping you ought to know about."

"What?"

"He left his house an hour ago. Our boys tailed him to the mall. They lost him, but not long after that we got a charge notice from one of his credit-card companies. At Books 'N' Java he bought six books. We don't know exactly what they were, but the product code from the store listed them as travel books. Then he left the mail and spent thirty-eight dollars for two boxes of nine-millimeter ammunition at Tyler's Gun Shop."

"Jesus. I always figured him for a shooter. The guards at Anco're lucky they didn't hear him breaking in; he would've taken them out, I know it . . . Did the surveillance team pick him up again?"

"Nope. They went back to his house to wait."

"Got something else," called a young policewoman nearby. "He charged forty-four dollars' worth of tools at Home Depot."

Carnegie mused, "So, he's armed, and sounds like he's planning another heist. Then he's going to flee the state." Gazing at one of the computer screens, he asked absently. "What're you going after this time, Muller? A business, a house?"

Hager's phone rang. He answered and listened. "That was the babysitter in front of Muller's. He's back home. Only something funny. He was on foot. He must've parked up the street someplace." He listened some more. "They say there's a painting truck in his driveway. Maybe that's why."

"No. He's up to something. I don't trust anything that man does."

"Got another notice!" one officer called. "He just went on-line . . ." The police had no court order allowing them to view the content of what Muller downloaded, though they could observe the sites he was connected to. "Okay. He's on the Anderson & Cross Web site."

"The burglar alarm company?" Carnegie asked, his heart pounding with excitement.

"Yep."

A few minutes later the officer called, "Now he's checking out TravelCentral dot com."

A service that let you make airline reservations on-line.

"Tell surveillance we'll let them know as soon as he goes off-line. They should be ready to move. I've got a feeling this's going to happen fast."

We've got you now, Carnegie thought. Then he laughed and looked at the computers affectionately.

Big Brother Is Watching You. . . .

In the passenger seat of his car, Jake Muller nodded toward a high fence in an alleyway behind Tremont Street. "Sam, pull over there."

The car braked slowly to a stop.

"That's it, huh?" the nervous kid asked, nodding toward a white house on the other side of the fence.

"Yep. Now, listen. If a cop comes by, just drive off slow. Go around the block but turn left at the street. Got that? Stay off Tremont, whatever you do."

The boy asked uneasily, "You think somebody'll come by?"

"Let's hope not." Muller took the tools he'd just bought that morning out of the trunk, looked up and down the alley, then walked through the gate in the fence and disappeared around the side of the house.

He returned ten minutes later. He hurried through the gate, carrying a heavy box and a small shopping bag, disappeared again, and returned with several more boxes. He loaded everything in the back of the car and wiped sweat from his forehead, then dropped hard into the passenger's seat. "Let's get outta here."

"Where're the tools?"

"I left 'em back there. What're you waiting for? Go."

The kid hit the accelerator and the car jumped into the middle of the alley.

Soon they were on the freeway and Muller gave directions to a cheap motel on the far side of town, the Starlight Lodge. There Muller climbed out. He walked into the lobby and registered for two nights. He returned to the car. "Room One Twenty-nine. He said it's around the side, in the back."

They found the spot, parked, and climbed out. Muller handed the boy the room key. He opened the door and together they carried the boxes and the shopping bag inside.

"Kinda lame," the kid said, looking around.

"I won't be here that long."

Muller turned his back and opened the grocery bag. He extracted five one-hundred-dollar bills and handed them over. He added another twenty. "You'll have to take a cab back downtown."

"Man, looks like a good haul." Nodding at the bag of money.

Muller said nothing. He stuffed the bag into a suitcase, locked it, and slipped it under the bed.

The kid pocketed the bills.

"You did a good job today, Sam. Thanks."

"How'll I find you, mister? I mean, if you want to hire me again?"

"I'll leave a message at the Starbucks."

"Yeah. Good."

Muller glanced at his watch. He emptied his pockets on the dresser. "Now I gotta shower and go meet some people."

They shook hands. The boy left and Muller swung the door shut after him.

In the bathroom he turned the shower on full, the water hot. He leaned against the wobbly basin and watched the steam roll out of the stall like stormy clouds and wondered where his life was about to go.

• • •

"There's something screwy," Sergeant Hager called out.

"What?"

"A glitch of some kind." He nodded at one computer. "Muller's still on-line at his house. See? Only we just got an advisory from National Bank's credit-card computer. Somebody using Muller's card got a room at the Starlight Lodge on Simpson about forty-five minutes ago. There's gotta be a mistake. He—"

"Oh, Christ," Carnegie spat out. "There's no mistake. Muller left his computer on so we'd think he was home. *That's* why he parked the car around the corner. So our men wouldn't see him leave. He snuck through a side yard or out the back." Carnegie grabbed the phone and raged at the surveillance team that their subject had gotten away from them. He ordered them to check to make sure. He slammed the receiver down and a moment later a sheepish officer called back to confirm that the painters said Muller had left over an hour ago.

The detective sighed. "So while we were napping he knocked over the next target. I don't believe it. I just—"

"He just made another charge," a cop called. "Eighteen gallons of gas at the Mobil station on Lorenzo and Principale."

"Tanked it up." Carnegie nodded, considering this. "Maybe he's going to drive up to San Francisco to catch a flight. Or Arizona or Las Vegas, for that matter." Walking to the wall map, the detective stuck pins in the locations Hager had mentioned. He was calmer now. Muller may have guessed they'd be monitoring his on-line activity, but obviously didn't know the extent of their surveillance.

"Get a county unmarked to tail him."

"Detective, just got a report from the speed-pass main computer," one of the officers across the room called. "Muller turned onto the Four-Oh-Eight at Stanton Road four minutes ago. He entered at the northbound tollbooth."

The little box on your windshield that automatically paid tolls on highways, bridges, and tunnels could report exactly when and where you used it.

Another pin was stabbed into the map.

Hager directed the pursuing officers to that interchange.

Fifteen minutes later, the cop monitoring the speed-pass computer called out once again, "He just turned off the tollway. At Markham Road. The eastbound tollbooth."

Eastbound into the Markham neighborhood? Carnegie reflected. Well, that made sense. This was a tough part of town, populated by rednecks and bikers living in ramshackle bungalows and trailers. If Muller had an accomplice, Markham would be a good source for that sort of muscle. And nearby was the desert, with thousands of square miles in which to hide the Anco loot.

"Still no visual yet," Hager said, listening on his phone to the pursuing officers.

"Damn. We're going to lose him."

But then another officer called, "I just got a ping from Muller's cell phone company—he's turned on the phone and's making a call. They're tracing it. . . ." A moment later he called out, "Okay. He's headed north-bound on La Ciena."

Another blue-tipped pin in the map.

Hager relayed this information to the county cops. Then he listened and gave a laugh. "They've got the car! . . . Muller's pulling into the Desert Rose trailer park. . . . Okay . . . He's parking at one of the trailers. . . . Getting out . . . He's talking to a white male, thirties, shaved head, tattoos. . . . The male's nodding toward a shed on the back of the property. . . . They're walking back there together. . . . They're getting a package out of the shed. . . . Now they're going inside."

"That's good enough for me," Carnegie announced. "Tell 'em to stay out of sight. We'll be there in twenty minutes. Advise us if the suspect starts to leave."

As he started for the door, he said a silent prayer, thanking both the Lord—and Big Brother—for their help.

The drive took closer to forty minutes, but Jake Muller's car was still parked in front of the rusty, lopsided trailer.

The officers on the scene reported that the robber and his bald accomplice were still inside, presumably planning their escape from the jurisdiction.

The four police cars from headquarters were parked several trailers away, and nine Annandale cops, three armed with shotguns, were crouching behind sheds and weeds and rusty autos. Everybody kept low, mindful that Muller was armed.

Carnegie and Hager eased forward toward the trailer. They had to handle the situation carefully. Unless they could catch a glimpse of the Anco payroll money through the door or window, or unless Muller carried it outside in plain view, they had no probable cause to arrest him. They circled the place but couldn't see in; the door was closed and the curtains drawn.

Hell, Carnegie thought, discouraged. Maybe they could—

But then fate intervened.

"Smell that?" Carnegie asked in a whisper.

Hager frowned. "What?"

"Coming from inside."

The sergeant inhaled deeply. "Pot or hash," he said, nodding.

This would give them probable cause to enter.

"Let's do it," Hager whispered. And he gestured for the other officers to join him.

One of the tactical cops asked if he should do the kick-in but Carnegie shook his head. "Nope. He's mine." He took off his suit jacket and strapped on a bulletproof vest, then drew his automatic pistol.

Gazing at the other officers, he mouthed, "Ready?"

They nodded.

The detective held up three fingers, then bent them down one at a time.

One . . . two . . .

"Go!"

He shouldered open the door and rushed into the trailer, the other officers right behind him.

"Freeze, freeze, police!" he shouted, looking around, squinting to see better in the dim light.

The first thing he noticed was a large plastic bag of pot sitting by the doorway.

The second thing was that the tattooed man's visitor wasn't Jake Muller at all; it was Carnegie's own son, Billy.

The detective stormed into the Annandale police station, flanked by Sergeant Hager. Behind them was another officer, escorting the sullen, handcuffed boy.

The owner of the trailer—a biker with a history of drug offenses—had been taken down the hall to Narcotics and the kilo of weed booked into evidence.

Carnegie had ordered Billy to tell them what was going on, but he'd clammed up and refused to say a word. A search of the property and of Muller's car had yielded no evidence of the Anco loot. He'd gotten a frosty reaction from the Orange County troopers who'd been tailing Muller's car when he'd raged at them about misidentifying his son as the businessman. ("Don't recall you ever bothered to put his picture out on the wire, Detective," one of them reminded him.)

Carnegie now barked to one of the officers sitting at a computer screen, "Get me Jake Muller."

"You don't have to," an officer said. "He's right over there."

Muller was sitting across from the desk sergeant. He rose and looked in astonishment at Carnegie and his son. He pointed to the boy and said sourly, "So they got you already, Sam. That was fast. I just filled out the complaint five minutes ago."

"Sam?" Carnegie asked.

"Yeah, Sam Phillips," Muller said.

"His name's Billy. He's my son," Carnegie muttered. The boy's middle name was Samuel, and Phillips was the maiden name of the detective's wife.

"Your son?" Muller asked, eyes wide in disbelief. He then glanced at what one officer was carrying—an evidence box containing the suitcase, wallet, keys, and cell phone that had been found in Muller's car. "You recovered everything," he said. "How's my car? Did he wreck it?"

Hager started to tell him that his car was fine but Carnegie waved his hand to silence the big cop. "Okay, what the hell is going on?" he asked Muller. "What'd you have to do with my boy?"

Angry, Muller said, "Hey, this kid robbed *me*. I was just trying to do him a favor. I had no idea he was your son."

"Favor?"

Muller eyed the boy up and down. "Yesterday I saw him steal a watch from Maxwell's, over on Harrison Street."

Carnegie turned a cold eye on his son, who continued to keep his head down.

"I followed him and made him give me the watch. I felt bad for him. He seemed like he was having a tough time of it. I hired him to help me out for an hour or so. I just wanted to show him there were people out there who'd pay good money for legitimate work."

"What'd you do with the watch?" Carnegie asked.

Muller looked indignant. "Returned it to the shop. What'd you think? I'd keep stolen merchandise?"

The detective glanced at his son and demanded, "What did he hire you to do?"

When the boy said nothing, Muller explained. "I paid him to watch my car while I moved a few things out of my house."

"*Your* house?" the boy asked in shock. "On Tremont?"

To his father Muller said, "That's right. I moved into a motel for a few days—I'm having my house painted and I can't sleep with the paint fumes."

The truck in Muller's driveway, Carnegie recalled.

"I couldn't use the front door," Muller added angrily, "because I'm sick of those goons of yours tailing me every time I leave the house. I hired your son to stay with the car in the alley; it's a tow zone back there. You can't leave your car unattended even for five minutes. I dropped off some tools I bought this morning and picked up a few things I needed and we drove to the motel." Muller shook his head. "I gave him the key to open the door, and I forgot to get it when he left. He came back when I was in the shower and ripped me off. My car, my cell phone, money, wallet, the suitcase." In disgust he added, "Hell, and here I gave him all that money. And practically begged him to get his act together and stay clear of drugs."

"He told you that?" Carnegie asked.

The boy nodded reluctantly.

His father sighed and nodded at the suitcase. "What's in there?"

Muller shrugged, picked up his keys, and unlocked and opened the case.

Carnegie supposed that the businessman wouldn't be so cooperative if it contained the Anco loot, but he still felt a burst of delight when he noticed that the paper bag inside was filled with cash.

His excitement faded, though, when he saw it held only about three or four hundred dollars, mostly wadded-up ones and fives.

"Household money," Muller explained. "I didn't want to leave it in the house. Not with the painters there."

Carnegie contemptuously tossed the bag into the case and angrily slammed the lid. "Jesus."

"You thought it was the Anco money?"

Carnegie looked at the computer terminals around them, cursors blinking passively.

Goddamn Big Brother . . . The best surveillance money could buy. And look what had happened.

The detective's voice cracked with emotion as he said, "You followed my son! You hired the painters so you could get away without being seen, you bought the bullets, the tools. . . . And what the hell were you doing looking at burglar-alarm Web sites?"

"Comparative shopping," Muller answered reasonably. "I'm buying an alarm system for the house."

"This is all a setup! You—"

The businessman silenced him by glancing at Carnegie's fellow officers, who were looking at their boss with mixed expressions of concern and distaste over his paranoid ranting. Muller nodded toward Carnegie's office. "How 'bout you and I go in there? Have a chat."

Inside, Muller swung the door shut and turned to face the glowering detective. "Here's the situation, Detective. I'm the only prosecuting witness in the larceny and auto-theft case against your son. That's a felony, and if I decide to press charges he'll do some serious time, particularly since I suspect you found him in the company of some not-so-savory friends when he was busted. Then there's also the little matter of Dad's career trajectory after his son's arrest hits the papers."

"You want a deal?"

"Yeah, I want a deal. I'm sick of this delusion crap of yours, Carnegie. I'm a legitimate businessman. I didn't steal the Anco payroll. I'm not a thief and never have been."

He eyed the detective carefully, then reached into his pocket and handed Carnegie a slip of paper.

"What's this?"

"The number of a Coastal Air flight four months ago—the afternoon of the Anco robbery."

"How'd you get this?"

"My companies do some business with the airlines. I pulled some strings and the head of security at Coastal got me that number. One of the passengers in first class on that flight paid cash for a one-way ticket from John Wayne Airport to Chicago four hours after the Anco robbery. He had no checked baggage. Only carry-on. They wouldn't give me the passenger's name, but that shouldn't be too tough for a hard-working cop like you to track down."

Carnegie stared at the paper. "The guy from the Department of Public Works? The one the witness saw with that suitcase near Anco?"

"Maybe it's a coincidence, Detective. But I know I didn't steal the money. Maybe *he* did."

The paper disappeared into Carnegie's pocket. "What do you want?"

"Drop me as a suspect. Cut out all the surveillance. I want my life back. And I want a letter signed by you stating that the evidence proves I'm not guilty."

"That won't mean anything in court."

"But it'll look pretty bad if anybody decides to come after me again."

"Bad for my job, you mean."

"That's exactly what I mean."

After a moment Carnegie muttered. "How long've you been planning this out?"

Muller said nothing. But he reflected: Not that long, actually. He'd started thinking about it just after the two cops had interrupted his nap the other day.

He'd wire-transferred some money from an investment account to one of his banks in France, to fuel the cops' belief that he was getting ready to flee the country (the French accounts were completely legit; only a fool would hide loot in Europe).

Then he'd done some surveillance of his own, low-tech though it was. He'd pulled on overalls, glasses, and a hat, and snuck into police head-quarters, armed with a watering can and clippers to tend to the plants he'd noticed inside the station the first time he was arrested. He'd spent a half-hour on his knees, his head down, clipping and watering, in the hallway outside the watch room, where he'd learned the extent of the police's electronic invasion of his life. He'd heard, too, the exchange between Billy Carnegie and the detective—a classic example of an uninvolved father and a troubled, angry son.

Muller smiled to himself now, recalling that after the meeting Carnegie had been so focused on the case that when he nearly tripped over Muller in the corridor, the cop never noticed who the gardener was.

He'd then followed Billy for a few hours until he caught him palming the watch. Then he tricked the boy into helping him. He'd hired the painters to do some interior touch-up—to give him the excuse to park his car elsewhere and to check into the motel. Then, using their surveillance against them, he'd bought the travel books, the bullets, and the tools, and logged onto the alarm and travel agency Web sites in order to fool the cops into believing he was indeed the Anco burglar and was getting ready to do one last heist and flee the state. At the motel he'd tempted Billy Carnegie into stealing the suitcase, credit cards, phone, and car—everything that would let the cops track the kid and nail him red-handed.

He now said to Carnegie, "I'm sorry, Detective, but you didn't leave me any choice. You just weren't ever going to believe that I'm innocent."

"You used my son."

Muller shrugged. "No harm done. Look on the good side—his first bust and he picked a victim who's willing to drop the charges. Anybody else, he wouldn't've been so lucky."

Carnegie glanced through the blinds at his son, standing forlorn by Hager's desk.

"He's savable, Detective," Muller said. "If you want to save him . . . So, do we have a deal?"

A disgusted sigh was followed by a disgusted nod.

Outside the police station, Muller tossed the suitcase into the back of his car, which had been towed to the station by a police truck.

He drove back to his house and walked inside. The workmen had apparently just finished and the smell of paint was strong. He went through the ground floor, opening windows to air the place out.

Strolling into his garden, he surveyed the huge pile of mulch, whose spreading had been postponed because of his interrupted nap. The businessman glanced at his watch. He had some phone calls to make but decided to put them off for another day; he was in the mood to garden. He changed clothes, went into the garage, and picked up a glistening new shovel, part of his purchases that morning at Home Depot. He began meticulously spreading the black and brown mulch throughout the large garden.

After an hour of work he paused for a beer. Sitting under a maple tree, sipping the Heineken, he surveyed the empty street in front of his house—where Carnegie had stationed the surveillance team for the past few months. Man, it felt good not to be spied on any longer.

His eyes then slid to a small rock sitting halfway between a row of corn stalks and some tomato vines. Three feet beneath it was a bag containing the $543,300 from Anco Armored Delivery, which he'd buried there the afternoon of the robbery, just before he'd ditched the public-works uniform and driven the stolen truck to Orange County airport for the flight to Chicago under a false name—a precautionary trip, in case he needed to lead investigators off on a false trail, as it turned out he'd had to do, thanks to compulsive Detective Carnegie.

Jake Muller planned all of his heists out to the finest of details; this was why he'd never been caught after nearly fifteen years as a thief.

He'd wanted to send the cash to his bagman in Miami for months— Muller hated it when heist money wasn't earning interest—but with Carnegie breathing down his neck, he hadn't dared. Should he dig it up now and send it off?

No, he decided; it was best to wait till dark.

Besides, the weather was warm, the sky was clear, and there was nothing like gardening on a beautiful spring day. Muller finished his beer, picked up the shovel, and returned to the pile of pungent mulch.

The 2002 Edgar Allan Poe Mystery Fiction Short-List

Alexander, Gary, "Georgie Porgi," *Alfred Hitchcock's Mystery Magazine,* February

Allyn, Doug, "The Jukebox King," *AHMM,* June

Armstrong, Michael, "A Little Walk Home," *The Mysterious North*

Charles, Hal, "Moody's Blues," *Ellery Queen's Mystery Magazine,* November

DuBois, Brendan, "By the Light of the Moon," Crippen & Landru Supplement

DuBois, Brendan, "Richard's Children," *Much Ado About Murder*

Freeman, Mary, "The Path of Bones," *EQMM,* September/October

Healy, Jeremiah, "Just Kryptonite," *Flesh and Blood*

Hennessy, Mike, "Murder in Chinatown," Orchard Press Online

Lippman, Laura, "What He Needed," *Tart Noir*

Lutz, John, "Lily and Men," *Flesh and Blood*

Mortimer, John, "Rumpole and the Primrose Path," *The Strand*

Oates, Joyce Carol, "Angel of Wrath," *EQMM,* June

Oates, Joyce Carol, "The Deaths," *EQMM,* December

Owens, Barbara, "In My House" *EQMM,* January

Rusch, Kristine Kathryn, "Heroics," *EQMM,* April

Scholfield, Neil, "Mine Hostage," *EQMM,* May

About the Editors

Ed Gorman has been called "one of suspense fiction's best storytellers" by *Ellery Queen,* and "one of the most original voices in today's crime fiction" by the *San Diego Union.*

Gorman has been published in magazines as various as *Redbook, Ellery Queen, The Magazine of Fantasy and Science Fiction,* and *Poetry Today.*

He has won numerous prizes, including the Shamus, the Spur, and the International Fiction Writer's Award. He's been nominated for the Edgar, the Anthony, the Golden Dagger, and the Bram Stoker Awards. Former *Los Angeles Times* critic Charles Champlin noted that "Ed Gorman is a powerful storyteller."

Gorman's work has been taken by the Literary Guild, the Mystery Guild, the Doubleday Book Club, and the Science Fiction Book Club.

Martin H. Greenberg is the CEO of TEKNO•BOOKS, the book-packaging division of Hollywood Media, a publicly traded multimedia entertainment company. With more than nine hundred published anthologies and collections, he is the most prolific anthologist in publishing history. His books have been translated into thirty-three languages and adopted by twenty-five different book clubs. With Ed Gorman, he edits the 5-Star Mystery line of novels and collections for Thorndike Press, and he is copublisher of *Mystery Scene,* the leading trade journal of the mystery genre.

In the mystery and suspense field, he has worked with at least fifteen best-selling authors, including Dean Koontz, Mickey Spillane, Tony Hillerman, Robert Ludlum, and Tom Clancy.

He received the Milford Award for lifetime achievement in science fiction editing in 1989, and in April 1995 he received the Ellery Queen Award for lifetime achievement for editing in the mystery field at the 50th Annual Banquet of the Mystery Writers of America, becoming the only person to win major editorial awards in both genres.

Dr. Greenberg received his Ph.D. in political science and international relations from the University of Connecticut, and was the founding chairperson of those departments at Florida International University from 1972 to 1975. He retired as professor emeritus of political science and literature after a twenty-year teaching and administrative career at the University of Wisconsin—Green Bay, where he served as the university's first director of graduate studies.